the
DEVILS

BY JOE ABERCROMBIE

The Devils

THE FIRST LAW TRILOGY

The Blade Itself

Before They Are Hanged

Last Argument of Kings

Best Served Cold

The Heroes

Red Country

Sharp Ends: Stories from the World of the First Law

THE AGE OF MADNESS

A Little Hatred

The Trouble with Peace

The Wisdom of Crowds

THE SHATTERED SEA TRILOGY

Half a King

Half the World

Half a War

JOE ABERCROMBIE

the DEVILS

TOR

TOR PUBLISHING GROUP • NEW YORK

THE DEVILS

Copyright © 2025 by Joe Abercrombie

All rights reserved.

Endpapers, map, and interior illustrations by Joel Daniel Phillips

A Tor Book
Published by Tom Doherty Associates / Tor Publishing Group
120 Broadway
New York, NY 10271

www.torpublishinggroup.com

Tor® is a registered trademark of Macmillan Publishing Group, LLC.

The Library of Congress Cataloging-in-Publication Data is available upon request.

ISBN 978-1-250-88005-5 (hardcover)
ISBN 978-1-250-88006-2 (ebook)

Our books may be purchased in bulk for promotional, educational, or business use.
Please contact your local bookseller or the Macmillan Corporate and Premium Sales Department
at 1-800-221-7945, extension 5442, or by email at MacmillanSpecialMarkets@macmillan.com.

First Edition: 2025

Printed in the United States of America

0 9 8 7 6 5 4 3

For Gillian,
Dragging fantasy fiction into the sewer
Since 2006

NORWAY

Brittain?

BURGUNDY

BAVARIA

FRANKIA

LEON

ARAGON

Venice

SERBIA

Bage

CASTILE

ATLANTIS

CORDOVA

Holy City

NAPLES

SICILY

DEVASTATION
of
CARTHAGE

THE·HOLY·CITY

TROY

part

I

WORST PRINCESS EVER

Saint Aelfric's Day

It was the fifteenth of Loyalty, and Brother Diaz was late for his audience with Her Holiness the Pope.

"God *damn* it," he fretted as his scarcely moving carriage was buffeted by a procession of wailing flagellants, their backs streaked with blood and their faces with tears of rapture, whipping themselves along beneath a banner that read simply, "Repent." What one was called upon to repent *of* wasn't specified.

Everyone's got something, don't they?

"God *damn* it." It might not have been numbered among the Twelve Virtues, but Brother Diaz had always prided himself on his punctuality. He'd allowed a full five hours to get from his hostelry to his interview, sure that would leave him with at least two to piously admire the statues of the senior saints before the Celestial Palace. It was said all roads in the Holy City led there, after all.

Only now it seemed all roads in the Holy City led around and around in chilly circles crawling with an unimaginable density of pilgrims, prostitutes, dreamers, schemers, relic-buyers, indulgence-dealers, miracle-seekers, preachers and fanatics, tricksters and swindlers, prostitutes, thieves, merchants and moneylenders, soldiers and thugs, an astonishing quantity of livestock on the hoof, cripples, prostitutes, crippled prostitutes, had he mentioned the prostitutes? They outnumbered the priests some twenty to one. Their glaring presence at the blessed heart of the Church, screeching smoking come-ons and displaying goosefleshed extremities to the uncaring cold, was shocking, of course, disgraceful, undoubtedly, but also stirred desires Brother Diaz had hoped long buried. He was obliged to adjust his habit and turn his eyes heavenwards. Or at any rate towards the jolting ceiling of his carriage.

That sort of thing was what had got him in trouble in the first place.

"*God damn it!*" He dragged down the window and stuck his head into the frosty air. The cacophony of hymns and solicitation, of barter and pleas for forgiveness—and the stench of woodsmoke, cheap incense, and a nearby fish market—were both instantly tripled, leaving him unsure whether to cover his ears or his nose while he screamed at the driver. "I'm going to be late!"

"Wouldn't surprise me." The man spoke with weary resignation, as though a disinterested bystander and not charging an exorbitant fee to convey Brother Diaz to the most important appointment of his life. "It's Saint Aelfric's Day, Brother."

"And?"

"His relics have been hoisted up the steeple of the Church of the Immaculate Appeasement and displayed to the needy. They're said to cure the gout."

That explained all the limps, canes, and wheeled chairs in the crowds. Couldn't it have been scrofula, or persistent hiccups, or some malady that left the afflicted capable of flinging themselves out of the path of a speeding carriage?

"Is there no other route?" Brother Diaz screeched over the gabble.

"Hundreds." The driver directed a limp shrug at the swarming crowds. "But it's Saint Aelfric's Day everywhere."

The bells for midday prayers were starting to echo over the city, beginning with a desultory dingle or two from the roadside shrines, mounting to a discordant clangour as each chapel, church, and cathedral added its own frantic peals, jockeying to hook the pilgrims through their doors, onto their pews, and up to their collection plates.

The carriage lurched on, flooding Brother Diaz with relief, then immediately lurched to a halt, plunging him into despair. Not far away two ragged priests from competing beggar-orders had been cranked up in telescopic pulpits, swaying perilously above the crowd with a groaning of tortured machinery, spraying spit as they argued viciously over the exact meaning of the Saviour's exhortation to civility.

"God *damn* it!" All that work undermining his brothers at the monastery. All that trouble preventing the abbot's mistresses from finding out about each other. All his bragging about being summoned to the Holy City, singled out as special, marked for a great future.

And this was where his ambitions would die. Buried in a carriage stalled in human mire, in a narrow square named after a saint no one had heard of, cold as an icehouse, busy as a slaughterhouse, and squalid as a shithouse, between a painted enclosure crammed with licensed beggars and a linden-wood platform for public punishments, on which a set of children were burning elves in straw-stuffed effigy.

Brother Diaz watched them beating the pointy-eared, pointy-toothed dummies, sending up showers of sparks while onlookers indulgently applauded. Elves were elves, of course, and surely better burned than not, but there was something troubling in those chubby little children's faces, shining with violent glee. Theology had never really been his strong suit, but he was reasonably sure the Saviour had talked a lot about mercy.

Thrift most definitely was numbered among the Twelve Virtues. Brother Diaz always reminded himself of that as he gave the beggars outside the monastery gates a wide berth. But sometimes one has to invest to turn a profit. He leaned out of the window to scream at the driver again. "Promise to get me to the Celestial Palace on time and I'll pay double!"

"It's the Holy City, Brother." The driver barely even bothered to shrug. "Only madmen make promises here."

Brother Diaz ducked back inside, tears stinging his eyes. He squirmed from his seat onto one knee, slipped out the vial he wore around his neck, its antique silver polished by centuries against the skin of his forebears. "O Blessed Saint Beatrix," he murmured, gripping it desperately, "holy martyr and guardian of our Saviour's sandal, I ask for only this—get me to my *shitting* audience with the Pope on time!"

He regretted swearing in a prayer at once and made the sign of the circle over his chest, but while he was working his way up to pinching himself in the centre by way of penance, Saint Beatrix made her displeasure known.

There was an almighty thud on the roof, the carriage jolted, and Brother Diaz was flung violently forward, his despairing squawk cut short as the seat in front struck him right in the mouth.

How It Goes

Alex nailed the jump from window to carriage-roof, rolled smooth as butter and came up sweet as honey, but botched the much easier jump from carriage-roof to ground, twisted her ankle, blundered off balance through the crowd, bounced mouth-first from the dung-crusted flank of a donkey, and went sprawling in the gutter.

The donkey was quite put out and its owner even more so. Alex couldn't be sure what he was yelling over the wails of some passing penitents, but it was *not* flattering.

"Fuck yourself!" she screamed at him. A monk gawped at her from the carriage, with a bloody mouth and that look of sweaty panic tourists get in the Holy City, so she shrieked, "And you can fuck yourself, too! Fuck each other," she added, half-hearted as she hobbled away.

Swearing's free, after all.

She whipped a prayer-cloth from a stall while the merchant wasn't looking—which wasn't so much theft in her book as just good reflexes—wrapped it over her head scarf-like, and slipped among the penitents, doing her best pitiful moan. Not difficult given the pain throbbing up her leg and the prickle of danger tickling her neck. She raised her hands towards the jagged strip of blue between the mismatched roofs and mouthed a smoking prayer for deliverance. For once, she almost meant it.

This is how it goes. Start the evening looking for fun, end the morning begging forgiveness.

God, she felt sick. Stomach churning, burning up her sore throat, and there was the rumour of trouble at her arse-end, too. Maybe last night's bad meat or this morning's bad prospects. Maybe the money she'd lost or the money she owed. Maybe a little dung on the lips, still. Then the unholy stench of the pilgrims—forbidden from washing on their long treks to the Holy City—wasn't helping anyone. She twitched a corner of the prayer-cloth over her mouth and stole a glance backwards, peering through the thicket of arms raised to heaven—

"There she is!"

No matter how she tried, she never could quite fit in. She elbowed past a blindfolded pilgrim, shoved over another shuffling on his scabbed knees, and lurched up the street as quick as she could with a bad ankle, which was nowhere near as fast as she'd have liked. Over the noise of someone belting out hymns for coppers she could hear chaos behind. A fight, if she was lucky, those penitents could get pretty frisky if you came between them and the grace of the Almighty.

She skittered around a corner into the fish market in the shadow of the Pale Sisters. A hundred stalls, a thousand customers, the clamour of bad-tempered barter, the salty sea-reek of the morning's catch, gleaming in the watery winter sunlight.

She glimpsed a flash of movement and dropped on a reflex. A clutching hand ripped a loose hair from her head as she went sliding under a wagon, was almost clubbed by pawing hooves, rolled away to wriggle between someone's legs, through the chilly slather of guts and bones and slimes beneath the stalls.

"Fucking got you!"

A hand clamped around her ankle, her fingernails leaving worming trails through the fish mulch as she was dragged into the light. It was one of Bostro's thugs, the one suffering from a three-cornered hat made him look like a failed pirate. She came up punching, landed one on his cheek with a sick crunch that she'd a worry was her hand not his face, and he caught her wrist and wrenched her sideways. She spat in his eye, made him flinch, booted him in the groin and made him stumble, flailing about with her free hand. They might put her down, but she'd never stay down. Her fingers found something and she shrieked as she swung it. A heavy pan. It smashed the pirate across the cheek with a sound like the bells for evening prayers, knocked his stupid hat spinning, and laid him out lengthways, customers diving away as hot oil showered everywhere.

Alex spun around, a fishy wad of her own hair stuck across her eyes. Staring faces, pointing fingers, figures forcing through the crowd towards her. She sprang onto the nearest stall, planks bouncing on their trestles as she kicked through the ocean's bounty, fish flopping, crabs crunching, merchants roaring abuse. She sprang for the next stall, slipped on a huge trout, and reeled one more desperate step before she crashed down on her shoulder and went sprawling in a shower of shellfish. She struggled up gasping, limped for a rubbish-choked alleyway, and was about four steps down it before she saw it was a dead end.

She stood there in a horrified crouch, staring at the blank wall with her hands helplessly opening and closing. Ever so slowly, she turned.

Bostro stood in the mouth of the alley, big fists propped on hips, big jaw jutting, a blank slab of menace. He clicked his tongue with a slow *tut, tut, tut*.

One of his thugs joined him, breathing hard from the chase. The one with the grin full of brown teeth. God, they were a sight. If you had that grin, at least clean your teeth, and if you had those teeth, at least don't grin.

"Bostro!" Alex produced the best smile she could while panting for breath, which was a poor one, even by her standards. "Didn't know it was *you*."

His sigh was as weighty as the rest of him. He'd been collecting for Papa Collini for years and must've heard every trick, lie, excuse, and sob story you could imagine and no doubt quite a few you couldn't. This one didn't impress him.

"Time's up, Alex," he said. "Papa wants his money."

"Fair enough." She held out her bulging purse. "Here's the whole sum."

She tossed it to him then made a dash for it, but they were ready. Bostro caught the purse while his shit-toothed friend caught Alex by the arm, swung her around, and flung her against the wall so her head smacked the bricks and she went rolling in the rubbish.

Bostro opened the purse and eyed the contents. "Here's a shock." He dangled it upside down and dirt showered out. "Your purse is as full of shit as you are."

The aspiring pirate had joined the party with a pink pan-mark down his face. "Watch it," he grunted, knocking a dent from his fish-smeared hat. "She's vicious when cornered. Like a starving weasel."

She'd been called worse. "Now look," she croaked as she clambered up, wondering if they'd broken her shoulder, then when she tried clutching at it wondering if she'd broken her hand. "I'll get him the money. I can get him the money!"

"How?" asked Bostro.

She pulled the rag from her pocket and unfolded it with suitable reverence. "Behold the fingerbones of Saint Lucius—"

The one with the hat slapped them out of her hand. "We know dog feet when we see 'em, you swindling bitch." Which was quite upsetting after all the work she'd put into filing the claws down.

"Now look," she said, backing away with her battered, throbbing, fishy hands up but fast running out of the alley, "I just need a bit more time!"

"Papa gave you more time," said Bostro, herding her backwards. "It ran out."

"It's not even my debt!" she whined, which was true, but entirely beside the point.

"Papa warned you not to take it on, didn't he? But you took it on." Which was also true, and very much on the point.

"I'm good for it!" Her voice was getting higher and higher. "You can trust me!"

"You're not and I can't, and we both know it."

"I'll go to a friend!"

"You don't have any."

"I'll find a way. I always find a way!"

"You haven't found a way. That's why we're here. Hold her."

She landed a punch on Shitty Teeth with her good hand, but he barely noticed. He caught her arm and the pirate caught the other, and she kicked and twisted and wailed for help like a mugged nun. They might put her down, but she'd never stay—

Bostro thumped her in the stomach.

It made a thud like a stable boy dropping a damp saddle and the fight fell straight out of her. Her eyes went wet and her knees went floppy and all she could do was hang there and make a great long vomity wheeze and think actually it might be best if she stayed down after all.

There really is nothing romantic about a punch in the gut from someone twice your size, specially when the best you've got to look forward to is another. Bostro caught her around the throat with one great fist and cut her wheeze off to a slippery gurgle. Then he took his pincers out.

Iron pincers. Polished from lots of use.

He didn't look happy about it, but he still did it.

"Which'll it be?" he grunted. "Teeth or fingers?"

"Now look," she slobbered, near swallowing her tongue. How long had she been playing for time? A week or two more. An hour or two more. She was down to playing for moments. "Now look—"

"Pick," snarled Bostro, his pincers getting so close to Alex's face she went cross-eyed staring at them, "or you know it's both—"

"One moment!" The voice rang out, sharp and commanding, and everyone looked around at once. Bostro, the thugs, and Alex, too, far as she could while half-throttled.

A tall, handsome man stood in the mouth of the alley. In her line of work, you learn to tell how rich someone is at a glance. Tell who's rich enough to be worth swindling. Tell who's too rich to be worth the trouble. This was a very rich one, robe worn around the hems, but good silk, stitched with dragons in golden thread.

"I am Duke Michael of Nicaea." He had a trace of an eastern accent, it was true. A bald fellow with sweat on his forehead hurried up beside him. "And this is my servant Eusebius."

Everyone took stock of this surprising turn-up. The so-called duke was looking at Alex. He had a kind face, she thought, but then she could put on a very kind face and she was a thieving bitch, ask anyone. "I understand your name is Alex?"

"You understand correctly," grunted Bostro.

"And do you have a birthmark beneath your ear?"

Bostro shifted his thumb and raised his brows at the piece of neck revealed. "She does."

"By all the saints . . ." Duke Michael closed his eyes and took a very deep breath. When he opened them, it looked like there might be tears there. "You're alive."

Bostro's grip had loosened enough for Alex to wheeze, "*For now.*" She was shocked as anyone, but the winners are those who get over their shock quickest and start working out where the profit is.

"Gentlemen!" announced the duke. "This is none other than Her Highness the Princess Alexia Pyrogennetos, long-lost daughter of the Empress Irene and rightful heir to the Serpent Throne of Troy."

Bostro must've heard every trick, lie, excuse, and sob story you could imagine, but this one lifted even his eyebrows. He squinted at Alex as if someone had told him the turd he'd just watched squeezed from a goat's arse was actually a gold nugget.

All she could do was shrug her shoulders very high. She'd been called a scammer, a fleecer, a cheat, a thief, a bitch, a thieving bitch, a ferrety fuck, a lying weasel, and those were only the ones she'd taken as compliments. She'd never, far as she could remember, been called a princess. Not even in the least funny jest.

Shitty Teeth's face twisted so violently that even shittier teeth came into view towards the back. "She's fucking *what* now?"

Duke Michael considered Alex, hanging there like a cheap rug halfway through its annual beating. "I will admit she does not appear . . . *terribly* princessy. But she is what she is and we'll all have to live with it. I must therefore insist that you unhand her royal person."

"Unhand?" asked the would-be pirate.

"Let go of her." The duke's pleasant manner peeled back a touch and Alex caught a glimpse of something flinty underneath. "Now."

Bostro frowned. "Lying weasel owes our boss."

The pirate twisted a tooth from his bloody mouth. "Ferrety fuck knocked out one o' my teeth!"

"Shame." The duke raised his brows at the tooth. "It looks a really good one."

The man angrily tossed it away. "Well, I bloody liked it."

"I see you have suffered some inconvenience." Duke Michael reached into a pocket of his gold-threaded robe. "God knows, I am well aware how inconvenient princesses can be, *so* . . ." He held some coins up to the light. "Here is something . . ." He put a couple back, then tossed the rest onto the dirty cobbles. "For your trouble."

Bostro peered down, scarcely more impressed than he had been by the dirt in Alex's purse. "Thought she was a fucking princess?"

"When announced by a herald it is typically without the *fucking*, but yes."

"And that's what her life's worth?"

"Oh, no," said Duke Michael. His servant sank gracefully to one knee beside him, pulled open his coat, and produced a large sword, its stained sheath chased with shining wire, its battered gold pommel tilted towards his master. The duke rested one fingertip upon it. "That's what *your* lives are worth."

The Thirteenth Virtue

I ... am ..."

Brother Diaz let fall the hem of his habit, which he'd been obliged to gather up around his knees like a flustered bride arriving late to her wedding, his flapping footfalls echoing from mirror-polished marble as he scurried around the labyrinthine hallways of the Celestial Palace in ever greater extremes of sweaty panic.

"I ... am ..." He'd slipped on a patch of fresh saliva where a party of high-ranking penitents were licking the floor clean and thought he might have done himself a mischief around the groin area. It was all a very long way from the towering dignity with which he'd dreamed of sweeping through these hallowed halls to finally have his quality acknowledged. God, his head was spinning. Was he fainting? Was he dying?

"Brother Eduardo Diaz?" asked the immensely tall secretary.

The name sounded familiar. "I think so ..." He leaned on the desk with both fists, struggling to control his wheezing and appear worthy of a respectable post in the middle of the Church's hierarchy. "And I can only ... apologise ... for being late." He managed, with a heroic effort, to prevent himself from vomiting. "There was a damned gouty crowd out for Saint Aelfric's Day! And the driver—"

"You are early."

"—was no help whatsoever, and I—What?"

The secretary shrugged. "It's the Holy City, Brother Diaz. Every day is at least one saint's day, and everyone is always late. We shift all the appointments to allow for it."

Diaz sagged with relief. Sweet Saint Beatrix had come through for him after all! He might have dropped to his knees to weep his thanks on the spot, had he not feared he would never rise again.

"But never fear." The secretary clambered down from what must have been a very high stool and revealed herself to be surprisingly short. "Cardinal Zizka has cleared her schedule and asked that you be shown in the moment you arrived." And she gestured to a door with a showman's flourish.

A large man, craggy-faced and crooked-knuckled, sat on a bench beside it, perhaps awaiting his own interview. He sat with his grey eyes on Brother Diaz, in such perfect stillness it seemed the Celestial Palace might have been built around him. His clipped hair was iron-grey with two great scars through it, and his clipped beard was iron-grey with at least three scars through it, and his grey brows were more scar than brow. He looked like a man who had spent half a century falling down a mountain. Perhaps one made of axes.

"Wait," muttered Brother Diaz. "Cardinal Zizka?"

"Indeed."

"I understood I was meeting Her Holiness the Pope . . . to be assigned a benefice—"

"No."

Could it be that things were starting to look up? Her Holiness might be the Heart of the Church, but she assigned a thousand irrelevant positions, offices, and blessings to a queue of irrelevant priests, monks, and nuns every day, presumably with as little thought as a grape picker gives each grape.

A meeting with Cardinal Zizka, the Head of the Earthly Curia, was another matter entirely. She was undisputed mistress of the sprawling bureaucracy and colossal revenues of the Church. She only took note of the noteworthy. And she had *cleared her schedule* . . .

"Well, then . . ." Brother Diaz wiped sweat from his forehead, dabbed at his fat lip, tugged his skewed habit straight, and began to smile for the first time since he entered the gates of the Holy City. It was starting to look as if sweet Saint Beatrix might have positively *outdone* herself. "By all means announce me!"

Considering it represented the very pinnacle of ecclesiastical power, Cardinal Zizka's office was something of a disappointment. A huge space by the standards of a rural monk but made to feel positively cramped by dizzying piles of paperwork bristling with tassels, markers, and seals, deployed on benches to both sides with the precision of rival armies about to do battle. Brother Diaz had expected splendour—frescoes, velvet and marble with gilt cherubs crowded into every angle. But the furniture wedged into the strip of floor between those twin cliffs of bureaucracy might best have been described as dull and functional. The back wall was one blank expanse of stone, strangely rippled as if it had melted, flowed, then set in place, presumably some vestige of the ancient ruins on top of which the Celestial Palace was built. The only decoration was a small and rather violent painting of the Scourging of Saint Barnabas.

A first glance at Cardinal Zizka herself was honestly something of a disappointment, too. She was a sturdy woman with a shock of greyish hair, engaged in taking papers from a pile on her left, signing them in a disappointingly untidy hand, then adding them to a pile on her right. She appeared to have slung her golden chain of office over one of the prongs on the back of her chair, the front of her crimson vestment adorned instead with a scattering of crumbs.

Had it not been for the red cardinal's hat abandoned upside down on the desk, one could have taken this for the office of some junior clerk, engaged in a junior clerk's humdrum business. Still, as Brother Diaz's mother would have said, that was no excuse to let his own standards slip.

"Your Eminence," he intoned, delivering his best formal bow.

It was wasted on the cardinal, who did not so much as look up from her scratching quill. "Brother Diaz," she grated out. "How have you been enjoying the Holy City?"

"A place of . . ." He politely cleared his throat. "Remarkable spirituality?"

"Oh, without doubt. Where else can one buy a desiccated pizzle of Saint Eustace from three different stalls within a mile of one another?"

Brother Diaz was desperately unsure whether to treat that as a joke or a searing indictment, and ended up straining to do both by grinning and shaking his head at once while murmuring, "A miracle indeed . . ."

Fortunately, the cardinal had still not looked up. "Your abbott speaks very highly of you." He'd bloody better, after all the favours Brother Diaz had done him. "He says you are the most promising administrator his monastery has seen in years."

"He does me too much honour, Your Eminence." Brother Diaz licked his lips at the thought of bursting free from the smothering confines of that very monastery to claim all he deserved. "But I will strive to serve you, and Her Holiness, in whatever capacity you might desire, to the very limits—"

He jumped as the door was noisily shut behind him, spinning about to see the scarred grey man from the bench outside had followed him into the cardinal's office. Baring his battered teeth, he lowered himself into one of the hard chairs before her desk.

"To the very limits . . ." persevered Brother Diaz, uncertainly, "of my abilities . . ."

"That is a tremendous comfort." Her Eminence finally tossed down her quill, placed the latest document carefully on top of its heap, rubbed her inky forefinger against her inky thumb, and looked up.

Brother Diaz swallowed. Cardinal Zizka might have had the bland office, drab furniture, and stained fingers of a junior clerk, but her eyes were those of a dragon. A particularly formidable example that suffered no fools.

"This is Jakob of Thorn," she said, nodding at the newcomer. That chopping-block of a face had been troubling in the hallway, but thrust into Brother Diaz's private interview it was positively distressing. Rather in the same way that finding a beggar in your doorway would be merely distasteful, while finding one in your bed would be cause for considerable alarm.

"He is a Knight Templar in the sworn service of Her Holiness," said Cardinal Zizka, which was far from an explanation and even further from a comfort. "A man of long experience."

"*Long.*" The one word growled from the knight's immobile mouth like a handful of old gravel between new mill wheels.

"His guidance and advice, not to mention his sword, will be invaluable to you."

"His . . . sword?" Brother Diaz was no longer sure where this interview was taking him but did not at all care for the notion that he might need a sword when he got there.

Cardinal Zizka narrowed her eyes slightly. "We live in a world beset by perils," she said.

"We do?" asked Brother Diaz, and then, having considered it, changed the question into a sad observation. "We do." And finally to a grim assertion. "We *do*." Not personally, in his case, of course.

He lived in a small but actually—now he really thought about it—quite comfortable cell with a view of the sea, and a breeze washing through the windows that at this time of year was rich with the scent of juniper. He had a creeping suspicion the scent of juniper was not among the perils to which the cardinal was referring. That suspicion was all too soon confirmed.

"The Eastern and Western Churches are in schism." Her Eminence seemed to be glaring right through Brother Diaz's head into a distance crowded with threats.

"I understand the Fifteenth Grand Ecumenical Council did little to resolve the outstanding issues," lamented Brother Diaz, hoping to impress with his knowledge of current events and theology at once. He knew the Church of the East had male clergy, that they wore the wheel rather than the circle, that there was some furious row about the date of Easter, but he honestly had almost no understanding of what the deeper divisions were. Few did, these days.

"The many grasping princes of Europe ignore their holy duties and squabble with each other for earthly power."

Brother Diaz rolled his eyes piously to the ceiling. "They will all face judgement in the hereafter."

"I would prefer they faced it a great deal sooner," said Cardinal Zizka, with an edge on her voice that made the hairs on Diaz's arms prickle. "Meanwhile we are plagued by a veritable infestation of sundry monsters, imps, trolls, witches, sorcerers, and other practitioners of the many foul faces of Black Art."

Words temporarily failed him, so Brother Diaz contented himself with making the sign of the circle on his chest.

"Not to mention even more diabolical powers, plotting the ruin of creation from the eternal howling night beyond the world."

"*Demons*, Your Eminence?" whispered Brother Diaz, making the circle with even greater enthusiasm.

"And then, of course, there is the apocalyptic threat of the elves. They will not stay in the Holy Land forever. The enemies of God will boil out of the east again, bringing their unholy fire, and their unclean poison, and their *accursed appetites* with them."

"Damn them," croaked Brother Diaz, in danger of wearing a circle into the front of his habit. "Is it certain, Your Eminence?"

"The Oracles of the Celestial Choir have been consulted and leave no doubt. We live in a world sunk in darkness, in which our Church is the one point of light. The one hope of humanity. Can we that are righteous suffer that light to be extinguished?"

Here was an easy one. "Absolutely not, Your Eminence," said Brother Diaz, vigorously shaking his head.

"And in this battle of what can only be described as *good*, against what can only be described as *evil*, defeat is inconceivable."

"Absolutely so, Your Eminence," said Brother Diaz, vigorously nodding.

"With God's creation and every soul it contains at stake, restraint would be madness. Restraint would be craven dereliction of our holy duty. Restraint would be *sin*."

Brother Diaz had a creeping suspicion that he was somehow straying onto wobbly theological ground, like a clumsy bear chasing rabbits onto a half-frozen lake. "Well . . ."

"A time comes when the stakes are of such enormity that moral objections become themselves immoral."

"Do they? I mean—they do? That is—they *do*. Do they?"

Cardinal Zizka smiled. A smile somehow more troubling even than her frown. "Are you familiar with the Chapel of the Holy Expediency?"

"I . . . don't think that I—"

"It is one of the thirteen chapels within the Celestial Palace. One of the oldest, indeed. As old as the Church itself."

"I understood there to be twelve chapels, one for each of the Twelve Virtues—"

"It is sometimes necessary to draw a curtain over certain regrettable facts. But here, at the very heart of the Church, we must look beyond the mere *appearance* of virtue. We must tackle the world as it is, with the tools available."

Was this some kind of test? God, Brother Diaz hoped so. But if it was, he hadn't the slightest idea how to pass. "I . . . er . . ."

"The Church must, of course, remain faithful to the teachings of our Saviour. But there are tasks that must be undertaken, and methods used, to which the faithful and unimpeachable . . . are not suited."

Brother Diaz supposed, if you really squinted, you could make that argument, but he didn't want to be anywhere near it himself. He glanced towards Jakob of Thorn, but found no help there whatsoever. He looked like a man whose methods were *deeply* impeachable. "I'm not sure I entirely follow—"

"Those tasks are undertaken, and those methods used, by the congregation of the Chapel of the Holy Expediency."

"By the congregation?"

"Under the direction of its vicar." And Zizka raised her brows significantly.

Brother Diaz was helpless to prevent his own rising to match. He touched one hesitant fingertip to his chest.

"Her Holiness has selected you for this honour. Baptiste will introduce you to your charges."

Brother Diaz spun about for the second time to find a woman leaning against the wall behind him, arms folded. He couldn't have said whether she'd slipped in silently or been standing there the whole time and didn't care for either possibility. Her origin was hard to place—one of the many shores of the Mediterranean was his closest guess—and she struck him as being every bit as much trouble as Jakob of Thorn, but of an opposite sort. Her clothing was as flamboyant as his was dowdy, her broad face as expressive as his was stern. She, too, had scars. One across her lips. One beneath the corner of her eye, which made him think of a teardrop, strangely at odds with the amused quirk constantly hovering at the corner of her mouth.

She swept off a gold-fringed hat and bowed low enough that her mop of dark curls brushed the tiles, then leaned back with one gold-buckled boot crossed over the other in a display of nonchalance that seemed positively offensive in light of Brother Diaz's own mounting panic.

"Is she . . . one of my flock?" he stammered.

That quirk became a grin. "Baaaaaa," she said.

"Baptiste is what one might call, within the unique context of the chapel . . ." Cardinal Zizka paused for a moment, considering her. "A lay minister?"

Jakob of Thorn made a strange snort. Had it emerged from any other face, Brother Diaz might have considered it a chuckle.

"Living in a nunnery for a few weeks is as close as I ever came to being ordained." Baptiste struggled to wedge her unruly hair back into her hat, leaving several stray curls dangling. "It didn't suit the nuns, but they needed the money."

"The nuns?" asked Brother Diaz.

"Nuns have to drink, Brother, like anyone else. Perhaps a bit more. It's been my *honour* to assist several former vicars of the chapel, including your predecessor."

"Assist how?" asked Brother Diaz, rather dreading the answer.

Baptiste's grin became a smile. Behind the scar across her mouth she had two gold teeth, top and bottom. "However was expedient."

"You seem perplexed," said Her Eminence.

Perplexed was the very least of it. Brother Diaz wasn't sure what he'd got into, still less how, but he was developing a strong sense that he wanted to get out of it, and if he didn't do it soon, it would be too late. "Well, you know . . . my thing is really . . . mostly . . . bureaucracy?" That windowless expanse of stone behind Cardinal Zizka was developing the look of a prison cell. "I reorganised the books. In the library. At the monastery. That was my big . . . contribution." He wrestled to minimise the very accomplishments he had spent months outrageously inflating. "Accounts. Paperwork. Bit of negotiation over grazing rights and so forth. Inky fingers." He chuckled, but no one else did, and his laughter died a death almost as painful as that of Saint Barnabas, in his plain frame on the wall. "So, erm . . ." he waved towards Jakob of Thorn, "*knights*, and . . ." he gestured towards Baptiste, "er . . ." then realised he had no idea what to call her and gave up, "and *devils* in the howling night beyond the world . . ."

"Yes?" asked Cardinal Zizka, with signs of growing impatience.

"It all comes across as a little . . . outside my experience?"

"Did Saint Evariste have experience when at fifteen years old she took up her father's spear and led the Third Crusade against the elves?"

"But didn't she end up getting . . . a little bit . . ." Brother Diaz winced. "Eaten alive?"

The cardinal's brow wrinkled. "We are at war for our very existence against merciless enemies. To win a war, one must, sometimes, make use of the weapons of one's enemies. To fight fire, one must be prepared to use fire."

Brother Diaz's wince grew even more twisted. "But wouldn't it follow, Your Eminence, that to fight devils . . . one must be prepared . . . to *use* devils?"

Jakob of Thorn rocked his weight forwards, bared his teeth, and stiffly stood. "You see it," he said.

"This is an enormous opportunity. For your own advancement. For the advancement of the interests of the Church. But most importantly . . ." Cardinal Zizka rose, plucking her chain from the back of her chair and slinging it skewed around her shoulders, the jewelled circle swinging back and forth. "To do *good*." And she jammed her hat on, indicating beyond doubt or hope that the interview was concluded and its outcome irreversible. "Isn't that why we all join the Church?"

Brother Diaz's mother had made him join the Church to spare his family further embarrassment. But he somehow doubted that was what the Head of the Earthly Curia wanted to hear. And if there was one thing that was *within* Brother Diaz's experience, it was telling people what they wanted to hear.

"Of course," he said, managing a watery smile. "To do *good*."

Whatever the hell that meant.

This Much Luck

A lex stood by the window, a cool breeze on her cheek and a warm fire at her back, rubbing her bandaged knuckles and looking down on the Holy City.

Way above it, rather'n crushed in its guts, it seemed a different place. A beautiful place, even. Gardens and pale palaces on the hilltops, with statues of angels on their gables. Grand streets and tall houses on the slopes, dozens of church spires and shrines capped with the Circle of the Faith. All dissolving into a haphazard maze of slum roofs in the valleys, shining wet from a chilly sleet that just stopped falling. You could see the ruins the city was built on, built around, built out of—towering blocks, shapeless blobs, tumbledown walls heavy with creeper, remnants of a fallen empire poking from the mass like the bones of a giant carcass. The Pale Sisters stuck up like fingers, two crumbling columns left over from a vast temple, on top of which some canny set of priests had built two rival bell towers, soaring high over the city and clanging away at each other at every prayer time like twin babies screaming for Mummy's attention.

From up here, you'd never have guessed the strife and struggle going on in their long shadows, where you'd as much chance of feeling a fresh breeze as an elf of feeling heaven. The human rubbish crawling all over each other like ants in an anthill. The lying and hustle and hurt to get one step ahead. Snatches of hymns and hawkers' cries drifted up, feeble on the cold wind, clamour of faith and fury dulled by distance, like none of it was much of her concern any more.

A set of nuns had bathed her, scrubbed her, wrapped her in a robe with the faces of saints stitched in silver, fur on the collar so warm against her cheek it made her want to cry. She hardly knew her own face in the mirror. Hardly knew her own hands with the dirt scraped from under the bitten-down nails. She doubted she'd ever been this clean before and wasn't sure she liked it, kept being ambushed by the feel of her own hair, now they'd cut out the thousand tangles and combed it till it shone.

They'd left the comb behind. Silver, with amber in the handle. She kept wondering what Gal the Purse might've priced it at, and how much more it was really worth. Her hand kept creeping towards it, one finger *tap, tap, tapping* at the windowsill. Wouldn't have been theft in her book, just picking up what was thrown away.

If you don't want your comb stolen, you shouldn't leave it alone with a thief—

Knock, knock at the door and she jerked her hand back, heart suddenly pounding, desperate to slither out the window and down a drainpipe, frantic voice in her head shrieking that she was the mark in some con and would soon enough be suffering for it.

But there was a colder, softer voice, too, whispering that she might squeeze more out of this than a nice comb. A *lot* more. All she had to do was sell a lie, and wasn't she a liar? She'd played so many parts she hardly knew which one was her. She was an onion made of only skins with nothing at the centre.

So she dragged in a slow breath, and unclenched her fists, and tried to wriggle free of her usual cringe and look like she deserved to be there. She tried to coo, "Come in," the way a princess might, but she ended up hooting the *come* then going too far the other way for the *in* so she sounded like a pigeon turning into a hog and was wincing at her own blunder as the door opened.

It was her unlikely saviour, the self-styled Duke Michael. He had an awkward smile, like he didn't quite trust her, which showed good judgement as she was a treacherous rat, ask anyone.

"Well," he said, "isn't that better?"

She pushed a strand of hair behind her ear in a way that aimed at winsome, but she hardly knew what *winsome* meant, let alone what it looked like. "Got the fish out of my hair," she said.

"They're treating you well?"

"Better'n those three bastards in the market. You should've killed 'em and kept the money." Or better yet, given it to her.

"The Almighty tends against killing," said Duke Michael, "if I remember my scripture."

"Far as I can tell he makes all manner of exceptions."

"God has that luxury, he's unlikely to get knifed in a fish market."

"You had a sword."

"If I've learned one thing in all my years of using one, it's that men with swords die every bit as easily as other men, and usually much sooner. Besides, I couldn't risk Eusebius. New dukes can be made with a word, but good servants are rare treasures. May I come in?"

Alex wasn't sure she'd ever been asked that before. Never had a place of her own. That and the folk she dealt with didn't tend to be the permission-asking sort. So she enjoyed the little pause before giving a haughty toss of the head and saying, "You may."

"I expect you have . . . some questions." Duke Michael eased himself into the room.

"One or two." She fixed his eye, businesslike. "First off, is all this a sex thing?"

He burst out laughing. "No. God, no. By no means."

"All right. Good." She tried not to show her relief. No need to discuss the terms she'd been considering if it *had* been a sex thing.

"I'm your uncle, Alex. I've been searching for you for a long time." He took a step closer. "You're safe now."

"Safe," she muttered, having to stop herself taking a step away. She was even less sure what to do with *safe* than she was with *may I come in*. Her rich uncle, popped out of nowhere to tell her how special she was. Too good to be true hardly seemed to cover it. "Are you really a duke?"

"I am, though . . . without a dukedom, for the time being."

"Bit careless. Losing a dukedom."

"It was stolen." He took another step towards her. "Do you know anything about the politics of the Empire of the East?"

She could've given him a solid rundown of the politics of the slums, but the Empire of the East had always seemed a long way off. "There may be a few gaps in my schooling . . ."

"You've heard of the Empress Theodosia the Blessed?"

"Obviously," lied Alex.

"She had three children. Irene, Eudoxia, and . . . me."

"Your mother was an Empress?"

"Your *grand*mother was an Empress. A great one. When she died, my elder sister Irene should have been crowned, but my younger sister Eudoxia . . ." he turned his face away, his voice cracking, ". . . Eudoxia murdered her and usurped the throne. There was a civil war." He stared into the fire, shaking his head like it was heavy with regrets. "There was war, and famine, and schism between the Churches of East and West, and the great fortress city of Troy rotted from the inside. Irene's servants spirited her infant daughter away to the Holy City, to the Pope's protection. But she was lost on the way. Killed, I believed, for a long time." He looked up at Alex. "Her name was Alexia."

"And you think . . . that's me?"

"I *know* it. There is the birthmark on your neck, and the chain you wear . . ." And he pointed to a few links showing inside that fine fur collar.

She pulled her gown tight over it. "It's not worth anything."

"You're wrong. Is there, by any chance, half a coin on it?"

Ever so slowly, she pulled it out. The bright half-disc of copper dangled on the end, polished smooth by years against her skin, its zigzag clipped edge glinting. "How did you know?"

He reached into his collar and pulled out a chain of his own, and she stared as she saw, dangling on the end, another half-coin. He came closer to hold his up to hers, and Alex felt all the hairs on her neck stand up as she saw the ragged edges were a perfect match. One coin.

"You were given this the day you left Troy. So there could be no doubt who you were. But I knew the moment I saw you." He smiled, and the awkwardness had faded, and it was so warm and open he almost had her believing. "Even with fish in your hair and a fist around your throat. You look *just* like your mother."

"I . . ." Alex swallowed. "I don't remember her—"

"She was the best of us. Always so brave. So *certain*." And he took her good hand and her bandaged one and held them in his. Big, strong hands he had, and warm, and once she'd smothered the instinct to wrench herself free, there was something weirdly reassuring about their touch.

"Look," she grunted, "I don't know anything . . . about being a princess—"

"All I want," he said, "is for you . . . to be you."

Alex very much doubted he'd have said that if he'd known her better. But Gal the Purse always said, *Don't interrupt the mark when they're making a mistake*, and he was frowning down at the floor now, so she let him keep talking.

"I learned a few weeks ago that my sister Eudoxia is dead. To no one's great sorrow. Some say poison. Some say an experiment gone awry . . . a last act of sorcerous hubris . . ."

"Sorcerous?" muttered Alex, doubtfully.

"Whatever the cause, her throne is empty!" Michael's eyes flicked back up and met hers. "It's time for you to return."

Her brows had gone even higher. "To a throne?"

"The Serpent Throne of Troy."

At their first meeting he'd declared her a princess. At their second he was putting Empress on the table. At this rate she'd be an angel by teatime and a goddess by nightfall.

"I can't wait for you to *see* it, Alex!" he said, eyes shining. "The Pillar—raised by the Witch Engineers of ancient Carthage—towers over the city, casting the whole harbour into its shadow! At its top, the famous Hanging Gardens, more beautiful than you can dream of, watered by mountain springs carried down the Grand Aqueduct."

He took her by one shoulder, holding out the other hand as though the view was spread before them.

"The Basilica of the Angelic Visitation rises over the greenery, crowded with pilgrims come to view the relics of the grand crusades! And the palace, too, the Pharos above all, the greatest lighthouse in Europe, at its top Saint Natalia's Flame, shining like a star, guiding the sons and daughters of Troy home!" He turned to her, catching her by the other shoulder, holding her at arms' length. "*Our* home, Alex!"

She blinked up at him. Her every instinct—learned several different hard ways down the years—was to treat everything as a lie, and had there ever been a more laughable set of clangers than this?

And yet here she was. In the Celestial Palace. Warm for the first time in weeks. With a comb worth more than her hands. In a robe worth more than her head. And there was something so damn *plausible* about this bastard. She was starting to think he might be who he said he was. She was almost starting to think *she* might be who he said she was.

Duke Michael seemed to remember himself and pulled his hands away. "I know this must be . . . a lot to take in. I know it must be frightening. But I will be with you, every step along the path."

"I never had . . . any family . . ." She hardly knew whether she was telling the truth or playing a part any more. Probably just as well. That's where you find the best lies.

"I'm so sorry, Alex. That it took me so long to find you. For many years . . . I gave up hope. Let me put it right. Let me help you now." He had some damp in his eyes, so she reckoned it'd suit her to do the same. She never had to search far for some sad memories.

"I can try." She sniffed, and blinked back tears, and put on a shy little smile, and was quite pleased with her performance.

"That's all I can ask." He wiped his eyes on his wrist. "There's so much to do. You must meet Cardinal Zizka! She can help us. Soon, Alex, we'll be back where we belong!"

And he smiled, without a hint of awkwardness now, and stepped away, shutting the door behind him.

Alex had been told where she belonged a few times. In prison. In a sewer. In a shallow grave. In hell, depending who you asked. This much luck had to have a razor hidden in it somewhere, but what were her choices?

She owed Papa Collini twice what she was worth, if you were very generous about what she was worth, and that wasn't even her only debt. She'd borrowed money from the Queen of Clubs at ruinous interest so she could cheat at cards against Little Suze, but Suze had turned out to be a better cheat than Alex, so she'd come out owing Suze, too, who'd cut her nose off for it, *and* the Queen of Clubs, who'd take her kneecaps off for it, *and* still owing Papa Collini, who'd take some teeth and fingers, and *then*—when he found out about the other two debts—likely her eyes into the bargain.

Many thanks, but fuck that.

Whatever her doubts about this whole princess business, it had come along at the perfect time. She'd play the part, and get what could be got, and when it started to look like trouble, she could ditch her so-called uncle somewhere on the crooked road to Troy and find some new name to wear and some new place to settle.

You have to treat people like oranges, Gal the Purse always said. *Squeeze what you can from the bastards, then waste no regrets when you toss away their wrung-out skins*. You have to treat people like stepping stones. Like rungs on your ladder. Or you'll wake up one day with nothing but a set of bootprints on your own back.

Alex couldn't stop the smile spreading across her face. Been a while since she'd tried one on and she liked how it felt. She was starting to think Duke Michael might be a stepping stone to somewhere very sweet. She wasn't sure where, exactly. Been a while since she looked too far past the next meal. But she'd work it out as she went. She was a quick thinker, ask anyone.

She propped her elbows on the sill, cool breeze on her cheek and warm fire at her back, and grinned towards the slums. You could just see people down there, if you really squinted. But they were so far below. She couldn't help rubbing that lovely fur against her face again, and giving a little giggle.

Then she slipped that comb up her sleeve.

Best to be on the safe side.

A Flock of Black Sheep

Brother Diaz turned slowly around, head tipped back and mouth hanging open, dizzy with awe.

"It's so beautiful . . ."

The Chapel of the Holy Expediency might have been four times as high as it was wide, an echoing well of varicoloured marble lit by angelic shafts from a cupola high above. Carved niches held sculptures of the Twelfth Virtues in human form, the walls crowded with paintings of the seventy-seven senior saints and a dizzying assortment of junior ones. There was a porphyry pulpit that wouldn't have been a disappointing centrepiece for a cathedral, a gem-studded copy of the scriptures open on the lectern.

His lectern, he realised, awe beginning to melt under a warming glow of satisfaction. *His* pulpit in *his* chapel. He'd never been much of a preacher, admittedly. But in a place like this? He would make do.

"It *is* beautiful." Baptiste draped an overfamiliar arm around his shoulders and pointed out a painting. "That Saint Stefan is by Havarazza."

"Really?"

"I knew him, in fact."

"Saint Stefan?"

"Havarazza." Baptiste modestly flicked a stray curl from her face and it immediately flopped back. "He painted me once."

"He did?"

"I was between jobs at the time, serving as a lady-in-waiting to the Queen of Sicily."

"You . . . what?"

"He was painting her during the days. I modelled for him in the evenings." She leaned close to whisper, "He wanted to do it nude."

"Er . . ."

"But I insisted he keep his clothes on!" Baptiste burst out laughing, then her laughter became a chuckle, and the chuckle petered out into awkward silence. She dabbed her eyes. "He died of syphilis."

"Havarazza did?"

"And the Queen of Sicily soon after. Make of that what you will. I think the Duke of Milan has that painting."

"Of the Queen of Sicily?"

"No, the one of me. He was a lovely man."

"The Duke of Milan?"

"Ugh, no. He's an absolute turd. I meant Havarazza." She considered that painting of Saint Stefan, smiling beatifically as toothy elves squashed his balls with red-hot tongs. "One of those truly pure souls you find now and again."

"I am . . . so sorry to hear that. About his death, that is, not his pure soul . . ." Brother Diaz took the opportunity to slither from under Baptiste's arm. He hadn't been in such close contact with a woman for many years, and the outcome then had been far from a happy one. He placed a fond hand on one of several dozen giant votive candles, twice his height at least and thick as a tree trunk, wondering what it must have cost. He'd scored an unsung triumph negotiating a new contract with the chandler on his monastery's behalf, so had a reasonable idea. "It really is a *beautiful* chapel . . ."

Pride was not numbered among the Twelve Virtues, but after being left to pickle in shame for so long he couldn't help picturing the faces of his so-called brothers in the refectory when they heard the news. Vicar? Of an opulent and exclusive chapel? *Inside* the *Celestial Palace*? He imagined the monstrous scale of his mother's boasting, the petty achievements of his actual brothers cast aside, the dishes passed first to him before they squabbled over the scraps—

The grating voice of Jakob of Thorn cut his daydreams off at the knee. "We won't be spending much time here."

"We won't?"

The knight had one hand under the lectern, wincing as he searched for something. There was a clunk, a grinding of gears, and the pulpit slid aside to reveal a hidden stairway, disappearing downwards.

"Your flock are below."

Brother Diaz swallowed as he peered into the inky darkness under the chapel, Cardinal Zizka's mention of the howling night beyond creation making the hairs on his neck prickle. "Why below?"

"Partly for their protection."

"Mostly for everyone else's," said Baptiste, taking up a candelabrum with three flickering candles.

It was while following her downwards that Brother Diaz noticed all the daggers about her person. One could hardly miss the huge one strapped to her right thigh, and the only slightly smaller one buckled to her left, but now he noticed a curved one in the back of her belt, and the telltale glint of a pommel in the top of one tall boot, and, Sweet Saint Beatrix, *two* in her other boot.

"You have a very great number of knives," he murmured.

"I've found it's a bad idea to run out." The candles gave her eyes a playful gleam quite at odds with the subject matter. "How could I stab anyone then?"

"Do you stab people . . . often?"

"I try to keep it to a minimum. Never stick your neck out, that's my motto." She sighed. "But a life well lived will, perforce, feature some regrets."

"Perforce," murmured Brother Diaz, pointlessly. Behind him, Jakob of Thorn made the slightest pained grunt with each scraping footfall.

The walls changed as they descended. Dressed masonry gave way to the carelessly mortared brick of the foundations, which gave way to that strangely seamless grey stone, like the back wall of Zizka's office, the candlelight throwing odd shadows from its humps and waves. Brother Diaz reached out, brushed it lightly with his fingertips. Very smooth, and very hard, and very cold.

"The remains of the ancient city," said Jakob of Thorn.

"Not much left above ground," tossed Baptiste over her shoulder, "but there are miles of tunnels below. No one knows how deep they go. All built by the Witch Engineers of Carthage."

Brother Diaz snatched his fingertips away, touched them nervously to the lump in his habit made by the vial of Saint Beatrix. He couldn't escape the irrational sensation that he was descending into the guts of a monster.

"Ironic, really." Baptiste chuckled. "Long before it was the Holy City, it was . . . well . . ." The light from her candelabrum fell on a weighty door, studded with iron, apparently scorched by flame and deeply carved with several interlocking circles of runes. "An unholy city?" And Baptiste grinned over her shoulder as she rapped on it with her knuckles.

Brother Diaz steeled himself for unknown horrors as locks rattled and the door swung open—but beyond there was only a storeroom containing a fireplace and cookpot, several crates and barrels, shelves holding crockery and cutlery, and a huge bald man with a whale-oil lamp.

Baptiste frowned towards another door, still heavier and more rune-scored than the last. "All quiet?"

"The wizard complained about his food," said the big man, in a thick accent, as he sat back down at a table and picked up a very small book. "But otherwise yes. This our new priest?"

"Brother Diaz," grunted Jakob.

"Ah, a Castillian?"

"Leonese . . ." Though insisting on the distinction seemed absurd under the circumstances.

"Good to meet you. I'm Hobb. I look after the devils."

Brother Diaz swallowed. "The what?"

"Didn't Cardinal Zizka give you the talk?"

"She gave him the talk," said Jakob of Thorn.

"They're not really devils." Baptiste had gone to a long rack from which dangled at least a dozen bunches of heavy keys. "Not *technically*."

"You have a very great number of keys," murmured Brother Diaz.

"Well, Brother," replied Baptiste as she plucked down one ring and began to sort through it, "we need a very great number of locks."

Hobb laughed. "You'll be fine. Just . . . stay back from the bars."

"From the what?" muttered Brother Diaz, watching Baptiste tackle one lock after another.

"Stay back from the bars, keep on your toes, trust nothing they say, and I'm sure you'll fare better than your predecessor."

"What?"

"That's the spirit," said Hobb, planting one boot on the table and turning his attention to his book. "And don't stick your neck out, eh, Baptiste?"

"Never." Baptiste finally slid back two hefty bolts and shouldered the second door open, a faint breath of cool air issuing from beyond.

"He looks after the devils," said Brother Diaz, in a kind of whimper.

"But he's from England." Jakob of Thorn ushered him over the threshold. "They're all devils there."

A hallway stretched off into the gloom, walls and ceiling a single semicircular vault of that melted-looking rock. The only light came from three ominously flickering candles in rusted sconces, falling on a set of archways in the left-hand wall. It might almost have felt like a wine cellar, had it not been for the grilles blocking the openings, bars of black iron thick as Brother Diaz's wrist, well secured with yet more heavy locks.

He swallowed. "Are these . . . cells?" Ancient ones, by the look of it. "What kind of prisoners did the Witch Engineers of Carthage keep?"

"The righteous?" Baptiste shrugged. "Or the *really* unrighteous?"

"Those they hated," said Jakob. "Those they feared."

"And those they failed to *understand*." There was a scraping of chains from the nearest cell. "And little has changed in *that* regard." A man shuffled from the shadows. "New *jailers*, perhaps . . ." He was an imposing figure, perhaps a patrician of northern Afrique, his black hair and beard shot with grey. "But petty injustice, hypocrisy, and oppression are *eternal*." His air of outraged dignity was undermined by two facts impossible to ignore: his ankles were fettered by a heavy chain of black iron, and he was entirely naked.

Baptiste leaned casually against the archway. "Might I introduce the most recent addition to our little family. His name is Balthazar . . ." She squinted at the ceiling, jingling her keyring on a fingertip. "I forget the rest of it."

"Balthazar Sham Ivam Draxi." The man flared his nostrils magnificently. "And it is a name that shall resound through *history*!"

"Bit lengthy for an echo, isn't it?" said Baptiste, giving Brother Diaz a wink. "These sorcerers and their names—"

"I am a *magician*, fool."

"Oh, I'm a dunce and you're a genius." Baptiste smiled wider, gold teeth glinting. "That's why you're naked in a cage and I'm holding the key."

"Laugh while you can!" The magician pressed his face to the bars and obliged Brother Diaz to take a cautious step back. "But no chain can restrain me! No spell can bind me! I shall free myself, and when I do my vengeance shall be the stuff of *legend*!"

He shook his fist as he worked himself to ever greater heights of outrage, and whenever he did his prick would swing about, and though Brother Diaz had no desire to see it, he somehow couldn't stop looking at it, and had to hold up a hand to shield his eyes. "*Must* he be naked?"

"He was scraping dirt from the corners of his cell and using it to write on his shirt," said Baptiste.

"Would writing have been bad?"

"It could've been *very* bad," said Jakob.

"He is an infamous practitioner of Black Art," said Baptiste, "pursued by the Witch Hunters for nine years and found guilty as hell by the Celestial Court."

"Don't they tend to . . . a little bit . . ." Brother Diaz cleared his throat, "burn people for that?"

"On rare occasions they are given a chance at redemption through a lifetime of service to Her Holiness."

"Redemption?" snarled Balthazar Sham Ivam Draxi. "Ha! The distinction between Black Art and White is a patent *artifice*, born of wilful *ignorance*. They are drawn from one well. They even emerge in the same bucket! Then you blockheads dip in two cups and declare what suits your petty prejudices *White* and what defies your pitiful understanding *Black* when in fact they are one and the same—"

"There was the matter of the dancing corpses," grated Jakob of Thorn.

"And the bargaining with demons," added Baptiste.

Balthazar threw up his hands. "You bargain with *one* demon and that's all anyone talks about!"

"I need to sit down," muttered Brother Diaz, but there was no chair on offer.

The next cell was neatly furnished with a narrow bed well made, two faded rugs, and a shelf stacked with books, including a fine copy of the scriptures. But there appeared to be no one in it.

"Sunny?" Baptiste tapped at the bars with a man's signet ring she wore. "You can come out."

She didn't jump from the shadows or wink suddenly into substance. She must've been standing there, in full view. But, for no reason Brother Diaz could explain, it was only when she turned towards him, breathing out with a long sigh, that he noticed her.

One could not possibly have overlooked that face otherwise. It was recognisably female, dusted with very ordinary freckles, but resembled a face reflected in a carnival mirror: impossibly narrow across the jaw and impossibly wide across the sharp cheeks, the nose far too small and the unblinking eyes far, far too big.

"Saviour protect us," he breathed, making the sign of the circle over his chest. As if the magician hadn't been bad enough. "It's an elf."

She stepped forwards, long fingers curling spider-like about the bars. "New priest?" One might have expected an enemy of God to speak with a devilish hiss. The elf's flat, high, normal little voice was quite the anticlimax.

"This is Brother Diaz," said Jakob of Thorn.

The elf studied him, unblinking as a lizard. "Charmed," she said, and was no longer there.

"Why . . ." whispered Brother Diaz, his throat so tight he could hardly make the words, "is there an elf under the Celestial Palace?"

Baptiste waved towards the next set of bars. "For the same reason there's a vampire under the Celestial Palace."

This cell contained the most ancient-looking man Brother Diaz had ever seen. His body was hunched, face a withered mask, neck a flopping wattle, a few floating wisps clinging to his wrinkled pate. But his voice was rich with culture and refinement.

"To undertake the labours," he said, "that those upstairs will not contemplate. I am Baron Rikard, and I can only apologise for my wretched decrepitude." He glanced towards the walking stick on which he leaned with one crooked, trembling hand. "I would bow but, with the stiffness in my back, I fear I might never rise . . ."

"Pray don't trouble yourself!" Brother Diaz had never met a baron, had no notion where he might rank in Europe's labyrinthine aristocracy, but felt the need to be on his very best behaviour. "It is my honour to—"

As he stepped towards the bars, Jakob of Thorn held out an arm to stop him. "Best keep your distance."

"You have no doubt already realised that Jakob can be *exceedingly* tiresome." The baron hobbled closer, flashing a smile. He had superb teeth for a man of his age, so pearly white and delicately pointed, Brother Diaz yearned to inspect them more closely. "I cannot tell you how desperately I am in need of good conversation, not to mention spiritual instruction. Your predecessor was no use whatever in such matters—"

Jakob of Thorn's grating voice cut in. "Don't get too close to the bars." Brother Diaz was surprised to see that, almost without noticing, he had taken another step towards the cage.

"Honestly, Jakob, few people are more keenly aware than you how much blood a healthy young man contains. We all know he can spare a pint or two, eh, Brother Diaz?" His eye had a playful sparkle and Diaz could not but chuckle. What a spirited and amusing old gent he was! How proud his mother would be, to learn he had a friend of such status! Whyever should he be kept in a cage? He had half a mind to wrestle the keys from Baptiste and unlock the gate—

Jakob's voice was a warning bark. "Step back from the cage!"

Brother Diaz found, to his amazement, that he had stepped right up to the grille and was on the point of slipping his arm between the bars, right beside the baron's withered face. He snatched it back as if from a blazing fire.

Baron Rikard curled his tongue around one pointed tooth and dragged it away with a disappointed sucking. "Well, you can't blame a boy for trying."

"Did you ensorcel me just now?" demanded Brother Diaz, gripping one hand to his chest with the other. "Was that ensorcelment?"

"Manners might seem like magic in this company," grunted the vampire. "The two are not so far apart as some would prefer to believe. Rather like good and evil, in that regard."

Brother Diaz gave an outraged gasp. "We can probably agree that feasting on the blood of innocents is on the evil side of the line!"

"I will bow to your expertise. Or would if my back permitted." The baron gave a papery sigh as he turned away. "If vampires made sound moral judgements, after all . . . why would the world need priests?"

The next cell contained only dirty straw, a bucket, several sets of rather worrying scratches, and an animal odour that reminded Brother Diaz of a visit he once made, and instantly regretted, to a slaughterhouse in Aviles.

"We had to place the last of our flock in more secure lodgings due to . . ." Baptiste scratched her throat as if searching for the right words, which in someone who produced as many as her did not strike him as a good sign.

"Unacceptable behaviour," said Jakob.

"To put it *very* mildly. Sometimes we have more charges, sometimes fewer. The tasks assigned to the Chapel of the Holy Expediency lead to a certain . . ."

"Churn," said Jakob.

Brother Diaz had no words. Honestly, he was finding it difficult to breathe down here. He was feeling dizzy. As if the ground might suddenly fall away. He struggled to loosen his collar once again. All he'd wanted was a comfortable living, somewhere sunny. To be taken seriously by the frivolous, regarded as wise by the unwise, and considered important by the unimportant. Instead, for reasons he couldn't comprehend, he found himself called on to consort with scarred knights and part-time painter's models, to face unspecified perils dire enough to threaten creation, all while not getting too close to the cages in which his congregation were kept.

"I spent many years in a monastery," he almost whined, at no one in particular. "Away from everything, in the library, mostly, and a bit of work on the accounts, some weeding in the herb garden . . ." God help him, he was starting to wish he was still there. "I really have . . . no experience with . . ." Brother Diaz's gesture encompassed the Witch Engineers' dungeon housing the naked magician, the vanishing elf, the geriatric vampire, and whatever had been too badly behaved to be kept in such company. "All *this*."

"Your predecessor had experience," said Jakob of Thorn.

"No one more," said Baptiste, sadly swinging her keys around one fingertip.

"What became of them?" asked Brother Diaz, desperate for a glint of light at the end of what was starting to seem a very dark tunnel. "Some new assignment?"

Baptiste winced. "Mother Ferrara was a very . . . *rigid* woman. Full of faith. Full of zeal."

"Huh," grunted Jakob.

"But rigid things are prone . . . under extremes of pressure . . . to shatter."

"Extremes," echoed Brother Diaz, "of pressure?"

"You see it." Baptiste placed a hand on his shoulder. If it was meant to reassure him, it failed spectacularly. "The Chapel of the Holy Expediency is no place to get . . . all dogmatic."

"Hmm," grunted Jakob.

"In my experience—and my experience, did I mention . . ." Baptiste slid her arm across Brother Diaz's shoulders in an unsolicited embrace, the grip of one of her many knives poking him in the side, ". . . is *considerable*—if you treat everything like a fight you will, sooner or later, and probably sooner . . ."

"Lose one," growled Jakob, glaring off grimly into the shadows.

Brother Diaz cleared his throat. He never used to need to clear his throat, but lately he was having to do it before every sentence. "I wouldn't presume to challenge the breadth of your experience—"

"Then we'll get along famously!" said Baptiste.

"—but you don't seem to have explained what, specifically, *became* of my predecessor."

Jakob turned his grey eyes back to Brother Diaz, as if only now remembering he was there. "She's dead." And he started to limp back the way they'd come.

"Dead?" whispered Brother Diaz.

"As *fuck*." Baptiste gave his shoulders a parting squeeze. "She's dead as fuck."

Born in the Flame

N o one has doubts," said Cardinal Bock, who was tall and kindly but seemed always to have her mind on other things. "What was her name?"

"Alex," said Duke Michael.

"No one has doubts, Alex."

It wasn't quite true to say no one had doubts. Alex had massive ones. She was nothing but doubts. Any moment now they'd realise that instead of a long-lost princess they'd found themselves a piece of shit. But Gal the Purse always said, *Never give up the lie*. Admit the truth, you're fucked. Cling to the lie, you never know. Lie all the way to the scaffold, lie with the rope around your neck, let them bury your lying corpse still sticking to its story. *The truth is a luxury the likes of you can never afford.*

"There is your half-coin," said Cardinal Bock, leading the way through the chilly maze of the Celestial Palace at a hell of a pace, "and your birthmark, and your uncle is entirely convinced—"

"Entirely," said Duke Michael, giving Alex a grin she was quite grateful for.

"—so no one *here* has doubts, but when you get to Troy . . . *if* you get to Troy . . . they'll want to be absolutely sure. I mean, one can understand it. You're not inheriting granny's cheese shop, are you?"

"No," said Alex, with a slightly wistful chuckle. Cheese shop would've been nice. She reckoned she could handle a cheese shop. That was about the right level of responsibility.

"So it's just that extra little *certainty*. Just the icing on the bun." Bock thoughtfully patted her stomach, then glanced towards one of the silent priests hurrying after them. "Sister Stefanu, could you make a note to go out and fetch me a bun? I've given myself a hankering. Anyone else? Bun?" Alex had a policy of never turning down food, but before she could say yes Cardinal Bock stopped dead before a hefty door flanked by armoured guards. "And here we are."

She began to wave her hand around. "*Azul saz karga* with this rod this oil this will this word I sanctify the portal. *Droz nox karga* I shall permit no unclean thought to pass amen. Locks, please."

Each of the guards turned a wheel and there was a grinding as toothed bars slid back. Funny, to have the mechanism on the outside. Like it was made to keep something *in*. The door opened with a hiss of escaping air and Bock stepped through. Alex didn't care for magic one bit, whether it was White Art, Black Art, or some grinning liar with a pack of cards. There'd been that mess when she was hired to steal that book off that sorcerer and it had *not* turned out well. This felt like a much bigger and more serious business altogether and her short hairs were all prickling. But when she looked back Duke Michael was giving her that smile again, so encouraging, like he actually *believed* in her, the damn fool, and she reckoned he'd be disappointed if she made a run for it. What could she do but go in?

Right away she wished she hadn't. The room on the other side was huge, round, domed, all painted white, so bright it was almost painful after the gloom of the corridors. The polished floor was set with a crazy confusion of rings, and lines, and symbols of polished metal. Nine monks stood evenly spaced against the walls, each holding something in their clasped hands: a candle, a sickle, a bunch of some herb, each face beaded with sweat, each set of lips constantly moving, the heavy air full of the echoing whisper of their ceaseless prayers. Alex jumped as the door crashed shut behind her, bars on the far side grinding back into place.

For someone constantly thinking about running for it, it was amazing how she always missed her chance.

Cardinal Bock was already striding across that expanse of sorcerous floor, past a very nervous-looking clerk sitting at a portable desk, towards a priest with a shaved head near its centre who was kneeling with a book open in the crook of her arm, obsessively polishing the floor with a rag, then breathing on it and polishing again.

"Lovely," murmured Bock. "Lovely, lovely, good good good . . . seals all triple-checked?"

The priest clambered up, tucking her rag away. "And triple-checked again, Your Eminence." And she handed Bock some sort of crystal on a handle.

"Braziers full, in case of another *incident*?"

"They won't get past us this time, Your Eminence."

Bock shut one eye to peer around the room through the crystal. "Those bastards are always picking at the seams, remember. *Always.*"

The shaven priest swallowed. She shaved her eyebrows, too, Alex noticed. "How could one possibly forget, Your Eminence?"

"Good, lovely, *excellent.*" Cardinal Bock waved Alex over. "Now don't worry, there are no wrong answers here."

Alex tried to smile. In her experience, there were always wrong answers, and she'd very likely soon be giving them.

"One thing, before we begin . . ." Bock took her by the shoulders and guided her forwards a few steps, then back an inch or two, until she was satisfied. "Stay inside the circle." Alex followed her eyes down, and saw her rather lovely borrowed shoes had been positioned within a circle of brass in the very centre of the floor. "Stay inside the circle, *at all times*." Bock stepped backwards, towards the priest with the book, beckoning to Duke Michael. "And if you could join me here, Your Grace, we need to be south of the principal of course. Don't worry a bit . . . what was her name again?"

"Alex," said Duke Michael.

"Don't worry a bit, Alex, this is all entirely standard. Even if standard still represents colossal risks, of course, we are all *well* aware of the risks . . ."

Alex swallowed. "Er . . ."

"Just stay inside the circle. *Whatever happens.* You can bring them in now!"

Two doors at opposite sides of the hall were opened and two teams of four guards shuffled in, each carrying a chair on poles. Alex had a feeling the nine monks were sweating more, praying more, looking more pained than ever.

In the chairs, in white shifts, blindfolded and with wrists and ankles chained, were two people. One was a man, she thought, one a woman, though it was hard to tell, they looked so starved, skin and bone, and unhealthy skin at that, scabs about their withered lips. They were limp as rags, heads lolling, bouncing slightly with the movement of their chairs. They looked like paupers' corpses. Things she'd been close to more often than she'd have liked. Things she'd been close to *being* more often than she'd have liked.

The guards set the chairs down, one on each side of Alex, and hurried back. As if they'd carried in two barrels of oil and Alex was the spark. Eight hard-bitten veterans, and they all looked terrified.

"Er . . ." muttered Alex, glancing around for some way out. But, you know. Locks on the *outside*.

"Begin," said Bock.

Chains rattled as the blindfolded man and woman lurched forwards in their chairs together, clutching Alex's hands. She flinched, almost stepped back, then realised she might step from the circle, and stayed where she was.

In a ringing voice, the woman spoke. "I see the elves!"

"The elves come!" wailed the man. "Their blind mad hungry gods come!"

"God save us, the elves come!" screeched the woman, gripping Alex's hand painfully tight. "Hungry, hungry, hungry, laughing."

Alex stared wildly at Bock, but the old woman waved it away. "Don't worry. They always say that."

"And that's a good thing?" squeaked Alex.

Bock hooked a finger to scratch under her crimson skullcap. "Long term it is *definitely* a concern, but for the time being—"

"I see a great building!" The woman twitched, head flitting this way and that. "An ancient building with buildings upon it with buildings about it feet in the sea head in the clouds I see rivers in the heavens gardens in the sky."

"The Pillar of Troy," said Cardinal Bock, with a significant glance towards Duke Michael. Her priest had pulled a stub of pencil from behind her ear and was scribbling furiously in her book.

"I see an ordeal," whispered the man, in a papery wheeze, "I see tests and trials."

Alex didn't much like the sound of that. But if these withered ghosts had talked about cake, it likely would've come over sinister.

"A tower a high tower the highest tower and there burns a light a light to guide the faithful a false light a true light a light reflected."

Cardinal Bock stood, eyes narrowed intently, like a miner sifting gravel for gold.

"A hunt within a hunt without a crooked path by land by sea."

"I see teeth," said the man.

"I see teeth," said the woman. Was it getting hotter? Alex was sweating. "I see a monk and a knight and a painted wolf I see death and no death I see blood I see a circle."

"I see a wheel."

"I see flame!" barked the woman, making Alex jump. "I see fire I see fire I see cleansing fire I see fire at her end."

"I see fire at her beginning," said the man, softly, hard to hear over the prayers, whispered louder and louder.

"Fire at her beginning." Bock and Duke Michael exchanged another glance. "Born in the flame . . ."

"Pyrogennetos . . ." And Duke Michael began to smile.

"The elves!" wailed the man, gripping Alex even tighter. God, his hands were burning. She had to bite her lip. His blindfold was smoking, two charred brown spots spreading over his eyes. "The elves come!"

"Enough!" snapped Bock, and the Oracles' fingers went limp at once and dropped away, and their faces went slack, and their heads rolled back, and they were two starved corpses again. The initiates hurried forwards with buckets to throw water across the floor, and where it hit metal it went up in hissing steam. The shaven priest checked something that looked like a compass and made another note in her book, then puffed out her cheeks with relief and gave Bock a nod.

"Good, good!" Her Eminence peered thoughtfully up at the distant ceiling. "Great . . . so . . . on this day, the twenty-first of Loyalty . . ." The clerk's pen began to scrape on paper. "I, Cardinal Bock, being certified of sound mind uncorrupted by Black Art or demonic powers et cetera, et cetera, assert that the candidate has been examined in a purified pale chamber under nine seals by paired Oracles of the Celestial Choir. Blast it!" she called over. "What's her name again?"

"Alex," said Duke Michael.

"You can leave the circle now, Alex, we're all done!"

Alex backed away from the limp Oracles, nervously rubbing her hands, fingers still pink and tingling from the heat of their touch.

"You did well." Duke Michael was smiling as he squeezed her shoulder.

"All I did was stand there."

"That's nine-tenths of what an Empress does." And he led her across the echoing floor towards the desk.

"What's Pyrogennetos?" she whispered.

"The title granted to royal children born in the Imperial Bedchamber, high in the Pharos of Troy, directly beneath Saint Natalia's Flame. Only Empresses and the firstborn of Empresses are permitted to give birth there. It is the ultimate mark of legitimacy."

Bock was leaning down over the clerk, one hand on his desk as she continued to dictate. ". . . Her Holiness Benedicta the First, therefore, invested with the full authority of the college of cardinals and speaking by papal bull and holy writ with the sanctified voice of God on earth and so on and so on, proclaims her to be none other than the Princess Alexia Pyrogennetos, born in the flame, eldest offspring of Irene, eldest offspring of Theodosia, and the one and only rightful and legitimate heir to the Serpent Throne of Troy."

Alex blinked as she watched Bock pluck the pen from the clerk's hand and scribble out a flamboyant signature.

"And there . . . we . . ." She slung pen back into inkwell, spraying black spots over the clerk, and gave Alex a beaming smile. "*Go.*"

"Right." Alex swallowed. "Fuck."

"They will eat us all . . ." whispered one of the Oracles as she was carried

past, tears leaking through her singed blindfold and trickling down her hollow cheeks.

Alex kept her face near her plate and her fork moving between the two fast
as she could. She'd have loved to use her fingers as stuff kept falling off the
cutlery, but as long as she was getting something down her gullet she called
it a win. Duke Michael watched, slightly pained, from the opposite side of
the table. Likely this was no one's idea of eating like a princess. But once you
know what proper starving feels like, when someone offers food, you eat all
you can quick as you can in case they change their minds.

"The elves will rise again," Cardinal Zizka was saying, from the big chair
at the head. "That is the terrible inevitability we must all face. Against that
implacable, insatiable, unholy enemy, Europe must stand together . . . or forever fall into darkness."

"Uh," grunted Alex, around her latest mouthful. She'd no doubt the elves
were real bastards. Who wasn't? But they seemed a long way off. Hadn't been
their pliers in her face the other day, had it?

"All I want—all Her Holiness wants—is to close the great schism, heal the
great wound, and bring the Empire of the East back into the loving embrace
of her Mother Church."

Schism and Church and blah, blah, blah. Alex couldn't have given a smaller
shit about all that if she'd gone at a turd with tweezers, but she knew better than
to say so. She could tell this Zizka was high up, from the big, dark furniture in
her dining room, polished by centuries of holy arses. From the great paintings
of martyrs piously suffering on the high, high walls. From the plate, and the
cutlery, and the candlesticks, and the candles in 'em. Gal the Purse would likely
have pissed her pants at the sight of it all. Then there was the gold chain with
the jewelled circle she'd so carelessly slung over the back of her chair.

You have to be rich to have a thing like that. But to be *careless* with it? That
meant power.

Alex wouldn't have minded sleeving a couple of pieces. Wouldn't have
been thieving *at all* in her book, just a noble effort at redistribution. But sadly,
the dress they'd belted her into was cut more for sitting still and smiling than
redistribution, and had tight sleeves.

Might be she'd spot a chance to palm a spoon or two when dessert arrived.

"The Saved must be united against the enemies of God," the cardinal
was burbling on. "Beneath the banner of the Saviour. Beneath the banner
of the Pope. Ready to march all one way when the heavenly trumpets herald

a new crusade, so we may drive the elves back into the abyss from whence they came!" She glared over, making Alex pause with her fork halfway to her mouth. One long drip of gravy spattered on her plate.

The cardinal had this way of looking at Alex that was making her worry this might be a sex thing after all. Priests might not be allowed to fuck, but that only seemed to encourage some of them. A servant kept drifting in from behind and pouring more wine and Alex had the same policy on drink as food so she'd sunk a few glasses. Now the room was a bit spinny and her ears were all hot and her nose had a dewy sweat on it she kept having to wipe on the back of her sleeve.

"Happy to help," she muttered around her latest half-chewed mouthful. Much better to agree with powerful folk then weasel out later than to risk vexing 'em up front. "With the crusades . . . and all . . ."

The cardinal raised one brow. "Your commitment to the cause of the Church will be rewarded, in this world and the next."

Alex coughed as she tried to swallow too much in one go and had to thump her breastbone then slurp some wine to wash it down. "You can hold off on the heavenly rewards," she said, grinning, "if I can cash in on the earthly ones now, eh? Eh?" No one laughed.

Oh God, she was drunk. She thought the answer might be to drink more, and drained her glass.

"We should set out for Troy as soon as possible," Duke Michael was saying. "My dear friend Lady Severa stayed in the city after the civil war, she served as Warden of Eudoxia's Chamber." He held up a folded little sheet of paper. "She's risked everything to keep me informed ever since." And he did what Alex had been afraid of, which was to hand the paper to her.

"Lady Severa," she muttered, "very good. *Very* good." She shook the paper open and frowned at the writing, the way she'd seen priests frown at the writing in holy books. It all looked very neat and careful but meant about as much to her as the patterns the pigeon shit made on her windowsill. "Mmm. Hmm."

Duke Michael looked slightly pained as he leaned close, took the letter from her hand, and turned it the other way up so he could read it. "She tells me Eudoxia's sons are moving to cement their positions. If it wasn't for their own bitter rivalries, one of them might already—"

"What?" Alex stopped waiting for the last drops of wine to trickle into her mouth and lowered her glass. "I've got cousins?"

"Eudoxia's sons. My nephews. Four dukes, and each a bigger bastard than the last. Marcian, Constans, Sabbas, and Arcadius." He bit the names off with narrowed eyes, the way a preacher might've listed the deadly sins.

"Don't they want the throne?"

"They will stop at *nothing* to get it," said Cardinal Zizka.

Alex sucked half-chewed food from her teeth. Wasn't tasting so fine as it had. "They're dangerous?"

"Powerful men in the Empire of the East," said Duke Michael. "Men who delighted in inflicting Eudoxia's reign of terror on the people."

"Men with land, and money, and influence." The cardinal forked a piece of meat with deadly precision. "Men with soldiers, spies, and assassins at their command. Men with no care for their immortal souls. Men who will not balk—if the rumours are to be believed—at employing forbidden magic, trafficking with devils, and worse."

"Worse?" muttered Alex.

Duke Michael was looking uncomfortable. As well he might. He'd said nothing about cousins till now, let alone forbidden magic. "My sister Eudoxia not only murdered your mother and usurped her throne, she was also a sorceress of terrible power. After she won the civil war, she founded a coven in Troy."

"She and her apprentices performed Black Art." Cardinal Zizka scowled down the table. "*Openly*, mark you! Offences against God, committed within sight of the hallowed ground wherein the heroes of the grand crusades are buried!"

Duke Michael shook his head. "Eudoxia was always obsessed with the soul."

"That sounds . . ." Alex squinted. "Sort of pious?"

Zizka gave a snort of disgust. "The soul is that part of himself that God puts into each one of us. To tamper with it is the worst heresy."

"How do you tamper with a soul?" muttered Alex, definitely not wanting the answer.

"She conducted . . . experiments," said Michael.

"Obscene experiments," said Zizka.

"She began . . . to combine man and beast."

"Like a dog's head on a man's body?" Alex was about to laugh, then saw Zizka and Duke Michael exchange a glance to kill all humour dead. "Wait . . . like a dog's head on a man's body?"

"People are given souls," said Duke Michael, "beasts are not. Eudoxia believed . . . that by fusing the flesh of the two, she could locate the soul. Release it. Capture it. *Harness* it."

"She sought to enslave a splinter of God." Cardinal Zizka glared down the table. "In fifteen years as Head of the Earthly Curia, it is the most depraved sacrilege I have heard."

"Oh," croaked Alex.

"Now you see, Your Highness, why we cannot suffer one of Eudoxia's sons to sit on the Serpent Throne. Why her cursed legacy must be ripped up by the roots, and the holy ground of Troy purified once again." She watched Alex while she chewed, looking like a woman who never bit off more than she could swallow. "It is *such* a brave thing you are doing, Your Highness. A noble, a righteous, and a brave thing."

A breeze seemed to whip through the room, or at any rate Alex got goose-flesh up her arms, tight sleeves or no. "No one said I'd need to be brave," she muttered.

"In an Empress," said Duke Michael, "I think it goes without saying."

"But bear in mind you are a step ahead of your cousins," observed Cardinal Zizka. "No one outside the Celestial Palace even suspects Princess Alexia is alive, let alone found. You will approach Troy in secret, under the protection of a handpicked group. Copies of the papal bull confirming your identity will be sent ahead of you to Lady Severa, to be circulated shortly before your arrival. Until then Eudoxia's cursed brood will be engrossed by their struggles against each other. You will fall on them like a bolt from the heavens!"

Alex didn't feel much like lightning. "What if one of 'em wins before I get there?"

"No one denies there are risks," said Duke Michael. "It is near a thousand miles to Troy, and we cannot be certain what support you will have when you reach the city. The stakes are huge, and our enemies powerful, and they will move heaven and earth to stop us—"

"Look, I grew up out there." Alex jabbed at the window with her fork and a pea flew off and stuck to the wall. "In the slums. I've done . . ." None of what she'd done seemed quite right for the surroundings. "All sorts . . . of stuff, but I don't know a fucking thing about being a princess—"

"I sense you are a quick study," said the cardinal, unmoved. She struck Alex as a woman not likely to be moved by anything short of an earthquake. And probably not far even then.

"But these four cousins, with all the soldiers and the money and the land, won't I have to fight them, sooner or—?"

"I'll fight for you." Duke Michael gave her an encouraging smile that made her want to pee. Or maybe that was all the wine.

"A famed hero taking your part!" said Zizka. "And you will enjoy the support of Her Holiness the Pope, and with her," and she rolled her eyes towards the ceiling, painted like a cloudy sky at twilight, hopeful rays breaking through the gloom, "the aid of the Saviour, blessed daughter of the Almighty. They may have spies and assassins, Your Highness, but you have saints and angels in your corner!"

In Alex's experience, the Almighty sides with the favourites, and once you're hoping for angels to even the odds you're proper fucked. But she had a sinking feeling she'd been proper fucked for a while and had only just re-alised.

Duke Michael leaned towards her. "And never forget that you have some-thing those four usurping dukes never will."

"What's that?" asked Alex, sounding very small.

"The *right*!" He thumped the table with his fist. "You are the Princess Alexia Pyrogennetos, born in the flame, and through the Oracles of the Ce-lestial Choir endorsed by *God himself*!" And he hit the table even harder, making the cutlery jump. Would've been a good moment to palm one of those little forks but Alex hadn't the heart.

"I've got the right . . ." She was pretty sure the right would fetch nothing on Gal the Purse's table. She'd known there must be broken glass hidden in the cake, but she'd chomped into it even so. She'd been dazzled by the big score, so fixed on reaching for it she'd tripped over her own feet. Tripped over and straight down a mineshaft. A mineshaft filled with deadly cousins, heretical sorcery, and stolen souls.

She made one more whingeing effort. "But they've got sorcerers, you said, and folk who are somewhere between man and beast, and, you know, *devils*—"

"They do." Cardinal Zizka smiled. It was the first time she'd done it and Alex reckoned, on balance, she'd preferred her frown. "But we have devils of our own."

The Start of a Bad Joke

Balthazar delivered a weighty sigh, but nobody noticed.

His current predicament gave him a great deal to sigh about: the ghastly mattress, the dreadful food, the frigid damp and unspeakable odour of his lodgings, the outrageous denial of clothing, the abominable absence of intelligent conversation, the heart-rending loss of his beautiful, beautiful books. But after long reflection he had come to the conclusion that the very worst thing about being forced to join the Chapel of the Holy Expediency . . . was the mortifying embarrassment.

That *he*, Balthazar Sham Ivam Draxi, learned adept of the nine circles, suzerain of the secret keys, conjurer of unearthly powers, the man they dubbed the Terror of Damietta—or at least had dubbed himself the Terror of Damietta in the hope that it would stick—one of the top three necromancers in Europe, mark you—possibly four, depending on your opinion of Sukastra of Bivort, who he personally considered an absolute hack—should have been apprehended by buffoons, tried and condemned by dullards, then pressed into humiliating servitude alongside such abject morons as these.

He glanced sideways with an expression eloquently communicating his utter disgust, but nobody was looking. The ancient vampire, presumably rendered decrepit by being starved of blood, slumped in a chair looking as fashionably bored as a wisp-haired skeleton could. The elf stood, thin as a length of pale wire, face obscured by a shag of unnaturally ashen hair, motionless but for a constant and deeply irritating nervous twitching of her long right forefinger. Their chief jailer, Jakob of Thorn, looked on from the corner with arms tightly folded: a war-worn old knight who appeared to have spent a sizeable portion of his life being crushed in a mangle, an experience that had clearly squeezed all sense of humour out of the man. Then there was the supposed spiritual shepherd of this congregation of the disappointing: Brother Diaz, a perpetually panicked young idiot from a little-known and less-regarded monastic order, who wore the expression of a man who cannot swim on the deck of a rapidly foundering ship.

An ineffectual priest, an enervated knight, a misanthropic elf, and an antique vampire. It sounded like the start of a bad joke to which the tragic punchline was yet to be revealed. One might at least have hoped for an awe-inspiring venue: some sculpture-crusted sanctum whose marble floor was in-set with the ideograms of saints and angels. Instead, they got a draughty little box in the guts of the Celestial Palace, whose one window had a view of a nearby wall sporting a muddle of leaky drainpipes.

The choice at Balthazar's farce of a trial had been atonement for his tres-passes through service to Her Holiness or burning at the stake. At the time it had seemed a no-brainer, but he was beginning to suspect that, in the long run, immolation might prove to have been the less painful option.

That *he*, Balthazar Sham Ivam Draxi, who had made the dead his play-things and the storm his steed, who had forced back the borders of mortality itself and bent the arch-demon Shaxep to his will—or at any rate wheedled a few favours from her and survived—was not only reduced to wretched slav-ery, but slavery of this intensely banal and brainless variety.

He was preparing a sigh so explosive that someone would be forced to finally acknowledge his discomfort when locks rattled and the door was thrown wide.

A gaggle of acolytes trooped in, each wearing a white habit, a countenance of otherworldly piety, and a prayer-shawl stitched with phrases from the scrip-tures. One struggled beneath a heavy wooden frame strapped to his back, a giant book held open upon it, a second scattering ink as he strove to follow and write on the towering pages at the same time. A third had a great round wreath of flowers about her neck that almost brushed the floor. A fourth clutched the silver circefix he wore in one hand, a sheaf of prayer-sheets in the other, glassy eyes rolled to the ceiling, lips in ceaseless motion as he burbled an endless orison for the blessings of Almighty, Saviour, and all the Saints.

"Here come the clowns," wheezed Baron Rikard, wobbling upright on his cane—if one could use the word *upright* when he remained so hunched his nose was barely above his belt.

The acolytes parted to reveal two grey-haired women: cardinals, by their crimson sashes and skullcaps, not to mention the jewelled circles they wore on jewelled chains. One was exceedingly tall and graceful, gazing beneficently about like a rich woman come to distribute alms to the poor. The other tended towards the short and solid, with a wrinkled brow and flinty gaze. These, Balth-azar deduced, were none other than Cardinals Zizka and Bock, the opposite poles of the leadership of the Church, Heads of the Earthly Curia and of the Celestial Choir. At first glance, he was less than impressed.

"D'you mind?" The two old women were elbowed aside by a ten-year-old girl in simple white, who planted her hands on her hips and surveyed the unwilling congregation with a critical cocked eyebrow.

Here she was, then: Benedicta the First, the Child Pope. The election of a new Holy Mother was never without controversy but this particular choice, being decidedly under parenting age, had caused widespread fury and denunciation, the excommunication of three rebellious cardinals and some dozen bishops, and nearly ushered in yet another full schism in the Church, whatever her supposed magical potential.

"From folly to farce," murmured Balthazar under his breath. He had never had much patience for religion. What was it, really, but superstition with money?

"Sorry, everyone!" sang Her Holiness, not sounding sorry at all. "The Frankish ambassador brought me a bird and it was so funny-looking! What was it called?"

Cardinal Zizka looked almost as humiliated by this pantomime as Balthazar. "A peacock, Your Holiness."

"Lovely colours. Have you been waiting?"

"No, Your Holiness." Brother Diaz flashed a servile smile and bowed as low as any penitent. "No, no, no, no—"

"Yes," drawled Baron Rikard, examining his yellowed fingernails. "But what choice do we have?"

Her Holiness only smiled the wider. "Well, if you were Pope people might bring *you* a peacock but you're a vampire so tough."

The baron issued a long sigh. "Out of the mouths of babes . . ."

There was a barely audible groan from the corner and the mumbling acolyte tottered, prayer-sheets sliding from his nerveless fingers and flapping across the floor in the draught. He slumped onto his side in a faint and one of his colleagues instantly took over, clasping her hands and rolling her eyes to the ceiling, smiling lips moving in ceaseless prayer. Balthazar was caught where he spent much of his time: somewhere between contempt and envy. He might know it was all flimflam, but to believe a lie was as comforting for the believer as to know the truth. For an instant he could not but wonder—is it truly better to be a woebegone cynic than an ecstatic dupe?

Bock was fanning the insensible acolyte with a sheaf of the fallen prayer-sheets, but one, by chance, had come to rest beside Balthazar's bare foot. It was scrawled with pieties on one side, but he noted with no small measure of excitement that the other was entirely blank. In the confusion it was a simple matter to slip his foot sideways and cover that scrap of paper. He could not quite keep the triumphant smile from his face as he felt it crackle beneath his sole. He would free himself from this humiliation and extract a vengeance to

make the martyrs weep! They would all rue the day they dared cross Balthazar Sham Ivam Draxi!

Zizka cleared her throat as the unconscious acolyte was manhandled into
the corridor. "Shall we administer the binding, Your Holiness? You have a
busy day."

"Pffffft," snorted Benedicta the First. "They're all busy days. Being Pope's
not half the fun you'd think."

"Most things aren't," murmured the elf, which, despite their occupying
adjacent cells, more or less doubled the number of words Balthazar had ever
heard her utter.

One of the acolytes knelt with a bowl of red ink, into which Her diminutive Holiness dipped her forefinger, then drew a simple line across the vampire's wrist. With her middle finger, she did the same to the elf.

The Pope took one more step, and Balthazar looked into the face of the
very representative of God on earth. A pale little girl with a large mole above
one eyebrow, whose white skullcap struggled to contain a mop of brown curls.
Balthazar had heard her described as the greatest arcane power to be birthed
into the world for several centuries and been incredulous. He had heard rumours that she was being celebrated as the Second Coming of the Saviour
herself and wanted to laugh. Now, looking upon her sacred person with his
own eyes, he tended more towards weeping. If this unpromising child was
truly the last, best hope of the world then it appeared the world was every bit
as doomed as everyone said.

"Who's the new boy?" She cocked her head as she looked up at Balthazar,
putting her skullcap in imminent danger of falling off entirely. One of her
acolytes hovered nervously, perhaps in hopes of catching it.

Brother Diaz cleared his throat. "This is Balthazar . . . er . . ."

Balthazar's sigh of disgust bordered on a full groan. "Sham . . . Ivam . . .
Draxi."

"A sorcerer—"

"*Magician*," he corrected, biting off each syllable. It might have come with
greater gravitas had he not been wearing only a threadbare nightshirt provided for the interview, but he did his best to appear formidably mysterious
even so, lifting one eyebrow to its full magisterial height and regarding the
supreme leader of the Church down his nose, which was not difficult since she
barely reached his stomach.

She tried to snap her fingers but she did not have the trick of it and made
no more than a soft *thwup*. "Wait! You're the one who makes corpses dance?
A whole opera, I heard!"

"Well . . . only a first act, in truth. I was making amendments to the li-
bretto when the Witch Hunters descended and, if I am entirely honest, I still
cannot get the cadavers to sing. Certainly not in a manner that would please
a connoisseur. More of a tuneful groan—"

"I'd love to see that!" cried Her Holiness, clapping her hands, and Balthazar had to admit her childish enthusiasm was rather charming.

"It would delight me to put on a performance—"

"Perhaps another time," said Cardinal Zizka, drily.

Her Holiness rolled her eyes. "God forbid we should have any fun around
here." And she dipped the tip of her little finger in the ink and drew it across
Balthazar's extended wrist, by all appearances exceedingly pleased with her
handiwork. "There!"

He waited expectantly for the rest. But there was no rest. That, it appeared,
was the entire inscribed element of the enchantment. A line. Not even a
straight line. Not even an even line. The blob of ink had at one side become
a drip that was gradually sliding down his wrist. No circles within circles, no
runes of the highest and lowest, no spiral of Sogaigontung with the sacred
passages inscribed at the correct angle at each of the fifteen corners. A child's
finger painting, quite literally. Balthazar could hardly decide whether to feel
delighted at how easily he would shrug free of this pathetic effort, or affronted
that anyone might imagine it could contain a practitioner of his potency.

The prepubescent Pontiff had stepped back to consider the risible congregation of the Chapel of the Holy Expediency, one red fingertip pressed to her
lips where it left a noticeable stain. She leaned towards Cardinal Bock. "What
should I say?"

The Conductor of the Celestial Choir smiled upon her like an indulgent
grandmother. "I don't suppose it matters much . . ." It was the most Balthazar could do to stop his jaw falling open. This woman was supposed to
rank among the most learned magicians in Europe! Now it turned out she
was a worse hack than Sukastra of bloody Bivort. "But perhaps something
like . . ." She took up the jewelled circle she wore around her neck and began
to absently polish it on her sleeve, squinting to the ceiling as though she was
only at that moment considering it. Balthazar outwardly goggled, inwardly
boggled. The old bitch was making up the verbals on the fly! The wording of
a solemn binding! The *papal* binding, no less! He struggled to imagine what
his competitors, rivals, and outright enemies in the arcane fraternity would
make of *this* when he told them. "I require you to conduct Princess Alexia
to Troy . . . to obey the instructions of Brother Diaz . . . and to see her enthroned as Empress of the East."

On the words *Princess Alexia*, she waved towards a young woman trying to hide behind the acolyte with the book. Balthazar narrowed his eyes at her as he swiftly assembled the sorry pieces of this unedifying puzzle. *This* resolutely unglamorous waif, with the starved and sickly air of a stray dog and the shifty eyes of a low-class pimp, was the long-lost Princess Alexia Pyrogennetos, daughter of Irene, now to be installed on the Serpent Throne of Troy as a papal puppet?

"From farce to fantasy," he murmured in disbelief.

"I think that'll do it," mused Bock, breathing on her circefix before giving it another polish. "Anyone else have any thoughts? Cardinal Zizka?"

The Head of the Earthly Curia sourly worked her mouth, then sourly shook her head, as if she had a very great number of thoughts but forbore to give them voice.

"Here I go, then." The Pope bunched her fists and squinted as she concentrated on the words. "I require you to conduct Princess Alexia to Troy, to obey the instructions of Brother Diaz, and to see her enthroned as Empress of the East!" She clapped her hands. "I got it in one!"

"Wonderful!" said Bock.

"Wonderful!" said the Pope, clapping again. "And then come straight back, of course."

"Good point, Your Holiness," said Bock. "Well remembered."

The Pope's face turned suddenly grave. "If you don't give it your best, I expect you'll feel very sick. *And*—" she wagged a stern finger at each of them in turn "—be nice to each other on the way. Because being nice . . . is *nice*. Is it lunch yet?" she asked, turning towards the door.

"Soon, Your Holiness," said Zizka. "You must first apply the binding to the . . . *missing* member of the flock."

"Oh, I love Vigga! You think she'll let me ride on her shoulders again?" The Pope departed with a bouncing gait that bordered on skipping. "Then lunch?"

"As soon as you have given audience to that delegation of bishops from the Hanseatic League. They desire a ruling over the relationship between God, Saints, and Saviour—"

Her Holiness gave a long groan. "Boring!" And she was gone into the corridor, her acolytes trailing behind, one still praying, one still desperately trying to scribble in the giant book, one frowning furiously as she attempted to manoeuvre her huge wreath sideways through the door. The world's most disappointing princess gave everyone in the room one last worried glance, then skulked after.

Balthazar rubbed gently at the red mark on his wrist. "That . . ." he could not help saying, "is all?"

"That's all," said Bock, simply. "You'll leave tomorrow morning, with an escort of Papal Guard." She waved one hand in a vague benediction. "May God bless your endeavour and so on."

The baron flopped back into his chair, looking up from beneath his drooping lids. "Can God really bless such devils as we are, Cardinal?"

"In his hands, they say all tools are righteous." Bock pushed her skullcap down towards her eyebrows so she could scratch the back of her head. "You know, I have always found it a paradox: there is nothing more freeing than being bound to a common purpose." She gave Balthazar an oddly enigmatic smile, settled her cap again, slightly skewed, and left.

It was the most he could do to suppress an incredulous chuckle. A set of extremely dangerous fools, entirely incapable of working together, undertaking a journey of a thousand miles or more with the utterly impossible aim of installing that sulking milksop on the Serpent Throne of Troy? Thanks all the same, but Her infant Holiness could count him out. He would shrug off this tissue of a binding and be gone on the wings of the wind before anyone knew it!

He had to swallow a sudden, acrid burp, no doubt the result of the indigestible slop they fed him here. He entertained himself by imagining the moronic look on the moronic face of that smirking bitch Baptiste when she learned of his escape. When she realised she would be looking over her shoulder every moment of her life for his inevitable vengeance. He wondered what form of occult retribution would give him the greatest satisfaction, provide the most appropriate warning to others and the best metaphor for the humiliation he had suffered at her hands. This dunce of a princess could find her own way to—

—had Balthazar been punched in the stomach he could not have given vent to a more forceful fountain of vomit. It hit the floor perhaps four strides away, producing a crooked line of spatters all the way to his bare feet, and ended in an agonised, shuddering wheeze. He was left slightly bent over, tongue out, eyes watering, strings of drool hanging from his nose and his cupped hands full of his own sick.

"That's the binding." The elf had turned to regard him expressionlessly with those huge, unblinking eyes. "Works better than you'd think."

Hold on to Something

Alex clung to the reins so hard her hands ached and concentrated mostly on not falling off.

She'd ridden donkeys before, that autumn when she'd gone north to work at the harvest. Someone had told her it was good money for light labour and they'd been dead wrong on both counts. The horse they'd put her on was better smelling and a lot better behaved than the donkeys had been but also *way* higher, and riding side-saddle seemed like an open invitation to a broken skull. Every jolt had her panicking she'd slide off and get mashed under the monstrous box of a wagon rumbling along behind, which would've been a fitting end to this fairy tale.

Her lips were dry like she was running a badly thought-out swindle. Had to keep stopping herself tonguing them like a lizard. She could play a princess, couldn't she? Far as she could tell, all they did was get scrubbed and combed and dressed and talked over like they weren't there. A block of wood could've done the same job. She could play a block of wood, couldn't she?

She'd played a cripple cured by a miracle and a simpleton cured by a tonic and an orphan who'd found a purse and an ever-so-helpful pilgrim's child who knew a shortcut to a nice, cheap room. Just down that dark alley no don't worry just a bit further it's a really great room just a *bit* further. She'd even played a nobleman's daughter once, though she'd overworked the accent and the mark had seen through it and she had to jump in the canal to escape a kicking.

She'd a worry there was worse than a kicking waiting at the end of this particular caper. She kept checking for ways out, but there were armed men all around—hard bastards with hard faces and lots of hard metal to hand, the circle of the Saved on their surcoats. Duke Michael said they were there to protect her, but her history with men—and armed men especially—and armed men of the Church *especially*—left her far from reassured.

In fact, if you wanted to see the goddamned opposite of reassured then look no further, here it sat, riding a giant horse side-saddle.

She took a hard breath. Tried to settle her nerves. *Panicking bakes no cakes,* as Gal the Purse was likely even now telling a new batch of orphans. We all need something to hold on to. For Alex it was sharp wits and never staying down. So her plans had done like turds in a storm and turned to stinking slurry. Plans do that. That's when you squeeze out some new ones.

All she had to do was bide her time and get what could be got, stay on her toes, and be ready to vanish. There's no talent like not being there when things turn sour. She'd always liked to think of herself as a loner, self-reliant as an alley cat, but everyone can use a friend from time to time. Who knows when you'll need someone to soak up the blame?

Her uncle, if he really was her uncle, was riding at the head of the column with the baffled-looking priest and the grey knight who never smiled and the woman with all the hats who smiled too much. Alex couldn't see what use the ancient bastard on the roof of the wagon could be. He looked like a corpse in a coat. Not even a fresh corpse. Not even a nice coat. And the man with the ridiculous sneer who'd talked about making the dead dance spent all his time glaring at his wrist. There was a maid along, who rode like she was born side-saddle, but she combed and powdered and dressed Alex with such silent disdain you'd have thought she was the princess and Alex the maid.

Which left the elf.

Alex never saw one before, in the flesh. Folk said they were the enemies of God, and that they ate people, and scared children with stories about them, and preached new crusades against them, and burned dummies of them on holidays. When it came to getting blamed, elves were the best. She was a pointy-eared blame-sponge, right there in easy reach. So Alex gripped on tight and nudged her horse over.

"So . . ." she began. Usually, once Alex set her mouth off, it pretty much kept going on its own. But when those strange eyes turned on her, so big they hardly looked real, the only words she could find were, ". . . you're an elf."

The elf's head dropped to one side, swaying gently with the movement of her horse, her neck long and slim as a bundle of pale twigs, and she opened those eyes even wider. "What gave it away?"

"Oh, I am a very perceptive person," said Alex. "Something about the accent, maybe?"

"Aaaah." The elf looked back to the trees. "Another reason to keep my mouth shut."

If Alex could be put off that easily she'd have starved years ago. "I'm Alex." She risked letting go the reins to hold out her hand, wobbled and had to grab her saddle-horn, then held it out again. "Or . . . Alexia Pyrogennetos? Not really sure who I am right now . . ."

The elf considered her hand. She considered the guards. Then she reached out and shook it. For some reason Alex had expected those long, thin fingers to feel cold. But they were warm, like anyone else's.

"Sunny," she said.

"Really? Short for something . . . elf-y?"

"Sunnithilien Darktooth."

"Really?"

The elf slowly raised one thin white eyebrow.

"Not really," said Alex.

"Sunny's what they called me in the circus."

"You were in a circus?"

"I trained lions."

"Really?"

The elf slowly raised that thin white eyebrow even higher.

Alex winced. "Not really."

"I was dragged around on a chain and people booed and threw things at me."

"That . . . doesn't sound like much fun."

"They seemed to enjoy it."

"I meant for you."

Sunny shrugged. "Even bad shows need a villain."

They rode on in silence, the guards clanking in their saddles, the axles of the big wagon grinding away. Alex was a loner, of course. But she found she was enjoying the company. "I'd heard elves were all bloodthirsty savages," she said.

"I'd heard princesses were all beautiful fools."

"Give me a chance. I've only been a princess for a few days."

Sunny raised that brow again. "And already so good at it."

Balthazar glared at the binding. He had been glaring at it almost without interruption since the moment of its application. It appeared to be no more than a rusty smear, but his constant bubbling nausea, occasional bouts of projectile vomiting, and on one memorable occasion—when his thoughts turned to how he might escape its magical shackles by engineering the death of Princess Alexia by poison—a truly explosive episode at the other end of the digestive tract, left him in no doubt as to its considerable puissance. There was *nothing* Balthazar hated more than a riddle he could not unravel.

He held that unprepossessing smudge ever closer to his face until he squinted at a blur. Might there be tiny runes disguised there? Inscribed onto the girl Pope's fingertip *before* she touched him and by some unknown method transferred? Imprinted elsewhere upon his body while he slept? Between his shoulder blades or on the soles of his feet or maybe on the rear of his scrotum where no one was likely ever to check? Certainly no one had checked there lately, it galled him to admit. Inkless runes, impressed with a brass wire? Finger-figures that had not even made contact with his skin? Might that wilfully enigmatic ass of a cardinal, Bock, have woven some extra enchantment while he was distracted? However absent-minded she had seemed in the moment, she was reputed to be a formidable practitioner. It would not have been the first time he had committed the error of judging too much on appearances.

He took a hard breath, tried to pare away all emotion and apply unflinching logic. We all need something to hold on to. In Balthazar's case it was his mastery of the magical sciences and his formidable powers of reason. For everything there is an answer! He sifted once more through every instant of that interview, bitterly wishing that he had his pristine copy of al-Harrabi's *Six Hundred Abjurations*, and those superb German lenses, and was not perched atop a bouncing wagon.

It was the type of lumbering, absurdly over-engineered conveyance in which one might safely convey a valuable cargo, with a rail about its high roof, a seat at the front for the sullen driver, and a bench behind for passengers. It was difficult to be sure over the whirring of the iron tyres, but Balthazar occasionally fancied that he felt something large shift in the windowless compartment under his feet. They had not even bothered to chain him to the bench, apparently relying on the binding to prevent his escape, a decision they would come *deeply* to regret. It would take more than some precocious infant's finger daub to keep *him* down—

The thought caused another wave of nausea, obliging him to tear his wrist away from his face, struggling manfully to keep his breakfast on the inside of his body while he assessed the rest of the convoy. There were twenty-one well-armed Papal Guardsmen in attendance, but Balthazar made little room for them in his calculations. Men of violence are easily outwitted. Strength, after all, can be found in plenty among the beasts. It is thought, knowledge, science—and of all sciences the harnessing of magic—that mark mankind as superior.

He glanced towards the head of the convoy, but that gloomy plank Jakob of Thorn, that smirking pirate Baptiste, and that wilting dishrag of a monk were busy blabbing away to the Duke of Nicaea. The cut-price princess, meanwhile, appeared to be striking up an unlikely friendship with the taciturn elf. The princess and the elf sounded like a cautionary fable Balthazar had no interest in reading, let alone witnessing in the flesh.

The vampire, now apparently asleep at the other end of the bench, was a different prospect. Plainly he was a venerable example, which made him powerful, cunning, and deeply dangerous at a minimum. The only member of this laughless farce that Balthazar judged to be a threat as an enemy . . . and therefore the only one who might be of any real value as an ally.

He leaned over, making sure to maintain a prudent distance, held up his wrist, and murmured, "What is the trick of it?"

One of the baron's dim eyes opened a slit, one snowy brow edging upwards, its excessively long hairs fluttering in the breeze. "Pope Benedicta's binding?" he croaked.

"Yes, the binding."

Baron Rikard closed that eye again. "It is said that she is the most promising arcane power to be born into the world in centuries."

"Huh." As a highly promising arcane power himself, Balthazar saw no evidence of it.

The corner of the baron's mouth twitched in amusement. "I have even heard it suggested she is the Second Coming of the Saviour herself."

"Very droll," grumbled Balthazar, who was in no mood for levity.

"Well, you're the magician." The vampire's eye opened that slit again. "You tell me the trick."

Balthazar sourly worked his mouth. Something he was doing a great deal lately. "Have you tried to break it?"

Now the vampire's other eye eased open. "Pope Benedicta's binding?"

"Yes, yes, the binding!"

"I have not."

"Why not?"

"Perhaps I am exactly where I would like to be."

Balthazar snorted. "Starved, withered, and in transit to Troy by arse-numbing wagon?"

The baron took a creaking, crackling breath, and let it sigh away. "Estella of Artois was sure she could break it."

"The name is not familiar."

"A sorceress who occupied your cell beneath the Celestial Palace for a time. She spent months trying. Yammering charms night and day, swearing she'd find the secret. When she wasn't being sick, that is."

"Did she succeed?"

"Do you see her here?"

"So she *did* succeed!"

"Oh, no." And the baron stretched out with a faint clicking of aged joints and shut his eyes again. "She died, and they burned her corpse, and said, 'We must get a new sorcerer.' And here you are."

"Magician," growled Balthazar. "The binding *killed* her?"

"Oh, no. A giant fell on her."

This seemed to pose more questions than it answered, but before Balthazar could formulate another he was distracted by the elf.

"Hold on to something," she said as she rode past, then cantered on towards the head of the column.

Balthazar frowned after her. "What did she mean by that?"

"Not everything is a riddle." The old vampire wrapped the gnarled fingers of one liver-spotted hand firmly around the rail, regarding Balthazar from beneath his withered lids. "Sunny is, in some ways, your opposite."

"Meaning?"

"She doesn't say much. But when she does, it's worth listening to."

"And tell me," said Duke Michael, "how did a monk come to minister to this particular flock?"

"Honestly, Your Grace . . ." There had been a time, not so very long ago, when Brother Diaz would have fumbled for a self-serving falsehood, but frankly his heart wasn't in it any more. "I've no idea."

Duke Michael smiled. "I hear the actions of our Lord are mysterious. Sometimes, it seems, his Church is even more so."

"A month ago, I thought myself quite a clever man . . ." Brother Diaz remembered with painful clarity how clever he had felt in that final interview with the abbot. How pleased with the outcome of all his scheming. How pettily triumphant as he swept past his brothers in the refectory, doomed to remain prisoners in that solemn temple to boredom. Now he wondered if the abbot had known what was coming. If his brothers had been in on the joke, laughing behind their roughspun sleeves at him the whole time. "Now I realise I'm a fool."

Duke Michael's smile grew wider. "Then you're wiser than you were a month ago, Brother Diaz. For that you can be thankful."

He saw precious little else to be thankful for. Since he was made Vicar of the Chapel of the Holy Expediency, Brother Diaz's whole mouth had erupted with a plague of ulcers that might've served as a martyr's ordeal. They were unfeasibly, unreasonably painful, yet he somehow couldn't stop tonguing at them to remind himself just how painful they were. He'd dabbed them with holy water from the font in which Saint Anselm of the Eyes had been baptised, but if anything, they hurt more afterwards. It seemed ulcers were another nuisance he would have to accept now, as a routine part of life. Like saddle-sores, damp clothes, and ensorcellment by vampires.

"I thought they died in sunlight," he murmured, wistfully.

"A myth," growled Jakob of Thorn. "Baron Rikard quite enjoys it."

Indeed, the ancient vampire was virtually basking on the wagon's roof, head back and swaying on a brittle-looking neck. It was an exceptionally heavy wagon, riveted with iron, its whole back one windowless door secured by a great bolt at each corner, operated by a single lock.

He didn't want to ask but couldn't help himself. "What is . . . *in* the wagon?"

"A last resort," said Baptiste, showing her gold teeth. She rode the way she talked, which was to say loosely and with a perpetual smirk. "If our luck holds, you'll never need to know."

Brother Diaz's luck hadn't been the best of late. He took a hard breath, pressing at the lump under his habit where the vial of Saint Beatrix's blood lay against his skin, and offered the keeper of the Saviour's sandal yet another silent prayer for his survival. We all need something to hold on to, and he determined to make *faith* his anchor. He was an ordained monk, after all, however little he'd wanted to be one, so it was probably high time. Was it not the foremost of the Twelve Virtues? The one from which all others flowed? He would keep faith. That the Almighty had a plan. That he had a role in it. Probably not a leading one. An untaxing walk-on would be fine. He managed a watery smile, but it made the ulcers hurt, so he stopped.

"Are you related," Duke Michael was asking, all airy good humour to Jakob's stony gloom, "to that Jakob of Thorn who was Champion of the Emperor of Burgundy?"

The knight's already narrowed eyes narrowed by the smallest fraction. "Thorn is a large city. Lots of Jakobs there."

"True," said Brother Diaz, who vaguely remembered reading the name himself in a dusty account of the Livonian Crusades he'd come upon while reorganising the library. "I believe there was a Jakob of Thorn who was Grandmaster of the Golden Order of Templars."

"And wasn't there one who was the Pope's Executioner?" Baptiste looked faintly amused, as if enjoying a private joke. "Or was that a Janusz of Thorn? Or a Jozef?"

"Jakob." Brother Diaz recoiled as he found himself looking into the wrongly proportioned face of the elf at uncomfortably close quarters. It seemed she could even ride in uncanny silence.

"Sunny," said Jakob.

She spoke in a bland drone, hardly moving her lips. "We're being followed."

"What?" Brother Diaz spun one way in his saddle, got stuck, then spun the other, staring wildly into the trees behind them. "I don't see anyone!"

"I try to give the warning before everyone can see the danger," said the elf.

Duke Michael's smile had faded. "How many?"

"Three or four dozen. They're keeping pace half a mile back."

The only hint of concern Jakob showed was the working of a muscle on the side of his scarred face. "Anyone ahead?"

The elf pursed her strangely human lips, narrowed her strangely inhuman eyes, and cocked her head on one side for a moment. "Not yet."

Brother Diaz chewed at one of his ulcers. "Surely you don't expect . . . *trouble* . . ." Saints and Saviour, why did he have to use that word, it was as if saying it made it more likely, "so close to the Holy City?"

"I expect everything and nothing," said Jakob, "especially since I took this position. Baptiste! Is there anything defensible on this road?"

"A walled inn south of Calenta. The Rolling Bear. Couldn't tell you the origin of the name. They say the Emperor Karl the Unsteady slept there on his way to be crowned by the Pope. Interesting story, in fact—"

"Maybe later," said Jakob.

"If we're still alive," added Sunny.

Something untoward was happening. The column had accelerated, the wagon jolting even more wildly than before. Duke Michael had dropped back to whisper urgently to his hapless niece. The guards were loosening weapons and scanning the trees. Balthazar had planned to wait for darkness and a halt, but the wise man stands always ready to seize the moment.

He turned his back on the driver and surreptitiously slipped the prayer-sheet from his sleeve.

"What are you about, magician?" murmured Baron Rikard, with a flicker of interest.

Balthazar smoothed the paper out on the wagon's roof, placing his red-streaked left wrist precisely in the centre of the circle of power he had in-scribed upon it. "I am breaking this *risible* excuse for a binding."

A wave of nausea swept over him at the thought, but he was fully prepared and fought it down.

"Where did you get the paper?" enquired the vampire.

"That fainting acolyte dropped a prayer-sheet. I secured it."

"Nimble. And the pen?"

"I improvised with a strip of toenail."

"Resourceful. The ink is of an unusual consistency."

Balthazar paused in calibrating the angle of the diagram relative to his wrist and frowned over at the vampire. Blood would have been the obvious choice, with the advantage of a certain gothic charm, but after an exceedingly uncomfortable half-hour spent trying to scrape, scratch, and abrade himself on the walls of his cell he had given up and gone in a different direction. "We are the Chapel of the Holy Expediency," he snapped. "I did what was expedient."

The baron further wrinkled his already wrinkled nose. "I thought there was an odour."

"No doubt you have smelled worse," grumbled Balthazar. It was hardly his usual immaculate penmanship, everything somewhat lumpy and crooked. But when one is forced to employ a toenail to draw runes with one's own excrement one must settle for less-than-optimal results.

He choked back another surge of nausea as he made a final tweak to the orientation. A circle of this crudity, unquartered and lacking a ritual tablet, should ideally point north, of course, but that was rather difficult to ensure atop a moving wagon, especially with the driver heartily snapping the reins for more speed, wind plucking at the corners of the prayer-sheet. Balthazar wished he had his silver pins, his lodestone and plumb lines, his glorious clock and compasses, the set of bronze conjurer's rings he had commissioned from that metallurgist in Baghdad, but he supposed the Witch Hunters had destroyed it all, the utter barbarians—

"Is it raining?" murmured Baron Rikard. The sky was indeed beginning to spit, and soon enough fat drops were whirling down from the strip of grey between the treetops.

"God *damn* it," hissed Balthazar. The limitations of human faeces as ink were becoming starkly apparent. Several of the runes were already in danger of becoming blurry. It would have to be now or never.

He formed the sign of command over that cursed red stripe and began to pronounce the three charms he had devised: one of softening, one of untying, one of cleaving. Simple and to the point, there was no one here to impress. A modest three words each, each thrice repeated, elegant in their crystalline simplicity. He drew the letters in his mind's eye, felt them gather power, an excited pressure in his chest, a tingling at his fingertips. Even under these circumstances he felt the intoxicating joy of working magic, of using his wit and his will to bend the very rules of reality. He closed his eyes tightly as he spoke the last word, raindrops cold on his face, heartbeat loud in his ears, hissing out each syllable with furious concentration.

"Did it work?" asked the baron.

Balthazar lifted his arm, glaring at that rusty mark on his wrist. "I think so." And he began, for the first time in some time, to smile. "I think so!" His delighted cackle was torn away by the rushing wind as the wagon sped ever faster. He was Balthazar Sham Ivam Draxi, not only one of the top three necromancers in Europe, but the man who broke the papal binding, outwitted Cardinal Bock, and strolled away from—

The vomit showered from his mouth, sprayed the roof, spattered his shirt, and clipped the baron's sleeve before he was able to twist and direct the lag-end down the wagon's side. His stomach was wrung out in an agonising knot, his eyes bulging as he choked, drooled, wheezed his insides out onto the rushing road.

"Apparently not," observed Baron Rikard.

Balthazar tumbled back onto the bench with a whimper, his shit-daubed prayer-sheet crushed in one fist, sick burning every passage of his face. Gods and devils, was it coming out of his eyes?

"Fucking *fuck*!" he screeched.

The driver twisted in his seat. "Settle down back—" And an arrowhead burst from his throat, stopping a mere few inches from the tip of Balthazar's nose, thick streaks of blood caught by the wind and snatched away.

The driver tottered up on his speeding wagon, peering down cross-eyed at the arrow's red point. He spluttered blood into his beard, then his knees crumpled. He toppled sideways, bounced once in the road, then flopped bonelessly over and over, one of the guards having to swerve his horse around him.

"We're under attack!" gasped Balthazar.

"Mmmm." Baron Rikard had somehow managed to maintain his leisurely sprawl all the while, as if enjoying a pleasant ride in the country. He nodded towards the empty driver's seat. "Perhaps you should take the reins?" The four horses were still going at a gallop, straps and harness flapping wildly, urged on by the frantic riders all around them.

"God *damn it*!" gasped Balthazar as he scrambled over the bench, slipped, and was caught for a moment splay-legged, its vibrating back battering him in the balls. A couple more arrows shot from the trees, one zipped overhead, another stuck wobbling into the side of the driver's seat a moment before he slithered into it.

Fortunately, the reins had snagged on the brake lever and, straining with his bouncing fingertips, he was finally able to catch them. Unfortunately, he had not the slightest idea what to do once he had them. "What do I do?" he shrieked.

"I'm a vampire!" roared the vampire. "Not a coachman!"

The trees rushed past at a frankly terrifying speed, the horses' manes streaming, Balthazar's teeth rattling in his head. He bit his tongue at a particularly savage jolt, the taste of blood joining the taste of sick and doing nothing to improve it.

One of Duke Michael's servants was shot from his horse and tumbled across the road, the wagon's heavy wheels crunching over the man before Balthazar could even decide not to bother trying to avoid him.

The wind was whipping tears from his eyes now, the road a sparkling blur. Up ahead Duke Michael had his niece's bridle while she clung to her saddle. Balthazar caught a glimpse of her horrified face as she stared over her shoulder. He glanced back, too, and saw riders behind them. There was something odd about their shape. Were those horned helmets?

The wagon bucked wildly and he was obliged to turn from the terrors behind to the even more pressing ones ahead. He saw a wall among the trees, its gate bouncing wildly along with the rest of the maddened world, on the outside of a bend they surely had no chance of taking.

Baptiste was screaming at him over the screaming of the wheels. "Slow it down!"

"Fucking *how?*" screeched Balthazar.

"Hold on to something." Baron Rikard reached past him and, with both liver-spotted, knobbled fists, gripped the brake. There was a shrieking of tortured metal as he hauled on it, sparks spraying.

Balthazar glimpsed a man in the gateway, mouth and eyes wide open, before he dived aside and they were through into the yard, mud showering up as the wagon tipped onto one set of wheels. One of the horses tripped, twisted, then went down in a chaos of flapping straps and flying dirt. Its partner charged on, dragging the team sideways, and the wagon plunged past them, unstoppable.

"Oh God," mouthed Balthazar. He'd never cared much about God, but no other words seemed quite to fit the circumstances.

The half-timbered wall of an inn came charging at them. Balthazar's rump ended its brief and uneasy partnership with the driver's seat . . . and he was flying.

No Room at the Inn

Bar the gates!" bellowed Jakob.

He wondered how often he'd roared that order. The besieged castles, the surrounded towns, the desperate defences. But that led to wondering how many had turned out well.

In a leader, no one wants to see doubts.

His teeth were always gritted but he gritted them harder. He gathered himself for the hero's effort of lifting his right leg over the saddle, lunged at it too hard, got it caught, and had to drag it the rest of the way with both hands. He slid down with all the control of a felled tree going over and with about as much bend at the joints, stumbled as his boot hit the dirt and his throbbing knee threatened to buckle.

God, riding hurt these days. Almost as much as walking.

He straightened with a snarl. He hobbled on through the flitting rain. His flesh, so battered and broken, so often torn and stitched back together, was prone to fail. It was only a stubborn refusal to fall that kept him limping on. His refusal to fall, and his oaths.

"Arm yourselves!" he barked as two guards heaved the gates shut on screeching hinges. At least his voice still worked. "Or get indoors!" A boy with a grooming brush stood frozen, and Jakob took his collar and steered him scampering towards the inn. "See to the wounded!" It was an old habit, to take command. "Tether these horses!" To crush chaos into order with any tool available. "Anyone with a bow to the walls!" He'd always had something in him that men would obey, and that was lucky.

It was only keeping them going that kept him going.

The wagon had gouged a ragged scar through the mud as it tipped over, then crashed through the front of the inn on its side. But the locks had held, thank God and Saint Stephen. They were very good locks. Jakob had made absolutely sure of that. One horse was still kicking weakly near the wreckage, hooves scraping the ground. Too dazed to realise it had run out of road. Or too stubborn to accept it.

States of mind Jakob understood all too well.

It had been his task, long ago when he was a squire, to give the wounded horses mercy. Templar's mercy, that was: one blow, between the eyes. You learn to spot the lost causes and cut them loose. Like anchors from a foundering ship. Reckon up the strength you have left and save what can be saved.

"Where's the baron?" Jakob caught Baptiste by one embroidered lapel. "What about the new boy? The corpse-tickler?"

She shook her head bitterly. "I should've quit after Barcelona."

Jakob frowned towards the gate as the guards wedged the mossy bar into the rusted brackets. Frowned at the creeper-coated walls, the crumbling battlements. Frowned at the one leaning tower, the ivy-coated stables, the inn itself. He considered the few strengths of their position, the many weaknesses. "We should all have quit after Barcelona. Did you see who was chasing us? Your eyes are better than mine."

"I saw them," she said, jaw working.

"How many men?"

"Enough." She must've lost her hat on the road along with her sense of humour, mass of curly hair glittering with raindrops. "But I'm not sure they were men . . ."

The captain of the guards was trying to untangle himself from his surcoat. The gold thread that made the circle of the Saved had come unravelled, caught on his armour. "Who'd dare attack us?" he was muttering, fingers trembling as he fussed at the knots. "Who'd *dare* attack us?" He was a young man, too young for this, with one of those wispy moustaches young men grow, thinking it makes them look older when really it makes them look younger than ever. But Jakob tried not to judge people for their poor choices.

He'd made a lifetime of them, after all.

"We'll soon know." He slid out his dagger and sawed through all that loose thread with one decisive cut. "Bows on the walls, Captain, right now." The man stared back, blinking, and Jakob caught a fistful of his surcoat and dragged him close. "No one wants to see doubts."

"Right . . . bows." And he started pointing men towards the stairways. Shove tasks in their face so they don't notice death waiting, just beyond.

Jakob slowly stooped. Scraped up a handful of dirt. Rubbed it between his sore palms, between his aching fingers.

"What're you doing?" asked Princess Alexia.

She looked even less like royalty than usual. Her wet hair had come loose and stuck to her pale cheek, clothes mud-spattered and one bony hand twisting the other. But Jakob learned long ago that you can't judge someone's quality by looking. They can find grace and greatness in the strangest ways, at the strangest times. Grace and greatness were out of reach for him now. Sunk in the past. But perhaps he could make the room in which others could find them.

"An old habit," he said, slowly straightening. "Learned from an old friend." An old enemy. He thought of Han ibn Khazi's face as he rubbed the desert dirt between his palms. That impossible smile while all around him men raged and wept. An eye of calm in a hurricane of panic. "Know the ground where you make your stand. Make it your ground." Jakob gave her the closest thing he could to Khazi's smile. Even if it hurt that old wound under the eye. The one Khazi had given him. "Courage, Your Highness."

"Courage?" she whispered, then flinched at a great bellow outside the walls. It hardly sounded like a man's voice. More like an angry bull's.

"Or better yet, fury."

"Good advice," said Duke Michael, drawing his sword. You could tell from the way he held it—loose and easy like a joiner holds his hammer—that it was far from the first time.

"Protect your niece." Jakob clapped him on the shoulder as he headed towards the gates. They rocked under a great blow from outside, the bar jumping in its brackets.

It reminded him of the siege of Troy, in the Second Crusade. The earth-shaking blows of the ram against the thrice-blessed doors. Splinters flying from the bars, thick as ships' masts. Witch-fire flickering between the timbers as Bishop Otho, soon to be Saint Otho, roared out prayers to each archangel in turn, the battle-songs of the elves outside the walls providing an unearthly accompaniment.

It reminded him of the battle in the Ratva Bog. The roughness of the dirt against the grip of his sword. The flitting rain in his face and the air cold and sharp and clean in his lungs.

It reminded him of the day they stormed the tower at Corgano, that acrid, acid smell of burning thatch, the squeals of the wounded, the panic of the dying.

But you reach a certain age, everything reminds you of something.

The gates shuddered again.

"What shall I do?" asked Sunny, falling in beside him.

"Live through it." Jakob grinned at her. Grinning at an elf. How things change. "It always turns to shit, eh, Sunny?"

"Usually takes a bit longer than this." And she pulled up her hood, sucked in a deep breath, and vanished. For a moment he could see a kind of space in the rain where she was. Or where she wasn't. Then even that was gone. It was coming harder, now, wind swirling through the yard and making the cloaks of the guardsmen flap, making the sign of the Rolling Bear dance on its one creaking chain.

Jakob shrugged his shield from his back. Winced at the twinge in his shoulder as he slid his left arm through the straps. "Steady!" The half-roar, half-growl he'd honed to a deadly edge on a hundred battlefields. "Steady!"

You can stack your doubts high before. You can polish your regrets up after. But while the fight's on, your purpose must be pure. Kill the enemy. Don't die yourself.

He drew his sword. Winced at that old ache in his fingers as he gripped the hilt.

How things change. But how things stay the same.

Another bellow from beyond the gates. Another crashing blow on weathered wood.

"Ready!" he bellowed.

The oaths would keep him standing when his flesh failed. When his courage failed. When his faith failed.

The world could burn to ash and blow away and all could be lost, but his word would still stand.

The gates rocked again.

"Alex, are you hurt?"

She heard the words but couldn't make the bastards mean anything. She stared dumbly at Duke Michael, or her uncle, or whoever he was. "Eh?" And she flinched as mud flicked her face.

The yard was chaos. Horses dragged to the little stable that couldn't hold half so many, manes tossing, hooves thrashing, soldiers yelling and yammering, rushing to the walls.

One guard might've been younger than her and his helmet had a broken buckle. Kept falling over his eyes, and he'd push it up, and straight away it'd fall again.

The rain was pissing down now, spattering from a broken gutter. A guard was pulled from his saddle, hands gripping a snapped-off arrow-shaft in his belly.

"Is it bad?" he was snarling. "Is it bad?"

Alex was no surgeon but she was pretty sure an arrow in you wasn't good. Arrows are really sharp and your body's just meat.

Her uncle had her by the shoulders, was giving her a shake. "Are you hurt?"

He was staring at her saddle, and she saw it had an arrow sticking out of it, too. Dark wood, and surprisingly long, the flights with a beautiful stripe to them.

"Oh," she said. If she'd been sitting astride, it would likely have gone through her leg.

They had that guard on the ground, were dragging his mail coat up, padded jacket underneath sodden with blood, white skin slick with blood, and her uncle's servant Eusebius was wiping the wound with a rag, and more blood was welling out, and he was wiping it, and more blood came, and more.

"Oh," she said, again, and she found she was gripping her own belly, right where his wound was. Her knees were all wobbly, and her hair was stuck across her face, and she felt sick. Every instinct was screaming to run, but where to?

"How many of them?" someone shrieked.

"Where are the arrows?"

"God help us!"

"Steady!" roared Jakob of Thorn, and Alex flinched as the gate shuddered, and took a nervy step backwards to nowhere, then spun about as something crashed into the ground behind her.

One of the guards had fallen from the wall. Or been thrown. Because now someone jumped down on top of him. Dropped spear-first, nailing him to the ground through the chest.

Someone. Or something. It straightened before Alex's smarting eyes, leaving its spear stuck where it was. Instead of a man's nose it had a long snout, covered in tawny fur, one pointed ear sticking up and the other flopped over with a black tuft on the end. It glared at Alex with amber eyes. The eyes of the foxes she used to see on the rubbish tips at night, watching her outraged, as if to say, *What are you doing in our city, bitch?*

"Saviour protect us . . ." she heard Brother Diaz breathe.

Alex stood frozen as the thing swept a curved sword from a belt bristling with weapons, bared vicious little teeth, and gave a high yip of hatred as it swung at her.

There was a scrape of steel as Duke Michael barged her sideways, catching the sword on his, steering it wide so the point just missed her shoulder. With a flick of the wrist, he switched from parry to thrust, stepping forwards so his blade punched through the fox-man's studded leather jerkin, then whipped back out.

Hard to tell his expression, on account of the brown fuzz on his face, but he made a sort of squeal and fell to his knees. His sword clattered down as he clutched at the wound, blood flooding between his furry fingers.

"Into the inn!" Duke Michael jabbed a finger at two of the guards. "You and you, with us!"

He bundled Alex through a doorway, into a low common room with crooked rafters, smelling of onions and disappointment. A miserable place even by Alex's standards, which till a few days ago had been some of the lowest in Europe. Didn't help that the wagon had smashed a ragged hole through the wall and brought down a chunk of ceiling. A chubby man cringed behind a counter covered in broken plaster.

"What's happening?" he squeaked.

"A man," burbled Alex, mindlessly, "and a fox."

"Eudoxia's cursed experiments," spat her uncle. He caught the innkeep by his stained apron and dragged him close. "Where's the back door?"

The man pointed a trembling finger into the darkness beside the fireplace, where a couple of logs sputtered in the blackened hearth. Eusebius padded towards it, sliding out a hatchet.

Duke Michael pressed something into Alex's limp hand. A dagger, crosspiece like a snake, red jewels for its eyes. "Take this." He squeezed her fingers closed around the grip. "And be ready to use it."

He led her across the common room, his sword gleaming red in his other hand. Two patrons cringed under a table. A serving girl with a big birthmark was pressed to the wall, gripping a jug in both hands.

Someone was screaming outside, metal scraping, honks and bellows like a farmyard on fire, the crashes of whatever heavy thing was beating on the gates, the smaller of the two guards flinching at each blow. The maid was sticking close behind him, her bonnet all skewed and tears streaming down her face, clutching the bag that held the combs and oils and pretty powders that were suddenly a relic of a vanished world.

Seemed Alex wasn't the only one whose plans had turned to shit.

Eusebius had made it to the back door, was leaning against the chimney breast with one hand on the bolt. Ever so cautiously he eased it open, a strip of light down the side of his bald head as he peered out. He gave his master a nod.

Duke Michael licked his lips, spoke softly. "Stay close to me." He looked around as Eusebius eased the door wider. "And get ready to run—"

The two-log fire blazed up suddenly and the door blew off its hinges.

Alex's hair was lashed in her face by the draught, the low room flooded with crazy light.

Duke Michael was flung away like a toy, his sword clanging into the corner.

The maid shrieked, dropping her bag, bottles and powders spilling.

A woman slipped in through the scorched doorframe. She was very tall, and very lean, and she wore robes stitched with arrows and circles of runes, and her eyes shone with the reflections of the little fires now burning all about the room, and no one ever looked more like a sorceress.

"Not interrupting, am I?" she asked as Alex stumbled back, tripped over the hem of her dress, and went sprawling.

The big guard shouted something as he stepped forwards, then all at once went up in flames, his circle-marked surcoat on fire, his hair curling and twisting and drifting off him like burning straw.

Searing lines shot through the dark. The serving girl screeched, thrashing on the ground, legs on fire. The smaller guard turned to run. The sorceress pointed at him and he fell, crawled, his armour glowing like horseshoes on a smith's anvil, then his surcoat caught fire and he wriggled and howled and clawed at himself, steam clouding from his back.

Alex scrabbled away on her arse, through the mess of the maid's broken bottles, not even able to get the breath to scream, choked by the stink of char and burned flesh and the flowery notes of spilled perfume.

She still had the dagger in her sweaty hand but she never thought of using it. She only held on 'cause she'd forgotten how to make her hand come open.

The sorceress's bright eyes flicked towards her, and she smiled.

"Where do you think you're going?"

Brother Diaz prayed.

It was hardly the first time. Prayers are to a monk as stones to a mason, after all—you really can't do the job without them. Back at the monastery he'd filed into the church dawn, noon, and evening, occasionally led a service for the locals, a couple of baptisms, one slightly anticlimactic funeral. But he'd done plenty of private praying, too—that he might finally make a mark, make his brothers jealous, make his mother proud—and he liked to believe he was really rather good at it. Congratulate himself on his thorough knowledge of the psalms.

It was only in this moment of mortal terror that he realised: his mouth might have said the words, but his heart had never really been in it.

His heart was in it now.

"O God," he gasped, clasping his hands to make one trembling fist and turning his eyes to the spitting heavens, "O Father, O light of the world, bring down your cleansing fire and deliver us from darkness."

The inn's gates were rocked by a crashing blow, another great splinter flying from the back and bouncing across the yard to clatter into the stricken wagon.

"Steady!" growled Jakob of Thorn.

How could anyone be steady while under attack by creatures that were neither man nor animal, but some unholy fusion of the two? The misshapen corpse of the one Duke Michael had killed lay in a slick of blood. It had surely stood on two legs, surely wielded human weapons, but those eyes, still goggling at the sky, were undeniably fox-like. Saviour's breath, those fuzzy ears!

Brother Diaz fell to his knees in the mud, clutching the wooden circle he wore around his neck, symbol of the Saviour, through which one finds the passage to heaven. "O Holy Daughter, O blessed sacrifice, in your infinite mercy, protect us."

A huge figure, strapped with plates of spiked armour, had climbed onto the parapet and was swinging a great axe at two of the Papal Guards. Brother Diaz had thought at first he wore a horned helmet but now, squinting through the drizzle, it was evident the horns grew from his head. He bellowed into the rain, and with his next swing smashed one of the guards screaming off the wall in a shower of blood.

If humanity was fashioned in the image of God, what monstrous corruptions of his holy purpose were these? Brother Diaz had read rumours of such things in the monastery's more fantastical volumes, but always far from the righteous light of the Church, lurking at the edges of the map where the cartographer was just squiggling guesses.

He fumbled in his collar and drew out the silver vial, the sacred blood of Saint Beatrix, and gripped it and the holy circle together. Clearly, he needed every scrap of divine assistance he could get. "O Blessed Saint Beatrix, lend me your unconquerable faith, your dauntless courage. Forgive my weakness and stand by me in my time of trial."

Someone screamed. One of the guards, shot with an arrow, and he toppled from the wall and crashed through the thatched roof of a lean-to shed to lie weakly groaning in its wreckage. Something sprang over the battlements and onto the walkway where he'd stood. A woman with a bow in her hands, another over her back, and at least three quivers of arrows slung about her person, but with great, long, folded legs like a rabbit's.

This was no crusader fortress, bolstered by the White Art of the Faith, merely a badly maintained inn, its crumbling wall scarcely taller than a man. Brother Diaz squeezed his eyes shut and prayed more fervently than ever before, tears squeezed from beneath his prickling lids.

"I know I am an unworthy vessel, stained with lust and lechery, but fill me with your blessed light, let me not fear, let me not—"

At a final crashing blow one of the brackets tore from the wall in a shower of dust, the splintered bar flew back, the broken gates shuddered inwards, and the prayers died on Brother Diaz's lips.

Jakob of Thorn stood framed in the open gateway, grey and stubborn as a wind-bent tree, dwarfed by the monster that now stooped under the high arch.

A towering beast, draped in rusty chain mail and with a great studded club in its furry fists. A goat-legged, goat-headed, goat-horned abomination, bristling with weapons. It stretched out its neck, slotted yellow goat eyes popping, and gave a furious, thunderous, earth-shaking bleat.

Wrath

Balthazar pushed himself up with a piteous groan. Where was he? Darkness, lit by flickering flames, an acrid stench of burning. Was this hell?

The left side of his body ached appallingly. His head pounded. He remembered something about a trial. Wait, had he met the Pope? A spray of sparks as Baron Rikard hauled on a lever . . . the binding, the vomit, the wagon, the *ambush*! It all rushed back. He was just starting to wish this was hell after all when his vision was seared by a brilliant flare and a wash of heat made him cringe.

He sagged against a counter, noticed a smouldering, apron-clad cadaver behind it, lurched away and nearly tripped over Princess Alexia. She was wriggling helplessly backwards, clothes in ash-smeared disarray, across the floor of a low common room scattered with broken furniture, charred corpses, bits of fallen ceiling, and several fires. Her terrified eyes were fixed on a tall woman who, from her arcane robes and knowing smirk—not to mention that she was in the act of stepping unharmed through a sheet of flame—Balthazar deduced to be a pyromancer of no small potency.

It appeared that the plans of Cardinals Zizka and Bock to bring the Empire of the East back into the loving embrace of the Church were about to—quite literally—go up in flames. Under normal circumstances that would have been a matter of the most profound indifference to Balthazar but, for the time being, he found himself irresistibly constrained by the papal binding.

So it was that, as the sorceress raised her hands to tear flame from nowhere, Balthazar went in entirely the wrong direction: throwing himself *between* her and Princess Alexia. By some scrap of good fortune, he was still clutching his excrement-daubed prayer-sheet and, as fire bloomed towards him, he thrust it forwards like a shield, inscription outwards, hissing a charm of protection through gritted teeth.

He was at first immensely relieved to see the flames repelled, roaring around him as if around a glass dome, setting fire to the counter, a couple of stools, a section of the already ruined ceiling, and the circle-embroidered papal tabard of one of the dead guards. Sadly, whether due to the poor quality of the paper, the prayers on the back, the slight soaking with rain, or the imprecise drawing of the runes in shit with a piece of toenail, his relief was short-lived. The prayer-sheet began first to brown, then to blacken, then to curl at the edges, and finally burst into flames.

"Ah!" he squeaked. "Damn it! Ah!" As the fires subsided, he flung the burning scrap down, alternately sucking and blowing on his scorched fingertips, struggling to blink away the fizzing streaks etched into his vision. The princess scrabbled back, slapping at a patch of flame on the hem of her dress, and Balthazar swallowed as the sorceress stepped forwards, lip curled and eyes narrowed.

"You are a sorcerer?" she demanded.

"Magician," he muttered apologetically, scraping away like a disgraced chamberlain from an angry monarch, "though I hold sorcery in the *highest* esteem." He had always considered it a decidedly inferior methodology, the preserve of reckless fools who valued instinct over intellect, but now was hardly the time for absolute candour. "Do I have the honour of addressing one of the mentees of the Empress Eudoxia?"

The sorceress proudly tossed her head. "You do." Vanity was all too common a weakness with her kind. Balthazar deplored it but was not above exploiting it.

"I understand she was a most puissant practitioner!" he frothed.

"The greatest of the age," pronounced the sorceress, narrowing her eyes. "I once saw her throw lightning."

"Magnificent," breathed Balthazar, while reflecting on what a ludicrous exaggeration it must be. "My name . . ." And he delivered the most elaborate introductory bow he could manage while sweating profusely in a burning building surrounded by burning corpses and with his fingertips still singing with pain. "Is Balthazar Sham Ivam Draxi."

He had been hoping her look of furious contempt might dissipate. That proved optimistic. If anything, it intensified. "I have heard of you."

He found himself marooned between fear and gratification. "Good things, I hope?"

"Things." The fires in the inn were hot, but it was the waves of heat coming off *her* that were truly making Balthazar cringe, his face turned sideways and his eyes narrowed to slits while the spit on his lips was cooked dry. The air around her was shimmering, her sleeves scorching black, her hair wafted into a floating cloud by the updraught. She was powerful, that was plain. But those who give themselves to the fire become like the fire: reckless, destructive, and lacking all subtlety.

The princess scrambled for the doorway, the sorceress stepped after her, and Balthazar, with a helpless shrug, simply could not prevent himself from stepping between them once again. The woman's eyes, glowing like coals, flicked towards him.

"You dare oppose me?" she breathed.

Balthazar was not without pride, but it had never prevented him from grovelling when his life was on the line. "I make *abject* apologies for any perceived slight, personal or professional. I have not the *slightest* wish to obstruct you, or any member of your highly regarded coven. I would positively *revel* in the opportunity of watching you reduce that ferrety specimen to ashes, with lightning or otherwise, but—" Balthazar nearly tripped over the singed corpse of one of Her Holiness's finest in his haste to back away then stumbled up with hands high in submission. "I have been placed under this *bloody* papal binding!"

"*That* . . . is a papal binding?" The sorceress glared at the red smear on his wrist. "It looks pathetic."

"You give voice to my very thoughts! But it is *vastly* more effective than it appears!" The serving girl had only blackened twigs for legs, but the upper part of her might still serve a purpose. "I *will* discover its secrets, and I will *break* it—" he gave vent to an unsightly burp and had to swallow some sick "—but for the time being—urgh—I fear I am compelled to do everything in my much-diminished power to protect the little weasel—"

The sorceress raised her hands. "Then burn."

"Does it *have* to be fire?" squealed Balthazar, shrinking from another wash of heat and holding his trembling palms even higher, playing for time as he stretched his will, ever so subtly, towards the two dead guardsmen. "It has never been my strong suit!"

The shimmering around her hands had become even more intense. He could see her bones, glowing like red-hot metal within the flesh. "Do you have a strong suit?" she sneered, stepping between the smoking cadavers.

"Well, since you ask . . ." Balthazar began subtly to move his fingers, threading through the familiar incantations in his mind, feeling out the joints, pinching up the sinews, stroking the fluids into motion. "It's corpses."

The larger of the two guardsmen lurched up with a gurgle and a loud fart. He had a look of lopsided surprise on his blistered features but, rather gratifyingly for Balthazar, nothing compared to the shock on the face of the sorceress.

She gave a hoarse scream, fire shooting from her fingers and sending the big guard up in flames again but, since he was already partly cooked and entirely dead, he was not greatly inconvenienced, grappling incompetently with her like a drunken lover.

"Me, burn?" snarled Balthazar, all the petty frustrations of the last few months spilling forth at once. "I will snuff you like an overgrown *candle*."

Given the less than auspicious circumstances, he conducted those charred bodies like a string quartet. He whisked the small guard up to trembling attention and sent him flailing at the sorceress, pummelling her back. At the same time, he beckoned to the innkeep, whose eyes were cooked and so had to feel his way to the ale-casks like a blind man at a wine-tasting.

The smaller guard swung a fist, tottered on a stiff leg, missed, hit the big guard, and broke his burning hand off. But there was still plenty to work with. The sorceress shrieked as the big guard bit her arm, farting intermittently, which is a common problem with the recently dead unless one really concentrates on the relevant sphincters and, really, who has the patience? Fire spurted up and set the rafters alight, the sorceress stumbled under the big guard's weight, the upper half of the serving girl caught her ankles in a tight embrace, and she gave a despairing howl as she was brought down hard on the charred boards.

The small guard had become confused, wandering around in circles with his clothes on fire, but the big one was still holding on, pinning the sorceress however she twisted, while the serving girl gnawed viciously at her legs, cooked skin sloughing off her shoulders while she did it.

"I am Balthazar Sham Ivam Draxi, you incandescent *drudge*." Balthazar lifted his clenched fist high and the innkeeper reared up, hefting a barrel over his charred head with undead strength. "If someone kills that turd of a princess it will be *me*!"

The innkeep dashed the cask down and stove the sorceress's skull in with the rim, timbers bursting apart and beer spraying out to forever quench her flames with a satisfying hiss. A rather pleasant yeasty odour joined the smells of cooking meat and, for reasons Balthazar could not immediately discern, rather fine perfume.

He let his hands fall and the recently deceased flopped down in a smouldering heap, except for the small guard who tottered on towards the back door a few steps, one pointing hand extended towards daylight, before issuing a final fart, tripping one foot with the other, and pitching onto his face.

The goat giant ducked under the archway to tower head, shoulders, and chest over Jakob. With human hands it hefted a monstrous club sprouting with rusty nails, opened its maw, stuck out its tongue, and gave a braying scream to freeze the blood.

But Jakob had stood unflinching before worse horrors than overgrown livestock.

He shrugged off the instinct to shrink back, stepped forwards as the club plunged towards his head, and at the last moment angled his shield so the blow didn't crush him, but glanced off with a painful jolt, nails gouging wood before thudding into the mud beside him. The goat-thing lurched off balance on its skittering goat hooves, triumphant bleat turned to a honk of alarm.

Whack.

There's a sound a sword makes cutting into flesh. A slick, quick *whack*. Not that loud, if your technique's good and your steel sharp. Jakob never let his sword go dull.

Shocked honk became agonised squeal as the blade smacked deep into the thing's furry thigh, just below the flapping hem of its undersized mail coat, and it lurched sideways. Goats are really meant to have four legs. Very unsteady on two, especially when one's chopped near in half. It slumped against the archway, trying to lift its club again.

Jakob had been far stronger once. Too many wounds half-healed. Too many fights fought and lost. But a sword doesn't need strength if you have the skill and the will.

Whack.

He could've taken the beast's horned head off with one blow in his youth. Now he only cleaved its neck halfway, blade lodging in its spine. It crumpled in the archway, blood flooding from the yawning wound.

A man sprang over it. A squat man covered in black-and-white-spotted fur like a hunting dog, a heavy mace in each hand.

When you have a shield there's an urge to stay back. To hide behind it like a gate. But Jakob had never liked retreating. An enemy with a shield pressed in his face can't attack and can't defend—he's weakened, demoralised, prone to slip and fall. A fallen enemy is a dead enemy, and a dead enemy was Jakob's favourite kind.

So he made his shield a ram instead, drove it into the hound-man's chest, crowding him against the side of the gateway. He flailed with one mace around the rim but there was no venom there, it bounced harmlessly from Jakob's shoulder. Now Jakob rose up over the shield, sword angled down, looking the hound-man in his white-furred, black-spotted face. Dog's fur, but man's eyes.

The edge of a sword needs little strength. The point needs hardly any. You wouldn't have called them thrusts, just firm prods. The first took the dog in his furry cheek, scraped across his teeth. The second punctured one eye. The third slid through his throat. Dark blood welled from the holes, and when Jakob stepped away the hound-man crumpled like an empty sack, face in the mud and arse in the air. He had a hole cut in the back of his trousers for his dog's tail to stick out of.

Another beast was already charging through the gateway, grey hair woolly as sheep's fleece, spiral ram-horns curling from it, one of his eyes with a human pupil, the other with a sheep's keyhole. Even more off-putting was the great axe he was swinging with both hands. Jakob tottered back, the blade missing him by a hair and knocking a chunk of stone from the archway.

The ram-man hefted his axe again. Plates of beaked iron were strapped to his arms, but aside from tufts of wool his hands were bare. Pick one piece of armour, make it a helmet, but gauntlets had always come second on Jakob's list. His sword clanged against the haft of the axe, sent two woolly fingers flying off and left a third hanging by a flap.

The ram bellowed in fury, snapping forwards over Jakob's shield, horns crunching into his face. Jakob reeled back, fell gasping to one knee. The ram-man screeched as he hoisted his axe high in his good hand—

Thud.

Jakob caught a glimpse of Baptiste's snarling face as she buried a dagger in the side of the ram's neck. He drooled red blood into pale wool, axe dropping in the dirt, fumbling at his belt for a sword. Baptiste nailed him through the top of the skull with another knife before he got there, right between the horns. He flopped sideways, mute testament to the greatest fighting technique of all: a friend behind your enemy.

Jakob growled as Baptiste dragged him up, flinched as a horse flashed past, spattering mud. Half the mounts hadn't fitted in the stable and now they'd formed a panicked herd, frisking riderless out of the gate, harnesses flapping, trampling the misshapen corpses Jakob had left there. Beyond them, hazy through the rain, Jakob saw figures. Lumpen, animal figures, furred and horned and hoofed and bristling with weapons, and leading the way a man in bright armour.

"Where did these things come from?" hissed Baptiste.

Jakob wiped blood from under his throbbing nose. "Troy, maybe?"

"Your nose is broken."

"Hardly the first time."

"We're in trouble."

"Hardly the first time."

"I should've quit after Barcelona!"

"We should all have quit after Barcelona." The walls were falling, beast-men springing and wriggling and clambering down into the yard to press the last few guards. Their young captain was sitting against the well, wheezing as he was stabbed again and again with a spear. The moustache hadn't helped. The stables had caught fire, patches of flame all over the thatch, the few remaining horses plunging and screeching inside. Brother Diaz was on his knees, clutching his holy circle and mouthing prayers.

"Here's a pickle," breathed Jakob, and he ripped the shield from his arm and snapped his aching fingers at Baptiste. "Key."

She stared at him, eyes wide and white, hair black and bloody. "You sure?"

"Key!" No one wants to see doubts. You make your choice and live with it. Or die with it.

"God help us all . . ." She shrugged the chain from around her neck, the iron key dangling. Jakob snatched it from her and ran for the wagon. Not that fast, since his left knee didn't move too well and his right hip barely moved at all and it was hard these days to say which of his ankles was more buggered, but he ran still, past a guard with an arrow in his back, mud smeared down one side of his twisted face, crawling to nowhere.

You learn to spot the lost causes. You save what can be saved.

He slid the key into the lock but his crooked fingers were slick with blood and it slipped, dropping in the mud.

"*Shit!*" he groaned, bending to fish it up by the chain, reaching, reaching—

"Uh!" He sagged against the wagon, a burning pain in his side. An even worse one than usual. He'd a good guess what would greet him when he peered down, but it was still somehow a shock to see the arrowhead sticking out above his hip. He turned to see a woman kneeling on the walkway. She had great, tall ears like a hare, one of them flopped over, dozens of earrings dangling from it. He might almost have laughed, if it hadn't been for the bow she was already drawing again. One of those vicious little recurves they use in the desert. "Oh," he grunted, "fucking—uh!"

The second arrow punched through his lung, from the way his breath started to crackle. God, the pain.

Baptiste had vanished as neatly as Sunny might've. *Don't stick your neck out*, she always said. Good advice. His neck was always stuck out. His whole life, a succession of last stands, lost causes, and bitter ends.

But he had his sword in his hand still, and his oaths to consider. He made of his pain a spur, growled through gritted teeth as he gathered what strength he had left, blood on each breath.

The man in bright armour strode through the broken gates of the inn. He was tall and handsome, a warrior in his prime, a drawn sword in each hand and at least four daggers sticking from his belt, the only hint of animal his gilded helmet crafted like a lion's mouth. He roared as he hacked the crawling guard between the shoulder blades, and again, then stabbed him through the back for good measure and left one blade stuck there.

"This is it?" He glowered around the yard. "An old knight, a young monk, and a handful of the Pope's hirelings?" The captain of the guards was dead already, but the newcomer hacked at him savagely anyway, carved his head open in a shower of blood, then kicked the corpse over on its side. "Bock must be losing her fucking marbles."

"Can I kill th'monk?" snorted a man with a bull's face, the words not quite fitting in his animal mouth.

"Killing priests is bad luck," snapped his master, sounding quite disappointed about it.

"Damn ith!" blew the bull, in a mist of angry spit. He kicked Brother Diaz between his shoulders and the monk went down with a muddy boot-print across the back of his habit.

The key was the only chance, but it was in the mud, a stride or two away. Jakob gritted his bloody teeth, and with the faintest groan pushed himself from the wagon, clinging to his sword's hilt as if it was the last rung on a ladder.

"Do we have to?" asked the man with the lion helmet, one side of his sneer spotted with blood.

"I swore . . ." Jakob wheezed in one more bubbling breath, took one more wobbling step, "some oaths." He swung as best he could.

"For God's sake." The man stepped disgustedly around Jakob's sword so it clanged into the corner of the wagon and bounced away. "This is fucking *embarrassing*!" And he ran Jakob through the chest.

"Ooooof . . ." he groaned. That had definitely got the heart. So many times stabbed, and still he was never ready for the feeling of metal entering his body uninvited. He stood trembling a moment longer, then the blade whipped out of him and he crumpled to his knees.

His pulse surged in his ears. A sound like the sea. At Parnu, where they'd said their last goodbyes. Waves draining through sand stained black by all the pyres. He tried to get up, one more time. He had his oaths, and the oaths must keep him standing when his flesh failed, when his courage failed . . . when his faith failed . . .

He flopped on his face.

Alex scrambled from the nightmare in the inn and straight into a nightmare in the yard.

The stables had caught fire in spite of the rain, horses inside plunging in a frenzy. One of the guardsmen screamed as a woman with a great bushy tail like a squirrel's clawed and chomped and worried at his guts, snout speckled with blood. Most of the others lay hacked, stabbed, or broken. The maid was face down with an arrow in the back of her head. A woman with great tall hare-ears sat on the walkway, an arrow nocked to a bow, legs dangling playfully off the edge. They ended not in shoes, but dainty little rabbit paws.

A big man in bright armour stood near the wagon. He'd run Jakob of Thorn through with a jewel-hilted sword. Now he looked over at Alex like a bloodhound caught scent of the quarry.

"Ah! How nice of you to *join us*." He strode towards her, not even bothering to wipe his sword, a trail of dark spots dripping from the point. "I'm Duke Marcian. Youngest son of the Empress Eudoxia."

Behind him, the old knight flopped on his face in the muck. Alex looked into the eyes of the monsters around her. The pitiless animal eyes, and the even more pitiless eyes of the man who led them. She didn't say anything. She wasn't sure her mouth still worked.

"I apologise for these . . . *creatures* of my mother's." Marcian elbowed a man with slitted cat's eyes and crossed belts bristling with knives out of his way. "They smell as bad as they look, but they're as savage as you'd expect, and surprisingly loyal. And you can't really put a price on loyalty when you have the family *we* have."

"We?" Alex managed to stammer. "You've got me confused . . . with someone else." She tried to smile, but it ended up a wobbly grimace. "I'm nobody. I'm nothing—"

"The Pope doesn't think so." Marcian pulled something from between the two daggers thrust through his belt. A roll of paper. He held it up, letting it unfurl by the weight of its elaborate seal. Alex couldn't read it, of course, but she knew what it said. She'd heard Cardinal Bock dictate it. The papal bull confirming who she was. One of the copies no one was meant to know about till she got to Troy.

Alex could actually hear the *glug* in her own throat as she swallowed.

"That's right." Marcian's eyes flickered scornfully over the paper, then even more scornfully over her. "*You.* The long-lost Princess Alexia Pyrogennetos. *Her.* My cousin, born in the flame. *This.* The one rightful heir to the Serpent Throne of Troy." He curled his lip. "Fuck *me.*"

Duke Michael was dead. The Pope's guards were dead. Jakob of Thorn was, if not dead, then certainly on the way. Brother Diaz hunched in the mud, hands clasped and faintly rocking, probably dead but not realised yet. To be fair, he hadn't seemed much use at the best of times.

"I know." Alex realised she was still clutching the snake-hilt dagger and tossed it away, backing off, holding up her hands. "It's a joke." Begging for her life again. At least she'd had plenty of practice. "No one thinks it's a bigger joke than me!"

She tripped on a corpse, caught one fur-trimmed riding boot with the other, and went down hard on her arse. Marcian snorted laughter. The really sad thing was she laughed, too. A cringing little titter. They were going to kill her, and she was laughing along.

"I'm not a princess!" She wriggled back in the filth, voice rising to a pathetic little whine. "I'm a thief! I only came to run from a debt. Three debts! I'm a piece of shit. What would I do with a throne?" She was laughing and crying at once, heels scuffing the bloody dirt. "I sell fake relics in the Holy City! I trick pilgrims, and send 'em to be robbed. I stole a comb! Look!" And she shook it from her sleeve into the mud. "I didn't know what else to do with it. You don't have to worry about me. No one has to worry about me—"

"Unless you're a pilgrim, eh?" said Marcian, and the creatures gave a clamour of honking, snorting, squawking, gibbering, like laughter mixed with feeding time at the farmyard. Eudoxia's youngest son stalked after her, red sword resting on his shoulder, the way a digger might rest his shovel, the vicious-looking spurs on his armoured heels clinking with each step. "Thing is, you're offering me heaps of wretched desperation and contemptible cowardice, but what I'm not getting is any *trace* of a reason not to kill you. *Obviously,* you have to die." Her back hit the wall of the tavern, and there was nowhere left to go. Marcian sneered down at her, face speckled with blood. "You can shuffle off with some dignity, at least. You're royalty, aren't you?" And he tossed the papal bull into her lap.

"Please. You don't—"

"Get up!" he screamed, spraying spit.

Her knees trembled so badly she had to drag herself up by the wall behind her. But somehow, the further she got, the stiffer her joints became. She ended up standing tall. As tall as she got, at least. And she lifted her chin and looked her handsome, awful cousin in the eye.

"*Fuck you*, then!" She spat at him.

"Huh." His smile faded, leaving him looking thoughtfully at her. "I see it now. The resemblance." And he lifted his sword.

"Wait!" Brother Diaz blundered between them. "Just a moment!"

Marcian caught the monk by the front of his habit, lifted his sword to tickle him under the chin. Brother Diaz swallowed, wincing as his Kane's apple brushed the red point. Alex followed his staring eyes. She could've sworn she saw a footprint appear from nowhere in the sloppy mud.

"For *what?*" demanded Marcian.

Sunny stepped from empty air beside the wagon, plucked the key from the mud, nimbly turned it in the lock, took a deep breath, and was gone. The four bolts sprang open.

"That," said Brother Diaz.

The back of the wagon slowly tipped forwards then splashed down into the puddle-pocked filth beside Jakob's corpse.

Inside there was only darkness.

Or . . . did something shift in there? A deeper shadow in the black.

Marcian frowned towards it. "What's in the wagon?"

A low growl came from inside. Like the fighting dogs Alex spent one summer taking bets on, but deeper, bigger, far more frightening. The bull-man stepped back a pace, fingering his axe.

"No one would tell me . . ." whispered Brother Diaz.

And with a blood-chilling howl something burst from the darkness in a wash of foul-smelling wind, a mass of snarl and claws and whipping hair, of teeth and bunched muscle.

It fell on the bull-man and crushed him into the mud, blood spraying from his snout in an agonised bellow. It ripped him from throat to groin and he came open like an old coat, insides sliding out in a red-black slurry.

"Oh God," whispered Alex.

The Good Meat

The Vigga-Wolf screamed with fury and delight to be out of the horrid wagon and once again at her work, which was murder, and her hobby, too. Also murder.

She didn't know or care why this bastard had a bull's head. Folk all have their own different heads don't they? She slipped under his axe, ripped it from his fists, smashed off one of his horns with it, then flung it at the rabbit girl on the wall and split her skull in half. Then she clawed the bull's guts out with her fists, snarling, weeping, spraying drool, snuffling for the good meat, the nice bits, the tasty morsels.

People's heads might all be different but their insides are much alike.

Her jaws snapped shut on a woman with a piggy head, got head and arm together, squeezing, squeezing. The arm snapped first, went floppy as a sock of porridge, and she squealed piggy squeals and beat away with a shield, clobbered with the rim as the Vigga-Wolf snarled in frustration, the bits of arm still wedged in her teeth, and wriggled her head to get the best grip, biting, twisting, biting, wrenching, biting.

Squeals became screams then *crack* the skull popped and the Vigga-Wolf sucked the meat out and ugh, what a horrid salty mouthful. She choked and coughed and ripped at the foul-tasting pig bitch with her back claws and tore her so hard the other arm came off then flung what was left into the bull-man who was struggling up wailing with guts all hanging out and the pair of them went reeling across the yard all the horrid bad meat mashed up together.

"Where's the good meat?" she screamed, but her teeth and tongue weren't made for man-words and the rain was tickling her nose so all she could do was howl and growl but the fuckers got the gist. They'd thought they were the animals, they were the scary ones, but now they bore witness to the beast indeed and reeled about eyes rolling and fell and scrambled away whimpering with terror. The Vigga-Wolf remembered through a mist that everything that walked, crawled, or flew was always terrified of her.

This was the proper state of things.

She caught a horse by the rump, not sure if it was man-horse or horse-horse only knowing it was meat, brought it down while her hind claws raked and tore and sent the insides showering across the yard to spatter the wall with glistening shreds. She crammed a mouthful down, choking and gargling, but that was not the good meat.

The terrible hunger burned like a hot coal down her throat, like a hot brand up her arse, a great void inside choking and goading her, making her dance and twist and scream like she'd rip at her own tail.

Did she have a tail?

She spun around and around to try and see but her hind legs were always out of reach the fuckers and she ended up turning a tumble and skittering arse over tit across the yard, spraying mud and blood all over.

She caught one who was running and flung him against the wall and his head broke open, flung him again so hard the wall cracked, flung him again, flopping like rags and the broken stones crashed down on top of him, too much shattered to even be a corpse but just mess with fingers on the end.

She slit and tore and twisted them open as though each one had a special secret inside, but all they held was steaming slop and disappointment no matter how she snuffled for treasures.

She rooted about in a sheep one all fleecy but she got wool up her nose and had to twist and yelp and sneeze it all about. She screamed at the sky. Would've ripped the sun down and eaten it if her claws could've reached. She hated these meat-bags, hated the trees, the walls, the sky, the rain, herself most of all, filthy hungry thing that didn't even have a tail probably. She wanted to rip herself inside-out and eat herself, so endless was her monstrous appetite—

But who was this?

A man with shiny, shiny armour and a shiny, shiny sword and a bit of stubborn grit in the terror on his face. Such a handsome face. Oooh, what a brave one. The Vigga-Wolf wanted to bite it and find out if the good meat was hid inside.

She slunk towards him with a sultry slither all up on her tippy-toes, her jaw hanging open and feathering the mud, the rain cold pinpricks on her lolling tongue, leaving a zigzag trail of bloody drool.

"Die, fiend!" he squealed.

"Die yourself, you shitty bastard," answered she but the wit was wasted 'cause it came out as a slurping howl so she slapped the sword from his hand instead, snapped his arm bones even in their iron case. The blade spun twittering away to clang into the wagon and she caught him around the neck and bit on his head.

That shiny helmet was most annoying, it wouldn't break straight away, her teeth scored and scraped it and maybe his face a bit as well. Perhaps his nose came off.

Before she could really work her jaws around it something bashed her back and knocked her rolling over and she twisted around to see a man with slitted eyes like a cat had hit her with a halberd and her side was all bruised and burning and though she hated everything she hated cats particularly. Who'd he think he was?

He looked shocked as a cat could when she sprang on him and ripped a chunk of his ribcage out then flung him upside down into the burning stables, roof caving in and burning thatch sliding over his still-kicking corpse and a horse burst free and frisked sideways across the yard all wild and maddened with its tail on fire.

Shiny was up again which you had to admire since he was sobbing away with one arm bitten all floppy. There's a lesson. One moment you're king of the yard the next your face is all red strips and blood's bubbling from your empty nose hole. She pounced on him and this time got her jaws around his head, not just the nibblers but the crushers at the back, and she shook him flopping and flailing, his armour clanking like a pan-seller's wagon going off a cliff which she thought maybe she'd seen happen once.

He burbled and screeched and clawed at her face with his hand and dragged at her jaws with his nails but he'd have had better luck stopping the tide with his fingers. She gnawed and worried and the steel had to give, give all at once, and she crushed his skull like a nut and all the juice squirted out and she stuck her tongue inside and snorted up the bits, then flung the broken rags of him away, high over the wall.

The horrible hunger was withering, the wonderful need was shrivelling, and she spat out mangled shreds of helmet, prowling and growling. Maybe she needed the good meat still or maybe a lie down, back in the wagon, where it was dark and smelled comfortingly of herself.

Lie down and snooze.

What was that nagging noise though? She cast about with the drool dripping from her jaws and saw a girl sat with that wobbly-slack face they get when they're past crying and a trembling priest kneeling in front of her and the Vigga-Wolf could smell piss and perfume and she wasn't sure which of them or both had pissed or maybe pissed perfume it was a puzzle. He was dribbling prayers the way they do, *O God, O Saviour, O Saint Beatrix*, like God cares about such meat as this, like God cares about anything but himself.

She bared her teeth and gave a grinding growl because the Vigga-Wolf and God did not get on at all and she found it . . .

Very . . .

Irritating.

Brother Diaz knelt, still partly shielding the cringing Princess Alexia with his body, though it could only be by accident. He couldn't have moved had he wanted to, utterly frozen with terror as the thing crept ever closer, blurred through the tears in his eyes, its growl seeming to make the whole yard throb.

It looked sometimes like a vast and terrible wolf, a wild dog big as a horse, but the rags of human clothes trailed from it as it slunk low to the dirt, its forelimbs like arms, great muscles clenching beneath coarse fur, curving claws sprouting from almost human fingers, grasping hands squelching at the mud.

Through a mane of black hair clotted with blood he saw a snuffling wolf-snout. A glimpse of an eye. A devil's eye, burning with hateful malevolence. A giant mouth, black lips curled back in a frenzied snarl, teeth big as butchers' knives, steaming with gore.

"Father protect us . . ." he breathed. One of his knees was trembling. He could hear it flapping inside his habit.

"Though we stand at the gates of hell . . ." The beast gave a great bellow, blowing a mist of blood in his face, and he closed his eyes, wincing as he turned his head away.

"Though death's breath . . . is upon us . . ." He felt it hot on his cheek indeed and his prayers became meaningless whimpers. Here was death, and an utterly horrible death, and he gripped Alex's hand, felt her grip him back with desperate strength—

"*Vigga!*" roared a voice.

Brother Diaz prised one eye open.

Jakob of Thorn was, as Baptiste had put it, dead as fuck. He still had the bloody rent in his gambeson that Marcian's mortal thrust had left, not to mention two arrows sticking through his body. Yet there he stood, impossibly upright, with the expression of a furious schoolmaster dressing down a wayward pupil.

"Vigga!" he bellowed, stepping in front of the beast. "This behaviour is *unacceptable!*"

The monstrous thing shifted back. Away from Jakob and—thank the Saviour—away from Brother Diaz. It seemed somehow less a thing now, more a person, crouching on two feet rather than crawling on four claws.

Behind the tangle of hair he saw less muzzle, more face. There was a strange silence, with only the ongoing death-rattle of one of the butchered creatures in the background.

Then the thing leaned forwards, opening its maw, making Brother Diaz shrink away even though it showed less beast-fangs, more human-teeth, and shrieked in a broken growl. "I'm thirsty!"

More silence, with the faint spattering of rain from a broken gutter, and the snuffling gurgle of the man with the bull's head as he dragged himself towards the gate, unfurling a glistening trail of guts behind him.

The woman crouched, breathing hard, bloody hands dangling. It could not be denied now that it *was* a woman, albeit an extraordinarily tall, muscular, and entirely naked one, skin rather than fur slathered in mud and blood.

"I'm thirsty." Did her lower lip wobble? "I'm thirsty and . . . I've got blood up my nose." She dropped on her backside and started to sob. "I'm thirsty. And I hurt my hand!"

She dragged aside two handfuls of bloody black hair to reveal an angular face, broad-browed, heavy-jawed, and scrawled with tattooed writing in several alphabets. The word *beware* in bold type down her cheek. The word *caution* in large letters on each forearm, smaller messages pricked in other colours and languages around, and between, and inside the letters.

"You put me in the wagon," she said, rubbing tears on the back of her painted wrist. "I *hate* the wagon!"

"I'm sorry." Jakob planted his fists on his hips and surveyed the devastated yard. He still had those two arrows in him. "But I think . . . we can see why."

"I ate something bad." The woman lurched onto her hands and vomited up a great stream of blood and half-chewed offal at Jakob's feet.

Alex prised her hand from Brother Diaz's clammy grip, raising a trembling finger to point. "He . . . has arrows . . ."

"Yes," said Brother Diaz, hopelessly.

The big woman who a few moments before had been a giant wolf rocked onto her haunches. "That's bad meat," she groaned, wiping her mouth. "Where'd I get it?"

Jakob of Thorn considered the torn-open bodies. "Here and there."

She heaved again, more black lumps splatting onto the heap in a widening bloody puddle, and she worked her tongue, and let a couple of shreds of twisted metal drop from her mouth.

"Blessed Saint Beatrix . . ." Brother Diaz forced his eyes away. "What *is* she?"

"Rather obviously, a werewolf." An elderly gentleman stepped from the inn, calm as a patron after a meal, holding a walking stick but not really leaning on it. "And not one of those crappy little German ones, mark you, dancing about and wanking at the moon." He was very upright, and spry, with a twinkle in his eye. "A proper Norse blood-and-lightning werewolf! I see she has made another mess." He shrugged. "It's what Vigga does. But I suppose, sometimes . . . a mess is what you need."

It was only by his clothes, and something around the eyes, perhaps, that Brother Diaz was finally able to place him. "Baron Rikard?"

The vampire looked, if anything, faintly amused. "The very same."

"You have something . . ." Alex pointed at the corner of her mouth. "Just here."

"Ah." He whisked out a handkerchief, licked one corner, then dabbed away a bloody smudge. "How *incredibly* gauche of me."

"You look twenty years younger," said Alex, eyes wide.

"How delightful of you to say so. Perhaps you're not such a charmless cluck as I first suspected. We may make a princess of you yet." The baron gave Brother Diaz something close to a conspiratorial wink. "I know it's a great deal to take in, Brother, but trust me, it's amazing what one can get used to."

"For the Chapel of the Holy Expediency . . ." The elf had reappeared from nowhere, leaning against the wall of the inn, arms folded, "none of this is that remarkable."

Brother Diaz took in the burning buildings, the retching werewolf, the knight full of arrows, the dead guards, and the half-goat, half-sheep, half-dog corpses tangled in the inn's broken gateway. "So *this* . . ." he managed to croak, "is a typical day?"

"Well." Baron Rikard raised one grey brow. "It's not *un*typical."

Empress or Death

Alex sat on a damp bench, Empress of a yard full of muddy corpses.

The fires were mostly out, at least. The rain had mostly stopped. She wriggled her shoulders under the scratchy shirt she wore. She'd swapped clothes with the girl who'd been drawing water by the well, who looked way better in Alex's slightly singed but very fine dress than Alex ever had. Though it did spoil the cut a bit that her body was facing down while her head was twisted all the way around to stare baffled at the sky.

Jakob's idea. So anyone else sent to murder her might think she was dead. That was her highest ambition, right now. Everyone thinking she was dead. She'd never had the manners of a princess. Now she'd even lost the clothes.

All she had left were the enemies.

Baptiste had cut the old knight out of his tunic and he sat hunched, sinewy and lopsided, a stick wedged in his jaws, grimacing as she dug the arrows out of him. The man was more scar than man. Star-shaped punctures, criss-crossed gashes, mottled burns. Alex doubted this was his first impalement, let alone his first arrow-wound. There was one mark she kept coming back to, all the way around his arm. Gave her the mad feeling it had been cut clean off then stitched back on.

"So . . . you're one of them?" Brother Diaz was still mud-caked, still gripping his holy circle white-knuckle tight. Like he was hanging off a cliff and that was his one handhold. "One of my . . . congregation?"

Jakob of Thorn prised the stick from his mouth. "I was cursed by a witch and—*God* damn it!" As Baptiste wrenched one of the arrows out.

"Sorry," she said, tossing it away.

"I was cursed by a witch, and I cannot die. God knows I've tried—gah!" And he wedged the stick back in his jaws as Baptiste started to slit the skin around the other shaft.

It hardly bled. Like cutting a wax dummy. Any other day, being cursed by a witch so you couldn't die was a story that would've left Alex with a question or two. Today she just sat there, staring at nothing. She felt something pressed into her hand.

"Here." It was Sunny. Giving Alex that snake-carved dagger she'd thrown away. "You might still find a use for this."

It felt strange in her palm. Everything felt strange. Like a dream. Or maybe she'd been dreaming till now, and this was how waking up felt. She wiped some tears on her sleeve. She didn't really feel like she was crying, but water kept coming out of her face. And her nose. And her mouth. She was leaking all over, like a pauper's roof.

"You hurt?"

Alex shook her head. Scuffed and bruised. Few scratches on her arms where she'd crawled through her dead maid's broken bottles. Nothing compared to the dead maid herself. Nothing compared to most of the survivors. She wiped her eyes again. She'd always thought she was so tough. "Can't stop crying," she muttered.

"You get used to it," said Sunny.

Alex's eyes crawled over the burst remains of animals, men, and things in between. A couple of enterprising crows had flapped down to make an early start on the windfall. "Not sure that's a comfort," she whispered.

Only one of the guards had lived through the carnage, likely by hiding, and now he sat huddled beside the stable boy, both staring at the woman—or the wolf—who'd done most of the killing. Vigga, they called her. She stood by the well, stark naked, but with shoulders back and feet planted wide like she couldn't have cared less, humming tunelessly to herself, washing blood from her great tangle of black hair. Pink water streamed down a muscle-knotted back tattooed with wolves, dragons, trees, suns and moons, circles and snaking lines of runes, every gap filled in with warnings. One muscular arse cheek had *DANGER* written across it.

Brother Diaz shielded his eyes with one hand. "For Saint Agnes's sake, could she dress herself?"

She flashed a great grin showing four glistening, dog-like fangs. "If your God made all things, didn't he also make . . ." And she turned to give everyone a full view of her front, as densely muscled and painted as the back. "All *this*?"

"Have you no *shame*?" The monk clapped his hands fully over his eyes, though Alex did wonder if he might've left a gap between the fingers to peer through.

"What's wrong? Worried you might forget your vow of . . ." Vigga frowned at the sky, scratching her tattooed stomach, which had a streak of black hair down the centre. "What's the name of it?"

"Chastity," murmured Sunny, rooting through the saddlebags of a dead horse.

"God, no!" squeaked Brother Diaz, turning his back entirely. "Just . . . *please*, cover yourself, before I have to invoke Her Holiness's binding!"

"Fine, fine, take a fucking breath." And Vigga dumped the rest of the bucket over her head, blew a mist of drops, shook herself like a dog, and strode off to sniff at the corpses.

"Is she . . . *safe?*" whispered the monk, peering horrified around one hand.

Baron Rikard snorted. "*Absolutely* not. Can't you see all the warnings?"

"I have a survivor!" Balthazar stumbled from the ruined inn, half-carrying Duke Michael, both of them smeared with ash and blood.

Alex caught his hand, a new wave of snot leaking from her face. She'd been thinking of him as a mark in a swindle. Now she was pathetically pleased to see he was still breathing. He'd saved her life twice now, after all. He was on her side, and she couldn't say that of many people. Or any, really.

"Alex," he gasped, sagging on the bench beside her. "Thank God!"

"I ran," she muttered, pointlessly. "Well, *crawled—*"

"You're alive. That's all that matters."

"Saving wounded men?" Baptiste cocked an eyebrow at Balthazar as she knelt beside the duke. "Didn't have you down as the type."

"Far from my typical modus operandi." The magician glared at the red mark on his wrist. "But Her Holiness said we had to be *nice*."

"Are you trained as a healer?" asked Brother Diaz doubtfully as Baptiste flicked out the blade of a tiny knife.

"Spent some time as assistant to the barber of a mercenary company." She started to slit Duke Michael's trouser leg. "Which is why I give a very passable wet shave, as it goes."

"And *that* . . . qualifies you . . . for *this?*"

"We did the surgery, too, but mercenaries much prefer facial hair to fighting, so we weren't often called on for that. Still, if you reckon you're more qualified . . . feel free to step in."

She peeled open Duke Michael's trouser leg. His calf was stained black and purple all over, bent one way below the knee, bent back the other above the ankle.

"I will stick to the prayers . . ." murmured Brother Diaz, queasily shielding his eyes again.

"I think it's broken," croaked Alex.

"We need no barber to tell us *that*," said Baron Rikard.

Balthazar was busy bragging. "The princess was set upon by a member of the deceased Eudoxia's coven, a pyromancer of *considerable* puissance, but, fortunately for our royal charge, and indeed our entire endeavour, Balthazar

Sham Ivam Draxi was on . . . hand . . . to . . . there appears to be a very large naked tattooed woman over there."

"Werewolf," said Baron Rikard.

"Ugh." Balthazar wrinkled his nose. "A proper Norse one?"

"The massacre was in large part her handiwork."

"Urgh!" Balthazar rolled one of the corpses over with his boot, where it goggled at the sky with unnatural fox eyes. "What are these hybrid monstrosities?"

"Eudoxia's experiments," said Duke Michael through gritted teeth as Baptiste felt at his crooked shin with her fingertips. "She wished to discover the location of the soul."

"A conundrum that has confounded philosophers for centuries . . ." Balthazar squatted over the creature, eyes narrowed with curiosity. "So she merged human and animal in an effort to solve it. Ingenious . . ." He dragged back the lids to peer at one of the creature's bulging eyes at close quarters. "I have seen sarcomancy practised before but never with such precision . . ."

"People have accused Eudoxia of pretty much everything," muttered Duke Michael, "but never of being imprecise—" He gave a ragged moan as Baptiste snapped his leg straight below the knee. Alex pressed his hand, and he pressed hers. Wasn't much more she could do. Nothing needed stealing, and no one needed lying to, and it was hard to see how losing at cards would help, so that was her whole skillset exhausted.

"We need to move." Jakob was up, growling as he stiffly worked his blood-stained tunic back on.

Brother Diaz nodded eagerly. "I could *not* agree more. We head back to the Holy City at once—"

"No!" gasped Duke Michael. "They knew where we were. Someone in the Celestial Palace may have betrayed us."

"Well, we have to send for help, at least—"

"We don't know who we can trust." Jakob fished up the bloodied copy of the papal bull. "No one was meant to know the princess was even alive until she arrived in Troy." And he crushed it in his hands.

"Every time." Baron Rikard gave a long sigh, stretching his arms above his head. "*Every* time."

"Marcian's brothers may know about Alex, too." Duke Michael forced the words through his gritted teeth. "There's only one place she'll be safe now." He looked at her, and the silence stretched, and a broken gutter drip, drip, dripped.

"On the Serpent Throne?" she said, in a very small voice.

Brother Diaz gave a desperate snort. "Well, *we* can't get the princess to Troy!"

"You must." Duke Michael waved towards the one surviving guard and the one surviving stable boy. "These two can help me back to the Holy City. The rest of you will have to go on. Oh *God*!" And there was an ugly *crunch* as Baptiste wrenched his foot into position.

"We seven?" Brother Diaz waved at his flock. "A vampire, an elf, a werewolf—can she *please* dress herself?"

Vigga had been stripping the clothes from a dead guard but she'd got distracted catching raindrops on her tongue.

"A knight who can't die, a sorcerer—"

"Magician."

"—a monk who never even wanted to be a bloody monk, and . . ." Brother Diaz waved helplessly at Baptiste, "a former assistant barber to a mercenary company!"

"Among other things," she muttered as she fixed two broken lengths of spear to either side of Duke Michael's leg with dead men's belts.

Baron Rikard frowned. "You never wanted to be a monk?"

"Are you all *insane*?" howled Brother Diaz.

"I reckon none of us planned to attend a *fucking massacre*!" Alex screeched back at him, starting up off the bench with her fists clenched. "But here we are!" Suddenly everyone was looking at her. "They want me dead? Well, *fuck them*! I'm going to Troy!"

Brother Diaz had turned very pale. "But, Your Highness—"

"It's *fucking* decided!" she snapped.

Sunny shrugged. "There it is, then." And she started to round up the surviving horses. As luck would have it, the sun chose that moment to break through the clouds and bathe the scene of slaughter in warmth.

Baron Rikard turned his smiling face, a good deal less lined than an hour before, towards it. "Nice weather for a trip."

"She swears a lot, for a princess," said Vigga. "I like it." She'd finally got some trousers on, muscles squirming in her painted arms as she did up the straining buttons on a studded leather vest. She grinned down at Brother Diaz, who must've been half a head shorter than she was. "Look at that! Modest as a nun."

He squeezed his eyes shut. "Oh, sweet Saint Beatrix . . ."

Alex swallowed, the brief flood of anger or courage or whatever it had been quickly draining, leaving her with the dangers, and the enemies, and the miles to go, and a growing suspicion she'd made one of the worst mistakes of her life. And she'd made some real howlers.

Every time. She was the cunning loner, the selfish user, the ruthless swindler, till anyone did the smallest thing for her. Then she'd have to be their hero, and end up shitting all over herself.

Her knees felt weak as she dropped down beside her uncle. "Go back. Heal up." She forced on a smile. Did her best to sound confident. "I'll see you in Troy."

"My dear friend Lady Severa will be waiting for you there. I'd trust her with my life." Duke Michael smiled as he touched Alex's cheek with his fingertips and, God help her, she wanted to press her face into his hand. "I knew you had it in you," he whispered.

He didn't say what she had in her. Shit, maybe. Lies, probably. Doubts, definitely. But she, the stupid arse, had to make the big gesture. So, at least till she found some way to wriggle out of it, she'd cut her choices down to two.

Empress or death.

She regretted it already, of course. Just like always.

But now she was stuck with it.

Just like always.

part II

THE
BEST
MONSTERS

Least Worst Choices

The rain came down.

It had been coming down for hours, turning the track they'd taken to avoid the main roads into a crooked bog, dripping from the foliage that overgrew it on both sides, and gradually soaking the unfortunate congregation of the Chapel of the Holy Expediency to the skin. It had worked through Brother Diaz's hood, trickled down the small of his back, collected around his balls and, in unholy alliance with the endless movement of his damp saddle, chafed them raw. He didn't remember chafing being mentioned among the torments inflicted upon the martyrs. It bloody should've been.

"I'm *not* at my best in the rain," he grumbled, glaring towards the iron-grey skies.

"It was sunny a while back," said Princess Alexia, who rode beside him with a perpetual drip on the tip of her nose and all the royal dignity of a drowned cat's carcass. "You were grumbling then, too."

"I'm not at my best out of doors at all," he grumbled.

"Don't think anyone's enjoying it," she grumbled back.

"I'm enjoying it!" called Vigga from in front, holding high one tattooed arm. The wetter it got, the more clothes she'd taken off, until she was riding barefoot in a leather vest with a hood she hadn't even bothered putting up. The way the unfortunate garment clung to her muscular back was deeply distracting, her good humour in the face of all hardship exceedingly aggravating. Especially since the worst danger around, as far as Brother Diaz could tell, was her. He lived in constant terror that she might transform back into a toothy nightmare and rip him apart. Or, indeed, skip the transformation and rip him apart while in human form. She looked entirely capable of it.

He made one more futile effort to work his sore balls into a more comfortable position, and failed. "How *bloody* far is it to Ancona?"

Brother Diaz was in charge, of course, appointed by the Pope herself. But Jakob of Thorn was actually *in* the lead, sitting stiffly, a man locked in a mortal battle with the weather. One in which there could be no retreat, no surrender, and no victory. "We're not going to Ancona," he grunted.

"What?" Brother Diaz felt the grip of serious alarm. For perhaps the fiftieth time since they'd left the inn. He reined in his unhappy horse—no great task since they were moving at a crawl. "Ancona was very distinctly Cardinal Zizka's plan—"

The old knight turned his mount in preference to turning his head. "Plans must bend to the situation," he growled.

"Ours usually turn shockingly floppy within a few miles of the Holy City." Baptiste leaned from her saddle and tipped her hat with one finger, letting a stream of water pour from the brim. "After which we tend to improvise."

"Marcian knew where to find us." Jakob winced as he worked his fist into one of the spots where, not that long ago, he'd sported an arrow. "He's likely not the only one familiar with our plans. We need another port."

Brother Diaz sagged yet further into his damp saddle. "If not Ancona, where?"

"The Kingdom of Naples is out, obviously."

"Obviously."

"Genoa or any of the western ports—"

"Genoa has its charms in the spring," mused Baron Rikard.

"—would mean sailing past Sicily. The place is alive with pirates."

"Ugh, pirates." Baptiste shuddered.

Brother Diaz had no warm feelings for pirates, but they could hardly be worse than his current company. "You spent no time in the profession?" he asked, with heavy irony.

It missed the mark. "Three voyages, maybe?" said Baptiste. "It only came about through a bad throw at dice. I admit I started with some romantic notions, but they were soon shattered, I can tell you. The thing you don't realise, is . . ." She gave an elaborate shrug. "Pirates are fucking horrible."

Princess Alexia raised her dewy brows. "You don't say?"

"They're just really, really horrible thieves on the sea. They're not funny, they're not charming, the food is awful. If someone offers you the chance to be a pirate, tell them you're busy. That's my advice."

"I probably will be busy," said Alexia. "Being Empress of the East. Or, more likely, dead. Those are the two options I'm looking at, really, long term."

"Of course, you say that now, but in my experience—and it is—"

"Considerable?" offered Brother Diaz.

"—life takes strange turns. *Strange* turns. I mean . . ." And Baptiste waved one hand towards their current company, on horseback in a dripping excuse for a clearing. "Look around you."

"Why have we stopped?"

Brother Diaz wrenched about in terror to find Sunny haunting his elbow, those unnaturally huge eyes upon him. Whatever Black Art she used to pass unobserved seemed to apply to her horse as well. He eyed the beast with considerable suspicion.

"Considering the route," muttered Alex.

"Can't risk the Tyrrhenian coast." Jakob picked up where he'd left off with the weary air of a man forced to do it often. "So it has to be the Adriatic. The Kingdom of Naples is out, obviously—"

"Obviously."

"—and the docks in the Papal States will be watched, passengers documented—"

"The Church does love paperwork," observed Balthazar, hunching bedraggled in his saddle with a stretch of dripping tarp held over his head. "Even more than God."

"The Church is not that keen on God, in my experience," said Baron Rikard. "They think of him much as a lawyer thinks of the law. Something to be got around."

"You're a vampire," snapped Brother Diaz. "Of course you hate the Church."

"On the contrary, I am a great admirer of the tenets of your religion. I merely find it a shame that the Saved are, as a rule, so little like their Saviour."

"Must we really endure a vampire's opinions on theology?"

"Or law," added Baptiste. "I spent two months arguing a case before magistrates in Navarre, so I feel I've got one foot in the profession."

"Like every other," observed the baron.

"How many feet can one woman have?" asked Vigga, and she laughed. Alone.

"The docks in the Papal States will be watched," repeated Jakob, even more wearily.

"Which rules out Ravenna, Rimini, and Pescara," said Baptiste, counting the cities off on her fingers.

"Pescara's awful anyway," threw in Baron Rikard. "Wouldn't be caught dead in Pescara."

"You are dead," said Vigga.

"But I wouldn't be *caught*."

"It needs to be a busy port," grunted Jakob. "Somewhere we'll fade into the background."

"That's what I do," said Sunny, almost wistfully.

"And me." Vigga dragged her mass of hair to one side and pulled up her hood. Her sinewy shoulders, tattooed with runes and warnings, were still very much visible, along with the doglike fangs in her smile.

"You look like a werewolf with a hood," said Sunny.

"*So . . .*" Jakob delivered the word with the brutal finality of a cleaver on a butcher's block. "We're going to Venice."

"Venice?" Brother Diaz grew even more alarmed. "*That's* your plan?"

Jakob ignored him. "Anyone know people in Venice?"

"I know people everywhere," said Baptiste. "I can't promise they *like* me—"

"Does anyone like you?" asked Balthazar.

"They're lukewarm at best. And yet I'm the most popular among us *by far*."

The baron swept the group with a scornful eye. "The definition of a low bar . . ."

"People rarely remember me fondly," said Vigga, grinning. "But they rarely forget me."

"Speak for yourselves," said Balthazar. "I am one of the top three, possibly two, necromancers in Europe. Success leads to jealousy, of course, and jealousy to resentment, but people have no choice but to at least respect me."

"Point out *one* person who respects you," said Princess Alexia.

There was a silence filled only by the patter of rain.

"Venice," said Jakob, turning his horse. "We'll find a ship there to take us on."

"But the Serene Republic is at daggers drawn with the Papacy!" blurted Brother Diaz. "The Dogeressa's been excommunicated! *Twice!*"

"Some very fine people have been excommunicated," said Balthazar.

"It's well known she poisoned her husband!"

"Some very fine people have poisoned their husbands," murmured Baptiste.

"The place is a pit of vice!"

Vigga pushed her hood back again, one brow raised. "That a fact?"

"We're not going there to pray," said Jakob.

"And if we were," said Baron Rikard, "surely it is the prayer that counts, not the place in which it is given, for, lo! To the Saviour the lowliest midden was a cathedral."

"Venice is a nest of gangsters! They're no better than the Sicilians!"

"They're worse," said Sunny. "They're better organised."

Jakob shut his eyes, rubbing at the scarred bridge of his nose. "Which is why the last place anyone will look for a princess supported by the Pope . . . is Venice." And he bared his teeth, and turned his horse to leave.

All Brother Diaz could think of was the stench of burning thatch. The sensation of a bull-man's boot in his back. The murderous scorn on Marcian's face. The crunch of bones in the jaws of the wolf-monster now riding happily alongside him cracking abysmal jokes about the rain. He never wanted to experience anything like any of that ever again, and he could feel a bubble of trapped panic rising in his gullet that must burst out either as vomit or a desperate squeal for help.

"We are *not* going to Venice!" he shrieked. "I am Vicar of the Chapel of the Holy Expediency and if you recall the terms of the binding—"

"There's a gathering place for pilgrims." Princess Alexia interrupted as if he hadn't spoken at all. "Near Spoleto. Hundreds go through every day."

"What took you there?" asked Balthazar. "Concern for your immortal soul?"

"I'm guessing," said Baptiste, brightly, "she stopped by to swindle the Saved."

"They band together and head to Venice for the voyage towards the Holy Land." The supposed heir to the Throne of Troy didn't confirm Baptiste's accusations, but she didn't deny them, either. "We can all get hoods. Fall in with them."

"But that might take weeks!" squawked Brother Diaz.

"I'd rather get her to Troy late and alive than quick and in bits," said Jakob.

"Can't disagree on that one," muttered Alex.

"Your Highness . . ." Brother Diaz was caught halfway between lecturing and wheedling and ended up doing neither well. "Her Holiness picked me for a reason—"

"Cardinal Zizka picked you." Alex gave him a surprisingly withering look. "Because she knew you'd do as you're told. Venice is the least worst choice." And she clicked her tongue, and moved on up the track.

"Sometimes," growled Jakob as he turned his horse to follow, "least worst is the best you can hope for."

"Off to the Holy Land," sang Sunny, and she followed Alex and Jakob.

Brother Diaz stared miserably after them. Half a dozen monsters, yet it was the princess who'd slain him. "It seems our charge can be rather high-handed."

"It's virtually a requirement in royalty," said Baptiste, "but shouldn't you be pleased? What could be more pious than a pilgrimage?"

"Merciful Saviour," breathed Brother Diaz.

From this place, the faithful set forth to tour the tombs of the saints, the blessed shrines, the hallowed monasteries and cathedrals of Europe. Hoping to persuade the martyrs to intercede with the Almighty on their behalf. Cripples to be healed. Sinners to be made pure. Trespassers to be washed clean.

From this place, pilgrims journeyed in sacred fellowships, bound together by the hope that, through humble suffering and honest repentance, they could touch the divine.

From *this* place.

It was a city of tents, seething with a blundering throng, stinking of woodsmoke, incense, rotten cooking, and old dung. A canvas metropolis floating on a sea of filth, flickering points of lanterns and campfires stretching into the dusky distance. It was not a track they rode down but a river of rutted mud, scattered with half-buried rubbish.

"The Last Judgement's coming!" screeched an old man from the back of a mired wagon, voice broken from preaching, tearing at his hair in the desperate urgency of his mission. "Could be tomorrow! Could be tonight! Get on God's good side now, you bastards, 'fore it's too late!"

Brother Diaz swallowed, and refused to meet his eye, and his words were soon drowned in the drunken babble and desperate laughter and bawdy music and slobbered prayers, with here or there a sobbing or a roar of rage. A man squatted at what passed for a verge, listlessly watching them ride by. It was only as they passed that Brother Diaz realised he was in the act of emptying his bowels.

"You were saying something about a pit of vice?" murmured Baron Rikard, raising his brows at a set of scantily clad young women and men, awkwardly posed before a large tent decked in bedraggled ribbons.

Brother Diaz could think of nothing to say. Here was a pit of vice indeed, not confined to sinful Venice but within a few days' ride of the Holy City, catering to the weak flesh of those supposed to be embarking on a holy trek to save their souls.

"Looks like the pilgrims are getting all their sinning done before they set off," murmured Baptiste.

Baron Rikard looked faintly amused, as it seemed he was by more or less everything. "The more he has to absolve, the happier the Lord shall be."

"My question," murmured Vigga, "is can I get a taste?"

"Of the absolution or the sin?"

She showed him her fangs. "How d'you get one without the other?"

Jakob brought them to a halt beside a stall selling pilgrims' habits. Scarcely more than hooded tents of rough sackcloth, but Brother Diaz supposed they might hide the worst excesses of his monstrous flock. Sunny had melted into nothingness in her usual fashion, at least, but he was forced to wonder whether—in the midst of this carnival of the grotesque—even an elf would have excited much comment.

"To work, then." And Baptiste slung one leg over the saddle and sprang down.

"Find us a group to travel with," said Jakob. "Not too small, not too big."

"Got you." She nodded, turning away.

He brought her back around. "And make sure it's one of the able-bodied ones, we need to get to Venice this side of Saviourmas."

"Got you." She nodded, turning away.

He brought her back around again. "And leaving soon. This place is . . ."

Baptiste glanced around and wrinkled her nose. "Got you."

Jakob gently patted his horse's neck as he surveyed the scene of moral carnage. "Then we'd better sell the horses."

"We're walking to Venice?" muttered Brother Diaz.

"It's a pilgrimage." Jakob let go a grunt of pain as he hauled his left leg over the saddle and frowned down at the lamplit mud like an old enemy he doubted he could defeat. "Everyone walks."

Blessed Is a Stretch

Every step was its own little ordeal.

You'd have thought, on a long march, the legs would hurt worst. And yes, all the usual niggles were there. The aches, the stings, the twinges. The right hip. The left knee his horse had rolled over in the desert. Both ankles, obviously. His foot where the troll's club crushed it that time. And the toe, of course. Oh God, the toe.

But after the morning routine of groaning, testing, kneading, stretching, wishing for death, praying for death, then a mile or two of lurching torment, the waist-down discomfort settled to an almost manageable throb. Then, like the flames on that enchanter's tower they'd burned near Wroclaw, the pain would spread upwards.

There was the lower back, the upper back, and the stretch of back between. That constant sawing at the bottom of the ribs from that bastard Swede's axe. Three or four assorted stings in the neck. Some weird cramping under the right arm and that space between the shoulder blades that always felt twisted, however he wriggled. There was the ache in the lung from the Smiling Knight's lance, neither quite in the back nor the front. But that only hurt when he breathed in. Or out. Then there were the latest wounds, from the inn, the arrows and the sword, still with that ugly sharpness of the new. The new ones were always worse than they deserved. Till they got settled into the routine. Further footnotes to a life of violence.

Every step was painful, but every step had been painful for two lifetimes, now. Jakob kept taking them. The paces don't have to be quick, or long, or pretty. They just have to keep going.

Keep the steps coming. Someone had told him that, on the long retreat from Ryazan. So tired and hurt he couldn't remember who. He remembered the smell of it, though. The shimmering sun hanging on the black horizon. The thirst and the flies. The parched steppe stretching into infinity. The faces of the men they left by the way. The endless terror, grinding as a mill wheel. The sudden panic, brutal as a flash of lightning.

He'd learned, then, what men are. He'd seen grand betrayal, towering folly, endless greed, and bottomless cowardice. But he'd seen tiny, stunning heroics, too. A crust shared. A cracked voice raised in song. One man carrying another on his back. Another refusing to be carried. A hand on the shoulder and a voice saying, *Keep the steps coming.*

Each man found out who he was, on that endless expanse of mud and torment.

Jakob found out who he was. And he hadn't liked the bastard very much.

"Your *Eminence.*" Brother Diaz likely would've scraped the ground with his nose if he could've managed it while walking.

Bishop Apollonia of Acci, leader of their so-called Blessed Company, wore the smile of a woman who'd never had to beat a desperate retreat. She was a famed theologian, reputed to be marked out for future sainthood. Jakob had yet to see a theologian solve a problem they hadn't themselves created. As for sainthood, he'd known four people beatified after death, and at least one had been an utter shit while alive, and at least one other an absolute lunatic.

"To what do we owe the honour of your visit?" wheedled Brother Diaz.

The bishop waved off his fawning. "While I am away from my diocese, I am but one humble pilgrim among many." To be fair to her, aside from a silver Circle of the Faith, she put on no airs, wearing the same filth-hemmed sackcloth as the rest of them. "I am introducing myself to everyone in the company. I can tell you from experience, this is a journey on which one can use every friend."

"You've been on pilgrimage before?"

"This will be my third."

"Can't stop sinning?" muttered Jakob.

"To be human is to sin," said the bishop, mildly. "To sin, and to strive for redemption."

"Amen to that!" sang Brother Diaz. "Amen, amen, indeed."

He was quite the kiss-arse, but that's monks for you. Pay a man to grovel to God three times a day and he'll soon be grovelling to everyone.

"You are clearly suffering." Bishop Apollonia was considering Jakob with what could only be described as quiet concern. "Might I guess at a war wound?"

"You might guess at several," grunted Jakob. He hated sympathy. He knew he didn't deserve it.

"You should visit the Shrine of Saint Stephen when we pass. He is a patron of warriors."

"Protectors, in particular," murmured Jakob. "I carried his likeness for many years. An icon, screwed to the back of my shield."

"But no longer?"

"I buried it." Jakob winced. At his knee, or the memory, or both. "With a friend. Someone who deserved it more."

Bishop Apollonia thoughtfully nodded. "Appropriate. Stephen was a fearsome fighter, but after a vision of the Saviour he chose to bury his sword and turn his talents to healing. His relics have been known to ease the pain of wounds."

"I fear my ills won't be so easily cured."

"A wound to the body pales beside a wound to the soul."

Jakob wasn't sure he agreed. Borys Droba certainly wouldn't have. He'd received a pike in the genitals in the press around the gates of Narva. Took him seven months to die of it, and *not* good months. But Jakob doubted that particular parable would be to the bishop's taste. If he'd learned one thing during his many years on earth, it was that words are rarely better than silence. Particularly when it comes to genitals. So he gave a weary grunt, and left it at that.

By then, Bishop Apollonia was shading her eyes with one hand to glance back down the road. "Might I ask your opinion of our Blessed Company?"

Jakob had often been called on to judge the size of a body of people— sometimes while it charged at him with a blood-curdling war cry—and he reckoned this band at some two hundred souls. In the vanguard, accompanied by half a dozen soldiers and a disgruntled nun, was the bishop's horse-drawn portable pulpit, an invention that might have impressed Brother Diaz even more than the bishop herself.

The wealthiest of the pilgrims followed, including two portraits, carried by servants, of a merchant of Anagni and her fourth husband. They'd yearned to tend to their immortal souls, apparently, but a bit less than they yearned to tend to business, so they'd bought dispensation to send likenesses in their place. The Saviour had said one could not buy one's way into heaven, but most agreed that was just a negotiating tactic on her part.

Smallholders, craftsmen, and farmers made up the bulk of the fellowship, several labouring under some affliction. A blind couple was led by a little girl. A hollow-faced woman bounced groaning on a litter. All praying dutifully for a miracle at the many shrines along the way.

The poor were towards the rear, with fewer pack animals and worse footwear. There were several prisoners doing Church-mandated penance, some wearing fetters or signs proclaiming their offences. A shifting tail of hangers-on trailed behind: beggars and thieves, pimps and prostitutes, dealers in all manner of vices, including a tent set up every night from which music and laughter floated till dawn. There was even a softly spoken moneylender with a pawnshop in a wagon and several hard-eyed guards. A time-proven business plan, Jakob didn't doubt. A group fixed on forgiveness must, after all, include a decent number of habitual sinners.

What did Jakob think of their Blessed Company? He thought it was society in miniature, with its mean and its mighty, its grand hopes and petty ambitions, its rivalry, privilege, greed, and exploitation, topped and tailed by a portable pulpit and a foldaway brothel.

"I think *blessed* is a stretch," he said, and struggled on. Stop too long, you'll never start again.

Brother Diaz glared towards the stragglers with pious disapproval. "There are some unsavoury elements in attendance . . . could your guards not encourage them to move on?"

"Virtue is found in the resistance of temptation," said the bishop, "rather than its absence. And are not the lowly and abused in as much need of God's grace as the privileged?"

"It's certainly a lot harder for them to afford it," grunted Jakob.

The bishop chuckled. "A warrior *and* a thinker? Two qualities all too rarely combined. Tell me, my son, what trespass are you atoning for?"

It was around this point Jakob usually regretted swearing a vow of honesty. Like murdering a count, marrying a witch, or accepting a post as the Pope's Executioner, it had seemed like a good idea at the time. "Well . . ." He stretched the word out as long as possible. "When it comes to atonement . . . it's hard to settle on any *one* thing—"

"Jarek doesn't like to talk about it." Alex slung a friendly arm around Jakob's crooked shoulders, looking earnestly up into the bishop's face. "He's one of those strong and silent types. Brooding away on a dark past, I daresay. Maybe he'll break down and confess it all in tears, but I wouldn't hold my breath, eh, Jarek?"

Jakob had sworn not to lie. He'd made no promises about others lying on his behalf. So he gave another weary grunt, and left it at that.

Bishop Apollonia opened her mouth but before she could make a sound Alex slung her other arm around Brother Diaz's shoulders. "Brother Lopez has a special commission from Her Holiness the Pope!"

"I do?" muttered the monk, eyes wide.

Alex nodded towards the rest of the group. "To accompany these poor convicted sinners on pilgrimage and see them brought to the grace of our Saviour."

"Ah, yes." Brother Diaz looked over his flock with scant enthusiasm. "*That* mission."

"We have Basil of Messina." Alex jerked a thumb at Balthazar. "A merchant of Sicily. Far as I can tell, his main sin is a gigantic opinion of himself. Though he also made a deal with pirates."

Balthazar raised one brow at her. "In my line of work, one is sometimes forced into unsavoury company."

"Rikard is my name," said the baron, offering Bishop Apollonia his hand.

"He has a . . ." Alex narrowed her eyes slightly. "Drinking problem?"

Rikard displayed his pointed teeth. "You could say that."

"It is a powerful gesture of piety . . ." The bishop raised her brows at Vigga's bare feet, one tattooed around the toes with a snaking of runes, the other clearly marked *beware*. "To walk the road to redemption barefoot."

"Just like the feel of the mud between my toes." And Vigga gave a shiver and a giggle at once as she wriggled them, which could almost have been charming, had Jakob not seen her do the things he'd seen her do.

"Vigga was a Viking," explained Alex.

"Plainly," murmured Balthazar, with a look of scorn.

"A pagan."

"Plainly," murmured Brother Diaz, with a look of regret.

"A feared shield-maiden who went on raids against the English . . ."

"Surely no one blames her for that," observed the bishop.

". . . but Brother Lopez has brought her to the light of the Saviour!"

"Praise be," muttered Baron Rikard, rolling his eyes.

"And you, my child?" asked Apollonia, looking now at Alex. "For someone so talkative have you nothing to say for yourself?"

Alex ruefully hung her head. "It shames me to admit I was a thief, Your Eminence."

"Well. Saint Catherine was herself a thief, before she renounced all worldly things. By admitting your trespasses, you have taken a fine first step. Perhaps you, too, can claim redemption and turn your undoubted talents to higher purposes."

Alex piously fluttered her lashes. "Who doesn't hope for that?"

"I have always felt hope to be the foremost of the Twelve Virtues."

"The one from which all others flow," said Brother Diaz, nodding along.

"To turn such damaged souls towards grace?" The bishop placed a hand on his shoulder. "Truly, Brother Lopez, you are doing God's work."

"I try, Your Eminence." He looked up to the heavens. "He does *not* make it easy."

"Where would be the value in prizes easily won? It must be close to lunch. We should halt for midday prayers." And she steered Brother Diaz towards the head of the column. "I thought perhaps you might like to give a reading to our virtuous legion! The tale of Jonah and the dragon, perhaps?"

"One of my favourites!"

Vigga watched them go, scratching thoughtfully at her stretched-out throat with the backs of her fingernails. "I like the sound of shield-maiden."

"Shield-maiden, please." The baron snorted. "Axe-bitch, maybe."

Vigga grinned. "I really like the sound of axe-bitch."

"Brother Diaz seems very taken with the bishop," said Alex, watching him strut off beside her.

"Doubt she'll fuck him," said Vigga.

Balthazar pressed at the bridge of his nose. "Not everything is about fucking."

"'Course not." Vigga cheerfully sniffed up snot and spat it into the mud. "Only three-quarters of it."

"Hope it doesn't end in tears," said Alex.

Jakob pressed at his aching shoulder with his thumb, then limped on.

"Everything ends in tears," he muttered.

See to the Holy Land

Everyone's scared all the time. That's the thing you've got to tell yourself.

They might be scared of different things from you. Things that don't scare you a bit. Like heights, or failure, or wanting to piss then not being able to go. But everyone's scared of something. And even if they're not, it helps to think they are. The brave ones are just good at pretending, and pretending's just lying by another name, and when it came to lying, Alex was up there with the best. Ask anyone.

So she made straight for the place she least wanted to sit. Stuck one leg between Vigga and Baptiste, plumped her arse on that narrow stretch of firelit log, and wriggled her shoulders between them.

She'd been hoping they'd give her room, but the log was only so long. Baptiste couldn't move without falling off, and Vigga didn't shift at all. She might as well have shouldered a tree. A hot, clammy tree covered in warnings with an earthy piss smell.

So that's where bravery gets you. Wedged like a cork in a bottle between the most experienced woman in Europe and a proper Norse werewolf.

Baptiste peered down her nose at Alex with one black eyebrow high, like a shepherd at a sheep she was thinking of selling for mutton. "Pray join us, Your Highness."

"Just did," said Alex, digging at her stew and shovelling in a mouthful, having to pretend to be comfortable as well as brave, then having to duck as Vigga waved lazily into the darkness. She managed to dodge the flailing arm but was nearly knocked off the log by the sour waft from her hairy pit.

"Where the fuck are they all going anyway?" asked Vigga, peering towards the other fires, the other groups of pilgrims, the other sets of fears.

"Most to Cyprus," said Brother Diaz, who wasn't even pretending at courage, and had settled on a damp but generous patch of turf between Baptiste and Baron Rikard. "To the Basilica of Saint Justine the Optimist. They mean to climb the four hundred and fourteen steps up the Campanile. They will touch the great bells, which were cast from the armour of the righteous soldiers of the

First Crusade. It's said that from its roof, on a very clear day, one can see to the Holy Land."

"You eating that?" asked Vigga, her toothy grin only a few inches from Alex's nose. Maybe it was the smell, or the bunched and tattooed mass of her so close, or maybe it was the teeth, or the clear memory of what those teeth had done to Marcian's head, but Alex couldn't help thinking that pretend heroes might feel good, but honest cowards likely last longer.

Everyone's scared all the time. She wondered what a werewolf might be scared of, and decided she'd rather not know. She clutched her bowl very close.

"I'm eating it," she squeaked.

"Uh." Vigga stuck out her bottom lip, which had a line of runes tattooed down the centre to the scarred cleft in her chin. She started licking out her own bowl with a shockingly long tongue. "If they want to go to the Holy Land . . ." And she turned it and licked it again, then tossed it into the bushes. "Why not go to the Holy Land?"

"Well . . ." Brother Diaz left off prodding at his own food to stare in outraged amazement. "There is the *tiny* issue that, for the best part of the last century, to the great dismay of every right-thinking person in Europe, the Holy Land has been *infested* with elves."

"Uh," grunted Vigga, as if an elf infestation was something she'd tried and had no strong opinions on.

"No one could call Vigga Ullasdottr right-thinking," murmured Baron Rikard. "Or even wrong-thinking. Still less a person."

"We're talking about the greatest catastrophe of recent times!" said Brother Diaz.

"And with some stiff competition," said Baptiste. "I've taken part in several catastrophes that are right up there."

Jakob gave a grunt of reluctant agreement.

"Holy Land. Roly-Poly Land." Vigga waved it away, wildly enough that she almost spooned Alex in the face. "Ain't it all just sand? I'm a pagan."

"Oh, please," snorted the baron. "Calling you a pagan is an insult to actual pagans. You don't believe in anything beyond your own twat."

"My twat is a *fine* article of faith!" snarled Vigga, spraying spit into the fire and making Alex flinch.

"You can't deny it exists," murmured Baptiste.

"Anyone with a working nose is well aware of it," drawled the baron. "Dogs, from half a mile away or more."

"My twat has done more good for the world than any saint I know of!" Vigga waggled her eyebrows at Brother Diaz. "Only say the word, it shall perform for you a miracle."

"Please," the monk flashed a nervous smile towards a group of pilgrims frowning over from a nearby fire, "can we have fewer *twats*, miraculous or otherwise? The point is elves can't swim—"

"They can," said Jakob.

"They *bloody* can," said Vigga. "I've seen Sunny swim and it is a thing of wonder. When she swims, she has a queue of fish behind her hoping for lessons. You eating that?" She got up to peer hopefully towards Balthazar's bowl and the whole log lurched, so Alex had to clutch at Baptiste to keep from falling.

Balthazar shook his head disgustedly. "A queue of fish, I swear." And he tossed Vigga his bowl so she had to juggle it in the air.

Brother Diaz was gripping at his temples with both hands. "We have strayed far from the point!"

"You will get used to that in this company," said Baron Rikard. "The point will become so distant a memory you will wonder if it ever truly existed, or was but a mirage, glimpsed from afar in a dream."

"There was a point?" grunted Vigga, treading in the fire with one bare foot and apparently not even noticing, then dropping back down on the log and making it lurch again.

"The *point*," snapped Brother Diaz, "is that, occasionally, one can see the Holy Land from the Campanile of Saint Justine the Optimist. It's the closest one can get since the elves captured Aleppo."

"Infested it," growled Jakob. "The Church tells us the elves are unclean."

"*Official* doctrine is that elves are neither clean nor unclean. They have no souls. They are animals, like goblins or trolls."

"We had a troll once," said Baron Rikard.

"God, yes." Baptiste wrinkled her nose. "What an arsehole."

"What happened to him?" asked Alex.

"Vigga killed him."

"Arsehole," snarled Vigga, chopping at the air with her spoon and spattering the front of Balthazar's habit with stew.

"We had a goblin, too," said Baptiste, grinning. "You remember?"

"Iris." The baron smiled into the fire, eyes shining with reflected flames. "She was *quite* the joker."

"A riot!" said Vigga, grinning broadly.

"What happened to her?" asked Balthazar, brushing stew from his front.

Baptiste sighed. "Vigga killed her."

"I miss her," said Vigga, two fat tears rolling down her cheeks. Then she sniffed, and stuffed in another mouthful of stew.

"Are the elves . . . really all that bad?" asked Alex. "I mean, I've met loads of people, and a lot of them were horrible."

"Uh," grunted Vigga, nodding along.

"I won't say most . . ." Alex thought about that, "but, maybe most. I only ever met one elf—" Brother Diaz noisily cleared his throat, nodding towards the other fires, and Alex leaned forwards, dropping her voice to a whisper. "I only ever met one elf and, honestly, she seems pretty likeable."

"Umm," grunted Vigga, nodding to that, too.

"I won't say the most likeable here . . ." Alex glanced around the company. "But, you know . . ." She trailed off into awkward silence.

"Well?" Baron Rikard glanced over at Jakob. "*Are* the elves really all that bad?"

The old knight looked into the fire for so long it was a surprise when he finally spoke. "I fought in the Second Crusade."

Brother Diaz snorted. "That must've been a hundred and fifty years ago!"

"A shade more," said Jakob. "After the siege of Troy was lifted, we re-captured Acre. Didn't look like a city that had been sacked. Nothing broken, nothing burned. Cleaner than before the elves came." He considered the flames, unforgiving shadows in the hollows of his scarred face. "But no people. William the Red led us into the cathedral. I remember looking up, and seeing a forest of chains, and dangling from them, hundreds of carcasses. They had turned the place into a slaughterhouse. And I mean that literally. It wasn't bloody. It wasn't cruel. It was clean, and calm, and . . . efficient. There was no hatred in it. No more than the butcher has for the cattle." Jakob gave a long sigh. "We heard the elves sent some of the citizens east. To breed, maybe. To fatten up, maybe. As gifts, or slaves, who knows? None ever came back to say. But most they ate."

"Saviour protect us," whispered Brother Diaz, making the sign of the circle on his chest.

"Considering how skinny they are," the baron gazed thoughtfully up at the stars, "they have grand appetites."

"It's a holy duty, for the elves." Jakob raised his scarred brows. "To eat us. A righteous mission. To consume all humanity."

There was a silence. "So . . . I think we can say Sunny's one of the better ones," said Baptiste.

Alex set down her bowl. "I've lost my appetite."

"Magic!" Vigga snatched it up and began to shovel the leftovers into her mouth. "So, they go to fucking Malta—"

"Cyprus."

"—and into this church—"

"Basilica."

"—and they slog up Saint Justin's tower—"

"*Justine's Campanile.*"

"—and, you know . . ." Vigga showed her pointed teeth as she grinned, "they handle his bells. Then what?"

"Then . . . well . . ." Brother Diaz fumbled for the right words and sagged ever so slightly. "They come back."

Vigga squinted across the fire at him. "Eh?"

"They come back. Absolved of their sins."

There was another silence, while they all considered that.

Baron Rikard stared into the flames, looking almost wistful. "If only vampires could be so easily redeemed," he murmured.

Everyone's scared all the time. Alex wondered what a vampire might be scared of.

She decided she'd rather not know.

What Can Be Spared

Balthazar hardly even knew why he was bothering to pick his way around the puddles. His boots were saturated, every footstep a waterlogged squelch. His repulsive hessian habit was spattered to the waist with filth. The pilgrim's garment was, like so much that the Church produced, both functionally useless and aesthetically bankrupt, with the added indignity of making him appear to be fundamentally the same as everyone else, a misapprehension he had been striving to correct since a child. When he thought of his roomful of marvellous vestments, the pentagrams picked out in thread of precious metals—oh, the apron with all the little mirrors for the repulsion of demonic powers!—he felt moved to weep. Though, ever since his conviction for the crimes of creativity, free thinking, and increasing the sum total of human knowledge, he had felt moved to weep on an almost permanent basis.

No one would have noticed had he wept, of course. Firstly because the switchback tracks as their so-called Blessed Company climbed into the mountains were littered with treacherous drops and required one's constant attention; secondly because his enforced companions from the Chapel of the Holy Expediency were a cabal of self-centred misanthropic monsters who cared for no one's comfort but their own; and thirdly because his tears would have been instantly obliterated by the thin rain that had been sprinkling the pilgrims' gloomy procession for days, turning the already uncertain footing to claggy glue.

He had never been one for walking, opting mainly for a sedan chair if he really *had* to leave the house. Prayer had never ranked among his leading interests, either. He *believed* in God, of course, but, as a magician, they had never particularly *got on*. He believed in goats but desired no interaction with them. It was fair to say, therefore, he found a pilgrimage a bit of a slog.

In fact—once one had factored in the singing, the clapping, the mud, the blisters, the overweening smugness, the overwhelming hypocrisy, the mud, the rain, the interminable preaching, the atrocious mixture of hymns and crusading marches, the abhorrent slops served from the common cauldron, the mud, the constantly worrisome, frequently offensive, and occasionally repugnant company, and, of course, always, the mud—the whole business was more a peregrination to hell than to heaven.

The humiliation! That he, Balthazar Sham Ivam Draxi, luminary of the necromantic community, should find himself wedged into this procession of imbecility, this unholy trudge from nowhere to nowhere, this unmerry march to physical discomfort, spiritual disappointment, and intellectual impoverishment. He caught the mournful clangour of a bell up ahead, its music muffled by the rain. A death knell for his deceased hopes and dreams, perhaps.

"Let's hurry it up," grunted Jakob of Thorn, frowning back with his sparse grey hair stuck to his scarred grey pickaxe of a head, doggedly determined to wring the maximum pain from every step so he could manfully conquer it.

"You hurry it up, you deathless dunce," muttered Balthazar, though obviously not until the knight had limped well out of earshot.

"You may wish to speak even more softly," murmured Baron Rikard, leaning close enough that Balthazar could feel the chill of his breath, even in the mountain air. "His pet elf is likely somewhere among us. One of her ears may be clipped but she misses *nothing*."

"Sage advice," murmured Balthazar, glancing suspiciously about. The vampire appeared a shade younger and more pleased with himself every day, and had the aspect now of a hale and handsome aristocrat in his early sixties, the once dangling wattles of skin tightened around a noble jawline, dark hairs beginning to show in the silver of his beard. "You have plainly been indulging your particular appetites."

The baron flashed the sorry-not-sorry smirk of a spoiled heir caught diddling the maid. "Is it so obvious?"

"I have noted telltale pinpricks on the necks of several members of the company, and people do not as a rule *get younger*."

"Well . . ." Rikard dropped his voice to an intimate purr. "I *am* a vampire. Drinking blood does rather come with the territory. But I am *very* gentle when I dine these days, I assure you." Merely the slightest hint of fang showed in his easy smile. "I only take what can be spared."

"The self-serving justification of every burglar, slaver, racketeer, and tyrant throughout history."

"Role models for the ages indeed. I would hardly have expected a leading member of your profession to object to a little . . ." the vampire glanced back towards the file of pilgrims labouring up the steep path below them, "judicious exploitation of the cattle."

"As long as I notice no fang-holes about my own throat, why would I?"

"Oh, I would *never* feed on someone to whom I had been formally introduced without express permission. It would be like eating a pet. Once they have a name it feels . . ." The baron gave a fastidious shudder. "*So* crass."

"Still with us, then?"

Balthazar frowned up to see Baptiste sitting above him on a crumbling wall overlooking the path, one leg gently swinging. She had cinched in her pilgrim's habit with a worn hunter's belt cocked at a slant, and added brass-buckled knee boots, a chain sporting holy circles of several different materials, and a hat improvised from a folded scrap of waxed canvas. The effect should by all rights have been absurd but, to his great irritation, she looked sleek as a witch's cat. She never appeared to exert any effort, but nonetheless arrived everywhere first, and always with that damned supercilious smirk that felt like a living reminder of all his recent humiliations.

"Were you hoping I had slipped and plunged to my death?" he grumbled.

"A girl can dream." She reached behind her head, tipped her hat forwards with one finger, and directed a stream of water from the brim to spatter down the front of his habit.

Balthazar ground his teeth as he fumbled for a rejoinder. Her *brazen* boasting. Her *limitless* self-aggrandisement. Her *tedious* harping on her matchless experience. Once he was free of this damned binding he would give her an experience she would not soon forget. She would experience his ruthless retribution! A stern chastisement! A veritable *spanking*, bent helpless across his knee. And she would look back, over her shoulder, still with that smirk, most likely, and *beg* for more, and they would nip and bite and scratch at one another like witch's cats coupling, and she would whisper his name, pronounced correctly, her breath hot on his ear, and—

"Wait . . ." he muttered, "what?"

She looked suspicious. "What do you mean what?"

"What do *you* mean what!" he demanded, far too loud, as if one could turn abject drivel into triumphant repartee by volume alone, then strode on up the path towards the latest false summit before Baptiste could reply, hoping no one noticed the stiffness of his gait or the sudden colour in his cheek. He would keep his silence. Yes. He would not take the bait. This was not retreat, it was victory through towering dignity! No matter the provocation, Balthazar Sham Ivam Draxi *always* took the high road!

Though it seemed rarely to lead him anywhere that anyone would want to go. "Another bloody shrine?" he groaned.

This one, wedged into the sodden saddle at the highest point of the pass, consisted of a squat bell tower beside a cave, likely used as a temple by worshippers of other gods long pre-dating the Saviour's teachings. Say what you like about the Saved, they were masters of setting up in other people's houses and pretending they were the architect. Lying was a sin, apparently, unless you did it outrageously and persistently enough, in which case it qualified as scripture.

"Another bloody shrine," echoed the baron, a picture of suave disdain. "I would pray for God to have mercy upon us, but I fear he takes little note of the entreaties of vampires."

"I fear he is equally deaf to necromancers," grunted Balthazar.

"I fear he is equally deaf to everyone. Will you be queuing up to view the relics?"

They laughed together. The world was, it hardly needed to be said, divided into enemies and those that could be made use of. The baron might well have been the most dangerous monster in this monstrous company, but if Balthazar had learned one thing during his storied career in the magical sciences, it was that the worst monsters often made the best allies.

"Once the discerning spectator has viewed one jar of holy dust," he observed, "he finds little to entrance him in another dozen."

"And yet I note you have not abandoned our Blessed Company. Do I take it you have given up on breaking Her Holiness's binding?"

"Given *up*?" Balthazar glared down his nose at the vampire. "*Giving up* is not something I do." And he worked his wrist deeper into his ragged sleeve, where that infernal rusty streak could no longer offend his senses. "Though I will concede, reluctantly . . . as far as the power of Her infant Holiness's binding is concerned . . . I may have made a minor misjudgement."

"I believe humility stands among the Twelve Virtues." Baron Rikard pressed pious hands to his heart. "Perhaps our pilgrimage is already working wonders upon your immortal soul."

"I will overcome this enchantment, *believe me*." Balthazar glanced carefully about, but no one was listening. They never were, lately. "I merely need the correct tools. Appropriate books, charts, reagents, habiliments, conjurer's circles, and so on. Possibly . . . a staff."

"Robes, rods, magic rings?" The baron glanced significantly towards the many walking sticks, holy symbols, and sackcloth habits to be seen among the crowd of pilgrims. "Well, you're the wizard . . ."

"Magician."

". . . but one is forced to wonder if there is quite so much water between magic and religion as its practitioners would like one to believe . . . ?"

"The difference," snapped Balthazar, "is that magic *works*."

"Yet here we have one of Europe's foremost necromancers, obliged by the Pope's binding to attend a pilgrimage." The vampire strolled on towards the cave, where the queue of faithful was beginning to diminish. "I may give the relics a passing glance after all . . ."

Like a Treat

Alex set the lantern on a tree stump, and unfolded the cloth beside it, and pushed the cheese and the bread around a bit till it looked pretty.

Pathetic really. It was only cheese and bread, but she'd a lot of practice at making a meagre meal feel like a treat. Her Holiness had said they should be nice, after all, and this seemed a nice thing to do. Sort of thing she'd want someone to do for her, if she'd been left out in the woods on her own.

Sort of thing no one ever did do for her.

"Boo."

Alex jumped. Even though she'd been expecting it. Because she'd been expecting it, maybe.

"Every goddamned time," she muttered, one hand to her pounding heart.

Sunny padded past her to the stump. Padded was overstating it. A cat in fleece slippers would've made a din by comparison.

"How d'you do it?" asked Alex.

"I make a sudden noise in your ear."

"Not the boo. The vanishing."

"I hold my breath . . . and do it." Sunny squatted beside the stump, pushing back her hood, and gave the food a lookover. "A feast."

"It's bread and cheese."

Sunny made a circle with her long fingers in the air above it and peered through. "But look how it's *arranged*."

"Just . . . how it happened."

Sunny glanced over, and Alex got that nervous flutter she always did when the elf looked her right in the eye. "Then I like how it happened." And she picked up the cheese and nibbled it between her front teeth. Elves in stained-glass windows were always armed with terrifying fangs, often being sunk into some saint or other. But Sunny's didn't really look like teeth that'd rend the flesh from the bones of mankind. There might even have been an oddly childlike little gap between the front two.

"How is it?" asked Alex.

"Cheesy."

"Is that bad?"

"In many things it would be, but in cheese it's essential."

Alex watched her eat. There was something fascinating in how she moved, so neat and quick. Maybe it was rude to stare, but Alex's manners had never been the best, and probably Sunny was used to folk staring. Had a starring role in a freak show, hadn't she?

"Balthazar didn't like it," said Alex, once the silence started to feel like a weight. "Thought it was beneath him, I guess. He thinks most things are beneath him." Certainly he thought Alex was beneath him. He looked at her like she was a piece of shit. But then she was a piece of shit, ask anyone.

"He'll get less picky," said Sunny.

"Can't see it."

"Then he'll get more hungry."

"I reckon he's up to something."

"Everyone's up to something."

"He's teaching me the history of Troy."

Sunny looked up. Again, that little flutter. "How did such a thing come to pass?"

"I asked about the place and Baptiste offered to tell me and Balthazar said he couldn't stand to hear it done so badly. He knows all about the Empire of the East, he says. He knows all about everything, he says. He speaks twelve languages. He says."

"That's good."

"Is it?"

"You can learn twelve ways to tell him to fuck himself."

Alex spluttered laughter, then couldn't tell from Sunny's face whether it was meant to be a joke and tailed off. "Jakob thinks I should know about Troy. At least a bit. If I'm going to . . ."

"Sit in the Serpent Throne?"

"Mmm." That was right near the top of a growing list of things Alex didn't want to think about. Along with the smell of cooking flesh in the inn. The way the blood welled from the hole in that guard's belly. The sound Marcian made when the wolf's jaws closed around his head . . .

The wind came up chill, and Alex folded her arms around herself. She missed Duke Michael. She hardly knew the man, and he was the best friend she had. He'd made her feel like she might not be a piece of shit. Or might not *always* be one, which was a nice thought to entertain. However wrong it was.

"Maybe you should go back to the others?" said Sunny.

Alex stood up, wiping her eyes, pretending something had blown into them. "I'm annoying you."

"No. Thought I was annoying you." Sunny broke off a piece of bread and held it out. "Stay."

"Thanks." Alex took the bread and dropped back down on the stump. "All Vigga and the baron do is squabble."

"Sounds like them."

"And Baptiste and Balthazar try to outboast each other, while Jakob frowns into the dark."

"Jakob's a good man."

"Is he?"

"I've known some very awful men so probably I'm a bad judge. But I expect Jakob would die for you. If he could."

That didn't make Alex feel any better. "I'm hoping no one else will have to die on this trip," she said, then added in a whisper, "especially me."

"Hope can't hurt."

"But it can't help, either?"

Sunny just raised her white brows and nibbled more cheese with her strangely ordinary gappy front teeth.

"The camp's mostly empty anyway," said Alex. "Everyone went for evening prayers at some monastery. Holiest place in Romagna, they're saying. They've a list of all the miracles that happened there pinned up on a big board outside."

"Anything juicy?"

Alex shrugged. "Couldn't say. Can't read. But I can count, and there's a lot of 'em. They've got Saint Bartholomew's foot there, apparently. The foot he first stepped into the Holy City with. He was declared a heretic, apparently, but returned to the grace of the Saviour. So there's hope for everyone. Apparently."

"Even elves?"

"Well . . . no, probably not for them. Brother Diaz says elves don't have souls, so . . . The Church is really . . . not a fan of elves. In my experience."

"Nor in mine," said Sunny. "You didn't want to see it?"

"What? The foot?" Alex shrugged. "One dead man's foot is much like another, I expect. And you have to pay."

"Just to see it?"

"For extra you can touch its case and for even more extra you can drink from some holy spring. Burst forth from the ground the foot touched."

Sunny's smooth forehead crinkled a little. "You pay to drink water that's had a dead man's foot in it?"

"And they give you a badge to wear."

"Why?"

Alex shrugged again. "Tell everyone you're holier than average, I guess. Stick some saint's name on it and pilgrims will pay for fucking *anything*. Hell of a racket, if you can find a way in. Get a good relic signed off by the Papal Inspectors and the punters throw money at you."

"You'd like that?"

Alex shrugged one more time. "Guess there's worse they could throw."

The silence settled. An owl tooted. The gabble of the camp away in the night. The wind blew up again and shook the leaves.

"Don't you get . . . lonely?" asked Alex. "Out here? On your own."

Sunny looked up at the sky. A tear in the clouds where the stars were showing. "Why would I?"

"I don't like people much, and they certainly don't like me much, but . . . I sort of need 'em."

"Who would I miss?"

Alex thought through their group. The prissy priest. The pompous magician. The nit-picking vampire. The brooding knight. The tattooed woman who might at any moment become a massacre. Halfway down the list, her shrug was right up around her ears. "Me?"

"But you're here."

Alex hunched into her pilgrim's habit. It wasn't warm and it wasn't comfortable, but she'd hunched into worse.

"I'm so glad we have these talks," she said.

Clean Not Clean

"This way," said Vigga, striding on towards the river.

"Right," squeaked Alex, hurrying to catch up. She had to take three steps for every two of Vigga's, partly 'cause she was a stringy little scrap and partly 'cause she treated every step like it was saying sorry for something.

Vigga did not say sorry. Ever. Never had, even before the bite. She liked to walk. Feel the mud press the soles of her feet like a handshake. Jakob had said something about *incognito* and she got the feeling that was someone stealthy, but she'd never heard of him. Sneaking about was well enough for Sunny who was built like a length of wire, and well enough for Baptiste who could smirk her way through a keyhole, and well enough even for Alex who didn't look like anyone in particular so you almost missed her when she was right in front of you.

But it wasn't going to work for Vigga. Disguises weren't made in her size. So she pushed her hood back and shook her hair out and stood her full height. Some fucker wanted her to shrink they could try and make her, see how that turned out.

People stared, of course. *That's a very big woman*, they were probably thinking, and they were right. So?

Why be ashamed? her mother always said. If people don't like you, it's their problem, don't make yourself suffer for it. *Fuck 'em*, she'd always said. *You'll find enough folk want you to suffer, there's no need to help the bastards.* They never got Vigga's mother to drop her eyes, and Odin's beard, they'd tried. So Vigga didn't drop hers, either. Not for anyone.

"Fuck 'em," she said.

"Who?" asked Alex.

"Oh." Vigga had forgotten she was there. "Everyone. Fuck 'em. That is my . . . what's the word?"

"Philosophy?"

"Motto," said Vigga, then frowned. She was thirsty. She tapped at her breastbone with a finger. Felt like the thirst was a thing alive under there, niggling and gnawing. "Need a drink."

"You just drank," said Alex, hurrying to catch up again. "You drank all the water we had."

"That was then." Vigga didn't think about the past much. The past was nutshells. Once they're cracked off what use are they? Toss 'em away and walk on, why hoard the bastards? Also her memory was poor and digging up anything but the vaguest impressions further back than a week ago always felt like hard labour. Fucking yawn. She hadn't the patience for it. Never had any patience, even before the bite.

Why worry about it? her mother used to tell her. Maybe while she was smiling, and braiding Vigga's hair. The thought made Vigga smile. Made her push her fingers into her hair, trying to remember what it'd felt like. The tugging on her scalp. The being taken care of. The gulls calling on the dock and the smell of fish. Hadn't she been thinking she didn't think about the past much? Now here she was thinking about the past again. Maybe she remembered all the time, then forgot she'd remembered.

Vigga frowned again. Now she'd got herself a bit confused.

"You all right?" asked Alex.

"Why wouldn't I be?"

"Why have we stopped?"

"Oh. Right." Vigga walked on. She liked walking. "What was I saying?"

"You weren't saying anything."

"Oh. Right. Was I thinking something?"

"How would I know that?"

"Oh. Right. Hot, isn't it?"

"Not really."

"Uh." Vigga wiped sweat from that hollow at the base of her throat. Always collected there, for some reason. "I'm thirsty."

"You said."

"Did I? We should get water."

"That's . . . what we're doing."

"Ah! Hence the river. Good, then. Perfect. We should get a bucket."

Alex raised her brows, and rolled her eyes downwards, and Vigga followed them.

"Ah." She had a bucket in her hand.

"Jakob gave it to us."

"So he did. Jakob's a very practical man." He'd made sure to strip all the corpses back at the inn for coins and rings and what have you, so now they could buy food and blankets and things. Not that Vigga needed blankets. She ran hot. Hot as Brokkr and Eitri's crucible. The weather wasn't made that could make her cold. She'd probably have wandered off and left that plunder. Jakob was good for thinking ahead. Good on the details. Vigga was terrible on the details. Always had been, even before the bite. *You're terrible on the details, Vigga*, her mother used to say.

"Good," she said. "Money smooths things out. Can't buy things without it. You get debts and whatnot."

"Believe me, I know. Left a few debts behind me, in fact—"

"Need a piss." And Vigga hitched up her stupid bloody cloak-thing, took a step from the track, and squatted in the grass.

Alex blinked. "You just going to—" Vigga was already wriggling her trousers down. "'Course you are."

Couple of pilgrims walking towards the river were staring over at her now. "Morning!" called Vigga, but they hurried on. "What's got up their arses?"

"Couldn't say," muttered Alex, scratching the back of her head. "Maybe you—"

"And . . . there we go. Ha! Don't stand downhill of me, you'll be swep' away in the flood! Like when the sons of Bor slew Ymir! It's like a river in spate down here."

"Yep." Alex squinted off at the horizon. "It's a real fountain. All that drinking surely paid off."

"I knew it would!" And Vigga forced out a last dribble with a shiver, shook her arse and pulled her trousers up and was off, leaving Alex hopping along behind. Why hang around?

"You forgot the bucket!"

"Aye, but look, you've got it." And Vigga clapped Alex on the back, and near knocked her over, and had to catch her shoulders to whisk her up straight again.

The Pope said look after Princess Alexia, and Vigga loved the Pope. Such a laugh! They would chat about this and that. Vigga was usually in a cage at the time, but she was in a cage most of the time and had to accept there were good reasons why. They understood each other. Both missed their mothers, maybe. Her Holiness said look after Princess Alexia, so Vigga had decided to like her. If you have to look after someone what's the point in not liking them? Makes everything a pain in the arse. And *life's painful enough without getting in your own way*, as Halfdan always used to say. Before she killed him.

Don't look too far ahead. That was what Olaf used to say. Before she killed him, too. Or did she kill him first? The order was hazy. Probably best not to look too far back, either. Specially if your memory was as poor as Vigga's and had all the horrible shit in it hers had. Next breath, next step, next meal, next fuck. Get what you can from the moments then let 'em go. Don't hoard your nutshells. Travel light, light as wind, scrape off the mud of grudges and regrets. Stay clean.

"Vigga?"

And Vigga realised she'd stopped again. Just standing there, staring at the dirt.

"Wha?"

"We shouldn't be . . ." Alex glanced about. "Drawing attention."

"I cannot help that I'm a striking woman."

"Jakob said—"

"Jakob's all right," she said, striding on. "You can trust him. All the oaths and whatever. He's like a rock. Not much give, but he's a man who does what he says he'll do. Bloody past and blah, blah, 'course, but we're none of us along for our virtue. 'Cept Brother Whatsface, I suppose."

"Diaz."

"Is it? Priests like to be virtuous. Or at least like to pretend to be. Or at least like other people to pretend to be." She stopped to snarl the words. "Fuck that bastard Rikard, though! He has a fucking *stink* on him, can you smell it? That evil stink he has! Dead and wrong and rotten old blood." She realised she was standing over Alex and spitting in her face, and took a step back, and tried to smile, which was hard with that lumpy throbbing, that scratchy scratching under her breastbone. "But, you know, you can hate a shipmate and still row the same way." And she took the bucket from Alex's limp hand and set off again, towards the river.

Erik used to say that. Had she killed him? Or was he one of the ones that got away? Hard to remember, now, it was all in a mist, hints and whispers and bits and pieces. Take a breath, and open your fist, and let the mistakes fall out like nutshells and . . . there! You're clean.

"After all, look at me. How many folk have I killed?" And she laughed, and threw an arm around Alex's shoulders. "Boatloads. Imagine if you stacked them up into a hill. Into a mountain. Blot out the sun." And she laughed again, but she could hear it cracking, like it might turn to a scream any moment. She'd a worry the wolf was awake. Could feel its pitter-patter footsteps, up and down inside the cage of her ribs, slinking and slobbering, whining to be let out.

"What's the point of counting, after a while? Once you're over your head in blood, what's the difference?" And she realised she had tears tickling her eyes, and she wiped 'em, then laughed again, and made a better fist of it this time. You have to laugh it off. Nutshells. Pretend you're clean.

Here was the riverbank, and trees in the sun on the far side, and light all a-sparkle on the water with the little flies drifting in the chilly sunny morning and Vigga took a long, sharp breath through the nose and let it sigh away and things weren't too bad. Downstream a ring of women had gathered in the shallows, all facing out in their wet shifts, while one or two of their number washed hidden from view in the middle.

She nudged Alex with an elbow. "Look at these, I ask you. Didn't God make your twats?" she shouted at them. "He knows what's under there and the rest of us can guess!" She tossed the bucket down and started to wriggle out of her cloak-thing. "I'll show 'em how it's done—"

"But everyone'll see, you know . . ." Alex was peering at Vigga's hands, and Vigga turned them over, and saw the marks on the backs.

"Ah. The warnings."

Hard to feel clean, when they'd pricked her crimes into her. Warned the world about her, for ever. Chained her, and goaded the wolf out with hot iron. She could feel it, snapping and scratching in the cage of her ribs, ever-so-niggly, ever-so-sharp. She squeezed her eyes shut and tried to get the breath in. It was gone and done and washed away. No need for regrets. She flapped her hands about a bit, put 'em where she didn't have to see the writing on the backs.

"You all right?" asked Alex.

"Fine. Fine. I'm clean."

"You're what?"

"Like nutshells."

"What?"

"Fucking nutshells!" snarled Vigga, spraying spit. "Aren't you fucking *listening*?" And she saw her hands were up like they'd catch Alex and rip the meat out of her and the hair on the tattooed backs of them and the tendons standing stark and *shit* the points of claws popping her nails off and she hid them behind her back 'cause Alex looked very pale and who could blame her.

"Sorry," said Vigga. "I am so sorry for shouting. How rude." And she was sort of smiling and sort of crying at the same time. "My mother would be very disappointed." She touched Alex's cheek with her hand, and it was just a person hand with the nails a bit bitten down, and if you could look past the runes and what have you actually very gentle, and Vigga stroked Alex's hair and pulled a leaf out of it. She looked quite scared while Vigga was doing it but oh well at least one of them felt better.

"I like you, Alex," said Vigga.

"Why?" asked Alex, which sounded strange and almost a bit sad, but who knows why people say things?

"Don't know. You swear a lot, maybe? Here's the thing." Vigga tried to smile, but it was hard. "A time may come when I tell you to run away from me." She took a breath, but it felt like the wolf swelling in her chest hardly left room for it. "And if I say run, you have to run. You hear me? Don't argue. Don't dither. 'Cause the Pope's binding binds me . . . but not the wolf. Run away and maybe climb a tree? Or ride away fast on a horse. Or jump down a well."

"Down a well?"

"Yes. Good idea." Vigga took another breath, and got this one all the way in. The wolf was shrinking, shrivelling away. "Phew." She scratched her neck, and patted her breastbone, and wriggled her shoulders. "Fine, fine." She took another breath. "I'm clean."

Not far from the bank a man was changing a wheel on a wagon, down beside it on one knee, pilgrim's hood back and hair dark with sweat and his sleeves rolled up, sinews shifting in his forearms as he wrestled with the axle.

You couldn't have called him pretty, but no one ever called Vigga pretty and it wasn't about pretty. What was it about? Always something different. Never what you'd expect. Something in the way he knelt there so easy, the way he looked at the wheel to be changed, like it was the whole world. Something in that stillness, in that patience, and Vigga felt the tickle, and she pressed her tongue into her teeth and made the growl in her throat and thought about going over. Thought about how the tickle would become an itch and the itch would need scratching.

Not the time nor the place, Jakob would say, but he was wrong. The place and time was here and now. It had to be. Claw what you can from the world while it's on offer 'cause we're all meat, all dust, written on the sand, gone in a twinkle. You can't keep it for tomorrow, 'cause tomorrow your hopes won't all bloom of a sudden, tomorrow will be just like today. Not the time nor the place.

She took one step towards the man changing the wheel and felt someone grab her wrist.

"Vigga?"

"Uh?" She stared around. She'd forgotten Alex was there. Took her a moment to remember who she was. "Oh. Right. Princess. Who'd have thought?"

"Not fucking me," said Alex, puffing out her cheeks. "Where are you going?"

"Nowhere." Vigga shook herself. Shook the tickle off. "Not the time nor the place, is it? Ah! The river." She loved a swim! Always had, even before the bite. Water in your hair and whatever.

So she strode down the bank and slopped into the river in her clothes and felt the lovely chilly kiss of the water and drank it down and spat it out in a little fountain and laughed and splashed about and laughed again.

"The bucket!" shouted Alex from the bank.

"The what?" She did see a bucket, floating away on the current. Someone must've dropped it. That was careless.

She stood up in the river, water streaming off her sodden clothes. Now she was confused again.

"What was I saying?"

More About Those Dumplings

Dearest Mother,

I fondly remember the long evenings we spent discussing the pilgrimage you took to the Basilica of Saint Justine the Optimist, leaving me for six months in the care of your maid and groom. Imagine my delight, many years later, to find myself retracing your steps, and accompanying no less a personage than that celebrated theologist and philanthropist, Bishop Apollonia of Acci!

I confess the great figures I have recently encountered have not always measured up to their reputations, but I feel sure even you would admire Her Eminence. She strikes me as the very model of a servant of the Almighty, not only eloquently preaching, but stoically practising all Twelve Virtues and—dare I say—many more besides. On several occasions now she has asked me to contribute to her thrice-daily improving lectures, delivered from the remarkable innovation of a portable pulpit—what a time to be alive!

I pray to the Saviour and our own Saint Beatrix for the strength to follow the bishop's example, and fear I may need it in the days to come, for we have now reached Venice and

Brother Diaz paused, pen hovering over paper, and looked towards the city.

The river flared out across the plain, splitting into a hundred channels, flowing sluggishly about a thousand islands, all encrusted with red roofs, stitched together by bridges of stately stone and ramshackle wood. He could just make out the crooked twigs of wharves at the swarming docks, the shifting forest made by the masts of moored ships, the pinprick spires of the many churches, the white spike of the Campanile of Saint Michael's. He could hear the city's voice, when the salty wind shifted. A distant hum of commerce and industry over the outraged squawking of the gulls.

Boats plied the wide lagoon. Distant specks, leaving streaks of wake on the blue water, under the blue sky. He wondered what passengers they were carrying to what ports. Not princesses to Troy in the company of monsters, that was sure. He issued a long-suffering sigh. In through the nose, and out through the mouth. The way his mother taught him.

"That's Venice, then?"

Princess Alexia stood above him, at the top of the rise, hands on her hips, unremarkably coloured hair flicking about her pilgrim's hood in the breeze.

"Unless we've lost our way entirely," he said, reflecting that he'd lost his way entirely.

"Pretty."

"Surprisingly so, given her ill reputation."

"Guess things aren't always what they seem."

"I'm beginning to realise that."

"Who's the letter to?"

Brother Diaz wondered about lying but he'd never been any good at it. Even in his misspent youth, when he'd been called on to do it all too often. "My mother. I confess I haven't shared *all* the details."

"Doubt you'd be believed. Doubt anyone I know would believe it." And she snorted in a thoroughly unregal manner. "Princess Alexia."

"You should write and give them the news."

"No one wants to hear from me. Even if they could read. Even if I could write."

"You never learned?"

"Who'd teach me?"

"I could." They blinked at each other, equally surprised by the offer. "I am—I was—a librarian, after all, and someone who is to be . . . with any luck . . . Empress of Troy should, probably, know her letters?"

She frowned at him with her customary suspicion.

"I'm here, you're here." He glanced towards the track, where the candle-holders that topped the portable pulpit were only now wobbling into view. "We have some time before the Blessed Company catches up. Why don't we make use of it?"

With the watchful reluctance of a mouse approaching a trap, Alex perched on the rock beside him. He slid a sheet of paper from his satchel and handed her the pen.

"Hold it loosely, resting on the middle finger, like so. Exactly. Now dip it in the ink, not too deep, good. Make a line at an angle, yes, then another, so they meet, like a mountain, don't worry, everyone spatters at first, now a third line joining the two, halfway up, straight across, like that, and . . . there! You have formed the letter 'A.' The first letter of your name. Alex."

She looked at him, then at the paper, then snorted up a surprisingly girlish little giggle. "Easy as that?"

"It isn't magic."

"Feels like magic." She dipped pen in ink and tried again, tongue-tip pressed between her teeth with concentration, and Brother Diaz smiled. She looked very young, suddenly, and very much in need of guidance, and he felt oddly pleased to be able to give it. He wondered when he last felt truly useful. He wondered if he ever had.

"You couldn't keep your legs closed for one day?"

There was no mistaking the most gravelly voice in all creation. Jakob of Thorn was limping over with Vigga and Balthazar, a peculiar trio of pilgrims indeed.

"I could not," answered Vigga, proudly. "When the mood's on me they spring apart. I've got desires and refuse to be shamed."

Brother Diaz shifted uncomfortably. God help him, he'd got desires, too. Desires he had fondly imagined smothered in the tomb-like atmosphere of the monastery, but which turned out merely to have been throttled unconscious and were now starting to awaken, sharper than ever after their long torpor. Only last night he'd dreamed of something powerful and tattooed and woken with a raging stiffness of the member.

"One could more easily shame a gatepost," Balthazar was saying. "Venice?"

"Venice." Alex handed Brother Diaz back the pen. "What's happened?"

"Our werewolf has been . . ." Balthazar lifted the holy circefix Brother Diaz wore around his neck, and poked two fingers through it in a gesture more eloquent than any words. "Doing what werewolves do."

"Again?" asked Brother Diaz, snatching it back, clearly outraged, and absolutely neither jealous nor aroused.

"This . . ." Jakob rubbed wearily at the crooked bridge of his nose, "*person* you—"

"People." Vigga jerked her head down the track. "From the *back*. Lot more fun than these fools at the front."

"Venice?" asked Baptiste, strolling up. She had the sleeves of her pilgrim's habit carelessly rolled to display a selection of dangling bracelets. Brother Diaz suspected she'd won them gambling, but wouldn't have been shocked had theft or murder played a role.

"Venice." Alex proudly held up the paper. "I wrote an 'A.'"

"And it's a beauty. What's Vigga done?"

"What Vigga does."

"Again?" asked Baptiste, sounding impressed.

"These *people* saw . . ." Jakob waved a hand at Vigga, whose pilgrim's habit was far from fully fastened, displaying rune-covered collarbones and no small quantity of rune-covered chest into the bargain, "all this?"

"It wasn't dark," growled Vigga, "and *all this* makes an impression." It was certainly making an impression on Brother Diaz's restless member, he was obliged to shift his satchel into his lap and avert his eyes lest it be noticed. Sadly, however, one cannot avert one's ears. "Let me tell you the story—"

"Should Alex hear the story?" he asked, somewhat shrilly, though in truth he was more worried about the danger to his own immortal soul.

"How can one choose a life of virtue," asked Baptiste, piously clasping her hands, "without understanding the alternative?"

"I grew up on the streets," said Alex, waving him away. "This won't shock me."

Vigga cracked her tattooed knuckles. "Don't *fucking* count on it. So the tall one caught my eye first but I got a feeling about the short one . . ."

"Morning, Brother Lopez!"

"Your Eminence!" Brother Diaz jumped up, deeply grateful for the distraction, though he suspected his imagination would be filling in the details for the rest of the day regardless.

"Pray dispense with the honorifics." Bishop Apollonia flashed that humble smile Brother Diaz had determined to practise the moment he had access to a mirror. "They feel inappropriate at the cathedral in Acci, doubly so out here, where we are all siblings in faith, striving to save our souls."

"Fine words!" Brother Diaz drew the bishop away, fumbling his writing things back into his satchel and laughing awkwardly in a futile attempt to drown out Vigga's rapidly progressing tale of sexual conquest. "As yours always are."

"I could say the same of yours, my son." The bishop headed for the portable pulpit, which her guards were in the process of unhitching so the horses could graze beside the track. "I hoped you might help me lead our Blessed Company in midday prayers again? I had in mind the Saviour's exhortation on the Twelve Virtues."

"I only wish I could, today and every day, but it pains me to say I and my companions must leave the Blessed Company here." To step from the path to redemption and skulk off with the devils towards who knew what depths of depravity. "Important . . . indeed *vital* business calls us away."

"Try as we might, duty will find us out. You leave with my blessing." The bishop had an almost apologetic quirk to her brows. "All of you but one."

"How do you mean?"

"The Princess Alexia Pyrogennetos must come with me."

Brother Diaz actually felt the colour drain from his face as he glanced towards Alex, who chose that unfortunate moment to give a splutter of high-pitched laughter. At least any stiffening of the member was swiftly put to rest. "I . . . but . . . don't . . . isn't . . . *Princess*?"

The bishop sighed. "Must we?" Brother Diaz realised her six well-armed guards were all close by. Closing in, one might almost have said.

"Your Eminence—"

"Plain Bishop Apollonia, please."

"I *beg* you," and Brother Diaz held up a calming hand as he backed towards the others. That same calming hand which had so utterly failed to prevent a massacre at the inn. "In the name of the Saviour, can we not avoid violence?"

"I am giving you the chance to do exactly that, Brother Lopez," said the bishop mildly, "or should I say Diaz."

"Oh God," he murmured. He was starting to think he might not be the best judge of character.

"What's happening?" asked Jakob, frowning over.

"Bishop Apollonia . . . would like Alex . . . to stay with her."

There was a pregnant silence. Vigga straightened, eyes narrowing. Alex paled, eyes widening. Most people would have perceived no change in Jakob of Thorn's flinty features, but having known the man for several of the least pleasant weeks of his life, Brother Diaz was sensitive to the tiny adjustments in his frown that bespoke deep displeasure.

"That will not be happening." And he eased back his habit to reveal the battered pommel of his sword.

"I fear I must insist," said the bishop, and her guards lowered spears, put gauntleted hands on hilts, in one case levelled a wicked-looking crossbow. Most likely no crossbows look nice when they're pointed right at you.

"Please . . ." Brother Diaz tried raising the other hand, as if his own empty palms might somehow prevent everyone else from filling theirs with iron-ware. "My companions are *very* dangerous people."

"I have some dangerous people of my own," said Bishop Apollonia.

Perhaps a dozen denizens of the rear section of their company were closing in from the other direction, as slouched and ragged as the bishop's men were polished and upright. Among them were the moneylender, three pimps, and a fellow with a big facial boil who earned a living chopping wood for the evening fires. At the fore were two of the moneylender's thugs, one very tall and the other exceedingly short.

"Ah!" Vigga grinned over at them. "Back for seconds?"

"I reckon it's a different kind of rough and tumble they've come for," said Baptiste.

"You should know that a *very* great reward has been offered," said Her Eminence. "By Duke Constans of Troy."

"One of my fucking cousins," muttered Alex, peering out from behind Vigga's arm.

"Money?" Brother Diaz could only stare at the bishop. A woman who, until a few moments before, he had thought destined for future sainthood. "Where is your *faith*?"

"Gold might not follow one to heaven," and Bishop Apollonia nodded to the rogues spreading out around them, "but it can make a very great difference to these gentlemen while yet on earth. My own motives are not so base, of course. Duke Constans has promised me relics of the highest order, currently held in the Basilica of the Angelic Visitation in Troy. A fragment from the wheel on which our Saviour died. A scrap from her robe and a lock of her hair." She put a hand to the holy circle on her breast, looking to heaven with pious self-satisfaction. "Relics that will bring glory to our beloved Church."

"Not to mention their custodian," breathed Brother Diaz. "That might see her to a cardinal's chair, perhaps? Or can it be that your ambitions reach higher yet?"

Bishop Apollonia did not even have the decency to look guilty. "Setting our corrupted Church back on the righteous path is worth any sacrifice." She turned her scorn on Alex. "And do you really believe you can install this ferrety creature on the Throne of the East?"

"Ferrety?" snapped Alex.

"Hand her over now and you can all just . . . go home."

Brother Diaz stood with his mouth open. To just . . . go home. Ever since leaving the Holy City that was everything he had wanted. Perhaps it was because he wanted so much to accept it that the offer made him so utterly furious.

"And to think," he breathed, "I saw in you the model of what a priest should be. I *praised* you in a letter. To my *mother*! What a fraud you prove to be! What a penny hypocrite! Rather than prating from your moving pulpit in the vanguard of our sacred company you should've been bringing up the rear with the rest of the whores!"

"Ouch," said Vigga with a snort.

"We have been entrusted with a *sacred mission* by Her Holiness—"

"Her Holiness?" Bishop Apollonia's lip curled. "Cardinal Bock has stuffed an *infant* into the Throne of Saint Simon! Your ilk have made of our Holy Church a laughingstock and of the Celestial Palace a shameful sty! Better to have a piglet for a Pope—"

"How *dare* you!" bellowed Brother Diaz. "Her Holiness may be . . ."

"Inexperienced?" offered Baptiste.

". . . but she is the *Mother of the Church*!" An odd phrase applied to a ten-year-old, but the thought only threw fuel on the fire of his righteous fury. "She doesn't *suit you*? The *arrogance*. The *insolence*. The self-serving *hubris*! Bishop, cardinal, or King of fucking Araby, you don't get to *choose* a Pope." He stabbed at the sky with a finger. "That choice *is for God!*"

"Think Brother Diaz found his balls," murmured Vigga.

"The thing about God, *my son*," sneered Bishop Apollonia, "is that he often needs a nudge in the right direction. Brothers and Sisters!" she called, turning towards the track.

Caught up in his sermonising, Brother Diaz had failed to notice that many of the richer members of the fellowship had reached them and were drifting over to see what the shouting was about.

"There are *monsters* among us!" The bishop's voice rang out as clearly as the bell for midday prayers, her accusing finger outstretched. Brother Diaz was not the only one who could work himself up into a righteous fury, it seemed. In fact, he was nowhere near the best at it. "Heretics and heathens, recreants and recusants!"

"She's not exactly *wrong*," murmured Baptiste, sliding one hand into her habit and the other behind her back.

One of the portrait carriers set down his painting and produced a stick. It was a large stick, with a distinct knobble on the end.

"We're . . . very fine people!" ventured Brother Diaz, but as he looked across the scarred, tattooed, and ferrety faces of his companions his conviction ebbed away like holy water from a broken font. "The best people . . ."

More of the company was filtering up to join what was steadily taking on the character of a mob, pressing in on three sides, grumbling and jostling. Brother Diaz saw an old woman he'd been cheerfully discussing footwear with that morning pick up a rock.

"Here's a pickle," muttered Jakob.

The Chapel of the Holy Expediency had formed a little knot, facing outwards, with Princess Alexia at the centre. Balthazar and Baptiste were pressed shoulder to shoulder which, given how much they despised each other, didn't seem a good sign.

"They are malefactors and fugitives!" called Her Eminence, and the crowd edged in. "It is every pilgrim's duty to bring them to the righteous justice of our Mother Church!"

"Take another step and I will make *ashes* of you!" And Balthazar whipped something from his habit.

"Ugh!" Brother Diaz took a horrified step away, realised that took him towards the bishop's guards and was obliged to step the other way, realised that took him almost into Vigga's arms and was obliged to sidle awkwardly around her. Balthazar had produced what appeared to be a severed hand, the skin mottled and the nails black.

"Where'd you get that?" asked Vigga, no more than curious.

"From a sorceress who no longer needed it." Balthazar waved it towards the pilgrims like a torch at wolves and it jerked horribly into life, fingers wriggling.

"Ugh!" said Brother Diaz and Alex at the same time, shrinking back against each other. A little flame puffed from the blackened fingertips and there was a strong odour of sulphur.

"Sweet Saviour," whispered one of the pilgrims, making the sign of the circle over her heart. "He's a sorcerer!" A round of gasps, curses, angry jeers.

"*Magician*, God damn it!" snarled Balthazar.

Vigga had begun to growl in the back of her throat as poorer pilgrims shuffled up to join the rest, first curious, then furious, the anger spreading from the bishop like a plague.

"Witness!" she thundered. "Do you need any further proof of the debasement of our Holy Church? Cardinal Bock has lain down with monsters!"

"You want monsters?" Vigga ripped her habit off and flung it aside, crouching in her vest with her fists clenched and muscle popping from her tattooed arms. "I'll show you *monsters*."

"Take the girl alive but—urgh!" The bishop's head was wrenched back by the hair and Sunny stepped from nowhere, pressing the curved blade of a dagger into her throat.

There was a moment of breathless silence, the pulse thudding almost painfully hard in Brother Diaz's head, the air heavy with the promise of violence.

"What's your plan here, Sunny?" murmured Jakob.

"Hadn't got to that," she murmured back.

"An elf!" someone screamed. "A fucking elf!"

"Drop the knife!" squawked the chief of Her Eminence's guards, waving his crossbow around in a frankly dangerous manner.

Baptiste's eyes darted from one of the thugs to another as they closed in, her hands sliding from her habit with the telltale gleam of steel.

"Kill it!" screeched one of the pilgrims, pointing at Sunny.

"Wait!" gasped the bishop as Sunny's knife pressed into her throat. "Wait!"

A mild-mannered shoemaker who'd been hoping for a cure for his piles prepared to use a holy circle on a pole as a bludgeon.

"Oh God," whispered Alex, clutching tight to Brother Diaz's sleeve.

"Oh God," whispered Brother Diaz, clutching tight to hers.

The pimps, the guards, the pilgrims all edged forwards. Jakob eased an inch of steel from his scabbard.

"Who's got the *good meat . . .*" hissed Vigga, drool spilling from her lips as they twisted back from lengthening fangs.

Brother Diaz shut his eyes and turned his face away—

"Your attention, please, everyone!"

He looked around. He couldn't help it. The prayers died on his lips and his mouth dropped foolishly open.

A figure stood in the portable pulpit, hands gripping the lectern. A handsome man in his late fifties. A man of astonishing dignity and presence. A man from whom no one could for a moment tear their wondering eyes away.

"My name is Baron Rikard," he said, placing a humble palm on his breast. "I have been with you on the road since we gathered near Spoleto."

"He has!" gasped one of the pimps, and a hatchet dropped from his limp hand as he raised it to point. "I recognise him!"

"I was not born a nobleman." Rikard's voice overflowed with quiet authority and rich compassion. "The position was in some ways thrust upon me. By my wife, Lucrezia. A woman it was . . . *very* hard to say no to."

"What's he doing?" muttered Alex.

"Hush!" snapped Brother Diaz. He couldn't afford to miss a breath of this. He knew these were the most important words he would ever hear. The pilgrims had turned as one, attending more closely than they ever had to the bishop's sermons.

"When she first brought me to Krosno I was . . . so naïve. Frankly, I was no better than a pretty idiot. Perhaps I am unfair. A *very* pretty idiot. I think it was late spring, maybe early summer . . ." The baron frowned, scratching his neck. "No! Mid-spring, definitely, I remember the trees were coming into leaf . . ."

"My God," breathed Brother Diaz. The revelation burst upon him, a mind-expanding epiphany. If the trees had been coming into leaf . . . that *would* have been mid-spring!

Bishop Apollonia was similarly moved. "Trees . . . in leaf." Tears ran freely down her cheeks. Sunny took the blade from her throat and stepped back. No one even seemed to notice, so transported were they by the oration. One of the portraits fell from nerveless fingers and splashed into a puddle.

". . . though a lot of evergreens, also, in that part of Poland, of course, sometimes referred to as the garden of Eastern Europe. Perhaps you would like to put down your weapons while I talk?"

There was a clattering as guards, thugs, and pilgrims instantly divested themselves of swords, spears, axes, and knives. One pimp hopped around as he struggled to tug a dagger from his boot. People began to fall to their knees as the baron's awe-inspiring address continued.

"Lucrezia's castle was a bit of a pile if I'm honest. Been in the family for generations—that wallpaper in the dining room, ugh—and I was set on bringing the place up to scratch. Bit of plastering, new paint, the roofs were in need of attention but there's a certain kind of slate they use that had to be shipped in. Then there was a whole to-do over a new chandelier, the people there were exceptionally set in their ways . . ."

Someone was pulling at Brother Diaz's shoulder, hissing, "Let's go," in a gravelly voice, but he tore free. He understood now how it must have felt to hear the Saviour speak. Baron Rikard was close to touching the very secret of existence. Everyone there knew it. One woman—a coal merchant from Grosseto—was making a whimper of almost sexual ecstasy with every breath.

". . . my favourite food had been a stew of beans and sausage my father made with goose fat, but it soon became the dumplings local to my wife's estates." The baron's eyes were fixed on the far horizon. Fixed beyond the banal and everyday, fixed upon a divine revelation he was somehow moulding into earthly words. "Pork, I believe. Done with a little oil . . . some onion . . . those were the days." He gave a sad smile that cut right to the heart and left Brother Diaz breathless. "When I still chewed things."

"Merciful heaven, it's true," whispered the moneylender, hands clasped.

"It is *the* truth." One of the pimps had wet himself, standing transfixed while a dark stain spread across the front of his trousers. "The only truth."

Brother Diaz understood. What did it matter? What did anything matter, but to hear Baron Rikard's next words?

"So, everyone, if I have your absolute attention . . ." The vampire scanned the gathering to make sure all eyes were turned towards him, and they were, unerringly, in awestruck reverence. "And I believe I do . . . coming to my *point*." His beard had turned white, and his hair had turned white, and his face looked very lined, but those eyes . . . it was as if he stared directly into Brother Diaz's soul. There was utter silence. Even the birds and the insects were still. "You will continue to Cyprus, forgetting this speech, forgetting me, definitely forgetting the elf and any suggestion of sorcery, forgetting that any person such as I or my associates or anyone faintly resembling *a princess*, even a ferrety one, were ever members of your Blessed Company. Yes?"

There was a kind of wave through what had recently been a bloodthirsty mob as every person eagerly nodded their heads.

"Yes," gasped the coal merchant, eyelids fluttering. "Yes. Yes. Yes . . ."

"I wish you joy of the journey," said the baron. "May you all find what you are looking for." He turned away, then turned back. "Apart from you, Bishop Apollonia."

"Me?" asked the bishop, tears still streaming down her face.

"You will experience a frustrating itch that you cannot quite reach, all the way to Cyprus and back."

"I will," said the bishop, and she dropped on her knees in the mud and raised her hands joyously to the heavens. "God love me, I will!"

"Thank you, everyone." And the baron clambered down—a difficult undertaking at his advanced age, knotted knuckles wobbling on the handle of his cane.

And so they left the Blessed Company behind, most of them still staring at the empty pulpit, others gazing blankly about, still others wandering off, directionless. Brother Diaz allowed himself to be steered away, stumbling down the long slope towards Venice, into the dappled shade of the trees, most of his mind still lost in the sublime wonders of the baron's address.

"What was that?" Alex was asking.

"Glamour," said Baptiste through tight lips, glancing back up the slope with a dagger in one hand. "It'll fade in an hour or two."

"Should've let me kill the bastards," said Vigga, kicking through the brush.

"Not *everything* must be killed or fucked," observed Balthazar, tossing the severed hand away into the bushes and wiping his own on the front of his habit. "It was turning ripe anyway." And he shrugged the habit off and left it draped over a bush.

Brother Diaz had no time for such weightless distractions. "The most profound oration I have ever heard," he breathed. He was actually plucking at the vampire's sleeve, so desperate was he to understand. "Could you tell me more, Baron Rikard, about those dumplings?"

"Perhaps later." The aged vampire winced as he gently peeled Brother Diaz's hand away. "I am feeling quite fatigued."

No Smiles at the Monastery

It was a great big door fit for a castle, and after much scraping from the other side as locks were undone and bolts pulled back, it was heaved squealing open by an unsmiling doorman.

Marangon, the silent fellow Baptiste had first approached, gave an unsmiling nod in return, and led the congregation of the Chapel of the Holy Expediency through into an anteroom where two unsmiling thugs glowered at them each in turn.

All except Sunny, of course.

They paid her no mind because she was invisible.

Well, she wasn't *actually* invisible. She could still see her own hands. She could still see her own shadow. But no one else saw them. She wasn't even sure why, really. She couldn't have said how she did it.

She just held her breath and . . . did it.

Sunny had a lot of practice so she could hold her breath for a very, *very* long time, even when she was running or swimming or, on one memorable occasion, hanging from a wizard's ceiling, but even she couldn't hold her breath for ever, which was why she was always thinking about where her next breath would come from, and where people were looking, and where it was light and where dark, so life became a little dance from corner, to cupboard, to bush, to shadow, to under the bed, to behind someone's back, to between someone's legs.

And not usually in a good way.

Folk could still hear her—as she'd very definitely found out when she was following that witch and she fell off a roof into a pot and pan stall—so she padded along barefoot at the back with her boots tied around her neck by the laces, looking out for danger and trying to make sure no one blundered into her or shut a door on her or smacked her in the teeth with the butt end of a rake, which a gardener did one time. She'd been quite annoyed about it but could hardly blame the man.

Wasn't as if he could see her.

Sunny tried not to blame anyone if she could help it. *Blame lights not candles*, Mother Wilton used to say. Sunny had quite liked Mother Wilton, even though she'd been pompous and English, which were two black marks against the woman for most. Maybe Sunny had liked her because no one else did. Made her feel special. Though her liking had in no way been reciprocated. Mother Wilton had looked at Sunny like she was a dirty latrine floor. Then she'd died when that bridge collapsed and they'd got Mother Ferrara who looked at Sunny like she was an open sewer.

There's a lesson. Things can always get worse.

The anteroom led to a hallway with two more unsmiling thugs at the end. No one here smiled much. Sunny didn't smile much, either, mind you. But mostly because her mouth wouldn't seem to bend that way. Never felt right on her face, and people didn't like it when she tried. Made them think she was plotting something. Plus a lot of the time no one could see her, of course.

Made smiling rather a waste of effort.

Alex certainly wasn't smiling. She shuffled along head down as if she was trying to turn invisible herself. Sunny liked Alex. She'd brought Sunny food on the road, which was rare, and actually tried to be pleasant about it, which was even rarer. Sunny would've liked to ask her if she was all right but there was no way now and probably it would've gone wrong somehow. She'd practise in the mirror for hours but her face was all pointy and just wouldn't twist the same ways as everyone else's. When she tried to be sincere, she'd come over sarcastic. When she tried to be generous, she'd come over superior. When she tried to be friendly, she'd come over as a dirty elf bitch.

Dirty elf bitch, they used to shout at her in the circus, and make a chant of it, and it didn't seem all that funny to her, but everyone would roar with laughter. Maybe the joke worked on levels she didn't get? Nothing she said was ever funny, it was either horrifying or offensive. She'd stood up, once, in the circus, and told a joke, and it had made everyone furious. *You're here to be hated, not to make jokes*, the Ringmaster had told her. Still, it'd gone over better than when she tried to sing a song that time. *The villain doesn't sing.* Best if she kept her mouth shut. *Keep your fucking mouth shut*, the Ringmaster always used to say.

Which was why she generally kept her mouth shut and did little things to cheer people up. Things they'd barely notice, like even up the laces in Jakob's boots so he didn't have to bend down or fold Vigga's clothes while she was fucking or tuck Alex in a bit at night because she tended to thrash around and kick her blanket off and end up shivering. Made Sunny feel useful. Like she was in a family.

It was nice to try it out.

Jakob was the grumpy grandfather, Rikard the mysterious uncle, and Baptiste the put-upon mother. Balthazar was the overconfident older brother,

Brother Diaz the underconfident younger brother, and Alex the pretty child everyone liked 'cause she hadn't been around long enough to disappoint anyone yet. Vigga was maybe some weird third cousin who kept fucking everyone when she wasn't turning into a giant wolf-thing and by that point the metaphor had really fallen apart because how many families have an invisible elf?

None.

They rounded a corner and Sunny stayed back, pressed against the wall to treat herself to a couple of nice long breaths before holding the next one and ducking after them into a colonnade. It was built around what must've once been a garden, but successive floods had turned it into a brackish pond. Which was what a lot of Venice came down to, far as she could tell. A worn statue stood marooned up to its knees in the centre, holding up a handless arm as though begging God for rescue. That didn't work in Sunny's experience. Not on God, not on anyone.

You want rescuing, you'd better get ready to rescue yourself.

Maybe God will congratulate you afterwards, or something.

"Was this a monastery?" asked Brother Diaz.

"Yes," said Marangon, who spoke almost as little as he smiled.

"Where are the monks?"

"In heaven, maybe? You're the expert."

Jakob was gripping his leg as he walked. Weeks of marching with the pilgrims must've cost him. Sunny would've liked to help him, but she had no way to help and he hated the whole idea of help. For reasons of his own he wanted to make life as difficult as he possibly could.

She really didn't understand people at all, they were so weird. Dealing with them was like being slapped in the face over and over.

Another unsmiling thug stood beside another heavy door. Sunny would've usually nipped in first or slipped in among the others but they were packed too tight so she waited till they were through and the door was shutting, then lightly flicked the doorman's earlobe and when he jerked around darted under his arm, whipped around the door, and was in before it shut, which was very nimble even if she did say so herself.

Shame no one saw it.

The great high room on the other side had been built as a chapel, with a gallery halfway up the walls and rafters above with old cobwebs fluttering in the draught. There was lots of stained glass with saints getting murdered in imaginative ways. There was Saint Simon in his red-hot throne, and Saint Jemimah under her rock, and Saint Cedric with the nails in him, which always gave Sunny a shiver when she thought about it.

That was *not* a nice place to get nails.

Why the Saved wanted to see their heroes being mauled and drowned and hammered and squished she'd no notion. Maybe they thought if Saint Cedric had got nailed hard enough, they wouldn't have to get nailed themselves. In this she thought they were likely mistaken.

There are always more nails around.

It had been built as a chapel but they'd made a kitchen out of it since, with an oven at one end big enough to fit a corpse in. Nearby a man was pounding dough on the altar stone, flour dust puffing through the shafts of coloured light. There was something very firm in the way he did it made Sunny think that oven might well have held a corpse or two in its time. A little girl stood beside him in an apron that matched his and a sneer even Balthazar might've been proud of.

"Frigo!" sang Baptiste, swaggering up with her arms wide like she'd hug the whole place. She had this way of talking that made people like her somehow. Always seemed much more like magic to Sunny than just disappearing.

Baptiste's magic fell flat on this occasion, mind you. Frigo's eyes were very cool. "Baptiste," he grunted, the way you might talk about an ongoing mould problem, and he looked down at his dough again, and kept working. "I knew you'd be back. Like a fox at the bins."

Baptiste shrugged. "I've been called worse."

"Stick around," said Frigo. "You will be."

"This that fucking bitch Baptiste?" snapped the little girl, propping her floury fists on her hips. Sunny wished she knew how she could scrunch her face up so much, like it had no bones in it at all. "You that fucking bitch Baptiste?"

"My granddaughter," said Frigo, nodding towards her. "Best judge of character I know. I'm teaching her the family business."

"Baker or crime lord?" asked Baptiste.

"Why can't I be both?" sneered the girl. "I hear you're a liar *and* a thief."

Baptiste's smile wasn't even dented. "And those are just my hobbies," she said.

Sunny tiptoed around the outside of the room while they talked, the old flagstones so smooth and cool against her bare feet. She went carefully, though, on the shadowy side of the chapel 'cause folk might not see her, but in those shafts of coloured light they might see the dust motes washing in her wake.

They might not see where she was, but sometimes they noticed where she wasn't.

Frigo was still pounding his dough. "What are you after, Baptiste?"

"Do I have to be after something?"

"Yes. You can't help yourself."

A door in the far wall stood open a crack, and tiptoeing close Sunny could see a man against it, listening, with a knife in his fist, and two more beyond, and they had knives, too, which was no surprise, it was a knifey sort of place.

She climbed up the side of a window where there were good fingerholds and peered over the rail of the gallery. There were two men hunched out of sight on the other side, and they had bows. She dropped, soft and silent, flattened herself against the wall to slip behind Frigo's glowering granddaughter and over to a broken window. Three more men in the colonnade, at the door they'd come through. If things went the wrong way, they could get messy fast. But that's how it was, being in the Chapel of the Holy Expediency.

Things got messy fast.

Baptiste was coming to the point. "We need passage. To Troy. Me and my friends."

"You don't have friends, Baptiste." Frigo cast a patient eye over the group. All except Sunny, of course. "Only folk you can make use of."

Sunny slipped around Vigga, had to jerk out of the way 'cause the woman couldn't keep still for two breaths together, and pressed herself tight against Jakob's back.

Jakob was very handy to have around 'cause he was wide, and tall, and never got flustered, not even when he suddenly felt an elf pressed against him having a quick breather.

"Three on the left," she whispered, "three outside the door, two bows in the gallery."

Jakob gently cleared his throat to show he'd heard. It would've made Sunny smile, that they had an understanding. If she'd been better at smiling.

She held her breath again and slipped around him.

"These are them, are they?" Frigo was pointing at them one at a time with his floury forefinger. "The Pope's pets. Don't take a genius to guess she's the werewolf."

"That's what a fucking werewolf looks like?" sneered the little girl.

Between the hood and all the hair, the only bits of Vigga's face on show were her fangy smile and a hint of tattooed cheek. "It's what this one looks like," she said.

"And he's the vampire," said Frigo.

"That's what a fucking vampire looks like?" sneered the little girl.

Baron Rikard saluted lazily with his cane. "Enchanted, my dear."

"Which makes this Jakob of Thorn." Frigo scratched thoughtfully at his throat leaving some flour in his stubble. "I'm an admirer of yours, as it goes."

Jakob, still as a statue with arms folded, gave a weary grunt. "I'm not."

Posturing was another of those person things Sunny had never really understood, so she left them to it and sidled over to the oven to bask in its lovely shimmery warmth. An old cat had the same idea, though, and now it looked up, tail tip flicking. Cats always saw her just as plain as day. Dogs were blissfully oblivious. Sunny had no idea why.

She didn't understand how anything worked and herself least of all.

This cat got up, curious, wanting to rub against her leg. Sunny would've liked to stroke it because cats feel lovely against the palm. She liked it when their tails slipped through the webs between her fingers, so soft and tickly. But now wasn't really the time, so she mouthed sorry as she nudged the cat away with her foot.

"And who's this?" Frigo was asking, narrowing his eyes at Alex.

She frowned back at him. "I'm no one."

"Everyone's someone."

"Not me."

"How about you?" Frigo narrowed his eyes at Balthazar. "Bet you're someone."

The wizard gave that proud head toss of simultaneous scorn and offence. "I am Balthazar Sham Ivam Draxi."

"He sounds a fucking prick." The little girl pulled a knife from her apron and set to scoring grooves in the dough. Sunny once heard it said that loaves are all about the grooves. They won't rise properly without them. Maybe people are the same.

They'll never come out well unless they're cut a bit.

"Oh, she really *is* a good judge of character." Baptiste folded her arms as she grinned over at Balthazar. "He's a new boy. A warlock."

"I swear she does this to annoy me," murmured Balthazar, glaring back.

Frigo narrowed his eyes even further. "A good one?"

"Among the top three necromancers in Europe! Possibly two, depending how you feel about—"

"What are you after, Frigo?" asked Baptiste.

Frigo peeled one of the loaves onto a shovel with a skillful flick of the wrist and headed towards the oven. "Do I have to be after something?"

"Of course. You can't help yourself."

"Oh, touché." Firelight flared across Frigo's face as he leaned close, close enough for Sunny to have reached out and touched his pockmarked cheek. "There's a thing I want. In a house." Which was troublingly vague.

"Your people can't get in?" asked Baptiste.

"Oh, they got in." Frigo turned, leaning on the shovel. "They just never came out."

"No one comes out o' that place," said the little girl, spinning her knife in her fingers and flashing a grin almost as nasty as Vigga's. "Folk say it's cursed."

"Belonged to an illusionist." Frigo was shovelling up the next loaf. "Left Venice long ago but the house is still . . . protected."

"Protected how?" asked Balthazar.

Frigo slid the next loaf into the oven and shrugged. "You're the warlock."

Balthazar's lip curled but Jakob cut in ahead of him. "What is it we're looking for?"

"A white box, about so big, with a star on the lid."

"What's in it?"

"That's my business."

"I like to know what I'm getting into."

"Aye, but something tells me you tend to wade into it regardless. I've told you what I can. You don't like the terms—"

"—you know where the fucking door is!" finished his granddaughter.

Baptiste glanced at Jakob, brows high. Baron Rikard tipped his head back and gave a sigh. Sunny edged a little closer to the warmth of the oven.

"That it should come to this," murmured Balthazar bitterly. "Running errands for a baker and crime lord."

"And those are just my hobbies," said Frigo, mildly.

"I will need equipment."

"Marangon can get you anything."

"*Highly* specialised equipment."

"Marangon can get you *anything.*"

"We bring you this box." Jakob took one deliberate step forwards, towards the altar stone. One step and he stopped. "You organise us passage to Troy."

"Done." Frigo nodded towards the oven. "Wait a bit, you can take a fresh loaf as a bonus."

"We'd sooner get started."

"Suit yourself." And Frigo shovelled up another.

Marangon beckoned them towards the door, and everyone turned to follow, or watched them go, so Sunny grabbed the chance to take a quick breath, then with some reluctance had to leave the warmth of the oven behind. Frigo's granddaughter had put her knife down near the corner of the floury altar stone.

Looked like it might fall and hurt someone, so Sunny pushed it back safe on the way out.

Every House an Island

The heart of Venice was a half-drowned place, every building its own island, every street its own canal, swarming with people and teeming with boats. Boats made into houses, boats made into shops, boats where young lovers lazed, boats where furious rows took place, a boat turned into a chapel, from the forecastle pulpit of which a red-faced nun screeched for repentance. There was water around the buildings and water inside them. People swam through their front doors. People fished from their balconies. It smelled like beaches and bad drains, gulls endlessly bickering overhead, dashing everything with the ceaseless hail of their droppings.

"A perfect opportunity for a lesson," said Balthazar.

Alex sagged back in the prow and groaned. "Thought I was learning the history of Troy, not Venice."

The magician rolled his eyes, something he did more or less whenever she spoke. "All things are connected, child. Troy and Venice, and all the states and cities of the Mediterranean, for that matter, are branches grown from one root, which is . . . ?"

"The Empire of Carthage," she grunted.

"Why else would the varied peoples of southern Europe and northern Afrique speak one tongue, derived from ancient Punic?"

"Because the Carthaginians burned everyone who wouldn't," murmured Baron Rikard, lazily watching three little boys pole a raft past.

"Burning people may not be to everyone's taste," observed Balthazar, "but it cannot be denied that it is a viable route to improved efficiency. When the armies of Carthage conquered southern Italia, they built the vast temples on which the Holy City itself now stands. When they conquered northern Italia, their peerless Witch Engineers dammed the Po and the Piave, drained the lagoon, and founded this great city on the fertile land beneath."

"Greatest city in the world," murmured Marangon from the platform at the stern, flinging the pole up through his hands, water dripping from it onto the boat like spotty rain.

"The denizens of Krakow, Atlantis, Dijon, and many others would make their own claims, of course," said Balthazar, "as the denizens of Europe's great metropoleis so love to do, but you would have a case. Certainly in her heyday. The Carthaginians built great villas here, and swarming markets, and lofty temples, and civic projects to eclipse anything we dream of in these petty latter days. As their Empire spread around the Mediterranean, even as far as Troy, this was their northern capital."

"So what went wrong?" asked Alex, hoping to put off answering questions by asking her own.

"An enemy boiled out of the east unlike any Carthage had faced before, whose fanaticism and mastery of magic matched their own. Can you guess who?"

Sunny blinked suddenly into view, perched on the very stern of the barge behind Marangon, out of sight of Balthazar. She opened her eyes very wide and pointed to herself with both hands, then took a breath and blinked away again.

"The elves?" ventured Alex.

Balthazar looked faintly put out. "Gratifying that *something* at least is going in. Repelling the elves sapped all the strength of mighty Carthage, and their many human enemies took advantage of their weakness. The greatest Empire the world has seen, riven by internal struggles and pressed on every border, collapsed under its own weight. Its western parts tottered on for a century or two, then flew into fragments. Venice elected themselves a Doge and clung on to a few splinters of territory. Bits of the Dalmatian Coast, Ragusa . . ."

"Ragusa's lovely," murmured Baptiste.

"Everyone likes Ragusa," said Baron Rikard.

". . . some islands in the Aegean. Even as the cult of the Saved rose and bound the feuding tribes of Europe together. Even as the elves boiled from the east again, and into the Holy Land, and even as the crusades against them proudly flared up and ignominiously died down. Even as war, and plague, and famine swept the continent, and the big heads traded the big hats of the world, some vestige of lost glories remained here."

Again the slapping as Marangon flung the pole up, hand-over-hand, again the patter of fat drops from the wood.

"So . . ." Alex pronounced each word carefully. "What went wrong?"

Balthazar sank smugly back. "It might be fifty years ago, now—"

"Fifty-two on the thirteenth of Mercy," said Marangon.

"There were storms all through spring and into summer. More rain than anyone could remember. And the great dam across the Po, a thousand years old and more—"

"Burst," grunted Jakob.

Balthazar bared his teeth. "Honestly, I don't even get to deliver my own punchlines any more. The lagoon flooded again. The poorer districts, on the higher ground, were mostly spared, but the best parts of town, close to the water . . ."

"Became the worst parts of town," said Jakob.

"Up to their necks in the drink," added Baptiste.

"The great achievements of the ancients." Baron Rikard smiled faintly as he let his hand trail in the water. "Undone by rain."

"Sometimes, in a dry year, the waters drop, and the mosaics of the great forum are revealed once again, and people get their ground floors back." Balthazar waved towards old tidemarks striping the nearest corner. "In the wettest years every house becomes its own little island."

"I understand Saint Michael's Cathedral is usually flooded," said Brother Diaz. "They have little barges instead of pews."

"Can't they fix the dam?" asked Alex.

"Easily," said Balthazar. "All one need do is bring the matchless architects of ancient Afrique back from the dead. Otherwise, forget it. The elves toppled the Tower of Numbers in Antioch, and the English burned the Library at Calais, and the Witch Engineers of Carthage, daring any risk in their attempts to turn the tide, opened a gate to hell and destroyed their own city."

"I've yet to see a gate to hell turn out well." Vigga sadly shook her head. "Makes you wonder why they keep opening the bastards."

"Fragments of the Empire remain, scattered about the Mediterranean. The famous Pillar of Troy, most notably, and the knowledge gathered in its storied Athenaeum. But, by and large, the wisdom of that age is blown away as if it had never been." Balthazar settled back smugly. "Those in power prefer to remain sunken in ignorance."

"It's not the wisdom to build that was lost." Jakob caught a mossy post beside the boat. "It's the will." And he dragged himself up onto a rickety little jetty with a growl.

"They won a lot of battles," Baptiste considered a crumbling temple across the way, its tide-stained pillars half-sunk in the sea, "and built a lot of grand things, so people always forget."

"Forget what?" asked Alex.

"What absolute wankers the Carthaginians were. How many dead slaves are sunk in the drowned foundations of this city, do you think?"

"Lots." Balthazar shrugged. "But you can't build big without a few bodies."

If Alex had been picking somewhere to rob, and it would *not* have been the first time, the illusionist's house wouldn't have been her first pick. Or even her tenth. Next to the crumbling palaces in the neighbourhood it was squat and boxy, unadorned except by a riot of dead creeper, with narrow windows and steps leading up out of the water to a pillared porch on the first floor.

Alex looked down at it from a balcony across the flooded way, her elbows resting on the pitted parapet and her chin planted on her fists. "Doesn't look too magical," she muttered.

"Not to the naked eye." Balthazar had a set of coloured lenses on a ring like a bunch of keys and was peering at the house through them, one after another. "Certainly not to the naked eye of an idiot."

"No one comes near it," said Jakob, frowning down with his arms folded. No boats in the flooded streets around the building. No people at the shuttered windows facing it. No birds even, on the roofs.

"Folk say it's cursed," grunted Marangon.

"And they are correct." Balthazar turned to face them. "If only in the crudest of senses." He still had one lens to his face and it made his eye look ridiculously small. And orange. "The aura is quite exceptional, especially around the north-eastern corner, though that is of course to be expected, considering the prevailing wind." He riffled through the lenses and held another up to his eye. "There are at least three separate and quite powerful enchantments woven into the building, as well as some traces of a bound entity."

"Entity?" grunted Jakob, wincing. "Never liked the word."

"Then I am," droned Balthazar, "*as usual*, finding the correct one for the circumstance."

Baptiste glanced at Alex, and they rolled their eyes at the same time.

"There is something in the walls . . ." Balthazar had moved on to combinations of lenses now. "Copper wire? Lead in the plaster? It is quite impossible to see inside from this vantage point."

Jakob glanced sideways. Just with his eyes, as if turning his whole head would be too much effort. "But you can handle it?"

"Twice before breakfast." Balthazar swept from the balcony and, puffing her cheeks out yet again, Alex followed him.

Their apartment was on the top floor of a great damp pile that might well have been built by the Carthaginians but hadn't been given much attention since. There wasn't a right angle anywhere. None of the doors fitted their frames and the slanted floors groaned at each footstep as if one person's extra weight might make the whole place subside into the lagoon. You couldn't grumble at the scale, mind you. The main room could've held a whole fish market. Which would've been handy, since you could've caught the fish in the flooded street outside.

"I *suppose* this will serve as an adequate stage for the relevant rituals." Balthazar glanced about the decaying room with his nose wrinkled. "But I cannot do *everything* myself."

"Don't tell me." Jakob gave a gravelly sigh. "Someone will have to go inside."

"So you *are* cleverer than you look."

"Not much," murmured Baptiste, from the corner of her mouth.

"Don't get too smart," grunted Jakob. "You're coming with me."

She planted her hands on her hips and muttered at the ceiling. "I should've quit after Barcelona."

"There are a *very* great number of things I will need," said Balthazar, taking Marangon by the lapel, "foremost among them *punctuality* and *precision*. Tell me you have a notebook. Good. I trust you write quickly because I am *never* in a mood to dawdle. A full set of conjurer's circles, of course—bronze, not brass, obviously, we're not primitives—and a better set of lenses, salt and candles of the highest quality . . ."

"You and Brother Diaz stay here." Jakob was looking at Alex like a docker at a crate he couldn't see how to shift. "Baron Rikard will keep you company."

Alex glanced over at the baron, apparently asleep on a battered couch with the back of one hand over his eyes, like a fainting matron. "Don't tell me he doesn't bite."

"I won't bite you, anyway," he droned, without moving his hand. "I have *some* standards."

"But you should be ready," said Jakob. "In case something goes wrong."

"That does seem to happen a bit . . ." muttered Alex.

"Do you have a knife?"

She slid it out with some reluctance. The crosspiece shaped like a snake, the little red jewels where its eyes should be.

Jakob looked it over with the kind of approval she never got herself. "Fit for a princess."

"Duke Michael gave it me. At the inn." And all she'd done with it was toss it away. While crawling in the muck and begging for her life, as it happened.

"You know how to use it?"

Alex frowned back at him. "If I really don't like someone, I stick it in the bastard."

"This end first." Jakob rested a fingertip gently against the point. "Have you done that before?"

"I've been in a few fights." She licked her lips. "Lost most of 'em."

"I've been in *quite* a few. Even won some. And take it from me, because it might save your life—a fight is always a gamble." Jakob stepped close, so his shadow fell across her, and she had to look sharply up into his craggy face. "And you are small, and weak, and unskilled. Your chances of beating a strong man in a fair fight are close to none."

"If you're trying to talk me up you need some practice."

"So you make the fight as unfair as you can. Trickery and surprise are your weapons. Those and a lack of pity. Show me how you'd grip it."

She'd seen her share of knife fights in the slums, so she knew how the bravos did it. She held it tight, forefinger around the crosspiece, and bent her knees, and stuck the blade out in front of her and swished it about a bit, baring her teeth and making a hiss that aimed at viper but likely fell well short.

Jakob, certainly, was unterrified. "Very . . ."

"Don't say ferrety."

". . . *fierce*, but I think, for you . . ." He took her wrist and pushed it down, turning the dagger all the way around so the blade was pressing up against the underside of her forearm. "The first time they know you have a knife should be when it's in their guts. Now maybe shrink down, and cringe a bit more. Can you cry?"

It wasn't difficult. She'd felt close to tears for a while now.

"Nice. Beg for your worthless life."

"Wouldn't be my first time." Or even her tenth.

"Use what you have, then. Make them careless, draw them close. Then strike with all the rage you can muster. We all have some."

"Reckon I can dig up a little."

"Good." He waved at his own body like a butcher showing the cuts on a carcass. "Gut, groin, throat all work. And never stop at one. You'd be amazed by the wounds men'll keep fighting with."

"Oh, I've seen some things you wouldn't believe, recently."

"Keep stabbing till you're sure they're dead." Jakob gave her an awkward pat on the shoulder, then turned away. "Brother Diaz! You ever swing an axe?"

Balthazar was still droning out his shopping list. ". . . apothecary's scales, proper ones, a full set of alchemist's spoons, a good alembic and an oil burner, some nightshade, of course, and it must be fresh, none of that dried rubbish, and do you know of any twins who died recently?" There was a silence while everyone glanced over. "Well, if you are in there, and I am out here, we will require some method of communication. Or were you planning to just . . . shout across the street?"

Marangon scratched thoughtfully at his stubbly throat. "The Visentins. Brother and sister. He went a couple of months back. Her last week. Think they were twins."

"Excellent," said Balthazar brightly. "Put them on the list, too."

The Magic of Deportment

T he difference between a true magician and a mere sorcerer is, it needs hardly to be said, the proper apparatus.

The conjurer's circles had been calibrated with compass and callipers, and fastened to the warped floor with silver screws cast at midnight—a flourish Balthazar had by no means expected a gangster to provide. Genuine Eritrean myrrh candles had been set at the seven stations, and Balthazar was halfway through inscribing the heavenly verses around them in Punic *and* ancient Greek. He was a man who had always *insisted* on the best of both.

His delight at being engaged in a serious arcane undertaking after so long trapped in the banal was prodigious, wielding awl and hammer, inscribing the symbols, really drilling into the details. He *loved* runes. Runes never disappointed, or answered back, or made constant acid comments designed to strip away the few shreds of dignity one had managed to retain.

It was hardly his own private laboratory, but considering the time he had been given to work, the circumstances he had been forced to work under, and the wretched companions he had been obliged to work around, he considered the results remarkable. These last few months had, without doubt, been the most testing of his life, but Balthazar had finally procured everything he required.

Everything required to gain entry to the illusionist's house.

And everything required to break the Pope's binding.

He had to force down an acrid burp at the thought. He found it helped calm his continually churning stomach if he steered his mind away from escape or revenge and focused instead on the present task. Enabling this mismatched company of horribles to burgle an unspecified object from an enchanted building, in order to render it into the hands of a leading member of the criminal fraternity occupying a stolen monastery, in order to secure passage to Troy with a view to installing an orphaned urchin with a strong air of street trash upon its throne. So much for holy missions.

He glanced towards the chosen puppet, but the so-called Princess Alexia Pyrogennetos was entirely absorbed in laboriously forming letters on some scrap paper, bottom lip wedged behind her upper teeth with concentration and an inky smudge on one lightly freckled cheek from her efforts. Brother Diaz watched this performance with the gormless grin of a parent in raptures over their own offspring doing something entirely unremarkable. Small wonder that he was utterly ignorant of what Balthazar was really up to, the man was the very epitome of incognizance. Not that his congregation were any less oblivious, what a shock they would receive when—

This time he actually regurgitated some bitter grit and had to slap his breastbone. Baron Rikard glanced up from his book with his habitual look of wry amusement, as if he was party to some joke that everyone else would only later discover. Perhaps he alone of the group had sufficient arcane expertise to guess at Balthazar's true intentions. If so, he made no move to expose the subterfuge. Hedging his bets, no doubt. Hoping to copy Balthazar's method when he finally did manage to break this cursed binding—

He coughed up more bile and was obliged yet again to direct his thoughts away from freedom. Princess Alexia on the throne, Troy returned to the arms of Mother Church, the elves flung back into the east in disarray, Her Holiness clapping her little hands with delight, et cetera, et cetera—

"I'm *shit* at this!" snapped Alex, crunching the paper up in her inky fist and flinging it away.

"Nonsense, Your Highness." Brother Diaz dutifully crossed the room to retrieve her pitiable scrawlings and began to smooth them out. "You're making marvellous progress."

The baron gave an explosive snort. "Towards what? If she is to rule an Empire, she does not need to learn how to write, she needs to learn how to *be*. Are you not the granddaughter of one of history's greatest Empresses? Show some pride, girl!"

Alex frowned back at him. "What have I got to be proud of?"

"Find something, or *invent* it." Baron Rikard tossed his book aside and sat up. "For someone who made their living lying you are remarkably bad at it."

"Well, it wasn't a very good living."

"Ha! Amusing. A quick wit is a fine start and cannot be easily taught. But you must have some grandeur, too. Some *stature*."

Alexia frowned down at herself. "I'm short as a shit."

"You do not have to be *tall*. My wife Lucrezia was smaller than you but, sweet Saviour, she *towered* over any room lucky enough to receive her! Up, I will show you. Up, up, up!"

As Alex stood, looking faintly scared, Baron Rikard began to prowl around her, then to prod at her with a pointed finger.

"In there. Out here. Up. No! God, no. You do not merely thrust your chest at the sky, believe me, you have *very* little there to offer. The *head* rises, the *neck* becomes long—your neck is very fine, you see, so slender, you are a swan, not a seagull, not a duck, do not quack." And he touched her under the jaw and pushed up. "Imagine you are lifted by the crown. Your head is light, not full of weighty filth, not doubts and suspicions, but only high hopes and good wishes." He took a strand of hair between finger and thumb and pulled her head upwards. "There, there, there."

"Ow, ow, ow!"

"A mere fraction of the pain it has caused me to see you skulk into a room. The shoulders then come back—sweet Saint Stephen, no! You are not cracking a nut between your shoulder blades, they scoop under, there is a *structure*. You are not *hiding*, imagine you are there to display your clothes—to sell them to a discerning customer! Yes, better, strong but soft."

"Strong *and* soft?"

"Exactly! Now, the pelvis tilts—good grief, not back—arse *in*, such as it is, groin *up*, such as it is, stomach *tight*. At least pretend you have a spine. You are not uncooked tripe, you are sculpted from marble! And we walk. No, we *walk*. No, erect, like a human rather than a beast of the fields, imagine that. No, not clomping on your heels like Vigga Ullasdottr, no, not swaggering like Baptiste, on the balls of your feet! They caress the ground with the tender touch of a lover, weightless. Yes! Your big toes follow one another in a direct line from here to your desires. Own the room! This is your ground! Yes! Here she is! Her Highness the *Princess* Alexia Pyrogennetos has at last arrived!"

"Huh." Balthazar paused in his work to look over. The girl did indeed appear to be undergoing a dramatic transformation. "What is this magic?"

"The magic of *deportment*!" sang Baron Rikard, with a twirl of his fingers. "How does it feel?"

"Like torture," croaked Alex, prancing across the room with the expression of someone being tortured.

"Good! It's working."

"Can it stop?"

"The moment you stop being a princess."

"Er . . ."

"Oh, you are a princess all the time? Then you must hold yourself like a princess all the time. You must eat, sleep, and defecate with imperial dignity. It becomes instinct. Then people cannot but catch an intoxicating whiff of royalty whenever you approach, rather than . . ." and the vampire wrinkled his nose, "your accustomed air of the gutter."

"This can't be natural."

"Only because you, a thoroughbred racehorse, have been kept in a sack for seventeen years. We must *make* it natural, and we must therefore attend to this self-pitying wreckage *above* the neck." Baron Rikard patted her cheeks firmly enough to make a faint slapping sound. "So! We smile. No, we *smile*. Not a skull's rictus, you are not graded on acreage of teeth. Less with the mouth, more with the *eyes*. Not comedy, my dear, not pratfalls, but the happy end to a drama. Earnest and emotional. It has all turned out *exactly* as you hoped. Whoever you are with is the very person you *most* desired to see!" The vampire pranced, and smiled, as if surrounded by beloved well-wishers, and Alex pranced, and smiled, matching him step for step. "The world is a box of treats and you are humbled to be asked to pick one. Oh, which shall it be? Everything looks so fine! Yes! Very good, with the lashes. Her Highness, so dignified but so accessible. Her Highness, such humility, such grace, all Twelve Virtues in one! Charm them! Delight them! Steal their hearts!"

"Brother Diaz," said Alex, a hand to her chest, her face all quiet concern. "I am *so* glad that you could accompany me to Troy, and truly grateful for your instruction in penmanship." Balthazar was almost as surprised as the monk. Even her voice was changed: higher, cleaner, clearer.

"Marvellous!" The baron clapped his hands, eyes twinkling. "I almost believe you myself! If only I had been so quick a study as you I would never—"

The door of the apartment clattered open and Jakob of Thorn blundered through backwards, dragging something wrapped in sackcloth. Marangon, with a sheen of sweat across his brow, had the other end. The foot end, one might have said, because Balthazar knew a shrouded corpse when he saw one. Few people better.

"Jakob of Thorn!" sang Alex, clasping her hands and fluttering her lashes. "The hero of the Rolling Bear, to whom I owe my life. I could not be more glad to see you returned!"

Jakob dumped the body and straightened, kneading his back. "What?"

Now Vigga blundered in, manhandling a second corpse-shaped bundle with an unhappy Baptiste at the foot end.

"And Vigga Ullasdottr!" The princess pranced over to her. "What a wonderful vest. Is that new? Is that silk?"

"Fuck, no." Vigga looked from her stained vest to Alex, baffled. "Are you drunk? Is she drunk?"

"I wouldn't be surprised," murmured Baron Rikard. He had already slumped back on his threadbare couch, focused on his book with his usual lazy disinterest.

Princess Alexia looked somewhat crestfallen, but Balthazar had greater concerns, already squatting eagerly beside one of the shrouded bundles and beginning to unwrap it. "The Visentin twins, I presume?" He pulled the sacking away to reveal the face. A rather noble visage, in his opinion, with a prominent nose.

"Ugh," muttered Alex, stepping back with one hand over her mouth. "That reeks."

Balthazar ignored her. A necromancer cannot afford to be put off by a mild fragrance of putrefaction, after all. The skin had the expected greenish-blue tinge and some marbling of early decay, but the flesh beneath appeared sound.

"Excellent!" he murmured, beginning to unwrap the sister, who had a size-able wart on her cheek but if anything was in even better condition than her sibling. "You have outdone yourself, Marangon."

Marangon was unmoved. As if he had been congratulated on procuring a bag of plums. If the man ever tired of organised crime, he really would make an exemplary necromancer's assistant. Baptiste was less phlegmatic. She looked thoroughly disgusted by the whole business, which represented a con-siderable reward in itself.

"Whatever you're about here," she said, backing away, "you can leave me out of it."

"I am *entirely* happy to leave you out of *all* my dealings going forward." Balthazar was fully occupied gripping the male twin's neck, feeling out the position of the vertebrae with his thumbs. "Could you assist me, Jakob? I have a sense these will not be your first decapitations."

The old knight frowned slightly more than usual. "You want their heads off?"

"Unless you plan to lug a whole corpse around a cursed house with you?"

There was a silence.

"I was feeling like a fuck," mused Vigga, rubbing absently at her crotch with one hand. "But this has killed the mood."

Talking Heads

Wood scraped on stone, and Jakob watched with a bitter jealousy as Baptiste hopped breezily across to the steps. The boat heeled hard as Vigga planted one big bare foot on the side, then rocked wildly as she took the stride to dry stone, leaving Marangon struggling with the pole to hold it steady.

Jakob gritted his teeth as he wobbled up to standing, all the usual joints aching with the effort of keeping his balance. No one wants to see doubts. He thrust one boot out boldly, but as it reached the step he felt a brutal sting in his groin, and with a helpless groan lost all momentum. He ended up trapped with one foot on the steps and one in the boat while the two drifted gently apart, windmilling his arms to try and keep his balance, the agony between his legs sharpening with every moment.

"Ah," he grunted. "Fuck. Fuck it—"

Sunny caught his arm, leaning right back, teeth gritted, to haul with all her weight, and finally managed to drag him onto the steps.

He bent over to catch his breath, gently working his hips to check for damage. Sunny was still holding his arm with both hands, and he pulled it free.

"Thanks," he grunted. As if thanking her quietly meant he hadn't really needed the help.

"You say it like you didn't need the help," said Sunny.

"I didn't," he snapped, then added, even more quietly, "I could've just torn in half."

Marangon was staring up at Sunny. "Where did she come from?"

"Before this I was with a circus," she said.

"I love the circus," said Marangon. Mild surprise at an elf appearing from nowhere was the most feeling Jakob had seen him display during their entire acquaintance. "Why'd you leave?"

"It's not as much fun on the inside."

Marangon slowly nodded. "What is?"

The illusionist's house didn't look much fun on the outside as Jakob limped up the steps, its gloomy facade coated in dead creeper and its narrow windows tightly shuttered.

Baptiste stood at the top, hands on her hips. "Think I've found the first problem," she said, waving towards the door.

There was no door.

There were steps, a porch, a little roof. Everything to suggest an entrance. But no door. Jakob ran his hands over the stonework where it should have been. A little clammy, like everything in Venice, but very firm.

"This is going well," said Sunny.

"No worse than usual," said Vigga.

"Not even in the building," said Baptiste. "Already we need the sorcerer."

"Magician," said Jakob, and winced. "Bastard's got me doing it now. Best bring the head out."

No one looked delighted at the idea. Vigga reluctantly swung the sack off her shoulder and the four of them gazed down at it. "Well, I'm not touching the bloody thing," she said, wrinkling her nose.

"If there was one woman comfortable around bits of corpses," said Baptiste, "it should be you."

"It's not so much dead bits that bother me as them coming back to life," said Vigga. "No doubt you've got experience with this sort o' stuff?"

"I'm not touching the bloody thing," said Baptiste with a shudder. "You're a walking corpse, Jakob. You do it."

Jakob was busy pressing two fingers into his groin, which was still throbbing, and not in a good way. "It's not so much the corpses or the necromancy that bother me," he said, "as the bending down."

"Tsk." Sunny squatted beside the sack and took the head out by the ears. Its hair was a grey tangle. A leather patch had been sewn over its neck stump. A circle of crabby runes had been drawn on its forehead with a silver nail hammered into the centre.

"Balthazar?" asked Sunny. "Are you there?"

"Of course," said the head, "where the bloody hell else would I be?"

"Ugh," said Baptiste, taking a step back. The mouth moved but the face stayed horribly slack. The whole thing was about as pleasant as you'd imagine talking to a severed head would be.

"It's not his voice," mused Sunny, "but somehow you can tell it's him."

Vigga glared up towards the balcony of the crumbling building where the others were waiting. "I can smell an arsehole a mile off."

"I heard that," said the head.

"Good," said Vigga, "then it didn't go to waste."

"It's leaking," said Sunny.

And there was indeed a kind of goo dribbling from the corner of the mouth. Sunny held the head with one hand, pulled out a handkerchief with the other, and started dabbing it like the face of an elderly relative who'd lost their faculties.

"Why do you have a handkerchief?" asked Baptiste, as if that was the strangest part of this situation.

"For wiping things," said Sunny. "Why else would I have one?"

"Is it monogrammed?" asked Baptiste. There did appear to be an "S" neatly stitched into the corner.

Sunny turned up her nose. "An un-monogrammed handkerchief is just a cloth."

"What's that?" asked the head, dribbling more goo. "Handkerchief, did you say? Everyone's talking at once! Are you inside the house?"

Jakob gritted his teeth as he tried to shake one leg out. "Not . . . entirely."

"You're either inside or you're—"

"There's no door."

"There'th no door," said the head, which was propped against a stack of books on the table in front of Balthazar. Whether the mild speech impediment had afflicted it since birth or only since death, it was hard to say. Honestly, that was far from the most serious of Brother Diaz's concerns.

"Sweet Saviour protect us . . ." he breathed. The blackest of Black Art practised right before his disbelieving eyes. The most solemn strictures of the Church not merely stretched but entirely ripped to bits, then those bits flung down and trampled gleefully in the filth. It certainly put his own youthful indiscretions into sharp focus. Perhaps, as Cardinal Zizka said, one must sometimes use the weapons of the enemy against them, but if the righteous will stoop to any depths, what separates them from the wicked? Where was the *line*? *Was* there a line? Brother Diaz really didn't want to live in a world without lines and yet, through no apparent fault of his own, here he was, wondering if a severed head had always had a lisp.

Perhaps there had never been any lines. Perhaps the whole idea of lines was a consolatory fairy tale it had suited him to believe.

"Ugh," said Alex, almost as disgusted as he was, "is it leaking?"

"No more than expected," grumbled Balthazar. Here was one detail Brother Diaz would definitely be leaving out of his letters to Mother. His letters left out almost everything, mind you. It was likely a blessing for all concerned that he had so far found no way of sending them. "Does anyone have a cloth?" snapped the magician.

"I've got a handkerchief," said the head, and then, "she doeth, it'th fucking monogrammed."

"Not you!" snapped Balthazar at the head. "How could I wipe *my* head with *your* handkerchief, you're not here!" He gave a groan of frustration. "How much longer must I suffer these wretched creatures?"

Brother Diaz rubbed at his sweaty temples. "I have been asking myself the same question for some time now."

"Safe to say that none of us is in our chosen company." Balthazar twitched up his sleeves, stretching out his hands as though to pluck the strings of an invisible harp. "Already they need the magician."

"I would expect you to be pleased," said Baron Rikard, sprawled on his battered couch. "A golden opportunity to demonstrate your formidable arcane skills."

"*Please*," said Balthazar, though he seemed to have turned even more smug at the word *formidable*. "Dispelling one asinine illusion is no test of my powers."

"Though you need the stock of two junk shops to get it done," said Alex, looking over the magical paraphernalia covering the table and spilling onto the floor.

"Who knows what arcane obstacles our hapless colleagues might face?" snapped Balthazar. "What separates a true magician from witches, sorcerers, hedgerow fairies, and those most self-important pedlars of empty superstition . . ." and he curled his lip at Brother Diaz ". . . *priests*, is thorough preparation for *any* eventuality."

There was a pause. "Shouldn't you have a cloth, then?" asked Alex.

Baron Rikard sank back with a chuckle and Balthazar sourly worked his mouth. "Amuse yourselves, by all means." He reached out again, with all the drama of a conductor about to summon a grand harmony from a choir. "Some of us have *work* to do . . ."

"I was hoping for fireworks," grunted Vigga.

Like most things, magic was never quite the fun you'd been after. The stones didn't slide away or drift apart like smoke. The door was simply there of a sudden. A studded one covered in flaking paint with a tarnished ring for a handle.

"My turn." Baptiste rubbed her palms together as she knelt beside the lock, wriggled her fingers, slipped out a set of lockpicks, and started to prod away. She must've had a dozen of 'em, bits of wire all toothed and hooked, so fiddly it made Vigga's hands ache just watching.

"You sure you can open it?" asked Sunny, dropping the head back in the sack.

Baptiste made an annoyed *tsk*. She was good at sounds. Could tell a whole story with a sigh and eyebrows. "I've teased open tougher locks than this. Did I tell you the one about that wine merchant's safe in Ravenna?"

"At least twice," muttered Jakob, who was gripping his groin, and not in a good way.

Baptiste slid another pick into the lock. "What about that time I blackmailed the Bishop of Calabria?"

"One of your best," said Sunny.

"Do you have a door yet?" came muffled from inside the bag. "Are you in the house yet? Could someone answer me?"

"Patience," purred Baptiste, dragging the word out so long you needed patience just to listen to the end. "This takes . . . clever fingers . . . and patience—"

Two things Vigga never had, even before the bite. She grabbed the ring and wrenched it around. It turned and the door swung open with a loud creak, leaving Baptiste frozen, four picks still in her fingers and a couple more gripped in her teeth.

"The Chapel of the Holy Expediency has its drawbacks," said Sunny, "but I take pride in being part of an elite team. Including the man who can't step off a boat and the woman who can't unlock an open door."

"Guess sometimes you need clever fingers and patience." Vigga shook a hand through her hair and tossed it out behind her as she swaggered in. "But sometimes only a beautiful fool will do."

Like most things, her first look at the inside of an illusionist's house was on the disappointing side. A shadowy hallway with a floor tiled black and white, like a chessboard. Olaf tried to teach her chess once, but Vigga couldn't work it out. Little horsies and bishops and castles and queens, all things she didn't like full size. Even thinking about the different ways the fiddly pieces had to move made her want to slap the little bastards into a fire. A smug woman with a weasel in her hands smirked down from a cobwebbed painting. A couple of tarnished suits of armour stood to wonky attention.

"This it?" she muttered as Sunny slipped around her. "I was hoping for—"

"Less dust?" The elf ran her finger down the panelling, then blew a grey fluff of it from the tip.

"More magic, I guess. Maybe it gets more magicky further in?" Vigga started walking but Jakob caught her arm.

"We should go carefully." He frowned down the hallway, drawn sword in his fist. "We know the place is dangerous."

"But it ain't a swordsman's house, is it?" Vigga flicked the blade's point with her fingernail. "You going to sword an illusion? You'll likely do more harm than good."

"Swords always do more harm than good," murmured Sunny, already padding down the corridor on her silent tiptoes. "That's the point of them."

"Come on!" Vigga yanked her arm free and gave Jakob's cheek a pat before he jerked away. "What's the use of never dying if you're not going to live a little?"

"Charge off, then," said Jakob, slapping his sword into its sheath. "Won't bother me when we all fall in a spike pit. I can't die."

"You could be stuck down a pit for a decade with a spike up your arse . . ." Vigga trailed off. Sunny stood a few steps on, head cocked to the side. "You hear something?"

"Flies," said the elf.

It was a grand dining room with a high ceiling, a gallery all the way around, and a chandelier with a dozen candles. A long table was lit by a shaft of light like an actor on a stage, sixteen chairs around it, one knocked over as if someone had jumped up in a hurry. Dinner had been served but never eaten, laden plates crowding the tabletop and a carving fork still sticking from a mould-furred joint. Flies crawled about the rotting banquet, zipped and swam in the overripe air, their buzzing almost painful on Sunny's ears after the tomb-like silence of the hallway.

Vigga showed her pointed teeth. "*Bad* meat."

Two corpses lay in the corner, flies busy about each mottled face. "There are dead people," said Sunny.

Jakob puffed out his scarred cheeks. "There are dead people wherever we go."

"And if not when we arrive," said Baptiste, wrinkling her nose at the table's centrepiece of rotted flower stalks, "then surely when we leave. They Frigo's men?"

Sunny squatted beside the bodies. Looked like they'd died in each other's arms, which was sort of heartwarming, till she realised they were both holding knives, which was the opposite. Heartcooling? "They stabbed each other."

"That's good," said Vigga.

"Is it?" asked Jakob.

"Well, they won't be stabbing us."

Baptiste raised a brow. "I hear some people can get through a day without stabbing anyone."

Vigga shrugged. "Some people, maybe. What do these mean?" She waved at some symbols hastily daubed on the walls with streaky paint. "They look magicky."

Sunny held up the sack. "Shall we ask the expert?"

No one celebrated the suggestion.

"Let's leave that till we have to," said Jakob.

"Which way?" Baptiste was considering the four doorways in the four walls, panelled hallways stretching into the gloom in each direction.

"Weren't you a navigator?" asked Jakob.

"A pilot. For a month or two. Hanseatic shipping, mostly. Know the Rhine delta like the back of my hand."

Sunny glanced around the dining room. "Don't think this is the Rhine delta."

"I do remember it being wetter." Baptiste pulled off her hat to give the back of her head a scratch. "And I did run a ship aground on a sandbank one time. Funny story, actually, the cargo was in part live pigs—"

"So much for her sense of direction." Vigga strode off towards the nearest hallway. "How about this one?"

Jakob got a shoulder in front of her. "We need to go carefully, remember?" He nodded towards the two bodies. "Clearly it's dangerous."

"Then the quicker we're out, the better."

Jakob paused with his mouth half-open but couldn't find a ready answer.

"See?" Vigga swaggered past him. "Some of us are leaders. Most are followers."

"You hear that?" asked Sunny as they followed Vigga towards the light, between the old suits of armour, under the gaze of the mediocre portraits.

Jakob strained at the silence but all he could hear was the slapping soles of Vigga's feet on the chequered tiles. "My hearing isn't all it was . . ." Along with his sight, memory, joints, bladder. Honestly, his ears worked far better than most of him. "What do you hear—?"

But by then he could hear it himself.

"Flies," murmured Baptiste as they stepped into a grand dining room, a chandelier with a dozen candles hanging high above. The long table was laden with a rotten meal and one of the sixteen chairs lay on its back on the tiles.

"How many dining rooms does one illusionist need?" asked Vigga.

"It's the same room," said Sunny, squatting again beside the two corpses in the corner.

"Huh. How did I not see that?"

"Some of us are leaders." Sunny fluttered her eyelashes. "Most are follow-ers."

"I asked for that." Vigga stared wistfully up at the chandelier. "I bent over and begged for it. It's no worse than I deserve."

"What could be worse than *you* deserve?" asked Baptiste.

"We walked straight . . ." Vigga peered into one hallway, then the identical one opposite, ". . . but we came a circle."

"I've been ending up back where I started for decades," said Jakob, wincing as he pressed at his groin again. If anything, it was hurting more with time.

"How do we get further in?" asked Vigga.

"How do we get out?" asked Sunny, still frowning at the corpses.

They all thought about that for a moment.

"This is starting to feel a lot like sticking my neck out," said Baptiste.

"Get the head," said Jakob.

It didn't look out of place, balanced on its neck stump in the midst of that rotten food. "I take it you need me again," it said.

Jakob rubbed at the bridge of his nose. He doubted he would much miss Balthazar Sham Ivam Draxi when he inevitably went the same way as all the other sorcerers, conjurers, witches, and wizards who had come through the Chapel of the Holy Expediency over the years.

"We've found a dining room full of rotten food, but every door out seems to lead back here."

"How will you get further in?" asked the head, which Jakob reckoned was Brother Diaz talking.

"How will they get out?" asked the head, which Jakob reckoned was Alex talking.

They all thought about that for a moment.

"Is there writing anywhere?" asked the head.

"Runes on the walls," said Vigga, squinting at the sloppily painted sym-bols.

"What runes?" asked the head, as a fly settled on the goo at the corner of its mouth.

"I can't read," said Vigga.

"I am all amaze," said the head. "Who can?"

"I can," said Jakob.

"So we're making progress."

"But not runes."

"Do any of you know runes?" The head managed to sound frustrated despite the bubbling monotone, three or four flies now buzzing around its mouth.

"I know some," said Baptiste.

"And . . . ?" asked the head.

Baptiste squinted up at the runes, lips pressed thoughtfully together. "Not these ones."

"God . . . damn it," muttered the head.

"God . . . *damn* it." Balthazar pulled a long breath through his forcefully gritted teeth. If he was obliged to participate in this doomed quest for very much longer, and avoided murder at the hands of one of his repellent colleagues, and further avoided murder at the hands of one of their vast and constantly multiplying array of enemies, he would surely die of simple frustration at their monumental ignorance.

"I could dethcribe 'em to you," the head was saying. "First one's got two lines and a curly bit between, lookth thomething like a cock—"

"Everything lookth like a cock to you," said the head.

"Never mind!" snapped Balthazar. "You *people*—and I realise I am stretching the word beyond the fullest distortion of its meaning—can have a rest, or tell *jokes*, or *kill* each other. I doubt anyone will appreciate the artistry it will require, but Balthazar Sham Ivam Draxi will handle this alone!"

"You know what's going on in there?" asked Alex, with the innate suspicion of the practised swindler, always suspecting their own low character in others.

"I could explain it to you, but I fear the details might . . . go over your head."

She planted her hands on her hips and added obstinacy to her show of undesirable traits. "Try me."

Balthazar gritted his teeth yet more forcefully. "As a person of Your Highness's prodigious arcane expertise will have already deduced, the flies are the heart of it. They have, of course, six legs and two wings, eight being the number of stations on Geiszler's lesser key, a base favoured by illusionists for its strong influence over memory and the senses."

"Obviously," drawled the baron, with a careless wave of one hand.

"We are dealing with an insect-based warding involving a limited folding of space, fuelled by the harnessed energy of putrefaction. Clever, in its own way, but juvenile in execution and also rather pleased with itself—"

"Now *that* is unforgivable," observed the baron.

"The self-evident remedy is to destroy the insects, and with them the enchantment. *So.*" Balthazar twitched up the embroidered sleeves of the robe Marangon had procured for him, leaving his hands unimpeded to tap into the very essence of creation. "If the audience have no further questions, perhaps they will permit me to proceed?" And without waiting for the ferret princess he began the somatics, hands weaving with practised grace the opening forms of the ritual he had been planning ever since their arrival in Venice.

A ritual that had, of course, absolutely nothing to do with this ridiculous illusionist's house, and everything to do with breaking the cursed papal binding. It was almost a shame that he would never be able to discuss the precise methodology, because it was one of which he was particularly proud. Once he was free, this would be an interlude no one would be permitted ever to mention, on pain of an excruciating death. Once he was free—

He burped again, another acrid tickle at the back of the throat.

"Trouble with the stomach?" asked Baron Rikard.

"Merely the odour of these candles," grunted Balthazar. With a gathering movement he began to draw, the conjurer's circles twitching at their screws and beginning to thrum with energy. He could feel the tickle in his fingertips, the buzz in the soles of his feet as he spoke the first words, a seven-movement incantation of his own devising.

In spite of his mounting digestive issues, he could barely suppress his smile. He was a magician once again. He had reclaimed his full powers, and soon enough all those who had dared wrong him would *pay.*

In Circles

They'd taken the right-hand hallway this time, or maybe it was left, Vigga was getting mixed up, and what was the difference anyway? Every hall led back to the same room, the same rotten food, the same flies. Jakob and Baptiste squabbled, just like always, and Sunny fretted, hoping to stop Mummy and Daddy fighting, just like always. Vigga enjoyed a good squabble as much as the next werewolf and normally would've got stuck right in there, but now and again she'd come over all listless and leaden and now was one of those flat, grey times.

"What's the fucking point?" she grunted, dropping into one of the chairs, across the table from her mother, who was busy sewing. She'd always been nimble as Brokkr with a needle, took in mending work from around the village for an extra coin or two.

Her mother didn't look up, which was very like her. So organised, so patient. One thing at a time. Not like Vigga at all, always flying off in every direction.

"Where have you been?" she asked.

Thinking about that seemed to hurt, and a salty sea tang breezed in from the gloomy hallways and kissed Vigga's sweaty forehead, which was nice. "Around, maybe? I'm a bit confused."

"You always were confused. Flying off in every direction."

"Even before the bite. Life just . . . comes at me. Like a wasps' nest breaking open in my hands. Shocking and frightening and painful. And maybe makes you swell up a bit."

"Don't pick up wasps' nests, that's my advice."

"I never was very good at taking advice."

Her mother glanced up. "Even before the bite."

"Aye." Vigga flopped forwards with her arms on the wharf's rickety rail and her head on her arms, watching the waves slop against the barnacle-crusted timbers. "I'll let the others deal with this for now, I reckon."

"Others?" asked her mother, fingers busy with Vigga's hair, tugging and braiding. "Deal with what?"

Vigga watched a self-important seagull waddle down the wharf, looking beady-eyed for scraps the fishermen might've left. "Not sure," she said.

Lot of flies around.

"Ready?" asked Vigga, knitting her fingers together to make a step.

"Usually," said Sunny, setting her bare foot in Vigga's tattooed hands where it looked all thin and pale, like a child's drawing of a foot.

The werewolf counted, nodding with each number. "One, two, *three*."

Sunny jumped as Vigga heaved her up and she flew as if she weighed nothing. She didn't weigh much more than nothing, to be fair. She gave the rail the lightest touch in passing and dropped in a crouch on the gallery in total silence.

"Always impresses me," she heard Jakob say, below.

"The throwing or the jumping?"

"Honestly? Both."

"Aye, well," said Vigga, "either must look like magic to a man can't get off a boat without help."

"You're not going to let me forget that, are you?"

"Man of your age," said Baptiste, "I'm surprised you haven't forgotten it already."

There were four doorways off the balcony, and Sunny padded to the nearest, pressed her back to the wall, and peered around the corner, showing as little of herself as she could. Force of habit.

The more of her people saw, the less they liked it.

Another hall. Chequered tiles, dusty panelling, leaning suits of armour. How many had they walked down now? It felt like dozens.

"You should join the circus, you two," Baptiste was saying.

"Sunny tried that already," grunted Jakob. "Didn't work out."

"Maybe if I'd been an acrobat," called Sunny, "instead of a freak." She waited, but there was only silence. People rarely laughed at her jokes. It was the way she told them, they said. *Work on your fucking delivery.* But she'd been hoping for something. She went back to the rail and peered down. The room below was empty.

"Jakob?" she hissed. There was an ugly creeping of nerves up her throat.

"Vigga?" Her words sank into silence, such buried quiet it tickled her ears.

"Baptiste?" But even the flies were gone.

———

"That's . . . strange?" murmured Jakob, limping out of the hallway yet again.

How many times now, the same room? The same chequered tiles. The same table, laden with fly-blown food, one chair tipped over. The same chandelier holding a dozen candles. But the table was on the tiled ceiling now, and the chandelier stuck up from the wooden floor.

You'd be surprised if you saw nothing surprising in an illusionist's house, but this, he was pretty sure, wasn't right. He prodded at one of the strings of glass beads on the chandelier, sticking straight up, and it tinkled faintly as it waved back and forth, like rushes on the bed of a river.

"It's upside down," murmured Jakob.

"Or we are?" said Szymon, as though this happened all the time. Szymon Bartos, large as life, which in his case was large indeed, carrying the shield with the double eagle and the holy circle Pope Angelica had permitted them to add to their arms, turning the Iron Order into the Golden. How proud they'd been, to wear the circle when they marched out with hymns on their lips to set the world to rights. He had a bad feeling he knew how that had turned out.

"Where's Sunny?" he asked.

"Who?"

"And what's-her-face. Werewolf."

"Werewhat?" Szymon frowned. The other Templars were all frowning, too. The spell of command was so easily broken. The structure they all relied on could crumble, and that meant chaos, and death, and the failure of the sacred cause. The Grandmaster had to seem more than a man. Harder. Stronger. Above all, more *certain*.

From your certainty would grow their certainty, and the company united in a righteous purpose could not fail.

No one wants to see doubts.

"Never mind." Perhaps he'd dreamed it. It sometimes seemed he couldn't close his eyes without seeing the past. Jakob rubbed at his throbbing temples. A greasy sweat kept gathering there. "I thought you lot were dead. Long ago."

"I'm as alive as you are, Chief," said Szymon.

"Bad as that, eh?"

"So many choices," said Elzbieta, turning slowly about as she scowled up towards the upside-down gallery, and the upside-down doors that led off it, each one the same.

Jakob couldn't meet her eye. He was sure she was dead. He remembered strangling her himself. There'd been no choice. Doubt was like plague in a city, it had to be burned out before it spread. Only there she stood, with that

fat bottom lip and the braid coiled around her head, which had always faintly
annoyed him though he'd never been able to say why.

The buzzing of flies was everywhere. It made his teeth hurt. It made his
knees hurt.

"Which is the right door?" asked Elzbieta.

"There is no right door," muttered Jakob, closing his eyes. "They all lead
to hell."

A hell they would break their backs to build for themselves.

"There is no right door," muttered the head. "They all lead to hell."

"That doesn't sound hopeful." Brother Diaz was growing increasingly
alarmed. His moral compass might be spinning wildly of late, but he was reasonably sure hell was still in the wrong direction. "Does that sound hopeful?"

"No," snapped Alex, glaring at Balthazar.

The magician clawed at the air again, as if he was struggling to pull up an
invisible team of horses, and this time an answering breeze washed through
the room, making the candle flames dance, the pages of the weighty books
flutter. Baron Rikard sat up a little, not quite so fashionably bored as usual.

Balthazar was starting to look ill, in truth, hands and lips moving cease-
lessly, a sheen of sweat appearing on skin with a slight greenish tint. The
severed head was now babbling and leaking almost constantly, though whose
words were in its dead mouth it was becoming impossible to say.

"I don't like this," said Alex as the wind died back.

"Well, no one *likes* it," said Brother Diaz.

"I don't trust him."

"Well, no one trusts him!"

"Never fear . . ." Balthazar forced one eye open a slit and hissed through
a fixed and deeply unreassuring smile, "this will all be over soon." And he
winced as he swallowed a burp, then dragged angrily at the air again.

That unnatural wind swept through the room, stronger this time, making
the torn wallpaper flap, whipping up swirls of dust, the metal rings rattling
angrily against their screws. For perhaps the thirtieth time since he'd sat on
that bench outside Cardinal Zizka's office, Brother Diaz had the sense that
things were going profoundly wrong, but he was utterly powerless to prevent it.
For perhaps the hundredth time since he'd sat on that bench outside Cardinal
Zizka's office, he pressed the vial on its chain beneath his habit and closed his
eyes. "O Blessed Saint Beatrix, see me safely through my trials and deliver me
into the grace of our Saviour . . ."

"No, no," the head was saying. "I'll be good."

Somehow, that sounded less hopeful to Brother Diaz than ever.

"No, no! I'll be good!"

But everyone knew she wouldn't be. She'd never given the slightest hint that she even knew how. They dragged her on across the village square, a chain tight on each wrist and ankle, iron links biting at her, two grim men on the end of each one, hauling so hard it felt like her joints would pop apart.

Folk watched, peering scared around doorways, or cursing as she was bundled past, or hard-faced with arms folded, careless as empty suits of armour on a stand. Friends and neighbours become a gloomy jury and not one spoke up for her. She couldn't blame 'em.

"Ah, my shoulder! Ah, my knee!" But they didn't care how bad they hurt her. The more the better. They dragged her through the mud and dung and chilly puddles, torn trousers falling halfway down her arse, then all in the air, then hopping on one foot, then bouncing off the corner of a cart, sobbing and spitting and choking on a mouthful of her own hair.

They dragged her towards the square of shadow that was the doorway of the longhouse, and she caught one of the posts beside it, clung to it, hugged it like it was her last friend in all the world. It was.

"No, no! I'm safe! I'm clean!" But everyone knew she wasn't. The men hauled with all their weight, chains snapping taut, and she squealed as a woman started beating her with a broom, smack, smack across her back. They finally tore her free, arms ripped and bleeding, and she smashed her face against the side of the house and was into the darkness, smelling of herbs and smoke.

"You're not safe and you're not clean," said Sadi, laying out the ink. "You're the very opposite of both."

"I'm sorry!"

"So am I. But sorry will give no one back their lives." And they looped the chains around stakes in the straw-scattered dirt so she was dragged face down over the stained rock where the sacrifices were made.

"It was the wolf," whimpered Vigga, straining and struggling but trapped fast as flies in candle wax. "I couldn't help it."

Sadi lifted Vigga's face and held it with both hands, more sad than angry, and wiped Vigga's tears away with her thumbs. "That's why we have to mark you. Folk must know what you are." She took up the bone needle, and nodded, and they began to cut Vigga's dirty clothes off. "It is the only decent thing to do. And you know how we are here. We always try to do the decent thing."

"You can't," whimpered Vigga, "you can't."

"We must." *Tap, tap, tap*, as Sadi began to prick the warnings into her, and Vigga cried.

Not because of the pain. But because she knew there was no way back.

"You can't," the head was mumbling, "you can't."

Balthazar neither knew nor cared whose words it was parroting. He had always considered illusion an inferior discipline, the very definition of fraud, the province of crass pick-up artists rather than of self-respecting magicians. It was an opinion only reinforced when—after sharing it with her at a meeting of the Friends of the Numinous—Covorin of the Nine Eyes had tricked him into kissing a goose in front of the entire gathering, a humiliation neither forgotten nor forgiven, neither by Balthazar nor, he imagined, by the goose.

Probably the unkillable idiot, the unseeable elf, the unspeakable werewolf, and Europe's most experienced smug harpy were even now blundering in circles through an imagined maze of their own horribly clichéd worst fears. There they could indefinitely remain, as far as Balthazar was concerned. He had been living his own worst fears for the past few months already, and was entirely focused on liberating himself, thank you very much. That task, it turned out, was proving more than demanding enough.

He was required to perform two taxing rituals simultaneously: a lesser to suppress the nauseating effects of the binding and a greater to break it, all while maintaining the pretence that he was dispelling some hack illusionist's cumbersome home defence mechanism. That rusty streak on his wrist, however, was proving more stubborn than he could possibly have anticipated, notwithstanding one failed attempt already at his back. The more force he brought to bear, the more tightly it seemed to grip, the more the nausea bubbled up, the more effort he had to expend to force it down. He was running with sweat beneath his borrowed robe and was beginning to wonder how much these conjurer's circles could take before ripping their screws from the floor, warping in the heat or, indeed, simply melting.

The results of a sudden miscarriage could be explosive—for Balthazar, for everyone in the room, potentially for the entire neighbourhood. He remembered his disbelieving laughter when he discovered that Sarzilla of Samarkand had blown herself up attempting to turn tin into silver—since no one tried lead into gold after that fiasco with the lizards—along with two and a half reasonably prosperous streets and a fabric market.

What the hell would possess someone to take such a chance? he had wondered aloud. To his birds, obviously, since he had been living alone. Now here he was, making an even riskier gamble. But there could be no backing down. Here was his opportunity, not only to win his freedom, but to make an indelible mark as one of the great arcane practitioners of the age! He would show those sanctimonious hypocrites Bock and Zizka, and that smirking bitch Baptiste, and Covorin of the Nine Eyes and every other envious rival who had ever dared underestimate him!

He overcame his rising nausea as he had overcome all the obstacles, the injustices, the misfortunes. He would show the whole world! History was not made by the cautious!

He gritted his teeth and drew again, sucking air in through his flared nostrils, sucking power into the conjurer's circles, ringing now, singing, starting, like iron in the forge, ever so faintly to glow.

"This is wrong," muttered Jakob. "We shouldn't be here!"

And he ran from the dining room and its endlessly buzzing flies. As close to running as he got, anyway, gripping his right hip, left leg held nearly straight. He lurched back down the shadowed hallway, tiled with black and white skulls, panelled with shields hammered flat, dozens of suits of ruined armour standing at butchered attention. He ducked under the broken portcullis, past the shattered gates, and out onto the battlefield.

They were cut off. They were outflanked. He heard drums and horns and wailing battle-songs. The drone of the "Our Saviour" from a thousand mouths. The elves were everywhere. Ghosts in the forest, shadows at the corner of your eye, gone like smoke when you grabbed for them. Their black arrows flitted from the trees, poisoned whispers. To lose your way was death, to lower your guard was death, to turn your back was death.

"Forward!" Jakob held his sword high, or as high as he could with the pain in his shoulder. Courage is catching. If one man shows it, it spreads. Fear is the same. Retreat becomes rout. So one more time he made himself the point of the spear, into the melee, rain hammering down, leaking through his armour to soak the gambeson beneath, turning it to cold lead.

He wasn't sure who they were fighting any more. Was it the elves? Or the Lithuanians? Or the Sicilians? Or the Castillians? Or the Picts, or the Irish, or the witches from that tower they burned, or the monks from that church they burned, a century and more of enemies, flowing together like paints on a madman's palette.

He shoved and stomped, crushed shoulder to shoulder, snarled and shoved, hardly knowing whether the fighters around him were dead or alive, each helpless as a cork in a flood. Men groaned and screamed and bit and elbowed and punched and howled and fell to be trampled into the mud.

He could taste blood, he could taste death.

"Kill the bastards!" he snarled, struggling to free his sword arm. "Kill them all!"

The party was in full swing when Sunny stepped out of the hallway and made her grand entrance.

"Ta-da!" she sang, but no one noticed, which was a shame, because she'd spent hours dressing and was all sparkly for the occasion. Everyone was, a happy crowd packed into the high-ceilinged dining room under the chandelier. Up on the gallery, too. All knotting together and breaking apart and swirling around with a band playing somewhere.

Sunny loved bands. Always seemed like magic how they could make a piece of wood sing like that. She would've liked to dance but was incredibly bad at it. She'd practised a dance once but when she showed it to the Ringmaster, he'd looked like he was sucking on a lemon and said, *I thought all you fuckers were supposed to have an alien grace.*

When did she last get invited to a party? Never. Obviously. Everyone despised her. But she'd always wanted to go to one. One where she wasn't eavesdropping, or stealing something, or trying to poison somebody, that was.

Parties. Amazing. People dancing and laughing and flirting and saying one thing but somehow meaning another. Making the moves with the smiles and the eyes and the hands flapping around. Like a high-stakes game of social chess on that black and white tiled floor. Sunny loved people, they were so weird.

She wished she was one.

She was clutching the invitation tight. She'd been so excited to get it. *To our dearest Sunny, you are cordially invited . . . blah, blah, blah, or something.* Though she didn't remember opening the envelope, now she thought about it. Was she drunk? She'd got drunk once before. One glass of wine, and it tasted like feet, and she'd got dizzy very soon afterwards, then been sick and lost her dignity, and Vigga had to put her to bed.

Who was Vigga, anyway? She scratched her head. Very odd.

She tossed her cloak to the doorman, but he didn't notice and it just crumpled on the floor where someone promptly trod on it.

"I am here," she said, but the doorman ignored her, the rude bastard, busy taking a coat from some woman who'd crowded in after her, the rude bitch. Sunny noticed she was wearing a mask. Then she noticed *everyone* was wearing masks. Everyone but her.

She stared in panic at the invitation. *You are cordially invited to a masked ball . . . blah, blah, blah.* No! If anyone needed a mask it was her. Her face was appalling. The sight of it made people puke. She clapped her hands over it, and found she was blushing so hard it was almost painful, which was strange because she'd never blushed before, she'd seen it done and thought it was excellent but had tried for hours in the mirror and couldn't manage it.

"Sorry," she said, slipping sideways through the press, but no one made space for her. "Excuse me!" But they all acted like she wasn't there, and someone barged into her and someone else trod on her foot then as she was gasping someone told a joke and flung a careless elbow and caught her right in the mouth.

"D'you fucking mind?" she snarled at him, but he carried on and everyone burst out laughing at the punchline. A woman with great muscly shoulders and wild dark hair and writing on her cheek sat in one of sixteen chairs at a dining table, talking very animatedly to someone despite being alone.

She looked at the invitation again, but now it was an old, dog-eared bill from the circus, printed badly on bad paper. *Look in horror on the only captive elf in Europe!* Third down behind the living statue and that man with a giant wart on his face. It wasn't even true. About being the only captive elf, not about the wart. But *you get no crowds for the commonplace*, the Ringmaster always said. She wished he was there, even though he'd hated her. Even being hated was something.

Proof you'd made an impression.

Everything was too bright and too loud. She could hear flies. Was she drunk? She didn't feel sick but she'd certainly lost her dignity. Not that it mattered. What use is dignity if no one knows you're there? What use is anything?

If no one knows you're there, are you really there at all?

The band was playing that music with the honking trumpet they used to play at the circus when she came on to be booed and knocked over with a slapstick. She didn't like that music so much.

There was a circle of masked revellers pointing and laughing and a man standing bent over in the centre. A grey, scarred, worried man and he looked so familiar, but Sunny couldn't place him.

"This is wrong," he was saying. "We shouldn't be here."

"Hello?" Sunny snapped her fingers in his face. "Do I know you?"

But he didn't know her. He didn't even see her. She crushed the bill in her trembling fist. She was furious, and no one noticed, and she was terrified, and no one noticed, and she was miserable, and no one noticed, or would've cared if they had.

She found a corner and wedged herself into it. She slid down to sit and drew her knees tight into her chest.

She could make herself invisible. That was her thing.

But could she make herself visible?

There was the problem.

Nothing but the Truth

Wind sucked through the room, snatching at the candle flames, blowing dust into strange patterns. The bronze circles were humming, smoking. The severed head's burblings made Alex think her friends inside the house were losing their minds. If they'd ever had them.

So what did Balthazar have to grin about?

"Something's wrong," she said.

"Everything's wrong!" Brother Diaz gestured at the leaking head, at the rattling circles, at the muttering wizard. "It's been weeks since anything was right—"

"He's trying to break the binding."

"Now you're an expert on magic as well as deportment?"

"I can spot a liar," she snapped. "I heard him talking about it on the road." And she nodded at the baron. "To him."

The vampire draped limp fingers over his chest with an air of injured innocence. "To *me*?"

"Is this true?" Brother Diaz actually looked a bit wounded.

Baron Rikard sighed. "People can confide in me without fear of judgement. I am a vampire. I leave the moral adjudications to those . . ." And he waved lazily at the monk. "With less capacity for reason and more for hypocrisy."

Balthazar was smiling wider, his movements growing sharper. The wind was snatching papers from the tables, whipping Alex's hair in her face, torn wallpaper flapping at the rotten plaster.

"Why didn't you say something sooner?" squealed Brother Diaz.

Alex licked her lips. Mostly 'cause she'd been hoping to be miles away by now, slunk off in the dead of night to begin a brand-new life that she definitely wouldn't fuck up like the old one, with werewolves, vampires, and magicians just another set of ugly memories to pretend to have forgotten about.

Then Marcian and his man-beasts attacked, and it turned out the rest of Eudoxia's sons likely knew about her, and she started to think her best chance was to stay with the others. Jakob, and Vigga, and Sunny, say what you like about them, and you could say a *lot*, but they'd shown they were in her corner.

Been a long time since there'd been anyone in her corner but her. Her corner was a fucking desert.

"Tell him to stop!" She had to shriek over the racket.

The monk looked vaguely desperate. The kind of man who'd sooner let the boat sink than give an order to bail it out. You had to say he was a shitty choice of leader. But then Alex was a shitty choice of princess.

She caught a fistful of his habit. "Her Holiness put *you* in charge! Those were the words of the binding! *Order* him to stop!"

"Oh, sweet Saint Beatrix . . ." He set his jaw and turned towards the circle. "Balthazar Sham Ivam Draxi!" Without stopping his constant mumbling, the magician prised open one eye to glare at them. "I *order* you to—"

Balthazar snatched at the air with one hand and the monk's words were cut off in an awkward splutter. He bent over, clutching at his neck. He stared at Alex, eyes bulging.

"The magician has stopped him breathing," said Baron Rikard, calmly.

Alex caught Brother Diaz as he sank to his knees, veins popping from his temples.

"Let him go!" she shrieked at Balthazar, but aside from his self-satisfied lectures on the history of ancient Carthage, he'd been ignoring her for weeks. Would've been quite the shock if he'd chosen to start paying attention now. He stood with lips curled back, somewhere between a grimace of pain and a smile of triumph, his robes torn by a wind from nowhere.

"Help me!" she shrieked at Baron Rikard, one hand up to shield her face from the whipping grit.

The vampire didn't help one bit. "You're supposed to be taking a throne. You can't bring one wizard into line?"

The circles were glowing now, scorching the floorboards. The severed head kept shouting nonsense. Brother Diaz knelt, face turning purple.

"What do I *fucking do*?" screamed Alex.

"Heave . . ." called Erik, calm at the tiller, pipe clamped in his yellowed teeth. "Heave . . ." Calling the pace, chopping time into moments, his voice calming her thudding heart to its slow rhythm. "Heave . . ."

Gods, just the sea-smell and sail-snap and chill spray fresh on her skin. She'd forgotten how much she loved this. Forgetting was a talent of hers. Forgetting could be a gift. But it could be a curse, too. Who told her that? Some grim-faced knight she knew. But where'd she met him? She'd stopped looking for the patterns in things. She let it wash over her now, like the tide after dusk.

"Row, then," said Halfdan, frowning down at her. "Life's painful enough without getting in your own way."

"Aye. Row. 'Course." She always pulled her weight. She wrapped her calloused hands around the time-polished oar and set all her strength to it.

It was growing dark, the sky bruised with stormy colours. They'd best pull for shore, but she couldn't remember where the shore was. Couldn't remember if there was a shore, even. Had they always been out here? Out on the unquiet sea, with all that vast and unknowable deep beneath them?

"Don't look too far ahead," said Olaf, beside her, and Vigga laughed, but when he turned the far side of his face was gouged with claw marks and his eye was a red and weeping hole.

"What happened?" she whispered.

"You did," he said, and his cupped hands held a slop of his own guts.

"You can hate a shipmate and still row the same way," said Erik.

"Aye." Vigga nodded hard, fighting to swallow her terror and stay hopeful. "That's true. I say it often."

"But you rowed us off the edge of the fucking world." The words smoked from his blue-black lips. Maybe he got away from her but froze out in the snow? She'd always known the ones who got away couldn't have got far.

"It wasn't me," said Vigga, and she was crying, "it was the wolf."

She floundered from the surf onto the shore, salt spray and salt tears on her face. A dark shore under a dark sky, angry waves chewing at black sand. A track led off the beach, overgrown with thorns, between two great stones set up on end as if by giants' hands, and on the stones were warnings carved. The same warnings on her face, on her arms, on her back.

"I know this place," she whispered.

"Of course," said Halfdan, making for the stones. His throat was a great dripping red wound, and when he spoke, he blew bloody bubbles from his nose.

"I don't want to go," she said.

"But you did go."

She tried to run but her feet took her the other way, towards the path. Towards the wolf.

"Get inside and stay inside." They jabbed at her through the bars of the cage, iron glowing hot and stink of burning, and she scrambled for the corner, trying not to see the blood all up her arms and feel the blood under her nails and taste the blood crusted to her lips. She burrowed into the stinking rags, trying to hide herself, trying to hide from herself.

"I am wrong," she whimpered, huddled. "I am evil." Like she could curl up so tight she'd vanish into herself and hurt no more. "I am filthy. Mama, please. I love you."

"I love you, too," said her mother, tugging at her scalp as she braided her hair, and Vigga thanked the gods she was home. Though it was strange they had such a grand dining table. She didn't see how it could even fit in the little house. "I love you, and I'll always be with you." And she finished a braid, and patted it, and sighed. "But see where it got me. Loving you is gold down a well. Loving you is a death sentence. The wolf is an excuse, and not even a good one. You were an animal before the bite."

"Don't say that. You never said that."

"But you know I always thought it."

That hurt. She bit her lip and turned away with the wasted tears tickling her face. Clenched her fists and scowled into the dark country beyond the wrecked boat, its wind-sculpted timbers like the bones of a dragon's carcass.

The wolf prowled, outside the ribs of the wreck, inside the ribs of her chest. She saw the gleam of its eyes, in the blackness beyond the torchlight. The slinking, smouldering fury of them. The terrible hunger of them, never satisfied.

"Fucking wolf!" she screamed at it. "Fucking thief! You stole my life!"

Wolves have no use for words. Only howls and hunger. Padding, padding, so soft on its paws, stalking her, biding its time. Waiting to give her the terrible gift, the wonderful curse, the bite that would be the end of her and the start of her.

She crouched among the mangled corpses of her shipmates. "You won't make a slave of me." She stood, fists clenched. "I'll make you wear the muzzle! I *swear* it!"

And the rage burned up hot and fierce and irresistible, and she rushed into the dark.

The sun was sinking. A bloody sunset over a valley of blasted mud, of splintered stumps. Columns of dark smoke towered into the wounded heavens. Specks of ash rained down like snow.

"State of this," muttered Jakob, limping on.

The path slunk into a forest. But not of trees. Of sharpened stakes, hammered into the earth, point up. Of swinging gibbets and studded racks and dangling chains. Of great wheels like the one on which the Saviour gave her life for all humanity.

In the distance there was a tapping. *Tap, tap, tap.*

On some of the stakes, corpses were spitted. Displayed as warnings. Elves at first, who'd come to bring terror to mankind, and found terror. Enemies of God, who'd come to teach bloody lessons, and never guessed how apt a pupil would await them.

But God has many enemies, and not all are elves. As Jakob struggled on, he saw men among the skewered. Then women. Then children. More of them, and more. Here was where the holy path had led them. The conclusion of the righteous cause. The better world they'd set out to build. A forest of the dead.

The hammering drew closer. *Bang, bang, bang.*

Jakob's wheezing breath was raw with smoke. The road was become a sea of rutted mud, swimming with corpses, with parts of corpses, so he couldn't move without treading on a leg, a hand, a face. He wished this was the worst he'd seen. The worst he'd done.

Light through the gloom, the fingered shadows of stakes stretching towards him, a bonfire burning in a clearing ringed by impaled bodies, twisted and tortured bodies, bodies in the armour of the Iron Order and the Golden Order. His order. For the enemies of God are everywhere. Are everyone.

The hammer pounded louder, each blow a pulse of pain at his temples.

A wind whipped up, dry and scalding, ripping at the torn clothes of the dead men, the torn hair of the dead women, sucking the flames sideways to reveal an armoured figure, squatting by a stake, hammering wedges at the base to keep it steady.

One last blow of the hammer and he stood, his back to Jakob.

He wore the grand white cloak, embroidered with the double eagle, and the Circle of the Faith that Her Holiness had begged them to add, and the chips of blessed mirror to reflect Black Art back at its accursed practitioners, but the hem was stained red. Knee-high, as if it had been soaked in blood. It had been.

"Thought I'd find you here," said Jakob.

"Where else would I be?" The Grandmaster of the Order turned, and they looked at each other, across that graveyard, that slaughteryard, that gathering of lessons. Jakob had forgotten what he'd once been. At his best. At his worst. How handsome and how proud. How strong and how straight. Certainty shone from his younger self like a beacon. A man other men would follow into hell. Which was exactly where he'd led them.

"I've been waiting." The Marshal of Danzig stepped slowly across the clearing with the faint *click-clack* of gilded armour. Moving with such ease. Such authority. Such lack of pain. "It's *so* hard to get the help. Who knows that better than you?" And he raised his arms towards the impaled Templars ringing the clearing. "So few people have the vision, and the courage, and the *will* to pursue what they know to be . . ." He closed his eyes, as if searching for the word. "*Right* . . . all the way to its end. All the way *here*." And he opened his eyes again, bright with belief. "But you do. We both know you do."

"What have you done?" whispered Jakob.

"What have *we* done? We have dug out the filth. We have burned out the rot. You cannot make a better world by sitting there and crying about it, old man. You have to get your hands dirty."

"Bloody, you mean."

"Don't play the innocent with me," sneered the Emperor's Champion. "There's nothing worth a damn that has no blood on it. Don't you dare pretend there is some great gulf between the two of us. A few years, and a few wars, and a few corpses—"

"And a curse."

"A curse? You cannot die! What a *gift*. What an *opportunity*. What became of your dreams?"

"They became this nightmare," growled Jakob. "It must end."

"Doing right has no end. You were a great man with a great purpose. Now you are a twisted tree in the service of a little girl. Choked by guilt. Chained by regrets. No one wants to see *doubts*, Jakob of Thorn."

"I have my oaths to sustain me."

"Just words. Just breath." He snapped his fingers. "Like *that* you can be free of them."

"I will redeem myself," snarled Jakob, voice cracking. "I have sworn it. I will live by the Twelve Virtues."

The Papal Executioner snorted. "Twelve surrenders, listed by cowards, so they could sell bones to fools." And he set one hand upon the pommel of his headsman's blade. A silver skull, a reminder that death awaits us all. "The Saviour did not stop the elves with virtues. She did it *with the sword*."

Jakob slowly wrapped his fingers around his sword's grip, and slowly drew it. "Then I will stop you with the sword."

And steel rang as the blade slid free of the scabbard and glinted with the colours of fire.

He had known it would come to this. It always did.

And he was glad it had come to this. He always was.

"At last." A smile twitched the mouth of the Grandmaster of the Order. "*There* is the man I know."

Balthazar's head spun, his mouth watered, his vision blurred. From his efforts to fight the binding, or to control the forces he was conjuring, or the added necessity of pinching Brother Diaz's windpipe shut, or the distraction of the severed head babbling the deluded gibberish of the idiots flailing about in the magic box, it was impossible and frankly unnecessary to decide.

All that mattered was that he hold his nerve, and his stomach, and his makeshift apparatus together for a few moments more.

Princess Alexia hunched over Brother Diaz's huddled shape just outside the conjurer's rings, one arm up to ward off the tornado of grit and splinters whirling about the room. Over the roar of wind, the clatter of rubbish, the high-pitched singing of the circles, glowing red-hot as the gathered energy threatened to rip their screws from the floor, he heard her squeal, "Let him go!"

"I *refuse!*" screamed Balthazar, making the sign of command over his wrist and bringing all those years of study, all those stored-up resentments, all that hard-won power together in this one instant.

There was a flash of blue-white fire, a searing pain, a smell of burned flesh, and the brown streak across his wrist was singed to a charred blister.

"I'm free of you!" he screeched, detritus whipped up by his double ritual raining down around him, the flush of triumph overwhelming the throbbing pain in his wrist. "I'm free, you stupid—"

Vomit fountained from his mouth, his nose, more than likely his ears, sprayed the wall, spattered hissing and bubbling on the still-glowing rings, and left a long trail of splats and dashes all the way across the old floorboards to his very toes. He dropped to his knees, breath driven out in an agonised wheeze. He heard a footstep and looked up through watering eyes to see Princess Alexia had stepped into the circle with him.

"I—" he croaked.

Her fist cracked into his nose and sent him sprawling in his own sick where he was promptly sick again, all over himself. Beyond his own groaning retches he could hear Baron Rikard laughing.

"At last!" gurgled the vampire. "*There* is that regal authority, Your Highness!"

"Fucking *help* them!" snarled Princess Alexia, standing over Balthazar with her small but shockingly hard fists clenched.

"I order you . . ." wheezed Brother Diaz, who had struggled purple-faced to his knees, "to *help* them."

"I will!" sobbed Balthazar. "I obey, I submit, ever your humble servant." He felt his gorge—and it was astonishing that any gorge remained within him— rising once again, a long string of bitter bile dangling from his lip as he swept the rubbish from the table, knocking the still-mumbling head rolling across the dusty floor, fumbling desperately though the pages of *Kreb's Illusions* with two vomit-covered fingers, whimpering at searing twinges in his burned wrist and his knotted stomach and, worst of all, his mangled pride.

He began to suspect he had soiled himself.

One moment, Vigga was wrestling with the wolf. The next, she was strangling a grey-faced old man with a bloody nose.

"Wait . . ." she grunted. "I know you." It came out a bit snarled, like there were too many teeth in her mouth for talking.

"Ccchhhh," he rasped.

"Ah." She let her hands relax, which took some effort, and he dragged in a breath.

"Vigga," he whispered, and started to cough. Vigga tried to clap him on the back, felt a stab of pain in her shoulder, and saw her arm was streaked with blood. He was holding a sword, and that was bloody, too.

"You sworded me!" she said.

"Well, I thought you were me." Jakob hooked a finger in his twisted collar and tried to tug it loose.

"Huh. I thought you were me."

"So." Sunny tore a strip from one of the old corpses' clothes and started to bind Vigga's shoulder. "At least you hate yourselves more than each other."

"The cornerstone of any friendship," said Vigga. She preferred to bleed till it stopped by itself, but if a bandage made Sunny happy, she could indulge her. "Why do you care about being throttled so much? You can't die."

"Breathing's one of the few pleasures I have left," said Jakob, voice fading to almost nothing at the end.

"I'm retiring after this," said Baptiste, bent over in the corner with her hands on her knees. "I'm out. I'm done."

"You say that every time," wheezed Jakob. He looked over at Vigga, and there was something haunted in his eyes. Even more than usual. "What did you see?"

Vigga licked her lips. "My mother, who I let down. And my shipmates, who I killed. They said folk had to be warned about me . . ." She felt a lump in her throat, hard to swallow. "I've let the wolf be my master. I think, starting today, I must put a muzzle on it. What did you see?"

Jakob was frowning even more than usual. "Only the truth," he whispered.

Vigga wasn't listening, though. Among the rotten food on the table was something she hadn't noticed before. A white box, facing that one fallen chair. Like someone got quite the shock when they opened it.

"Would you look at that?" She grinned as she walked over, making Sunny cluck as she hurried after, still trying to tie the bandage. The floor was covered with a crunchy carpet of dead flies, sticking to the soles of Vigga's bare feet with each step.

There was a star inlaid on the box's lid. Felt light when she picked it up. Like it was empty. She gave it a good shake but nothing rattled.

"Careful!" snapped Jakob, and straight away fell into a coughing fit.

"Ah, stop carping!" said Vigga as Baptiste took her turn clapping him on the back. "Always comes out all right, doesn't it?"

"It never does." Jakob narrowed his eyes at her as he slowly, painfully straightened. "Have you forgotten what we saw already?"

Vigga looked puzzled. "What did we see?"

"My God . . ." He stared at her, awestruck. "What a gift."

Too Much Trouble

H ope it wasn't too much trouble," said Frigo, oven's glow on his face as Sunny watched him slide another loaf in with his shovel.

"Please," said Baptiste. "Long as you get what you want you don't give a shit."

Frigo shrugged. "Who does? Long as they get what they want? I was being polite. That's what politeness is. Not quite acknowledging the unpleasant truths that we both know we both know."

"I'm a little tired for dancing," growled Jakob, offering him the box.

Frigo wiped one floury hand on his apron and took it. Only Jakob didn't let go. "Must confess, I've a worry you might double-cross us."

"Well, that's a very sensible worry to have," said Frigo, looking levelly back.

"What assurance can you give us?"

"None but my impeccable reputation."

"So none," said Baptiste.

Frigo glanced at his granddaughter and gave a weary sigh. "Why do people insist on arguing when everyone knows they've got no choice?"

"'Cause they wish they did have a choice," said his granddaughter.

Frigo grinned. "Oh, she's sharp, this one. As sharp as her mother was. Your boat's waiting. Hand over the box and take the boat. Or keep the box and find some other way to Troy. Up to you."

Jakob gave a sour grunt and let go of the box.

"Wonderful," said Frigo, grinning at it. He weighed it in one hand, then gently shook it, then looked up at Jakob. "How do I open it?"

"No idea," said Jakob, already heading for the door.

"Long as I get what I want," said Baptiste, swaggering after him, "who gives a shit? Till next time, Frigo."

"Don't hurry back!" called Frigo after them, then the door was pulled shut, and there was silence. So quiet Sunny would've felt the need to hold her breath if she hadn't been holding it already.

Frigo set the box down. "You can come out now," he said, and started pounding his dough again.

Sunny blinked, wondering if he could be talking to her.

He paused in his pounding. "Yes, you. You can come out."

Sunny wondered whether to play dumb. But she was curious now, and once curiosity got hold of her, she never could wriggle free. So she slipped over the railing, and dropped down lightly on her feet, and breathed out.

Frigo's granddaughter took a shocked step back. "Shitting hell! It's an elf!"

"Doubtless." Frigo didn't look surprised in the least. "One with a *very* light step."

"How did you know I was here?" asked Sunny.

"Because knowing things is my real business. Because the girls and the gangs and the gambling are just ways to get to know things. Because knowing things is the only currency that counts. What's your name?"

"Sunny," said Sunny.

"Do you have elf ears?" asked the girl, getting over her surprise. "Show me your elf ears."

"Fuck off," said Sunny, "you little turd."

The girl angrily folded her arms. Frigo gave a snort. "You know, I've a sense this little sojourn to Troy will not turn out well."

Sunny sat down on the floor, then took her boots from around her neck and untied their laces. "I'm used to that."

"Well, you ever tire of the feeling of disappointment, you know where to find me. I'll always have work for someone of your talents."

"What kind of work?" she asked, pulling on one boot.

"All kinds."

Sunny pulled on the other and stood. She could rarely be bothered with doing up the laces anyway. "Maybe I'm happy where I am."

Frigo considered her for a moment, with those slow, careful eyes. "No, you're not. I think you're very lonely. Do you know how I know?"

Sunny swallowed so hard she could almost hear the spit move in her throat. "How?"

He kept looking at her, and it seemed for a moment as if he truly saw her. Not what she was, but *who* she was. "Because no one's really happy where they are, Sunny." And he sighed, and carried on working his dough. "And everyone's lonely."

Greed

Alex made the final letter, nice and neat, then looked up doubtfully at Brother Diaz.

"Troy?" she asked him.

"Undeniably," he said, smiling. First time she met the man she'd reckoned him a pompous prig whose approval was worth about as much as a paper bag of piss. Time hadn't much changed her opinion of the pompous prig bit, but his approval was starting to make her feel oddly proud of herself. It was a feeling she didn't get very often. In fact, it was hard to remember the last time. She found, to her surprise, she quite liked it.

"The Empress of Troy," she said, running her fingertip over the letters. She smudged one, but her hands were always inky these days. "I can write it, at least."

"Huh," grunted Jakob. He stood with scarred fists on the rail of the aftcastle, frowning into the wind. Frowning towards the coast. Frowning hardest of all at any other ships.

"You still worried?" asked Alex, putting down the paper to lean beside him.

Now he frowned at her. "It's my job to be worried."

"Lucky you. Your job and your hobby are the same!" And she bumped him playfully on the shoulder with her fist, which she got the feeling neither of them enjoyed, since her knuckles were still sore from punching Balthazar in the face. Which was another thing she felt quite proud of, come to think of it. "What country's that?" she asked.

Jakob nodded off to the right, the hazy rumour of a far-off coast under an iron-grey sky. "That . . . is the Kingdom of Naples."

Alex winced. "Enough said."

"This . . ." and Jakob nodded to the coastline sliding past on the left, rugged and rocky, "was Troy, until the Trojans retreated, then Bulgaria, until the Bulgars were forced back, then part of Venice, until the Venetians lost interest, then the Princedom of Serbia, until the Long Pox came."

"And now?"

"Splintered pieces of a land without law or leader, blasted by war, ravaged by plague, riddled by bandits."

"Well, who hasn't been riddled by a bandit or two?" Alex turned to rest her elbows on the rail and let the salt breeze tug at her hair, the seabirds circling carefree in their wake, the problems of land feeling far away. Everything's better at sea. "We're four days on the water without a whiff of trouble."

Jakob narrowed his eyes. "It's when there's no sign of trouble you most need to watch for it."

"But . . . it's not, though, is it? That's just one of those things folk say that sounds good but when you think about it doesn't really mean anything."

Jakob frowned. What else would he do?

"Oh, come on." Alex thought about bumping his shoulder again and decided against. "I haven't seen anyone killed in *weeks*. I've a feeling we might actually get to Troy." She somehow didn't want to say it out loud, so she leaned close to mutter out of the corner of her mouth. "Never mind writing it, I'm starting to think I could actually *be* an Empress."

Baron Rikard heard her, of course. Baron Rikard heard everything. "Anyone can be an Empress, given the right parents and a crown." He smirked knowingly at the handle of his cane. "It's whether you're any *good* at it that's the question." The vampire was looking younger than ever the last few days. He only seemed to carry the cane now so he could smirk knowingly at it.

"Well, I know how to read and write." Alex pushed herself from the rail and swaggered towards the mainmast, leading with her throat the way the vampire had taught her, like she was a throat salesman and hers was a perfect sample she was showing off. "I know how to walk. I know how to hide a dagger. I know the history of ancient Carthage, Venice, and Troy. I already knew how to spot a liar. What else does the Empress of the East really *need* to know?"

"You're across the essentials," murmured Vigga. She was sitting back on the deck, hands propped behind her, tattooed, sunburned shoulders hunched around her tattooed, sunburned ears and her eyes fixed on a couple of sailors busy in the rigging above. "Look at 'em climb. Wonder if they could swarm up me so nimbly."

"It's a crew," grunted Baron Rikard. "Not a menu."

"You can fucking talk," grumbled Vigga. "There are fang-holes all over half these lads already. How you get people to agree to being chewed on is beyond me."

"I listen, I understand, I sympathise. I act, in short, with simple grace and good manners, and so people are drawn to me, rather than repulsed, as they are by you."

"Oh, you'd be surprised."

"Horrified, perhaps. It amazes me how many men *willingly choose* to bed a werewolf."

"Well, most men will bed anything, and I don't usually *lead* with the were-wolf thing."

"What do you lead with?" asked Alex.

Vigga slid one foot across the deck until her legs were wide open, display-ing the slightly stained crotch of her trousers.

"*That*," she said.

"Sweet Saint Beatrix . . ." murmured Brother Diaz, though Alex noticed he'd glanced up from his letter to look and hadn't looked away.

"If there's a secret . . ." mused Vigga, who'd either forgotten she still had her legs wide open or didn't care, "it's to never be shy about asking the ques-tion, and never fear what the answer will be, and waste no tears over the refusals, and clutch with both hands at any flicker of warmth that can be clawed from the uncaring darkness of existence."

Alex slowly nodded. "Only that, eh?"

Balthazar lay in the darkness, listening to the creaking of the ship's timbers, and feeling profoundly sick.

He could not have said whether his constant nausea arose from his at-tempt to break the binding, his disgust at his chastening failure, or simple seasickness. How could one even tell? And what difference would it make? He loathed boats. He detested bindings. He abhorred cunning cardinals, infant popes, grim knights, supercilious vampires, and oversexed werewolves. He hated the fists of princesses. He despised everything.

He heard the door creak open and, with great reluctance, twisted around to look. Baptiste stood in the doorway, regarding him in the manner with which one might regard a blocked latrine.

That *he*, Balthazar Sham Ivam Draxi, the man who had occasionally re-ferred to himself as the Terror of Damietta, should be treated with such scorn. His life had become one endless, excruciating downfall.

"Oh," he said. "It's you."

She raised her brows. "Always nice to get a warm welcome."

"I daresay there are people I would less like to see." He faced the wall again, embracing his pillow. "But no names immediately occur." Though he stopped short of telling her to leave. He was trapped between his desire to wallow alone in clammy despond and his desire to complain bitterly about it. "I suppose you are here to gloat over my misfortunes."

"To change your dressing." He heard her step into the cabin. The click of the door shutting. "But maybe I can squeeze in some light gloating while I'm at it."

"Then do your worst. On both counts." He thrust his bandaged left arm out behind him.

The bed creaked as she sat. He felt her slip the pin from his dressing and winced as she began to unwrap it.

"Ow," he muttered, without much conviction. "Is this what I have come to? Medical attention from an ex-pirate?"

"I was a butcher's girl for a while, too, if that's any comfort."

"I daresay they are all enjoying a chuckle at my expense." He glared up towards the planked ceiling. "Up *there*. On *deck*."

"It may amaze you to learn . . . that not everything . . . is about *you*."

"Not even worthy of discussion! As though my abject failure in breaking the binding was not humiliation enough."

"You impressed me."

He could not help glancing over his shoulder. "Really?"

"Don't think we've ever had a sorcerer who got as far as badly burning themselves then being punched in the nose by a seventeen-year-old girl."

He had not even the strength to point out that he was a magician. After the scale of his failure could he truly claim the title? He turned to face the wall again. He allowed himself to be handled as though he were indeed a side of meat. He would never have admitted it, of course, but there was something soothing in submitting to that businesslike treatment. In being . . . taken care of.

"Could be worse," said Baptiste, after a while. "We had one sorcerer . . . what was his name? Been doing this too long. But he took his hand off to be free of it. Well, ice was his thing—"

"Cryomancy."

"—so he froze his hand then smashed it off with a brick."

Balthazar should probably have been horrified. But it rather blended into the high background level of horror he was experiencing lately. After a brief pause, his curiosity won out. "Did it work?" he asked, twisting over to look up at Baptiste.

"No. You magical types are so used to bending the world to your will you never see the value in just . . . letting things happen. Giving in to something bigger than yourself. There."

He held his arm up to such light as there was and worked his fingers. "Thank you," he said.

"Pardon?" She stuck a finger behind her ear and bent it towards him. "Couldn't quite make that out over the thunder of self-pity."

"It is a serviceable bandage. *Competent,* even. Your time with the butcher was well spent."

"High praise indeed."

"I have never found it . . . easy . . . to acknowledge the talents of others." Quite against the prevailing circumstances Balthazar found he was smiling, ever so slightly. "I have not the practice."

It could not be gainsaid that Baptiste had considerable defects of character. But who is pure in that regard? He was forced to concede that even he might be concealing a few trifling flaws. And it was pointless to deny that there was something . . . attractive about her. That aggressive confidence. That self-possessed swagger. That scar on her lips, which had initially struck him as so unsightly, seemed on reflection to add . . . a dash, a danger, a fascinating air of . . . what could only be called *experience.*

Some people impress one instantly. Others are only appreciated with time and prolonged exposure. Like a vintage cheese, perhaps. And, in the long haul, it is often the acquired tastes that one comes most to savour—

"What?" she muttered, suspiciously narrowing her eyes.

He opened his mouth to reply.

Which was when, with an explosive cracking of wood and a cloud of stinging splinters, a spearhead big as a spade came crashing through the ceiling.

It was a warship. Even a man as ignorant of both war and ships as Brother Diaz could have been in no doubt.

A great galley in the Trojan style, long and deadly and fast as a spear, rich gilding glinting on its rails and timbers, bristling with two tiers of fast-dipping oars. A stylised lighthouse glittered in gold thread on each of its three great triangular sails and a massive bronze ram, carved like a hawk's head, skimmed the waves at the prow to throw up clouds of glittering spray. It might have been a glorious sight. Had the ram not been aimed right at them.

"Sweet Saint Beatrix," breathed Brother Diaz, staring at the ballista bolt that had arced gracefully over the few hundred strides of water between the

two ships to bury itself in the deck mere inches from where he had been sitting, composing his latest unsent letter to Mother.

"Don't worry," said Vigga, clapping him on the shoulder and making him
stagger. "It was just a warning shot."

"What if it had hit me?"

"Then . . . I guess . . . it'd just be a shot?"

"We can't outrun them!" the ship's captain was screeching. "We're no warship! We have to surrender!"

"Can't surrender," grunted Jakob.

"Papal binding," said Baron Rikard, apologetically displaying the streak
on his wrist.

"And I swore some oaths."

"Oh God," Alex was saying, clumps of hair sprouting from between her white
fingers as she clutched her head. She'd gone from being pleasingly pleased with
herself over her improving writing to wholehearted terror in an instant.

"I suggest you take your men and abandon ship." Baron Rikard gave the
captain a reassuring pat on the shoulder. "I strongly suspect things are going
to get . . . *ugly*."

"Abandon ship?" The captain threw an arm towards the sea on every side.
"And go where?"

"I always enjoyed the south of France at this time of year. You have something . . ." Rikard reached up with a handkerchief and dabbed at the captain's
neck, where one of a pair of pinprick holes was leaking a red streak. "*Just*
there. Much better."

"*What* is happening?" Balthazar was scrambling up the steps from
deck to aftcastle, Baptiste behind him, pointing with an outraged finger
towards the giant ballista bolt buried in the planking. "That thing nearly
killed me!"

"A shame," observed the baron. "We can only hope their next is more
accurate."

Balthazar pointed past the bolt now, to the towering galley beyond. "Who
the hell are *they*?"

"Yet to formally introduce themselves."

"They were hiding in an inlet," said Jakob.

"Waiting for us?" snapped Baptiste.

"Well, they're not ramming anyone else. You think Frigo betrayed us?"

"I'd be shocked if he didn't."

"You said you knew people in Venice!" whined Brother Diaz.

"I never said they were trustworthy!"

The galley was still bearing down on them. Given its sheer mass it would doubtless have kept bearing down on them even if its crew had stopped rowing entirely. If anything, they were rowing harder than ever.

"We're trapped!" squawked Alex. "It's just like the inn!"

"No, no," said Vigga. "The inn was on land. You could run away from it. The inn wouldn't *sink*."

Alex stared at her. "So it's *worse* than the inn?"

"Oh, it's *way* worse." And Vigga grinned as the ship hit a wave and they were all showered with spray.

Jakob had found a shield, was dragging its straps tight about his forearm. "We'll have to fight our way out."

"Sweet Saint Beatrix," murmured Brother Diaz, "sweet Saint *Beatrix*, *sweet* Saint Beatrix," as if the key to their deliverance was finding precisely the right emphasis on that phrase.

"Bring up some straw!" Jakob roared at the captain. "Wet it and set a fire on the deck."

"Fire?" muttered Alex. "On a ship?"

"It's the smoke we want," said Baptiste.

"It's the chaos we want," said Jakob, glaring towards the rapidly closing galley. "When you're outnumbered and outclassed, chaos is your best chance."

Another great bolt whizzed past maybe forty strides away, but Brother Diaz still found himself ducking. A second warning shot, perhaps. He wondered if he could possibly have felt more warned than he did already.

"Turn!" the captain was shrieking. "Turn!" He flung his weight against the tiller beside the helmsman, the ship tipping as it shifted towards the coast. Brother Diaz had to catch the mast to keep from falling, seeing one of his pens roll away across the leaning deck. He could hear the galley's great drum calling the rhythm as it bore down on them. Could see the oars dipping smoothly, gilded decorations flashing in the sun, the great ram coming ever closer. The stretch of waves between the two vessels dwindled with an awful inevitability. The closer it came, the bigger it looked, towering over their toy ship, its great triangular sails blotting out the sun.

"*Sweet Saint Beatrix*," he breathed, clutching for the blessed vial.

The ram caught their boat around the waterline and there was a screaming of tortured timbers as it crashed through the hull and carried them sideways like a harpooned fish. The deck lurched, tilted, a great curtain of spray going up on the far side. A sailor toppled shrieking from the rigging, hit the ship's rail with a sick crunch, and flopped into the sea.

Brother Diaz clutched the mast with both arms, shut his eyes, and prayed.

"Ahoy there!"

Jakob looked up. A man stood on an arrow-shaped platform at the prow of the galley, leaning out to wave wildly, as if trying to catch a friend's attention in a public square. He had a soft, round face, a lot of flashing jewellery including a dangling diamond earring, and a floppy shock of curly golden hair. "I can only apologise for the whole ramming thing, but I find negotiations run smoothest following a strong statement of intent, don't you?" He placed a limp hand on the front of a scarlet jacket heavy with gilded honours. "I am Duke Constans, et cetera, et cetera, and so on, no need to kneel."

"Don't tell me," Alex snarled, "you're one of Eudoxia's sons."

"Her third, as it happens, though I like to think of myself as her sole heir. And *you* must be my cousin, the famed princess . . ." He slid something from inside his jacket and began to unroll it. "What was it, now . . ." A scroll with a heavy seal. Jakob gritted his teeth. A copy of the papal bull. The one nobody was meant to know about until they arrived in Troy. "The famed Princess Alexia Pyrogennetos," read Constans, "endorsed by paired Oracles of the Celestial Choir, no less!" He peered down at her, wrinkling his nose. "Bit of a mousey little thing, isn't she?"

"I'm working on my deportment!" she snapped back.

"Really? I expect you can stop now." Constans tossed the scroll over his shoulder. "Doubt you'll be needing it where you're going. But I must say it's *marvellous* of you to bring her straight to me like this. Now be a good sport and hand her over or I'll have to take her."

"Your brother Marcian tried the same thing," said Jakob.

"Oh, I am *so* sorry." Constans looked as if he tasted something sour. "The boy was always prone to tantrums. I used to think to myself, how *exhausting* it must be, to be so constantly *angry*. But then we had different fathers. His was an absolute arse. Mine, too, as it goes. Mother had terrible taste in men, she really was married to her arcane experiments but that's . . ." he waved it away, "honestly, straying rather from the matter. Where is Marcian now, might I ask?"

"Oh, you know. Bit here, bit there."

"He's dead?"

"As fuck," growled Vigga.

The duke's look of shock resolved, ever so gradually, into a beaming smile. "So there's another job you've saved me! For enemies you really are wonderfully obliging!"

"All my life I wanted a family," muttered Alex. "Now I've got one they turn out a real stack of turds."

"I sympathise," murmured Baron Rikard.

"Judging from your formidably scarred aspect and whole," Constans waved a chubby finger with an enormous ring vaguely towards Jakob, "*mood* I get the sense you've seen some battlefield action?" And he prodded at the air, lace cuff flapping, in a manner presumably meant to represent military manoeuvres but which looked more like pointing out his favourite cake.

"Couple of scrapes," grunted Jakob.

"Then I'm sure you have enough tactical acumen to recognise when you are at a *considerable* disadvantage."

Jakob made himself not flinch when he felt Sunny pressed against his back for a breath. "Five archers on the platform with him," came her whisper. "Maybe ten more up on the masts." And she was gone.

"It's far from my first time," he growled up at Constans.

"Let's not make it your last. You can all see this is a thoroughly lost cause."

"I know they're bad for me," said Jakob, "but I can't stop taking 'em."

"They're the only kind'll have us," said Vigga.

"Oooh." Constans gave a little shiver of excitement. "You're some of those grimly heroic types." He thumped one of his archers on the shoulder and roared up towards the rigging. "They're grimly heroic types!"

His soldiers did not reply.

Jakob worked his aching fingers. He hated fighting at sea. No soil to rub between his palms. No solid ground to plant his boots on. Everything shifting on the unquiet water.

Reminded him of that time they tried to cross the Danube before dawn on those little boats, the arrows flitting down. Had half of them made it to the far bank? Or that skirmish on the beach, charging up through the sea spray, bodies bobbing on the tide. Or that battle off the coast of Malta. The stink of smoke. The flap of sailcloth. Men throwing themselves from the burning hulks. He didn't know if that stretch of water even had a name. But you don't need to know the name of a place to die there.

"How many, on a ship like that?" he heard Alex mutter.

"Enough," said Jakob. All the advantages stood with Constans. The height. The numbers. The arms. The fact his ship wasn't holed and flooding with

water. But you don't always get to choose where you fight. Sometimes the fight
finds you, and you have to meet it as you are. At least the straw on the deck
was alight now, acrid smoke billowing up to cast a hazy pall over both ships.

"You sure about this?" muttered Baptiste.

"I'm open to better ideas."

To say the crew were in disarray was doing them too much credit. A couple
were arming themselves with boathooks and axes but more were diving over
the sides to take their chances with the Adriatic. Less comfortable with lost
causes than Jakob, maybe.

It made no difference to him. Ten to one. A hundred to one. A thousand
to one. He'd be fighting to the death and beyond, as always. He had his oaths
to consider.

He took a long breath, stifled a cough, and slowly drew his sword. "At least
there are no bloody goat-men this time."

"No," murmured Baptiste, tapping him on the arm, "but . . . er . . ."

Jakob never liked turning his head, but on this occasion he thought he'd
better. He took in Brother Diaz, eyes wide. He took in Princess Alexia, teeth
bared. He took in the captain, stepping away from the tiller with his hands
dangling. They were all looking the same way. Towards the back rail.

Someone was slithering over it. A woman in an extravagant uniform like
the one Constans wore, albeit soaked with seawater, dripping braid flapping,
and some sort of helmet—or no. That was her head, silvery, like the scales of
a fish, and coming strangely to a point.

She stared at Jakob with huge, wet, fishy eyes, and the gills on her neck
fluttered and opened wide as she gave a shrill scream, showing two rows of
skewer-like teeth.

Jakob sighed. "Fucking marvellous."

Fire on the Water

It'd been a busy few weeks for Alex. She'd been declared heir to the Throne of Troy, met the Pope, been attacked by pig-men and a burning sorceress, watched a mob calmed by a speech about dumplings, and seen a severed head talk. You'd have thought she would've been past surprises.

But somehow she was always caught trousers down.

It was a woman. Two arms. Two legs. But her skin had a scaly, shiny look. Her way too wide-set yellowy eyes and her flattened nose and her down-turned pouty mouth all had a fishy air, too. Oh, and there were the gills. Flaring open with each breath to show the frilly pink insides of her throat. It was ridiculous. Almost a joke. Not a funny one, mind you. The barbed sword she held in particular raised no laughs.

"Oh God," moaned Alex. Noises came through the thickening pall of smoke. Steel, pain, fear, and fury, just like at the inn. But on the sea. Everything's worse at sea!

"Can you swim?"

Alex whipped around. Sunny squatted on the rail, one hand on the net of ratlines that led up the mast, calmly as if she'd been born in the rigging of a ship under attack by fish-women.

Alex swallowed. "Not very well."

"Not very well or not at all?"

"Not at all!"

Why hadn't she been learning to swim in Venice instead of learning to walk, write, or talk about Carthage? It's hard to impress with your knowledge of ancient history as your lungs fill up with seawater.

Ahead of her Jakob backed off, shield up. Beside her Vigga backed off, Brother Diaz cowering at her shoulder. Behind her Balthazar and Baptiste backed off, fishy figures lurching through the haze of smoke beyond the tightening crescent, bedraggled braid glittering on sodden uniforms. Nothing would've pleased her more than to back off herself, but there was nowhere to back off to.

"Where do we go?" she squeaked.

Sunny looked upwards.

With very great reluctance Alex tipped her head back, too, following the wonky grid of ropes vanishing up into a dizzying nightmare of flapping sailcloth, cobwebbed cables, and creaking spars. Her knees felt weak just looking.

"You're joking," she whispered.

"I have no sense of humour," said Sunny, holding out her free hand.

Alex stood a moment longer, making a kind of desperate mew as she watched the fish-people close in. One seemed to have a piece of coral growing out of his head. Was there an eye on the end? It was looking right at her!

"Go!" growled Jakob, over his shoulder.

"Oh God." Alex caught Sunny's hand, wobbled up onto the rail and, with one glance down at the churning sea, swung herself around the net of ropes and started to climb.

Up the ratlines. What could be more fitting for a rat like her?

The fish-man loomed forwards, huge lips wobbling, making a weird blubbing sound. To Brother Diaz it sounded a little bit like, "*Help me,*" but that was a sentiment at odds with the huge axe it was raising high. Or was it more of a hook on a pole? Not that it matters what shape the metal is once it's buried in your skull.

Brother Diaz tottered one way and the blade whistled past, chopping splinters from the rail on his right. He reeled back the other way as it hacked into the rail on his left. He blundered into the mast, bounced off with a gasp, slipped on the tilted deck, his satchel flopping open and scattering unsent letters. The railing hit him in the backs of the legs, he made a despairing grab at it and achieved nothing but to tear one of his fingernails half-off before he tumbled over.

He was readying a scream as he plunged towards the sea, but had only got as far as a breathy whoop when he crashed side-first into wood. He sat up, one hand to his throbbing skull, squinting into the smoke. He must've tumbled off the aftcastle and only fallen the few feet to the deck.

He was about to count that quite a piece of luck when the fish-man sprang, nimbly as a leaping salmon, and thumped down before him, hook raised high.

He wriggled back, heels kicking at the planking, struggling to scramble away and get up at once and achieving neither, raising a hopeless arm to fend off the inevitable blow—

"That's my *fucking monk*!"

Vigga crashed down on the fish-man knees first, ramming him into the deck in a crumpled heap. She must've got at some carpenter's tools, a heavy hatchet in each fist. Now she brought them whipping down with a double thud, blood spotting her snarl.

Brother Diaz blundered up, coughing, blinking, coughing again. Could he see figures in the murk? Two wrestling on the floor. Another pair struggling over a spear. A glint of metal—

"Left!" he screeched. Vigga dropped, a halberd sailing over her head, the spike on its end missing Brother Diaz's nose by a whisker. A soldier charged at him, a hint of a gilded helm, greaves, bared teeth.

Vigga darted in, impossibly fast despite her bulk, hooked his leg away with the head of one axe, reared up as he flew squealing into the air, hacked him down into the deck with the other so hard his head shattered the planking.

"Right!" shrieked Brother Diaz. Vigga dodged around another soldier, axe whipping in a circle, staving in his helmet and flinging him cartwheeling past Brother Diaz to take a chunk out of the rail and flop bonelessly into the sea beyond.

"Italian crap," grunted Vigga, tossing the splintered haft of one of her axes over her shoulder.

"Archer!" screeched Brother Diaz. Vigga spun and threw in one movement, hatchet twittering end over end to bury itself in the forehead of a bowman on the platform with a sharp smack. He loosed his arrow high into the sky as he toppled backwards.

"You see that throw?" she yelled, grabbing Brother Diaz's habit and giving him a triumphant shake.

All he could say was, "Eeek." Rising from the smoke behind her with arms outspread was the most revolting thing he'd ever seen.

It had the body of a man, its smart uniform stained about the embroidered collar with goo, since instead of a head it had a great damp jellied blob with two orange eyes the size of collection plates, a mass of curling tentacles dangling from the front. Could he see through its skin? Was that its brain floating about like a nut in jelly? As it bore down on Vigga the tentacles flared wide to reveal rows of purple suckers, and where they met a great black beak popped out, and opened, and gave a furious, agonised, ear-splitting wail—

Cut off in a resounding *thud* as Vigga sidestepped and punched the thing in its gut, folding it in half and lifting its highly polished boots clear of the ground. It staggered a step or two, dribbling black vomit from its beak, then Vigga caught it by one wrist and a tattooed fistful of tentacles, and in a flash heaved it off its feet and rammed it upside down into the mast.

It dropped in a writhing mess of jelly and Vigga fell on top of it, sinews straining from her tattooed neck as she sank her teeth into its throat where human met sea creature, twisting and growling, until she finally tore free, wiping her ink-black mouth on the back of one arm, spitting out a lump of rubbery meat.

"Ugh," she snarled. "I *hate* seafood."

Balthazar had little fondness for the decks, cabins, or messes of ships. Cramped, squalid, malodorous places in which the least appealing members of society were crammed together, constantly drunk and grunting at one another in streams of incomprehensible nautical jargon. So it was saying something that he was even *less* enthusiastic for their holds, and this one in particular, since the galley's giant ram had made an unwelcome visit right in its midst, seawater gushing through the splintered hull around it in bubbling fountains.

Belowdecks had seemed a superb notion when above decks was a smoke-shrouded battlefield, but Balthazar was forced to wonder whether it was really such an improvement on a ship that was patently sinking.

"This does not appear promising . . ." he murmured. An utterance he could equally well have applied to any moment over the past few months. The hold was already knee-deep in brine and the foaming waters were rapidly rising, bobbing with wreckage, loose barrels, and the corpse of an unfortunate cabin boy who must have scurried down here for safety. Balthazar hoped they would have better luck but would not have liked to gamble his life on it.

"This way!" hissed Baptiste. "Maybe we can climb out through the breach!" She waded towards the rays of daylight coming in around the ram, shoving floating cargo aside with one hand, a drawn dagger in the other.

"*Damn* it," muttered Balthazar. Throwing oneself into the open sea is not a plan, it is what one is forced to do when all other plans have utterly failed, but he was obliged to follow, cursing noisily as he waded out into freezing water, through a complete absence of any better ideas and an overpowering reluctance to be left on his own. Baptiste was abrasive, but considerably less so than the barnacle-encrusted unions of person and sea creature that had invaded the vessel. Empress Eudoxia's sarcomantic experiments were undeniably impressive from a theoretical point of view—and Balthazar was deeply curious to see what necromantic possibilities her blurring of the line between human and animal might offer—but he really had less than no interest in associating with the live specimens up close. They appeared to have next to no conversation and smelled appalling.

"Here." Baptiste put one hand on the hawk-cast head of the ram as she ducked around it. "Help me with—"

Someone slipped from the shadows beyond and tapped her on the forehead. A tall, long-limbed man whose soaked robes clung to his body. Balthazar took a shocked step back, getting partly tangled with a loose cargo net, but Baptiste stood frozen, water foaming around her hips.

"Balthazar Sham Ivam Draxi, I presume?" asked the man, raising an elegant eyebrow.

"You know my work?" Balthazar could not help asking.

"No . . ." The man grinned. A particularly sinister and threatening example of the form. "But your name did come up . . ." Baptiste slowly turned, wet hair plastered to her frowning face, to glare towards Balthazar with even greater hostility than usual. "On a list . . ." There was a needle stuck in her forehead, and hanging from it a little scrap of bloody cloth with a single rune stitched into it. "Of people I have been asked to *kill*."

And on the words "asked to kill," Baptiste spoke them, too, in perfect time.

"God *damn* it . . ." murmured Balthazar, reluctantly backing off the way he had so reluctantly come, colliding with a floating barrel and nearly going over in the chilly water.

The man was a phrenomancer. A manipulator of minds. A discipline Balthazar found particularly loathsome not only because its practitioners stole the free will of others, slipping into their flesh like a maiden into a new dress, but also because they invariably believed their insight into the realm of the mental made them cleverer than anyone else. He was Balthazar Sham Ivam Draxi. Cleverness was his stock-in-trade! Although, granted, he felt less than perspicacious as Baptiste waded towards him with daggers in her fists, murder in her eyes, and a rune of control pinned to her forehead.

"Might I assume," said Balthazar, playing desperately for time as he stared about the flooding hold, surely the most unhopeful venue imaginable for a magical duel, "that I have the privilege of addressing a member of the Empress Eudoxia's coven?"

"You have," said Baptiste and the sorcerer, together.

"Such a loss to the arcane community!" frothed Balthazar. Preparation was the key to victory, and for weeks now he had found himself endlessly off balance, endlessly improvising, endlessly forced to rely on whatever rubbish chance handed him. "I understand she was among the leading practitioners of her generation. I have even been told she could throw lightning!"

"I saw it with my own eyes."

Balthazar believed it even less than the last time he had heard it. "I only wish I could witness such a feat," he muttered.

"Unlikely," said Baptiste, "since Eudoxia is dead." Behind her, like a tall shadow, the sorcerer mouthed the words. "And you soon will be."

He smiled, and Baptiste smiled. A smile that somehow did not fit her face.

Climbing the ratlines was harder than you'd think. Like climbing a ladder made of jelly. Didn't help that the ship had heeled over when it got spitted on the ram, its decks made slopes and its masts leaning towards the gilded galley on a dizzying slant.

"Oh God," Alex whispered as she climbed, "oh God, oh God." Divine intervention seemed like a long shot, honestly. God had folk packing into his churches and filling up his collection plates and living by his Twelve Virtues every saint's day, and far as she could tell he rarely stepped in on their behalf, so the chances of him sending down an angel for a faithless piece of shit like her must've been close to nil. But she kept saying the words even so. "Oh God oh God oh God," hand over hand, foot over foot, her arms burning and her legs burning and her lungs burning, higher and higher.

"Here." Sunny squatted on the yard above her. The lowest yard, which the bottom sail hung from. She caught Alex's wrist and heaved with all her weight. She weighed about as much as a bag of carrots, but Alex was very grateful for the gesture. She finally clambered up and stood there, teetering on what was basically a big stick creaking with the wind, gripping the mast like it was her most prized possession.

"Don't look down," said Sunny.

"What?" Alex looked down right away, of course. Straw burned in the middle of the deck, smoke billowing from their ship, the wind carrying it sideways over the great galley. She could see men between its benches. Soldiers in bright armour, clambering towards its prow, jumping across and into the haze on the sloping deck. Constans was there, on his platform, waving them forward. Did he look up at her and smile? Saviour, you could've seen those fucking teeth from a mile away.

"That *bastard*," she snarled, but it turned to a desperate squeak as the mast lurched, tilting a little further. "Is the ship sinking?"

"Well, there's a big hole in it." Sunny peered down towards the galley's ram, impaled in the hull. "And it's below the waterline, so . . ."

"We're climbing the mast . . ." Alex squeezed her eyes shut, trying not to take in the din of murder below. Trying not to notice the smoke scratching her chest with every breath. Trying not to think about the long drop. "Of a sinking ship."

"Best part of a sinking ship to be on."

"How do you work that out?"

"It'll be the bit that sinks last?" Sunny shrugged, bony shoulders up around her ears. "Am I helping?"

"Oh God," whispered Alex. They weren't alone in the rigging. There were figures following them up the ratlines, moving fast. One was halfway to the yard already, and it was horribly clear, even with all the smoke, that he wasn't quite human. He wore a uniform jacket, but it was all twisted and splitting at the seams around a bony oval body, with no neck and not much head. And he had claws. One little one and one huge one. Claws that seemed surprisingly well suited to climbing ropes. Or to crushing the heads of would-be princesses.

"Crab-men," breathed Alex.

"There's one over there who's more of a lobster, to be fair."

"Well, it's nice to know exactly what kind of shellfish you've been *murdered by*," shrieked Alex. "Where do we go?"

Sunny was looking upwards again. Up an even flimsier set of ratlines, past another set of flapping sails, narrowing towards the little split platform of the crosstrees at the very top of the mainmast, black against the blue sky high above.

"Oh God," whispered Alex.

Jakob's blade chopped into the fish-woman's ribs with that familiar butcher's block *whack*.

She dropped to her knees, her barbed sword clattering across the deck, blood welling from between her webbed fingers and turning her wet uniform an even darker red. Jakob swayed back, grabbed at the ship's rail to keep from falling, every breath its own wheezing effort.

"Blufutherbluther," she spluttered, blood bubbling from one gill and streaking from the corner of her mouth. "Blufuther."

"Wha?" Jakob couldn't tell if she was speaking a different language or couldn't form the words for the fishy shape of her mouth, or if he couldn't hear them for the thudding of blood in his ears.

A pendant had fallen out of her collar. A little enamelled flower on a silver chain. The sort of thing a lover gives as a gift. He wondered if she'd been given it before she became a fish, or after.

"Bluth," she said, and flopped sideways, pointed head clonking against the deck.

Jakob would've quite liked to join her there. His shoulder was on fire. He could hardly hold his shield up. There were fishy corpses everywhere. The whole aftcastle was slippery with blood. It stank like a disreputable fishmonger's.

He'd no clue what had happened to the others. The smoke made it hard to see, which had been his intention, and hard to breathe, which hadn't. But once you set the chaos rolling, you can't know where it'll end. That's the whole point of it.

"Oh, for God's *sake*."

He saw a flash of movement, couldn't do much more than lift his shield as something thumped into the deck.

Duke Constans, leaping from his galley and landing in a ready crouch on the aftcastle.

"I've heard it said . . ." Eudoxia's third son slowly stood. "That if you really want something done . . ." He picked an invisible speck of fluff from the jewelled honours crusting his crimson jacket and rubbed it away between finger and thumb. "You have to be prepared . . . to do it yourself?"

Jakob ran his tongue around the salty-sour inside of his mouth, teeth bloody from a shield in the face, and spat into the sea. It didn't quite make it and spattered on the rail beside him. "Uh-huh," he grunted.

"I will confess my mother's creations aren't the *most* competent soldiers." Constans pranced between the fishy bodies, and the corpses of a couple of dead sailors. He was bulky, crimson fabric straining about the highly polished buttons on his jacket, a little roll of flushed fat around his gilded collar, but he moved with a twinkly grace even so, up on his toes like a dancing master. "To be fair they were a theoretical exercise for her, she was fascinated by the soul, you know. Where it was located. How to release it. What became of it when you did . . ."

He stopped beside the creature with coral growing out of its head, on its back in a pool of blood. "She never intended them for military use. That was Marcian's idea." He dropped his voice, putting on a baleful frown and weakly shaking one fist. "Repurpose the bastards! Fearsome half-animal warriors! Breed an unstoppable legion! Reconquer the Holy Land and show the elves true horror!" He sighed as he squatted beside the malformed thing. "My brother wanted to turn everything into weapons. Ever since

we were boys. He'd make an unstoppable legion of the peas on his plate,
I swear."

He somewhat sadly adjusted the coral man's uniform, which had an embroidered hole around the shoulder for a nub of coral to grow through. "I
tried to give them a bit of pride, you know. Bit of class." He patted the polished buttons, very much like those on his own jacket. "What the Carthaginians used to call legion's honour!"

Jakob took a long wheeze in, produced a long wheeze out. He'd lost track
of the number of megalomaniacal speeches he'd had to endure down the
years. But if it gave him a chance to catch his breath, have at it. "Uh-huh,"
he grunted.

"Well. A work in progress, I suppose." Constans stood, glancing around
at the bodies. "I must admit, this is all . . . terribly impressive work on your
part, though. Is that . . ." He wagged his finger, a hefty ring glinting as he
counted the huddled, sprawling, leaking shapes. "Seven? No—eight! I do you
a disservice. That's two more over there."

The helmsman had done for one of those two, in fact, before they killed him,
and Vigga for the other, but Jakob saw no pressing need to correct the arithme-
tic. A couple here or there wouldn't make much difference to the butcher's bill
he'd run up down the years. "Uh-huh," he grunted.

"*So.*" Constans drew his sword, jewels glinting on the gilded hilt, steel
gleaming mirror-bright. "A duel to the death?" He raised his arms, sword
dangling languidly from one plump hand. "On the listing deck of a stricken
ship that's burning and sinking *at once*? I mean, it's a little lurid, but you can't
deny the *drama.*"

Drama made little impact on Jakob these days. He'd been through burn-
ings and sinkings aplenty and the phrase *to the death* didn't carry quite the
same thrill for him that it did for other men. "Uh-huh," he grunted.

Constans looked mildly disappointed. "I must admit I was hoping for a
little badinage while we were at it."

"Once you've done as many of these as I have . . ." Jakob waved at the
corpses scattered about the aftcastle. "It's just the same jokes over and
over."

"A sad indictment of the world we live in that we run out of jokes before
we run out of enemies." Constans twitched the legs of his tight-fitting
trousers up with his free hand and bent his knees into a waiting crouch,
sword point perfectly levelled. "I should warn you . . . I fear this will end
badly."

"Well." Jakob pushed himself away from the rail. "If you leave it long enough . . ." And he took one more breath, and blew it out. "Everything ends badly."

People often rushed to conclusions about Sunny. They spat at her or called her an enemy of God or tried to cut her ears off, and it was no fun at all. So she tried hard to be polite and not judge people on their appearance.

But you could not have called this crab-man a looker.

From the waist down he seemed normal-ish—he even had some trousers and a belt with a brass buckle. But things went off course about the ribs. He'd had a nice jacket like the Ringmaster used to wear at the circus, but it was all torn up by the rough edges of his shell-like body, which appeared to have a load of barnacles stuck to it, too. One overlong arm had a couple of fingers and a big pointy thumb on the end. The other was a great serrated claw, though he used it nimbly enough on the rigging. His head was a neckless lump, furry mouthparts quivering, one eye a bit like a human eye but the other sticking out on a stalk. The whole effect was really quite horrible. Especially since Sunny was within a few inches of him, clinging unseen to the other side of the ratlines.

Oh. He had strange little hairy legs sticking from his stomach. She really didn't want to use the word *underparts* about anything right in front of her face, but what else could you call them? All wriggling and squiggling, so she had to squeeze her eyes and her mouth tight shut as he clambered past. Did he drip on her a bit? Did she have crab juice on her?

Crab juice was almost as bad as *underparts*.

Even with her breath held she caught a sense of his stink, one part burial at sea to two parts fish market on a *very* warm evening. He stepped on her hand as he passed with a big bare foot that had a length of moist seaweed trailing from one of the three hard toes, and Sunny had to bite her lip. But he didn't notice as she swung around to his side of the ratlines. Didn't notice as she climbed up behind him. Didn't notice when she slipped the dagger from the back of his belt. He was fixed on Alex, not very far ahead at all, now, muttering, "Oh God," to herself over and over.

Sunny paused.

The Saviour had definitely tended against killing, and she heard priests talk about murder like it was really the worst, but when she finally read the scriptures herself, she found God couldn't go a page without smiting the shit out of someone. Then dead people might be a tragedy but dead elves are a punchline. No quicker shortcut to heaven than up a mountain of elf-skulls. You could be the most terrible bastard in the world but go on a crusade and fill a cart with pointy-eared corpses you came out a hero, fresh as daisies.

Alex glanced back, eyes wide and wild through the hair stuck across her face, only a stride or two between her heels and the bigger of the two claws.

In the end, it seemed to Sunny that right or wrong is mostly a question of what you can get away with.

So when the crab-man lifted one leg to find a new foothold Sunny stabbed him up the arse.

He gave a great bellow, but she was already swinging around the ratlines to the other side and swarming up past him, using what passed for his head as a step. She climbed up next to Alex, who looked very scared, which made sense since they were high up on wobbly ropes on a sinking ship crawling with murderous fish-people. Not everyone takes that sort of thing in their stride. Sunny let her breath out so Alex could see her, and she gave a gasp.

"You're there!"

She resisted the urge to ask where else she might be. "Yes."

"There's a crab-man after me!"

"I know. I stabbed him up the arse."

"He's gone?"

Sunny peered down. Being stabbed up the arse would definitely make most people think twice, but perhaps not most crabs, because he was coming faster than ever, albeit leaking more juice even than before.

"No, he's still coming," said Sunny. She had to give him some credit for it, really. "Don't look down."

Alex twisted around to look right away. "Oh God!" she whimpered, getting all panicked and tangled, which was why Sunny told her not to look in the first place. Why did no one ever listen to her? It gave the crab-man time to close right in, and Alex started flailing at him with one foot, the ratlines jerking and wobbling, and at quite an angle, too, since the ship kept tipping further over.

The crab-man reached for Alex with his claw, mouthparts all opened up and hissing, and Sunny grabbed for the first thing she could, some heavy metal thing hooked to the mast. She leaned past Alex as she kicked again and flung it in the crab-man's face, or where the face would be on someone who had one, and it caught him right in the eyestalk. With a despairing squawk he lost his grip and toppled from the rigging.

He fell onto the sail, flailing about, there was a great noisy ripping of cloth as his claw caught, slowed him a bit. Then he hit the yard at the bottom and went tumbling, the thing Sunny had thrown falling with him.

Which was when she realised it was a ship's lantern. One of those they light at night to let other ships know where they are. The kind all filled with sweet-smelling and highly flammable whale oil.

She watched it tumble towards the smoking fire on the deck below, and bit her lip.

"Oops," she said.

You Did It Now

Brother Diaz spun around at an almighty crash to see a bloody mess of broken shell had plummeted into the smouldering heap of straw from high above, one barnacle-crusted claw twitching.

"Holy—" he gasped as something else fell on top with a tinkling of glass.

He recoiled as burning oil shot out, spraying the deck with fiery puddles. He stumbled back, trying to slap away a flaming patch on the crotch of his habit, and blundered into Vigga.

"Fire!" he gasped.

"Weapon," she growled, waving her empty hand towards him.

"What?"

She snapped her fingers as figures began to form beyond her, at once shrouded in murk and lit by flickering flames. The whole episode was feeling more and more like hell with every moment. "Weapon!" she snarled.

Brother Diaz cast about the wreckage on the tipping deck, clawed a fallen hatchet from a dead sailor's hand, and slapped it into Vigga's. She flung it at a soldier as he came from the smoke, catching him in the shoulder and spinning him like a child's top.

"Weapon!"

Brother Diaz fumbled up a fallen sword and tossed it, she snatched it from the air and bent it in half around a man's head. He managed a few steps before he fell in the fire, which was spreading rapidly up the rigging nearby.

"Weapon!"

Brother Diaz threw her a fallen shield and she swung it, knocked a mace flying from a man's hand, smashed his knee sideways with the rim, smashed his teeth out with it as he fell, then flung the splintered wreckage away.

"Weapon!"

Brother Diaz groaned as he dragged up a huge axe with a pick on the back, wedging the haft into Vigga's hand as an armoured figure lumbered from the smoke.

Vigga shoved Brother Diaz clear so hard he sat down, a sword flashing past and hacking into the deck where he'd been standing. Vigga rolled away, came up quick as a snake, chopped at the soldier's side and made him totter, chopped at his leg and made him stumble, ducked under a wild sword swing then reared up, spinning the axe so the head was backwards, and buried the pick-end in the top of the man's helmet with a metallic thud.

"Saviour protect us," breathed Brother Diaz, scrambling clear as the man crashed onto the deck beside him, blood spreading from his ruined helmet in a widening pool.

"Weapon," growled Vigga, snapping her fingers again. "Weapon!"

Alex dragged herself up, frayed rope scraping her arms, weathered wood digging at her chest, spraying spit as she groaned through her clenched teeth, and finally tumbled onto her back, gasping for air.

Blue sky above, and clouds moving, and a little frayed flag snapping at the very top of the mast.

"Alex," came Sunny's voice.

"I'll just lie here," she whispered. "Here's fine."

"Here's not fine." Sunny caught Alex's elbow and hauled her up to sitting. "Not fine *at all*."

So this was a crosstrees. One of those things you've heard of, sounded vaguely interesting, but you'd never, *ever* want to actually visit. Like England.

A couple of weather-worn planks clinging to the top of the mast and a tangle of ropes. That was all it was. God, it was windy. Dragging at Alex's hair, tugging at her clothes, chilling the sweat on her face. She could hear the mast creaking. Feel the mast swaying. It was at quite the angle now. She hooked one arm around it and clung on tight, stomach rolling.

"We have to move," said Sunny.

"Move?" Alex would've laughed if she hadn't been so terrified. "Where?" Wasn't like they could go up again. There was no up. Not unless they both sprouted wings. Which, come to think of it, wouldn't even have been the most surprising thing to happen that afternoon.

"Along the top yard." Sunny nodded sideways. "Then across to the galley."

So matter-of-fact, she said it. Like directions to the inn. Down the street and second on the right.

"Along the *top yard*?" breathed Alex, staring at the cross-beam the topsail hung from. A narrow spar, netted with ropes, stretching away to end in empty air maybe ten strides off. At that moment it looked like ten miles.

"Across . . . to the *galley*?" Her voice faded to a reedy croak on the last word. With their ship leaning over, the very end of the yard was close to the sloping spar that held the great front sail of the galley. How close exactly was hard to say. But the empty air between the two was undeniable.

Very empty, and very, very high.

"You're fucking *mad*," muttered Alex.

Sunny shrugged. "And I'm probably the least mad out of us." She looked so calm, crouching there with her white hair flicking in the wind. Like she was crouching by a campfire. "If you've got a better idea, I'm . . . *all ears.*"

Alex stared at her for a moment, then forced through her gritted teeth, along with a quantity of spit, "Was that a *joke?*"

Sunny looked pleased. "Yes! All ears. I'm an elf. We have big ears and skinny bodies, so—"

"I fucking *get it*!" screeched Alex.

"I thought it was a good one." Sunny looked slightly crestfallen. "People are so weird. You want to go first or second?"

"Neither!" shrieked Alex. She was crying again, and she had snot leaking from one nostril, but she didn't dare peel her aching hands from the mast to wipe it. "Fucking neither."

Sunny raised her pale brows as she peered downwards. "So . . . crab-men, then?"

Baptiste lunged and Balthazar floundered back, one blade whipping past his ear.

Had this sorcerer been half the knife-fighter Baptiste was, Balthazar would already have been carved like a sabbath joint. Fortunately, he was not, and Baptiste with characteristic obstinacy was clearly making some effort to resist his control, the lashes of her blades stiff and wild at once. Stiff, and wild, but still highly deadly. Balthazar gasped as he slopped clear of another thrust, the knife thudding into a crate beside him. Baptiste abandoned it, buried in the splintered timber, and instantly drew another. He deemed it unlikely she would run out of daggers before she managed to stick one of them into some vital part of him. Honestly, he regarded none of his parts as expendable.

He was reduced, as so often of late, to humiliating retreat, clutching at any object he found floating and flinging it at her—scraps of planking, a coil of soaked rope, a cabbage—in the faint hope of jarring that cursed needle loose. Baptiste knocked this junk mechanically away, apart from the cabbage which she sliced neatly in half, a demonstration of the extreme keenness of her weapons that did his confidence no favours whatsoever.

"Let's get this over with," snarled Baptiste and her puppeteer, together. She lunged, a blade hissing past Balthazar's hand and leaving a distinct stinging sensation across his fingers. His back hit the curving wall of the hold as she raised both daggers to stab at him and he had no choice but to throw himself forwards, her wrists slapping into his wet palms.

They struggled, his eyes wide as he tried to focus on the waggling points of both knives at once. He squealed as one nicked his shoulder, squawked as the other pricked his neck, then groaned as Baptiste dragged him in a floundering circle and flung him into the ram, his head cracking against its metal cap.

She was long and lean and shockingly strong. It was like grappling with a great eel. That *he*, Balthazar Sham Ivam Draxi, should be wrestling over a pair of daggers while up to his waist in salt water in the hold of a sinking ship with a possessed jack of all trades, and *losing*. He had always harboured a ready contempt for the physical, of course, but as he wheezed with effort, every muscle trembling, he began to wonder whether taking occasional exercise might have been a sensible use of his time down the years. Baptiste bent him back, both blades aimed at his face, both his fists around her slippery wrists, a patch of daylight illuminating the side of her oddly immobile face.

The water lapped first at his shoulders, then at his neck, then at his ears as, with a terrible inevitability, he was driven downwards. He twisted his face sideways, struggling to put an extra inch or two between his skin and those gleaming points—and saw the corpse of the cabin boy bobbing in the water.

He clenched his teeth as he stretched his will towards it, running quickly through the verses in his mind, squeezing the fluids into motion. That was never straightforward with a drowned corpse, especially for a magician in the process of being drowned himself, there was *far* too much fluid around altogether, and more flooding into the hold with every moment, but he flatly *refused* to die in such a humiliating manner!

The cabin boy jerked up with a look of profound shock. His eyes bulged from the pressure and one popped out and dangled about on the front of his pale face. He reeled around, arms flailing, bounced off Baptiste, clutched stiffly for the needle with both hands, caught her ear and tried to pull that off instead, only succeeded in twisting her head slightly, needle and rune still very much attached.

Her expression did not change as she wrenched one arm free of Balthazar and stabbed the cabin boy's corpse cleanly through the one eye still in his head. He toppled back, clutching uselessly at nothing with some vestigial desire of the unstabbed half of his brain.

"Quiet now," said Baptiste, working her knee against Balthazar's chest and forcing him down into the water, forcing her remaining dagger down towards him. A long, thin dagger, point glinting in a shaft of sunlight. He strained his free hand towards it, taking a choking mouthful of salt water as the sea lapped over his face, missed entirely and, far more by accident than planning, plucked the needle from Baptiste's forehead.

She dropped like a scarecrow with its stick pulled out, and he caught her as he came up, spluttering for air, hardly able to see for the wet hair stuck across his face.

"Baptiste?" he gasped, for some reason wishing he knew her first name. Removing the needle without preparation was a risk. There was no way of knowing how long it would take her to return. Or even *if* she would return. "Are you—"

Which was when he felt a stabbing pain in the middle of his own forehead, where the little bead of blood was even now forming on hers.

Their blades clashed, Jakob lunged with his shield and missed, stumbled against the rail, pain lancing through his knee, saw the glint as Constans's sword whipped at him, barely got his up in time to steer it wide, flinched as it hacked splinters from the rail beside him, chopped clumsily back but hit only smoke.

Eudoxia of Troy's third son was already dancing away.

Not the best start. But Jakob had fought a lot of duels. A lifetime of them.

He remembered the first time he fought Heinrich Gross, on that bridge over the Rhine. Nobody thought he'd win that one. But he had. Even if, in the long run, it turned out badly for all concerned. You can't always pick a winner from the opening moves.

He covered, knowing his own shortcomings, and using every advantage he could winkle out, sticking to the highest corner of the sloping deck, conserving his strength, shield up and knees bent. That cost him, in pain. But an awful lot less than being stabbed would've.

"That shield isn't terribly sporting," grumbled Constans. "Care to set it aside?"

Jakob eyed him over the rim. "If you wanted sport you didn't have to send your fish-people first." And he planted his boot on one of their heads, blood welling from the great gash he'd left in it.

Constans grinned. "Fair point." He danced forwards, which Jakob was ready for, then whipped sideways, which Jakob wasn't. He only just got his shield over, sparks flying from its rim and sending him stumbling back. By the time he countered, Constans had found a comfortable range again, and only had to lean back an inch and smile as Jakob's point whisked harmlessly past.

"A brave effort," he murmured, "but a doomed one." He darted in and Jakob shuffled back, staving lightning jabs away with his shield, smoke scraping at his lungs with every breath. The fire was spreading, the rigging in flames above, maybe one of the sails, too, ash floating down. Constans didn't seem worried, though. Always smiling, his sword held so loose it looked as if it might slip from his plump fingers, but always ready to flick up as deftly as a painter's brush.

A fancy and ridiculous sword, but also, plainly, a very good one. As Constans was a fancy and ridiculous swordsman, but also, even more plainly, a *very* good one. The duke grinned wider, as if he guessed exactly what Jakob was thinking.

"I never enjoyed swordsmanship, but despite making very little effort, I've always been truly superb at it. My fencing masters were consistently astonished. Marcian tried twice as hard and was half as good. It always infuriated him. Even more than most things. My uncle used to say I had a God-given talent. I've really never found anyone who could match me."

"Maybe I'll surprise you," growled Jakob, starting to severely doubt it.

"I almost hope so." Constans circled, feeling out Jakob's considerable weaknesses. "I do hate a tale with a predictable ending."

He pounced again, quick, so quick, Jakob parried, thrust, sure he had the centre, but Constans had already sidestepped, catching Jakob across the sword arm. He willed his ankle not to give as he spun about, sinking behind his shield again, fending off a flurry of jabs that pecked splinters from the wood. He could feel the sticky warmth of blood inside his sleeve, the throb of the new wound starting to come on. Constans watched, sword's point utterly still, utterly ready, the only evidence of his efforts a slight pinking of his plump cheeks.

Jakob had fought many duels. A lifetime of them.

Enough to know when he wasn't going to win.

"Here," said Vigga, offering Brother Diaz her hand.

"Am I . . . alive?" He could feel wetness down the front of his habit, scrabbled at it in a desperate effort to locate the fatal wound, then realised the inkwell had shattered in his satchel and soaked him from the waist down in black dye.

"So far." Vigga hauled him from the tangle of bodies. They saw at the same time the hand she'd used was slathered with gore. "Oh." She wiped it awkwardly on the front of her leather vest, but that was slathered with gore as well. "Ah. Bit messy . . ." Who ever would've thought, a few months ago, when he was diligently reviewing the monastery's accounts, that *slathered with gore* would be a phrase he routinely employed?

He blinked at the corpses. The one with the sword bent around his head and the one with his guts unwound across the deck and the big one with the front of his helmet smashed right in. "You saved me," he gasped.

"Let's not get ahead of ourselves." Vigga narrowed her eyes as she peered into the smoke. "Where did our princess get—" She flinched, then gave a low growl. "Ah, Loki's *tits*." Brother Diaz realised there was an arrow stuck through the meat of her tattooed shoulder, the bloody head pointing right at him.

"You're shot!" he squeaked.

"You think?" she snarled, backing towards him. There were figures ahead of her, in the smoke. "That way." She jerked her head at the steps up to the forecastle. "Go."

She backed off, and behind her, he backed off. It was becoming something of a habit. Up the sloping deck they crept, towards the prow. Her right arm hung limp, blood dripping from her dangling fingers and spotting the planks.

"How many are there?" he whispered.

"Enough," she hissed, reaching up to grip the arrow-shaft and snapping off the flights with a grunt. "Pull it out."

He licked his lips. Who ever would've thought, a few months ago, when the definition of a harrowing task had been reorganising one of the high shelves in the library, that he would be called on to pull arrows out of werewolves?

"Our Saviour . . ." he gripped her shoulder with one trembling hand, "light of the world . . ." and gripped the shaft just below the head with the other. "Deliver us from—"

"Arrows," Vigga snarled as he wrenched it out, dissolving into a throbbing growl deep in her throat. He tried to grip the wound, but blood squelched around his hands, between his inky fingers, running down his wrists and into his habit.

"It's bleeding!"

"You think?" Her voice sounded strange. Sweet Saint Beatrix, were her teeth even more pronounced than usual? "I'm safe," she whispered, breathing hard. "I'm clean." An odd choice of words from someone covered in gore. "I've got . . . the wolf muzzled." She stumbled and fell to one knee.

"God help us . . ." squeaked Brother Diaz, half-squatting beside her, half-hiding behind her, plucking weakly at her bloody shoulder. The wind wafted the smoke away for a moment and he glimpsed soldiers crossing the deck. More clambering down from the galley. He'd no idea where the others were. If they were still alive, even. "I think . . ." He could hardly believe he was going to say the words, then an arrow flitted down and stuck wobbling into the deck beside him, and he blurted them in a rush. "We might need the wolf!"

Vigga's eye twitched towards him. "The wolf's a traitor. A devil. Once it's loose—"

"But can you fight all those?" He nodded towards the shapes rising from the murk, flinched as another arrow stuck into the deck on their other side. "With one arm?"

"'Course I can," she said, swaying slightly.

"Can you *win*?"

"Eh . . ." She dropped forwards onto her hands, blood soaking through her vest, running down one tattooed arm in streaks.

"Sometimes . . ." There was no escaping Cardinal Zizka's conclusion. "A devil is what you need."

Vigga's breath came crackly. Her eyelids flickered. "Then you . . . had better *hide*." With all the blood, smoke, and tattoos it was hard to be sure, but he'd a sense dark hair was starting to sprout from her shoulders.

"Sweet Saint Beatrix," whispered Brother Diaz. What had he done? He started to back away, tearing off the ink-soaked wreckage of his satchel and flinging it into the sea, but he was running out of deck in every sense, creeping towards the triangle of planking as it narrowed to the bowsprit.

He teetered onto it, crouching at the stricken ship's very prow, trying not to think about the drop to the sea on both sides. He snatched a glance back, saw the figures closing in on Vigga, weapons levelled.

Her head jerked sideways, one shoulder hunched, swelled. There was a sickening crunch as a spasm twisted her back into an impossible shape.

"*Sweet* Saint Beatrix," whimpered Brother Diaz, tearing his eyes from the unholy transformation and clambering down below the bowsprit, out of sight. He clung tight to the weatherworn figurehead. He pressed his face into the flaking gilt on her woody bosom. Not for the first time, he wished he was with Mother.

And oh, how lovely to be back!

The Vigga-Wolf let her tongue flop out and lie heavy on the woody salty planks where smoke and blood and the rumour of violence tickled at her nose-holes.

There were many questions rattling in her mind. What had she been doing? Why was her foreleg sore? Why was she on a boat and why was the deck
so slantwise? But the Vigga-Wolf's mind was not very big, there was barely
room for one question at a time, and the one that bubbled to the top and
squished all the rest was the one that always did.

Where *was* the good meat?

Then another.

Who were these fuzzy fuckers pointing toothpicks at her?

Smoke drew a coy little veil across the deck so they couldn't get a proper
look at each other. So they couldn't tell her shape, pressed to the deck as she
was with her claws gouging the wood, wriggling back and forth with shoulders low and haunches high, itching to spring, all quivery with anticipation.

And then an ever so playful breeze snatched the smoke away and they were
all of a sudden introduced. Three men with spears and helmets on all prettily
trimmed with gold and full to the eyebrows with meat.

She was very pleased to see them, her smile of welcome so hugely wide and
slobbery. But they were not equally happy to make her acquaintance.

"Oh God," said one.

People often said that when they met the Vigga-Wolf, which was a puzzle
because she doubted she and God looked much alike. So she pounced on the
man and clawed him and shook him so his insides came out in a red slither.

One of the others stabbed at her with his spear and she tiptoed over it, then
when he stabbed again, she slithered under it, but after a few stabs she got
bored of being where the spear wasn't so plucked it from his hand and ripped
his chest open with her jaws and snuffled and licked at the slop inside but it
was unsatisfactory.

The last one tossed his spear away and ran but only got a step before the
Vigga-Wolf was on him, quick as regrets, catching him by the neck and jerking him about so furiously his head flew off and bounced across the deck. She
was starting to snuffle the bits from his throat-hole when she had a thought.

She'd had a monk, hadn't she? A monk of her very own.

And she spun around but couldn't see him and it came to her perhaps
they'd killed him and that cooked her to the extremes of quivering fury 'cause
if anyone was going to kill anyone it'd fucking well be her. The rage pulled
her head right back and twisted her spine like a corkscrew and tore a ripping
howl from her so loud it scoured her on the inside and blew a great mist of
blood from her gaping jaws.

Vengeance, now, filled up her whole mind and boiled over.

She whipped and skittered across the slippery deck, gouging a couple of soldiers on the way and leaving them slit and screaming, and she bunched up and sprang, first onto the ram, then the platform above, and slunk over the top and onto the other ship. The big, bad, fishy-smelling ship.

Are ships alive? Do ships dream? Do ships hold meat? She would find out. She would break it open.

She would gnaw upon it till she found the good meat.

Wherever it was hid.

A Draw Is Enough

Balthazar Sham Ivam Draxi was not a man to be taken entirely by surprise. He had seen the needle, recognised the rune, at once understood the methodology. The instant he felt the pinprick, and with it the chilly intrusion of the sorcerer's mind, he began to mouth the first verse of Jahaziel, a reliable all-rounder. He stamped the symbols into his consciousness, arranged in the proper hexagon, and made them blaze forth with all his outrage. He fashioned from them an impenetrable rampart, then—dismissing the distraction of an unearthly howl echoing through the flooding hold from somewhere above—focused all his will upon a single point, and in the centre of that hexagon began to drill a hole.

For the needle and the rune were not like the galley's ram: a weapon striking in one direction only. They were a breach through which an assault could be mounted, but from which canny defenders could also sally forth. They were a conduit between two minds, and through it Balthazar now reached, ready to turn the tables on this bumptious body-burglar . . . when he felt himself stopped.

Moving his actual physical eyes was exceedingly testing, but he forced them to roll upwards. The sorcerer was mouthing his own verses, eyes narrowed with furious concentration, finger and thumb rooted to the needle, frozen, like Balthazar, at the very moment it had punctured his skin.

To have been rendered a slave by the Mother of the Church was embarrassment enough; to be made a marionette by some sideshow trickster was a humiliation too far. Balthazar redoubled his efforts. He swept everything else away, ignoring the rushing water as it poured in around the ram, ignoring the chill up to his stomach as it lapped ever higher, ignoring the stabbing pain in his forehead. He forced his will back down the needle, through the rune, and into the sorcerer's mind.

Balthazar was gaining the upper hand, could feel, through a prickling fuzz, the man's finger and thumb trembling on the needle as if they were his own. A little longer. A hint . . . more . . .

Something was wrong. He was having trouble mouthing the syllables. His image of the charm was growing blurred . . . was he breathing, still? He was not! While Balthazar had been struggling to grip this sorcerer's slippery brain, the sneaky bastard had outflanked him and seized control of his diaphragm!

His sight was dimming, he could not maintain the verses. The chilly presence of the phrenomancer crept into his head, like the cold into the blood of a man stranded on a glacier. He felt the needle twist and his legs were forced to bend. His back slid down the ram, his knees hit the deck, up to his shoulders in the chilly water.

Balthazar strained to lift his hands. Move his fingers, even. But he was still holding Baptiste, arms locked rigid around the soaked dead weight of her.

Pale and blurry in the shadows above him he saw the slack face of Eudoxia's student twitch. Saw his mouth curl into a thin smile.

"A brave effort." Balthazar realised it was not the phrenomancer's voice that spoke, it was his own. "But a doomed one. Now, if we have cleared up the question of who controls whom, it is time to lie back and accept the sea into your lungs, so we can urggggh—"

Baptiste's arm jerked from the water and buried a blade in the sorcerer's throat.

The icy intrusion began to drain from Balthazar's mind as Baptiste's other hand caught a fistful of the sorcerer's soaked robe. Black blood trickled from the corners of his mouth, ran from the grip of the knife as he pawed at it with fumbling fingers.

"Prick me in the forehead?" she hissed, twisting free of Balthazar's rigid arms. The sorcerer's eyes rolled up as she slid out another dagger and lifted it high, wet-beaded blade gleaming. "Let me return the *favour*."

The blade made a pop like a log splitting as she buried it right between his eyes. Probably not the easiest place to stab a man, but Balthazar had to admit that for poetic justice it would take some beating.

Eudoxia's apprentice slid down into the water and Balthazar felt his body suddenly released. He heaved in a breath, coughed, and heaved in another. He ripped the needle from his forehead, nearly falling, his legs a jelly.

Baptiste caught him under the arms and heaved him up against the ram. The two of them leaned against each other for a moment, both breathing hard.

"Magic . . . may be the ultimate expression . . . of man's triumph over nature," she forced through gritted teeth. "But sometimes you've just got to stab a bastard."

"For once," gasped Balthazar, "we are in accord. One could even say . . . that we make quite the effective . . ."

Baptiste was not listening. She had let go of him and was frowning towards the entrance. It was lost beneath the rushing waters, which now came as high as her chest, and were still rising.

"Ah," said Balthazar.

"Do you need a moment?" asked Constans.

Jakob's problem was that he'd had too many moments, not too few. He'd tried every trick he could think of. Tripping the duke over corpses, slipping him on their blood, distracting him with talk, then with silence, using the steepening slope of the deck, the rail, the mast, the smoke, the sun, the ballista bolt wedged into the floor. None of it had worked. None of it had even come close to working.

"Better finish up," he managed to mutter. "Ship's sinking."

"And burning." Constans glanced at the ash floating down around them, as if at an unseasonal snowfall that would entirely ruin his plans for the afternoon. "What happened to that cheeky waif Alexia? Did I see her up in the rigging somewhere?"

Jakob took the opportunity to lunge and Constans flicked it contemptuously away. "You really should've handed her over. It would've been easier for everyone."

"No doubt," grunted Jakob, "but I always find myself taking the hard way."

The duke grinned. "I am the *exact* opposite."

He darted forwards, made Jakob lurch back, wincing as his weight went through his bad hip, his bad knee, his bad ankles. He managed to parry the first cut on an instinct, managed to block the second with his shield, bitter edge raking the rim as Constans flitted past, already out of range of a counter, and back on his guard anyway.

Jakob hadn't so much as touched the bastard. Too fast, too skillful, too damn *young*. He was every bit as good as he'd said. If anything, he'd been modest. Jakob was bleeding from a dozen little slashes, nicks, and scratches. Could feel the stickiness of blood against the grip of his sword. Trickling down his cheek. One boot squelching with it at every step. It was getting difficult to breathe, let alone fight. He hardly even had the strength to disguise the fact any longer.

"Would you care to tell me your name," asked Constans, "before it's all over?"

"Do you care?"

"Well, not a lot. But it's the done thing in a duel, isn't it?" He feinted and made Jakob stumble back, shield up. "And I thought you might appreciate my asking. Appreciate the sense that this all . . . means something." He feinted again, and again Jakob fell for it. "Rather than just . . . Tuesday afternoon?"

Jakob had fought many duels. A lifetime of them. Enough to know when he was losing. But he told himself he didn't have to win. Only buy time. He thought he'd heard Vigga's howl, so anything could happen. And he trusted Sunny. With luck, she'd already got Alex to safety.

"Oh God," whispered Alex.

She'd always thought she was good with heights, but this wasn't some shuffle down a roof-ridge.

She could feel the space yawn beneath her. The plunging emptiness. The wind making the sailcloth flap, her clothes rustle, the mast creak as it leaned ever further.

She focused on the wood right in front of her, on the ropes on top that she clung to, the ropes underneath she shuffled her feet along. She kept going, dogged, till she reached out and found there was nothing to grip.

"Good!" she heard Sunny say. "You made it to the end." The elf was perched a few strides away on the great sloping beam that held the galley's front sail. "Don't look down."

Alex looked down right off, of course. A dizzying drop to the channel of foaming water between the two ships. Mast dwindling away towards the distant deck. Figures there, some moving, some definitely not, and . . . were the sails on fire? The ratlines, too, turning into flaming nets, smoke billowing in grey clouds.

"Oh God," she squeaked, then heard a blood-curdling howl down below. "Is that Vigga?"

"Never mind. Stand up on the yardarm."

"On the what?"

"The timber that holds the sail is called the yard, the end of the yard is called—"

"Is this the best time for a lesson in fucking *nautical terminology*?" screamed Alex, the wind whipping the spit from her bared teeth.

"Fine, we can go through it later."

"What?"

"If you're alive."

"*What?*"

"Stand up and jump!" Sunny held out her hand. "I'll catch you!"

"How can you catch me? You weigh a third of nothing!"

"All right." Sunny took her hand back. "I won't catch you."

"You won't catch me?" screeched Alex.

"Well, make your mind up!"

The one like a lobster had made it to the crosstrees, was clambering out along the yard towards her.

"Oh God," whimpered Alex. Slowly, surely, gripping with her hands, she shuffled her feet up onto the yard. She told herself it was like a roof-ridge. Long as you didn't look down. Or back. Or anywhere. She inched her feet towards her trembling fingers. The timber creaked under her, swayed, nothing flat, nothing straight. The smoke was making her cry. That or the abject terror.

"Just jump!" shouted Sunny.

The flames were spreading. She took one hand from the wood, lifted it, wobbling. She wanted to look back. Made herself stare ahead, fixed on Sunny's hand, fixed on the sloping beam. She told herself that was safety.

"Oh God, oh God, oh God." She took the other hand away. She made herself do it. She straightened, arms out wide. She stood. Balancing.

On the end of the yard. The yardarm, or whatever.

Far, far above the sea.

She bent her knees, gathering herself, eyes fixed on where she was going. Fixed on safety. Fixed on freedom.

"Fuuuuuuck!" she screamed at no one, and it became a howl as mindless as Vigga's as she jumped, the wind plucking at her clothes, her hair, plucking her voice away. She flailed wildly with every limb, as though she could swim through air. Which she could. Every bit as well as she could swim through water, anyway.

The beam rushed up at her and—

"Ooooof . . ." Breath driven out in a ragged wheeze as it punched her in the groin, then an instant later the chest, then an instant later right in the face, filling her mouth with blood and her skull with blinding light.

"Alex!" A hand grabbed at her shirt. She grunted, annoyed, waved them away. Wanted to sleep in. She was sliding down, though. Sliding out of bed. Everything on a tilt. Her eyelids fluttered, all bright and sparkly, and—

She dragged in a great breath. A glimpse of the reeling deck of the galley, little benches and little oars, so far below. A glimpse of the churning sea below that. Smoke billowing from their burning ship.

"Oh Goth," whispered Alex, her face numb, her legs wrapped around the sloping yard like she'd hump the damn thing. Arms hugging it like she'd marry it afterwards. She'd had less considerate lovers, to be fair.

"Oh Goth." Her mouth was one great throb. She tried to check whether she still had all her teeth but her tongue was too battered to tell. Her skinned hands were full of splinters and her arms were grazed to the meat and her sore chest was bruised like she'd done a bare-fist bout with Bostro, wheezing and sobbing with her salty teeth gritted and her eyes squeezed shut.

She could hear something, though, over the fumbling wind and the billowing sailcloth and her own pounding heartbeat. Crashing, and snarling, and terrified screaming.

"Don't look down," said Sunny.

The Vigga-Wolf padded between the benches of the nasty fishy ship, where the oarsmen sat.

They weren't sitting there any more, of course. They were screaming and blubbering and scrambling over each other to get away from her. She remembered everything that walked or crawled or flew was terrified of her. This was the proper state of things. But another memory came with it. Pulling an oar of her own at a bench of her own, smiling while they rode the whale road, singing with the crew on the way to adventure. The Vigga-Wolf couldn't sing, so whose dream was this?

She sank back on her haunches, confused.

What had she been doing?

Ah! Vengeance and good meat! And she dived among the fleeing oarsmen, ripping and biting and showering a mess of blood and bits. There were lots of them, though, and it was her tragedy that she never could kill everything however hard she tried. Most got away, scrambling over the benches and scurrying up the sides of the ship to fling themselves into the sea. The sea is bitter and vengeful but nowhere near so bitter nor so vengeful nor so furry as the Vigga-Wolf.

She was very furry. She paused to admire the clotty clumps of it on the backs of her leg-arms. Arm-legs? So bristly and warm, like a lovely sticky cushion. She tried to hug herself but got all twisted and went crashing and thrashing through the benches.

"I want a hug!" she screamed, and a man came clanking and rattling at her. A great big man covered in metal and swinging a sword so the answer on hugs was likely a no. She slithered away, over the oars and under them, and he chopped nothing but benches.

She could hear him roaring at her from inside his metal head, could smell his mouthwatering scent floating from his metal body. He had a plume on top all feathery and purple and she bit at it but got the feathers up her nose and danced away sneezing.

He clomped after her, lifting his sword high, and she sprang on him and rammed him against the mast so hard the whole ship shook. The iron case was very knobbly, but she smashed him with one claw and the other, made him ring like a bell, dented him and punctured him and raked the mast with claw marks, too.

She ripped at him, and she ripped at the mast behind him, sparks and splinters, blood and splinters, till one of his arms dangled by a flap with blood spurting about. He fell leaking and she smashed at the mast, gouging the wood deep with her claws and distant through a mist another remembering—chopping, chopping, *tock tock* of the axe, breath smoking, sent into the forest to find a new mainmast, smiling as it toppled in the snow, and Olaf clapping her on the shoulder and saying, *No one brings 'em down like you.*

The memory made the fury boil and she'd bring this tree down too the bastard and she gripped it with her front claws and raked it with her back claws and wrapped her jaws around it, ripping and tearing and worrying with her teeth and she—

"Vigga!" someone roared, and there was the monk! She hadn't dreamed him, he was a real true thing, very sweaty and ash-stained but quite stern. He stood up tall to her and bellowed, veins starting from his neck, "Vigga! This behaviour is *unacceptable*!"

The Vigga-Wolf stood frozen with her jaws around the mast, blinking at him. It was very rare for anyone to stand up to her like that and for a moment she wasn't sure how to feel. Then she unhooked her teeth, bloody splintery slobber spattering the deck. Then she narrowed her eyes. Then she made a lovely throbbing growl deep in her throat as she slunk towards him because it struck her . . .

As rather . . .

Rude.

"Good wolf . . ." murmured Brother Diaz as he backed away, his mouth gone very, very, very dry.

Saviour, what an immensity of lie. This was not a good wolf. This was a murderous demon of a wolf. This was the worst wolf in creation. A slinking, slavering, spiked and bristled, shifting and flowing monstrosity with more teeth than a crocodile and more muscle than a bull.

It seemed now he'd made two very serious mistakes. The first when he told Vigga to let the wolf free. The second when he drew its attention.

He'd watched horrified as it left a trail of destruction through the crew, then set about destroying the mast, when he'd been amazed to notice someone clinging to the yard high above, then even more amazed to realise it was Princess Alexia. He hadn't the slightest idea how she could've got up there, but as things stood she'd soon be coming down, via a long and likely lethal drop. And so, without thinking, he'd stepped forwards.

Some hope had perhaps lurked at the back of his mind that the wolf might turn back into Vigga, the way it had at the inn, when Jakob of Thorn roared the same words. But it was becoming increasingly clear that this expedition was no place for hope.

"Good wolf . . ." He hardly dared look into those orange eyes, flaming like the very pits of hell, but neither did he dare look away. He sensed that it was only by meeting them that he limited the accursed beast to stalking him rather than ripping him apart. Burning bits of rope or sail had wafted across on the wind, scattering patches of fire among the empty benches and abandoned oars, among the ruined bodies of the unlucky oarsmen.

"Easy . . ." he murmured, not sure if he was talking to his own pounding heart or the wolf-thing, its growls making the deck throb, the soles of his feet buzz, his very bladder vibrate, his boots slipping on spilled blood, squishing through spilled guts as he backed down the galley's deck.

"Easy . . ." he wheedled, and the beast's mouth curled into an even more bestial snarl, bloody slaver spattering the planks—

Crack! The ruined mast lurched, the beast whipped around with impossible speed, and Brother Diaz spun almost as quickly, sprinting away between the last benches, ink-stained habit flapping wildly.

He heard the outraged bellow behind, the skittering of claws on wood. He thumped up the sloping deck towards the galley's stern, back tingling with the horrible expectation of monstrous teeth.

He sprang!

And for a moment he was free, the wind blowing cold around his undergarments.

Then the foaming sea rushed up to meet him.

"Oh God," whispered Alex as another great jolt went through the spar. She clung to it with her skinned and aching legs, her skinned and aching hands.

There was a pinging sound, then another, a trembling through the wood, then a creaking shiver.

"Oh God." The whole mast was tipping. Tipping sideways into the void, sailcloth billowing beneath her like the train on some vast wedding dress.

"Oh *God*." She squeezed her eyes shut as the mast ground to a teetering halt, squeezed her teeth so hard together they creaked, praying it would swing back.

Crack. Another jolt and the mast shifted again. The same way. More pings, more cracks, and it leaned further. Faster. Like a tree felled and toppling.

She gave a helpless whimper. She plastered every part of herself against the pitiless wood. She did everything short of bite it with her teeth. You can't stop yourself falling by holding on to something that's falling. But it was all she had.

Faster she swung, stomach reeling, the last fibres of the mast splintering down below, and faster she fell, cloth flapping, ropes lashing, and faster she plunged, towards the boiling sea, wind ripping her hair, whipping tears from her eyes, hurtling from on high and she opened her mouth to scream.

They say your life flashes before your eyes at a time like that. It didn't for Alex.

Just as well, maybe. Doing it once had been bad enough.

The water hit her hard as a speeding wagon, chill bubbles rushing around her, and suddenly nothing mattered.

Didn't have to move. Didn't have to breathe. Didn't have to lie.

She let the sea suck her down, into the silence.

Jakob lashed with his sword and missed again. Missed even more than last time. Constans was a smirking, taunting, plump ghost in the fog of smoke.

The ship was going down, timbers groaning. Jakob knew exactly how it felt. He lunged again but he was so tired now, every breath an acrid rasp. He could taste fire. Could taste blood. All so familiar. When it came to fire and blood, he was a connoisseur.

His foot slid on the bloody deck, his ankle gave, and he lurched onto one knee with an agonising twinge in his groin, still not right after stepping off that boat in Venice. Constans had already flitted around him. He tried to twist, tried to lift his shield, but he was too late.

So much of his overlong life—that little bit too late. Too late he'd learned his lessons. Too late he'd sworn his oaths.

He felt the cold sting of the point between his shoulder blades, then the crushing lance of pain through his chest. He would've screamed if he'd had the breath, but all that came out was a tortured wheeze, then a kind of half-cough, half-puke, then a bit more wheeze.

He knew what he'd see when he looked down. Nothing surprising. But no better for being familiar. His shirt tenting to a point. A point from which a dark stain spread. Then the gleam of metal showed. Then the fabric came apart and the tip of Constans's blade peeked through, bright steel red with Jakob's blood.

Stabbed in the back. They say in the end every man gets what he truly deserves.

His sword slipped from his limp fingers and clattered to the deck.

He heard light footsteps as Constans pranced around him.

"So." He bounced back into view. "No last-minute surprises, after all?" He lifted the embroidered sleeve of his jacket and gave it a disapproving sniff. "Everything's going to *stink* of smoke now. I warned you this would end badly."

Jakob gasped blood, coughed blood, dribbled blood. "And I . . ." he mouthed, but it was hard to get the breath around the steel in his lungs.

Constans stepped towards him, leaning down. "What was that?"

". . . warned . . ."

Constans touched a beringed finger to the back of one ear and nudged it forwards. "Beg pardon?"

". . . you . . ."

"You'll have to speak up, my friend. You're really just blowing bubbles at this—"

Jakob caught him around the back and dragged him into a tight embrace.

Constans gasped as his own sword's red point scraped his chest, clutching at Jakob's shoulders, eyes wide with disbelief.

"*Everything ends badly,*" hissed Jakob.

He'd fought many duels. Enough to know when he wasn't going to win. But when you can't die, a draw is enough.

He dropped backwards. Not hard to do. It had been taking all his effort to stay kneeling. Their own weight did the rest.

The gilded pommel of Constans's sword struck the deck. The blade slid through Jakob till the crosspiece hit his back. The duke gave a shrill squeal as the point was driven into his chest, burst out beside his spine, and went straight through the meat of Jakob's right forearm.

Not an honourable end to a duel, maybe, but Jakob had sworn no oaths to be honourable. He'd better sense than that.

Duke Constans stared into Jakob's face, eyes bulging, veins popping, pink cheeks trembling, then he blew a bloody gasp and went limp.

Which left Jakob, one more time, where all men will ultimately find themselves. Alone, with the consequences of what they've done.

He lay there, skewered. The sword's hilt was trapped against his back. Its blade was right through him. Constans's dead weight was on top. He fished weakly with the arm that wasn't pinned, but he could scarcely breathe, let alone start to free himself. The pain was utterly excruciating, of course.

Fragments of burning sailcloth fluttered down. Water was beginning to lap across the deck as the ship sank, the chill wetness of brine replacing the hot wetness of blood.

He'd been in tight corners before. He'd taken a lead role in some infamous calamities. But this was right up there. This was a real peach.

He gave a helpless little laugh.

"Here's a pickle," he whispered.

And the sea surged across the aftcastle and swept him away.

part

III

HIGH ROADS, LOW ROADS

Strange Bedfellows

Brother Diaz crawled from the bitter Adriatic on his skinned hands and knees, like Saint Bruno vomited forth by the shark, chastened and repenting of his sins.

He struggled up the gently sloping beach as if it were a mountain, stung by spray and buffeted by breakers, the passages of his throat all pitilessly scoured by salt. He knelt quivering on all fours, gaping at the rubbery stripe of weed at the high-water mark, retching and spitting as the waves sucked greedily through the shingle. He slumped back on his knees, naked but for the vial of Saint Beatrix and his clinging braies, their still slightly ink-stained wool turned so baggy by water he felt like a babe in a man's drawers. Exhausted, aching, disbelieving, his leaden head rolled about on his jelly neck as he took mute stock of his surroundings.

They were not promising.

To either side grey sweeps of beach stretched into hazy obscurity, chewed at by the grey sea, scattered with patches of grey rock, streaked with breeze-rippled puddles in which the grey heavens were uneasily reflected. Ahead, rising shingle gave way to scrubby dunes, wind-whipped grass, a few crippled trees all bowing one way, like a procession of geriatric monks abasing themselves before a cardinal.

He felt a chilly prickling on his shoulders. It had begun to rain.

"*Seriously?*" he screamed at the heavens.

The only reply was the careless gulls calling, up on the high wind.

He took a few heaving breaths. Sobs, if he was for once being honest. Then with a groan he fought his way up first to one foot, then the other. He stood swaying, arms hugged about himself, and turned groggily to look out to sea.

God, how far had he swum?

The galley still burned near the horizon, the column of smoke streaking into the white sky to drift off as a watercolour smear. He turned back to the beach and frowned. Was there a pale speck, among the rocks? He began to totter forwards, grimacing as the pebbles jabbed at his soles, narrowing his eyes against the wind—

It was a foot. A bare foot, tattooed with a line of runes.

"Vigga!" And he broke into a lurching run. If recent experience should've taught him anything it was that the best direction to run in relation to a werewolf is always *away*, but he found himself instead sprinting *towards*, scattering shingle with every stride. Maybe, at that moment, anything seemed better than being left alone on that blasted shore.

She lay face down in a rock pool, one foot up on the limpet-speckled stone, torn cloth hanging from her ankle, hair floating around her in a black cloud.

"Vigga!" He slopped into the pool beside her, caught one tattooed shoulder with the intention of heaving her over.

"God!" The *weight*. How could she float? He couldn't even get her face clear of the water at first. He had to brace his legs, hook her under one arm and around her neck, his chest pressed against her back, slippery skin slapping like pigs in a puddle, less a rescue than a wrestling match with no winner.

"Sweet . . ." he wheezed, straining, "Saint . . ." he moaned, heaving, "Beatrix—gah!" He finally managed to roll her and flopped back on the rocks, partly smothered by her dead weight, partly smothered by a faceful of her salt-wet hair.

"Vigga!" He wriggled halfway out from under her, barnacles ripping at his bare back. "Wake up!" He twisted to scrape the hair from her face, her head tipped back and her mouth wide open. "Vigga!" His voice getting higher and higher as he slapped at her tattooed cheek. "Don't be dead!"

"Uh." He was shocked by the surge of relief as she twitched, grunted, lifted one scabbed hand to brush him away. "Uh." Her face crunched up, and she started to tremble. "Uh!" And she cried, heavy shoulders shaking with sobs, fat tears leaving streaks through the sand stuck to her face.

Fear, shame, and disgust were undoubtedly among the alloy of emotions Brother Diaz felt at that moment. It would have been a lie to say he gave no thought to desperately wriggling free. But in the end, he stayed where he was, patting Vigga awkwardly on the shoulder. Only an hour before he had wrenched an arrow from that spot, but somehow the only trace of it was a little star-shaped scab. He made deeply unconvincing calming hoots, like a man who'd never held a baby left holding the baby.

Was not a priest's first duty to help those in need, after all? Were not the Saviour's mercy and forgiveness infinite, and should her followers not strive to imitate her? Were not the cursed and outcast in need of compassion? More than anyone, indeed. Somehow, in the fog of his own disappointments and ambitions, he had lost sight of that. Like some ancient denizen of his monastery to whom all beyond the page he was illuminating was a blur.

He realised now, at this desperate pass, that there was comfort in giving comfort.

Also, she was the only source of warmth within ten miles.

"I'm thirsty," whimpered Vigga, after a moment, and blew a snotty bubble.

"Well, you know how it is," said Brother Diaz, lying on a rock in the thickening rain in his soaking-wet underwear with a naked werewolf sobbing in his arms. "God loves to test us."

"We should head on down the coast," he coaxed, squinting up at the sky. The light was very definitely fading. "The others are likely scattered on these beaches." He forced himself not to add, "The ones that survived, anyway," and then to further add, "if any."

"You go," mumbled Vigga, fumbling with the buttons on her damp shirt. "Leave me." Each button grew more difficult. "You'd be better off . . . without me." And she gave up, and let her hands flop hopelessly in her lap, and her lip wobbled, and she started to blub again. "I'm so thirsty!"

Brother Diaz issued a pained sigh and let go of his trousers to rub at his temples, but that allowed his trousers to slump down his arse, and he was forced to hitch them up yet again.

They had stripped the corpses of two drowned oarsmen washed up on the beach, while Brother Diaz tried not to look at their faces. Tried not to wonder if they had families back home waiting for them. His newfound compassion for his allies was causing him enough trouble, compassion for his enemies was a luxury he could ill afford. The smaller oarsman's trousers were too big for him, wet cloth flapping loose but still managing to chafe. The larger oarsman's shirt, meanwhile, was too small for Vigga, cheap material strained across her chest to bursting.

"God almighty," he muttered, "what a pair."

She glanced up at him.

"Of people!" he said, hurriedly. "You and I." Making sure he was gazing purposefully off towards the dunes and not at all towards her overworked shirt. "That is the pair I was thinking of. We *really* should head on down the coast—"

"You go. Before I kill you, too." Vigga mournfully dipped her fingers in the rock pool. "I'm not safe." And she wretchedly raised them to her mouth and miserably sucked them. "I'm not clean." She tipped her head back, closing her eyes, tears squeezed down her cheeks, and howled at the spitting skies. "It's all salty!"

"Yes," said Brother Diaz through clenched teeth, "it's *the sea*. Why am I having to explain how the shore works to a Viking? Scandinavia is *all shore*!"

He pressed at the bridge of his nose. Losing his temper wouldn't help. The one thing it might achieve, in fact, was making Vigga lose *her* temper, and that *definitely* wouldn't help. Someone would have to be calm, strong, and confident. Someone would have to actually *lead*. It said everything about the lamentable failure of their mission thus far that the person best equipped to do it . . . was him.

"Listen to me." He squatted beside Vigga, and reached out, paused, and finally patted her awkwardly on the arm. God, it was firm, like patting a warm tree. "I couldn't leave you even if I wanted to. Her Holiness made you my responsibility, and . . . I owe you, and . . . the truth is I'm utterly lost, and . . . these trousers don't fit *at all*, and . . . without you I'll likely get killed ten strides off the sand." Vigga gave a great sniff and blinked at him with wet eyes. "I'll admit you're an embarrassment at a dinner, and far from helpful on a pilgrimage, but we likely have fights ahead of us and no one could deny . . . in a fight . . ." He puffed out his cheeks. "You're magnificent."

Vigga gave a last, thoughtful sniff. When she wiped her face, she was left looking slightly smug. "*Magnificent* is a good word."

"It *is* a good word." Brother Diaz grinned ever so slightly, too. He felt a sensation he only dimly remembered, from the time before he took his vows. Was he . . . *proud* of himself? He gripped Vigga's shoulder a little more firmly. "Now. Did you see any of the others get off the ships?"

She winced, as if thinking back was a painful effort. "I remember blood . . . I remember oarsmen running . . . more blood . . ."

"That does tally," Brother Diaz licked his lips, "with my recollection—"

"Wait." Vigga frowned at him. "Did you stand up to the wolf?"

"Well . . . when Jakob did it, at the inn—"

"Jakob can't die. You can."

"I am . . ." Brother Diaz ever so gently peeled his hand from her shoulder. "Acutely aware of that fact."

Vigga considered him through narrowed eyes. "You are much braver than I thought."

His turn to look slightly smug. "Oh. Well—"

"Also much stupider."

"Oh. Well—"

"Don't tempt the wolf, Brother Diaz. Not ever. You cannot trust it. You cannot bargain with it." Vigga clapped a hand onto his shoulder so hard she nearly knocked him on his back. "I will keep that bastard muzzled from now on. But you need to stop this whining!" She pushed herself up so firmly she nearly dragged him onto his face. "We have to head on down the coast. The others . . ." She planted one bare foot on a rock and glared off southwards, jaw set. "Are likely scattered across these beaches."

"Thank God you're here," muttered Brother Diaz, only a little sour. "You think they're still alive?"

"Alex is, at least." Vigga held up her wrist, the brown streak across it barely visible between the various scars and tattoos. "Pope Benedicta's binding. Still tugging on me."

"That's good news!" said Brother Diaz, jumping up.

"I know! Thank God I'm here. I mean . . . she could be *about* to die."

Brother Diaz felt the distinct sinking sensation that always came hard on the heels of any relief. "Right."

"She could be bleeding from a dozen wounds, or horribly burned, or in the clutches of . . . I don't know . . . goblins?"

"Goblins?" asked Brother Diaz, alarmed.

"If you say so. But she's alive!" And Vigga strode off purposefully towards the dunes. "For now."

Not the First Time

Alex came to being slapped in the face.

Sad to say, it wasn't the first time.

She tried to utter an, "Ugh," but coughed up a mouthful of salty water instead, rolled over, groaning, and coughed up another.

She lay on her face, clutching two fistfuls of sand, just breathing for a while. Even her lungs hurt.

"Ugh," she managed, in the end. Hardly seemed worth it, for all the effort.

"You're alive, then."

Alex managed to lift her head far enough to get some hint of her surroundings. Sand, stretching up towards a rocky shore. Her face throbbed. Every part of it felt twice the usual size. Except her tongue, which felt three times the usual size.

"Where arth we?" she croaked.

Sunny stepped into view, wind stirring the white hair about her face. "On the beach."

Slowly, painfully, Alex rolled onto her back. "What beach?"

"Nearest one. Couldn't really be choosy, under the circumstances." She seemed to think a moment. "I don't often get to be choosy."

"Thircumthtances?"

"You know, ship sinking, you drowning, everyone drowning."

"Wait . . ." Slowly, painfully, Alex propped herself on her elbows. Two grooves stretched from the end of her legs down the sand, then faded into nothingness where the highest waves lapped. "How did I get here?"

Sunny shrugged. "I'm a strong swimmer."

Slowly, painfully, Alex sat up. Her arms were covered in scrapes. One leg of her wet trousers was ripped to the knee. Her chest felt like someone had taken a battering ram to it. But she was starting to suspect she wasn't dead. "Everyone says elveth are awful."

"I've heard it said."

"But all the elves I've met have been fantathtic."

"Have you met a lot?"

Slowly, painfully, Alex twisted around onto her hands and knees, then paused there to catch her breath. "Jutht you."

"Oh. That's . . . nice." And Sunny frowned. Like she trusted a compliment far less than an insult.

Alex tried to sniff and didn't enjoy it much. "Think my nose is broken."

Sad to say, it wasn't the first time.

Sunny squatted in front of her and put her fingertips on her cheeks, so gently Alex hardly felt it, and pressed at her nose with her thumbs. Looking into those big, calm, careful eyes made Alex feel a little calmer herself.

A little. Not a lot.

She was a bit disappointed when Sunny took her hands away and stood. "It's just bumped."

"It got smashed with a mast," grumbled Alex.

"Do you want it broken? I could get a rock."

"Pray don't trouble yourself. You've already done *so* much." She gave a pained grunt as she worked one leg under herself. "They might put me down . . ." Then a weary groan as she stood. "But I'll never stay down—woah!" And she had to catch hold of Sunny's arm as a gust nearly blew her over. The windswept sand, the balding dunes beyond it, the wooded hills beyond them, held no more appeal from a slightly higher angle. Less, if anything. "What now?"

"Get whatever we can use." And Sunny nodded towards a scattering of junk washed up at the high-water mark.

"Steal stuff?" Alex took a breath and blew it out. "That, I can do."

Took a while to unravel a tangle of rope still attached to a splintered spar and drag away a stretch of singed sailcloth, but there was an inlaid chest underneath that got the old thief's palms tickling. The lock was nowhere near as good as the inlay, only took a few bashes with an oar to get it open.

Alex pulled out the first thing in there and held it up. A red jacket with epaulettes and shiny embroidery, its gilded buttons shaped like griffins' faces.

Sunny eyed it doubtfully. "There is a strong flavour of military arsehole about that jacket."

"Must be Constans's clothes. He'd a strong flavour of military arsehole about him, too." Alex started undoing the buttons. "You reckon he survived?"

"He was fighting Jakob to the death. So I'd guess no." Sunny shrugged. "Jakob is one man you should never fight to the death." She paused a moment. "Since he can't die."

"That's some good news," said Alex, pushing one arm into the jacket.

"I mean, he could be trapped in the wreck on the bottom of the Adriatic.

Or squished to mincemeat. Or burned to bacon." Sunny thought a moment. "Or all three."

"That's less good news," said Alex, pushing the other arm in.

Sunny shrugged again. "I've learned not to worry about what I can't change."

"Never had that knack," said Alex as she did up the buttons. "The less I can change it, the more it worries me."

"Aren't you worried about everything all the time?"

"Absolutely shitting myself. How do I look?"

Sunny raised one brow. "Like the Empress of Troy."

"Well, it's much like what I normally wear." Alex struck the sort of pose you might see on a general in a painting. "In the alleys of the Holy City." The jacket was way too big for her, but she did her best to fill it, swan not duck, the way Baron Rikard had shown her.

"Your strong flavour of military arsehole must have stood out among the beggars," said Sunny.

Alex stuck her chin towards the sky. "I stand out in any company."

"I fade away in any company," murmured Sunny. "Like a whisper in a hurricane."

"You've always made an impression on me," said Alex.

Sunny frowned. "Shush."

"I just meant—"

"Shush! Someone's coming."

Alex felt that familiar sucking in the pit of her stomach as Sunny caught her by the wrist and they ran for the dunes. That mingling of *oh no* terror, *not again* despair, and *why me* outrage. The same things she'd felt when she saw the galley slip from its hiding place and bear down on them, how many months ago?

That morning. It had been that morning.

Alex laboured up a dune, sliding back almost as far as she went forwards with each step, oversized jacket flapping around her, and finally threw herself over the crest on her stomach, spitting sand.

Dark figures moved, out on the pale shore. Her sight swam too much to count them. Then she saw the tracks she'd left. A pattern of dents leading straight up the dune, sure as a great finger pointing right to her hiding place.

She slid down below the crest, pressing herself against the sand, eyes closed. "Maybe they'll be helpful?" she muttered. Like a prayer. "Maybe they'll be nice, and have, I don't know . . . pastries?" She almost added an *amen* to the end.

"Best not bet your life on it," murmured Sunny, peering through the thin grass on the crest. "I count eight. Well armed. Can't see any pastries but one's got a thing . . . like a corkscrew."

"Big wine drinker, maybe?"

"*Way* too big for a cork."

"What's it for, then?" said Alex, a desperate whine to her voice.

"I almost feel . . . I'd rather not know." Sunny hunched down slightly, a hand on Alex's shoulder. "They're looking at the chest."

"Maybe that's what they're after," whispered Alex. "Maybe they're military arseholes, too." She could hear voices, faintly, on the wind. "What are they saying?"

"They're saying the Dane's on his way. They seem worried about it."

"Who's the Dane? Oh God. Who worries a man with a giant corkscrew?"

Sunny didn't bother to answer. "They're leaving the stuff on the beach," she murmured, narrowing her eyes. "They're looking for something else."

Alex swallowed. She didn't want to say the word, but there was no getting away from it. "Me?"

"Think we'd better move," whispered Sunny, slithering down the back-slope of the dune on her belly.

"Oh God," whispered Alex, slithering after her. "Did they see the tracks?"

"They're showing some interest in them." Sunny caught Alex under the arm and pulled her up. "Think we'd better run now!"

So Alex ran.

Sad to say, it was *not* the first time.

Prone to Turmoil

ick, damn it!"

"What *precisely* do you think I've been doing for the past few *exhausting* hours?" snarled Balthazar through chattering teeth. "Hanging here *limp*?"

"The word I'd use is . . ." Baptiste narrowed her eyes as a wave smacked the side of her head and plastered soaking hair across her face. She blew it away with an explosive snort. "*Flaccid*. Now kick!"

Balthazar issued a sound of elemental discomfort and redoubled his efforts to kick for the shore. Honestly, the use of the term *shore* was lending it too much dignity. It was a jagged jumble of rock that hemmed in a frothing inlet where the waves were funnelled and amplified, clapping against stone to send explosions of spray as high as a building, washing them straight back towards a watery grave whenever their raft made the slightest progress. Honestly, the use of the term *raft* was lending it *far* too much dignity, as it consisted of three of the stricken galley's great oars, bound together with Balthazar's belt at one end and Baptiste's at the other.

"Kick, I said!"

"I *am* kicking!" he snarled, immediately receiving a lungful of brine that left him choking. He had breathed more water than air since they entered this cursed inlet. It would have been a fitting irony had they wrestled with the freezing Adriatic for hours merely to drown within arm's reach of land.

A last desperate effort brought them close enough for Baptiste to cling to a protruding knobble and heave herself onto the rocks.

"Out!" she hissed, face twisted into a rictus as she strained to keep her grip on the raft.

"Do you suppose . . . I am trying . . . to stay *in*?"

A wave buffeted Balthazar against stone and he had just the strength of mind to cling on by his fingertips as it surged away. The rocks were slippery with seaweed, crusted with razor-sharp barnacles, and he scrabbled at them with his bare feet, slipping, sliding, struggling desperately for purchase.

"Ah . . . God . . . no . . . yes!"

He caught a stubborn limpet with his big toe and, trembling with effort, propelled himself upwards to finally roll gasping onto his back like a landed fish, shivering and quivering, thoroughly battered and bloodied from the ordeal. It was only with a stupendous effort of self-control that he was able to stop himself from weeping with exhaustion.

"Thanks *so* much for the help!" he screeched at Baptiste as he sat up.

"You looked like you had it," she snapped, heaving their raft up onto the rocks.

"It truly *warms my heart* to see you would rather salvage your *oars*—and without a boat to row with them, mark you—than help the man who moments ago *saved your life!*"

"Well, I like this belt," she growled, undoing the buckle and pulling it slapping free. "As for saving lives, I could've sworn I saved yours twice. Gratitude costs nothing, you know."

"Gratitude?" breathed Balthazar. She might be soaking wet and barefoot, but had at least emerged from the brine clothed from neck to ankles. Balthazar had kicked his own trousers off to move more freely in the water, and the wind was now giving him considerable cause to regret his choice. "I did not think it *possible* that I could be *colder* than I was in the *sea*. Now I discover my error!"

"Doubt it's your first, since you chose to hide in the hold of a sinking ship." And she glared at him as she wrung out a fistful of hair that immediately sprang into unruly curls. "Feel free to dive back in."

"Gratitude?" hissed Balthazar, waving towards the bleak interior, the chilly sea, the spitting sky. He had barely the strength to speak but did not allow that to stop him. "For being shipwrecked God knows where on the barren Dalmatian shore?"

"You're alive, aren't you?" she snarled, with the strong implication that he was only so on her sufferance.

"*Gratitude*, she says! One could not hope to *come* upon a more forbearing man than I—"

She planted her hands on her hips and arched right back to bellow, "Ha!" at the sky.

"—but I feel it only fair to *warn* you that even *my* patience has a *limit*." He stomped to the oars, furiously waving his arms. "I have a *belt*," and he ripped the damp thing free and shook it in her face, "but *no trousers*! What am I to *do*, might I *ask*, with a *belt* but no—"

"Belt your fucking jaw shut with it!" screamed Baptiste, then clutched at her head. "I am the most easy-going woman in Europe—"

Balthazar planted his hands on his hips and arched right back to bellow, "Ha!" at the sky.

"—I've made common cause with witches, rubbed along with pirates, co-operated with trolls," she stuck her fingers in his face one by one, "humourless cardinals, arsehole aristocrats, even that bloody rotten ghost thing that was haunting the sewers in Genoa—"

"Sad I missed *that* adventure."

"—I have yet to meet a *fucking* magician I liked and I've *always* found a way to work with the bastards, but I swear to *God* you . . . what?" she snapped, frowning suspiciously at him.

He had begun to smile. "I could not help noticing that you grouped me among the magicians."

She put her hands over her face. "I should've quit after Barcelona."

"You are *warming* to me! It was but a matter of time before you began to treat me with the deference due to one of Europe's foremost arcane minds!"

Baptiste glared at the ground. "Saviour, I wish you'd drowned."

"Before long you will be boasting of having had me, for a brief time, as a friend and colleague."

Baptiste winced at the sky. "Saviour, I wish *I'd* drowned."

"In due course, we will—urgh." Balthazar bent over at a surge of nausea, spit rushing into his mouth. "Feeling a little—urgh."

"It's the binding." Baptiste looked inland. "Princess Alexia must've survived."

Balthazar was obliged to hunch over at another spasm. "Glad tidings pile one upon the next."

"We'll have to find her."

"And how, *precisely*, do you suggest we do that? Any survivors could be scattered over fifty miles of shoreline! Urgh." And he was doubled over by an even more unpleasant pang, spit rushing into his mouth and his head spinning. "We would need a *miracle* to track her down."

Baptiste bent to snarl the words right in his ear. "If only I had one of Europe's foremost *fucking* arcane minds along with me!"

"Divination is far from my strongest suit . . ." Cold, sick, desperate, Balthazar did his best to remember what his strongest suit had been. To grope from the murk of his misery and, in spite of the adverse circumstances, the impossible task, the complete lack of resources, support, or even trousers, nonetheless grasp a solution. "But . . . *perhaps* . . . I could devise a ritual . . . given access to an appropriate confluence of energetic channels—"

"A what?"

"In layman's terms, a stone circle."

"Druids?" Baptiste looked far from delighted at the notion. "Those bastards take themselves *way* too seriously."

"I am *no* enthusiast for the moss-dwelling lifestyle, *believe me*, but needs must." He took a breath, straightened, shuddered as he swallowed the latest upwash of bile and sour salt water. With a plan of action that tended towards installing Princess Alexia on the Throne of Troy, the binding was loosening its singularly unpleasant stranglehold on his digestive tract. "There is an old circle near Niksic, if I remember correctly."

"All right, then." Baptiste nodded grimly. "We head east. Take our bearings. Find supplies." She glanced across. "Get you some trousers, maybe."

"Finally, you consider my needs."

"Can't look at the twin twigs you dare to call legs a moment longer."

"I have been told I possess very finely turned calves."

"You clearly know some outrageous liars."

"Indeed I am in the company of perhaps the most egregious *right now*." Balthazar tossed his belt over his shoulder, contemplating the woods ahead. "We should be cautious. The country hereabouts is prone to turmoil."

"Well, we're due some luck." Baptiste was already picking her way up the shore. "Maybe we've come at a peaceful moment."

"God *damn* it," said Balthazar.

The valley was a scene of carnage.

Corpses of men and horses were dotted on the slopes and clogged about a stream meandering through the boggy bottom. Balthazar counted several hundred, at a glance, and when it came to counting corpses, he boasted of no little experience. Arson had been inflicted on a nearby hamlet, reduced to tangles of charred beams and a few tottering chimney stacks. A veritable legion of avian carrion pickers had gathered in the air above, as well as several dozen of the human variety on the ground below, all keen to gorge themselves upon this unexpected bounty.

He looked sideways at Baptiste, also taking in the scene of what had evidently been a significant battle. "Peaceful moment, did you say?"

"I said we're due some luck. Never said we'd get any." And she strode off down the hillside, her hair, which had transformed, as it dried, into an unmanageable cloud, blowing wildly around her.

"Plainly there is a war in progress," muttered Balthazar as he hurried to catch up.

"What gave it away?"

He took a hard breath. "Who do we think is fighting?"

"Serbians?"

He took an even harder breath. "When in Serbia, a reasonable assumption. But which ones, against whom?"

Baptiste stopped, leaning towards a corpse. "Who are you fighting?" she asked, then turned her ear downwards. The corpse made no reply. "Can't get a thing out of him," she said, walking on.

"Is it your purpose in life to frustrate and annoy me?" grumbled Balthazar.

"Only a hobby." Baptiste struck from the path, between the cadavers now thickly scattered in the trampled grass. "Get yourself some clothes, some boots, and anything else we can use."

"From the dead?" asked Balthazar.

"Doubt they'll complain." She rolled a body as carelessly as a cooper might an empty barrel and began to root through the pockets with quick fingers. "You're the last man I'd have thought would get coy around a carcass."

"My interest in the dead is to plumb the very mysteries of creation, not to procure loose change!" But Baptiste was pretending not to listen. Balthazar gave a heavy sigh, hooked his hands under a corpse of approximately the right dimensions, and gingerly rolled it over. A young officer, clammy with morning dew, good looks somewhat spoiled by a yawning axe wound in his skull. Balthazar squatted and began to unlace one boot.

"Damn it . . ." The knots were exceedingly tight. Hardly surprising, perhaps. Balthazar would have tied his laces securely had he been charging into battle. Which he would, of course, never have been fool enough to do. "Damn it . . ." His fingers were exceedingly numb. Hardly surprising, either, since he had spent the afternoon being buffeted in the ocean and those few clothes he had managed to retain were still damp with chilly seawater. "*Damn* it . . ."

"Well?"

Baptiste stood over him, hands on hips. She had procured a pair of shiny horseman's knee boots complete with brass spurs, and an extravagant military coat only lightly splattered with blood from a hole above the breast, beneath which the hilts of four assorted daggers bristled from a purple sash. Apart from a few damp curls, which he suspected she had left loose on purpose, she had managed to contain her ever rebellious hair in a leather forester's cap sporting a bedraggled feather.

Balthazar gazed up, astonished. However much he might have wanted to, there was no denying that, yet again, she looked spectacular. "How the hell have you managed all this? I haven't even got his boots off yet!"

She worked the sash down her hips for a more rakish tilt. "I spent a bit of time as a corpse-robber."

"How incredibly unsurprising," he muttered, deeply conscious of how ludicrous he must look at that moment by comparison, picking angrily at the knots on the other boot then cursing as he bent a fingernail the wrong way.

"During some local unpleasantness in Prussia." Baptiste rolled up her embroidered cuffs. "It's more art than science, really, you're just . . ." And she narrowed her eyes and rubbed her fingertips against her thumbs. "Feeling out the good stuff." She slid an overblown man's signet ring onto her middle finger. "What d'you think?"

"I think you're ready to seal some very important letters."

"Not for the first time. I used to melt wax for the Duke of Aquitaine, in fact."

"You amaze me," he forced through gritted teeth, tugging harder at the knots.

"He'd sign hundreds at once," she said, bending over a face-down corpse. "Administrative nonsense, mostly. Couple of love letters. Got through a *lot* of wax." She gripped both trouser legs. "After a day of that you'd end up with sticky fingers, I can tell you."

"A regular occurrence for you, I have no doubt."

"Didn't last long at it." And Baptiste whipped the trousers clean off with one skillful jerk. "The duke could be rather handsy."

"Dukes often are, I understand—ah!" As the knots finally gave and Balthazar was able to work the second boot from its dead owner's foot.

Baptiste tossed the trousers to him. "Those should fit you."

He was obliged to sit in the sodden grass to wriggle into them, unpleasantly clammy about the thigh, then started dragging on the boots. "Damn it . . . blast it . . . bloody things are too small!" He flung one away and it bounced through the grass, rolling to a stop at the feet of one of the human scavengers: a particularly ill-favoured example of a generally ill-favoured profession, sporting a bumper crop of facial warts. He looked from boot to Balthazar with a belligerent scowl.

Balthazar scowled back with no greater affection as he stalked barefoot to another body and squatted beside it. "I generally adore receiving unexpected visitors, but I find burglarising the dead is like taking one's toilet, best done without an audience."

The man gave a squint of warty befuddlement. "This is all ours," he grunted.

"Impressive." Balthazar glanced about the valley. "You killed the whole lot?"

"No, but . . ." The wart collector folded his arms, waxing more bellicose by the moment. "We found 'em."

"It's a battlefield. You can't lay claim to it like a gold strike. We're not subject to mining law here. Baptiste, could you explain to this gentleman?"

"He with you?" growled the man whose warts had warts.

Baptiste produced an expression of intense innocence. No mean feat from a woman freshly decked out in dead men's finery. "Never saw him before," she said.

Balthazar gritted his teeth. "My thanks for your *unflinching* support."

Perhaps half a dozen corpse pickers had gathered now, a couple brandishing weapons salvaged from the fallen. A woman with an old cloth wrapped around her head pointed at Balthazar with a short sword. "Who the fuck does this bastard think he is?"

"Aye." The warts around the man's mouth performed an intricate dance as his lip twisted. "Who the *fuck* d'you think you are, bastard?"

Balthazar frowned. Perhaps finally putting trousers back on, albeit those of a dead man, had restored some hint of his old confidence. Perhaps Baptiste's many barbs had finally worn through his frayed patience. Or perhaps he had simply endured one humiliation too many, and the contempt of such contemptible dregs as these was too much to bear. A bubble of cold fury rose within his breast, while in the grass around his feet the dead began to twitch in sympathy.

"Who do *I . . .*" Balthazar slowly rose, and the thieves shrank against each other in predictable horror as perhaps two dozen corpses jerked, wobbled, and tottered up with him, all apart from one unfortunate trooper who had lost a leg and kept falling over. ". . . think I *am*?"

The blade dropped from the woman's limp fingers as the young officer turned towards her, fluid bubbling from his nose as his lungs spluttered into reflexive action with a sound like a punctured bellows, a string of brains hanging from the yawning wound in his skull.

"My name is Balthazar Sham Ivam Draxi." He pronounced each syllable with withering precision. "And you should know that I teeter on a lethal precipice at the very *limit* of my patience. Now . . ." He stepped towards the stunned wart collector, so close their toes were almost touching. It appeared, from a cursory assay, that their feet were of comparable dimensions. "I think you may be wearing *my boots*."

Bit by a Monk

"This way," said Vigga, striding on through the dunes, enjoying how the sandy grass and grassy sand felt 'twixt her toes. She'd always been happiest by the water. Beaches and coves and harbours and wharves. That crinkly ribbon of the world where land and sea meet, and fight, and fuck, and grind each other into new shapes like ill-matched lovers in an endless stormy romance neither can ever escape.

The thought of that style of romance set off a bit of a tickle, in fact.

She vaguely remembered being upset about something but it hardly seemed worth groping around in all the horrible mess in her memory just so she could feel upset about it again. Whenever she went looking for something in her head, she never came out with anything she wanted. Like diving for oysters in a fucking midden. Better to let it go.

"Like nutshells," she muttered.

"Nutshells?" asked Brother Diaz.

Vigga grinned sideways. "Exactly!" He'd a fine, long stride when he actually used all his legs, and didn't weigh himself down with his prayers and his doubts and his saints and whatever. "Who'd have thought, when we first met at that inn, we'd end up getting such an understanding?"

Brother Diaz puffed out his cheeks. "Life brims over with surprises."

"You look different," she said. "Out o' your monk sack."

"It's called a habit."

"Then it's a bad habit. Ha! Bad habit, 'cause, you see—"

"Yes," he said, "I see."

"You're not laughing."

"There aren't many jokes about the life of a monk that a monk won't have heard a thousand times." He gave a rather wistful sigh. "In the monastery, there's plenty of time to think of them."

"Well, whatever you call it, you look different out of it," said Vigga. "More . . ." She dug for the word but got distracted by the way his damp shirt kept sticking and unsticking to his side with each step. She could see the shape of his ribs through it, then they were gone, then they were back, then gone, like they were winking. Good ribs, they were, gone, back—

She realised he was watching her. "More what?"

"Exactly! It's like they put you in sacks to make you look bad."

"I imagine that's precisely why they do it. It's been a while . . . since I wore anything but the sack. I never even wanted to be a monk."

"Who'd have thought, when we first met at that inn, we'd have so much in common," said Vigga. "I never even wanted to be a werewolf."

"How did it happen?"

"Usual way. Bit by a werewolf." And she undid the top couple of buttons on her shirt, which honestly were more or less undoing themselves, so she could peel it back to show him her shoulder, and the mottled ring of scars with the rings of runes around it. "Still aches, sometimes. When the moon's full."

"It's true, then?" asked Brother Diaz, peering over. She might've been imagining it, but she could've sworn his eyes strayed away from the bite a bit. "What they say about werewolves and the moon?"

Vigga stopped, closing her eyes. Just the word. *Moooooooooon.* She saw it on the inside of her lids, at its roundest and most swollen, hanging in the black with its soft and sultry silvery glow like a great ripe fruit in the sky, ready to burst with the sweetest juice, and she made a little noise, not quite a howl but a sort of whimpery coo, and shivered all the way from her hair to her tippy-toes. "Oh, it's true," she whispered.

"Right," said Brother Diaz, and cleared his throat.

"And you?" she asked, setting off again, doing up the hard-pressed buttons.

"To me it's . . . only the moon."

"No, I mean, how d'you become a monk?"

"The usual way. Bit by a monk."

She stared sideways. "Really?"

"No. Not really."

"Ah! Ah-ha! Who'd have thought, when we first met at that inn, you'd turn out such a joker!" And she thumped him playfully on the arm which it looked like he didn't at all enjoy. She never could quite learn the lesson that punching people wasn't always a good thing. She made a note to remember that, then right off forgot and thumped him again.

"I took the vows," he said, rubbing his arm. "I chose to take them."

"Saw the light, did you?"

Brother Diaz kicked at the grassy sand. "Something like that."

"I'd like to see the light," said Vigga. "Folk keep trying to show it to me, but you can't just choose to see it, can you? And I can't help thinking, all the while I'm looking, that if you'll wake up one day and see the light, who's to say you won't wake up the next day and see a different one?"

"Well . . . a thing's either true or not," said Brother Diaz, but with a kind of puzzled frown. "It doesn't all depend on who you ask . . . does it?"

"It does a bit. I mean, even the Saved in the West and the Saved in the East are in spasm, or whatever."

"Schism."

"Like I said. What is one, anyway?"

"A great rupture and disagreement between the two arms of the Church! Over the tripartite nature of God, and the precise wording of the Creed, and whether one should take the circle or the wheel as the holy symbol, and whether priests should be women in the image of the Saviour, or men in the image of her Father and, of course, some particularly bitter arguments over the calculation of the date of Easter . . ." He sounded like he was getting a bit confused himself and he was a monk. "There's no point digging too far into the details—"

"Lord be praised."

"—but the Pope excommunicated the Patriarch then the Patriarch excommunicated the Pope . . . or was it the other way around . . ."

"Whichever. You've got two voices of God on earth shouting over each other right there." She held up two fingers then kept on counting 'em off. "Then you've got the Followers of the Five Lessons and the Doubters, too. Then there's cults of this saint or that and your angel or mine, and all kinds o' pagans and druids and shaman and spirit-worshippers and demon-worshippers before we even get to the elves and whatever dark and hungry many-faced fuckers they worship." She'd run out of fingers somewhere and was going back the other way, so she threw up her hands instead. "They're all certain as can be they've got the truth, but they've each got a different truth, don't they? Still, I'm a well-known fucking idiot, what do I know? If you've seen the light, I'm happy for you, the world's a dark enough place without—"

"I didn't become a monk because I saw the light!" snapped Brother Diaz, which was a timely refresher 'cause Vigga had fully forgot where this conversation began. "I made . . . a mistake."

"You became a monk by mistake? I would've asked what the sack was all about before—"

"No! I made a mistake, so I *had* to become a monk."

Vigga felt a faint tingling of interest. "Did you kill someone, Brother Diaz?"

"No!"

"I won't judge. I myself have killed several people."

"I've seen you kill at least three dozen with my own eyes! I didn't kill anyone!"

"What did you steal? Was it candlesticks? Was it pie? Was it . . . hold on, I'll get it—"

"Are you just going to list everything there is?"

Vigga shrugged. "We've got time."

Brother Diaz closed his eyes. "I didn't steal anything."

"Was it bacon?" The mention of pie had made her thoughts stray towards food.

"No."

"Cheese?" she asked, hopefully. "Peas?"

"I got a girl pregnant!" barked Brother Diaz. He gave a long sigh, and said, much more softly, "There you are. That's the awful truth. Why hide it out here?" He tipped his head back and bellowed it at the sky. "I got a girl pregnant!" Whipped away instantly on the wind and gone. "The wrong girl," he added, gloomily. "The most wrong girl available."

"Brother Diaz," murmured Vigga, "are you hiding a lustful past?"

"No." He looked straight back at her. "I'm telling you about it right to your face. I was reckless, in my youth, and I got the wrong girl pregnant. My mother said a monk's vows were the only way out. For my redemption. For my protection. To spare my family from embarrassment."

"Huh." Vigga still had some water squelching deep in one of her ears and she stuck her finger in and waggled it about. "I'm a bit disappointed."

"Who'd have thought," grunted Brother Diaz, "when we first met at that inn, you and my mother would have so much in common."

"Not by you, by your crimes." Vigga tried tipping her head one way, then the other, but the water wasn't shifting. "I mean, being what I am, I've heard of . . . and seen . . . and, you know, *done* . . . some really diabolical outrages." Vigga gave up waggling and thumped her ear with the heel of her hand. "Fucking the wrong girl? I wouldn't put it on the list of the most shameful secrets I've heard. I wouldn't even put it *near* the list. Ah!" The bubble burst in her ear and that delicious trickle of warm water came tickling out. "Hah! I got it! What were we talking about?"

"The wrong girl," murmured Brother Diaz.

"Right, yes. You've got to shrug it off. Toss it away." And Vigga wiped out her ear and flicked away the water.

"Like nutshells?" he grunted.

"Exactly!" And she thumped him again. "When you've eaten the nuts, you don't keep the shells, do you? Till you're dragging sacks of the bastards up every hill? Till you're sleeping in a great heap of the fuckers?"

The details of the story were already fading. As far as Vigga was concerned, there was just one important lesson to take away from it.

Brother Diaz's cock worked.

"Ah! Look!" she said, pointing to some rubbish scattered on the beach. "Must've floated from the wrecks."

"The others might've floated here, too!" Brother Diaz hurried towards it. A big chest sat on the sand, ringed by scattered footprints, lock broken and lid pushed back. "Clothes," he said, peering in.

Vigga dragged a jacket up, bright cloth all covered in glinting thread. "The clothes of a fancy bastard." She sniffed it, and she sniffed around the chest, and she bent down to sniff the footprints, too. "Alex was here."

"You know her smell?"

"I know everyone's smell."

"Everyone has a smell?"

"Oh yes."

Brother Diaz glanced down at himself. "Do I?"

"*Oh* yes. Sunny was here, too."

"What does Sunny smell of?"

"You know, sort of salty. That salty elf smell. They weren't alone, either." She dropped to her hands and knees to get her nose to the ground and her tongue out so she could really taste it. "Men . . . several men . . . several badly washed men."

"What were they after?" asked Brother Diaz. "Were they chasing Princess Alexia?"

"I'm a werewolf," said Vigga, frowning up at him, "not a clairvoyant."

"No. Right. Sorry."

"We did have a clairvoyant, once, but not for long. The thing I learned is . . . it's usually better *not* to know. They went this way." She loped on a few paces, still bent over, then sat on her haunches to sift at the wind. "Maybe being careful. Maybe being chased." She crept up a dune and snuffled at the scratty grass where the scent was stronger. "They waited here . . . then headed that way." She nodded towards the trees, then froze, narrowing her eyes.

"What is it?"

"Something else." She crawled sniffling around the hollow, pushing away salty sea and salty elf and scared princess and the distracting scent of Brother Diaz, and—

Her lips curled back. Her nostrils flared. She felt the wolf awake, prowling within the cage of her ribs, scratching to be released, and its growl came from deep in her throat—a long, low, warning throb.

"What do you smell?" whispered Brother Diaz, looking slightly scared.

Vigga glared up at him and snarled the word, turned to a slurred gurgle by the angry spit rushing into her mouth. "Werewolf."

The Current Set of Enemies

Sunny crouched in the damp brush, in the gathering darkness towards sunset, and kept watch on her current set of enemies.

Four men, a woman, and a werewolf.

She spent a lot more of her time than she'd have liked holding her breath while slinking, skulking, and slithering through wet vegetation. Also muddy crawlspaces, cobwebby attics, ditches, cellars, and sewers. She'd much rather have been sitting in plain sight in a dry room, in a comfy chair, breathing easily and having her opinions taken very seriously. Like Cardinal Zizka.

But Jakob had been right. They weren't going to make an enemy of God a cardinal and it was high time she accepted it. Who gets to pick their place, after all? You just get crammed into the slot the world finds for you on account of your luck and what you're good at.

Sunny was a natural spy with the shittest luck imaginable.

So she kept low, like usual, in the shadows, like usual, her breath mostly held and her shoulders mostly hunched against the cold, peering through the wet fronds towards the fire.

The four men and the woman sat on one side of it, talking a bit, passing a bottle, tending to a steaming pot, and sharpening quite the arsenal of weapons. The werewolf sat apart on the other side, and all he had was a little knife, firelight winking on its blade as he whittled a stick. Not a particularly sinister pastime, but he managed to make it off-putting as stacking skulls. Maybe once you know someone might at any moment turn into a slavering bull-sized monster, everything he does seems sinister.

Sunny sighed, from right down in her stomach.

For her, making a friend could take years, but new enemies popped up like mushrooms after the rain. Glance out your window in the morning and there they were, by the dozen.

Not that she had a window, of course. They mostly kept her in a cellar.

Talking of mushrooms, she tugged up a few more of the Nun's Worries scattered among the roots and added them to her handful. This many wouldn't kill anyone who ate them. But they'd be far too busy shitting water to chase any would-be Empresses.

Or any invisible elves, for that matter.

She was wondering about the best way to sneak them into the stew when her ears pricked up at hoofbeats, and she held her breath and wriggled deeper among the roots. The four men and the woman reached for weapons, but when they saw riders come from the trees into the light, they gave the sort of grins you give folk you're expecting.

More enemies, then.

Sunny gently shook her head. Given how hard she tried to be liked, it was amazing how she could stack 'em up.

She counted eight riders, led by a man with a great golden cloak, gathered up high across his shoulders and trailing over the hindquarters of a skittish warhorse. Sunny learned in the circus you can usually judge a person's character from how they treat their animals. The way this cloaked fellow wrenched the reins around made her reckon him quite the arsehole, and his comrades looked no better. There was a tall, gaunt, lank-haired bastard who glowered at everything like he was thinking of eating it, and a pair of smirking women with identical shaved heads, angular as anvils, who had quite the sorcerous flavour.

So she was up to fourteen enemies, purposeful, powerful, and prepared. Staying in the damp brush had rarely seemed so appealing, but if she did nothing, they'd catch Alex tomorrow, or maybe the day after. So Sunny dragged a breath to the deepest corners of her lungs, closed her fingers tight around her Nun's Worries, and scurried closer.

"Duke Sabbas!" called the bastard with the corkscrew, standing up with a salesman's grin.

"Where are the others?" asked the one with the cloak, and his voice was all silk and honey. So he was Sabbas. Alex's cousins certainly had some extravagance when it came to tailoring. Sunny would've liked more extravagance in her tailoring. But spying really demands a low-key look.

"Jenny the Promise and her boys are up the coast," said Corkscrew, "and Angelo's lot went searching the other way." As if the odds hadn't been bad enough already. "We've sent people to bring 'em back . . ." The man paused a moment, licking his lips as he glanced at the werewolf. "Now the Dane's got her scent."

"She's not alone," said the Dane, not even looking up from his whittling. His voice was icebergs crashing into an angry bear pack and it made Sunny's neck hairs prickle.

"Who's with her?" asked one of the sorcerous twins, firelight gleaming in her narrowed eyes.

"By the smell . . . an elf."

Werewolves have deadly keen noses. Vigga could sniff Sunny out even when she couldn't see her. She said she had a salty elf smell, which Sunny found rather unfair, as Vigga smelled like a damp haystack. So she made sure she stayed well downwind as she wriggled through the grass, closer to the fire.

"An elf?" sneered the gaunt man. "Here?"

Now the Dane peered up from his knife, firelight catching the warnings tattooed onto his craggy face. "I know what an elf smells like," he growled, now with an added hint of slobber. "That salty elf smell."

"God damn it . . ." mouthed Sunny, tempted to sniff her pits to prove him wrong.

"Well." Sabbas perched himself beside the fire, folds of golden cloth spilling around him. "I daresay you can handle one little girl and one salty elf."

"Oh, we'll see," breathed Sunny as the mercenaries competed to give the braggiest laughs, and she sucked in another breath, even longer, and held it as she stole across the open towards the horses.

A young lad had their saddles off and was roping them together, but they sensed her coming and stirred uneasily, Sabbas's big stallion nickering and nipping at the mare beside him. The lad patted them, shushed them fondly, and Sunny felt a bit sorry for him. Someone always ends up with the blame, she'd been lumbered with far more than she deserved in her time. But she felt less sorry for him than she'd have felt being ridden down by that warhorse. So she leaned forwards and took the grip of his dagger, then flicked his ear so he whipped around, taking the scabbard with him and leaving her holding the drawn blade. She ducked under his arm while he looked about, rubbing his ear, then got down on his knees with some rope to hobble the horses.

He did a very conscientious job of it, too, tugging the knots tight and checking each one thoroughly. His problem was that Sunny was following along behind him, ribs starting to ache from holding her breath so long, sawing through each one with his own dagger as soon as he finished it.

He stood, slapping his palms together, very pleased with his work. Sunny slipped up next to the stallion making it dance, one eye rolling towards her.

"What the—" The lad had spotted his empty scabbard. Then he saw the hobbles on the nearest horse were cut. Then he saw they were all cut. Stealing the horses would've been much the best thing, but now they were all riled and jostling and had no saddles and the bastards at the fire were looking over. Sometimes you've just got to toss your plans away and blow with the wind.

So as the lad started towards the horses Sunny gave an apologetic wince, stuck out one boot to hook his shin, and sent him sprawling in the grass. Then she gave an even more apologetic wince and smacked Sabbas's horse across the rump hard as she could.

It reared and was off like a shot, cut hobbles flapping. Roped together still, the others tore off with it in a whinnying crowd.

"You damn fool!" snarled Sabbas, jumping up, and Sunny had to do a little spin around him to keep from being barged. She could've stabbed him as he passed, but Sunny never liked to stab people if she could avoid it. In her experience, the more people you stab the sooner you end up stabbed yourself.

"Get the horses!" snarled the gaunt man, waving at the others.

"Not my fault," the boy was shrieking. "Someone stole my dagger!"

"She's here!" Of a sudden the Dane was looming over Sunny, big as a house, white shavings from his whittling scattered down his front. "The elf. I *smell* her."

Sunny could smell him, too. Even holding her breath he had a haystack reek more pungent than Vigga's. He jerked his head to one side, took a sudden step forwards, and Sunny had to duck under his sweeping arm and slip around behind him. Her lungs were bursting now so she grabbed one quick breath while his bulk was screening her from the others, who were fully occupied tearing after the horses in any case, then she tiptoed around in an arc, staying behind him as he slowly turned.

"Where are you, mischief-maker?" he growled, and she could hear him snuffling at the air, sniffling for her scent. "Come out, little Loki!"

"She has hidden herself," snapped one of the sorcerous women, "but I will reveal her . . ." She caught some crystal on a thong around her neck, shut her eyes, and started muttering, cut off in a squawk as Sunny shoved her hard in the back and sent her sprawling face first into the fire.

The werewolf hugged the air where Sunny had been with both huge arms but she'd already dropped, darted between his wide-planted boots, and slipped around the flames, tossing her handful of Nun's Worries in the stew on the way and hopping over the sorceress, who was rolling about trying to slap the embers from her flowing clothes.

Really, you wear robes to a hunt you deserve everything you get.

"Sister!" shrieked her twin, eyes flicking furiously this way and that, and she thrust out her palms, heels of her hands together. A wind from nowhere ripped a wave through the grass, sending stalks whirling. As luck would have it, Sunny was lurking at the very edge of the blast, and it only plucked at her sleeve, made her ears pop, and near dragged her off her feet.

She needed no more encouragement and scurried for the treeline quick as she could. She heard fast footsteps behind but didn't slow to look back, held her breath even though her heart was thudding and her ears ringing, and slid on her side into the brush where she'd begun.

The Dane was after her, bounding on all fours across the open ground, more animal than man. She took one quick breath then slithered away into the trees. She heard him crashing through the bushes behind her, his drooling snarl hardly a voice at all.

"Where are you, salty bitch?"

Baron Rikard might've considered it a breach of etiquette, but she decided against making an introduction. Instead she wove through the trees in widening circles, the cries of Sabbas and his mercenaries fading into the distance, leading a werewolf in a spiral dance through the darkened greenwood till he hardly knew which trail he was following. She snatched a breather pressed against the dark side of a tree trunk, winked from sight, and slipped away, leaving him snapping and snarling and snuffling at the dark.

The sun was almost altogether sunk, so there was no shortage of shadows.

"Alex!" snapped Sunny, catching her by the elbow.

"You're back." Alex grinned at her, which took some of the heat out of Sunny's panic. Must be nice, to have a winning smile. "This is Sunny. The one I was telling you about."

The man and woman huddled together on the seat of their cart, shocked by Sunny's sudden appearance. Or shocked by what they could glimpse of her face. She dropped her head, pulling the peak of her hood down.

"We have to go," Sunny grunted, marching Alex away down the road, away from the cart, away from the torchlight.

"We have to go!" Alex shouted over her shoulder. "Hope you find your boy!" Then softly, to Sunny, "Are you angry with me?"

"Yes." Sunny was angry she'd put herself in danger. Or maybe she was angry at herself for giving her the chance to put herself in danger. More angry than she had any right or reason to be. "You should've stayed hidden. Like I told you."

"We can't all turn invisible. Thought I could learn a few things. I wanted to be useful."

Sunny thought about saying that would be a first, but Alex looked a bit hangdog so she didn't have the heart. Her hangdog look was quite winning, too. "So were you?" she said instead, letting go of Alex's arm, then feeling a bit guilty and patting her dirty jacket ineffectually where she'd wrinkled it.

"There's a war on. Between the Count of Niksic and the Countess of . . ." Alex crushed her face up. "No. Forgot where."

"Fighting over what?"

"Rich people stuff, I guess. Not like the rest of us, are they?"

"Says the would-be Empress of Troy."

"And I'll be pouring scorn on the ruling class till the moment my arse hits the throne."

Sunny snorted. She couldn't seem to stay annoyed with Alex. "Anything else?"

"Troy's that way." Alex pointed towards the darkened hills. "I did get some bread." She held out a stale-looking heel and Sunny's stomach gave an audible squelch. She hadn't realised till then quite how hungry she was. "Thanks," she grumbled.

"Thank them, I guess." Alex jerked her head towards the cart, dwindling into the darkness behind them. "They didn't have much."

Sunny closed her eyes as she tore a bit off. It was tough. It was dry. It was delicious. She slowly chewed, and slowly swallowed.

"Did you find them?" asked Alex. "The ones who're chasing us?"

"Yes."

"How many?"

"A few." She thought about mentioning all the weapons, and the gaunt man with the hard eyes, and the twin sorcerers, and the Dane, but Jakob sometimes said, *No one wants to hear all the truth*, so she stuck to the good news. "I slowed them down a bit."

"How'd you do that?"

"Scattered their horses. Poisoned their stew."

Alex blinked. "Remind me not to annoy you."

"I wouldn't poison you for annoying me."

"Phew."

"I'd just leave you and let fate take its course."

"Oh."

"Your cousin Sabbas was there."

Alex glanced up. "What was he like?"

"Seemed very nice, actually, not at all like his brothers."

"Really?"

"No, not really. Every bit as bad. Likely worse. He had the stupidest cloak."

Alex scrubbed at the sides of her head with her nails. "All your life you dream of being special. Having a family somewhere. Then they find you, and it turns out you *are* special. So special they want to kill you so they can steal your inheritance."

"There's still your uncle."

"Duke Michael? If he made it back to the Holy City alive. And my cousins haven't killed him since."

"If he sailed from Ancona like we were meant to, he might be in Troy already," said Sunny, still trying to stick to the good news. "Getting ready for you to arrive. With that friend of his, Lady Whatsface."

"Severa. Maybe. I guess. I hope." Alex looked less than convinced.

"How do you do it?" Sunny glanced back towards the cart, a couple of twinkling torches in the darkness now. "Make friends?"

"Start talking and see where you get to. Tell 'em a story they want to hear."

"No one wants to hear my story."

Alex shrugged. "Then tell 'em a different one."

"I'm a bad liar."

"Then leave all the bad bits out till it's only good bits."

"If I left the bad bits out there'd just be silence." An owl hooted somewhere, off in the trees, low and lonely. "I never can make friends."

And there was silence as they trudged on through the gathering darkness. Sunny felt Alex glance across at her, then away.

"You've made one," she said.

Our Heavenly Calling

Jakob woke to a stab of agony and the taste of old blood.

So. Alive, still.

Every time he came to that realisation, it was with a hint of disappointment.

Agony and the taste of blood greeted him most mornings, of course, but his bed didn't usually shudder this way, and when he tried to shift, then gave up with a groan, the pain redoubled, every jolt like a lance through his chest. And Jakob knew what a lance through the chest felt like.

He noticed a noise—a grinding clatter with the odd squeak, as of badly oiled axles—then a smell—an all-too-familiar spoiling-meat and slaughterhouse odour—and finally a hardness, as of wooden slats battering his sore shoulder blades—and it all became clear. He was in a corpse cart. Again.

How had he got here? A vague memory floated up of his company ambushed on the road to Carcassonne, a scream from the rear of the column . . . no, no, that had been years ago. He remembered the long days healing, limping around the cloister, and the inquiry, and the panel of frowning priests he'd told to fuck themselves.

Had he fallen fighting that troll, then, on the borders of Brittany? Never fight a troll, it's the first thing they tell you. He remembered lying among the bodies, bloody fingers stretching for the little icon of Saint Stephen, broken from the back of his shattered shield . . . but that was even longer ago. Saint Stephen's look had somehow changed from understanding to accusation during those three bad winters, and he'd tossed the icon into Khazi's grave along with him. Told himself the dead needed its protection more than he did, when he meant they deserved it more than he did. That was before the oath of honesty.

Over the noise of the cart, he became aware of a cultured drone. ". . . all nations have their charms and I *always* loved Poland, but the rural life simply wasn't for me. I wasted away in isolation like an orchid in the dark."

"Where am I?" wheezed Jakob, but his voice was a croak, even he could scarcely hear it.

". . . Lucrezia saw it, of course—she was, for all her monstrous faults, a supremely perceptive woman—and she agreed to leave the estate. So our tour of the great cities of the Mediterranean began! Never too long in one place, for obvious reasons, my wife had a habit of wearing out her welcome. Sucking it dry, one might almost say . . ."

The wagon ground to a halt with a final jarring jolt and Jakob groaned, bloody spit flecking from his clenched teeth.

"Ah! He's awake!"

Baron Rikard's face swam into view. He looked younger than ever, with just a hint of silver in his moustache, his brows, the dark hair that hung around his face as he smiled, showing his elegantly pointed canine teeth.

Another face appeared, as shocked as the baron's was smug. A pockmarked man with an ugly hat. "Saint Bernard's *bollocks*," he said, making the sign of the circle over his heart, "he's alive!"

"I told you," said Baron Rikard.

"Thought you were mad!"

"Oh, I'm *entirely* mad. But rarely wrong."

"The count'll want to see this," muttered the driver, ducking away.

"A miracle indeed," murmured Rikard. "How do you feel?"

"About . . ." croaked Jakob, working his tongue around his mouth in an effort to make spit as desperate and doomed as most of his efforts, "like usual."

"As bad as that?"

Jakob felt his wrists gripped, and growled through an advancing regiment of throbs, stings, and stabbing pains as he was hauled up to sitting and squinted into the daylight.

The cart had pulled into a field hospital: a few sagging tents beside a stand of trees. He was sharing it with five others, all dead but still looking a good deal better than he felt. Nearby, a priest was giving water to a row of wounded men. Another was softly murmuring the last rites, licking her finger as she turned the page of a prayer book. Only the flies seemed happy with the arrangements. Somewhere behind he could hear the regular scrape of gravediggers' shovels, but couldn't bring himself to turn his head to look. Every grave looks much the same, after all. With the possible exception of your own.

"What happened?" he muttered, almost reluctantly, since the general answer was predictable and the specifics rarely comforting.

Baron Rikard leaned back against the cart beside him, grinning at the scene as though it was a village fair. "There was a fight."

"On the water?" whispered Jakob, gingerly touching his chest where the worst pain was focused.

"That's right, well done! I stayed out of it."

"Wish I had."

"Violence rarely solves anything."

"Can't disagree. Did I fight a duel?"

"On the burning aftcastle!" Rikard spread his hands to indicate a spectacle. "You always find the most dramatic stages for your battles to the death. You really are a loss to the theatre!"

"Who did I fight?"

"One of Princess Alexia's cousins. Lots of jewellery. Constans, was it?"

"Constans." Jakob shut his eyes. Their latest mission, or their most recent fiasco, was all coming back to him. The flames. The fluttering ash. The flickering steel. "He was good with a sword. No doubt he'd have won a fair fight."

The baron raised his brows. "But who wants to fight *those*?"

"Saint Bernard's *bollocks*!" Boomed out suddenly, in the tone of a man used to shouting over others and getting away with it. The speaker clattered heedlessly between the wounded in highly polished armour, one big fist propped on the hilt of an oversized sword.

"Your Excellency, please," complained a priest hurrying in his wake, holding the hem of a very fine surplice above the muck, in the tone of a woman used to issuing chastisements to no effect whatsoever.

"I'm sorry but, I mean . . ." The big man grinned as he stopped before the cart and held both meaty hands out to its contents. "He's alive!"

"I told you," said Baron Rikard.

"But, frankly," observed the priest, "we took you for a liar."

"The best liars don't lie about *everything*. Who would believe them then?"

"Forgive me," Jakob swallowed more blood, "but I'm still—"

"Forgive *me*! I . . . am Count Radosav!" And the big man clapped his palm to his breastplate as if his being Count Radosav was of itself an awe-inspiring achievement. "Of Niksic and Budimlja, and this is Mother Vincenza, Vicar General to the Archbishop Isabella of Ragusa."

Weighty titles for a man in Jakob's state to absorb. He touched his fingertips to the back of his head, the hair there sticky with blood, maybe his own, maybe from the cart's other passengers, and winced.

"Honoured," he said.

"No, no, the honour is ours. You, after all, are the celebrated Jakob of Thorn!"

Jakob winced harder. His vow of honesty didn't give him much wiggle room there. "I am," he confessed. And he repented of it daily.

Count Radosav wagged a thick finger. "Your friend Baron Rikard has told us all about you!"

Jakob winced harder still. "Good things, I trust?"

"What's good at a dinner party is rarely good in a fight."

"And . . . don't tell me . . ." Jakob glanced towards the wounded, feeling the familiar sensation that things might be even worse than he'd supposed. "You're in a fight."

"I am indeed! And you are a noted champion, knight, and general in the sworn service of the Pope!"

Baron Rikard leaned close to whisper in Jakob's ear, his breath chilly as a winter draught. "I was obliged to talk you up."

"Are you any relation of the famous Jakob of Thorn who lifted the siege of Kerak during the Third Crusade?"

Jakob cleared his throat as he wondered how to answer that one without lying. Luckily, the baron clapped him on the shoulder first. "They share some blood, I believe!"

"I knew it!" The count shook his fist in triumph. "My grandfather was in the fortress at the time and never tired of telling the story! He said it was the finest damn charge he ever witnessed! The elves put to flight! Illustrious forebears, eh?"

"Generations of military experience," said the baron, "and all at your disposal."

Mother Vincenza looked to the skies. "The Saviour has rendered unto the righteous the tools they require for their deliverance."

"She has a habit of doing that," muttered Jakob, through gritted teeth.

"Your associate has spoken to us of your holy mission." And Radosav piously circled his chest with a forefinger. "We understand you might be missing a princess."

Jakob wearily patted his pockets. "I do seem to have one fewer than when I set out from the Holy City."

"Naturally," said Mother Vincenza, "we stand ready to give all possible succour to an emissary of Her Holiness."

"But not for nothing?"

The priest spread her hands. "Alas, we have holy missions of our own to discharge."

"To bring to heel Jovanka, the troublesome Countess of Pec!" growled Radosav.

"And to frustrate the ambitions of her backers from the Church of the East," added Mother Vincenza. "Damned wheel-wearers! Is there no end to the arrogance of the Archbishop of Dardania?"

Baron Rikard sadly shook his head. "When will those blasted priests stop interfering in politics?"

"So, to sum up . . ." Jakob dragged himself from the cart. "You're in a border war . . ." His knees nearly buckled when they took his weight, but he managed to stay standing. "With a neighbouring noblewoman . . ." He painfully straightened, painfully clenched his buttocks, painfully worked his shoulders back, and stood as close to straight as he got. "One of you supported by the Western Church, the other by the Eastern."

The kind of ugly proxy war that the squabbling sibling Churches had been fighting for the last three centuries. The kind, in fact, that their mission to Troy was intended to stop.

"You see instantly to the heart of it!" frothed the count, thumping the side of the corpse cart and making it rock on its axles. He was one of those men who could say nothing quietly and do nothing gently. "Perhaps we can assist each other?"

"Let's hope," muttered Jakob.

"Help me humble the wayward countess on the battlefield, I'll help you track down your runaway princess! How does that sound?"

It sounded like a disaster waiting to happen. Or, maybe, one that had already happened. "Honestly, these days, I try to avoid battlefields."

Baron Rikard grinned. "But with *such* little success."

"However we might try to dodge our heavenly calling," said Mother Vincenza, "the saints will guide us back to it."

The priest with the prayer book had finished with one corpse and begun to croon over another. Jakob gave a heavy sigh, and grimaced at the stab of pain where Constans's blade ran him through.

"Great," he muttered.

The Wrong Way

Alex struggled on up the endless rise. Feet battered. Muscles aching. Dizzy with hunger. A stink of char put her in mind of that month she'd spent making charcoal, out in the woods, and left with nothing to show for it but black fingers and a bastard of a cough. She'd count herself lucky indeed if she got away from this with such riches. You'd have thought having the Pope proclaim you long-lost Empress of the East would mean a step up in the world, but as far as she could tell the only thing that'd grown was the size of her enemies.

She heard quick footsteps, turned with her heart in her mouth, but it was only Sunny jogging up. She breathed a sigh of relief. Her best friend was an elf. That was where she was now.

"They still behind us?" asked Alex.

"Closer than ever."

That sigh died in her throat, along with the relief. "Shit."

"I laid a fake track. They didn't fall for it."

"They got dogs or something?"

Sunny glanced back, the tip of her tongue pressed into that little gap between her front teeth. Alex had noticed she did that when there was something she didn't want to say. "Or something. And they're not alone."

"They're not?"

"They've got other parties out, looking for us."

Alex swallowed. She couldn't put into words how much she appreciated that *us*. She knew it could've been a brutal *you*. "What do we do?" she whispered.

"Keep going." And Sunny jogged on past. She never seemed to tire. It was like she was made of wire with shaggy white hair on top.

She stopped at the crest, hopping onto the wall beside the track for a better view, a thin figure chopped out black from the last dregs of sunset. Alex laboured up beside her, puffing away, and froze—

"Fuck," she breathed.

In the valley ahead, a town was burning. There was a church, maybe, its domed bell tower a black finger against the flames, and a river snaking through the buildings, shimmering with reflected fire. Twinkling pinpricks danced in the land about it. Torches, Alex reckoned, on the roads. A sack going on, before their very eyes.

"Well, it's not much of a war till something's burning." Ever since they'd washed up, Sunny had always seemed to know just what to do next, but now she glanced doubtfully about the dark country. "We can't double back, and I don't like north. Maybe south . . ."

"There's one other option." Even as Alex said it, she wished she hadn't, but now Sunny was looking at her, one pale brow raised. Alex nodded towards the town. The smoky silence hung between them for a moment.

"That town's on fire," said Sunny.

"I know."

"That town's being *sacked.*"

"I know! But we're hunted, and they're gaining on us, and they're not alone, and maybe in there . . . we might . . ." As Alex watched that town burn all conviction drained from her voice and it ended up a squeaky question. "Shake them off?"

Sunny narrowed her eyes, a muscle working on the side of her head, and didn't say anything.

"I don't see another way. Do you?"

Sunny set off again, with the same quick, light step as ever, down a track towards the fire. "No."

"Shit," said Alex, standing a moment longer, then hurrying after her. "I was really hoping you might."

"You could wait for that fellow with the corkscrew, I guess."

Uphill had been hard, but at least there'd been the hope of something good beyond the summit. Downhill Alex could see exactly what she was heading for and was already regretting opening her big mouth.

"This is a bad idea!" she called. "This is jumping off one side of a bridge so you don't fall off the other!"

"We ran out of good ideas in Venice," Sunny threw back at her. "Maybe a bit before that. But if you have a better one, I am . . ." And she turned very slowly to look at Alex with her huge, shiny, mirthless eyes. "All ears."

"Oh God," said Alex, clutching two fistfuls of her hair.

"All ears, because I'm an elf."

"Oh *God.*"

The track joined a road, and they started to pass people coming the other way. Miserable, terrified, dirty people. A woman crying and a child with dead eyes. A man shouting at the sky, a bundle in his arms might've been a baby.

"You're going the *wrong way,*" snarled an old woman grimly wheeling a handcart with three chairs in it, its one wheel squeaking off into the darkness behind them.

"I've a feeling she might be right," hissed Alex to Sunny.

"Baptiste says you can't turn profits by following the crowd," hissed Sunny to Alex.

"Forgive me if I can't hear her advice from the *bottom of the Adriatic*." Alex caught Sunny's shoulder. "It'll be chaos in there!"

"Chaos works for us." Sunny put her fingers ever so gently on Alex's, ever so gently peeled them away. "Chaos is our best chance." And she pulled her hood up even higher and put her head down even lower and walked on with her hands wedged in her armpits. "Chaos is our only chance."

There was an inn at the edge of town, an arch of timbers over the road beside it. The place was lit up bright and jolly and someone was playing a squawking violin and Alex could hear laughter. Soldiers stood around a bonfire at the gate, talking, drinking, warming their hands, heaping stuff onto a wagon. Then Alex saw things hanging from that arch of timbers. Bodies, strung up by the feet, arms dangling. One hung by one leg and the other stuck out at the strangest angle. Another might've been a monk. His habit had fallen down over his head to show his dirty underwear.

"This was an awful idea," whispered Alex. "This was a *terrible* idea."

"And still the best we've got." Sunny pulled Alex off the road, through a gap in a hedge, twigs scratching at her, into an overgrown orchard, wading through tall grass, the mad music from the inn fading into the night.

"Wait," whispered Sunny, holding her hand out, and Alex froze. Couldn't tell what she'd heard. Couldn't tell what she was waiting for. "Go."

And they crept on, through the outskirts of town, past thatched huts and ramshackle fences, past heaps of stuff dragged from houses. Broken furniture, trampled clothes. There were noises, in the darkness. Shouting. Smashing blows. Clapping footsteps. A distant roar of fire. Another day, Alex might've taken it for a celebration. Feast-day high spirits.

She wiped the cold sweat from her forehead. Her tongue felt thick in her mouth. "Where are we heading?"

"Towards the river," whispered Sunny. "There might be boats."

"So we'll just float away?"

"We'll try." Sunny frowned back the way they'd come. "They might lose our scent on the water."

"Seems like a lot of fucking *mights*," muttered Alex.

Sunny stopped at a crumbling corner, peered out onto a track filled with rutted puddles, hemmed in by bushes. "I'm going to disappear," she said.

Alex swallowed. "Don't blame you one bit."

"You might only see me now and then. But I'll be with you. Whatever happens." She reached out, and paused a moment, then very gently took Alex's hand. "Trust me."

"I trust you," whispered Alex. She regretted it right off. It's the moment you trust someone they shit all over you. But by then Sunny had vanished and Alex was whispering to the darkness. She felt herself pulled along, scuttling down the track, keeping low, trying to blend into the weeds. She passed a broken stretch of fence, saw soldiers gathered in front of a house, torchlight shining on helmets and weapons.

"Open this fucking door!" roared the leader. "Or we'll break it open!"

One of the men tossed his torch onto the roof of a shack. Others cheered as flames spread. Another started smashing at the door with an axe, blade winking in the glare of burning thatch, Alex flinching at each blow as she slunk past, sticking to the deepest shadows, praying they didn't see her as burning straw fluttered across the track. The would-be Empress of Troy, and her dearest ambition was that they caught someone else.

A noise beside her and she shrank away, slipping on her arse in the mud— just a big carthorse, nudging at a gate with its face.

"Fucking horse," breathed Alex.

"As scared as you are," said Sunny, pulling Alex up, pulling her on. She eased to the corner, peeking onto a cobbled way with houses on the other side, one with its door hanging off its hinges. Alex eased after her, desperate to stay close. Clinging on, almost. Her mouth was so dry she worried the sound of her tongue moving would give her away.

"Can you see—"

"Shush." And Sunny was gone again, her not very significant weight pressing Alex back into the shadows.

A clattering, then a flicker of light, and soldiers rushed past the mouth of the alley, two of them with lit torches, flames rustling in the darkness. Alex held her breath, tried to shrink away to nothing. She was a spear's length from them. If they turned their heads they'd see her.

But they didn't turn. Just charged off into the night. Alex breathed again, slightly ragged.

"Wait here," whispered Sunny.

"What?" But she was gone again. Alex edged to the corner and peered around it. Broken furniture scattered across the cobbles. Torn sheets in a tree, flapping with the breeze. She wondered what would happen if Sunny decided to run for it. Abandoned her in the midst of this madness. Alex couldn't even have blamed her. It was what she'd have done, in Sunny's shoes. What any reasonable person would've done, lumbered with a piece of shit like her—

"Sss." Alex felt a surge of relief as she saw Sunny, the briefest glimpse in a doorway, beckoning with one finger.

Alex dashed across the street, scrambled along beside the houses and into the shadows. She heard voices behind her, getting louder. She wriggled back against the door, sucking what was left of her stomach in, turning her face sideways on. The voices faded. She breathed again. For a moment, anyway.

"Sss." A glimpse of Sunny pressed against the pedestal of a statue. Some saint or other, arms raised in a pointless blessing over the ruined town.

Alex took a breath, picked a path through the rubbish, and dashed towards it. She saw soldiers further on, two of them hacking at a door with axes while others watched, bored.

She expected a shout, or more likely an arrow in her arse, but she made it, wriggling into the darkness next to Sunny, squinting around the edge of the pedestal towards the soldiers. They had the door open now, were bundling someone out of the house.

"I want to go home," hissed Alex. "I want to go home and just be slapped around by thugs after a debt."

"That ship sailed," said Sunny. "It's Empress of Troy or nothing. Over there looks good." And she nodded towards a wooden gate in a high wall, slightly ajar, maybe fifty paces down the road.

"Looks lovely," whispered Alex. "Apart from all the *fucking* soldiers in the way."

"Trust me."

Alex gritted her teeth. "I trust you." But she was gone again. Hell of a way to avoid an awkward conversation.

That poor bastard was huddled on the ground now and the soldiers were kicking the snot out of him. "What have you got for us?" one snarled. "What have you got?" And the thuds of the kicks, over and over, Alex twitching at each one, a little taster of what was waiting if they caught her. When they caught her.

"Up here, arseholes!"

The soldiers all turned, gaping up. Sunny stood on the roof of the house, feet planted wide apart and her arms spread to make the biggest star she could. Alex had no clue how she'd even got up there. But she was only half as shocked as the soldiers were.

"Wha' the fuck?" one of them muttered, and while they all looked at Sunny Alex gathered the tatters of her courage and slipped from behind the pedestal, tongue pressed into her teeth, padding along behind them.

"Look, I'm an elf!" Sunny pushed her hood back and waved her arms around. "I'm a fucking elf!"

One of the soldiers fumbled for a crossbow, but by the time he had it raised, Sunny was gone.

"Where'd she go?" he snapped, point of his bolt waving wildly around.

Alex slipped by, close enough to have touched him, every thudding heartbeat lasting an age. She was tingling with the need to sprint, but she had to stay careful, had to stay quiet.

"Over here!" And the soldiers all turned again, away from Alex, towards Sunny, who was up on the next roof, arms spread, wriggling her long fingers and sticking out her tongue. Alex scuttled along the wall without looking back, pushed the gate open with her fingertips and wriggled through, into a shadowy little courtyard behind a house, strewn with junk, with heaps of scattered books, a slashed mattress with its feathers flown everywhere. The ruins of a comfortable life puked across the flagstones.

She let go of the breath she'd been holding in a silent sigh. She saw Sunny drop from the wall ahead, pressing herself beside another gate, so still and slight you could hardly see her even when you could see her. Alex picked her way over, smothering a cough as smoke tickled her throat.

"Everyone should have an invisible friend," she whispered.

"Then what'd make you special?"

"My sense of humour?"

Sunny wrinkled her nose. "I've heard better. You ready for more?"

"Oh God," muttered Alex. But Sunny was already gone. A moment later she was in a doorway across the street, beckoning.

Alex licked her dry lips and scurried over, the sounds of the soldiers fading behind her as she slipped into the doorway, pressing herself tight to the wood.

"That way," muttered Sunny, peering down the street. "And don't get caught." And she was gone again.

Alex heard something on the other side of the door, frowned—

It whipped inwards and she stumbled over the threshold and nearly into the arms of a soldier with a chuckle dying on his lips. She caught a glimpse of a red beard, a shocked face, then she was swinging. He'd enough presence of mind to turn his head and her knuckles smacked hard into the side of his helmet. She groaned through gritted teeth as pain lanced up her arm, lurching back into the street, gripping her throbbing hand.

The bearded man came after her, his curse turning to a shocked yelp as he tripped over nothing and went sprawling on his face. Another soldier bundled after him, rotten teeth bared. Alex gave a little gasp as he raised an axe—

—which was plucked out of his hand and his helmet tipped forwards over his eyes. He gave a shocked gurgle and Alex stepped up and planted her boot right between his legs. He roared with pain, doubling over, and she was off along the street like a squirrel up a hot chimney.

She ran, footsteps clapping off the walls, no clue where she was going. She scrambled around a corner and saw soldiers, skittered to a halt and her feet went from under her. She scrabbled to a low wall on her arse, breath whooping, hauled herself over it, not sure if she'd been seen or not, blundering scratched and torn through a bramble patch.

Heat like a slap in the face. A church on fire, rafters black lines against the flames. A graveyard. A tumble of old tombstones, names lost to moss. She felt a clutch of terror when a figure loomed at her, but it was only a stone angel on some rich man's tomb.

Convenient place to die, at least. Timed right, she could save the undertakers some effort and just drop straight into a grave.

Torchlight flickered, shadows of the headstones reaching out across the wet grass, and she shrank against a tree. Was anyone following? Couldn't tell. She darted from one stone to another, hardly knowing which side to hide on. Glass shattered somewhere. Someone shouted. Someone laughed. Her head jerked towards every sound as if it was on a string. Her own heart pounded in her skull, almost painful, like it'd pop her ears off. God, her hand was hurting. Was it broken? Every breath came with a helpless little whimper.

Her good hand found something soft. A hunched shape. A corpse. She jerked her fingers back, sticky with blood, glistening black by firelight. A tree had caught fire, sap spitting and popping, burning leaves fluttering across the churchyard. Pigs were screaming somewhere. Was it pigs or was it people?

There was a crash as the church's roof fell in, flames gouting from the windows, sparks whirling into the night. Alex caught a breath of smoke and started coughing, tottering along, bent double, and each breath she heaved in made her cough again, and she coughed puke and breathed that in, fell against the wall of the churchyard, spitting and sobbing, eyes streaming so bad she had to feel her way, blundering through the gate and into the street.

People were coming at her. Men, and women, and children. No idea how many. By the flickering light they became one blubbering, screeching, jostling mass. Alex, halfway panicking already, caught their terror and ran with them, no idea where she was heading. She was barged against a wall, smacked her head, nearly fell, shoved somebody away. Something caught her elbow, she was dragged sideways. She made a fist to punch, gasped at the flash of pain through her knuckles, then saw Sunny.

"Don't look back," she said, so of course Alex looked back right off.

Through the scattering crowd she saw a group of figures, calm and hard and purposeful. A tall man strode at the front. Very tall, with a big shaggy beard, and a big shaggy fur around his shoulders. His eyes were sunk in the shadows of his heavy brows, but she could see marks on his face.

Tattooed writing.

Tattooed warnings.

"They've got a werewolf?" she whimpered.

Sunny gave the strong impression of having known already. "This way."

She was bundled into a building, a door slammed behind her, a bolt shot into place. It was a forge, an anvil gleaming dully, a rack of tools knocked over. A body lay still, hunched on its side. Alex padded closer. A soldier. His eyes were open, staring at nothing, blood everywhere, a hammer lying by his head.

"He got clonked," said Sunny, nudging his fallen helmet away with her foot.

"I reckon." Alex tiptoed after her to another door at the back. Or maybe the front. Who knew which way around anything was now?

It opened onto a town square with a fountain in the middle. Must've been nice on market day. Not so nice on looting night. Soldiers everywhere. Dozens of the bastards, rooting through the buildings one by one, thorough as locusts on a wheatfield. Some were beating at the door of a fine old house. Some were dragging things from a handsome place might've been a town hall. Some were loading their plunder onto wagons piled high with curtains and candlesticks and bedsteads and anything could be shifted without block and tackle.

"Steal some bastard's purse you're a thief," breathed Alex. "Steal a whole town you're a hero."

Broken furniture and the timbers from smashed market stalls had been heaped up and set fire to, lighting the scene of industrial robbery with a crazy glow, turning the grand old facades to hellish faces, making staring eyes from windows and screaming mouths from doorways.

"How the hell do we get across there?" she whispered.

"Too many soldiers." Sunny had the tip of her tongue between her teeth. "Maybe we circle back, try to get around—"

"Back?" whispered Alex. "No. Werewolves are bad enough when they're on our side." She thought she could see the glimmer of water down an alley across the square. So close. "Back? No."

"You can't turn invisible."

Alex took a breath and blew it out. "It'll have to be the next best thing." She went to the soldier's corpse, rolled him over and undid his cloak buckle. She grunted as she rolled him back, wincing at the pain in her hand, then dragged the cloak up and around her shoulders. "Looking like I'm meant to be here."

"There's blood all over it," said Sunny.

It was true, the cloak's shoulder was crusted up pretty good. Alex shrugged. "Everyone here's got at least a little blood on 'em."

She noticed the grip of a dagger sticking from the dead soldier's belt, and she leaned down and slid it out. A hard-used, unlovely thing beside the snake-hilted beauty Duke Michael had given her, likely now adorning the bottom of the Adriatic. But Alex had a soft spot for hard-used, unlovely things. Came from being one, maybe.

"This is a bad idea," said Sunny.

Alex slipped the knife into her own belt and scraped her hair back. Dirty as it was, it more or less stayed there on its own. "If you've got a better . . ." She fished up the helmet and planted it on her head. "I'm all ears." And she tugged at the cloak till it hid as much as possible without looking like it was hiding anything, shoved the door open before the second thoughts throttled her, and sauntered out across the square.

She tried to walk like a man, *clomp*, *clomp*, heavy tread, not too fast and not too slow, one thumb in her belt and the other arm carelessly swinging, like she'd take up as much room as she damn well pleased.

Some soldiers were rolling up a carpet. One of them glanced over and Alex gave him an offhand nod, then a careless sniff, then turned her head and risked a spit. Bit too much, maybe, but by then he'd looked away, eyes for nothing but the profit he stood to make.

She passed the bonfire, eyes fixed on that alley ahead. The glimmer of water at the end. All she had to do was get there. A couple of soldiers came clattering up and her every muscle quivered to make a run for it. But she forced herself slower, forced herself not to look, and she heard them hurry by behind her. Long as she stuck to the part, long as she didn't flinch, it'd all be fine, that's what she told herself. Just get there. *Just get there.* The mouth of the alley only twenty paces off. It's amazing how far you can go, if all you do is act like you're meant to be there—

"Oy!" came a voice.

Every part of her screamed out to run but she made herself stop. Made herself take a breath. Made herself turn.

"What?" she grunted, trying to put some gravel in her voice, praying she sounded like a boy trying to sound like a man rather than a girl trying to sound like one.

A great beefy bastard stood glaring at her beside a wagon, a nervous horse stirring in the traces. "Who the hell are you?"

"Alex," she said. As if it was something everyone should know. As if he should be ashamed of himself for not knowing.

He narrowed his eyes as he stepped over to her. "What you doing?"

"Got sent to find a boat," which was true enough, and she started to turn away.

"No." And he stopped her with a pointed finger. Poked her right in the middle of the chest, fortunately, so he noticed nothing unusual to either side. He frowned down and Alex frowned up, wondering whether her best chance was to punch him or run for it or pull the knife and stick him or scream out *elf attack*. Then he bent and grabbed one handle of a big trunk on the ground beside him. "Help me wi' the other end o' this bastard first."

Felt like it took an age of the earth. To lean down. To grip the other handle. To straighten up, grunting at the weight. All the time she was wondering how many soldiers there were around her. When they'd work out she didn't fit. When they'd spot the blood, and whip the helmet off, and set to hurting her.

The big man dropped his end of the chest on the wagon, and Alex shoved the other end and slid it all the way on. She paused a moment, bent over, catching her breath, which is when she saw Sunny, crouching behind one wheel. She silently pointed back the way they'd come. Alex followed her finger, and straightened up, mouth turning drier than ever.

They'd been hunting her for days, but she'd never seen them this close. Six men, maybe, dressed in black, and the werewolf in the lead. Half a head taller than the others, writing clear across his face, teeth shining in his smile, eyes glinting with the bonfire.

Alex smothered another almighty urge to run and cleared her throat instead, and shouted, nice and loud, so all the soldiers could hear, "Who're these bastards?"

The man she'd been helping looked over. "Aye. Who're these bastards?"

"Is that a fucking corkscrew he's got?" muttered one of the other soldiers.

"Look like thieves to me," said Alex, who ought to know, since she'd spent years in the profession.

"If there's one thing I hate . . ." The beefy soldier sprang down from the wagon he'd filled with plunder. "It's thieves. Oy!" Grabbing his spear and striding towards them. "Who're you bastards?"

Most of his comrades had turned to look. Some were wandering over. Those who'd set down weapons so they could go about the soldier's true business of mass robbery were taking them up again, forming an angry crescent about the newcomers. Alex started to sidle around the wagon. Best not to rush anything.

Then the werewolf tipped back his head and gave a great howl. The horse bucked, kicked out in terror, made the wagon lurch forwards on the brake. Soldiers started shouting, started running, and Alex followed suit, but in the opposite direction. She heard a crash behind her, a throbbing growl that was horribly familiar, but she kept her eyes on the water ahead.

A quay, and wharves, and boats at the wharves. A couple of big ones with furled sails. Little ones beyond. A rowing boat at the end, bobbing on the water. She bent to the mooring post, started tugging at the knots.

"Sunny?" she hissed at the night as she untied it. "You there? Sunny!"

"Way ahead of you." She was already hunched in the prow, hood up and jaw fixed.

"Should've known." Alex clambered in, taking the oars and starting to paddle out, quiet as she could. She'd done a bit of work for a smuggler one time, so she could just about keep from sinking.

The shouts and screams and crashes faded. The oars dipped with a calming *slap, slap, slap*. The centre of town slipped away. They passed a darkened warehouse, then a couple of shacks, one half-sunk in the river, then only shadowed woods on either side. The glow of the burning church on the western sky faded, and the glow of the coming dawn in the eastern sky began to show.

"We fucking did it!" Alex started to giggle. Might be she was crying a bit at the same time. She was fumbling the oars but didn't much care. Right then she was happy to drift whatever way the current was taking them. "Well. *You* fucking did it. I was just your luggage." And she glanced over her shoulder.

"We did it," muttered Sunny, but the best Alex could tell in the shadows, she didn't look too pleased, lying more than sitting in the prow now, curled up, hugging herself.

"You all right?" asked Alex, the sense of triumph quickly draining.

"I might've got . . ." Sunny's face was all crushed up as she breathed in. "A little bit . . ." And she gritted her teeth and gave a feeble little groan. "Kicked by that horse."

Reverses

God *damn* these goddamned boots!" snarled Balthazar, hopping along on one so he could rip the other off and shake out some particle of grit, the discomfort it caused in outrageous disproportion to its infinitesimal dimensions. "They are less footwear than devices of *torture*!"

"So speaks a man who's never been tortured," murmured Baptiste, the seed head on the stalk of grass she gripped between her front teeth waving as she spoke.

"And you have, I suppose?"

"I have."

Ordinarily, when she shared some aspect of her boundless experience, there was at least one elaborate anecdote attached. But on this occasion there was only silence, and Balthazar was forced, to his surprisingly intense discomfort, to imagine the circumstances for himself.

"That is . . ." *Awful. I am so very sorry.* The words teetered on his lips, but at the last moment he refused to give them voice. Was she not his jailer, after all? His bitter nemesis? Had he not sworn to exact a terrible revenge for her many slights? And here he was tricking himself into sympathy! It spoke extremely highly of his forgiving and empathetic nature, of course, but being dragged in opposite directions only made his anger flare up more brightly. "God *damn* this goddamned shirt!" He scratched savagely at one armpit, then the other. "If there is one thing worse than one's own lice, it is inheriting the lice of the deceased!"

"You can't always pick your travelling companions," murmured Baptiste around her grass, somewhat pointedly.

"No doubt some among us thrive in squalor," he snapped, "but I am *not* a man made for sleeping in hedges, nor for defecating in ditches, nor for subsisting on squirrels!"

"You don't like squirrel? You should've said so."

"A thousand times I said so!"

"Only a thousand? It felt like more. You still ate it, though."

Balthazar gritted his teeth. Teeth in which shreds of squirrel might very well still be lodged. He *had* eaten it, after all, and should no doubt have been praising the great ingenuity with which she had trapped the stringy little creature. It had been fascinating to watch her about it: so utterly still, so perfectly intent, so formidably patient, biting ever so gently on her scarred lip, the drizzle leaving glittering dew in the curls about her face . . .

He shook himself. Knowing that without her he would very probably have starved, frozen, or fallen prey to bandits out here in this war-ravaged corner of Europe only made his resentment simmer all the hotter.

"We should have reached the stones by now," he grumbled.

"Feel free to plot your own course, we can see who gets there first."

"We should have gone left at that fork!"

"Way too well travelled. It'd likely have taken us straight into an ambush. In case you haven't noticed, there's a war going on."

"The several devastated villages, torched vineyards, and burned farm-houses, not to mention the *large battlefield* from the corpses of which we stole my *lice-ridden clothes*, did rather give the game away in that regard. Had we taken the last left we would have been there already!"

Baptiste removed the stalk of grass from between her teeth to speak more freely. "You need to stop clinging to the notion that there's only one right path. You'll waste half your time panicking you're not on it, and the rest backtracking to find it. You know your problem?"

"That I am enslaved by this *bloody* binding—" he gave an acrid burp, and scratched angrily at the burned patch on his wrist "—and my life has become a succession of humiliating detours from a route I have no desire to take?"

"None of that'd hurt so badly if you weren't so *rigid*. You demand every-thing bend to your will and declare war on whatever doesn't." She took a deep breath through her nose, and let it sigh contentedly away. "You should be like water. Take the shape of wherever you are and make the best of what floats past."

She grinned over, gold tooth glinting, and for an instant Balthazar won-dered whether the smile he had always taken as mockery could as easily be interpreted as a playful invitation. Whether it had been up to him, all along, which way he took it. And despite his lice and his hunger and his entirely reasonable hatred of the binding, he could not help grinning back. Did he catch a tantalising glimpse of a world in which . . . he could look on the *bright side*? A world in which every reverse did not have to be a disaster, nor every offhand jibe a bitter score to settle. A world in which he could throw vanity and pedantry and suffocating self-regard to the wind and take wild chances. A world in which a man like him and a woman like—

"What?" she muttered, narrowing her eyes.

He opened his mouth to reply.

"Stop right there!"

They sprang from the bushes and slipped from the trees, closing in on every side. Soldiers, with uncompromising expressions, with drawn bows, with levelled spears. Perhaps Balthazar might have noticed them, had he not been fantasising about being an entirely different person. Perhaps Baptiste might have noticed them, had she not been encouraging his doomed effort. But it was a little late for either of them to notice now. She considered the soldiers and—presumably seeing that neither fight nor flight offered a compelling chance of success—displayed a winning smile and slowly raised her hands.

Balthazar propped his own on his hips, and stared at the sky, and forced the words through gritted teeth.

"God *damn* it!"

"Sergeant . . ."

Balthazar pressed his face to the bars. He had been pressing it there for some time. He would likely end up with a permanent imprint of those bars across his visage. If he ever left the cage, that was.

"Sergeant . . . ?" His voice wavered between needy croon and tetchy demand, and somehow ended up with an entirely unintended come-hitherish inflection. "Just a *moment* of your time?"

The lumpen jailer looked around. "Another?"

"This is no more than an honest misunderstanding. We were simply passing through, on our way to the standing stones near Niksic—"

"You're druids?"

"Druids? No. Druids? Ha! Do we look like druids?"

The man shrugged. "Being a druid's not a question of outward trappings, but of mindset and beliefs."

"Well . . ." That was a good deal more perceptive that Balthazar had been expecting. "You have a point there, but—"

"Same as being a spy, in that respect."

"Spies? No. Spies? Us?" Balthazar delivered a peal of slightly shrill laughter. "Do we look like spies?"

"Not looking like a spy is exactly what a spy would look like," said the sergeant, identifying a weakness in the argument Balthazar had himself realised the moment the words left his mouth.

"I spent some time as a spy, in fact," interjected Baptiste.

Balthazar turned to stare at her. She was lying on the bench at the back of the cell with one knee up and her hat over her face. "*Really?*" he demanded. "*Now?*"

"During that unpleasantness with the succession in Saxony a few years ago, but the lifestyle didn't agree with me." She nudged her hat back to frown at the cobwebbed ceiling. "I mean, maintaining one decent identity is hard enough."

Balthazar and the jailer looked at each other in silence for a moment, then the man shrugged. "Well, she's not wrong."

Perhaps fortunately, the door to the cellar was at that moment heaved open and a woman swept down the steps. She was very small, impeccably attired in a sapphire-blue dress with epaulettes and a gilded ornamental breastplate, her coils of golden hair gathered in a pearl-speckled net. A sort of *generalissima attends her arch-enemy's wedding* mood.

"Countess Jovanka!" snapped their jailer, jumping from his chair to stand at stern attention, while Balthazar assumed his most sycophantic smile. Here, after all, was the kind of elevated personage with whom he was in his element!

The countess peered into the cage like a discerning diner finding a severed toe in their pudding. "And what have we *here?*"

"Spies, I daresay." An exceptionally tall, gaunt, and humourless cleric accompanied the countess, made to look even more tall, gaunt, and humourless by a headdress almost scraping the cellar's ceiling that, along with the silver five-spoked wheel he wore, identified him as a senior priest of the Eastern Church.

"Spies? No, no." It seemed Balthazar was cursed endlessly to repeat the same conversation with ever diminishing results. "Merely simple sojourners, on our way to the standing stones near Niksic—"

"You don't look like a druid," said the countess.

"Druid? No, no, no." His chuckle died a slow death, alone. "Though . . . one might observe . . ." Good grief, what was he saying? ". . . that being a druid is not a question of outward trappings, but of mindset and beliefs . . ." Weeks of hunger, exhaustion, degradation, and the company of monsters appeared to have left him entirely incapable of cogent conversation. ". . . though I realise now that is . . . rather beside the point—"

"Saviour protect us," murmured Baptiste with the heaviest of sighs.

"I am as far from a druid as could be!" declaimed Balthazar, hoping to finish strongly.

"Then why the stones?" The priest narrowed his eyes in a manner that reminded Balthazar more than was comfortable of the jurors at his trial. "Are you a magician?"

"Magician?" Balthazar bit the tip of his tongue. For months he had been wilfully miscategorised at every turn. Finally addressed as befitted his talents, he was obliged to deny it. "Ha! No. Magician? Anything but. My name is Balthazar Sham Ivam Draxi, a humble . . . person, and I feel there has been a simple misunderstanding—"

"So you were invited to enter my domain?" The countess's painted lips made a round O of surprise. "I feel sure I would remember making out letters of transit with such a *very* long name."

Balthazar cleared his throat. "Well, perhaps, I confess, not *exactly* invited—"

"Not *exactly*? Or just *not*?"

"Well, not *invited*—"

"So whose misunderstanding was it?"

This, like most things over the half-year since his conviction, was not turning out quite how Balthazar had hoped. "I fear . . . we have somehow got off on the wrong foot—"

"Perhaps you misunderstood which foot you're on?"

"It may well be, it may *very* well be!" God, was he shuffling from one foot to the other? His chuckle had grown positively embarrassing. "I am really only here due to unavoidable circumstances involving an attack at sea, which itself was the result of an unforeseen diversion to Venice, a regrettable incident involving an illusionist's house—a discipline more suited to cheap tricksters than genuine magicians—"

"Though you're not one?"

"Me? No. Magician? Ha! Really, we should be halfway back from Troy already—"

"Troy?" asked the priest, his brow wrinkling in a manner that reminded Balthazar more than was comfortable of the judge at his trial. "What business have you in Troy?"

"Well . . . er . . . oh . . . hmmm." Balthazar rubbed at his temples, where a quantity of sweat appeared to have developed. "Could we perhaps . . . start again—?"

"So!" Baptiste sauntered over to put him out of his misery. By then it was a mercy killing. "This is what passes for a countess these days?" She peered down her nose, obliged to lift both hands, since they were chained together, to push up the brim of her hat with a forefinger. "They really will put a coronet on any old shit."

Such fleeting relief as Balthazar had felt at her interruption was swept away in a surge of cold shock so intense that his intake of breath made an audible squeak somewhere in the upper reaches of his nose.

The countess stared in shock of her own, first at Baptiste, then at Balthazar. Her nostrils flared with fury. "Open this gate *at once*," she breathed.

The key rattled in the lock and Baptiste swaggered out while Balthazar edged as far from her as the cell's limited dimensions allowed, wondering if he could conceivably get away with saying they had never met. Countess Jovanka stepped forwards, the toes of her highly polished riding boots, and the toes of Baptiste's filthy walking boots, almost touching.

"Well, aren't . . . you . . . a *tall* one," snarled the countess, glaring up, the top of her blonde head barely reaching Baptiste's chin. "I may have to cut you down to *size*."

"You should do it quickly," said Baptiste. "Before I accidentally *step* on you."

There was an exceedingly ugly pause, during which it appeared very likely that Balthazar had escaped being burned in the Holy City for a crime he most definitely *had* committed, only to be hanged in rural Serbia for a crime he had not even contemplated.

Then both women burst out laughing. The countess caught Baptiste's face and pulled it down to kiss her on both cheeks. "Baptiste, you glorious *shit*." She grasped her manacles with one hand and beckoned the sergeant over with the other. "Get these bracelets off at once, Sergeant. You wear them with *such* dash, but they really don't go with your ensemble *at all*. What the hell are you doing here?"

"It's a long and tragic story."

The countess raised one brow. "Do you know any short stories?"

"Wait . . ." murmured Balthazar, edging back into the light. "What?"

"This is Baptiste," the countess was explaining to her priest. "And this is Father Ignatios, Syncellus to the Archbishop Alypius of Dardania, a staunch supporter of my cause."

"And of all righteous causes," observed the priest, a pronouncement Balthazar did not doubt to be true, since righteousness tends to be self-defined.

"We were both ladies-in-waiting to the Queen of Sicily," said Baptiste.

"Queen of Sicily?" muttered Balthazar.

"She hasn't told you her story about Havarazza?" asked Countess Jovanka. Each exchange left Balthazar more confused. "The painter?"

"It was all long before I was a countess. But then there was the carriage accident, and then the fire, then my cousin Dragan was kicked by a horse, and my older brother took himself out of the running over that business with the nuns, and my younger started pissing blue and went completely mad, and before you know it everyone was kneeling to me and calling me Your Illustriousness so what *was* I to do?"

"You seem to have risen to the challenge," said Baptiste. "Jewels suit you."

"Jewels suit everyone." The countess raised a considering brow at Balthazar. "And what the hell have you brought with you? As I recall you liked poor athletic men and rich ones of any description. This one seems . . . bookish and aloof."

Balthazar would have liked to protest, but doubted he could fundamentally disagree, and in any case had a firm policy of not protesting to people who held the key to his manacles.

"He's a colleague, not a lover," said Baptiste, smirking as though the very suggestion was absurd.

"Not a lover *at all*," said Balthazar, making sure he smirked just as much while feeling, for some reason, deeply aggrieved.

The cellar was beneath a house packed with soldiers in blue livery, all competing to salute first as Countess Jovanka swept past. The house was on one side of a farmyard in which a team of butchers was slaughtering a penful of sheep, opposite a barn in which even more soldiers were stacking supplies. The farm proved to be at one corner of a sprawling camp pitched across several fields, swarming with more saluting soldiers, unhappy horses, smoking fires, stalled wagons, improvised forges, and more.

"I'm only an occasional soldier," said Baptiste, wedging her hair back under her cap and brushing the wilting feather to attention, "but I get the impression you're fighting a war."

"Not my first choice." The countess affectionately pinched the dirt-smudged cheek of a drummer-boy as she passed. "I despise marching music, but have been most outrageously provoked, and you know me, a provocation *must* be answered."

"Answered emphatically," murmured Balthazar, considering a large siege engine with carpenters crawling over its great arm, planing off the knots.

"Bloody Count Radosav!" spat the countess. "What a bore, what a bastard, what a menace to the public good, what a goat's anus, eh, Ignatios?"

The priest inclined his head. "I am forced to deplore the language but with the substance I must regretfully concur."

"A tyrant to his underlings, a sycophant to his superiors, and to his equals the most arrogant, stubborn, contrarian . . . ugh, ugh!" She mimed sticking fingers down her throat. "His demands, his disputes, *my* orchard, *my* wheat-field, *my* village. I swear if you gave him the world he'd want more. And now he's gone to *war* with me! Or me with him, one or the other, the *outrageous* bastard! The man simply does not understand the word *no* or the word *joke*, though he did, it appears, understand the words *arrogant shit* because that last letter of mine *did not* improve his mood."

She glared at Balthazar as though expecting a response. He cleared his throat. "A rebarbative oaf, beneath even the contempt of a noblewoman of your calibre. I will hope for your crushing victory."

"Huh." She considered him a moment longer, then strode on. "Your Draxi did not make much of a first impression, but I begin to warm to him. You're heading for the standing stones?"

"Indeed . . ." Balthazar had to swallow yet another surge of nausea. "And time is *something* of a factor—"

"You're very close, in fact. I can show you the way." And the countess headed on between the tents towards a row of sharpened stakes at the edge of the camp. "Though you may face some . . . difficulties in reaching them."

"Believe me when I say we have overcome some *considerable* difficulties already," observed Balthazar, tiptoeing through the mud to stand beside her. "I do believe there is nothing . . . we cannot . . ."

"Ah," said Baptiste.

The ground sloped away into a shallow valley, speckled with patches of sedge, scattered with sheep, or possibly goats, is there a difference? On the opposite slope a matching line of stakes had been planted. Tents were ranged beyond, with pennants fluttering overhead, smoke from cookfires drifting leisurely into the evening sky, steel glittering with the sunset. The camp of Count Radosav's army, Balthazar presumed.

And there, in the no-man's-land between the two sides, was the double ring of standing stones, small on the outside, large on the inside, a couple fallen over during the long centuries like missing teeth from a smile. Well within bowshot of two opposed armies numbering several thousand each, and in the perfect epicentre of what would, at some point on the coming day, very likely be a heaving battlefield.

Balthazar rubbed at the bridge of his nose and gave a long sigh.

"God . . . *damn* it," he muttered.

Famously Dove-Ish

"There she is," breathed Count Radosav, glowering across the valley towards the lines of the enemy, "almost close enough to touch." And he ground his gloved fist into his gloved palm. "With any luck, there'll be a battle tomorrow."

His knights competed to grunt the gruffest agreements and strike the most manful poses, while Mother Vincenza and three monks she kept to carry all the reliquaries nodded belligerently along.

Baron Rikard leaned close to Jakob. "Not sure a battle suits us," he murmured.

"No," said Jakob. The favour of a man like Count Radosav was a thin thread to hang your hopes on at the best of times. But in a battle, he might very well lose, or die, or be fought to a bloody stalemate, and end up in no position to help anyone. Even if he won a crushing victory there'd be prisoners to deal with, and terms to dictate, and a bumper crop of gloating to harvest. Jakob had seen it a hundred times. Good intentions can be buried in the graveyard of defeat, but they just as often sink in the bog of victory.

In a battle, their hopes of finding Princess Alexia would likely be the first casualty. "Peace would be better all around."

The baron smiled. "Ah, the famously dove-ish Jakob of Thorn once again seeks an end to hostilities."

Mother Vincenza was taking an opposing view. "Victory is assured!" she sang at the heavens. "The purity of your cause is sanctified by Archbishop Isabella herself. You are in her prayers, in the Cathedral of Ragusa, dawn, noon, and sunset." And her monks circled their chests, and fingered their relics, and murmured the names of sympathetic saints.

Jakob took a deep breath and stepped forwards. "It's a comfort to know that all the soldiers who die tomorrow will do so under sanction of the Church and reach the gates of heaven purged of their sins."

Count Radosav frowned over at him. "You expect casualties?"

Jakob glared across the valley. The long slopes of damp grass. The scattered goats. The mist in the bottom, and the standing stones poking through it.

When he judged all eyes were on him, and the silence had stretched long enough to make his words sound weighty, he spoke.

"I've known many powerful men, Your Excellency. Emperors and kings. Fought for some. Against others. Men who steered the course of history. Men like you." Count Radosav pretended not to be flattered, but he did it very badly. Men born to peace and privilege often crave the approval of the violent. Jakob was counting on it. "A problem for men that are much loved . . . or much feared . . . is that no one will tell them hard truths."

The count looked over his gaggle of military sycophants. "But you will?"

"I have sworn a vow of honesty. I've no choice but to be blunt."

"Speak honestly, then. I demand it!"

"A battle is always a gamble." Jakob took a long breath, and let it sigh away. Time might have sapped his strength and dulled his senses, but his sigh had only gained in gravelly dignity. "But as things stand . . . I don't like your chances."

Mother Vincenza's face grew dark while the officers muttered and spluttered, but the count held up a hand to still them. "How so?"

"I was in your field hospital. Heard your soldiers talk, unguarded. They admire you and your cause, but the campaign has been long while supplies run short. Their ranks are thinned by wounds and sickness. Frankly, they want to go home."

"Countess Jovanka's men are no fresher!"

Jakob glanced towards Radosav's ill-pitched tents, then across the valley towards their counterparts. "To me her camp looks very orderly. A sign of good morale and ample provisions."

The eager young knights whispered of cowardice, which is the word eager young knights use to describe good sense, but some of the older men began to grumble.

Mother Vincenza gave a cluck of upset. "Count Radosav, I know you for a pious son of the Church, a dauntless warrior in the Pope's cause. Countess Jovanka has enlisted the aid of schismatics and recusants! Her Eastern heresies cannot be permitted to stand!"

"What an inside-out world," murmured Baron Rikard. "The priest argues for war, the knight for peace."

Mother Vincenza waved towards one of her monks, who carried a sort of gilded lantern on a pole, but holding a shrivelled brain instead of a candle. "The relics of Saints Basil and Grigorije stand proudly among your host! How can victory be in doubt with such divine support?"

"In my experience of war . . ." Jakob thought, under the circumstances,

Baptiste wouldn't mind him borrowing a flourish, ". . . and I have a *very* great deal . . . the saints side with the numbers, and the equipment, and the ground."

Vincenza glared back at him. "You may have experience, Jakob of Thorn, but plainly age has drained your sap—"

"Have you ever been to Poland, Mother Vincenza?" asked Rikard.

"I fail to see—"

"There is a style of dumpling served there." The baron held her eye, unwavering. "Sublimely simple and yet . . . simply sublime."

The priest's mouth dropped open. "Dumplings . . . you say . . . ?"

"The purity of your faith brings to mind the chapel on my wife's estates." Baron Rikard gently drew her away. "Its door surrounded by honeysuckle. Do you know the smell of honeysuckle . . . ?"

"Your Excellency." Jakob put a comrade's hand on the count's shoulder and used the other to sketch the contours of the land, the likely lines of attack. "I know a man of your experience will have seen this at once, but the countess's camp is higher placed than ours. The slope on her side of the valley is steeper, that stream and those rocks would break up an advance."

"A small advantage," scoffed one.

Count Radosav gave a weighty sigh of his own. "Battles turn on small advantages."

"I have seen it," observed Jakob, licking a finger and holding it up. "The wind is against us. Their arrows will carry further."

"The wind can change," snapped one of the officers.

"The wind can change?" Jakob turned his eyes upon the man. If the years had made his sigh a lethal weapon, it had made his glare a more deadly one yet. "Is that your strategy?"

"But I have you!" said the count.

Jakob could not help a smile at that. When Emperor Odo had his doubts about battle with the Flemish, Jakob had convinced him to charge. *You have me*, he'd said, self-belief burning in him like a furnace. *You have me.*

"In my youth I dreamed one man could tip the balance of history," said Jakob. "Time has taught me that when one does, it can tip the wrong way as easily as the right."

The count turned back to the valley, rubbing worriedly at his jaw. "The men *are* weary. Her camp *is* orderly. And neither the ground nor the weather is favourable . . ."

"And they have the advantage in horse . . ." chipped in one of the older knights, giving Jakob the hint of a nod.

Count Radosav thumped his fist against his armoured thigh. "God, but I'd love to *beat* her!"

Jakob had spent years talking peaceful men into violence. It seemed his penance was having to talk warmongering fools out of it. He eased closer, close enough that no one else could hear. "But have you thought how it would feel . . . to be beaten *by* her?" The count blinked, then frowned across the valley once again. "The loss of prestige. The risk to your unimpeachable name. You want to humble her?" Jakob shrugged. "Do it at the negotiation table, where your shrewdness will give you the advantage."

Count Radosav raised his chin, jaw working. "I suppose, one way or another, every battle ends there."

"I've spent a lifetime at war," more than one, in fact, "and I can tell you only this. Nine times out of ten there's more to be won from peace."

"Yet you still wear a sword," said the count.

Jakob gave a weary smile as he rested his hand on the hilt. "A man of my age needs something to lean on."

Loophole

"What happened here?" whispered Brother Diaz, peering around the corner and out across the square.

They'd seen bodies as they slunk into the devastated town. Some huddled bloody in the street. Some charred in burned-out buildings. Some dangling in archways, from windows, from shop signs. But the square ahead was littered with them. Corpses so broken Brother Diaz had to turn his head sideways and really think about it to work out they'd once been people.

He dashed chill sweat from his face. It sprang back instantly. "It looks almost like . . ."

"My work?" offered Vigga, striding out across the stained paving.

"But without all the restraint . . ." He forced his quivering legs to yet another last effort and crept after her.

She was a killer, of course. God alone knew the extent of her butcher's bill. And yet, since they'd left the shore and followed Alex inland, she'd been the one thing keeping him alive. Dragging him on, sniffing out the track, finding him food, slapping him awake, dragging him on, his tireless guide, his fearless protector, his relentless tormentor.

She snuffled at the air, heavy with the stink of char and untimely death. "They came this way."

"Why straight through a town?" Brother Diaz stared at the remains of several soldiers, so thoroughly mashed together it was difficult to tell how many. "Especially one being sacked?"

"To shake off the bastards hunting 'em."

Brother Diaz blinked. That did, indeed, neatly answer the riddle.

She was an animal, he knew. Fickle as a magpie, blunt as a bear, forgetful as a sardine. But she was also rather good company, and would sometimes strike some spark of unorthodox insight that proved she was no fool at all. He couldn't see her adding much to one of his old abbot's theological seminars. But he doubted his old abbot would've been much use in a hunt across a battlefield for a princess and a renegade elf.

Good companions and bad ones—so much depends on the circumstances.

"D'you think it worked?" he whispered.

"Sunny's a nimble little scrap so I'm hoping." She poked through some spilled innards with her toe. "At least till I step in their corpses." She gave him that always slightly off-putting toothy grin. "Smile while you can, that's what I say. The world'll kick you in the twat soon enough." Vigga sniffed at a wagon, tipped onto its side with one shattered wheel in the air, snuffled underneath it, then padded towards a rubbish-scattered alleyway. "They were here . . . Headed over here . . ." He saw the river, at the end, followed Vigga towards a rickety pier, his heart thudding in his ears. She squatted at the edge of the wharf, peering off downstream. "Trail stops here."

"So they got away by boat?"

"Makes sense. Harder to track 'em on the water—" Vigga looked up sharply, then stood, glaring back down the alleyway. "Someone's coming."

Did he hear shouting, back in the square? He shrank closer to Vigga. "Whoever it is, I doubt they'll be friendly . . ."

The tendons started from the tattooed backs of her fists as she clenched them. "I can be unfriendly."

"That's what I'm afraid of."

"I mean I'll fucking kill 'em," she snarled.

"That's what I'm afraid of!" The door of a warehouse across the street stood ajar, and Brother Diaz caught Vigga's elbow and pulled her towards it.

She didn't move. Not even a bit.

"I don't want to die while you're doing it," he hissed, hauling at her elbow with both hands. "I don't want *you* to die." Could he see torchlight flickering in the square now? "*None* is the ideal number of deaths!" He leaned back with all his weight, like a man leading a team at high-stakes tug-of-war. "Don't make me use the binding—"

"Odin's *bollocks*." Vigga turned so suddenly he had to cling to her elbow or go flat on his face in the street. She kicked through the open door, bundling him into the warehouse with her, wrestling it shut behind them, shouldering it into the broken frame with a creaking of tortured wood.

The place was mostly darkness and a smell of damp, split sacks and empty barrels glimpsed in the chinks of light from the boarded-up windows. There was a scrape as Vigga slid something through the handles to bar the door and set her shoulder against it.

A moment later he heard noises outside. Hurried footfalls. Raised voices. A mob.

He shrank back as torches passed, a bar of flickering light crawling across Vigga's face as she frowned through a gap between the boards of the door.

Her heavy cheekbone, the scabbed nick beneath one glinting eye, the writing down her face. *Beware.* Advice he knew he would do well to keep in mind . . .

The voices faded to dull echoes, and were gone, and Brother Diaz ever so slowly let out the breath he'd been holding in a shuddery gasp, sinking down the wall on trembling legs until his aching buttocks hit the floor.

With the danger passed, exhaustion rushed in like the sea into a holed rowing boat, dragging him down. He hadn't felt so utterly spent since he charged through the Celestial Palace, late for his appointment with Her Holiness. It was strange to even think of that man now, with his smug little ambitions. A comfortable post in the church bureaucracy. Tutor to some appalling noblewoman's appalling brood. Chuckling at the bishop's jokes. These days his hopes barely extended beyond surviving the next horrifying interlude. Which, no doubt, would not be long in coming.

"You were right," grunted Vigga.

"You sure?" Brother Diaz shut his eyes and tried to slow his breath, the hammering of his pulse gradually fading. "Doesn't sound like me."

"Look for fights, you'll always find more. I never learn!" There was a thud in the darkness that made him flinch, as she punched some meaty part of herself. "I'd like to blame it on the wolf, but the truth is I was a fucking fool before the bite."

"You're no fool," muttered Brother Diaz. "You just have . . . your own way of seeing things."

"Good you're here." She turned from the door, slid down the wall until she sat. "Make sure I don't shit all over myself." His eyes were adjusting to the dark now. He could see her outline. Knees up, arms propped on top of them, hands dangling. "I need help keeping the wolf muzzled. Calmer heads."

Brother Diaz let his head fall back against the wall. "Cowards, you mean."

"Cowards run. You're scared. But you're still here." He saw her eyes gleam in the darkness as she considered him. "You've changed."

"Changed back, maybe. Closer to the man I was before . . ."

"You fucked the wrong girl?"

Somehow, in the darkness, it was easy to speak. He could say things he'd never have shared in confession. Say what you like about her, Vigga didn't judge. His sins seemed meagre indeed beside hers, after all. "There were things to like about that man," he said. "Doing whatever he pleased. Sparing no thought for the consequences. Like you."

Vigga held up her hands and fluttered her fingers. "It's got me everything I don't have."

"But you had fun on the way, didn't you? I buried myself in a monastery for ten years and followed every rule." Brother Diaz shrugged. "And I'm in the same place you are."

She was contemptible, of course. A pagan primitive, born into the darkness of ignorance beyond the light of the Saviour's grace. There were several of the Twelve Virtues to which she was an utter stranger. But when it came to some others—bravery, honesty, loyalty, generosity—she could have given lessons to most priests of his acquaintance. She was contemptible, and yet, even though he was nothing but dead weight for her to carry, she never showed contempt for him.

"Reckon they're gone," she muttered. It was silent now, outside, and she stood. "We should move—"

"Don't think I could even stand." Brother Diaz slowly stretched out his aching legs. "We're safe here."

"Ish."

"We've a roof over our heads."

"Ish."

"We'll do no good fumbling about in the dark."

"Hmmm . . ." Vigga sat back down beside him, and he wondered whether she might be sitting closer than before, and he realised of a sudden his unfortunate choice of words. He could hear her breathing, the soft rhythm of it, each breath ending in the slightest growl.

She was a savage, it couldn't be denied. Tattooed with warnings for the safety of the unwary. He had known it from the first moment he saw her in human form, naked and spattered with gore and puking up undigested bits of people. He wasn't sure whether it would be safer to move or to stay still. At that moment, safety was not first on the list of his desires.

"Monks . . ." came Vigga's thoughtful voice, "have a rule, don't they?"

"It sometimes seems rules are all they have."

"About fucking women, though?"

Brother Diaz swallowed. "There is . . . something of a *vow*."

"Though I tell you what, visit a brothel in a day's ride of any monastery you please and you'll find more monks than whores."

"I'll have to . . . bow to your experience there."

The silence seemed to press in heavy. "And I expect . . ." Vigga's voice began low but got higher and higher as she wandered to the end of the question. "The same goes double . . . for fucking animals?"

Brother Diaz swallowed with even more difficulty. "Definitely frowned upon."

"Though again . . ."

"Each churchman must answer to his own conscience."

"But . . . hear me out . . ." The air was thick with her smell, almost overwhelming in the confined space, once so foul, now somehow the opposite. "What's the position . . . on fucking things . . ." She was edging closer. "That aren't women *or* animals . . ." He could tell by her voice she was closer. "But somewhere . . ." The pause felt impossibly long. "*In between?*"

She was a monster. He'd seen her become an unholy horror with his own eyes and indulge in an orgy of slaughter. She was an accursed aberration hunted down, condemned, and imprisoned by the Church for the good of humanity. But it was hard to concentrate on that. It was hard to concentrate on anything but the sliver of warm and tingling darkness between them, filled with her heat and her sour-sweet smell.

That and the blood flowing rapidly to his crotch.

"I'm no legal mind, I know . . ." murmured Vigga, and he heard a creak. Her putting one fist on the floor beside him. "But d'you think . . . I might've found . . ." Another creak as she set the other fist on his other side. "A loophole?"

God, she was almost nuzzling at him. "Vigga . . . please," he whispered, shutting his eyes tight, for what good that did. "Even if there's no . . . *specific* restriction against . . ." He could hardly believe he was even saying the words. "*Lying with werewolves . . .* it would be . . . *wrong.*" So wrong. So incredibly wrong, in so many ways.

"No," he whispered. He had to be a rock. Like Saint Eustace, tempted with every earthly delight, but turning his face to the Lord. "No," he said. She was a killer, an animal, a savage, a monster. He slipped his hand into the narrow space between their mouths, touched a finger to her lips, pushing her gently away. "The answer must be no."

He heard Vigga sigh. Felt the heat of her breath on his fingertips. "All right." Her hair tickled his neck as she rocked back on her haunches. "No one'll twist your arm, Brother Diaz. But . . . you change your mind . . . my loophole will be ready whenever—"

"Fuck it!" he snarled, catching her behind the head and pulling her back. He missed, in the darkness, so terribly out of practice, started by kissing her nose, but he soon made it to her mouth.

He licked at her pointed teeth and she kissed him back, growling at him, nipping at him.

He felt the vial of Saint Beatrix's blood knock against his chest, as if making a desperate last plea. He slapped it angrily over his shoulder.

It was utterly wrong, deeply disgusting, entirely forbidden. She was a monster. And he couldn't help himself.

"Fuck . . ." he growled, pushing his fingers into her hair, pulling her close. "*It.*"

What You Can't Change

The door gave at one kick and shuddered open on wheezing hinges.

Sunny couldn't help a miserable whimper as Alex dragged her arm over her shoulders and half-lifted her, so they lurched over the dripping threshold together like some fatally wounded four-legged beast melodramatically creeping into a hole to die.

"Told you," muttered Alex, glancing about, "no one here."

"Surprising," hissed Sunny, "when it's so nice."

A ramshackle barn, or slaughterhouse, or stables by the smell, long abandoned. The back wall was stone, the crumbling carcass of some older building, the rest botched together from warped boards. Strings of ancient cobweb fluttered in the chilly draught. Rain spattered in through holes in the roof.

"I've stayed in worse." Alex lurched into the driest corner and started lowering Sunny towards the dirty straw.

"Careful," grunted Sunny through her clenched teeth.

"I'm being careful," growled Alex, trembling with the effort.

"Careful!" grunted Sunny.

"I'm being careful!" snarled Alex, then lost her balance and they flopped down together.

Sunny lay for a moment, on the prickly straw, in the fusty dark, trying to breathe shallow, nose all wrinkled as she waited for the pain, but after a moment she actually felt better. Alex was on top of her, on hands and knees. She smelled of sweat and fear and the smoke of the burning town, the name of which they still didn't know and likely never would.

"We shouldn't stay . . ." whispered Sunny, "too long." She never used a lot of words but right now each one was hard labour. "They'll guess . . . we were on the river."

Alex pushed herself up to her knees. "Unless they all got killed in that town."

"Really think our luck's that good?"

"On past performance, no. How're your ribs?"

"Fine," whispered Sunny. "If I don't breathe."

"Maybe I should look?"

"Why? Do you have healing eyes?"

Alex fluttered her lashes. "Maybe a little."

Sunny slowly pulled her shirt up. She was used to being a sideshow curiosity, but it still felt strange, having Alex shuffle closer. Touch her ribs, ever so gently, wincing in sympathy, just one fingertip so light and tickly it made Sunny shiver.

People didn't touch her often. Not gently, anyway.

"Well?" she muttered.

"Well, I'm glad they're not my ribs. Should we . . . I don't know . . . bandage them?"

"How will that help?"

"I can't do nothing."

"Nothing is the easiest thing to do." Sunny settled back against the straw, and tugged her shirt down, and lay very still. "You head on. Leave me here. I'll be all right."

Alex snorted. "Fuck yourself. We've got no food or water, and we're being hunted, and you're no complainer, so when you say 'ow,' I reckon you mean it."

"So I won't be all right. Leave me here anyway. You have to get to Troy."

"I don't give a shit about Troy. I've never even been there."

"I hear it's nice. You should go."

"Very funny. You've saved me how many times?"

Sunny couldn't help a little groan as she shifted. "A few."

"A lot. And you don't even make a big thing of it, which is even worse than if you did."

"Tragic dignity comes naturally to me."

"And I don't get to try it? When it looks so good on you?"

"How do you plan to get us both out of this?"

Alex clambered up, rubbing at her jaw, and said nothing.

Sunny had almost been hoping she'd have a plan. But finding out she hadn't was no surprise. "I thought so. You should go."

"The farm we passed," said Alex. "They had a stable. Maybe they had a horse."

"You're not going back. You might get caught."

"You wanted a plan, there's my plan."

"I didn't want a shit plan. You can't steal a horse."

"You're skinny but I can't carry you far."

"'Cause we need an angry farmer after us."

"On top of two dozen hired killers and a werewolf I doubt the farmer will make much difference."

"I can't let you do it."

"How will you stop me?"

"I'll think . . ." Sunny bared her teeth as she tried to get up. "Of something . . ."

Alex put a hand on her shoulder. "No need." Not exactly pushing her back but stopping her from getting up. "You can trust me."

Sunny looked up at her. "I trust you," she said.

Then Alex leaned in and kissed her.

Not a forceful kiss all tongues and teeth. Not some accidental brushing of the lips. Decided and patient and leaving no doubt at all what it was. She caught Sunny's top lip between hers, sucking at it ever so slightly, then her bottom lip with the faintest flapping sound, then the top again, and maybe actually there was a little bit of tongue on the end of that one, and Sunny was just about to kiss her back when Alex pulled away.

Sunny stared at her, whole face tingling. Alex's eyes flickered open, and she stared back. There were only a few inches of darkness between them. Silence, except for the hinge of the door creaking with the wind. The muscles fluttered in Alex's throat as she swallowed.

"Oh," said Sunny, slightly hoarse.

Alex jerked back. Like Sunny had been the one kissed her, which seemed somewhat of a rewriting of history, and very recent history at that. She stood up, and concentrated on slapping straw from her knees, as though the most important thing in all this was clean knees.

"You stay here," she said, turning towards the door. "I won't be long."

"Can't move." Sunny wondered whether wriggling for a more comfortable position would be worth the pain, and decided against it. She didn't panic. Panicking never helped.

She actually did trust Alex. At least to try and help her.

Whether she'd succeed was another question.

Sunny dreamed of kissing someone, pleasantly tingly in the deep, deep woods. Singing, and laughter, and the leaves fluttering in a yellow shower onto a bed of moss, so soft, and the shafts of emerald light through the high branches, the forest floor so far below it felt like being queen of an underwater kingdom.

Then she thought to herself, on the edge of waking—woods? What an embarrassing thing for an elf to dream about. What a cliché. Then a thumping and scraping intruded like the sound of riders and with a start she sat up and felt an awful flash of pain like she'd been kicked afresh and dropped back groaning.

Shafts of dirty grey came through the gaps between the boards leaving stripes across the straw, and by a smear of daylight the place looked even filthier.

Morning.

So Alex had stolen off in the night and abandoned her. Sunny had told her to, but she'd been sort of hoping she might decide against it. More fool her, of course.

When someone tells you they're a liar you'd better believe them.

The door wobbled open. Sunny tried to hold her breath but the pain through her side was so bad she just curled up, clutching at her ribs as if she had to hold herself together or blow apart, no choice but to lie there and take whatever came.

Not for the first time, sad to say.

"In, you big bastard. Get *in*." Alex's voice. And Sunny saw a black-and-white-patched shaggy horse being led into the warehouse while Alex tugged at its bridle.

So she wasn't abandoned after all, and she felt a giddy wash of relief and surprise pleasantly mingled.

"You got a horse," she said.

Alex looked around, still tugging at the reluctant beast. "You sound surprised."

"Little bit."

"Told you I used to be a thief, didn't I?"

"Thought you'd changed."

"I have." Alex finally got the horse through the doors and looked proudly up at it. "Now I'm a horse thief." And she patted its neck, and it dipped its head and gave a nicker. "He'll be way happier with us."

"Why would he be happier with us?" asked Sunny. "We're a fucking disaster."

"That's just it. We *need* him. With that farmer he can pull a plough. With us he can be a *hero*." And she looped the horse's bridle around a rail and stepped over to Sunny. "That's the story I'm telling myself."

"Guess I've heard worse lies . . ." muttered Sunny, but it turned into a spitty grunt as she tried to sit up.

Alex caught her under the arms, almost a hug, lifted her till she could lean on the rotten side of the stall. "Can you stand?"

"No problem." Sunny tried to catch her breath. Without breathing too deep. Or too shallow. "If you can hold me up."

Alex looked her in the eye. Not smiling. Not frowning. "For as long as you need," she said, and she started to help Sunny towards the horse.

"Well, ain't this nice?"

Two men stood in the doorway. One was a hulking big bastard, the other smaller but still likely twice Sunny's weight, entirely bald down to his hairless eyebrows.

"Oh fuck," said Alex.

Sunny felt more tired than anything, and wondered whether she should lie down again. She tried her best to be nice, but the world still took every opportunity to kick the shit out of her.

"Is that one even human?" asked the bald man, peering at her.

"It's an elf," said the big bastard.

"Which makes *her* the cousin," said a woman with a broken nose, stepping into the barn after the other two and pointing a thick finger at Alex. "Sab-bas'll be pleased."

So they were outmatched three to two in numbers, about five to one in weight, and about thirty to one in weapons, since these newcomers looked like they'd packed for war with Burgundy.

Sunny eased back, gripping her ribs, and Alex eased back, too, putting herself between Sunny and the three killers, who were all easing forwards, ever so slowly, like this was a dance with no music and a bad ending.

"So much for the magic nose, eh?" said the big man. "Can't wait to see the Dane's face when we tell him we found her first."

"You can tell him," said the woman. "Bloody Dane gives me the willies."

"Who d'you hate worst?" mused the bald one, still easing forwards. "The Dane, the twins, or the Man-Catcher?"

"I can hate 'em all equally, can't I?" said the woman. "Not like I'll run out o' hate."

Sunny tried to take a breath and hold it, but the stab of pain near made her faint and she had to let it out in an agonised wheeze. For years she'd been desperate for someone to see her. Now she actually wanted to disappear she couldn't manage it.

Alex had her right hand down near Sunny, behind her back, and she tweaked up the filthy hem of her crimson jacket and eased the dagger from her belt.

"Careful," said the woman. "Reckon she's got a blade."

"So?" said the bald man. "I've got loads." And he slid one of his own out, twice the length of Alex's, worn to a cruel, thin crescent by years of sharpening.

"Sabbas won't want her all cut up," said the big man.

"How about a *bit* cut up?"

"That he could probably live with."

Sunny took another step back and her shoulders hit the wall. Out of room. And now someone else was slipping through the door. Their odds getting even worse . . . except . . . a chink of light slid across the newcomer's face, showed tangled black hair, then a slice of pale cheek, then tattooed writing down it. Sunny had to stop herself grinning.

Werewolves are a real curse. Right up until they're the very thing you need.

"Best toss the knife, eh?" The big bastard planted his hands on his hips, blissfully unaware of what was creeping up behind him. "Honestly, I'm running short o' patience. You two have led us quite the merry dance."

"That shit in town was painful," said the bald man, no idea how painful things were about to get. "Fucking Dane went wolf-crazy. I nearly got arrow-stuck. Whose idea was that?"

Sunny pointed to Alex. "Her idea." All that mattered was to hold these two idiots' attention a little longer. Vigga's hands flashed around the woman from behind. One across her chest, pinning her arms, one across her shoulders, tattooed fingers locking about her throat. The woman's mouth yawned like she was screaming but no sound came. She twisted and wriggled but she was held tight as a wasp in honey, boots off the ground, kicking silently.

"But it was me poisoned your stew," said Sunny.

"I shat water for three days!" The big man pulled a barbed hatchet from his belt. "Maybe Sabbas will have to get you in pieces."

"Now wait!" Alex waved her open palm at the two men, making sure their eyes didn't leave her as Vigga squeezed tighter and tighter, streaks of blood running down her forearm and dripping from her elbow. "We can strike a bargain!"

The bald one chuckled. "With what?"

"*Jewels.*" Alex had this way of saying the word, stretching the *oooo* the way a priest might a saint's name, the answer to everyone's prayers. "I got 'em buried."

Doubt and greed battled on those two ugly faces while, right behind them, the woman's eyes rolled up and her kicks became twitches.

"Don't tell 'em about the jewels!" hissed Sunny, since folk always want to know what they've been told they shouldn't know.

That seemed to win a provisional victory for greed. The big one licked his lips. "You got jewels?"

"I'm a princess, aren't I?" said Alex, lifting her chin in a princess-y sort of way as Vigga lowered the woman's corpse to the straw, ever so gently, like a mother lowering a shallow-sleeping baby into its cot. "I've got *loads.*"

"Where?" asked the bald one as Vigga slid a dagger from the dead woman's belt and crept forwards.

"Close." Alex started to grin. "*Very* close."

"Where?" asked the big one, eyes all shiny with greed.

Alex leaned towards him, like they were all in on the same lovely little secret. "Up your *fucking* arse."

Which was when Vigga rammed that dagger into the top of the bald man's pate, stoving his skull right in with a wet crunch, popping one of his eyes out and sending blood spraying all over the big man's cheek.

He spun around as the corpse crumpled bonelessly at his feet. Vigga looked back at him, brows curiously raised, like she'd asked a testing question and was keen to have his answer.

The colour drained from his face. "Another Dane-Wolf . . ."

Vigga showed her pointed teeth. "I'm a *Swede.*"

The man swung his axe. With a *smack* Vigga caught his wrist, drove the heel of her hand into his forearm, and snapped it in half, like it had a second elbow. The axe tumbled from the man's limp fingers and he gave a roar of pain and rage, pulling a curved dagger with his good hand.

With another *smack* Vigga caught that arm, too, and broke it even worse, a shard of bone tearing through hairy skin and flicking blood around. He sank wailing to his knees, knife clattering down next to his axe.

Vigga leaned over him. "You going to kick me now? Kick me, I fucking dare you." She turned and yelled, "We're ready!"

A man burst through the door brandishing a large branch, still with a few leaves on it. Took Sunny a moment to recognise him without his habit— sinewy, wild, and unshaved.

"You're alive!" said Alex, starting to smile.

Brother Diaz stared at the two corpses. "It seems the Almighty may yet have some use for us."

Sometimes it's not till the danger's gone that you fall apart. Sunny felt her knees tremble, and her eyelids flicker, and a moment later she was slumped on her knees with someone patting her face and saying, "You all right? You all right?"

Vigga grabbed the last killer by the throat and gave him a furious shake.

"Did you fucking hurt her?" He moaned and squeaked, broken arms flopping hopelessly. "I'll rip you in two from your arsehole up!"

"Horse kicked me," muttered Sunny. Her head felt all light.

"Horse?" Vigga rounded on the horse Alex had stolen. "This fucker?"

"No, no!" said Alex. "Different horse."

"It better hope I don't get hold of it!"

"Calm, Vigga," Brother Diaz was saying. "Calm!"

"I can be useful!" squeaked the big man, who in Sunny's opinion was learning a strong lesson. However terrible you are there's always someone worse, and the more you throw your weight around the quicker they'll end up breaking both your arms. "I can tell you what Sabbas is planning!"

"Duke Sabbas?" asked Brother Diaz. "Empress Eudoxia's second son? He's here?"

"Chased us halfway across the Balkans," muttered Sunny through gritted teeth as she slumped back onto one elbow.

"He's on his way!" whimpered the big man, "with his sorcerers, and his Dane-Wolf—argh!"

"Vigga, please!" The monk struggled to prise Vigga away from the big man and only succeeded in being hauled around with him.

"I can help!" whimpered the man. "I can take Sabbas a message!"

"He's right!" said Brother Diaz, finally wrenching Vigga's fist from the man's now thoroughly ripped jacket. "I order you to let him go!"

"He *is* right," grunted Vigga. "I'll give you that."

Alex puffed out her cheeks, leaning on her knees, and Brother Diaz exhaled a long sigh, and slowly let go of Vigga, and the man with the two broken arms did his best to grin at her, which was quite impressive given the pain he must've been in.

Then Vigga punched him so hard her fist drove his nose right into his head, flung him against the wall so he bounced off, rolled flopping across the dirty straw, spat a sort of bloody gurgle, and was still.

Vigga sniffed. "That'll send quite the message."

Brother Diaz stared at the corpse. "I told you not to hurt him!"

"You told me to let him go. I let him go."

Sunny lay back in the straw and closed her eyes.

Why worry about what you can't change, after all?

A Splendid Occasion

Under other circumstances, Balthazar would have revelled in such pomp and ceremony.

Countess Jovanka sat side-saddle, painfully erect and sparkling with jewels, on a magnificent grey as towering as she was tiny, processing with an almost offensive lack of urgency from her lines towards the standing stones, where a highly polished table, large enough to have played centrepiece to a castle's dining hall, had been set up in the shade of a giant emerald awning on four gilded poles. She was the diamond point to an arrowhead of soldiers and servants, clerks and dignitaries, men-at-arms and maids-of-honour arrayed in their feast-day best. Syncellus Ignatios, in particular, had exchanged his already lofty headdress for another, encrusted with semi-precious stones, that the enemy could easily have mistaken for an approaching siege tower. The opposing delegation, meanwhile, paraded down the opposite slope with equal gravity, not to be outdone in numbers or opulence, pennants snapping, harness jingling, sunlight glinting on polished armour and golden thread.

Alas, while a glittering gathering is exactly the audience you might wish for at your triumph, it is the very last one you want bearing witness to your shameful degradation. Balthazar's boots, extorted from a grave robber, were in squelching ruins. His shirt, purloined from a corpse, was stiff with filth, stained with squirrel grease, and infested with a dead man's lice. He was famished and unwashed, testing the limits of physical and emotional exhaustion, and more closely resembling the assistant to the assistant dung-collector than one of Europe's foremost practitioners of the arcane.

So it was he skulked miserably after the countess and her entourage through the outer ring of stones, each taller than a man, then through the inner ring, twice as high and sprouting wildflowers in the cracks, and Balthazar felt that twitching of the small hairs, that tingling of the fingertips, that delicious presence of *power*. Here was a place where the mundane brushed the mystical, where many varieties of magic were at their most potent, where the energetic currents of the earth converged and the boundaries between worlds were at their thinnest. Once upon a time the possibilities it presented would have flooded him with excitement. Now he felt only the endless niggling of the Pope's insatiate binding upon his ravaged digestive tract.

Count Radosav heaved at his reins, forcing his sable charger to rear. As a counterpoint to his pomposity, Countess Jovanka halted her mount with dignified understatement. The two nobles faced each other, from opposite sides of the ring of standing stones, in full view of their massed armies. The grass rippled and the awning flapped in the breeze. A bird nesting somewhere among the stones, perhaps startled by this unexpected interruption to its peaceful morning, chirruped. Balthazar stifled a burp.

Each member of the bloated retinues picked out, as if by unspoken arrangement, some opposite number to glare at. Ignatios locked narrowed eyes with a female priest in equally opulent vestments. Balthazar scanned the grim faces and felt a sudden shock of recognition. He tugged gently at Baptiste's sleeve.

"Uh-huh," she murmured. "Most unkillable pair of bastards you'll ever meet."

Because there, loitering at the rear of Count Radosav's retinue, were Jakob of Thorn, more stony-faced even than Balthazar remembered him, and Baron Rikard, more apparently youthful even than at their last meeting. The vampire touched two fingers to his forehead in a jaunty acknowledgement.

"Let's get to it," snarled Radosav, swinging from his saddle, wrenching his jewelled sword-belt into position, then striding for the table.

Countess Jovanka snapped her fingers. One footman threw himself down on all fours to make a step of his back. Two more offered their hands to whisk the countess from her saddle like a diminutive angel from heaven, while a pair of ladies-in-waiting caught the corners of her train, allowing it to feather the grass as she glided to the table.

"They are making *quite* the exhibition of it," murmured Balthazar.

"Oh, this is nothing," said Baptiste. "You should've seen the peace talks between the twin Queens of Frankia and the Emperor of Burgundy. Went on for three months."

"You were there?"

"Neutral observer for the Duchess of Aquitaine."

Balthazar sourly shook his head. "You *always* have to go one better, don't you?"

"I don't *have* to." Baptiste fanned herself modestly with her hat, wayward curls fluttering. "It just always seems to happen."

Count Radosav planted his gloved fists on the polished tabletop with an audible thud, glaring up, lip scornfully twisted. Countess Jovanka examined her fingernails, sighed, then with an imperious toss of her head met his gaze with a formidable sneer of her own.

"Husband," she hissed.

"Wife," snarled the count.

Balthazar frowned. "Wait . . . what?"

"Wait . . . what?" grunted Jakob. He'd lost count of the parleys he'd stood watch over. Often disappointed at the end of the fighting. Sometimes trying to get it started again. But he'd never attended peace talks between a married couple.

Baron Rikard raised his brows. "I thought everyone knew?"

"Some of us aren't so sensitive to romance," muttered Jakob, adding somewhat bitterly, "lack of practice, maybe . . ."

"I have always been *painfully* sensitive to romance," said the baron as Radosav dropped into a chair and glowered at his wife. "And this, I sense, is one of those affairs in which one can hardly tell where the love ends and the hate begins," as Countess Jovanka perched on a chair opposite and glared at her husband down her nose. "Lucrezia and I were very much the same. Like cats and dogs, as they say, but with a bigger house and far more collateral damage. So many disagreements. Such apocalyptic arguments! But the rapprochements . . ." Baron Rikard closed his eyes. "She was a ruthless, reckless, self-serving snake. God, how I miss her."

There was a thud as Syncellus Ignatios dumped a heap of leather-bound tomes on the table, while Mother Vincenza spread out a huge map.

"I've a sense they'll be at this a while." Jakob folded his arms, shifting his weight from one leg to the other in a futile effort to work the aches out of his hips.

"The one thing the Churches of East and West prefer to an actual clash of arms is a protracted legal wrangle," said Baron Rikard, "but look on the bright side."

"There's a bright side?"

The vampire leaned close to murmur, "Neither of us is likely to run out of time."

The day wore on. The sun climbed. The shadow of the awning crept across the grass, the documents spread out to cover the table while the two priests struggled viciously over every detail, the cut and thrust of their verbal duel punctuated by the hissed comments of Countess Jovanka, the barked objections of Count Radosav. Both Churches might have lauded the charity of the Saviour from their pulpits, but they weren't giving much away at the negotiating table.

Count Radosav sent for wine for himself, and drank, and grew even more baleful, then tired of drinking alone, and sent for wine for everyone. Jakob had his vow of temperance so he turned it down, like he always did, and watched everyone else drink, like he always did, and regretted his vows bitterly. Like he always did.

His mood never loosened, but everyone else's started to. The guards gave up standing to attention, then leaned against the stones, then lazed on the grass, setting aside weapons, then helmets, then starting to mingle and greet old comrades on the other side.

"Jakob, you old bastard!" called Baptiste as she strolled over, fanning herself with her hat. "Fancy seeing you here."

"Baptiste." Jakob gave as much of a nod as his stiff neck would permit. "Glad you're alive."

They stood in silence for a moment, watching Mother Vincenza sketch a boundary on her map, then Syncellus Ignatios fling up his hands in a show of disgust.

"This is where you say you're glad I'm alive," said Jakob.

Baptiste shrugged. "You're always alive. How'd you end up in a count's retinue?"

"Usual way. Left for dead in one of his corpse carts then a vampire talked him into it. How'd you end up serving a countess?"

"Oh, she's an old friend."

"You've always had a lot of friends," said Jakob, struggling not to sound envious.

"Still a slice of luck to run into one out here."

"You've always had a lot of luck," said Jakob, struggling not to sound envious.

"What you call luck I call careful preparation, healthy caution, and never sticking my neck out."

"We're the Chapel of the Holy Expediency. Our necks are always out." Jakob glanced over at Balthazar, glaring at his burned wrist with the sourest expression imaginable. "I see you kept our magician alive."

"He didn't make it easy. Couple more days I might've killed him myself."

"No one could've blamed you." Jakob dropped his voice a little. "If his binding's bothering him, Princess Alexia must be alive."

"So it would seem," murmured Baptiste. "He thinks he can work a ritual to track her down. Here. At the stones."

"You'd count on him?"

"What choice do we have?"

"As much as ever," said Jakob. "Meaning none."

"We're the Chapel of the Holy Expediency," said Baptiste. "We never have any choice."

"Next . . ." The nib of Mother Vincenza's quill scratched as she crossed another item from her lengthy list, "we have the matter of the disputed pasture between the river and the shrine of Saint Petar the Blind—"

Countess Jovanka sat up. "I want the pasture!"

"Your Excellency?" Syncellus Ignatios ran his inky finger down a list in a ledger. "It is of no significance. Perhaps twelve roods of earth all told—"

"It has . . ." The countess glanced at her husband. "Sentimental value."

Count Radosav set down his goblet. "We met there. Some ancient willows grow on the bank." His face softened, ever so slightly. "A charming spot."

Countess Jovanka swallowed. "You told me it was your mother's favourite place."

"She wanted to be buried there, but . . ."

The countess put her hand gently on Ignatios's arm. "I would like the pasture . . ." she said, softly, looking across at her husband. "So I can have the willows cut down and burned." Her lips curled back and she spat the words across the table. "Just like you burned my town, you *shit*!"

"Saviour help us," groaned Baptiste, putting her head in her hands.

"God *damn* you, madam!" exploded the count, leaping up to send his chair flying over backwards. "How could any man make peace with such a *cursed harpy*!"

"God damn *you*, sir!" screeched the countess, slashing at the air with her hand and nearly chopping one of her guards in the face. "I can make no concession to such a *sack of spleen*!" She shoved past Syncellus Ignatios, striding imperiously alongside the table while her maids fell over each other to catch her train.

"Let us all remain calm . . ." begged Mother Vincenza, but the count shouldered her aside, stalking around the table with eyes locked on his wife.

"Uh-oh," muttered Baron Rikard, propping himself on his elbows. He had been lying on the grass, hands behind his head, watching the clouds.

All about the stones, guards who'd put thoughts of murder behind them and begun to look forward to a peaceful afternoon stirred unhappily. Gauntleted fists closed around grips, slid through the straps of shields, eased blades in their scabbards.

"Uh-oh," murmured Jakob. A moment comes. A tipping point, after which things can only slide one way. He could feel the violence approaching, like an old sailor feels the storm a few breaths before rain patters on the deck.

"Nothing less than your *total surrender* will satisfy me!" bellowed the count, rounding the end of the table and taking a step closer to his wife. Behind him, one of his officers lifted a nervous hand towards the ranked troops on the hill behind, ready to signal the charge.

"Surrender?" sneered the countess, taking a step towards her husband. "Ha! I will *crush* you beneath my heel!"

The armed retainers eased almost imperceptibly inwards. The unarmed retainers eased almost imperceptibly back.

"Uh-oh," said Baptiste.

"You will *beg* for mercy!" snarled Count Radosav.

"You will *squeal* for forgiveness!" hissed Countess Jovanka.

Everywhere teeth were gritted, prayers were mouthed, arses were clenched. The count glowered down at his wife, nostrils majestically flared. The countess glared up at her husband, bosom imperiously heaving.

For a terrible moment, the world held its breath.

Then that bird chirruped again, and Countess Jovanka seized her husband by the collar, and he grasped her by her ornamental breastplate, and they dragged each other into a tight embrace and began furiously necking, heedless of priests, retainers, armies, or anyone else.

Jakob raised his brows. "That was unexpected."

"Not for one sensitive to romance," said Baron Rikard, lying back down.

The two retinues let go their collective breath. Men on opposite sides shrugged at one another, rolled their eyes. Swords were eased away. Bloodshed was averted.

Jakob released the grip of his sword, tried to shake the aches from his fingers, and breathed a sigh of relief. Or was it disappointment?

Husband and wife broke apart just long enough to gaze into one another's eyes.

"I *love* you, you fool," spat the countess.

"My *God*, I love you," snarled the count.

And they set to kissing again. Syncellus Ignatios looked across at Mother Vincenza. "Perhaps we should repair to the chapel at Saint Gloria's and thrash out the final details?"

Mother Vincenza waved a weary hand. "By all means."

Baptiste frowned at her fingers, then up the slope towards the gathered armies, lips silently moving.

"What are you up to?" asked Jakob.

"I'm working out the price of one man, and a mail coat, and a halberd, sword, dagger, horse, tent, a few months' food . . ." She pushed back her hat. "And I'm wondering what all this cost."

"My wife Lucrezia went to war once," mused Baron Rikard, "against my advice, I might say, and we fought perhaps half a battle altogether, and won, as it happens, but the whole business proved utterly ruinous even so. Sometimes I think of the *decorating* we could have done for the same money and it makes me so terribly sad." He raised his hand, as though touching something beautiful. "There was a damask I had been considering for some drapery, in a shade of scarlet I can hardly describe, which I was forced to forgo." And he dabbed at one eye with a knuckle.

Radosav whisked Jovanka up and she clamped her legs about his hips, hands tangled in his hair, their mouths locked together in a duet of muffled grunts and moans. He stumbled back, barging into the table, a couple of goblets toppling, wine spilling over the maps.

"These two went to war . . ." Balthazar considered them with folded arms. "Spreading fire and murder across the region they are meant to care for, causing untold death and destruction . . . over a lover's tiff?"

Baron Rikard tipped his head back to consider the shifting clouds. "And they call *us* monsters."

My Greed Is a Famine

The count and countess had ridden off first, presumably to engage in a sexual escapade as intense as their recent hostilities. Balthazar could hardly have said which was the greater: his disgust or his jealousy. His own most recent sexual escapade was a hazy memory and, in all honesty, one probably best forgotten. The word *escapade* was, indeed, lending that particular misadventure *far* too much dignity.

The rival priests had departed still bickering over the legal jargon on an ancient deed, the centuries-long theological, financial, and political feud between the Churches of East and West a little too thorny to be settled in the bedchamber. The guards had dispersed to give notice of the cessation of hostilities and, on opposite sides of the valley, the two armed camps gradually collapsed in on themselves like punctured wineskins, soldiers streaming back towards their banal existences, lacking the imaginations to comprehend the privilege they enjoyed. Servants had finally carted away table and awning, labouring after their master and mistress, so that as the sun wallowed towards the hills and the shadows of the stones stretched long, the only evidence that the talks had ever taken place was a well-trampled area of grass and the skins from some exotic fruit the countess had at one point tossed aside. Balthazar wondered briefly about picking them up and scraping them out with his teeth, but decided that might still be beneath his dignity, even if that particular bar had sunk so low it was virtually subterranean.

As though to underscore that very point, Baptiste nudged Balthazar with the toe of one boot, the way a shepherdess might a stubborn goat. "Time to track down our wayward princess, then?" She glanced towards Jakob, arms grimly folded, and Baron Rikard, leaning against one of the standing stones and picking his fangs with a sharpened twig. "Doubt anyone here'll be put out by a little Black Art."

"It seems unlikely." Balthazar wearily stood, slapping the damp from the clinging seat of his dead man's trousers, and sighed. More of a groan, in truth.

Setting about a ritual, however pedestrian, would once have been the source of almost boundless excitement. What would be the risks, the challenges?

How could they be minimised, overcome? What was the most efficient form of words, the most potent arrangement of symbols, the most elegant set of gestures? Magic not just as a practical science but as an art, a spectacle, the highest form of self-expression!

Now he felt nothing but a faint irritation, a nagging disgust at how low he had fallen, and, of course, the ever-present sickly tug of the binding.

"I will need something with a point," he said, and then as Baptiste and Jakob both reached for one of their implements of death, "something that will float in water, or better yet milk. The pointer of our compass."

Baron Rikard held up his sliver of wood. "How's this?"

"A vampire's toothpick." Balthazar plucked it from his hand without enthusiasm. "Grimly appropriate, I suppose."

"And then?" asked Jakob.

Balthazar sank down at the very centre of the circle. "We bury it." And he began to tear at the grass with his fingers, ripping out a tiny grave in the damp earth, a few inches long, a few inches deep.

A grave for his hopes and ambitions. A grave for the man he had been. A very tiny one, of course, but then his stature was so very much reduced.

He lifted heavy hands to begin the gestures and could not but notice the filth under his cracked nails, smeared across his scabbed fingers, ingrained into the lines of his mottled palms, the angry scarring where he had, in Venice, attempted and spectacularly failed to cauterise the binding from his wrist. He used to have such beautiful hands.

"If we find Alexia," he murmured, "what then?"

"Get her to Troy," said Jakob, with his accustomed lump-hammer bluntness.

"Braving hardship and hunger, contending with more deadly cousins, the unholy results of Eudoxia's demented experiments, and assorted sorcerers, mercenaries, and monsters?"

"More than likely," said the baron.

"Without thanks, reward, or hope of release."

"I can tell you I don't get thanked much," grumbled Baptiste.

"A downward spiral," said Balthazar, "of loathsome humiliations."

"That's the job," growled Jakob.

"If I am not held captive in a literal lightless dungeon, I will yet face life imprisonment in the metaphorical oubliette of the papal binding, enslaved to the whim of a ten-year-old girl."

"She'll get older," said the baron, brightly.

"Being enslaved to the whim of a thirteen-year-old strikes me as little better."

"Likely a good deal worse," said Baptiste. "But you're far from the first to find yourself in this fix."

"As you have made *abundantly clear*." Balthazar slowly rose, slapping at least some of the dirt from his palms. "A veritable *procession* of warlocks, witches, and wizards have passed through the Chapel of the Holy Expediency, and on to glory, riches, and success." He glanced at the unpromising faces of his three colleagues. "Oh, wait, forgive me, they are all *dead*."

Baptiste rubbed impatiently at the back of her head. "You've been condemned by the Celestial Choir. What's the alternative?"

"The alternative?" Balthazar gave a sad smile. "Honestly, I have been considering that very question ever since my abject failure to break the Pope's binding in Venice was heaped upon my abject failure to break the Pope's binding on the road." He felt its familiar tug now, the ugly twist of nausea, the acrid taste of bile, as if to twist the knife of his despair at this lowest moment. "I am a slave to fools, a banquet for lice, a joke for the amusement of morons. Everything I once valued has been stolen from me. My books. My dignity. My freedom. My future."

"It's a tragic tale," said Baptiste, examining her fingernails.

"But is there a point to it?" asked Jakob.

"I have nothing left." Balthazar turned towards the tallest of the stones: two great uprights with a third balanced on top, forming a crude gate through which the setting sun now shone. Here, at this convergence of channels, in this place where the boundary between worlds was thinnest. "And so . . . I have nothing left to lose."

He thrust his hands high, making the sign of summoning with his dirty fingers, the form of welcome. Not really necessary, but why be a magician at all if one cannot indulge in a touch of theatre?

"Wait . . ." murmured Baron Rikard, the smooth skin of his forehead crinkling. "What are you—"

And Balthazar spoke the name.

There are, of course, excellent reasons why demonology is the most feared and hated of all the Black Arts. Even its most powerful practitioners, from the Witch Engineers of Carthage down, have frequently destroyed themselves, and not been shy over the quantities of innocent bystanders, animals, cities, and countryside they have taken with them. To *force* the least puissant infernal entity into the mortal world and bind it to one's will, even with the most painstaking preparation, is a task fraught with peril.

But to bring a demon who *wants* to come?

Why, you only have to stand in the right place . . . and ask.

Baron Rikard's expression turned in an instant to utter horror. "No—!" But it was too late.

The door between worlds opened and the sun went out. Daylight, and all beyond the edge of the standing stones, was in an instant cancelled.

The door between worlds opened, three times man's height, and still she had to stoop through.

A glimpse was all Balthazar caught. All he dared catch, before he wrenched his smarting eyes to the ground. A hint of the great antlers of twenty-nine points, black as phosphorescent ink, black as iridescent oil, dripping with finger rings and earrings and arm rings, festooned with glittering chains, flashing with pearls and jewellery, tributes, ransoms, and sacrifices from every culture beneath the night sky.

To bring a demon who wants to come, you only have to ask.

It is when they arrive that your problems begin.

With a gurgle of despairing terror Baptiste crumpled to her knees, clapping her hands over her face, rolled onto her side, and curled into a shivering ball.

Jakob stood frozen, mouth hanging open, scars picked out starkly on cheeks even more colourless than usual.

Only Baron Rikard retained the power of speech. "Stop, you fool," he gasped, one hand over his eyes, the other raised as if to shield him from the unholy spectacle, "send her back! Seal the door . . ." His voice grew higher and higher until it was nothing but a squeak, then silence, a silence utter and complete, with no bee's buzz, no bird's call, no wind in the grass. Like the icy sea bursting through the holed hull of a ship, the demon spoke.

"I . . . am . . . *invited*." Her voice was thunder, far off. "Would you un-invite me, you parasite, you maggot, you *leech*? Will you banish *me*? You *presumptuous husk*?"

"No," gasped the baron. "Oh, no."

"I am Shaxep, Duke of Beneath. My greed is a *famine*. My envy a *plague*. My lust a *flood*. My fury a *hurricane*." The last word was lightning close at hand, and the demon spread her mighty wings and cast the stones into an even deeper darkness, the wash of honey-smelling wind tearing at Balthazar's face, stinging tears from his eyes, leaving him gasping as black feathers and golden dust fluttered down around his feet and he wondered through his utter terror if perhaps this had not been his best idea.

"I'll be silent," whimpered Baron Rikard.

"*Excellent* choice," purred the demon, her satisfaction almost more terri-ble than her anger, and though Balthazar's smarting eyes were fixed on the ground, he felt her gaze turn upon him, and his knees trembled. "And so, Balthazar Sham Ivam Draxi . . . to *business.*"

Footsteps approached, soft, and slow, and at each one came the gentle crunch and crackle of frozen grass. "You have presumed to *call* me, and I have deigned to *answer.* Know that you teeter on the brink of *doom.* Know that you bargain with *infinity.* Know that your very existence dangles by a *filament.* So . . ." She stopped before him, and her wings clicked and rustled as she folded them, and the jewellery on her antlers jingled and rattled, and then was still, and there was silence. "What do you need?"

Balthazar licked his lips. He was, it hardly needed to be said, a man who always chose his words carefully. "I seek your—"

"Did your mother not teach you manners?"

"I never knew my mother," he whispered.

"That explains so much. When you ask a favour, look upon me."

"I dare not," he whispered, and he could feel the crackle as the tears froze on his cheeks. He could see her feet in the frost-rimed grass before him, her toes like a bird's, the colour of blood from a slit throat, the talons long as daggers, painted with darkly glistening golden designs. "Lest your unearthly beauty drive me mad."

"Mmmmm." Her feathers clattered as she adjusted her wings. "I love it. Imagine having such *delicious* sycophancy on tap."

"I offer you that and more." He wobbled down to his knees. He clasped his hands. "If you can free me from my bonds."

Shaxep clicked her tongue, *tut, tut, tut,* each one a nail hammered into his head. "My preference is for making slaves, man-child. If I free you from these shackles, you will have heavier ones to wear. An eternal debt to me."

"But those chains," he managed to gasp, holding out his trembling arm to show the burn on his wrist, "I will have chosen."

"As long as you never say . . . I didn't *warn you.* Now . . ." He felt her presence as she leaned towards him, and it was the best he could do not to void his bowels on the spot. "Let . . . me . . . *see.*" A bitter chill, the hairs in his nose freezing, and more than the cold, the abject terror, and the ecstatic thrill, of being in the presence of a power from beyond the world. A power before which the very rules of creation must bend. A power to challenge the angels themselves—

"No." There was a kind of irritated snort. "Sorry. Can't help you. Not with that."

"Wait . . ." whispered Balthazar. "What?"

"I could do you limitless wealth, or turn your enemies to salt, or something? Pretty much anything. Just . . . not this."

"But . . . you're . . ."

"Duke of Beneath, yes, but there are rules, and there are limits." Shaxep gave a sigh like a winter wind, and her wings shivered, and gilded dust floated down. "The ambitious never realise until it is too late. Power is a cage, Balthazar Sham Ivam Draxi."

"You can't do it?" he muttered. "*You?* Can't *do it*?"

"You think I'm *happy about it*?" And her voice was thunder once again, and he cringed in her towering shadow. "I did the whole 'greed is a famine' speech and *everything*."

Balthazar could not help one glance as she turned away. He glimpsed her back, crimson knots of muscle between the vast shadows of her wings, scored with gilded marks, rings, arrows, symbols, hypnotic spirals of impossible geometry, and in the midst a great wound, endlessly leaking tears of molten gold. She stopped in the doorway and turned back, the chains and crowns and bracelets chiming, and he tore his eyes away, lest he meet her gaze and see there the answers to questions no mortal should even conceive of, and at once be driven mad.

"I am interested in the soul, though," she said. "It's actually quite a good one. So, you know. Do call. If you need something else."

The door closed, and the sun was lit as sharply as snapped fingers, and it was once again a pleasant evening, bees, birds, and all, the warm sunset touching the western hills with rosy light.

The only change was the black feathers scattered everywhere. Black feathers, and golden dust.

"Oh God," sobbed Baptiste, and she crawled a little way through the grass and was noisily sick.

"What did you do?" snarled Baron Rikard, seizing Balthazar by his shoulders and giving him a furious shake.

Balthazar hardly saw him. Hardly heard him. "She couldn't do it," he whispered, holding up his wrist and staring at the burn.

"I saw her," whispered Jakob, tears leaking down his face, wide eyes fixed on the empty archway in which there was nothing now but the sunset. "I *saw* her."

"Even Shaxep . . ." breathed Balthazar, "couldn't *do* it." He blinked into Baron Rikard's face. "There must be some trick . . . it cannot truly have been her!"

"Not *her*?" screeched Baptiste. "The place is covered in *demon quills*!" And she threw a furious hand at the obsidian feathers scattered across the grass, even now melting into smears of iridescent pitch.

"She struck some other deal, then," muttered Balthazar. "With Cardinal Bock, maybe . . . to deceive me!"

"A cardinal struck a deal with a demon," muttered Baptiste, "because *that's* how important you are, you *reckless lunatic*!"

"I will find it out . . ." whispered Balthazar, scratching absently at his wrist. "I will get to the heart of it. I *will*. I *must*."

"The trouble with clever people," muttered Jakob, rubbing his scarred hand across his scarred face to wipe away the tears, "is they think everything must be clever." He looked over at Balthazar. "But this is simple. There is no scheme. There is no trick. Pope Benedicta's binding is too strong even for a Duke of Hell to break."

"Oh, *of course*!" screeched Balthazar, voice dripping scorn. "Because, I suppose, that ridiculous child really *is* the Second Coming of the Saviour, therefore her pathetic binding is the word of *God himself*!"

A joke, of course. The most ludicrous joke of which he could conceive. But no one laughed. Baptiste glared at him, wiping her mouth. Jakob glowered at him, hands on hips. Even the endlessly smirking Baron Rikard had not the hint of a smile.

"Wait . . ." Balthazar took a hesitant step away, the hairs on the back of his neck prickling. "You can't really believe that . . ." He stared at Baron Rikard, surely among the least credulous creatures he had ever encountered. "*You . . . can't* really believe that?"

"I still had my doubts." The vampire licked one pointed tooth with the tip of his tongue. "Until now. But the insane extremes of your efforts to prove the binding can be broken have ended up proving the exact opposite. Shaxep could not do it." He gave a helpless shrug. "What higher power is there?"

Balthazar felt dizzy. He wanted desperately to deny it. To heap scorn upon it. He opened his mouth to do it, but for a moment nothing emerged. In the end he forced out a bark of shrill laughter, and of all the false chuckles he had vomited up that day it was the least convincing. "Well, if the Saviour walks among us again," he said, less cutting barb than desperate squawk, "I suppose the Last Judgement must be at hand!"

The silence stretched.

"Finally," grunted Jakob of Thorn, wearily turning away. "He gets it."

End Times

Alex kept trudging, head down. Best to keep her eyes on the dirt. It was where they belonged. Look up and she'd see how far it was to the horizon, how shitty the journey was likely to be, and that there'd be nothing worth having when she got there.

Safe to say she was *not* in the best of moods.

"You need a turn on the horse?" asked Sunny.

"Me? No. Last thing I want. I hate horses." God, she'd have loved a turn on the horse. Her left foot had been buggered for days, just one massive blister, then she'd stepped in a rabbit hole and buggered her right foot, and now she hardly knew which leg to limp on.

Sunny looked dubious as well as hurt, shoulders hunched around her hood, arms hugged around her ribs.

"I'm fine," said Alex, in the same tone you'd say *I'm dying*, but though Sunny could see a mouse at half a mile, it seemed she was blind to any sub-text, even when it was hobbling along next to her with a face like a smacked arse. Or maybe Sunny saw the subtext plainly but didn't really want to get down on Alex's account, which was no surprise, since Alex had fucked up their friendship if they'd even ever had one. Who'd want to kiss a greedy piece of shit like her? The moment she got her fingertips to something halfway good she had to ruin it by grasping for more.

She frowned off, desperate for a distraction, towards the row of crooked posts on one side of the track, all wonky like they'd been put up by a drunk. Here an old sheep skull had been stuck on top of one, rotten wool blowing, and there an iron circle or a copper wheel hung, clattering and tinkling in the breeze. "What's all this business?" she asked.

"It's got quite the pagan flavour," said Vigga, stomping along barefoot but somehow having no trouble with her feet at all. "Reminds me o' home . . . and not in a good way . . . not that there's any good way to be reminded of home . . . or anything in the past, really . . ." She trailed off, looking puzzled. "What were we talking about?"

"The fence," said Sunny.

"It's notice of a joint Papal and Patriarchal Interdict," said Brother Diaz, scratching at the patchy beard he was developing.

"Papal into what?" grunted Vigga.

"*Interdict*," he snapped back at her, waving at the nearest post. Monks and werewolves likely don't make natural travelling companions, but the two of them seemed to be winding each other up worse than ever. "It must be the boundary of the Barony of Kalyatta. The place was devastated by the Long Pox thirty years ago. Killed a quarter of the population."

"Sounds bad," muttered Alex. She remembered the Long Pox coming through the Holy City. The guards herding the sick into the pest-houses. The reek of smoke from the burning bodies. Folk chanting lists of saints' names to ward off the vapours. The choirs wailing day and night for the forgiveness of the Almighty.

"The fourth plague to strike the region in a decade," said Brother Diaz. "The Sighing Sickness had been even worse. There was an account of it in my monastery's library. Too many dead for the graveyards, so they buried them in pits by the hundred. Buried them in every inch of consecrated ground, under every shrine, church, or chapel in the region . . ."

The landscape wasn't much different beyond the fence, but knowing the story lent it a threatening feel, somehow. A whole province wiped off the map. Alex shivered, and drew her stolen coat a little tighter around her torn jacket. "Sounds *really* bad."

"Bad enough to force the squabbling Churches of East and West for once to act together. They declared the whole barony cursed, ordered it evacuated, and had it placed off limits until reprieved by a certified divine intervention."

"Looks like God never showed . . ." murmured Sunny.

"He's got a habit of doing that," said Alex.

"Plague on one side." Brother Diaz gazed gloomily past the posts into the scrubby no-man's-land beyond. "War on the other." And he gazed gloomily back towards the burned-out wreckage of the village they'd passed not long before. "One could start to think these are the End Times."

Vigga snorted. "You priests are always announcing the End Times. Like the gothi in my village. Oh, the omens! Look how the crows fly! Ragnarok comes! Butchers sell meat, coopers sell casks, and your lot sell End Times, it's how you fill the pews."

"Pagans have pews?" asked Alex.

"Well, benches, I guess? Maybe with a sheepskin for the rich folk."

"Everything has a sheepskin in your stories," said Sunny. "To hear you tell it, Scandinavia is all blood, boats, and sheepskin."

Vigga waved that away. "That is just . . ." She scratched her head as she thought about it, ". . . not a bad summary, actually, but the *point* is . . ." She stared off towards the horizon. "What's the point?"

Brother Diaz rolled his eyes. "You make every conversation like this! You seize the reins, immediately drive the cart off the road into a bog, then sit there asking, 'How did this happen?'"

"But you have to admit it's not dull!" said Vigga, bursting out laughing. "Freya's shite, look at the long faces on you lot." She hooked an arm around Alex's shoulders and gave her a squeeze that made her groan. "Killed those bastards in the barn, didn't I? Can't see 'em bothering anyone again."

"It's not the dead bastards that worry me," wheezed Alex, wriggling her shoulders to loosen Vigga's crushing arm so she could glance back the way they'd come, "so much as the bastards still alive."

"Never look back, that's my advice." Vigga let go of Alex's shoulders, which was a huge relief, then grabbed her head with one big hand, which wasn't, and twisted it slightly painfully to face forwards. "Eyes ahead. Scrape off the mud of grudges and regrets. What good does worry ever do?" And she mussed Alex's hair with her fingers.

"I've always worried a very great deal," said Brother Diaz, "and it's amazing the number of massacres I haven't participated in."

"You've took part in a couple to my certain knowledge," said Vigga.

"More *witness* than *perpetrator* . . ."

"My point is you've got to shake off the past. Like nutshells." And Vigga shook herself so hard her hands flopped about on the ends of her arms and her hair all fell in her face, so she had to stick her bottom lip out to blow it away, then it got stuck in her mouth, so she had to spit it out. "My *point* . . ." as she walked up towards the top of the rise and stopped, hands on hips. "What's my point?"

"Cart in a bog," muttered Brother Diaz, stopping beside her. "Up to the axles." And Alex caught up to them and looked down into the valley beyond.

There was a village in the bottom. Not much of a settlement for a girl dragged up in the Holy City, but there were lights down there, twinkling in the chill twilight, and could she hear faint music on the air? Her mouth watered with a painful longing at a whiff of cooking.

"Look at that!" Vigga clapped Brother Diaz on the shoulder and near knocked him through the strange fence into the forbidden Barony of Kalyatta. "Civilisation! We've got money, don't we?"

"We do," said Alex. Those bastards Vigga killed must've been well paid to hunt her, and she had the silver scattered all about her person now in three different purses, both socks, and some folded rags wrapped under her shirt. She'd been tempted to slip the two little gold coins up her arse—a habit from her younger days when Gal the Purse would strip the children after they'd been robbing—but without a bit of olive oil it wasn't the most comfortable operation so she'd sleeved 'em instead.

"Might be we could find a hayloft," said Sunny, her eyes very big. "Spend a night out of the weather."

"Get us some fucking *dinner*," sang Vigga, almost dancing a jig on her tiptoes. "I could eat a lamb chop, couldn't you, Brother? Lamb chop in gravy!" she howled at the sky, and she licked at her pointed teeth with her long tongue. "Baldr's arsehole, I could eat a dozen of the shits!" And she trotted off down the slope.

Alex looked worriedly over at Brother Diaz. "Going in there might not be the best idea."

He winced towards the village, scratching again at his straggly beard. "It might not."

"Taking Vigga in there might *really* not be the best idea."

"It might really not." He turned to look at her and gave a helpless shrug. "But, sweet Saint Beatrix, I could eat a lamb chop."

Good Givers

─────────────

Sure I can't tempt you?" simpered the Pope, hitching up her skirts, painted lips gleaming by torchlight.

The Patriarch of Troy gripped the golden wheel he wore and turned his eyes towards heaven. "My virtue is not for sale at any price, devil!"

The crowd—if you could use the word about two dozen peasants, a couple of merchants, a monk, a princess, a werewolf, an uncomfortable elf sticking to the shadows, and a baffled-looking dog—dutifully clapped. Well, the dog didn't, because it lacked the equipment, but Alex clapped loudly enough for both of them.

"Always loved the players," she explained, over her shoulder.

"Hmmm," said Sunny. She was less keen. They'd opened this particular performance with John of Antioch bashing up some often-patched pointy-eared dummies, which was a good way to chisel a cheer from even the most sullen audience, as her old Ringmaster could no doubt have testified, but was a long way from her own favourite spectacle.

"All the silly stories," Alex was saying, "and the nimble talk and the costumes and clowning. Takes you out of yourself for a while. Away from your hunger and your debts and the shit people done to you and the shit you had to do to them and maybe the coins up your arse."

"Coins up your—?" asked Sunny. But Alex was already blathering on.

"Then the best players pull some big audiences all fixed on something else, so there's no better place for lifting purses."

"Hmmm," said Sunny, wishing she could think of something clever or funny to say, but the cupboard was bare.

"I used to dream of joining 'em when I was little. Looked like heaven to me. A company to belong to. Always on the road, always on the move, leaving your regrets at your back, never in one place long enough to be hated, getting paid for pretending to be someone else. That's all I wanted, when I was little. To be someone else . . ." And she petered out, frowning towards the stage.

Sunny wanted to say she liked Alex the way she was. Liked her more than anyone else she knew. She'd wanted to say it ever since that kiss. But having an audience didn't help at all, with Brother Diaz there to judge and Vigga to make jokes. Now somehow too much time had passed, like the way things were was mortar in a wall and had set hard.

Sometimes Alex would look at Sunny, like she was trying to smile, and Sunny would try to smile back but her stupid face wouldn't do it. Stupid face! And Alex would look away a bit crestfallen and that would feel actually painful.

Though maybe it was her broken ribs which were still very sore when she breathed in.

If there was going to be a next move Sunny would have to make it, but when you've spent so long building walls you can't topple them whenever you fancy. A few times every day she'd work herself up to do it, then she'd start thinking Alex was so easy, maybe kissing people was just something she did? Maybe she kissed all sorts of people all the time and she'd already forgotten about it. That thought made Sunny feel strangely miserable. People really fucking hate the elves, as John of Antioch could no doubt have testified, but in her experience, they also really want to have sex with them, so it was far from the first kissing she'd done, but it was the first in a while she'd had any wish to repeat.

The Pope whipped her skirts up again to give everyone a glimpse of a big fake muff and that made them all laugh which seemed like good cover. Sunny leaned forwards, reaching out with one hesitant finger to tap Alex on the shoulder—

"Here!" Vigga blundered past to stick another skewer of meat in Alex's hand. A big woman was cooking them over a sparky fire and they were covered in char and oily sauce and weren't to Sunny's taste at all.

"Looks like hell," said Alex, closing her eyes as she sniffed at it. "Tastes like heaven," and she took a bite from one of the lumps.

"I have my doubts it's lamb," said Brother Diaz, nibbling at his own skewer with his front teeth.

"If I found out it was human I'd likely keep eating," said Alex around her mouthful.

"Sunny?" asked Vigga, waving a skewer at her.

Sunny pulled her hood down lower and retreated back into the shadows by the wall. "I'm full."

"Well, you're no thicker'n a blade of grass." And Vigga stuck out her long tongue and slid the whole skewer into her mouth and sucked the lot off it while Brother Diaz watched her, very quiet, and she chewed away with her tattooed cheeks bulging and dragged out a bit of hair she'd got stuck in her mouth and stared happily mystified towards the stage. "What in the name of all that's unholy are these bastards about?"

"Fucking is bad," said Alex, "is the gist."

Vigga leaned over to spit out a bit of gristle. "And up's down and day's night. It's like they can't be happy till everyone's miserable. I swear they'd snuff the sun out if they could. Give us another coin, Alex."

Alex slapped a little silver coin into Vigga's palm and she went to get more meat. Sunny leaned close to her. "Tell me that hadn't been up your arse."

"I only put gold up there these days." Alex stuck her chin in the air as she turned back to the play. "I'm a princess, don't you know."

It all ended with the sinful Pope dragged to hell, of course. Or at any rate, behind some painted wooden flames stage left, the hands of whoever was wiggling them just about visible from where Sunny was standing. The Patriarch gave a booming oration on the importance of the Twelve Virtues, especially charity and generosity. Then, in an entirely unconnected move, he hopped down from the stage with his bowl out, at which the audience scattered quicker than they might've if Sunny had thrown her hood back and shown everyone her ears.

Alex made it worth the players' while, though. For someone who'd grown up finding new places to hide coins, she was open-handed when she had the chance. The Patriarch of Troy raised his bushy brows—one hanging off by a bit of failed glue—when he saw what'd tinkled into his bowl. "Blessings upon your generosity, my child," and he made the sign of the wheel on the front of his robes, which close-up were sprinkled with a goodly contribution of dandruff.

"Your sinful Pope was quite the laugh," said Alex. "Can't imagine it plays too well in the west, mind you."

The Patriarch leaned closer to murmur, "In the east it's a sinful Pope and a righteous Patriarch, in the west we swap over."

"What about the middle?" asked Brother Diaz.

"If you're not sure of the opinions of your audience, try to be as vague as possible."

The Pope had ambled over now, freed from eternal damnation and flapping her vestments to let some air in. "Been sent running from more than one village by a torch-wielding mob after misjudging the mood," she observed.

Vigga nodded thoughtfully along. "Who hasn't?" The players didn't seem unduly worried by her. Hard to perform in a travelling show without getting comfortable with the unusual, but there were limits, so Sunny made sure to keep her own hood well down.

Brother Diaz still seemed troubled. "Surely a good play does not merely indulge the biases of the audience, but guides them towards the Saviour's *truth*?"

"Sounds grand in theory." The Patriarch removed his crown to scratch at a wispy and slightly scabrous pate. "But, believe me, there's no good tips in it."

"Fornication is . . ." Brother Diaz cleared his throat. "A *sin*, of course . . ." He cleared his throat again. "But there are ample examples in the histories of . . . sinners of *that* variety repenting of their ways and returning to the bosom of the Saviour—"

"Pray leave the Saviour's bosom out of this!" intoned the Pope, looking piously to the skies.

"To the grace of the Almighty, then! It's just that being dragged to hell . . . well . . ." Brother Diaz cleared his throat even one more time. "I prefer to believe in a forgiving God than a vengeful one, that's all."

"Don't we all?" muttered Sunny, under her breath, though she wasn't sure the evidence was with him.

"I'm no priest, friend," said the Patriarch, "despite the robes. But it seems to me the sin she's punished for ain't so much the fornication as the hypocrisy."

"That's it," chimed in the Pope, in a display of unity between the Churches of East and West sadly absent off the stage. "The beasts in the field all fornicate, after all."

"When their luck's in," said Vigga, grease on her chin and cheeks bulging with meat.

"But they don't *lie*," said the Patriarch. "They don't preach one thing and practise another. They don't judge others while riddled with sin themselves."

"Right," said Brother Diaz, frowning at the ground as if that wasn't quite the answer he'd been hoping for. "Hmmm."

"But I do thank you most profusely for the contribution." The Patriarch bowed low. "Don't run into many good givers these days, sad to say."

"A sign of the times indeed." Alex glanced across at Sunny with the hint of a grin, and Sunny was trying to arrange her stupid face to do the same when the Pope spoke up again.

"Who was that fellow the other day?" She nodded towards the road east they were planning to take in the morning. "The one with the golden cloak." Sunny felt a prickling on the back of her neck. "Stupidest cloak I ever saw, but *he* was a good giver."

"What was his name?" asked Alex, trying to sound breezy but Sunny could hear the strain in her voice.

"Sad ass?" ventured the woman who played the Pope. "No! Sabbas." It wasn't an unpleasant surprise, exactly, because bad news never came as a surprise to Sunny, more a tiresome confirmation of what she'd somehow known was coming. "Said he was searching for a girl."

"That so?" asked Alex, almost a groan.

"And I replied that for a further contribution I'd play any part he pleased, but he said he was looking for a *particular* girl." The woman leaned close. "Her Highness Alexia Pyrogennetos! Long-lost heiress to the Throne of Troy!"

The Patriarch looked thoughtfully at his stage, which was a flat wagon with a few brightly painted boards around it. "Must admit I thought right then that'd make a fine play."

"Stretching credibility a little," said Brother Diaz, voice somewhat tight.

"If I've learned one thing in forty years on the stage, it's that folk will believe any old shit if you dress it up right. Don't suppose you lot seen a princess on your wanderings, have you?"

"We mix with royalty daily!" said Alex, forcing another laugh.

"Shame." The Pope sighed as she pulled the sock from her head, a surprising quantity of red hair spilling out. "This Sabbas was offering quite the reward. Enough for a man to become a good giver himself."

"If he was that way inclined," added the Patriarch, and he planted his headdress back on, at something of an angle, and waved a flamboyant benediction. Slightly less effective now he'd taken off the beard to reveal a rather weak chin, but the voice rang out nicely. "May good fortune follow you, my children!"

Alex met Sunny's eye for a moment, then looked away. "It'd be a fucking first," she muttered.

Cart in a Bog

somehow knew . . ." muttered Brother Diaz, "when I saw the forbidding plague fence . . . that I'd soon enough end up on the wrong side of it." He was picking his footsteps with irritating care, since half the road had been washed away by old storms and the rest turned to treacherous glue by the current one. "Knowing my luck I'll survive werewolves, crab-people, and sorcerers in order to slip into a ditch and break my neck."

"We can hope," murmured Vigga. She'd almost been warming to Brother Diaz at times—mostly while fucking him—but since they'd found Alex and Sunny, he'd backslid into the prickly whiner she'd first taken him for, with an added streak of stubborn bitterness. Bitter stubbornness? Both, maybe. As if he hadn't quite realised he'd been lying with a werewolf till there were other people to notice it.

Her patience had never been the strongest rope on the boat but since they struck off the road and into the forbidden Barony of Whatever, she could feel it fraying further with every step. When night came the moon would be almost full and she could feel it swinging around beyond the clouds, behind the horizon. Hot and cold and numb and tickly all at once. Her collar wasn't tight, but it felt too tight, so she was forever wriggling at it, desperate to pop the stitches and rip herself free of her clothes to charge snarling through the tangly undergrowth, wet fur glistening in the moonlight and her wet nose full of the sticky spoor of prey, slinking and slobbering in the endless hunt for the good meat.

But she'd promised herself she'd keep the wolf muzzled. She winced as she rubbed at her breastbone, blew out a breath in a puff of mist. Clean, clean, nothing to worry about.

"I swear I'm being punished." Brother Diaz shook his head at the streaming heavens, then glanced at Vigga out of the corner of his eye as if she was part of the punishment.

"Who made you the hero of the story?" asked Alex, peering down at her own squelching boots. One had split open at the end to make a sad, flopping mouth through which her broken toenails showed. "Maybe *I'm* being punished."

"Or me," said Vigga, glowering sideways at Brother Diaz. "I'm a stinking pagan, after all, and a murderous savage, and an unrepentant fornicator!"

There was an awkward silence. "Well, you wouldn't want to fornicate with someone who was busy repenting, would you?" asked Alex. "It'd kill the mood!"

Nobody laughed.

"Maybe it's a blessing." Sunny peered out from under the dripping peak of her hood. "The rain hides us. Masks our scent."

"You think they're still following?" asked Alex.

"If they've got a werewolf . . ." Vigga stopped to glare back the way they'd come. "It'll take more'n a few drips to shake 'em off . . ."

She could feel him out there, somewhere. Almost smell him. Squatting in the brush, bent over her muddy footprints, snuffling and sniffling at *her* scent. Following *her* track. Hunting *her*, the hairy fuck?

"We should turn the tables," she said, and her voice had the wolf's growl. "Hunt *them*."

"The four of us?" Brother Diaz snorted. "We'll be lucky if we can track down a dry spot to sleep. I may not be an expert in military strategy—"

"They don't teach that at a monastery?" snarled Vigga, having to wipe a little slobber from the corner of her mouth.

Brother Diaz took a step towards her, holding her eye for once, and she thought she saw a hint of scorn there. "But Her Holiness put *me* in charge, and even *I* know that when the odds are against you, you had better run—"

"Not when the odds are *long* against you and there's no help coming." Vigga stepped towards him now, baring her teeth. "Then you fall on your enemy when they least expect it, on the ground you choose, at the moment you choose. Kill their strongest, and break the spirit of the rest, and teach 'em a bloody lesson!"

"That sounds . . ." His eyelids fluttered slightly, as though he'd caught a waft of her scent, then he set his jaw, and spat the word in her face. "*Absurd.* We can't risk Princess Alexia's life!"

"Then you take her on while I go back—"

"No! I've lost half my congregation already and I *will* get the rest of us to Troy! No one's fighting!"

Vigga's turn to snort her scorn. "If you win, what a victory! And if you lose, you die gloriously, and, I don't know . . ." when the gothi talked about it she'd followed till the dying gloriously then lost the thread, "the Valkyries set a place for you in Valhalla . . . or something."

Brother Diaz lifted his chin to glare at Vigga down his nose. Since she was taller, he had to lift his chin quite a long way. "I don't believe in *Valkyries.*"

She glared back at him, nostrils flared. "I don't believe in *monks*, yet here you are."

They stayed there, while the rain pattered down, both clammy with wet, both breathing fast, and to have kissed him would've been no effort at all. It was almost an effort not to do it, the fury and the tickle and the moon all mingled. To suck at his tongue, and drag him down in the mud, and she started to make a long, low growl—

"Enough!" snapped Alex, poking Brother Diaz in the chest with a pointed finger and making him stumble back and nearly slip in the mud. "You, stop riling the werewolf!"

"Ha!" said Vigga. "You tell him—ow!" As Alex poked her in the chest.

"And *you*, we're going to Troy, not Valhalla! We're far outnumbered, Sunny's still hurt, and you're the only real fighter among us!"

"You properly poked my tit," grumbled Vigga, rubbing at the bruise.

"Behave yourself or I'll poke the other one!" Alex glared at her, then at Brother Diaz. "What the hell happened between the two of you anyway?"

There was an awkward silence.

Vigga licked her lips. "Well . . ."

Brother Diaz swallowed. "Er—"

"What's that?" asked Sunny, pointing up the road.

The rain had slacked off. Enough that through the grey haze to the south, Vigga could see a ridge above the trees and, at its end, a jagged outline that had to be man-made.

"Looks like a bell tower," said Brother Diaz, squinting into the rain.

Vigga pushed her hair back, sending a trickle of cold water down her spine, and set off towards the ruin. "Might still have a roof," she said.

Vows

"his looks nice," said Alex, squinting up at the ruinous facade. It gave the
strong impression that the dead creeper was the only thing holding it up.

"The Abbey of Saint Demetrius," whispered Brother Diaz. A statue of the
patron of healers stood in a dripping niche above the gateway, his hand once
raised in blessing, now snapped off at the wrist.

"He's one of my favourite saints!" said Sunny.

"Really?"

She and her bedraggled horse both gave him a long look. "For an elf they're
all much of a muchness."

Brother Diaz sighed. "The monks treated the sick here with selfless dili-
gence, until the order was given to abandon the place. It's said some remained
even then, to render last rites to the dying."

Vigga frowned at the overgrown graveyard crowding in towards the monastery's walls. The ground had sunk at some point in the last few decades,
nettle-shrouded gravestones all leaning in around a muddy puddle. "Will you
render me last rites," she asked, "if the place turns out haunted?"

"Thought you were heading for Valhalla?" asked Sunny.

"That's my first choice, but there's no harm hedging your bets."

"Heaven is for *repentant* sinners," grunted Brother Diaz, stepping close to
the abbey's door, which had long ago dropped from its hinges and now lay
rotting in the gateway. A wooden tablet was set into it, carved writing worn
away by time, but stamped with both the circle and the five-spoked wheel.
"The seals of Pope and Patriarch. Entrance is forbidden on pain of excommunication."

Sunny shrugged. "I've never been incommunicated."

"And I'm on small-talking terms with a Pope and two cardinals." Alex
stepped around Brother Diaz, clonking over the rotten door and under the
dripping archway. "Reckon I can get us a dispensation."

Water spattered from broken gutters in the overgrown courtyard, one corner turned into an impromptu pond, a cloister with a fallen roof running
down one side. It put Brother Diaz in mind of his own monastery—shuffling

along the colonnade in single file to morning prayers, breath smoking on the winter chill.

He stepped into a draughty hall, cobwebs floating among the rafters. Aside from one trickling leak the roof still held and the floor was dry. Dusty chairs and tables were set in rows, undisturbed in decades, so like the refectory in his own monastery they might have been built from the same plan. The tasteless food, the suffocating silence, the crushing routine, every day a copy of the last—

He jerked around at a noisy clatter. Vigga had thrown her soaked coat over a table and was shaking herself wildly, water flying. She blew a mist of drops and bent over, wringing her hair out with both hands, wet shirt stuck to her back so he could see ghosts of the designs beneath, wet trousers stuck to her backside so there was no need to guess at its shape, not that he had to guess, he knew exactly what it looked like, what it felt like, what—

"Sweet Saint Beatrix," he muttered as he turned away, surreptitiously adjusting his trousers with one hand while reaching into his shirt with his other to grip the blessed vial.

Sunny had led the horse in and was trying to unbuckle the girth and grip her ribs at once. He started over, eager for a distraction. "Here, let me," dragging the soaked saddle free and dumping it on the ground.

Sunny peeled her wet hood back, started to give the horse a rub, muttering softly to it. Aside from a few wild tweaks her pale hair was stuck to her skull and one of her ears poked through. Elves have pointed ears, of course, it's the first thing you learn about them. But the tip of Sunny's was cut off jagged.

She saw him looking. In the gloom her eyes were huge. "They clipped it off," she said, "with sheep shears."

Brother Diaz swallowed. "Who did?"

"They said I was an enemy of God so, I guess, friends of God?" She went back to rubbing the horse. "It bled way more than they expected, though, so they left the other one." And she turned her head to show him and flicked the pointed tip with her finger.

Brother Diaz swallowed. "That's . . ." He hardly knew what that was. She *was* an enemy of God, from a strictly doctrinal point of view, but without her their holy mission would've foundered in the Adriatic. He'd known plenty of humans who showed less evidence of having a soul. He turned somewhat guiltily away, hoping for another distraction.

Alex was peering into the dead fireplace, rubbing her pale hands together. "You reckon we can get a fire going?"

"No harm trying." Vigga plucked up a chair, whisked it over her head, and brought it whistling down on another to smash them both to bits. She showed her pointed teeth in a mad grin as she set about stomping the remains to kindling under one bare heel.

The effortless strength. The joyous savagery. The utter scorn for propriety or inhibition. Brother Diaz forced his eyes away, obliged to make another adjustment to his crotch. "*Sweet* Saint Beatrix . . ."

Pure thoughts. Boring thoughts! This was a monastery, for the Saviour's sake, there should be no shortage of purity and boredom to dwell on. He set a hand on the dusty stand where the lector would have droned out readings from the scriptures at mealtimes, discouraging idle chatter and improper thoughts, focusing the brothers' minds on higher things.

He pushed open a creaking door into a chapel, birds nesting in its vaulted ceiling, the ground streaked with their droppings. His own monastery had half a dozen shrines dedicated to one saint or another. This one had a fine stained-glass window, an image of the Saviour being broken on the wheel turned bloody by the sunset outside. All very pious and in *no way* arousing.

He dropped to his knees, miserably clasped his hands, miserably stared into the face of God's daughter. "O light of the world," he whispered, "what should I *do*?" The Saviour kept her silence, and Brother Diaz winced. "Well, I know what I *should* do, far as the rules go, don't bed the werewolf, obviously, or . . . don't do it *again*, anyway." He gave a pathetic shadow of a laugh, then choked it off halfway. The omniscient daughter of God was unlikely to be moved by a chuckle, especially one as false as that.

"It's just . . . why must I be *tempted* so?" The Saviour kept her silence, and he winced again. "Well, I know *why*, of course, in a general sense, so I can *resist* the temptation, I see that, I mean, anyone can stay strong if they're never tested, can't they? And I am being tested, and I am failing. Failing *dismally*." He was conscious that he was leaving prayer behind and moving into the realm of wheedling but couldn't help himself. The line between the two had always been blurry.

"It isn't the pleasures of the flesh . . ." The Saviour kept her silence, and he winced once more. What was the point of confession if you kept trying to wriggle around the truth? "Well, not *only* the pleasures of the flesh . . ." Oh God, saying the word made him think about the flesh, the tattooed skin, taut over a fearsome firmness of muscle, so warm, so tacky with sweat. "Though they are . . ." He fumbled for the right word. "Fleshy?" Bad choice. Really awful. "It's the opportunity to be a different man! Not a better man, not exactly, but . . . a man I preferred?" The man whose misbehaviour had landed him in a monastery in the first place. He winced yet again. He was wincing constantly, of late, it had simply become the standard shape of his face.

"I need . . . *guidance*." He was moving from prayer through wheedling to all-out whine. "My faith . . . is *shaken* . . ." It had proved considerably weaker than a werewolf's buttocks, in fact. Though it couldn't be denied that as buttocks went, they were truly formidable, the feel of them under his palms, as if they were carved from wood—"No!" he hissed. "No, no." Praying with an erection had not been unknown at the monastery but was definitely frowned upon, and he turned away from the Saviour's disappointment, and froze.

Vigga stood in the doorway, a damp blanket in her hand. They looked at each other, while outside the rain tapped and dripped and trickled.

"Praying?" she asked.

Brother Diaz swallowed. "Well, I am a monk."

"Oh, right. I sometimes forget that."

"Frankly, so do I." On his better days, at least.

"Did it work?"

"Being a monk? Not really, if I'm honest with myself."

"I meant the praying."

"Not really." He scratched at his beard, which was at the worst possible length and constantly itchy. "If I'm honest with myself."

Vigga sat on the ground, back against the wall. "Sunny's got a fire going in there." She shook the blanket out over her knees and looked towards the window. "The moon'll be near full tonight so . . . I'll likely get a bit frisky. Best I stay in here, where I won't annoy anyone—"

"You've done nothing wrong," said Brother Diaz.

Vigga narrowed her eyes doubtfully at him. "I'm a stinking pagan, Brother, and a murderous savage, and an unrepentant fornicator, not to mention a werewolf convicted by the Celestial Court."

"Well, yes, I'm sure you have . . . many regrets, but . . ." He glanced towards the door and lowered his voice. "I mean, as far as *we're* concerned—the fault's all mine. You've stayed true to yourself. You've broken no vows." He looked at the floor. Poked at the groove between two flagstones with the ruined toe of one boot. "God knows, you've treated me far better than I've treated you. Far better than I deserve. If you're a monster . . ." And he looked up at her. "At least you're an honest one."

"Huh." She narrowed her eyes a little more. "I thought you were disgusted with me."

"Worse than that." He took a slightly ragged breath. "The opposite."

They stared at each other, in a ruined chapel in an abandoned monastery, silent except for the ceaseless dripping of water. "Well, if you'd like to *stay* . . ."

And she lifted one corner of the blanket and gently peeled it back. "Reckon I can promise you a night you won't soon forget."

"*That* . . . I readily believe." Brother Diaz's eyes were fixed on the floor beside her. A patch of worn stone like any other, but somehow so very appealing. He took a deep breath and shut his eyes. "I appreciate the offer. More than you can know, but . . . it can't happen again." He glanced towards the stained-glass window. Towards the face of the Saviour. "It can't happen . . . *ever* . . . again."

"Brother Diaz?"

He groaned, dawn stabbing at him with such painful brightness he had to lift a limp hand to shield his eyes. Light of many colours glittered about a dark figure. An angelic visitation? Was he dreaming? Was he dying? He had a gnawing worry that an interview at the gates of heaven wouldn't go well for him.

"Brother Diaz?"

When he realised it wasn't an angel but Princess Alexia, his first feeling was relief at avoiding divine judgement, his second dismay as he remembered the miles and the danger that still lay ahead, his third confusion as he saw the princess had an expression of intense shock and he was lying on something very warm. Something gently rising and falling. Something that made the faintest throaty growl with each breath.

"Gah!" He tore free of the blanket, scrambling up only to realise, as Alex's eyes went even wider, that he wore nothing but the vial of Saint Beatrix, an absurdly inappropriate accessory under the circumstances. He grabbed for the blanket, then saw he couldn't whip it across his nakedness without exposing Vigga's in all its tattooed majesty and was obliged to cup his private parts with both hands instead.

"I can explain!" he said.

Alex looked to Vigga, starting to wriggle faintly under the blanket, then back to Brother Diaz, then down at his cupped hands, her face twisting into an expression of doubt so intense it verged on pity. "Really?"

He stood a moment, mouth open, hoping, perhaps, for divine inspiration. But no man had ever less deserved to be filled with the grace of the Lord. His shoulders slumped. "I absolutely cannot."

"Well . . . I just came to say the sun's up . . ." Alex backed off. "So . . . we'd better be leaving . . ." And she almost ran for the door, catching her shoulder against the frame and stumbling through with a choked-off squeak of pain.

"Shit," hissed Brother Diaz, snatching up his trousers, which he appeared to have abandoned in a patch of bird droppings.

"She knows now," grunted Vigga, blowing hair out of her face, then pushing her arms above her head and stretching luxuriously.

"Yes!" snapped Brother Diaz as he wriggled into his clammy shirt. "I'd say so!"

"Might as well stay, then." She gave him that grin, with so many teeth, which he'd once found so repulsive, and now, God help him, found . . . otherwise. "Got something for you, under here." From the way the blanket shifted there could be no doubt she was opening her legs.

"Oh God," he whispered, swallowing as he looked towards the stained glass.

Vigga waited a moment longer then, clearly losing patience, nodded downwards. "It's my twat."

"Yes, I believe I'd solved that riddle." He snatched up his boots, did his best to wedge his member down beside his leg, and tore himself towards the door. "Princess Alexia! Alex! Wait!" He tried desperately to sound contrite as he hurried into the dusty refectory. God knew, contrite was all he'd done for a decade. If anyone had the knack it should be him. "I know I have fallen . . . terribly short—"

"You could say that!" snapped Alex, shoving her things into her pack. "I mean, aren't you a *monk*?"

"Well, yes, I suppose . . ." Though he had to admit that he was feeling less and less like a monk with every mile they travelled. "I mean, of course I *am* . . . but I never really *wanted* to be one—"

"Ask me if I ever really wanted to be a princess. Go on, ask me."

"I'm not sure . . . that there'd be much—"

"I did *not*," said Alex. "Don't you have *vows*?"

"Well, yes, I suppose . . ." He pulled one boot on, which was hardly worth it since a hole in the sole had grown to encompass more or less the entire thing. It had become the mere pretence of a boot, as he had become the pretence of a monk. "But Vigga laid out quite a strong argument for a loophole . . ." Alex looked exceedingly doubtful and he had to admit he couldn't blame her. "Which seems actually, now, not *terribly* convincing—"

"Oh, you think? On the floor of a chapel?"

"Well, when you're talking about . . . what we're talking about . . ." Brother Diaz helplessly waved the other boot at nothing in particular. "I'm not sure it makes much difference *where*."

"What are we talking about?" asked Sunny, who was leaning against the wall with her arms folded and her hood down, almost invisible even when she was visible.

"Him . . ." Alex pointed at Brother Diaz, and then at the doorway. "And Vigga . . ."

Sunny wrinkled her nose, unimpressed. "Well, obviously."

"Really?" demanded Alex.

"Vigga's like damp. Give her time, she gets in everywhere." Sunny shrugged as she turned away. "I'll catch you up."

Alex threw her pack over her shoulder and strode for the archway.

"Please!" Brother Diaz hopped after her, into the dismal daylight of the courtyard, struggling to follow and pull his other boot on at the same time. "Let me try to explain—"

"I'd rather you didn't," said Alex, sharply, and then, after a weary sigh, more softly. "I mean . . . it's not up to me to absolve your sins, or whatever. I'm a thief. What's my forgiveness worth?"

"It's worth something to me," said Brother Diaz.

"Well, then." She waved her finger in a vaguely circular manner. "You're forgiven, my son, I guess." She glanced back towards the refectory, muttering somewhat bitterly under her breath. "Likely I'm just jealous 'cause you did what I haven't got the guts to try."

Brother Diaz blinked at her. "Lie with a werewolf?"

"Grab any shred of comfort you can find with both fucking hands." And she stopped for a moment, and gave a little snort. "Remember that prig of a monk I met back in the Holy City? Hard to imagine finding him . . . where I found you."

"No." That made him think of how she'd been when he first met her. Jumpy and suspicious as an alley cat. "It seems . . . nobody comes through a journey like this one quite the same."

"I don't know," muttered Alex. "Reckon I'm as much a piece of shit as I was then. No closer to a princess, anyway—"

"I respectfully disagree," he said. "I must admit you weren't *quite* what I expected. But I'm ever more impressed by your courage, your commitment, your good humour in the face of adversity, your . . ." He blinked, surprised to be using the word. "Leadership."

Alex frowned at him with a hint of her original suspicion. "Are you trying to win me round after what I just saw?"

"Is it working?"

"Little bit."

"The Empress of Troy should probably get used to flattery." He glanced sideways at her and tried a grin. "At the very least you're a piece of shit who can read."

"Even write." And she grinned back, sunlight splashed across her face from the doorless gateway of the monastery, one eye narrowed and the other closed against the dawn glare. "On a good day."

Pride

For the first time in a long time, Alex was smiling as she stepped through the gateway.

The Abbey of Saint Demetrius looked different by sunlight. A little less fortress of nightmares, a touch more tumbledown charm. Dew glittered on the cobwebs among the leaning grave markers like a hoard of diamonds, fallen stones shining with damp, birds twittering in the trees that hemmed in the overgrown road.

She hadn't asked for any of this. To be heir to an Empire. To be hunted by beast-men. To catch monks coupling with werewolves. To punch conceited magicians and kiss invisible elves. But she was starting to wonder—in her wildest moments—if it might not turn out too bad. Beat Bostro's pliers, anyway—

Brother Diaz shot out a hand to grip her wrist.

Which is when Alex saw him. Superbly mounted, nobly handsome, like a crown prince waiting for the horn to blow on the royal hunt, his gilded cloak gathered up high above his shoulders and spread across the hindquarters of his horse.

Alex's smile died the usual quick death, and as the corners of her lips sagged, the corners of his twitched up, as surely as if their mouths were linked by lines and pullies. If Marcian's smile had been all rage, and Constans's had been all greed, then this was a smile of pure pride, and it managed somehow to be the worst of the three.

He nudged his horse forwards. "Allow me to introduce myself—"

"There a way for me to stop you?" Alex muttered.

"—I . . . am Duke Sabbas." He said the name like it delighted him afresh every time. "Lord of Mystras and Iconium, Admiral of the Cretan fleet, Warden of the Royal Stable, and Master of the Imperial Hunt, son, and grandson, and great-grandson of Empresses." He spoke towards the sky, as if for the benefit of a wider audience, in the tone of a man who'd never had to ask for anything twice.

"I'd guessed," said Alex.

"And *you . . .*" He slipped out another of those damn scrolls, and let it unroll by the weight of the ever-so-predictable seal that ended up dangling from the bottom. The papal bull confirming her identity. Seemed everyone with an interest in the Throne of Troy had got a copy. ". . . according to the infant Pope's pet clairvoyants, must be my cousin. The exalted Alexia Pyrogennetos!"

Alex winced. "If I said I never heard of her?"

"I'd have to call you a liar as well as a pretender." He tossed the document down and nudged his horse forwards, trampling it into the muck. "Can you really believe that *you,* so *short,* so *shabby,* so lacking in *any* mark of distinction," and he curled his lip in disbelieving disgust, "have a better claim to the Throne of Troy than *I,* simply because of the room you were born in?"

Alex glared back at him. "This from a man given all his fancy titles by his mummy."

Sabbas paled with the special fury of those born with everything when they're told they haven't actually earned it. Brother Diaz pulled gently on Alex's wrist, edging back towards the gate. "Perhaps we shouldn't rile him . . ."

"This prick was born riled," muttered Alex, but seeing nowhere else to edge to, edged with him.

"It's getting late." A woman rode up behind Sabbas. A woman with a shaved head looked like it was hammered from bronze, a chain of many metals looped around and around her neck.

Another woman followed, so like the first they had to be twins, the links of her chain made of different-coloured glass. "We thought you'd never get up."

"You likely wish you hadn't." A tall man with a face like famine brushed from the undergrowth on the right side of the graveyard and leaned loose and easy on a spear with a forked end. Alex had seen its type before. Made to catch a man around the throat and hold him helpless at arm's length. It likely worked on princesses, too.

"Or at least . . ." A growling voice with a strange accent, and its owner stalked from the trees on the left. Alex had seen him before, lit by the fires of that burning town, but he looked even bigger by daylight, coat hanging open to show a patch of musclebound, hair-covered chest and belly, dark with tangled tattoos. Pointed fangs showed in his beard as he grinned. "You soon will."

More people crept from the woods all around the graveyard, with the hungry look of hunters who wrung out a living catching the thieves, killers, and heretics less ruthless folk couldn't. A diverse crowd, with swords, with axes, with bows, with strange weapons hooked and barbed and chained that made

Bostro's pliers seem quite comforting in hindsight. A pack of manhunters, a crew of land pirates, the bastards were everywhere.

All Alex could do was keep edging back, and hope Sunny could see a way to get them out of this.

Sunny could see no way to get them out of this.

They were outnumbered ten to one and the odds kept getting worse. There was a werewolf, so she had to keep well downwind of him, and not one sorceress but a matching pair, so she had to keep well out of sight of them, and she didn't care one bit for all the room under that great cloak Sabbas wore, it felt to her like there might be a surprise there, and not a nice one like a birthday cake. Not that anyone had ever got Sunny a birthday cake. Not that she even knew when her birthday was. But she'd heard of them and thought it must be nice to get one. Something to work towards, maybe.

If she lived out the hour.

She'd healed some since getting horse-kicked, but her ribs still stung when she held her breath, and her head throbbed from hunger and her guts ached because with classic timing these bastards had arrived just as she was squatting for her daily business. She'd even had a few nice shiny ivy leaves lined up for the wipe.

Ivy was her preference, so smooth but so tough to tear.

Sunny could see no way to get them out of this, but she did her best work blowing with the wind, so she took a breath, and winced as she held it, and slipped out around the edge of the graveyard looking for chances to take.

The first hunter she came to had a crossbow, loaded but lowered, so she leaned over a gravestone and eased the bolt from its groove with a fingertip, so the string was against the flights. The next man had a curved sword with a big leather loop over the hilt. As he stepped forward, he eased the loop back with his thumb, so Sunny knelt beside him and eased it straight back on.

"You've led us quite the chase!" Sabbas was gloating. "I hoped to be back in Troy weeks ago, claiming my birthright, instead of slogging through this godforsaken armpit of Europe."

"Haven't you heard, you gilded turd?" Vigga swaggered through the archway and slapped a weighty hand down on Alex's shoulder. "It's *her* birthright."

At the sight of her the Dane began to make a throbbing growl so deep Sunny could feel it in the soles of her feet, tattooed warnings squirming on the backs of his great fists as he clenched them.

"And as a point of theological fact," Brother Diaz peered over Vigga's shoulder to hold up a lecturing finger, the way he did when he corrected Alex's writing, "God is generally agreed to be everywhere."

Sunny had slipped behind a tree to grip her ribs while she caught a couple of shallow breaths. Now she clenched her jaw against the pain as she dragged air all the way in and slipped back into the open. A portly man in a jacket with polished brass buttons had ridden up beside Sabbas, his horse laden with packs, including several hunting spears in fine leather cases. He slid one out now and offered it eagerly, silver-chased butt first.

"Spear, Your Grace?"

"No need." Sabbas waved towards Brother Diaz the way you might brush crumbs from a tablecloth. "I have *exceedingly* little interest in the rest of you." His horse stirred uneasily as Sunny crept up beside it, but Sabbas stilled it with an impatient yank on the reins, which she quite appreciated as getting horse-kicked again really would've capped her morning off. "By all means we can kill you, if you'd prefer," like he was offering the choice between salt and no salt, "but you're welcome to piss off and live."

Brother Diaz grimaced as if stepping into a storm. "I'm afraid . . ."

"I wouldn't blame you," said one of the sorceresses.

". . . we must decline." And he eased in front of Alex, half-shielding her with his body, which likely wouldn't achieve much as he was quite a narrow man, but Sunny still appreciated the gesture.

"Papal binding." Vigga held up her wrist as Sunny, with a painful effort, worked the pin from the first buckle on Sabbas's saddle girth and carefully slid the strap through, leaving it loose. "But there are four other reasons."

The horse stirred again, again Sabbas yanked at the reins. "Pray enlighten us."

"I haven't had breakfast," growled Vigga, curling in one finger. "I don't like being told what to do," curling in another, "and I don't like your *fucking face*."

Silence stretched. A silence in which Sunny dragged the stiff strap from the pin on the second buckle then bent the pin out of the way.

"That's only three reasons," said the other sorceress.

Vigga frowned at her hand, and saw she was pointing at the sky. "Ah. Well, my thing isn't so much counting . . . as killing." She curled that last finger in to make a fist and gripped it with the other, cracking her knuckles. "So which o' your fucking clowns'll fight me first?"

"I'll be first." The Dane shrugged off his coat and let it drop. "And last."

He was every bit as covered in tattoos and scars as Vigga, but even more with dark hair and twisted muscle. The rest of the killers shuffled back, so Sunny had to hop out of one woman's way, perch on a gravestone, biting her lip, then whip her legs clear and drop down behind it to catch her breath. Here was a bastard even these fearsome bastards were scared of, and who could blame them? An angry werewolf would as happily rip apart friends as enemies . . .

Which gave Sunny an idea.

She slipped around the gravestone, breath held, and slid a dagger from the sheath on that woman's hip in passing. The blade was cruel and thin with a jagged edge. The very sort to make a werewolf properly furious if it got jammed, say, up his arse. Hadn't worked on that crab-man, but maybe she'd have better luck this time.

"I've had your *stink* in my nose for days," the Dane was snarling at Vigga, drool dangling from his mouth.

"You've something of a whiff yourself." Vigga sniffed thoughtfully at the air. "Smells like . . . *piss and cowardice.*"

The Dane sank into a quivering crouch, lips curled back. Sunny tiptoed closer, ribs aching, face burning, the grip of the knife slippery in her palm, her eyes fixed on the worn seat of his trousers. Like a diver for pearls, holding her breath just a moment longer, knowing she had to keep a bit for the swim back to the surface and not sure she'd have enough, except it wasn't an oyster she was after with her knife it was a werewolf's backside, and not a pearl she'd win but a berserk rampage.

"Werewolves, I swear." Sabbas wearily rolled his eyes. "Very well. Get it done quickly."

"Oh, don't worry." Vigga bared her own fangs in a mad smile as Sunny gritted her teeth, pulling back the knife. "This'll be over in *no* time."

With a roar the Dane sprang forward, one heel spraying Sunny with dirt as he tore across the graveyard. Vigga rushed snarling at him at the same moment and they caught each other with a thud like two bulls clashing, hit the ground, and rolled snapping through the wet grass in a cloud of flying leaf and dirt, shattering two headstones and knocking three more flat.

Sunny crouched, knife frozen, face spattered with mud. She did some of her best work without a plan. But this was not a good example.

She backed towards the trees, slipped the knife into the woman's sheath where she'd found it, then, since her attention was fixed on the duelling werewolves, slipped the knife back out and sawed through the back of her belt to leave her trousers hanging dangerously loose.

Vigga came up on top, lovely hot jolts up her arms as she rammed his skull into the dirt. She screamed as she punched at him, but he caught it on one great arm, flung her off with the other, and she rolled through the wet grass and came up grinning, forced one fist open long enough to beckon him on.

He sprang at her so fast leaves whirled in his draught, caught her jaw with a glancing blow made her ears buzz, her blood surge.

There's nothing like a good fight. No maze of arguments to stumble about in, no flitting memories to slip through your fingers. Only you, and your enemy, and your breath and your hands and your strength.

Her fist sank into his gut, hot breath on her face as he grunted, her other fist thudding into his ribs, twisting him. He was bigger, heavier, a woody mass of tattooed muscle. She'd fought a bear once and it had been slower and less angry. She smiled, saw him smile, too, a crescent of bloody fangs, eyes shining with love of life, love of death.

Her fist glanced off his shoulder and he wrongfooted her, caught her, hoisted her into the air, hair whipping in her face as the graveyard turned upside down, a blur of trees and crumbling walls and gawping faces. He brought her crashing down through a tomb lid, rattling the teeth in her head, but she kept her grip on his back and brought him down with her. They wrestled among the graves, and the wreckage of the graves, skin against skin, breath against breath, heaving and clawing and twisting, straining to tear each other apart.

Her heart hammered with the effort and the fear and the joy of the great gamble, the great ordeal in the eyes of the gods, the final test of grip and backbone, sinews threatening to rip with the effort.

She got one leg under him and had just the breath to kick him off, send him reeling back into a tree, little men scrambling out of his path. She punched at him but he ducked, her knuckles smashing a great wedge out of the trunk, filling the air with splinters.

Her wolf was awake and bristling, all snarl and slobber 'cause it could smell his wolf, so close it could be bitten, and tasted, and gnawed on, and swallowed.

She sprang on him, hard to make fists for the claws popping off her fingernails, hard to swear for all the tongue and teeth and bony jaw she had, her maw hanging open and dripping hot slobber on his hairy snarl.

"Our Saviour . . ." Brother Diaz clung so tightly to the vial of Saint Beatrix's blood the chain bit into the back of his neck. "At God's right hand . . ." He knew he'd lost any right to ask for himself. "Hear my plea . . ." But Alex seemed a halfway decent human, which made her the best within some considerable distance, and deserving of a chance at redemption. "Deliver us from evil—"

Cut off in a gasp as the Dane rammed Vigga into a statue of a miserable angel, showering chunks of mossy stone.

He couldn't have said which werewolf had the upper hand. He could hardly have said which was which, they moved so fast, a whirlwind of tattoos, hair, ripping clothes, and flying fists, or perhaps not even fists, as it seemed their transformations into something less than human were both well underway.

"What do we do?" whispered Alex, who kept jerking this way and that as she followed the fight.

"What *can* we do?" muttered Brother Diaz. One of the hunters had already been ripped wide open by a stray claw and he had no desire to be next.

He pressed himself into the gate as they rolled to a halt nearby, the Dane on top, his right hand on Vigga's throat and his left gripping her wrist, her right hand clawing at his face and her left gripping *his* wrist, both covered in blood, sweat, dirt, leaves.

Then Vigga twisted up, fangs bared, and Brother Diaz winced as they spat at each other, tore at each other, bit at each other's mouths . . . or . . .

"Oh," said Alex.

"Ah," said Brother Diaz.

They were still fighting. Sort of. But they were perhaps, also, doing something else.

"Are they . . . ?" One sorceress turned her face sideways.

Her sister wrinkled her nose. "Ugh."

It couldn't be denied that their movements had taken on a certain savage rhythm.

Sabbas rubbed at his temples. "For pity's sake . . ."

They rolled once more, Vigga's legs clamped around the Dane, shedding what clothes they still had, hair sprouting from tattooed skin, joints popping as limbs twisted, each writhing about the other so it could hardly be told what was wolf and what human.

One unfortunate hunter was forced to dive aside as the two beasts tore hissing past him, in the midst of transformation, in the midst of coupling. The sounds of them ripping through the undergrowth faded, there was a distant simultaneous howling, then an awkward silence.

The eyes of the manhunters swivelled back towards Alex and Brother Diaz, huddled in the empty gateway on the other side of the battered graveyard.

Sabbas sighed. "Werewolves, eh?" He waved to the nearest crossbowman. "You can kill them now."

Brother Diaz heard the twang of the bowstring, flinched in anticipation of the searing agony, but instead of punching through his ribs, the bolt shot diagonally from the bow and went twittering end over end to bounce harmlessly from the ruined walls ten strides away.

It seemed, in spite of Brother Diaz's manifest sins, the Saviour hadn't yet abandoned him. "A miracle . . ." he breathed.

"What the fuck?" said the archer, frowning baffled at his weapon, then stumbling back in horror. "What the *fuck*?" An arm was clutching at him. A blackened, bony arm covered in clods of earth. Nettles thrashed beside a gravestone, soil humping then bursting open to reveal more clawing hands, catching at the horrified man's legs.

"All of you!" snarled Sabbas. "Get—"

His horse reared with an outraged nicker, straps flapping loose from the saddle as a decomposing body clutched at it from behind, sinking decaying teeth into its hindquarters. There were corpses everywhere, slithering from the buckled ground, wrestling with the hunters.

The sorceress with the metal chain stepped forwards, fingers pressed into a diamond. She spoke a word and the earth jolted, broke apart, rising up in two trembling mounds full of roots and broken stones. They fell together like waves in the sea, catching a dozen corpses between them, crushing them back down into the earth. One blundered free, its jaw and one of its arms falling off, reaching for the sorceress with the glass chain. She chopped contemptuously and a gravestone was ripped from the ground, spinning through the air to slice the corpse in half at the waist. Its top half tumbled away through the grass, while its legs kept wobbling towards her.

She curled her lip and kicked them savagely away. "They have a necromancer!" she snapped.

"One of the *three* . . ." came a voice from the opposite side of the graveyard, "*best in Europe!*"

Balthazar Sham Ivam Draxi stood among the trees, ripped trousers held up by a length of frayed twine. He curled his fingers into trembling claws, dragging them upwards, the ground bursting open, gravestones toppling, the tortured earth vomiting up corpses.

Brother Diaz had never imagined he might rejoice to see the blackest of Black Art practised before his very eyes, but now he punched the air.

And the magician's tangled hair was whipped by the breeze as Jakob of Thorn thundered past him at a full gallop, sword flashing in the morning sun.

Our Latest Last Stand

The first man's eyes were just going wide as Jakob's sword split his skull open. Surprise is worth a thousand men. A sorcery that reduces the best-drilled company to a green rabble, the hardest-bitten knight to a pissing pageboy.

The next man could've raised his bow, could've turned and run, but all he did was stare. Only took a twitch of the reins to ride him down.

The Knights of the Iron Order had gone into battle with prayers on their lips, the "Our Saviour" endlessly repeated till it lost all meaning, droning over the battlefield like bees over clover. It had been a habit with Jakob for a lifetime, snarling a prayer for mercy as he waded through gore, but down the long years he'd given up on prayers, then even on curses. Now he gritted his aching teeth and saved his breath, and left the higher purpose to those with more faith and fewer old wounds.

A man with a red beard charged at him, sweeping out his curved sword—

But it stuck in the sheath. He'd forgotten to slip the loop off the hilt. Jakob hadn't made himself one of Europe's most hated men by turning down gifts like that.

He missed Red Beard's head but angled his swing so he still carved his shoulder wide open, flung him howling against a gravestone where rotten hands burst from the ground, rotten arms embraced him.

The dead were everywhere, eye sockets yawning empty, papery skin stretched over the bones, clutching, plucking, biting. Not the best fighters, but they surely gave a scare when they popped up uninvited. A man with the most ridiculous cloak Jakob ever saw—and he'd borne witness to some self-important drapery in his time—was jabbing at one with a gilded spear, but it was a poor choice of weapon against the already dead, and all he was doing was scraping shreds of rotten skin from its skull.

Jakob's mount jumped a crumbling tomb and he struggled to stay in the saddle, gripping his reins with his aching shield hand, the battle hardly begun and his body already singing with pain. He was a forever casualty, eternally wounded. Luckily, the horse he'd neglected to return to Count Radosav was a formidable beast, well trained for war and still eager for the bloody business. It did most of the work.

The cloak-wearer had finally kicked free of the corpses and wrenched his own warhorse about. He lifted his spear and Jakob raised his shield to meet him—

The man gave a helpless yelp as his horse started forwards, saddle and rider both sliding off its flank and narrowly missing a mercenary stumbling between the gravestones, struggling to hold her trousers up with one hand while she beat desperately at a shambling corpse with the other.

Jakob had seen the strangest things happen in battle—impossible luck, or the favour of the Lord, depending on who you asked—but this much fortune looked a lot like the work of an invisible elf.

The graveyard had become quite the scene of chaos. He'd carved a bloody path through the enemy, or clung to a horse while it carved one, at any rate. Balthazar galloped past, jolting wildly in his own saddle. Baptiste followed, couched low, one hand gripping the reins, the other gripping her hat to her head. She was a very experienced rider, after all. Spent a month racing horses at the Hippodrome in Alexandria.

The hammering of hooves made Jakob think of his charge to lift the siege of Kerak. That evening he'd led twelve hundred men-at-arms into one of the strongest fortresses in Europe. This morning he led a necromancer in an identity crisis and a disgruntled jack of all trades into a monastery without even a door. A fitting summing up of his career.

He clattered into the cobbled yard, meaning to vault from his horse the way he had at Kerak, while the famished knights fell at his feet to give thanks to God for his prowess. His mount had other notions, though, still dragging at the bit, keen for action. He managed by some miracle to swing one leg over the horse's hindquarters but his other foot caught in the stirrup, dragging him hopping through a great puddle in one corner of the yard, snarling curses.

"Shit! Stop!" He finally worked his foot free and crashed down on his side, taking a mouthful of weeds.

"You're alive!" blurted Alex, still about the least likely Empress of the East you ever saw.

"Well . . ." He bared his teeth as he clambered up. "You can't have everything."

"Thank the Saviour you're here!" Brother Diaz had lost his habit and gained a beard, shirt ripped and hair wild. He looked like a surprisingly upbeat beggar.

"Wouldn't miss it for the *world*," replied Balthazar, who looked like a surprisingly downbeat beggar.

"One more last stand," growled Jakob, hefting his shield.

"Our third on this trip alone." Baptiste peered over the sill of a ragged hole that had once been a window. "When do we start calling them *stands*?"

The battle thrill was fading. Like some aging drunk's revels, each time the joy was shorter lived, the pain and disgust rising quicker behind it. Jakob pressed himself to the stones beside the gateway, peering into the graveyard, where a score of hardened killers were getting over the shock and moving fast to fury as they hacked the last of Balthazar's corpse-puppets into twitching pieces.

"Oh God!" Alex gripped her head with her hands. "This is just like the inn!"

"No, no," said Balthazar, through gritted teeth. "The inn had a *door*."

Sunny dropped into a recently opened grave to catch her breath, back of her skull against the leaning headstone. Honestly, the catching her breath wasn't going great. Each in was a knife in the ribs, each out a hammer to the back. It'd be hard to hold it and move. It'd be very hard to hold it and fight.

But if you wait till everything's perfect, you'll never do anything.

For a generally dour man, Jakob of Thorn could surely make an entrance. His charge had left a couple of hunters dead and a few more rolling and howling and all in all sown quite the beautiful confusion.

Sabbas had snatched another spear from his valet—who was hurrying along behind his master trying to pluck free a corpse arm still clinging to his golden cloak—and was thrusting it angrily towards the monastery shouting, "Kill them all!"

Sunny would've very much liked to slip over and give him a kick in the sack, but she'd learned long ago not to force an issue. Patience was the foremost of the Twelve Virtues, the one from which all others flow, as Brother Diaz would no doubt have boringly lectured. In the end, time gives everyone the kick in the sack they deserve.

For now, those sorceresses were a far bigger worry.

They'd linked hands and were walking out among the graves with their eyes closed. Where they passed, rocks were plucked from the ground and sucked from the graves, whirling into the air until the two of them were surrounded by a spiral of flying soil and spinning chunks of tombstone, the dead scoured to the skeletons or smashed to bonemeal by the hurricane of gravel.

Sunny held a big breath, then sprang from the grave and ran for the monastery, which was what most of the hunters were doing. The one whose laces she'd tied together had just managed to get them untied, so she shouldered him into an open grave as she passed, squeezed between two men in the gateway, elbowed one in the face then ducked under the furious punch he aimed at the other and slipped into the courtyard.

Things weren't much less chaotic inside.

One hunter lay still, a red pool spreading around his head. Another crawled for the gate, gripping his leg and leaving a trail of red smears. Jakob was backing stubbornly across the cobbles towards the ruined cloister, crouching behind his shield, already with two crossbow bolts buried in the wood. The horse he'd ridden in was bucking wildly in the opposite corner, and from the glimpses Sunny got of Balthazar, Alex, and Brother Diaz, huddled together behind Jakob and his shield, they were every bit as panicked.

Two hunters—a big one and a small—were circling right and left, aiming to come at Jakob from two sides. The bigger was stepping over his dead comrade when the corpse sat up like he had a spring underneath him, brains spilling from his chopped-open skull, and sank his teeth into the hunter's thigh.

Jakob stepped to meet the smaller, rammed him back with his shield. Baptiste darted from behind it, slashing his leg with one dagger, slashing his face with a second, but that left Alex and Brother Diaz in the open, clinging to one another.

A hunter knelt beside Sunny, aiming his loaded crossbow at Alex.

"Got you, you little bitch," he whispered, and pulled the trigger.

Only nothing happened, 'cause Sunny had stepped up and wedged a finger behind it. She had to bite her lip as he squeezed furiously, grinding her finger between trigger and stock, but by then Jakob had shuffled back, his shield across the others.

"What the hell?" The archer lowered his bow to fiddle with the catch. Wasn't hard for Sunny to nudge it down the rest of the way with her other hand then pull the trigger herself. He gave a great howl as the bolt nailed his foot to the ground, then Sunny ripped it from his hands and heaved the heavy thing spinning into the air, and Baptiste popped from behind Jakob's shield to catch it, neatly as if it was an act rehearsed for the circus.

"This was your plan?" Sunny heard Brother Diaz squeal as she ducked around the stricken archer and headed for the others, lungs burning with the need for a breath.

"Why do I have to be the one with the plan?" growled Jakob, backing under one of the arches of the cloister. Its roof had long ago fallen in, leaving the bare rafters poking at the sky. "What's *your* plan?"

He set himself to meet a short, wide bastard pounding across the yard, but Sunny stuck out a boot and hooked his leg as he charged past, turning his war cry into a shocked whoop and leaving him tottering, so Jakob could sidestep and take the back of his skull off with one neat swing. Sunny slipped around the old knight, pressing herself against his back to take a breath. Felt pleasantly familiar, leaning on him. Like leaning on your favourite tree.

"Good to see you," she muttered.

"Good to not see you," Jakob grunted back.

She felt the jolt through his shoulders as he took a blow on his shield and she breathed in and spun away. A weasely hunter had got around his side, pulling his spear back to thrust, and Sunny caught the haft, digging her heels in hard. He got quite the shock when the spear didn't move and, since she couldn't hold the spear and her breath at once, an even bigger one when he looked around to see her dragging on the end of it.

He let go of the spear and Sunny stumbled back, smacking herself right in the mouth with the butt. The weasely one turned on her, pulling an axe. "You fucking—"

Baptiste clubbed him over the head with the stirrup on the end of the crossbow. He stumbled towards Sunny, dropping his axe to clutch his skull, and Jakob smashed him with the rim of his shield, flung him against one of the pillars to bounce off, reel straight into Sunny, and send her rolling through a puddle.

"You see that?" A tall one was looking right at her. Or right where she'd been when she snatched the last breath. He levelled his spear, frowning at the telltale ripples on the puddle's surface.

"Where'd it go?" snapped a short one, and he lashed at the air with a mace, one way then the other. The beaked head came within an inch of Sunny's nose as she jerked away, sloshing through the puddle again. Her back hit the wall and she only just held on to her breath, ducked under the darting point of the tall one's spear. The short one came at her swinging, but he favoured a wide-legged stance, so she could drop under his mace, slither between his boots, and come up behind him on dry ground, take a quick breath while his tall friend was looking the other way, then kick him right between the legs hard as she could manage.

Sunny did her best work blowing with the wind, so when he doubled over, she used those two as a human stepladder, planted her right boot on his backside, her left on the back of his head, then her right on the tall one's shoulder and sprang. She sailed through the air still with her breath held, caught the crumbling head of one of the pillars, swung herself up onto the top of the ruined colonnade, lungs bursting, then rolled onto her back and lay there, staring at the white sky, trying to breathe silently in spite of the aching through her ribs and the stinging through her mouth and the burning in her hands and the bruising across her chest where she'd caught the wall and hoping to hell no one saw her feet sticking up.

She could hear the fight still raging, weapons clashing, men swearing, wounded howling, Sabbas snarling, "For pity's sake *kill* the bastards!"

She took one more breath, held it, and scrambled up.

On her left the broken roof of the cloister, and between the rotten rafters she could see Jakob beside a doorway, shield up while the others scrambled through. On her right the yard, hunters pointing, shouting, converging on the congregation of the Chapel of the Holy Expediency.

Sunny snatched up a loose stone and threw it at a crossbowman. It missed but went close enough to his head that he flinched and his bolt flew wide. Another archer spun, waving his bow towards the rafters, and Sunny thought it prudent to move, scurrying along the roof of the ruined cloister, snatching every loose chunk of masonry she could find and flinging them among the hunters, making men reel about in surprise.

Folk don't always think to look upwards, but the narrowed eyes of one of those twins were fixed on the top of the colonnade. "Up there—"

The next stone caught her right on the forehead, sent her reeling back into a wall with a shrill cry. Sunny felt there was poetic justice in hitting a geomancer with a rock, but her sister didn't see the funny side.

She thrust her palms towards the wall with a scream of fury and summoned a storm of dust and splinters. Sunny had upped the pace, pounding along the top of the cloister, but the edge of the blast still raked her side, scratched her cheek, nearly tore her off her feet.

She tottered along that narrow strip of crumbling wall, each step more wobbly than the one before, then her foot landed on a loose stone and she nearly fell, no choice but to suck in a desperate breath.

"There!"

The colonnade flew apart under Sunny's boots and she was in the air, thrashing, falling, clutching at nothing. The ground did what the ground always does and rushed up to meet her, and she went rolling through a patch of brambly nettles and slid to rest clutching her ribs, gravel raining down on her while she gave a long groan.

They burst through the door, their desperate gasps falling muffled. The gloom was Stygian after the brightness of the yard, shafts of light from narrow windows swirling with dust. As Balthazar's eyes adjusted, he saw a long hall, crowded with decayed cots in cobwebbed ranks. The infirmary, he concluded, where monks had offered succour to the doomed victims of the epidemic until the bitter end.

Out of the frying pan, into the plague house.

Jakob threw his shield aside and his shoulder against the door, heaving it about as closed as a door in its condition was likely to get. It was every bit as ancient and gnarled as the knight himself, chinks of light showing through the warped planks and much of the ironmongery consumed by rust. Brother Diaz, scrabbling at the latch, was discovering that it had no functioning lock and only one extant hinge.

"It doesn't work!" blathered the monk.

"I see that," growled the knight. "Get something to wedge it with!"

Balthazar was scarcely listening. His mind was still racing after observing those twin sorceresses: practitioners of geomancy and aeromancy, two supposedly opposite disciplines, not only working in highly effective harmony, but apparently employing *identical techniques* to influence their chosen element . . .

"Anyone hurt?" grunted Jakob.

"Anyone not hurt?" snapped Baptiste. She had set down a large crossbow to plant one boot on Jakob's fallen shield and tug at the bolts buried in its face.

"The use of magic . . ." Balthazar put the heels of his hands together, thrusting them thoughtfully forwards, just as those twins had. "To create a wave though *matter* . . ." He had seen it done with water, but this . . . could it be that Hasdrubal and Cellibus, so long accepted as the highest authorities on the nature of the elements, had made a fundamental misapprehension? That earth and air were *not* in fact opposites, but somehow composed of the *same* stuff . . . ?

"Is Sunny in here?" Alex was squeaking.

"She's got better sense," growled Jakob.

"At least we're back together."

"Oh, yes," said Baptiste. "Would've been a shame to die separately—damn it!" One of the bolts snapped off in her bloody hands, and she pulled a dagger to dig at the other one.

"My God . . ." whispered Balthazar. He felt himself trembling on the brink of an awe-inspiring epiphany. Could it be possible . . . that *all* matter had some fundamental nature in common? That—

A powerful blow rattled the door on its one hinge and shook him from his reverie. "Sweet Saint Beatrix . . ." whimpered Brother Diaz, wedging himself against the wood beside Jakob, heels of his ruined boots scuffing tracks across the filthy floor as the door shuddered from further blows.

There had been an instant, on first seeing princess and monk huddled in the monastery's gateway, when Balthazar had felt an unexpected sense of pleasure to find them alive. Within a few mere moments of their reunion, however, he was remembering why he had liked this half of the congregation almost as little as the other.

"Oh, *sweet* Saint Beatrix . . ."

"I *very* much doubt she will get us out of this," snapped Balthazar. Many of the dilapidated beds were still occupied. Those beyond help, he supposed, when the monastery was abandoned. "Once again, it will be left to Balthazar Sham Ivam Draxi to save the day!" He ripped back the moth-eaten remnants of a blanket in a shower of dust to reveal the most unpromising, desiccated corpse, frozen in twisted death throes.

"Ugh," said Alex, shrinking back. "They died of plague?"

"If we get the chance to die of plague I will count it a *miracle*." Balthazar began to pull up the dead. He had no time for his usual respectful coaxing and was obliged instead to yank what remained of their organs into life, snatching them rudely from their last rest and onto their feet.

"Ugh," said Baptiste as a corpse floundered from its rotten bed beside her, leaving one leg behind. It hopped a step then tripped over another body, both of them sprawling among the cots.

"Ugh," said Brother Diaz as crumbling cadavers flopped against the door to either side of him. The jaw dropped from one immediately, falling on the monk's shoulder, and he brushed it away with a shudder of horror.

"I am doing the best I can with the materials available!" snarled Balthazar, plucking up more corpses to limp, lurch, and hobble towards the door. "Would a little *appreciation* be too much to ask?"

Sweat tickled his face at the effort, but they were too old, too dry, their tendons brittle as straw. One's head fell off while it was rolling out of bed. Another disintegrated as it walked, until it was one arm dragging a rag-covered ribcage. Perhaps if someone had needed their laces tied it could have lent a hand but was of minimal utility in a fight to the death.

"This is your best?" spat Baptiste, digging away at Jakob's shield with her dagger. "Thought you were Europe's top necromancer—ha!" As the last bolt came free and she thrust it up in triumph.

"These corpses are part *mummified*!" Balthazar dashed sweat from his face. "They're all *papery*! If I had some time to *prepare*—"

"Shall I ask them to *give us an hour*?" snarled Jakob as the door jolted open a crack and he twisted to try and heave it shut again. "Check that doorway!"

Alex scampered towards an archway at the back of the room then froze, staring at the ground. "That looks bad." Dust was rising, agitated by a draught that could not be felt. There was a faint hiss as the loose plaster scattered on the floor began to vibrate, and then to lift, too. "Is that bad?"

As if in answer there was a loud bang, cracks shooting across the wall. Five cracks, radiating outwards in the shape of a star. "Fascinating . . ." murmured Balthazar. One of those twins might have been the most gifted geomancer he had ever seen practise. If Eudoxia's students were capable of such feats, he began to wonder whether the Empress herself really had been able to throw lightning—

"Fascinating?" Baptiste shoved past with stolen crossbow in one hand and salvaged bolt in the other. "Or fatal?"

"A little of both," Balthazar was forced to admit. "We should perhaps relocate . . ."

"To where?" screeched Brother Diaz.

For once, the monk had a point. From what Balthazar had been able to tell as they hurtled towards the monastery—against his clearly expressed better judgement—it occupied the terminus of a ridge with precipitous cliffs on two sides. No doubt a marvellous position for the contemplative isolation of the monks who long ago inhabited the place, but by no means an advantage for a ragtag band of convicted heretics attempting to flee for their lives. In all likelihood, they were retreating towards nothing but a very long drop.

Still, as those cracks spread, vibrating splinters of stone and mortar floating free and whirling towards the ceiling, Balthazar found that he much preferred the idea of a long drop some distance away to a colossal weight of falling masonry right on top of him. They could worry about the drop when they were plummeting down it, which was more or less what they had been doing ever since they left the Celestial Palace. The Chapel of the Holy Expediency was a think-on-your-feet sort of institution.

"Anywhere!" roared Balthazar. "They are bringing the walls down!" And a couple of blocks shook loose and tumbled to the ground, where they continued to tremble.

"Go!" snapped Jakob at Brother Diaz.

"Sweet Saint Beatrix . . ." whimpered the priest, then he released the door and ran for it.

"You too," said Balthazar, grabbing Jakob's dagger-wounded shield by the straps. The weight of it took him aback for a moment, he had to admit.

The old knight still strained against the door, Balthazar's corpses crumbling around him, his boots sliding through a mass of their broken pieces. "Get the princess away."

"This is no time for *heroics*." Balthazar cringed as one of the rafters split with a deafening crack, light suddenly stabbing through holes in the roof. "Whatever sins you have committed will not be atoned for under a hill of rubble!"

Jakob's narrowed eyes glinted in the half-light. "Didn't know you cared about my sins."

"A purely selfish decision! My chances are better with you holding a shield for me." And he shoved the thing at Jakob. "Now can we *please* make an exit before the entire monastery comes down on our heads?"

Brother Diaz blundered through the doorway and straight into Alex, the pair of them sent sprawling on the buckled flagstone floor of an abandoned church. The heart of the monastery, into which the monks had trooped three times a day to chant psalms. The only songs now were from the birds nesting in the crumbling bell tower.

Most of the walls still stood to their original height, filigree stonework surviving in empty windows, patches of plaster showing traces of rich frescoes, but the roof was long gone. Some of the great vaults held above, black against the brightness. Others had fallen, reduced to scattered masonry overgrown with bramble. The altar stone was yet in place, a block of black basalt much like the one in the monastery where Brother Diaz had been imprisoned. Where he'd imprisoned himself.

Beyond the altar, in happier times, stained glass would have shown the ascent of the Saviour to heaven, or the acts of the saints, or the angels marching to righteous war, a glimpse of the divine brought to earth. Now there was only cloud-scattered sky. The monastery had plainly given way to subsidence since the Long Pox, and the entire back wall of the church had collapsed off the cliffside, ragged paving slabs hanging in empty air.

Brother Diaz scrambled up, then spun about as the grinding of the unquiet earth behind became a rumble that made his teeth buzz.

Alex clutched at his arm. "Where are the others?"

"Coming," grunted Baptiste, her salvaged crossbow bolt between her teeth, struggling with both hands to heave back the string. "Shit!" It snapped from her grip, leaving her flailing her grazed fingers.

The rumble became an ear-splitting crash and Brother Diaz stumbled back, coughing, as dust billowed from the doorway and out into the ruined nave. A few soft clatters followed.

They held their breath.

Then Jakob limped from the murk, battered shield on one arm and the other over Balthazar's shoulders, both of them covered in blood and dust.

"Thank the Saviour," breathed Brother Diaz, starting forwards to help them.

"Thank her when we're in Troy," groaned Baptiste, crossbow's stock wedged into her stomach in her latest effort to load it.

"This way!" Alex was running down the abandoned nave towards a low doorway where the back of the church had fallen away. Brother Diaz set off after her, past the altar, its surface worn to a glassy polish by centuries of services thrice a day.

"Careful!" growled Jakob from behind, dissolving into wheezy coughing as Alex picked her way along the ragged edge, the sky yawning wide beyond, a few flags still clinging on where weeds and sapling trees had taken root—

With a crash a whole section dropped into nothingness. Brother Diaz caught a glimpse of Alex's face as she slid with it, legs over the edge, hands scrabbling desperately at the buckled floor.

He lunged, jaw cracking the ground, and caught her wrist, the two of them staring helplessly at each other as he slid after her, the long drop swinging into sickening view before him, not entirely sheer, but more than sheer enough, jagged rocks falling away to the forest far below, Alex's boots sending stones bouncing down as she kicked desperately for a foothold—

Something cut into his stomach. Baptiste, catching his trousers. He heard her growl as she dragged at him, growled himself as he hauled at Alex's wrists, teeth furiously clenched. He heard Balthazar groan as he caught Baptiste and added his own weight to the human chain. Alex began to inch upwards—

There was a popping, a tearing—Brother Diaz might refuse to let go but his salvaged trousers were less bloody-minded, he could feel himself slithering free of their ripping waistband. He gave one more desperate heave. Alex snarled, wriggled, finally caught a solid foothold, and came slithering back over the crumbling brink.

The four of them collapsed against the altar stone in a sweaty, dusty, wheezing tangle, staring towards the long drop.

"The other way," gasped Alex.

"Don't think so," said Jakob, backing towards them, shield up.

Men were coming through the old main door of the church, and not to pray. Hunters. Some of them bloodied. All of them angry. At least a dozen. Brother Diaz was in no state for an accurate count. The twin sorceresses came with them, their identical deadly glares directed towards the altar. Slow clapping echoed from the bare stone walls, and Sabbas followed. He still wore that absurd high cloak, his valet scraping along beside him, covered in dust, clutching three spears to his chest.

"A brave effort!" called Sabbas as Alex dragged Brother Diaz down behind the altar, hard stone on one side and empty sky on the other. "But you appear to have run out of road!"

The Angel of Troy

Sunny sat up with a great deal of effort.

Her ribs throbbed worse than ever, with a bad mouth and a bad arm to boot, and she'd tumbled through a patch of nettles so to add insult to injury was stung all over, too.

She worked her way to her feet. Her trousers were torn and her leg skinned bloody but it still bent in the right places. She was in an old storeroom, maybe, roof long gone, storing nothing now but weeds and puddles. Angry noises echoed around her. Screaming and yelling, crashing and beating. The battle still going, then. She took a step towards the one doorway and froze.

"Where are you . . . ?" It was a deeply unpleasant voice, between growling and singing. "I know you're in here . . ." Crooning, maybe, and who croons if they can help it? "No need to hide . . ." She'd heard that voice before, around the fire when she first saw Sabbas, and she felt a pressing need to hide, and snatched the best breath she could, slipping into a ready crouch.

The end of his spear introduced itself first. That forked spear, edges of its twin blades jagged on the inside. Made her think of the hooks they used for catching the big fish, and she didn't care to get hooked, and she spread herself against the wall tight as fresh plaster.

The spear's owner appealed even less than his weapon. Very tall, and very lean, with lank hair hanging about his pocked face and a heap of mismatched stolen chains around his veiny neck.

"You're a tricky one, ain't you?" His eyes flickered about, horribly sly, horribly alert. Hard to move with all the weeds and the water, so Sunny stayed very, very still. "A *very* tricky one, but you're not the only one . . ."

He swung his spear in a great arc, tip scraping the walls, then another, lower, and Sunny ducked the first, then shrank back into a corner and watched cross-eyed as the points of the spear whirled past her nose, the wind of it leaving an annoying tickle on the tip, and she had to wriggle it desperately, which only made it tickle worse. God, she wanted to sneeze now, and was fast running out of air, her face hot, the ear-tip she still had burning.

"Where I come from . . ." crooned the hunter, turning slowly away, "they call me the Man-Catcher, 'cause there's no one I can't lay my hands on."

He lunged at the air, stabbing viciously left and right, high and low. She twisted sideways, sucking her stomach in, wincing at the pain in her ribs as the gleaming points whipped past her on one side, then even closer on the other, ever so nearly catching the loose tails of her shirt on one prong.

"Why don't you come out?" he crooned again, prowling the room. "Show yourself."

Why the *hell* would she do that? To a man with that croon? That grin? That spear? Not an attractive invitation *at all*. He began to turn away, slipping between the weeds, spear in one hand, each footstep soft and silent.

Sunny's ribs were singing with pain. Her head was pounding, bright spots swimming in her vision. She forced herself to hold her breath a moment longer as he turned slowly, so slowly away, till finally his back was to her, and she gasped in air.

Just a twitch of his head. A glimpse out the corner of his eye, maybe. She was already gone again, but with a bark of triumph he was spinning, whipping something from behind his back.

It spread in the air like a great cobweb. On a better day Sunny might've been quick enough to slip from under it. But she was battered and spent and hadn't eaten and couldn't get a proper breath. The net flopped over her, far heavier than it looked, and she thrashed and kicked but there was no getting loose. The more she fought the more stuck she became, huddled in the corner on her knees, and she felt something sharp prodding at her side, and she stopped struggling.

"Shush, shush, shush." He poked her with his spear again and made her grunt. No point holding her breath any more. Whether he could see her or not he could for damn sure see the net, so she let it wheeze away.

"Ain't that better?" Sunny definitely didn't think so as he squatted beside her and slipped long fingers through the netting. "Now will you look at this?" Fucker was crooning more than ever as he pushed her head back, pushed her hair back, pinched the ear-tip she still had painfully between finger and thumb. "Might be from now on . . . they'll call me the Elf-Catcher."

"I've an offer for you!" barked Jakob as the hunters spread out around the far end of the nave. The odds were desperate and his comrades were all cowering behind an altar with one crossbow bolt between them. The time had come to clutch at small chances.

"What do you have I can't prise from your corpse?" snorted Sabbas, and several of his lackies chuckled along.

Jakob puffed out his chest and stretched to his full height. "Honour!" he roared, the word bouncing from the ruined walls and bringing the laughter to a sudden halt.

There'd been a time Jakob had cherished honour more than virtue, valued honour higher than jewels. His lust for it had dragged him into the darkness, and there, among the bodies of his friends, he'd discovered its true value. But there are always men who need to learn that lesson for themselves.

"You and me!" He pointed down the ruined nave with his sword. "Here and now! To the *death*." He didn't mention death came easier to some people than others. He'd sworn an oath of honesty, not an oath of blabbing every detail.

Sabbas glanced towards his hirelings, all looking back at him. All judging. There was no good reason to accept the challenge. There was scarcely even a bad reason. Only pride. But Jakob knew more than most about pride. He'd suffered from a near-fatal case himself in his youth. And he'd never in all his long life seen a man more bloated with pride than this fool in the golden cloak.

Sabbas lifted his chin, narrowed his eyes, and there was a long silence.

"My lord," murmured his valet, "you cannot—"

"Shush." Without shifting his gaze, Sabbas reached out and snapped his fingers, and Jakob knew he'd reckoned right. Men born with every advantage often burn to prove they've deserved them all along. The valet took a sharp breath, then slid a spear into his master's hand.

"Your . . . *colleagues* . . ." Sabbas sneered towards the altar, "will not interfere?"

"On their honour," said Jakob. Since they included a confessed thief, a convicted heretic, and Baptiste, he doubted their honour would stop them doing much of anything.

One of the sorceresses grunted her disgust. "*Never* trust a necromancer. Let us—"

"If they try anything underhand," snapped Sabbas, "you may bring the church down on their heads. Until then, stay out of it." He turned back to Jakob with an imperious toss of his head. "To the death, then!"

"Not much of a duel without it." Jakob gave Sabbas's hired men a slow look-over, then took a long sniff and spat onto the buckled flagstones. "Bit disappointed by your henchmen, if I'm honest. Your brother Marcian had been recruiting in a farmyard, your brother Constans at the bottom of a rock pool." He settled into a fighting crouch. Or at any rate the closest his knees would get to it. "Didn't your mother give you any toys to play with?"

"Oh, I received my full share of Eudoxia's gifts." Sabbas had the smile of a man who never admitted to being wrong. "My brothers desired, like petty gods, to remake our mother's experiments in their own image. Marcian goaded them into butchers to conquer for him. Constans dressed them up as pirates to steal for him. Neither lacked ambition." With his free hand, he undid the clasp on his gilded cloak. "But they had no *vision* at all." With one movement he flung it off, and with a great rustle and a wash of wind, he spread mighty wings across the nave of the church, their white-feathered tips almost touching the creeper-covered columns to either side.

"*Now* . . ." Sabbas planted one fist on his hip and struck the butt of his spear on the ground with a clang. A man. With wings. In a pose from a statue. "You see why they call me the Angel of Troy!"

Jakob burst out laughing. He couldn't help himself. He coughed, burped a little sick, had to hold up his shield for indulgence while he swallowed it. "I've seen angels and demons, boy." He sighed, wiping his eyes on his sleeve. "The angels scared me more. I understood them less." He looked Sabbas up and down, and gave a snort of his own. "You don't become one by stitching the poulterer's offcuts to your back."

Sabbas's smile slowly faded into a glower.

"We shall see," he said.

During the last few months of Alex's life the insane had become standard, the horrifying unsurprising, and the impossible routine. But even she had to raise her brows at this.

"He's got wings," she muttered. Sometimes you just have to hear yourself say it. Explained the strange cloak, anyway. Probably had trouble finding anything that fit.

Sabbas rocked back then lunged forwards, fists clenched and legs braced while those impossible white wings beat, beat, beat, ever harder.

Alex narrowed her eyes against a storm of dust and grit and the odd loose feather. Jakob clung to his shield, straining to hold his ground in the gale, and Sabbas took a running stride and sprang into the air, wings giving one mighty flap as they bore him up over the nave.

He plunged down with an echoing screech, spear crashing against Jakob's shield, cracking the rim against the old knight's jaw and flinging him across the mossy flagstones.

Sabbas straightened, then with a snap of feathers spread his wings wide again. "I'll give you poulterer's offcuts, you ancient fucking *remnant*."

"What do we do?" hissed Alex, peering over the altar stone. A couple of hunters were easing down the sides of the church, slipping through the shadows from one pillar to the next. Others were cranking crossbows, pulling out arrows, generally preparing to deliver a hail of death. And then there were the two sorceresses, watching the duel impatiently with their arms folded, ready and willing to blast them off the cliff or shake the whole building to bits.

"Interfere and they'll kill us," grunted Baptiste, who'd rolled onto her back, one foot in the crossbow's stirrup as she strained at the string with both hands.

"And if we don't?" asked Alex as Jakob slowly pushed himself up. "They'll let us go? We can't just cringe behind an altar!"

"If you want to find somewhere else to cringe you have my blessing!" snapped Balthazar. "I could use the cringing space!" He jostled at Baptiste as she struggled with the crossbow. "Can you even bloody shoot one of those?"

"Spent a summer as a gamekeeper," she growled. "Came second in an archery contest, actually."

"Why don't you have your own bow, then?" asked Brother Diaz as Jakob and Sabbas began to circle each other.

"Because in case you *hadn't noticed*," veins popped from Baptiste's neck as she arched back, hauling at the string, "they're absolute *bastards to load*."

The so-called Angel of Troy darted forwards, wings beating so his toes barely brushed the ground, lightning thrusts of his spear gouging the face of Jakob's shield. The old knight growled as its point scraped from the rim and tore his shoulder, stumbled as it slipped under his guard and scratched his hip, slid onto one knee in front of the altar as Sabbas danced away, grinning.

"Very good, Your Grace!" called the valet, who'd tucked the spare spears under one arm so he could politely applaud.

"Obviously!" barked Sabbas, then turned to grin at Jakob as he clambered to his feet, spinning his spear nimbly in his fingers. "You don't yield easily. I can admire that." And he struck the butt end against the flagstones with a clang that echoed from the high walls. "But I think you see your time is up."

"Lots of men told me that down the years," said Jakob. "I'm still *here*." He lunged but Sabbas caught his sword, blade screeching against his spear's gilded haft.

"I won't deny you exist. So do ants and syphilis." Sabbas flung Jakob back. "And they're about as likely to save your princess."

Alex reckoned syphilis might well do for Sabbas, but not on a timescale that'd keep her alive. One of his wings flashed over, cracked Jakob on the shoulder and knocked him sideways, while the other struck him on the side of the head and sent him sprawling across the stones again. Sabbas rubbed at the bright scratch Jakob's sword had left through the gilding on his spear.

"Absolute *vandalism*." He leaned forwards, beating his wings again, whipping up a storm that made Alex shrink back, smiling like a boy at a trapped fly as Jakob strained into the wind with all his strength, feet scraping the broken flagstones, sliding towards the edge of the precipice—

Sabbas stopped suddenly and Jakob stumbled towards him, off balance, just as the Angel of Troy danced forward. "Take *this*!" Sabbas smashed Jakob's shield aside with the butt of his spear, ripping one plank loose from the bent rim, then lunged with the blade as Jakob blundered on, sticking the old knight right through his breastbone.

"Ooooof . . ." breathed Jakob as the spear's red point slid from his back. He wobbled a moment, eyes bulging. "That's . . . a bit sore." He coughed blood and dropped to his knees, battered shield and notched sword hanging limp in his hands.

Sabbas grinned as he ripped his spear free in a red gout, turning towards the altar. "Out you come, cousin . . ." he sang.

Alex held her knife behind her back, hand sweaty on the grip as she started to stand, getting ready to coax out the tears. Look weak. Make them careless, draw them close. Then gut, groin, throat, with all the rage you can muster—

"I said it was *sore* . . ." came a voice from behind Sabbas. Jakob was on one knee, his shirt stained red around the rent the spear had made. He spat blood, then, leaning on his sword, slowly pushed himself up. "I didn't say we were *done*."

"Never had one o' your kind in my net before." The Man-Catcher, or the Elf-Catcher as he now was, gave Sunny a blast of breath that did nothing to improve her opinion of him. "Reckon you'll fetch *quite* a price—"

"I'll make you an offer," came a voice.

The Man-Catcher whipped around, spear raised, quick as a scorpion with its sting.

Baron Rikard leaned against the wall, head back and eyes shut, a strip of sunlight across his smile. He looked a decade younger than when Sunny last saw him. A touch of grey in his neatly trimmed beard. A tasteful suggestion of crow's feet at the corners of his eyes. But very much a man at the peak of his powers. He rolled his head towards them, giving that look of detached, slightly melancholy amusement, as though none of this was terribly urgent.

"I'll give you your life for her," he said.

"*My* life?" The Man-Catcher began to circle, spear held high, while behind his back his hand slipped towards his belt. Probably Sunny should've been trying to get free of his net, but she was tired, and sore, and had been making a lot of effort lately, and thought she could let the vampire get off his arse for once.

The baron pushed himself from the wall, handsome features slipping from that strip of sunlight and into shadow, dark eyes gleaming as he swaggered forwards. "Seems to me you're getting a hell of a bargain but, really, I have *never* had any patience with—"

The Man-Catcher whipped another net from behind his back and threw it in one motion. It spread in the air, little brass weights on the edge making it a spinning circle.

"—haggling." Baron Rikard merely stood there as the net flopped over him. Through the cords across his face, Sunny saw him sigh. "So . . . that's a no?"

The Man-Catcher cackled with triumph as he lunged. His spear's jagged blades sank into the baron's chest—or would have, had he not in that instant become a cloud of black vapour, the net dropping suddenly, snagging on one of the spear's prongs and hanging limp.

"What the—"

The smoke whipped and spiralled, fanned by impossible breezes, formed tendrils that flowed towards the Man-Catcher, curled around him. He lashed out viciously, but how can you fight mist with a spear? It wafted about him, embraced him from behind, and suddenly was the baron once again.

"Now who's the Man-Catcher?" His smile was very white, and very wide, and his eyes were very black, and very empty. The hunter struggled, but though he was much the bigger man, the baron's arms scarcely moved. "I have defied God and his angels," he hissed. "I have bathed in blood and waded through gold. Kings . . . have *abased* themselves . . . at my feet. Do you truly imagine . . . you can stick me with a *fork*?"

He swelled, rose up, his black hair stirred as if by a wind, his neck twisting like the body of a snake, fretted with trees of pulsing veins. His mouth unfolded, too wide, and wider yet, bristling with impossible legions of shining teeth, and Sunny squeezed her eyes shut, and turned her face away.

She heard the scream, and heard it gutter out into a whimpering, ecstatic gasp, accompanied by an awful sucking and slobbering.

When she dared to open her eyes the Man-Catcher lay bonelessly on the ground, eyes sunken, cheeks hollow, tooth marks in his neck yawning red and dry.

"Ooooooh," purred the baron, eyelids fluttering, wiping the blood from his cheeks, "a heady draught . . ." slurping at his fingertips like a child licking away the last traces of some sweetmeat. His eyes flicked open, dark as a yawning grave, empty as the eyes of a stalking cat, and his blue lips twitched back from his fangs, and for a moment Sunny felt she looked into the pit of hell.

Then he smiled.

So radiant a smile that even she, who didn't much care for humans, or men, or vampires, and certainly not people whose faces were splattered with gore, felt a faint ache of attraction, and wondered what those white arms would feel like around her, wondered what those white teeth would feel like inside her meat, wondered if the most terrible monsters were among them, and had always been among them.

"One cannot expect manners from man-catchers. Still less from elf-catchers, apparently." She'd never seen the baron look so young, and even through her relief that felt ever so slightly worrying. He bowed gracefully, a sweep of raven-black hair falling across his face, and Sunny felt sad that so beautiful a thing should be hidden for even that long. "But for my own breach of etiquette, I can *only* apologise."

"Accepted." Sunny held up her hands, swags of netting draped off them. "Now do you think you could help me out of this bastard net?"

Sabbas stared at Jakob, impaled yet still alive, for just a moment. Then, perhaps understandably, he decided he'd had quite enough of that.

"Kill them all!" he screamed, wings flapping nervously as he scrambled backwards.

Alex heard a bowstring, shrank down as an arrow pinged from the corner of the altar and went spinning past her ear. The hunters were edging closer. One had made it to a pillar no more than ten strides off.

"Oh, fuck it," groaned Jakob as a bolt thudded into his thigh, and he tottered a step and went sprawling. Brother Diaz caught his wrist, Alex caught his back, and with a mutual groan they rolled him over, sprawling behind the altar together as a hail of dirt blasted its side, bits of shattered masonry bouncing over the brink and down the long drop.

"That damned aeromancer!" Balthazar squirmed back, hands over his head. "She'll blow us off the cliff!"

"I . . ." snarled Baptiste as she finally heaved the crossbow's string over the catch. "Think . . ." She slotted the bolt into place and rolled up to her knees, bringing the stock to her shoulder in one smooth motion. "*Not.*"

She pulled the trigger, there was a loud whipping sound, and as Alex slithered up to peer over the top of the stone, she saw the sorceress with the glass chain stumble back a step. She wobbled a moment. She blinked. Alex realised the bolt was buried right between her eyes. She toppled to the ground.

"No!" screeched her sister. Her lips curled into a furious snarl. Her fists furiously clenched. Her eyes furiously narrowed as she looked up at the altar.

"Oh God," muttered Alex as dust began to spiral up around the woman's robes.

The ground trembled. A few flagstones buckled upwards. Some loose masonry tumbled from the tops of the lofty walls. Alex twisted back around, sinking down between the others, squeezed in shoulder to shoulder, and watched a couple of ragged flagstones at the edge of the cliff shake loose and fall away.

"You shot the wrong sorceress!" wailed Balthazar. "That damned geomancer will shake this whole place to splinters!"

"It was your fucking idea!" snarled Baptiste, throwing down her empty bow. "If only we had a sorcerer of our own!"

"*Magician!*" he nearly screamed back at her. "But I need corpses to work with!"

Sabbas was waving his wings about to keep his balance, bellowing at the sorceress, but she was standing over her sister's body taking not the slightest notice. The ground was shaking too much now for archery and the hunters were scrambling for safety, one putting his shield over his head as more stones pinged down. On the upside, the arrows had stopped coming. On the downside, it looked as if the whole back half of the church would soon be crashing down the mountainside, and they'd be in it.

"We'll all be corpses soon enough," whimpered Alex.

"Corpses . . ." Brother Diaz's eyes went wide. He twisted to shriek over the altar. "Is that the best you've got? The ground shakes more when I *fart!*"

The sorceress gritted her teeth, sweat streaking her shaved head. She raised her trembling fists and the ground trembled with them, flagstones pinging apart with little showers of rising dust.

"Are you trying to make her *angrier*?" squeaked Alex.

"Four plagues in a decade . . ." breathed the monk. "Too many dead for the graveyards."

"You could pick a better moment for the *history lesson*," snarled Balthazar, hunching down as mortar began to shower from the vaulted arches above.

"They buried them in pits by the hundred. In every inch of consecrated ground they could find . . ."

Jakob's eyes narrowed. Balthazar's went wide. Alex's rolled to the ground.

Earth was shaking loose from the flagstones, worn by time, and weather, and the passage of monks' feet. But on some she could still make out the faded epitaphs.

"Plague dead?" muttered Balthazar. "Decades buried?"

Alex grabbed him by the shirt. "You're saying you can't do it?"

"They'll be too old." The magician squeezed his eyes shut. "They'll be too deep!"

"Too *deep*?" Alex dragged him close, giving him a savage shake. "Who does this bitch think she is?" His jaw clenched. "That she can get the better of Balthazar Sham Ivam *Draxi*?" His nostrils flared. "The best necromancer in *Europe*?" His eyes snapped open. "Above a giant fucking *tomb*?"

He slapped her hands away. "I . . . think . . . *not*."

Balthazar sprang onto the altar stone. Chest out, shoulders back, feet planted wide, he faced this glorified earth mover, thirty strides of shuddering flagstones between them.

He issued the bluntest of challenges. He dared all comers. With no subtlety and no subterfuge he forced his mind downwards, through stone, and soil, and root, into the foundations of the monastery, vibrating now with magic, and there he found the dead.

There was a grinding beneath his feet and with an almighty crack the altar stone split in two, one half tipping towards the brink. He stumbled, his concentration faltering—

Someone caught him around one leg. Princess Alexia, her jaw grimly set. Baptiste seized his belt on the other side, and her eyes met his for just an instant, and she gave him the slightest nod.

Balthazar turned to face the surviving sorceress. This would be a feat of necromancy discussed with awe in magical circles for decades to come! And this tower of geomantic self-regard never guessed that she was acting as *his* assistant. He let his lips curl back from his gritted teeth and put forth all his power.

The dead were reluctant. So deeply buried. So long entombed. But Balthazar would not be refused. He demanded. He *commanded*. He would do it without book or circles, without rod or rune or blessed oil, without even *words*. He would not stroke them up with tender caresses, he would rip them from the clutching earth by force of will.

"Obey!" he hissed.

One of the vaults above cracked apart, masonry crashing to the trembling ground. Sabbas tottered back, wings curled over his head as a shield. The shriek of one of the hunters was suddenly cut off as he was crushed under a boulder the size of a cow.

No dead thing was beyond Balthazar's reach. However deep. However ancient. Be they rotted fragments, he would yet knit them together. Be they nought but grave wax, he would yet mould them to his purpose.

"Obey!" he snarled.

Eudoxia's student redoubled her efforts, straining forwards, her face a snarling rictus, and the quaking of the ground grew yet more violent, stones raining down as the walls of the church shook themselves apart.

He did not even need whole bodies. He saw that now. He had fallen short, of all things, in *ambition*. He had allowed himself to be made *small*. He had given in to *doubt*. But that was *over*.

Cracks shot out across the ground, weeds thrust into the air, stones parting, toppling inwards.

"Obey!" he screamed.

With a noise like the end of creation the floor of the tortured nave collapsed inwards and, as if it was a breach in the ceiling of hell itself, the dead came boiling from beneath.

"Sweet Saviour," whispered Brother Diaz, hardly knowing whether to clap his hands over his eyes, ears, or nose.

God, the unholy sight! Jaws dropping from skulls, worms falling from eyeholes, shreds of clothes still hanging from mouldering bodies, or shreds of flesh still hanging from blackened bones. Buried together, rotted together, he couldn't say which limb belonged to what, a formless mass of teeth, nails, hair, corroded earrings, rusted belt-buckles, many fingered, many mawed, crumbling even as it rose and bursting up afresh.

Heavens, the unholy stench! He once attended a beatification investigation where one Brother Jorge had been exhumed, his corpse supposed to be incorruptible. It had proved otherwise, several monks of his order reeling from the tomb. That stench was the tiniest fraction of this one, a grave far older, far larger, closed in haste and violently rent open, its air unbreathable, unbearable, indescribable.

Saviour, the unholy sound! Did the cursed mass thunder like a stormy sea upon a bitter shore? Did it groan with infinite pain? Did it howl with mindless rage? Did it mewl through a hundred tongueless, lipless mouths to be released from this world and returned to hell? Or did Brother Diaz only hear the thunder of the collapsing church, the desperate wails and squeals of the hunters as they scrambled to escape the horror?

"Oh God," he heard Alex say.

The ground gave way beneath the sorceress and she plummeted into the pit along with her dead sister, the valet shrieking as he slid after them, and yet the earth kept shuddering, as if with revulsion at the spectacle, broken flagstones toppling from the ragged edge at the back of the church and down the long drop. The strip of floor between altar and cliff, on which Brother Diaz and his companions were cowering, was rapidly narrowing.

The stones fell away beneath three hunters and they dropped into the fetid vortex. Others scrambled back as arms reached blindly for them, as if in terrible jealousy, as if in terrible need. They were embraced, enveloped, dragged screaming towards the brink, clawing uselessly at the ground with their fingernails, hacking pointlessly with their weapons at what was already decades dead.

An ear-splitting crack came from above and the top of the church's bell tower broke free and plunged downwards, crashed into the wall of the nave, chunks of stone scattering across the shuddering ground, the wrought-iron holy wheel that had topped it clanging wildly away.

One pillar crumbled, the arch above and a whole section of wall sliding into the pit. The altar stone had already split, and with a grinding shifted further. Alex stumbled and Brother Diaz caught her, braced her as she was bracing Balthazar.

Sabbas gave a desperate screech, his great wings beating, sending a blasting wind through the ruin. He got off the ground as it fell away beneath him, a stride or two, perhaps, but from the blind hunger of the dead there was no escape.

Their flailing hands caught his ankle, pawed at his knees, clutched at his clothes, a writhing mountain of them, falling apart even as they clambered up each other. One came apart at the joints, leaving a rotted arm dangling from his belt.

He kicked furiously but they caught one wing and he screamed as they ripped fistfuls of feathers from it, the other still beating wildly. The legion of the long dead clawed at him, bit at him, and the self-styled Angel of Troy was dragged down, bloody and squealing, into the rotting embrace of the damned.

His despairing wail became a desperate howl, then a muffled groan as that corrupted mass of rot closed over him, and finally was cut off.

With a gasp Balthazar sagged onto his knees on the broken altar.

Corpses and bits of corpses, still writhing from the pit, flopped back, crumbled, and were still.

A hunter goggled from behind one intact pillar, then with a whimper flung his crossbow away and fled sobbing.

A few stones fell from the edge of the great pit that had once been the abbey's nave, and clattered down inside, and all was still.

Alex kept clinging to Balthazar's leg, tears running silently down her stricken face. Baptiste was on the necromancer's other side, eyes wild behind tangled curls, trying to say something, but each quick breath turned to a meaningless gasp.

Jakob grunted as he let his sword clatter down, then slowly toppled back to lie with arms spread wide, watching the clouds drift across the sky.

Brother Diaz realised he was still gripping the broken altar stone with one hand, desperately tight, and his mouth was locked as if in a silent scream, and with a mighty effort he forced his fingers to relax and dashed the tears from his eyes.

"Fuck," he breathed.

A Miraculous Medicine

I'm still alive," said Alex, but so doubtfully it was almost a question.

"It's true." Sunny reached up, and caught a pinch of her cheek, and shook it about with a faint flapping. "Far as I can tell."

They sat huddled together on Sabbas's carved bench, on Sabbas's plump cushions, with Sabbas's gilded cloak, which was surprisingly soft, wrapped around both their shoulders. They sat staring into Sabbas's fire, and drinking Sabbas's wine, and Sunny had drunk too much, which was about three sips.

She used to think any wine at all was too much, but she'd had an epiphany the last hour or two, and now considered it a truly miraculous medicine. Your first sip might taste like feet but the more you drank the better it got and now it was summer meadow in a bottle, sunshine for your tongue. Her many hurts had faded to whatevers with a slightly dizzy sense of contentment and a warm love for the world, which might hate her but what the hell. You can't choose how other people will be, only how you'll be, and she'd chosen to be a good thing.

At least till tomorrow.

"I wasn't stuck with a spear." Alex prodded at her stomach as though checking for holes. "Or hacked with a sword or shot with an arrow . . ."

"Well, I'm *delighted* for you," growled Jakob. "Gah!" as Baptiste dug at the great wound in his chest with her needle and pulled the thread through.

The monastery had held little appeal in the aftermath. Not to anyone but Balthazar, at least, who'd stared into the opened plague pit with the delighted disbelief of an architect seeing their grand cathedral finally realised. So they'd limped and blundered, leaning on one another and nursing their various injuries, from the destroyed church into the destroyed courtyard and through the destroyed graveyard, out into the woods where they'd come upon the camp of Sabbas and his hunters, looking much as the so-called Angel of Troy must've left it, complete with tents, horses, provisions, and a very great deal of wine.

Alex waved a bottle of it around now. "I wasn't ridden down, or crushed by falling masonry, or blown off a cliff by a winged man, or dragged into a plague pit by a legion of the dead."

"On balance . . ." said Sunny, "I'm glad."

"Think I might've survived as well." Brother Diaz frowned at the scabbed back of his hand, then turned it over so he could frown at the scabbed palm. "However little I deserve it. You could get to thinking . . . that God must have a purpose for you."

"Can't . . ." Jakob's scarred cheek twitched at each movement of Baptiste's needle, "recommend it."

"It's just a short hop," murmured Baptiste, scarred mouth pressed into a hard line as she stitched, "to thinking your every whim must be part of his plan."

"At which point any outrage is justified," said Baron Rikard. "As a man who has been justifying outrages for *centuries*, you can take my word for it." He slipped another bottle from the crate and studied it by firelight. "I must say, your cousin's valet kept an excellent cellar."

"Shame he fell in the pit, really." Alex held her bottle out to the baron. "My uncle once told me one can always make more dukes, but a good servant's a rare treasure."

"Most kind, but I already drank my fill." He glanced towards Sunny, firelight gleaming in his black eyes, on his white teeth. "A *most* intoxicating vintage."

Sunny nervously cleared her throat, and drew Sabbas's cloak tighter against the cold, and Alex offered her the bottle instead.

Their fingers brushed as she took it, and there was a strange heat there, and Alex caught her eye, and there was a strange heat there, too, and Sunny right off looked away, and sipped from the bottle, and slooshed it around her mouth, and swallowed it, and breathed it in, and her head filled with its fruity vapours.

"Aren't you worried they'll come back?" Alex was asking, glancing at the good gear abandoned in the camp.

"The ones who went into the pit?" Balthazar peered up at the stars. "I am not."

"I meant the ones who got away."

"After they saw those others go into the pit?" Jakob winced down at the ground. "I am not."

Alex's turn to pull the cloak tighter, and her shoulder rubbed up against Sunny's shoulder, a comfortable rubbing that made her want to rub back, like a cat rubs at things, and purrs. Sunny might've purred, a little bit.

"First time I haven't been cold in weeks," she murmured.

"First time I haven't been terrified in weeks," said Brother Diaz.

"First time I haven't been in pain in weeks," said Balthazar.

"Well, I'm *delighted* for you," muttered Jakob as Baptiste pulled the last knot tight and trimmed the thread with a dagger.

"Turn around, then." She licked a new length and started twisting it through the needle. "I'll do the back."

"God *damn* it." Jakob puffed out his cheeks, then stiffly clambered up, gripping his bandaged leg, and with a groan turned around, firelight catching the even larger spear-wound in his back.

"So what next?" asked Alex.

"A little more of this," said Brother Diaz, grinning at his bottle, "then bed."

"I meant in general."

"Well," grunted Jakob, "thanks to your winged cousin—"

"Such a generous soul!" observed Baron Rikard, raising his arms to take in the camp.

"—we have horses, we have supplies, we have money—"

"And a *very* nice cloak," said Sunny, pressing her bruised cheek against it.

"And wine!" Brother Diaz thrust his bottle in the air and a bit of wine slopped from the neck and spattered on the ground. "Lots of wine."

"Isn't temperance among the Twelve Virtues?" asked Balthazar.

"Down near the bottom, though. And who's got all twelve?"

"I can't even name all twelve," said Sunny. Though everyone said she had no soul to save, so it didn't make much difference whether she sinned or not. Probably she should be sinning more.

"We head for the coast," said Jakob, grimly soldiering on, as usual. "Make for a port. Not one of the busiest—"

"Kavala, maybe?" muttered Baptiste.

"Kavala is *lovely* this time of year," said the baron.

"—and then ship—"

"One that stays afloat this time," grunted Balthazar.

"—to Troy."

"And then what?" Alex blinked at the fire. "You drop me off at the gates?"

"Well . . ." Brother Diaz gave the strong impression he was considering that question for the first time. "Assuming Duke Michael made it back to the Holy City, and assuming he recovered from his wounds, and assuming Cardinal Zizka secured him passage, it's entirely possible . . . that he's in Troy already?"

Alex was far from reassured. "That's a lot of assuming."

"He could be with his friend, what was her name?"

"Lady Severa?" muttered Alex.

"Exactly! Preparing for your arrival!" Brother Diaz waved his bottle again. "Maybe cheering crowds will await us! Isn't hope the foremost of the Twelve Virtues? The one from which . . . all others flow?"

"Maybe." Alex looked less reassured than ever. "Can't say it's ever done much for me—"

"D'you hear that?" Sunny glanced towards the bushes, only to see them shake and rustle. Jakob twisted around, groaning as he pulled free of Baptiste's needle, and clutched for his sword, only managing to knock it over. Brother Diaz lifted his bottle as if he'd throw it, Sunny heaved in a breath to disappear but burped halfway through and ended up just sheepishly drawing the cloak to her chin.

A huge figure loomed from the shadows and lurched bow-legged into the light. A figure swathed in a coarse and filthy blanket. A blanket now pulled back to reveal a mass of black hair tangled with mud, leaves, twigs, and a strong-featured face marked here and there with tattooed warnings.

"Vigga!" Sunny barked out a laugh. "You're back!"

Vigga narrowed her eyes. "You've got wine?" And she plucked the half-full bottle from Sunny's hand. "Last time you had wine you lost your dignity."

"I'm fine. Look how fine I am." Sunny threw up a hand, but forgot it was under the cloak, and got it a bit tangled up. "What's the point of dignity anyway? Can you hug it when you're lonely?"

"You cannot." Vigga upended the bottle and started to swallow, throat working. Sunny wasn't sure if she'd grabbed for Alex's hand in the excitement, or if Alex had grabbed for hers, but she realised they were holding hands now, under a dead angel's cloak, and didn't want to let go.

"Wait." Vigga paused to look around the fire. At Jakob, stripped to the waist, Baptiste, with needle and thread, Balthazar, bottle in hand, and finally, with some disgust, at Baron Rikard. "Were these lot here when I left?"

"We charged in." Jakob, who'd finally fumbled up his sword, now tossed it back down. "Seemed like a good idea at the time."

"Well, I'm glad you did," said Alex. "What about the Dane? You kill him?"

Vigga sucked the bottle dry and slung it into the bushes from which she'd come. "I did not."

"Huh." Balthazar raised his brows. "Most unlike you, to not kill someone."

"We *rutted*," said Vigga proudly, and she plucked Balthazar's bottle from his hand and took a long pull, then burped, and wiped her mouth. "Like beasts of the forest. It was one for the songs."

Baron Rikard sighed. "Which songs are they?"

"The full moon and all." Vigga waved vaguely towards the sky. "Couldn't have stopped if I'd wanted to."

"One imagines you did not."

"Almost wish I had." Vigga perched herself gingerly on a log, grimaced, turned herself one way, then the other. "Feel like I've fucked the bell tower of Saint Stephen's."

Baptiste slightly narrowed her eyes. "An image to lodge in the mind."

"Gave as good as I got, though!"

"Who'd doubt it?"

"He'll be limping back to fucking Denmark to stick his cock in a glacier."

Baptiste winced. "And another."

"You would've been proud, Jakob!"

The old knight thought about that a moment. "Would I?"

"What became o' that tit Sabbas?"

"He had wings," said Alex, staring into the fire.

Vigga froze with her bottle halfway to her mouth. "Ah. Hence the cloak. Likely hard to find anything that fits." And she primly adjusted her filthy blanket around her shoulders. "I know the feeling. Could he fly, then?"

"Not well enough to avoid being dragged into a plague pit by a legion of the long dead."

Vigga thoughtfully nodded. "Huh." And she raised her bottle to Balthazar, and he gave a little nod in return, like two professional competitors recognising the quality of one another's work.

"God *damn* it!" hissed Jakob, twisting in his chair as Baptiste dug at his back again.

"You should have some of this." Vigga held her bottle up to the light. "There's no such thing as bad wine, but this is good wine. It'll dull the pain."

"He doesn't want the pain dulled," said Sunny. "He loves the pain."

"I swore . . ." grumbled Jakob, gripping his stool with his knotty-knuckled fingers, "an oath of temperance."

Vigga raised her brows. "Life's too short to commit to things for ever."

"*Your* life's too short?" Jakob snorted. "Well, I am *fucking* delighted for you—gah!"

"So what did you lot get up to?" asked Vigga.

"Usual stuff," said Baptiste as she pinched Jakob's wound closed and pushed the needle through again. "Spot of grave robbing, briefly jailed by an old friend, attended some peace talks. Balthazar summoned a Duke of Hell . . ." She snipped the last bit of thread free with her dagger and sat back. "Then another last stand, earthquakes, winged arsehole, plague pit. You're done."

"Thanks," grunted Jakob, pulling on a fresh shirt. It must've belonged to Sabbas, involved a lot of golden thread about the collar and cuffs, and made him look like a wealthy widower determined to throw himself back onto the marriage market.

"Is every one of your missions . . ." Alex waved vaguely at everything and nothing, "like this?"

Baron Rikard looked happily towards the night sky. "The missions assigned to

the Chapel of the Holy Expediency are like the members of the congregation—
each awful in its own special way."

"It could be a lot worse," said Sunny. Everyone looked over at her, and she
wondered whether she might be drunk. "I mean . . . we're all alive, and back
together."

"Hallelujah," grumbled Balthazar, whose delight at his own necromantic
achievement had not lasted even one day. "We remain stuck in the middle
of nowhere, in the cause of the world's least likely Empress, no offence . . ."

"Entirely fair," said Alex.

". . . at the behest of a ten-year-old Pontiff," and he waved towards Brother
Diaz, "under the command of the Celestial Palace's least effective monk—"

"Don't talk to him like that!" snarled Vigga. "He's a good man! An honest
man, and a brave man, and an excellent lover! Surprisingly bold and assertive—"

"Wait . . ." Balthazar's look of surprise turned to one of confusion. "What?"

"Oh." Vigga blinked. "Shit."

"Really?" Jakob of Thorn pressed the bridge of his nose between finger and
thumb. "Again?"

"When . . ." Balthazar glanced from the monk to the werewolf and back,
"where . . . how . . . ?"

Brother Diaz looked pained. "Could we . . . talk about something else?"

"You spend years illuminating manuscripts," said Baptiste, working off
one boot, "and singing hymns, and tending the monastery gardens, but all
anyone wants to talk about is the *one* time you fucked a werewolf."

"Three times," said Vigga, "in fact."

"Once could be considered a mishap," said Baron Rikard, in a sermonising
tone, "but *three* times begins to look like deliberate sin!"

"How can even once be a mishap?" asked Sunny, confused.

"Cardinal Zizka, I must confess," sang Baptiste as she pulled off her other
boot and leaned back, wriggling her bare toes at the fire, "that I slipped while
praying, my habit caught upon a stray nail, and my prick, engorged as it always is
while filled with the love of our Lord, accidentally went up a lycanthrope's twat."

"I have heard it all." Balthazar stared off wide-eyed into the darkened forest. "The universe holds no mysteries for me any longer."

"Fine!" shouted Brother Diaz. "The road to redemption begins with confession." He took a swig from his bottle, eyes closed, and then blurted out, "It
was *four* times!"

Vigga squinted up at the sky, then her eyes went wide. "Ah! You're right!"

"The heart wants what the heart wants," said Baron Rikard.

"As does the twat," said Sunny, "apparently."

"And I have no regrets!" shouted Brother Diaz. She'd heard that when you're drunk, it can be hard to tell whether other people are drunk, but she was reasonably sure the monk was drunk. "How about *that*? Vigga's an excellent lover." And he offered her his bottle. "Surprisingly tender and sensitive."

"Doubt the Dane would agree on that score." Vigga modestly flicked her twig-filled hair back as she plucked the bottle from Brother Diaz's hand and raised it to him in a toast. "But I have my moments."

"*Now* I have heard it all," murmured Balthazar, looking from Vigga back to Brother Diaz with an expression almost of wonder. "How can I be both disappointed and impressed, and with both of you at once?"

"It's a wonderful thing . . ." Jakob rubbed gently at his chest, where a spotting of blood was already marking his shirt. "That a man can live as long as I have, and see the things I've seen . . ." He wasn't exactly smiling into the fire but, for once, he wasn't exactly frowning, either. "And *still* the world can surprise him."

"It's a bitter place!" Sunny lurched up, feeling she had something very important to say. "And we must grasp . . ." was a bit difficult to organise her thoughts with her face so hot and the world drifting around so much ". . . at any joy we can." She shut her eyes, but that was even worse, so she opened them again, and raised one hand high. "So I would like to make a *toast*—"

And on the word *toast* she burped and was suddenly sick all down herself.

"You may have toasted too much," said Vigga.

"Oh." Sunny straightened up, her legs all wobbly, and wiped her wet chin. "Did I lose my dignity?"

"Some of it," said Baptiste.

Jakob stared off into the darkness. "But what's the point of dignity anyway?"

"Here." Sunny felt her arm lifted and Alex's head slipped under her armpit, which seemed a good place for it. She was held up, and helped along, which was a very good idea since each of Sunny's legs wanted to wobble off in a different direction.

It was dark in Sabbas's tent, which was almost as gaudy as his cloak. Just the glow of the fire through the canvas, and the gleam of gilt here and there, including the big bedframe that was fit for an Empress indeed and was probably the finest Sunny would ever lie on. Not that there was much competition. When she'd been with the circus she'd slept in a dog basket.

She tripped on something, and nearly fell, but Alex held her up, and she giggled a bit, which was very unlike her. Sunny had never been much of a giggler. Maybe she hadn't had much to laugh at.

"Thanks . . ." she said, suddenly a bit breathless and the tent dark and spinny and smelling of flowers. "For the help."

She felt rather than saw Alex shrug. "You kept me alive, when I was hunted."

"I did, didn't I?"

"Least I can do is help you to bed . . . now you're drunk."

"You think I'm *drunk*?"

Sunny flopped onto the bed on her back, and Alex flopped with her, onto her knees, hands either side of Sunny's shoulders.

They stayed there for a moment, in the darkness, with the sound of the others outside, Balthazar saying something, and Vigga laughing, and Alex was only a dark outline against the glow of the fire through the tent's side. Then she started to move away, and Sunny caught her. Caught her face with both hands, and craned up, which was a dangerous operation with her balance so far gone, and kissed her, very gently, and dropped back down, breathing hard.

Silence again, and Sunny's face was tingling, and the breath was tickly on her lips somehow, and Alex was frozen over her, her knee pressed up against Sunny's hip, her face hot against Sunny's fingers, and now it was Vigga saying something outside, doing a Jakob impression, deep and growly, and the others were laughing, and probably the kiss had tasted somewhat of sick and probably Alex hadn't wanted it anyway but she'd had to try.

"You can go back to the others," whispered Sunny. "If you want." Usually she couldn't find the words she wanted to say. Now she couldn't seem to stop. "I'll be fine. On my own. I'm used to it."

"The world's a bitter place," said Alex, a gleam in the corner of one eye made Sunny think she was smiling. Made Sunny hope she was smiling. "We've got to grasp at any joy we can."

"Wise words. So very wise."

"You're sure about this?" whispered Alex.

Sunny slid one hand around the back of her head. "Who's ever sure?"

She dragged Alex down, and Sunny closed her eyes as they kissed, lips and tongue and warm breath and fingers in hair and legs tangled together, and the tent spun pleasantly, and the laughter burbled outside—

And Sunny twisted free and was sick all over the floor.

part

IV

SAINT NATALIA'S FLAME

End of the Road

I t's *big*," said Alex.

In the darkness before dawn, the distant pinprick of Saint Natalia's Flame had seemed to float over the horizon, like an overbright star. Now, as the sun poured golden over the mountains in the east and their fat-bellied ship wallowed towards its final stop, the mystery was explained.

"It's *really* big," said Brother Diaz.

The Pillar of Troy was so colossal that it was less building, more landscape. A tree-stump-shaped mountain of masonry thrust out of the sea, a froth of green at the top where the famous Hanging Gardens grew, the spikes of smaller towers rising even higher above it, like the prongs of a crown.

"It's fucking immense," said Vigga.

And some genius had decided it'd be a great idea for a piece of shit like Alex to *rule* it. She pressed at her churning stomach, as if she could squeeze the nerves out. She'd always known it was a mad notion, but assumed sooner or later everyone else would see it too and come up with a better idea. Then they'd all have a good laugh. Remember that ferrety fool we were going to make Empress? What were we *thinking*?

Only here she was, about to arrive in Troy, and no one was laughing.

Certainly not her.

"There are so many things in life . . ." Balthazar had an oddly boyish look of wonder as he watched the sun rise over the city. "That have somehow acquired an overblown and undeserved reputation—"

"Like the third best necromancer in Europe?" asked Baptiste.

The third best necromancer in Europe gave a long-suffering sigh. "—but the Pillar of Troy is plainly not one such. A relic of a grander epoch, in the shadow of which ours appears a petty afterthought." He narrowed his eyes at Alex. "Who built it?"

"The Witch Engineers of Carthage," she said, instantly, "though it's rumoured they bound the demon prince Hoxcazish to serve as architect."

"Why was it built?"

"Depends who you ask. Merchants say to control trade routes by land and sea. Priests say as a temple to diabolical powers. Nobles say to strike awe into the hearts of the conquered. Soldiers say as an eastern fortress against the elves."

"We all see the world through the lens of our own obsessions," murmured Jakob.

Balthazar was giving Alex the faintest nod of approval. The highest praise he offered. "I am gratified to see that you were listening. According to the histories, ancient Carthage itself boasted three pillars on an even grander scale, but they toppled when most of the city was sucked through a gate to hell."

"A bad day for property values in general, one imagines," observed Baron Rikard, running fingers through his raven-black hair and letting the sea wind take it like a shining banner.

"When Carthage fell Troy's Pillar wasn't finished." Alex pointed out the line of tiny arches that linked it to the mountains east of the city. "It was Basil the First, later named Basil the Builder, who completed the Grand Aqueduct, planted the Hanging Gardens, and began work on the Pharos. Saint Natalia's Flame wasn't lit at its top until fifty years after his death. Not long after that the foundation stone of the Basilica of the Angelic Visitation was laid, following . . . wait for it . . . an angelic visitation."

Balthazar gave a sour grunt. "Now you're just showing off."

"Well, *that* I learned from the best," said Alex, staring towards the Pillar, one side in shadow, the other bright with the light of the rising sun, a spreading carpet of newer buildings, tiny by comparison, beginning to show around its base. "What if they despise me?" she murmured. "My . . ." She could hardly say the word. ". . . *subjects.*"

"Then you'll be no worse off than most rulers," said Jakob.

"It is not the role of an Empress to be *liked*," said Balthazar, "provided they are *obeyed.*"

"Maybe you'd feel differently about being liked," said Baptiste, "if you knew how it felt."

Balthazar opened his mouth, as if to disagree, then shut it, as if he'd realised he couldn't.

Alex wriggled at another surge of nerves, plucking at the gilded fabric of her dress again. Baptiste had been apprentice to a dressmaker in Avignon for a few weeks and had spent the morning with a mouthful of pins, swaddling her in cloth from Sabbas's cloak. It was too tight at the waist and too bulky at the chest, as if it had been cut for a better shaped version of her. Gal the Purse used to say, *Pretend to be what you want to be, one day you might find you're not pretending any more*. Always sounded wise to Alex, who spent a lot of time pretending, but she had her doubts it'd make anyone's tits bigger.

"I feel like a fucking birthday present," she muttered.

"And who doesn't like getting those?" said Baron Rikard. "Never fear, Your Highness, you could not be better prepared." He indicated himself with a flourish. "You have received expert instruction in etiquette," waving to Balthazar, "showing off," pointing to Brother Diaz, "letters," indicating Jakob, "frowning," waving towards Vigga, "indiscriminate slaughter—"

"Indiscrimmy what now?" she grunted back at him.

"It means thoughtless," said Baptiste.

Vigga opened her mouth, as if to disagree, then shut it, as if she'd realised she couldn't.

"Then there are whatever lessons Sunny has been giving you." The baron flourished his pale fingers towards nothing in particular. "Invisible cunnilingus, for all I know—"

"Cunny what now?" grunted Vigga.

"It means—" began Baptiste.

"We know what it means," said Brother Diaz.

"And last, but by no means least," finished the baron, waving towards Baptiste, "everything else." And she, as comfortable around high society as low, performed an exemplary curtsey, though it looked a bit odd in knee boots.

"Do bear in mind," the baron went on, "that some of the most charmless, talentless, luckless people in history have made quite passable monarchs once crowned. You really are no worse than average material."

"That's a huge encouragement," said Alex.

"Of course." He smiled, showing perfect white teeth, if not to say fangs. "Thank *God* for me."

"But I'm not crowned yet." Alex felt another ugly surge of nerves as she looked back towards the Pillar. "I still have one living cousin . . ."

"Arcadius," growled Jakob.

"The eldest," said Balthazar.

"And by all accounts most powerful," added Baptiste.

"The brothers were bitter rivals for the throne." Brother Diaz scratched worriedly at his beard. "Killing the others will only have made him more dangerous."

"Great," said Alex. "That's *great*." She'd been expecting his galleys to surge from every inlet, his mercenaries to shoot arrows from every town, or his winged lizard-men to swoop from every cloud they'd passed on their voyage. The fact they hadn't only made her certain there must be an even more horrifying attempt on her life to come. She pressed her hands against her bubbling stomach. "That is so great I might puke."

Like most things, it was worse close up.

Ships swarmed the harbour, jostling at the wharves like famished piglets competing for the teat. Beast-prowed ships of the north, lean and vicious, dwarfed by triple-decked galleys from Afrique, the Five Lessons stitched in golden thread into their sails. Greetings and threats were hurled between passing sailors in tongues Alex couldn't understand and hand gestures that left no room for doubt.

The Pillar towered over everything, casting one edge of the harbour into its mighty shadow and dwarfing the jagged line of foothills behind. In places its walls were like natural cliffs, great sheets of seamless rock, in others they were built from crumbling masonry on an inhuman scale—buttresses big as bell towers and arched vaults with whole streets huddling beneath—all rain-stained and dropping-streaked, splattered with rashes of green fern and red creeper, swarmed by flocks of multicoloured birds roosting in the heights.

Dwellings had been chiselled out up there, stairways and doorways and smoking chimneys cut from the stone, or built out on dizzying scaffolds, garlanded with ladders and teetering walkways, with ropes and chains dangling to the city on which breakfasts were winched up in buckets. Everywhere water flowed, channels in the Pillar's flanks made frothing sluices and glittering waterfalls, their spray darkening the roofs of the streets below and casting rainbows over the city. Within those channels Alex saw mighty wheels moving, monstrous gears turning, as though the whole had clockwork guts, as much machine as building.

The sails were brought in, the ship drifted closer, and Alex began to see the people. Mobs, wedged onto every roof, quay, and wharf. Closer still, and she began to fear those thousands of faces might be aimed directly at her. "Are they waiting . . ." she whispered, "for *me?*"

"Well, they're not waiting for me," grunted Jakob.

"Oh God." A city full. An Empire full. Alex chewed at her sore bottom lip, all dry and cracked, like an overdone sausage. As far from Empress lips as could be. Worst lips you ever saw. "Is it too late to head back to the Holy City?" she muttered.

"I'm wondering the same thing," said Vigga, peering out from behind the mainmast as timber scraped on stone and sailors hopped to the shore to make fast the ropes.

"Merciful heavens, we have a bashful werewolf." Baron Rikard's sigh was a chill breeze on Alex's neck as he leaned in. "Now remember, Your Highness, there are no strangers to you, only beloved old friends to whom you are *delighted* to be reintroduced."

"Oh *God*." There was a welcoming party, baking in the already fierce sun—sparkling guards, horses in glittering harness, led by a woman stately as an Empress. An actual Empress, rather than a laughable impostor.

"An *explosion* of generosity and good humour will ignite behind your eyes at each introduction. I want to see social *fireworks*. And straighten *up*, for pity's sake, you have come to lead a nation, not hunt for a lost earring."

"Sorry," mumbled Alex, forcing down her endlessly hunching shoulders.

"And never say *sorry*."

"Sorry. Shit!"

"And never say *shit*."

The gangplank slid across to the stones. There was a horrible silence.

And . . . we walk. Exactly the way the baron had taught her. As if she had a priceless jewel between her collarbones that everyone deserved the pleasure of seeing. She floated across the gangplank. She glided across the quay. The pitiless glare of the sun and the even more pitiless glare of hundreds of eyes and an ever-worsening itch in the small of her back that in this dress she'd never be able to scratch were *exactly* the things she most enjoyed.

And . . . we smile. Happiness and good humour and she was not at all worried she was going to shit herself in front of several hundred of her future subjects. *We smile.* Everything was just the way she wanted it, and she was absolutely not going to shit herself. *We smile.* Warmth and well-wishes and her bowels were absolutely under control, but if she *did* shit herself no one would be able to say she hadn't looked like she enjoyed it.

She swore this woman grew with every step she took. She was almost as tall as Jakob, but with way better skin. Empress skin if ever there was any. Best fucking skin you ever saw. Alex felt like a ridiculous beggar-child in her presence. Not even a piece of shit. A smear. A speck. God, could she feel her nose sweating? A speck of shit with the complexion of a wormy windfall squeezed into a golden sausage skin made from a dead man's cloak.

Alex was expecting the woman to burst out laughing as she stopped in her unnaturally long and slender shadow, then for everyone else to join her. *No, really, bring out the real one.* Instead, she sank into the most respectful of curtseys, skirts settling in a shimmering pool, as smoothly as if she'd been lowered on a hidden platform.

"Princess Alexia, it is my honour to welcome you home. I am—"

"You must be Lady Severa," said Alex. "Warden of the Imperial Chamber. My uncle spoke of you often."

"Not too harshly, I hope?"

"He said you were a dear friend. That you risked everything to send him letters. That he trusted you with his life, and I could trust you, too."

Lady Severa sank a little deeper, if that was possible. "Your uncle is too kind. But in my experience . . . an Empress is wise never to trust anyone *too* much. Might I rise?"

"What? Shit, yes! I mean, shit. Yes! Sorry."

"Your Highness need *never* say sorry." Lady Severa glided upwards to tower over her by at least a head, and what a head it was.

"Any chance you could . . ." Alex squinted up at her. "Rise a bit less?"

"Would Your Highness prefer that the soldiers of her guard bring her a box to stand on? Or dig me a trench to stand in?"

Alex began to grin. "I've a feeling you may be joking, Lady Severa."

"It has been known on special occasions. But there is no need for Your Highness to use the *Lady*. Severa is quite enough." She leaned down to murmur, "As Empress, Your Highness will be free to call me bitch, mare, sow, or harpy without fear of correction, indeed your predecessor frequently did, and I always thanked her for the kind attention. Whatever Your Highness desires, it is my duty and pleasure to provide. For now, it is my duty and pleasure to conduct you to Duke Michael—"

"He's here?" asked Alex.

"He has been here for several weeks, making arrangements for your entrance into the city. He is waiting for you at the Grand Lift of Heraclius, at the end of the cavalcade."

"Cavalcade?" Alex's voice cracked slightly. She'd been half-expecting to be beheaded the moment she stepped off the boat.

"The people of Troy wish to greet their Empress-to-be." Severa gestured towards an immense white horse. "Do you ride, Your Highness?"

"Very badly," muttered Alex.

Some bird's droppings noisily spattered the cobbles as she set off towards that fortune in horseflesh. The silence was going from odd to worrying. She thought she heard somebody murmur, "That's her?"

"Wait." Jakob held out an arm and Alex froze, heart in her mouth as she wondered what threat he'd seen. He stepped forwards, left hand gripping the hilt of his sword. He took a great breath, like a man about to order a charge against impossible odds, and roared at the very top of his gravelly voice. "A cheer for Her Highness, the Princess Alexia Pyrogennetos!"

"Princess Alexia!" A child's voice, shrill with innocent joy, and as if that was the raindrop that caused a dam to burst, whooping, whistling, cheering went up everywhere, birds clattering from the roofs in alarm.

Jakob gave an approving grunt. "They just needed a nudge."

A pair of bearded priests led the way with two icons on gilded poles, Saint Natalia and Saint Hadrian, according to Brother Diaz, who knew a saint when he saw one. Next came a pair of nuns, one carrying a crystal case with a mummified foot inside, the other wearing a golden breastplate with a pickled angel's feather set into it. Next tramped a dozen guards, the breeze stirring their purple plumes and the sun twinkling on their ceremonial weaponry. Next, exhibited side-saddle on a spectacular white horse with a jewelled harness, came the heavily sweating centrepiece of the whole event, a thief who once got badly beaten for trying to steal a leper's crutch, accompanied by a vampire, a werewolf, and an immortal mass murderer.

Only went to prove that other one of Gal the Purse's favourite sayings— *Tell the right story, people will buy any old shit.*

Troy was a city of dazzling sun and even more dazzling colour. Polished domes twinkled, burnished doors flashed, gold and silver tiles winked in the mosaics of saints surrounding chapel doors, at the feet of which beggars lurked. They passed through a market where everything on earth had its price: strangely striped and spotted animals prowling cages, gaudy plate and gleaming glassware, bowls of pungent spices big as baths in vivid green, brown, orange, gold, bolts of bright white linen and shining silk in every colour. They passed a great dye-works, where waters from the Pillar were channelled into pools stained strange shades, the near-naked workers wading in them stained strange shades, too. All about them on a forest of poles endless swags of cloth were gathered to dry like the sails of great galleys, seas of bright blue and vivid red and shining green billowing with the breeze. They took a curving boulevard around the base of the Pillar, new vistas of grinning faces endlessly revealed, sweltering in gaudy feast-day clothes till Alex was dizzy with their dazzle and their cheering. There were almost as many bells as in the Holy City, pealing from churches with green-streaked copper domes, echoing from chapels clinging to the top of the soaring aqueduct like barnacles to a harbour chain, clanging from shrines with flaking paintings of smirking crusaders putting elves to the sword.

That made her wonder where Sunny had got to. Weaving subtly through her honour guard? Slipping unnoticed through the crowd? Clinging to the underside of her horse? Maybe later she could get Sunny to cling to her underside. She found herself smiling at the thought. But the smiles were coming easier by then, as the parade passed into a wide square at the foot of the Pillar and the cheers grew even louder.

"Do they . . . *like* me?" she murmured to Jakob, whose scarred frown was a grey anchor in the multicoloured madness.

"Oh, they love you," he grunted. "The way you can only love someone you've never met and never will. They love the idea of you. The thought of becoming their best selves. Being redeemed. Made whole." He shook his head at the crowds lining the square. "No matter who rules, the world will still be the world. People will still be people."

Baptiste snorted. "Take no notice of this grumpy fossil."

"So it's happy endings all around, then?" asked Alex as the priests with their icons, then the nuns with their relics, then the gilded guards halted before a platform set into a channel in the Pillar's side, where a party of brightly dressed grandees watched her ride closer.

"Oh, I doubt it." Baptiste blew a kiss to the crowds. "Happy endings are just stories that aren't finished yet."

"Uncle!" Duke Michael's familiar face jumped from that party of rich folk, smiling more broadly even than the rest. Alex right away forgot all the proper etiquette, slithering from her horse while two footmen were labouring over with a set of gilded steps, running between two carved columns commemorating victories of long ago and straight into Duke Michael's arms.

He caught her, lifted her, swung her around, holding her tight.

"It's so good to see you," she murmured into his shoulder. Took her by surprise how much she meant it. She hadn't seen the man in months, had only known him for a few days then, but he'd always been on her side.

"I've been dreaming of this day for so long," he said. "There were times I thought it would never come. I know the road was hard. I'm so sorry I wasn't with you." He gave her a squeeze, then held her out at arm's length. "But I hardly recognise you! You have *grown*. I cannot tell you . . . how much you look like your mother . . ."

"Pray do not be greedy, Duke Michael," said a holy-looking old bastard whose beard nearly reached his belt. "Allow the rest of us to welcome the princess home!"

"Of course!" Duke Michael might've been dashing a tear from his eye. "May I introduce the Head of the Church of the East, Grand Patriarch Methodius the Thirteenth."

Alex was sorely tempted to nudge the Grand Patriarch and ask what had gone wrong with the other twelve, but for once she thought she'd better stick to Baron Rikard's script, and she sank to one knee, pretending very hard to be a princess. "Your Beatitude, Her Holiness the Pope asked that I convey to you her sisterly greetings, her wishes for your continued good health, and her hopes that two such servants of the Saviour, and the two branches of the one true Church you represent, may soon be united again as one family."

The Patriarch raised his bushy brows. "Pious sentiments, Your Highness, warmly expressed. It will be a profound relief, after a period in which our faith has been sorely tested, to have the rightful heir of Theodosia once more sitting the Serpent Throne. You were examined by two Oracles of the Celestial Choir, I understand?"

There was a calculating glint in the Patriarch's eye as he helped her up, but Alex kept smiling as if he was a dear old friend, and proof of her legitimacy was her favourite subject. "I was, Your Beatitude."

"In a properly purified pale chamber?"

"Well, I'm a princess, not a magician, but it was a big white room." Alex laughed, and sprinkled smiles around, and was pleased to see several of the noblemen laughing along.

"You have seen the bull confirming my niece's status as Pyrogennetos." Duke Michael unrolled a copy now to display its weighty seal and overwrought signatures. "Signed by Cardinal Bock and Her Holiness the Pope."

"The ten-year-old Pope?" asked the Patriarch, smirking slightly as he gave the bull a thorough look-over.

"The Pope," said Jakob, not smirking at all.

"And that is the birthmark?" Methodius peered at the skin behind Alex's ear. "I hope it is not too forward of me to ask, but might I see the famous coin?"

Alex pulled her half from her collar and lifted the thong over her head to offer it out. Duke Michael produced his half and handed it to the Patriarch. They didn't look much alike, as he held them to the light. Michael's tarnished dull brown, Alex's polished bright, Empress Theodosia's face worn to a blob by years against her skin. But you could see their ragged edges matched. One of the noblewomen gasped. A man with a huge moustache gravely nodded. A fellow with a heavy golden chain about his shoulders muttered softly to a neighbour.

Wasn't much proof of anything, really. Alex had run cleverer cons on pilgrims for the sake of a few coppers, let alone a whole Empire. But it doesn't take much to prove what folk already want to believe. Patriarch Methodius looked at Duke Michael, and Duke Michael looked back, and Alex could see that whatever her uncle was selling, the Patriarch had already bought.

The Head of the Church of the East thrust up the two halves of the coin in one hand and the papal bull in the other, for the crowds to see. Even if at that distance they could've been one of Brother Diaz's letters to Mother and two halves of a bull's bollock.

"Princess Alexia Pyrogennetos!" he thundered. "Firstborn of Irene, first-born of Theodosia, examined by the Oracles of the Celestial Choir and de-clared first in line of succession, has returned to Troy! Has returned to *us*. Has returned to claim *her birthright*, to protect the realms of men from the terror of the elves and lead our Empire into a new age of prosperity!"

Who could doubt something said so loud in such a deep voice? A great cheer went up as everyone in that crowd thought how they might benefit, and simply as that, Alex was acclaimed by Pope and Patriarch as rightful heir to the Serpent Throne of Troy. She did her best to pretend she believed it, and the high and mighty crowded in, beaming for the honour of being introduced.

To a piece-of-shit thief.

Strange world, eh?

To Duel with Giants

Guards slotted an iron railing into place at the edge of the dais. A woman sporting a chain of gilded cogs made a self-important performance of hauling on a long lever. There was a jolt that made everyone totter, then, not with a tortured grinding of gears but a smooth *whirr*, the whole platform, and the two dozen or more people occupying it, began to rise up the channel in the Pillar's side.

"Astonishing," whispered Balthazar.

The triumphal columns and grand buildings about the square dropped away, the brightly dressed well-wishers dwindled into an anonymous crowd, the azure Aegean showed itself on the far side of the harbour wall. Higher they rose, and higher still, the horizon stretching off, a maze of streets reaching to the crumbling city walls and beyond, an expanse of tiled roofs pimpled with verdigrised domes, and even a few freshly installed on the palaces of the wealthy, bright copper glinting in the baking sun.

Troy. Jewel of the East. Balthazar had once deemed it inconceivable they would ever arrive. Had been sure the ridiculous Princess Alexia would end up incinerated by sorcerous fire, consumed by crab-men, or interred beneath a collapsing abbey. But there she stood, in the place of honour, feted by the mighty. The Empress-to-be. And looking, one had to confess, almost convincing in the role.

Balthazar realised he was in danger of smiling and was obliged to avert his gaze lest it be noticed. Could it be that he felt the faintest flickerings of paternal pride towards the clueless waif? Whatever her considerable shortcomings, it could not be denied the girl had *grit*, not to mention a surprisingly agile and inquisitive mind, when properly stimulated by a conscientious instructor. Nor could it be denied that Balthazar had himself played a vital role in her survival. He rather suspected there would be no reward. No honours and no offices. But, when all was said and done, what was the acclamation of strangers truly worth? He knew what he had done. Perhaps that could be satisfaction enough? He watched the gears turning, beside the lift, and felt his smile grow wider.

"If you are impressed now . . ." He turned to find Lady Severa regarding him from close quarters. "Only wait until we reach the top."

"Well . . . er . . ." For months, Balthazar had dreamed of associating once again with persons of breeding and refinement. Now, addressed by an evident paragon of those very qualities, he found himself tongue-tied. "I fear I have been too long among barbarians . . . I can only apologise for my *wretched* appearance—"

"You have helped conduct the princess safely home, braving dangers we dread to imagine. You should wear every smudge like a medal. I am—"

"Lady Severa, of course. I overheard your exchange with Princess Alexia on the quay . . ." And he had been deeply impressed, not only by her immaculate bearing but, to his surprise, by her humility. Not a quality he had previously much celebrated, but he could not help noticing how, by making so little of her status, her status was only enhanced. What manner of person needs constantly to assert their own importance, after all? Only the truly unimportant. "I am Balthazar." He gave the simplest bow he could, while thinking how laughably pompous the elaborate ones he had once practised in the mirror would have been.

"Just Balthazar?"

"There is more to it, but . . ." He waved such affectations away. "Balthazar is quite enough."

"And are you an engineer?"

An engineer of the arcane. A tinkerer with the forbidden workings of the universe. A machinist of the delicately interlocking gears of life and death! Balthazar bit his tongue. "Merely a dabbler, and more in theory than in practice. Indeed, I observed some . . . phenomena, recently, that have me reconsidering the nature of matter." He absently put the heels of his hands together, as the twin aeromancer and geomancer had done. "I am forced to wonder whether the elements of earth and air might not in fact be opposites, but composed somehow of the same fundamental stuff . . ."

He realised he had wandered onto territory that few indeed would find as engrossing as he, but Lady Severa was regarding him with eyes thoughtfully narrowed. "So you would dare to do battle with Hasdrubal *and* Cellibus?"

Balthazar stared back. Merciful heavens, all this *and* a thorough grounding in the pillars of philosophy? "I have no desire to duel with giants . . . but the facts might force me to it . . ." Her piercing assessment was having a most unsettling effect upon him, and he cleared his throat as he forced his eyes away. "I knew some of the architecture of ancient Carthage survived here in Troy—your magnificent Pillar and Aqueduct—but never guessed that its machinery might still function."

"The Empress Eudoxia had her drawbacks." Severa counted points on the expressive fingers of an artist. "The coven of sorcerers, the overbearing off-spring, the summary executions, the abominable experiments."

"Ah, yes." Balthazar was relieved to happen upon so unromantic a topic. "We were accosted by some of them on our journey here. Hybrids of man and beast. Twisted creations, in many ways, though the sarcomancy was undeniably superb."

"You thought so?"

"I have never seen its equal. They made formidable fighters."

"It was not Eudoxia's intention to breed warriors. Or, at least, I understand it was the doing of her sons. She was afflicted from birth with a wasting sickness that left her . . . far from the imperial ideal of perfection. She sought a way to preserve her own weak flesh. Then she became fascinated by the soul." Severa gripped the railing tight, frowning out over the city. "With locating it. With releasing it. With *capturing* it."

"Fascinating indeed . . ." murmured Balthazar, wondering if the dead Empress had made any progress with the age-old riddle of locating the soul within the body, then realising his curiosity had once again dragged him onto dangerous ground, "and entirely insane! A crime against God, and so on. Eudoxia must have been . . . a most testing employer."

Severa moved a little closer to murmur under her breath, an occurrence for which he was highly thankful. "You could not guess the half of it. But she was an enthusiastic student of history. She repaired long-dormant machines within the Pillar, driven by the waters of the aqueduct, the three lifts among them. They really are the only way to the top. Unless you are a *very* confident climber."

"A noble project." Balthazar dared to venture a smile. "People, and great figures especially, are rarely all hero or villain."

"All things are relative." Did he dare to imagine that she had the faintest smile of her own? "I presume you are employed by Pope Benedicta?"

His smile twisted into a grimace, as his smiles often did. "I . . . find myself in her service . . ." He thought it prudent not to mention the multiple convictions for heresy, necromancy, and consorting with demons that had brought it about.

Severa leaned still closer. "Can it be true . . ." He fancied he could feel the warmth of her breath on his neck. ". . . that the child is the Second Coming of the Saviour?"

Balthazar swallowed. "If you had asked me a few months ago, I would have been obliged, despite the breach of decorum, to laugh in your face. You will not find a more committed sceptic than I anywhere in Europe, and on meeting the infant Pontiff in person I was . . . *not* impressed."

"I see."

"But . . ."

"But?"

"I have always desired, above all, to be thought a wise man. I have begun to realise it might even be a good idea to *be* one. And a truly wise man must accept that, however much he knows, there is always far more to learn."

"Wisdom indeed," murmured Severa.

"Events . . . have made me reconsider my position on the Pope."

With a lurch the lift stopped, he stumbled slightly, reached out involuntarily, and felt her firmly catch his arm. "You must find time to tell me more about these . . . *events*." Did she give his wrist the lightest parting squeeze? Or, as she glided away, did he only want desperately to believe it?

"So far out of your league . . ." Baptiste leaned in, speaking from the corner of her mouth, "you might as well come from different species."

Balthazar did not even bother to deny it. "Let a man dream," he whispered.

Rivers in the Sky

Brother Diaz stepped onto the top of the Pillar of Troy, and into another world.

The city below had been dry and dusty, walled in and paved over. Up here, in the royal grounds, all was shimmering green against dazzling blue. Trees majestic as any in a forest soared overhead, emerald lawns spread out in invitation, bushes offered up a treasure of blossom, all planted with such masterful artifice it seemed the seeds must have fallen from the hand of God.

A double row of immaculate guardsmen lined the paved road, and as Alex approached, they all stomped one heel with a single crash of military might, lowering gilded halberds to form a corridor of polished metal.

"So many guards," murmured Brother Diaz, nodding in approval at all that armour.

"So many guards," murmured Alex, peering nervously at the blades hovering overhead.

"Being afraid . . . is a hard habit to break, I know. I'd always imagined our hardest tests would lie at the end of the journey." Brother Diaz let his hand trail through a frond of greenery, dewy leaves tickling the webs between his fingers. "Dare we imagine the worst might be behind us?"

"Don't count on it," grunted Jakob of Thorn. But even his flinty frown showed signs of softening. The city below had been airless, baking, thick with reek and flies. Up here, in the Hanging Gardens, a cooling breeze caressed the skin, making the bright sun flash and sparkle through leaves of a thousand shapes and colours.

Brother Diaz took a breath heavy with the fragrance of flowers and resin and let it sigh away. "As near as I've come to paradise."

"I've heard during Empress Diocletia's reign, every plant God made was represented here." Alex held up her palms as a zephyr brought a fluttering rain of tiny pink petals down around her.

Duke Michael smiled as he watched. "Say what you will about Eudoxia— and she murdered my sister, usurped her throne, and was a tyrant and heretic who deservedly burns in hell—but she spared no expense on the Pillar and

Aqueduct, and gave us a glimpse of the majesty of old." He grinned at the babbling waters as they crossed a bridge over a snaking channel. "When I was a boy there was nothing but a brackish trickle here, the gardens were reduced to thirsty palms, just one of the lifts worked, and only when it was in the right mood. But now? Listen."

The city below had been raucous with cheering, the clatter of commerce, the bellows of beasts on four legs and two. Here there was only the murmur of foliage, the trill of birdsong, and everywhere the nearby chatter of running water, the far-off whisper of falling water.

"Rivers," murmured Brother Diaz, "in the sky."

"The water floods down the aqueduct from springs in the mountains," said Duke Michael, "and flows through hidden pipes beneath us, or spreads out in channels to cascade down the Pillar's sides, driving the lifts, flowing out through the districts below to water the gardens and fill the public baths. The scholars say it did much more, once, but those secrets are lost."

"The scale . . ." breathed Balthazar, "beggars belief . . ." Even he'd lost his usual detached superiority.

Duke Michael grinned. "The top of the Pillar is several hundred strides across. The Witch Engineers of Carthage did not lack ambition, and nor did my forebears, in building on their legacy. On the east side, they raised the Basilica of the Angelic Visitation." He pointed down a paved road, busy with hooded pilgrims. The towering facade of the Basilica at its end, framed by the blue heavens, was covered in geometric carvings and glittering images of the angels. The four spires at its corners were the size of bell towers, its two soaring bell towers taller yet.

Here was the grandeur Brother Diaz had hoped, and decidedly failed, to find in the Holy City. "Truly," he murmured, closing his eyes for a moment, "a place where one can feel the presence of God."

"On the Pillar's west side, they built the palace." Duke Michael pointed out a dizzying cluster of spires, striped with bands of dark stone, and set a fond hand on Alex's shoulder. "*Your* palace, and at its top, Saint Natalia's Flame, which for centuries has guided the children of Troy home." The Pharos gently tapered like the blade of a sword, the highest of all the great towers built on the great tower of the Pillar, the flame at its domed top gleaming brightly even in the sunlight.

Duke Michael pointed out more imposing architecture, glimpsed through the green. "They raised the grand dwellings of the noble families, and the headquarters of army and navy, fortresses to house the Emperor's elite, and all the machinery of a great Empire. A city within the city!"

"A city among the clouds . . ." Balthazar was gazing at a building rising from the gardens beside them, its pediment held up on ten lofty pillars, carved with scenes of art and learning. "The famous Athenaeum?"

"Desecrated and diminished." Duke Michael shook his head. "Eudoxia drove out the scholars, replaced them with sorcerers and alchemists, and gave the place over to the study of Black Art."

"The excavation of arcane mysteries," murmured Balthazar, "not cloaked in shameful secrecy, but proudly celebrated! Only imagine!" He cleared his throat as he realised everyone was staring at him. "And . . . be utterly *scandalised*, of course."

"We faced a few of Eudoxia's students on the road," said Jakob.

"They were bad enough in ones and twos. The thought of a *coven* . . ." And Brother Diaz hastily made the sign of the circle over his chest.

"Some swore loyalty to one or another of the Empress's sons," said Lady Severa. "The rest fled soon after her death."

"Like woodlice, they feared the light." Duke Michael smiled over at Alex. "No doubt they sensed the new dawn coming, and judgement with her! Like so much of the city, our Athenaeum yearns to be reborn. Its library remains one of the greatest in the world, by all accounts."

Brother Diaz had scarcely thought of books in months, but memories of happy hours among the shelves now flooded back. "How many volumes?" he asked.

"Counting them would be a labour of itself," said Severa, "but well over a hundred thousand."

Brother Diaz gaped. He'd often boasted that his monastery's library held a thousand books, and knew he'd been stretching the truth. He struggled to picture what *one hundred* thousand might look like. Imagine the index alone! Sweet Saviour, what system of sliding ladders might they employ?

"I would very much like to see that," he whispered.

"I will make arrangements to have it opened to you. You must promise not to wander within, though. There are still . . . *things* left behind, from Eudoxia's experiments . . ." Severa looked warily towards low vaults cut into the foundations to either side of the front steps and sealed with barred gates. They reminded Brother Diaz more than was comfortable of the cells beneath the Chapel of the Holy Expediency. "Things we dare not disturb . . ."

"My great-grandfather gathered a menagerie in the building's basement," said Duke Michael. "Strange and wonderful creatures, from the ice of the Arctic, the deserts of Afrique. He had planned to study, delight, and educate."

"Eudoxia put the animals to a different purpose," said Severa.

Jakob narrowed his eyes. "This is where the things that fought for Marcian and Constans were made." Brother Diaz took a nervous step away. He thought he had seen something shift, deep in the shadows beyond the bars.

"Where Sabbas got his wings," said Baptiste, "and set himself up as the Angel of Troy."

"The arrogance of those pampered dolts!" snapped Lady Severa, with sudden venom. "The gifts they squandered, squabbling over what was never theirs! I should have done more . . ."

"You can't blame yourself for their sins," said Brother Diaz, softly.

"If no one blamed themselves for the things they could not help . . ." She gave him a faint smile as she turned away from the Athenaeum and led them on towards the palace. "Wouldn't the whole Church go out of business?"

Before You Ask

The Imperial Bedchamber." Lady Severa swung open a magnificent pair of double doors. "As Pyrogennetos, *this* . . . was the place of Your Highness's birth."

"So the Pope's Oracles tell me," murmured Alex. "My own memory's a little hazy . . ." The cavernous room on the other side was where high-end brothel met cathedral to some evil god—all dark marble, gold leaf, and swags of silk the colour of a slit throat. Three great arched openings in the thick wall of the tower gave an almost impossible view of the western sky, clouds stained pink and gold by the setting sun.

Alex walked over, the breeze kissing her face, feeling a pleasant lurch in her stomach as the harbour came into view far below, ships drawing white letters across the dark page of the Aegean Sea. Almost made climbing all those steps worthwhile.

"It's quite a view." She turned back to consider the chamber. You couldn't learn etiquette from Baron Rikard without developing some opinions on decor. "Though it does look a *bit* like the room where you'd bed a demon."

"Given Eudoxia's reputation . . ." Lady Severa considered the colossal bed. "Nothing would surprise me. I will give orders to render it less . . . diabolical." She snapped her fingers and sections of the panelling were swung open so sharply Alex flinched, ready to run for her life from some new monstrous legions.

Instead, four very unmonstrous young women glided through the doors, heads bowed. They might've been Alex's age but came from a smoother-limbed and shinier-haired species. The one Lady Severa belonged to.

The rich.

From the range of skin tones, face shapes, and daunting jewellery, these four came from the rich in different corners of the Empire. None made any moves to attack. Unless you considered extreme demureness an assault. Which Alex did, a bit.

"These are your handmaidens," said Lady Severa. "Athenais, Cleofa, Zenonis, and Placidia. All selected from unimpeachable families."

"Right." Until Alex ran into Duke Michael while being beaten for small change in a fish market, the closest she'd come to family was a back-alley fence and her battalion of child pickpockets. "Wouldn't want anyone impeachable near the throne . . ."

"If they displease you there is no shortage of other candidates—"

"No!" Severa's tone was so careless Alex had a worry she might backhand any rejects out of the window and more than likely have their replacement in post before they hit the sea. "You all seem lovely." Not to mention tall. "I'm sure you'd make . . . much better . . . princesses than me . . ." And she petered out into awkward silence.

"Then, ladies, consider this a probationary period. You have seven days to make yourself indispensable to Her Highness." The girls bowed even lower, chins to throats, falling in behind Severa as she led Alex on the lengthy voyage across the room, further chambers glimpsed beyond open doors, dizzying hints of tapestries and paintings, pottery and plate, stained glass and candles.

"I've got a chapel?" she asked.

"Previous rulers had their own chaplain, too. A spiritual advisor and confessor. But that particular post has sat empty. Empress Eudoxia was . . . not the most devout of rulers. This chamber was more to her taste."

Alex peered into a room three times the size of the one she'd once shared with seven other thieves, dominated by a giant bronze bath.

"I took the liberty of having water brought up in anticipation of your arrival. I thought Your Highness might want to bathe after your journey."

"Oh God," whispered Alex, and for once in a good way. Steam rose from it, and flower petals floated on it, and some sort of oil was in it that was sweet on her tongue and peppery in her nose so her mouth watered and she wanted to sneeze together. "Can you read my mind?"

"It is my responsibility not only to provide you with what you ask for, but to know what you want before you ask."

The handmaidens closed in around Alex, their hands on her but not quite on her, undoing the fastenings of the dress Baptiste had spent all morning fastening her into.

"Oh, you're just . . ." She'd been feeling way out of her depth, so the very thing she needed was to be stripped naked by four strangers. "Getting right in there . . ."

"You will never have to undo another button, Your Highness," said Cleofa, or maybe Placidia.

"That's a relief. Buttons . . . have really been . . . my worst problem up to now." Alex awkwardly cleared her throat. She felt like a ferret being waited on by leopards. "You're all so . . . *long*."

"Empress Eudoxia was shorter than you," said Lady Severa.

"She was?"

"And had a withered left leg and had to walk with a stick for much of her life, and no one took her lightly, believe me. She was the terror of an Empire."

"I don't need to be a terror." Alex felt weird and bony and scarred, covered in the marks of a shit life full of losing battles, fought viciously over tiny stakes. The toes on her left foot were all crooked where a wagon ran over them. She had to stop herself sliding the other foot over the top to hide them. "I'd settle for not being a joke."

"No one here is laughing, Your Highness—"

There was a noisy clatter as one of the girls draped Alex's dress over her arm and the dagger she'd stolen from a brained soldier in a burning town dropped out and bounced across the marble floor to lie at Lady Severa's feet.

"Ah." Alex winced. "Forgot that was in there."

Severa took the battered pommel between finger and thumb and stood with it dangling, the way one might pick up a dead rat by the tail.

"A sensible precaution." She flipped the dagger in her fingers and slid it up her sleeve with a skill that implied it wasn't her first time. "But if Your Highness has no objection I will find her a blade that better suits the imperial aesthetic."

Alex cleared her throat. "No objection."

She gasped as she sank into the bath, the heat making her clench up, then gradually go soft to the tips of her fingers. Someone began combing her hair. Someone scrubbed at her blistered heels. Someone picked the dirt from under her fingernails. She'd barely ever picked her own fingernails, let alone had someone else do it for her.

She caught a glint at the corner of her eye, turned her head to see the girl with the comb had silently produced a knife of her own, its edge gleaming with the sunset.

"*Fuck!*" Alex floundered up with a stab of terror, spraying water.

The girl gaped, knife trembling in her hand. "I'm so sorry, Your Highness . . . I was only cutting out a tangle. I never meant . . ." Her lip wobbled and tears started leaking down her cheeks.

"Oh God. Oh shit." Alex stood, dripping naked, a few sad petals stuck to her, fragrant water sloshing around her knees, both fists clenched like a prizefighter willing to take on all comers. "I'm sorry."

"Your Highness need never apologise." Lady Severa stepped calmly forwards. "Duke Michael has told me everything."

Alex swallowed. "Everything?"

"Enough." She offered her hand. "To know that you have braved a terrible ordeal." Alex took it, so cool, so effortlessly assured, just touching it made her feel stronger. "But that is behind you now." Lady Severa helped her from the bath. "Like our blessed Saint Natalia, you have passed through the fire unscathed."

"I sometimes feel . . . a bit scathed."

"Singed but alive, then." She kept her eyes on Alex's while beckoning gently to the others. "You have in this room five servants who would give their lives for you."

Alex blinked at the girls as they closed in around her, each with a sheet. "Not sure I've earned your loyalty—"

"You have it already." They began to dry her, with gentle rubs, from every side, neither quite looking at her nor looking away, as if they were artists at work on a statue. "If you wish, you can earn it later."

"From what I've seen, that's not really how it works—"

"For Empresses, that is how it works." Two of the girls had split her hair between them, each drying one side. "Below you in the palace, throughout the towers and gardens on the Pillar, are hundreds of guardsmen sworn to protect you."

"Hundreds? What are they expecting to protect me from?"

"Expecting? Nothing. Prepared for? Anything." Lady Severa shrugged, and one couldn't but be fascinated by the way the hollows around her collarbones shifted. "You are safe."

Alex took a shuddering breath. "I'm safe." Her heart didn't quite believe it yet, still hammering in her ears. She'd been clinging on so long, like a rider on a runaway horse. The girls swished around her. That blade darted in and snicked away the tangle almost without her noticing.

"I'm safe," she whispered. One of the girls flicked her with wonderful-smelling water from a thing like a little silver mace, another blew glittering dust on her from a tiny bellows.

"I'm safe," she mouthed. Her skin buzzed pleasantly, raw and softened at once, and she began to wonder, the lightest tickle at the back of her mind . . . whether it might be true.

One of the girls wrapped her in a robe, so soft, while another reached to drain the bath.

"Leave it," said Alex, "please. I might soak my feet later."

"Of course." Severa snapped her fingers again. "Now I expect Her Highness would like some time alone."

Without turning their backs on her, the handmaidens somehow managed to shuffle from the room. Lady Severa paused in the entrance, one hand on each door so she looked like a priest, arms spread in benediction.

Baron Rikard would likely have rolled his eyes in despair at the day's performance, but Alex tried at least to finish well. "Your ministrations have been beyond reproach."

"We are at your disposal if there is *anything* you need." And Lady Severa swung the doors shut with the click of a smoothly oiled latch.

Alex took a deep breath, and let it hiss slowly away. "I'm safe."

She walked to the window. In fact, she allowed herself a bit of a strut. Felt good to walk like Alex again instead of Princess Alexia, even if it was only for a moment. She plucked some grapes from a dish on the way. God, they were sweet, she closed her eyes as she burst them against her palate one by one, then looked out towards the sinking sun. The sounds of the city floated up, faint. The tiny ships swept across the harbour, the even tinier people swarmed on the docks. It was easier to think of ruling it all from so high up that it looked like a toy city, filled with toy people.

She felt the slightest prickling of the hairs on the back of her neck and smiled.

"You can come out now," she said.

And just like that, Sunny was leaning against the window beside her, letting her breath go in a long sigh. She pushed back her hood and scrubbed her white hair with her fingers. "Thought they'd never leave."

"Wasn't it awful? I despise being waited on hand and foot, but it makes the little people feel needed, so I suffer it for their sake."

"Saint Alexia, so modest and so generous."

"They should give me my own chapel! Oh look, they did."

"Bit small," said Sunny, swaggering over to peer through the chapel's doorway. "You couldn't fit more than thirty in here."

"But if we run out of room," said Alex, leading her on across the wide expanse of floor, "there's space for another thirty in the bath." And she waved towards it. "I kept it full for you."

Sunny slipped past, leaned down to sniff the water. "So I get to soak in your dirt?"

"Oh . . . I can get them to—"

Sunny raised one white brow.

Alex sighed. "I still can't tell when you're joking."

Sunny was where demureness went to die. She shed her clothes like a child on a summer riverbank, spent a minute hopping around trying to drag one sock off, skinny as a pale stick. Alex stood in the doorway and watched her. Couldn't stop thinking how strange and fine it was that she got to do it.

"Thought you were going to punch that girl with the knife." Sunny finally hauled the sock off, tossed it over her shoulder, and poked one long toe into the water.

"I reckon I could've taken her," said Alex.

"Never doubted it. She had the reach but you're vicious when cornered." And Sunny slipped into the water, barely even making a ripple. "Oh." She closed her eyes as she sank up to her chin. "Oh God."

"I know."

"I mean, I've got mixed feelings on God, and he fucking hates me, but oh God." Sunny slid slowly under the water, white hair floating on the surface with the flower petals long enough for Alex to get a bit worried, then she burst up and spat out a fountain with a long farting noise. With her hair stuck wet to her skull Alex could see the pointed tip of one ear, the obvious lack of the other. She perched on the side of the bath, reached out to comb Sunny's hair back with her fingers. Couldn't stop thinking how strange and fine it was that she got to do it.

"That Lady Severa . . ." Sunny puffed out her cheeks.

"I know." Alex gave a faraway sigh. "Everyone should have one."

"Not sure everyone can afford one. She looks *expensive*."

"I could call her." Alex let one hand trail in the water, fingertips not quite deep enough to touch Sunny's skin. But almost. "Get her to scrub your back."

"I've a feeling elves are even less popular here than in the Holy City, what with the invasions and the massacres and the crusades and the eating people. Finding one in your bath might give her a shock."

"I don't know, she seems hard to rattle."

"And I doubt I'm the strangest thing . . ." Sunny caught the front of Alex's robe with both hands, knuckles brushing her chest. "That's been found naked . . ." Tipping her face up towards Alex as she pulled her down, their lips almost touching. "In these rooms . . ." And Alex smiled a little, breath coming fast, thinking how strange and fine—

Sunny yanked on her robe and Alex toppled face first into the water. She surfaced on her knees and shook herself, and scraped the wet hair out of her eyes. "They'll have to comb me again now."

Sunny had the tip of her tongue pressed into that gap between her teeth. "It'll make the little people feel needed."

Alex looked down at her soaked robe and, on some old instinct, wondered what Gal the Purse would've valued it at. Then she realised she could snap her fingers and get a dozen more. She peeled it off and tossed it onto the floor with a wet flap.

"Do you know . . ." said Sunny, as Alex slipped one leg over her, slithered into the bath on top of her, skin against slippery skin. "That's just what I was hoping you'd do."

"Well . . ." Alex leaned down over her and gently kissed her top lip. "It's my responsibility not only to provide you with what you ask for . . ."

She gently kissed her bottom lip. "But to know what you want . . ."

She pushed her fingers into Sunny's wet hair, pulled her close. "Before you ask . . ."

Tomorrow's Ghosts

With yet another final effort, Jakob forced his burning, clicking, trembling legs up the last few steps and into the glare at the top of the Pharos of Troy.

The dearest wish of his hammering heart was to flop down and roll screaming like a man on fire. From the way the remains of his knees felt, it would've been no surprise to see them wreathed in flames. Instead, he clenched his ever-clenched jaw, allowed himself only a steadying hand on the archway, and gave vent to something between a groan and a growl. As he had ten thousand times before, he made of his pain a spur to push him on. He raised his head and squinted through one eye towards the dazzling light of Saint Natalia's Flame.

It rose from a great bronze dish in the centre of the gallery and was sucked up through a flue above, a scriptural pillar of fire, constantly tended by a silent nun and never allowed to go out. The dome was set inside with a mosaic of shining mirror chips, held up by an arcade of stone arches, so that Saint Natalia's blessed light was reflected back redoubled, bringing comfort to everyone on land or sea for miles around.

Those who dared the steps to this highest point in Troy were greeted, once their eyes adjusted to the glare, by the kind of views an angel might have from heaven. To the west the sea and sky, struck red by the sinking sun. To the east, the Grand Aqueduct curving towards the darkened mountains. To the north the ragged coast and the black slit of the Hellespont through the dark country, pinpricks of light travelling the roads towards the city.

Duke Michael, who had far fewer serious leg wounds to recover from, stood a few strides off, fists resting on a parapet chiselled with the names of centuries of visitors, gazing off towards the south. Towards the Holy Land. Where the elves had come from, and at a terrible cost been turned back.

From whence they would come again.

"God damn them," whispered Jakob.

"The elves?" Duke Michael glanced over, Saint Natalia's Flame casting searing brightness down one side of his face while it sank the other into darkness.

"The steps," grunted Jakob, grinding a sore knuckle into his throbbing hip.

"The elves have the good grace only to visit once a century. The steps never give me a moment's peace."

"If you dislike steps . . ." And Duke Michael grinned out across the darkened country. "I fear you came to the wrong city."

"I belong to the Chapel of the Holy Expediency." Jakob forced himself to let go of the archway, forced his crooked back to straighten, his wheezing lungs to settle, his wobbling legs to take one step more, one step more. Past the Sister of the Flame in her nun's cowl, so still and silent on her stool she might've been a stuffed habit. Across that mixture of shrine, guardhouse, and eagle's eyrie. "We go where we're sent."

Duke Michael considered him like a cautious buyer working out the proper price for a carpet. "But you are not the same as the rest of the congregation. You were not tried by the Celestial Court."

"Perhaps I should've been."

"You were not condemned to service."

"Perhaps I should've been."

"You joined of your own free will. You could leave right now."

"If I could make it back down the steps," muttered Jakob, and he set his hands on the parapet, on the carved names of those who had stood here before him, faded over years, decades, centuries.

"I have no doubt you could achieve anything you set your mind to," said Duke Michael. "A warrior of your long experience deserves a place of honour. You could reclaim your *destiny*." And as he said the word he clenched his fist and ground it into the carvings, eyes shining.

"I believed in destiny, once." Jakob made a fist of his own, all scar and twisted knuckles. "That I was bound for great things. An instrument of God's purpose! That every obstacle must be swept aside, and any method used to do it. There were trials along the way. Tests of faith. Tests of commitment. I told myself I couldn't waver. What kind of great purpose, after all, is easily realised? So I sacrificed everything and everyone. I covered myself in glory and steeped myself in blood. And there, at the summit of a hill of corpses, I reached my destiny, and passed through it to the other side . . ." He slowly opened his aching fingers, and let his hand fall. "Where there was nothing. And I saw I'd never followed God's plan, only the lies I told myself to justify my greed and my ambition."

Duke Michael looked sideways at him. "So you have made of yourself an arrow shot from another's bow. You have trusted them to aim well and washed your hands of the right or wrong of it. Some might call that cowardice."

Jakob would've snorted, but it felt like too much effort, so he settled for a weary grunt. "Believe me, I am *long* past caring what some might call it." Saint Natalia's Flame was hot behind him, and he was grateful for the evening breeze on his face. "I've seen it all, Your Grace, then seen it all repeated. One man's cowardice is another's prudence. One man's treachery another's courage. One man's destiny another's disaster."

"So everything is a matter of where you stand?"

"And when you reach my age, you've stood everywhere. To be the arrow takes all the faith I have left. To aim the arrow . . . I'll leave that to those who still believe."

"Talking of which . . ." Duke Michael turned grinning towards the stairway as Brother Diaz came labouring from it, breathing even harder than Jakob had.

"Saviour, what a climb," gasped the monk, wiping his forehead on his sleeve. His eyes went wide as he took in the view beyond the archway, then wider yet as he leaned out gingerly to peer over the parapet, a murmuration of little birds billowing and twisting in the evening far above the city, and yet far below them. "And, Saviour, what a fall." He turned to the brazier, the flames surging up through the flue above. "So this is Saint Natalia's Flame?"

"And they haven't let it go out since Natalia lit it, centuries ago." Duke Michael nodded towards the nun, and the neat stacks of cedarwood beside her. "Or if they have, no one's admitting it."

"And the chain?" asked Brother Diaz, taking a curious step towards the one that hung beside the brazier, each link fashioned to look like a serpent eating its own tail.

"It drops a powder into the fire and makes it burn blue. A warning to any who see it that the elves are coming." Duke Michael leaned close to Brother Diaz. "Best not to send up any false alarms. It hasn't been used in my lifetime."

The monk took a cautious step back, drawing the sign of the circle over his chest. "Let us hope it never is again."

"Hope is a precious resource," murmured Jakob. "We shouldn't waste it against the inevitable."

The Sister of the Flame grimly nodded her agreement, and silently took up more wood, and tossed it into the basin, the flames roaring brighter.

"To business, then," said Jakob. The sooner he got to lie down the happier he'd be. "Princess Alexia should be crowned as soon as possible."

"I've dreamed of it for half my life," said Duke Michael, "and I am far from her only supporter. The people yearn for old glories restored and new hopes for the future, and she offers the promise of both. I still have friends here, was able to take back my old position as Commander of the Palace Guard. I've seen them reaffirm their oaths of service."

Jakob rubbed at his jaw. "An oath can be a useful thing. You're sure the remnants of Eudoxia's coven have been scattered?"

"To the winds. Resistance to Princess Alexia's rightful claim will be of a more mundane type."

"Mundane enemies can kill you just as dead," said Jakob. "The Church of the East?"

Duke Michael sighed. "Always hard work. The virtues of humility and generosity are not much in evidence among the wearers of the wheel."

"In my experience, the wearers of the circle are no better."

"The priesthood fear the Pope's influence. That they might fall under the control of Zizka and Bock and be stripped of their privileges. But the elves stir, and Patriarch Methodius is not unreasonable. I have been able to convince him that my niece's claim is legitimate."

"Or at any rate can be made to serve his own purposes," muttered Jakob, while Brother Diaz shook his head. "Where do the nobles stand?"

"As one of them, I can safely say you could not find a pettier set of backbiters anywhere in Europe."

"And with some ruthless competition."

"They will extract a high price for their support. They have already presented me with a list of what they call long-standing injustices, by which they mean petty grievances and brazen blackmail."

"Might I see them?" asked Brother Diaz.

"I *beg* you to free me of their considerable weight." Duke Michael slid out a sheaf of papers which the monk set to leafing through by the light of Saint Natalia's Flame. "But it is Eudoxia's sons that cause me the greatest concern."

"Marcian, Constans, and Sabbas are dead." Jakob winced as he touched the still-sore spot on his breastbone where the point of Constans's sword had emerged.

"Good news at last." The duke closed his eyes and took a deep breath. "You have done Troy a great service."

"An unfinished one. There's still Arcadius."

"The cleverest of the four, and the most influential. He is Admiral of the Imperial Fleet. He kept the sailors paid during the years of Eudoxia's neglect and they love him for it. He could mount a blockade of the city tomorrow and starve us out within weeks. If the merchants didn't rise up within hours at the interruption to business."

"A rule of politics always and everywhere," murmured Jakob. "Never stop the money. Arcadius is the greatest threat, then."

"Doubtless. But I have a plan for him—"

"The Athenaeum." Brother Diaz looked up from the nobles' demands. "Lady Severa spoke of records there?"

"Centuries of them," said Duke Michael. "For bureaucracy the Empire of the East concedes no equal."

"Might I consult them?"

"I see no objection, provided you do not stray from the books. Some extremely dangerous . . ." Michael seemed to grope for the right word. "*Leftovers* . . . from Eudoxia's time remain sealed beneath the place."

"I've witnessed some horrors, in recent months." Brother Diaz cleared his throat. "Believe me when I say I have *no* wish to witness more."

Duke Michael watched him head for the steps, still poring over his list, and leaned close to Jakob to murmur, "The monk always struck me as a curious choice of leader. Is there more to him than meets the eye?"

"There's more to everyone than meets the eye," said Jakob. "Brother Diaz is a man in search of a purpose. Without it, he is a curious choice. If he were to find it . . . who can say what he might do?" His body was calming after the climb, pangs softening to familiar aches, the heat of the flame soothing his back as he turned to the view. "Looking at this, you can believe anything is possible."

"I forget how it must strike someone who has never seen it before."

"I have seen it before. I stood at this very spot and witnessed the army of the elves, their fires spread out like stars on the black country." Jakob slowly brushed the carved names beneath his fingertips. "I think . . . this one is mine." It was hard to tell, the lines were so worn by the long years between then and now. Almost as worn as the man who carved them.

"I *knew* it." Duke Michael wagged a finger at him. "You *are* the same Jakob of Thorn who fought in the Second Crusade! But that was more than a century ago! How can it be?"

"It is a long and tragic story." Jakob traced more names. Thought of the men who had carved them. Strange, how strong those memories still were, forged in the white-hot crucible of his youth. "This is King William the Red of Sicily, and this his butler, Biordo Ambra, one of the most savage fighters I ever saw. This one is Sir John Galt, who they called the Pillar of the Faith. He carved it with his fingernail, and I thought it the finest thing I ever saw."

"Weighty names," murmured Duke Michael. "Heroes all."

"Yesterday's heroes." Jakob pulled his fingertips from the faded carvings. Soon enough there would be nothing left of them. "Tomorrow's ghosts."

"Yet you are still with us."

Jakob gave a chuckle so dry it was little more than a grunt. "I'm a ghost already."

"Oh, I suspect you have a few fights in you yet." Duke Michael frowned out towards the south and east. Towards the Holy Land. "Tell me . . . the elves. Are they really as bad as they say?"

"I have come to think . . . that they are no worse than men." Jakob took a long breath. "So . . . yes."

Close to Heaven

H ere we have philosophy," said Lady Severa, swinging the doors wide, "history, theology, astronomy and mathematics, the natural and arcane sciences . . ."

"Sweet Saint Jerome . . ." breathed Brother Diaz as he followed her. Who else could he appeal to at that moment but the patron saint of learning?

The rotunda at the heart of the Athenaeum was closer to heaven than he'd ever expected—or supposed that he deserved—to come. Shafts of angelic light filtered down from cupolas high above, set into a dome decorated with scenes from the history of Ancient Troy: Hector humbling Achilles, Cassandra tricking Odysseus, the burning of the Trojan Horse, the triumph of Astyanax and the sack of Mycenae. Dizzying ranks of shelves covered the walls below, a curving cliff of them, ten times a man's height or more, festooned with a madman's scaffolding of gantries, stairs, and ladders, bursting with books in mind-boggling numbers. Legions of them. Acres of them.

"Drama and comedy are through there . . ." Severa gestured to other doors as she led him down a flight of steps, since they'd entered at the lowest of several balconies ringing the hall, the rotunda's floor sunk into the ground.

"This isn't all of it?" he breathed, mouth falling open as he gazed upwards.

"Oh, no. Herbalism and physic are in the west wing, theology and scripture in the east, there is a separate collection of maps, and so on . . ."

"Incredible—" breathed Brother Diaz, cut off awkwardly as his eyes dropped from the shelves. If it was heaven above, perhaps it was hell below.

The wide circle of floor was more densely covered with markings than Vigga's back. Rings within rings, triangles within pentagons, spiralling diagrams of interlocking symbols so complex they gave him a sickening sense of vertigo. Cast from different metals, painted in different inks, chiselled into the marble, whole incomprehensible treatises in crabby handwriting. It reminded him far more than was comfortable of the apparatus Balthazar had prepared in Venice, but on the grandest of scales. That floor, one might have said, had Black Art written all over it.

Lady Severa glided across it, the swishing of her dress over those runes echoing in the heavy silence, and Brother Diaz had no choice but to follow. In the centre was a tall copper rod, wreathed in wires, blackened as if by fire, and on either side of it, ringed by particularly dense snakings of symbols, were two benches. As he came closer, he saw—to his even greater discomfort—that they were furnished with heavy straps, as if to hold a prisoner tightly in place.

"This was the apparatus . . . for Eudoxia's experiments?" he murmured.

"Her final one," said Severa.

Brother Diaz blinked down at the nearest bench. The padding looked scorched. "The one she died performing . . ."

"She had been dying for years." Severa frowned at the other bench. "She was born sickly. The runt of Theodosia's litter, with a saint for a sister and a hero for a brother. Small wonder she felt . . . some resentment."

"Hardly an excuse for stealing an Empire."

"She was protecting it," said Severa. "Or . . . I suppose that would have been her justification. So imperfect herself, she yearned to create something perfect. Her husbands disappointed her, betrayed her, one by one, and then her sons. So she retreated. Buried herself here, among her books. Hoping to find perfection in her magic."

"But that failed her, too, in the end . . ."

"So it seems."

There were two jars clamped to the copper rod. Brother Diaz's curiosity overcame his fear and he stepped closer, peering through the distorting glass of one. Did something float inside? A great, black, shiny feather? "What was she trying to do here?" he whispered, somehow reluctant to raise his voice.

"Free herself, perhaps. From her own decaying body. From her own mistakes."

"You sound almost as if you admired her."

Severa looked up. "She was a savage, vindictive, paranoid tyrant. Her efforts to save Troy brought it low. Her efforts to build a dream created a nightmare. She shunned her failures, whether they were her experiments, or her students, or her sons. But she could not stop making the same mistakes, right to the end. Admired her? No. But *understood* her? We all have our reasons, do we not? We are all the prisoners of our own flaws."

Brother Diaz slowly nodded. No doubt he had his own flaws to contend with. His own mistakes to atone for. He tightened his grip on the sheaf of demands Duke Michael had given him and squared his shoulders. "We will have a new Empress, now. A new chance. Our only option . . . is to do better."

"You are right, Brother Diaz." Severa lifted her chin, clasped her hands, and was once more the stately Warden of the Imperial Chamber. One could never have guessed that she had such things as feelings, let alone what they might be. "The archives are this way." She glided off across the rotunda and Brother Diaz strode after her, fixed on the task in hand.

Not at all reluctant to leave Eudoxia's mistakes—not to mention his own—behind.

Clean Inside

Vigga jerked awake with a sneeze that made her head throb and her belly ache.

She hawked and spat and scraped hay from her tongue. She could hardly tell where hay ended and tongue began, and she was stark naked and could taste blood. None of that was unusual, but one thing did puzzle her.

If she was awake, why was she snoring?

There was a snort, and the haypile shifted, then humped, then fell away.

"Ah," said Vigga as a man was revealed.

He had no clothes, either, and hay in his hair, and he stared down at himself with an almost tearful look of confusion. "What happened?"

Vigga narrowed her eyes. She hated remembering things at the best of times. "Did I lose at dice?" For her, to play at dice was to lose at dice. "Did I fall in a fountain?" For her, to go near a fountain was to fall in it. "Did I punch a camel?" For her—

"Who are you?" he whimpered, crossing his arms nervously over his chest.

"Sometimes . . ." Vigga gently patted his face. "It's better not to know." And she clambered from the hay and sprang down to the floor of the stables, the hard-packed earth covered in slits of brightness as that prying oaf the sun peered through the gaps between the boards.

One leg of her trousers turned out still to be rucked up around her ankle, which was lucky, but she slipped as she tried to get her foot in the other leg, which wasn't, as she rolled through something she thought was horse dung but could just as easily have been her own. Some style of dung, anyway. What's it matter, once it's in your hair?

"Damn it," she grumbled, pulling on one boot. She saw the other peeking from beneath a horse trough and she stepped over and dunked her head in, the cold water kissing at her face then streaming from her hair as she pushed it back, shivering most pleasantly. A horse regarded her from a stall.

"Mind your manners!" Vigga blew a mist of drops at it. "Has no one told you it's rude to stare?"

It turned away with a nicker she didn't know the meaning of, but she'd a worry the horse had won the argument. She became aware of a ripe odour, even for a barn. Sniffing at her pits she learned, to no one's surprise, that she was herself the source, so she had a quick splash and scrub before strolling for the doors.

A last sad and rumpled garment lay in the strip of brightness in front of them. Sometimes after she'd been fucking, she'd find her clothes all neatly folded up, which was strange, as she never remembered doing anything but leaving 'em where they dropped, but nice, 'cause it was sort of like putting on new clothes. But that hadn't happened this morning, sorry to say. She pushed her bottom lip out as she turned the straw-stuck thing this way and that, trying to make sense of it.

"This isn't my vest," she muttered. But it was the only vest to hand, so she struggled into it with a complaining creak of stitches, the leather threatening to split under her arms.

"Are there any clothes for me?" The man peered from the hayloft with his hands cupped around his balls.

"What am I?" grunted Vigga, catching the handles of the stable doors. "A tailor?"

"I don't know what you are!"

"Not a tailor." And she yanked them open. "Gah!" She shielded her eyes against the blinding sun, stumbling out with one eye shut and the other blinking wildly.

A canal, maybe? A cobbled roadway on each side, busy with people, little bridges over fast-flowing water. Buildings with tiled roofs and tall windows, shops and houses and there a church with the little faces painted around the door and there—

She began to give a long, low growl at the back of her throat, the wolf padding up ever so suspiciously behind her ribs and she couldn't blame it one bit. She brushed through the traffic and stomped over a bridge to a tavern of sorts, folk perched at tables outside.

"Why are you here?" she snapped.

"Waiting for you." Baron Rikard picked at a loose thread on his embroidered shirt, the cuffs rolled up loosely to his elbows, the front hanging open to his navel, exposing a slice of sinewy stomach, pale as polished ivory. "Someone had to make sure you perpetrated no outrages. Or should I say, no *further* outrages. What you did in that fountain last night . . . merciful Saviour." And he took a glass of wine between finger and thumb, swilled it for a moment beneath his nose like quite the fucking connoisseur, licked his lips with a kind of needy shiver, and closed his eyes to sip.

Not wine. Vigga caught a salty waft and the wolf dribbled hungrily, thoughts of the good meat flooding hot and guilty from the dark corners of her mind. Without looking, Baron Rikard slid a plate towards her with the back of his hand. A large joint sat on it, swimming in bloody juice. "I ordered for you."

Vigga's mouth flooded with slobber of her own, but her pride held her back. "So you think I'm a dog?" she snarled.

"Since when have you cared about my opinion?" Rikard arched one black brow. "The better question is—do *you* think you're a dog?"

Vigga glared back at him, but the joint kept smelling the way it smelled, and her hunger was vast and her pride extremely threadbare, so she stepped over a stool and sat, snatched up the joint, and began ripping into it with her teeth. The baron watched her with that smug grin, which was one of his most enraging looks.

"So that's one question answered," he murmured.

"Can I get you . . . anything else?" A serving girl leaned over the table, staring at Rikard with huge, damp, adoring eyes. "Anything at all?"

"No, no, my dear." The baron smiled as he leaned towards her. "You've done *so* much already." And he damped a handkerchief with the tip of his long tongue, and dabbed away two little specks of blood above her collar. The girl gave a kind of desperate sigh when he touched her, eyelids flickering.

Vigga growled with disgust around her latest near-raw mouthful.

"Pray don't mind my . . . associate." The baron sighed. "She is what she is."

"And proud of it," grunted Vigga, who couldn't have been less proud of it.

Rikard upended his glass, then licked out the inside, then carefully set it down, and tossed a couple of coins beside it. "Hard to believe those might have the face of our little Alex on their backside soon," he said, stepping from the table and walking on, leaving the serving girl staring after him, hands clutched to her chest.

Vigga shook her head as she followed, stripping every shred from the bone with her teeth, but something about the street was confusing her—it seemed to end, some distance ahead, at a riot of greenery with tall towers above, like the one on top of the Pillar. But that had been very high up, and this was if anything below them, and there was so much sky everywhere . . .

"Where are we?" She peered around the corner of the tavern and recoiled in horror. Beyond a low rail was a dizzying drop towards the city, the harbour wall beyond it, the sea beyond that, all far, far below, and Vigga felt a lurch of sickness, dropping her bone and clinging to the corner of the building.

"On the Grand Aqueduct, of course."

"I don't like heights!" She shuffled back from the brink and someone nearly walked into her.

"It has withstood civil wars, collapsing Empires, and invading elves," said the baron, airily. "I daresay it will bear even your considerable weight."

"Not all of us can turn into bats," snapped Vigga. She couldn't shake the memory of the aqueduct from below, how delicate the arches, how teetering the little houses clinging to the top. *These* houses.

"You don't like heights and you don't like crowds," said Rikard. "Honestly, you really have ended up in the worst city. But never fear, we won't be staying much longer. Our mission approaches its conclusion, after all! Unless there are some points of protocol you would like to review in connection with Princess Alexia's coronation?"

Vigga squinted at him. "Points o' what, now?"

"I will take that as a resounding *no*," said Rikard, swaggering on. What would you even call that walk of his? A flounce? A prowl? A prance? No weight in his heels, hips swaying, somewhere between snake and man. The most annoying thing was it gave Vigga no choice but to do the opposite, and lumber along slouching like a grumpy savage. The baron smirked at her as if he guessed her thoughts.

"You know, you stomping around like a bull with sore balls doesn't make me look worse. If anything, it only highlights my grace and refinement. The way pretty people often choose ugly friends so they'll stand out like a diamond in the dung."

"Don't tell me how to walk," grunted Vigga.

"Oh, I'd never try to change you, even if I dared dream it was possible. Entirely repugnant you undoubtedly are, but no one could deny you are a true original."

Vigga frowned. "That a compliment?" Should you be pleased or insulted at a compliment from someone you hate?

"Of a kind. We justifiably detest each other, but . . . wouldn't the world be dull without you?" A well-dressed woman stepping from a shop fainted against the doorframe with a breathy moan as the baron passed. "Look at the two of us. A pair of monsters."

"Speak for yourself," said Vigga. "I've collared and muzzled the beast in me."

"Is that a fact?"

"Do you see fur?" She held up her bare arms. Some downy hair below the elbows, true, but nothing you could call *fur*.

"You did not look especially collared at that inn near the Holy City," observed the baron.

"I'd been locked in that wagon for days." Vigga gave a dainty sniff. "Who could blame me for stretching my legs?"

"You did not look very muzzled on that galley in the Adriatic."

"Brother Diaz begged for help and I chose to save his life. *I* chose. That is the point."

"And at the Monastery of Saint Sebastian?"

"That Dane let out his wolf, so I let mine out to play with it." Vigga felt a little tickle at the thought, in fact. "The wolf's not gone and never will be gone, I know that, but *I* choose when to be the wolf. Not gothis with irons or cardinals with whips, not you or Jakob of Thorn, not even the moon," and she couldn't help a shiver at the lovely thought of it, so fat and silvery, "and *definitely* not the wolf. *I* choose. The rest of the time I will be nice, and safe, and clean."

"Clean?" The baron raised one brow at her. "Is that dung in your hair?"

Vigga scraped angrily at it, pulling a few strands out and getting them tangled up with the dung on her fingers then waving her hand around as she tried to flick the mess off. "Not on the outside! You can be clean . . . *inside*." And she jabbed at her breastbone with two fingers and may have got a bit of dung on her vest. Or whoever's vest it was. But the point was made, because the wolf slunk away when ordered, meek as a puppy. "See? That's not a wolf's chest, that's a woman's chest, and, as it goes, a pretty spectacular example, though I say so myself."

"Do you indeed?"

"I do," she said. "Indeed."

"Well, if you are clean inside . . ." A passing woman caught the baron's eye and tottered as if she'd been slapped, eyelids fluttering. "I congratulate you . . ." He leaned towards her, lips curling back, touching his tongue to the point of one fang, eyes fixed on her throat—

Then he tore himself away and walked on. Vigga heard him mutter under his breath.

"I wish I was."

The Beautiful Compromise

The Throne Room of Troy was a space carefully designed to inspire awe. As far as Brother Diaz was concerned, it worked.

First, there was its position. Supposedly, the throne had once been in a far larger audience chamber on the ground floor of the palace, but some canny councillor had recommended it be moved upwards, as upwards as possible, indeed, to the very highest floor of the Pharos, directly beneath Saint Natalia's Flame. Even the most arrogant ambassador could not but be impressed by the majestic view through the great windows. Even the most overweening magnate would be wordlessly reminded of the dizzying drop that awaited any that might incur their liege's displeasure. Even the most athletic supplicant would arrive cowed by the merciless stairs, their knees wanting nothing more than to bend.

Then there was the crushing display of wealth. Pillars of many-coloured marble, amber vases tall as a man, tapestries of cloth-of-gold, treasures given in tribute from the length of the Mediterranean competed to dazzle the eye. There were arms and armour, too, bracketed to the walls, enough to equip a legion. Slim-hafted spears from Afrique, gold-hilted sabres from the steppe, axes of the savage north, swords of the stubborn west, pointed reminders of centuries of Trojan victories over all comers. Even, in pride of place, barbed spears, jagged daggers, and cruel arrows whose alien design could not but produce a shiver of fear. Relics of the crusades against the elves, and testament to the possibility of victory.

Finally, there was the Serpent Throne itself: a towering edifice of coiled snakes carved from variously coloured translucent stones, glowing with the light through the vast windows behind so they seemed to writhe, fangs bared. A chair fit for a giant of legend. Which did rather render the idea of Alex sitting in it, even Brother Diaz had to admit, faintly ridiculous.

No one seemed more aware of that fact than the would-be Empress herself, sitting pale and worried in a far smaller seat at the foot of the throne's agate steps, at the head of a highly polished table, picking nervously at her fingernails.

On her left was Lady Severa, impeccable Warden of the Imperial Chamber, on her right Michael, celebrated Duke of Nicaea. Beside him the immortal crusader Jakob of Thorn sat stiffly, an oasis of grimacing grey in this desert of dazzling colour. Opposite *him* sat Brother Diaz. An assistant librarian from a monastery no one in Leon, let alone Troy, had ever heard of. He adjusted the heaps of ledgers, deeds, and documents he'd brought with him—as though success could only be ensured by lining them up perfectly parallel with the edge of the table—then after sending up a silent prayer to Saint Beatrix, he nodded to Alex.

Like an actor in the wings preparing to take the stage she rolled back her shoulders, slapped her own cheeks, stretched out her neck, flashed on a generous smile, and became a confident, comfortable, even a faintly *regal* presence.

"We're ready," she said.

The major-domo, a man who looked like he spent most of his life bent at the waist, bowed low. "Then may I present the assembled representatives . . . of the aristocracy . . . of the Empire of Troy!" And he scuttled sideways like a crab as a pair of armoured guards swung open the towering doors. "Duke Kostas Phrantzes Dukos of Aeolis and Ionia!" he boomed, as if announcing final victory over the elves rather than a small man with an enormous forehead. "Warden of the Isles of Lesbos and Pylos, Protector of Plomari, Admiral of the Imperial Fifth Fleet, Knight of the Rose in the third degree."

Duke Kostas, evidently less awestruck by the throne room than Brother Diaz, delivered the smallest nod to Alex that decorum would allow, and sauntered to a chair, nose in the air.

"Duchess Helen Tzamplakon Arsenios Guilland of Thrace . . ." An ancient woman with an immense wig shuffled over the threshold, angrily refusing the help of a concerned servant.

So it went on, a barrage of ponderous names followed by an assault of honorifics, titles, and distinctions. The chairs filled with painstaking slowness until the beaming Princess Alexia and her four retainers were outnumbered five to one by a disapproving throng of bejewelled noblemen and -women, and Brother Diaz was forced to wonder whether the moment they were all announced it would be time to break for lunch. Or possibly dinner.

"And finally . . ." called the major-domo.

"Oh yes," whispered Alex, hoisting her smile a little higher.

". . . Duke Arcadius . . ."

"Oh no," breathed Alex, her smile almost slipping off entirely.

". . . eldest son of Her Imperial Resplendence the Empress Eudoxia, Grand Admiral of—"

"They know who I am." Arcadius patted the major-domo on the shoulder and gave him a conspiratorial wink. He was tall, slender, handsome, and carried himself with the lazy confidence of a man who has rarely been confronted by the word *no*. He considered Alex with a heavy-lidded smile quite unlike his brothers' sneers of scornful hatred. Brother Diaz instantly trusted him even less. Their murderous intentions had been stated plainly from the start. What game Arcadius was playing had yet to be revealed.

"You must be my cousin Alexia." He snapped his heels together and delivered a bow far more respectful than most of the other visitors had.

She glared back at him. "Do I disappoint?"

"What, me? Not a bit!" He flopped into the chair at the foot of the table, tilted it back on two legs, dropped one boot on the polished top, and grinned around the room. "But I'm easily pleased, ask anyone."

"I speak for the whole gathering . . . I am sure . . ." A duke whose face was almost invisible behind immense moustaches clambered up. "When I say we are delighted . . . to have the daughter of Irene . . . among us once more." Though no one looked much delighted, not even him. "But before we can consider . . . Your Highness's ascension to the throne, there are certain . . . inequities . . . grievances . . . *debts* . . . that must be settled."

"The first in line is the first in line," said Duke Michael, stonily, "regardless of your grievances or anyone else's. She is Alexia Pyrogennetos!" And at the name, as though conscious she might not quite measure up to it, Alex cranked herself even a fraction more proudly erect in her chair. "Born of Irene in the Pharos of Troy, proclaimed the one legitimate heir to the Serpent Throne by both Patriarch and Pope. Are there not still such things as deference, loyalty, duty in the Empire of the East?"

"Of course. Duke Michael," said a countess whose lengthy neck and pecking sentences put Brother Diaz in mind of a stately wading bird, "but. They are double-edged swords. And cut both ways. An Empress has a duty. To her subjects."

"A duty of *care*," croaked the ancient duchess, weak eyes staring off somewhere to Alex's right, "a duty of *justice*."

"Eudoxia's reign. Was not easy on anyone—"

"Harder for some than others," grunted Michael.

"But we *all*," said an emollient count with a cloth-of-gold hat, "desire a new era of *stability* and *prosperity*, and that the path to the Serpent Throne be *smooth*—"

"Rather than an endless legal slog through a thicket of objections." Arcadius picked a speck of dust from the front of his uniform and rubbed it away between thumb and fingers. "Now, who's first to grumble?"

The ancient duchess pushed her chin forward, wattles wobbling beneath. "Perhaps . . . we go by seniority?"

"Or by *size* of holdings?" boomed a rotund count.

"Or number of titles?" From a duke whose grey hair exploded from his head at all angles.

Alex reapplied her smile and directed it towards the chair furthest left. "Why don't we just work around the table?"

"Very well, Your Highness," said the man with all the forehead. "I, as you are likely aware, am Duke Kostas Phrantzes Dukos. My family have, for centuries, held Aeolis and Ionia on behalf of your forebears. For much of that time, however, the crown has operated a naval base on the Isle of Lesbos. An ever-growing array of barracks, stores, and defences have prevented my family from exercising its rights to graze the land and fish the waters . . ."

As he droned on, Brother Diaz ran a fingertip down the list of demands, cross-referenced with his own notes, flipped through the appropriate ledgers to the appropriate markers, arranging his paperwork as a knight might prepare his harness for a tourney.

"Let me understand this," cut in Duke Michael. "You want my niece to pay for the privilege of protecting you?"

"I ask for fair recompense, no more! My steward has made an estimate of what my family is owed . . ."

Brother Diaz's heart was pounding now, as the knight's might on entering the lists. He'd never engaged in legal jousting against such eminent opponents, but he had far more relevant experience than when he flung himself from a burning galley, and he'd washed up after that alive. With stained drawers, admittedly. He gave the vial of Saint Beatrix one last squeeze, then lurched to his feet before he could think better of it.

"My lords and ladies!" he called, a little too loud. "If I may interject?"

There was a deeply uncomfortable silence in which all eyes turned towards him, apart from those of the ancient duchess, which peered over his left shoulder. "Who is this . . . *person*?" The way she pronounced the word *person* implied she had yet to be convinced that he qualified. "A monk?"

"Selected by Her Holiness," said Lady Severa, "to convey Her Highness safely to Troy."

"Ah!" boomed the rotund count. "A *warrior* monk!"

"Honestly, more of . . ." Brother Diaz cleared his throat. "A librarian."

"A bookworm?" Laughter.

"An *incurable* bookworm." He gave his most ingratiating smile. The one he always used before presenting an argument. "So you can imagine my delight to have been granted access by the gracious Lady Severa to the stacks in your astonishing Athenaeum." He set a loving hand on the books and papers he had collected. "I thought we knew a thing or two in the monasteries of the west, but I've learned more about filing in the last few days than in ten years as a monk!"

"What's he saying?" snapped an elderly count with an ear trumpet. "What are you saying?"

"No idea." The ancient duchess flopped back despairingly in her chair. "He's a blatherer."

"You're not the first to say so!" Brother Diaz chuckled as he spread his treasures across the polished tabletop. "I will come to the point—"

"If . . . you have one," grunted the duke with the moustaches to more laughter.

"These deeds, and corresponding entries in this ledger of holdings in the Duchy of Ionia, confirm the lands in question were always imperial property, only leased to the family of Phrantzes. You will see from the dates on the seals that the lease ran out two centuries ago."

"What?" Duke Kostas's immense forehead crinkled as he frowned at the documents.

"And I fear . . . not only those lands." Brother Diaz winced like a doctor delivering bad news. "You have been grazing on, even building on, considerable tracts of crown property for some decades." He slid his fourth paper across the table, adjusted it so it sat straight. "Here is my estimate of what you owe."

That forehead turned terribly pale as the duke examined it. "Can this figure be correct?"

Brother Diaz held up his hands. "Prepared in haste. It could *easily* go up." There was muttering as he dipped quill in ink, carefully drained the nib, and crossed out the first entry on his list. But the laughter had dried up. "Now then, Duke Eulogius of Paphlagonia?" He looked to the next man in line, a remarkably red-faced fellow. "You say the crown owes you several galleys? I fear there may have been a misreading of the original contract . . ."

Now legal battle was joined Brother Diaz felt no fear, the splendour of the venue only spurring him to greater prowess. He flipped pages in a blur, cross-indexed like lightning. The sums might have been far greater—at one point he took ownership of an entire city for the Serpent Throne—but the principles were much the same as arguing over monastic brewing rights back in Asturias.

He gave ground on repairs to a bridge then countered with a bill for road maintenance ten times the size. He struck with rebates and compound interest and excavated the finer points of mining law. The long-necked countess thought she'd caught him out on fisheries, then visibly wilted as she realised her own argument denied her a share in lucrative sea lanes.

One could almost feel the balance of power shift. Alex sat straighter and straighter in her gilded chair. Duke Michael went from baleful to smug. Did even Lady Severa allow an infinitesimal smile to trouble the corner of her mouth? He crossed the complaints from his list one by one, and the sun reached its apogee and began to fall. Brother Diaz did not break for lunch. He did not need to eat. He was fuelled by pure administration.

The last of the aristocrats, one Count Julian, was not at all pleased when Brother Diaz revealed his deeds to be forgeries, and not even good ones. He planted his clenched fists to either side of the doctored documents and administered a furious glare. "I swear to God, were you not a man of the cloth, I would *demand* satisfaction on the field of arms!"

The powerful often resort to threats when frustrated by those they think weak. Brother Diaz had been cowed that way, in the past. But the Saviour said, *One cannot grow without being tested*, and he realised then how much he had grown since he left the Holy City. He had witnessed the unimaginable and looked into the eyes of true monsters. Beside that, threats from these perfumed fools seemed almost laughable.

But humility is the first of the Twelve Virtues, the one from which all others flow, so Brother Diaz only spread his hands. "I am a mere man of letters. In a duel I could give you no worse than a paper cut. If you insist on making a challenge on the field of arms—"

"You can talk to me," growled Jakob of Thorn, "and my associates. When Her Holiness has a problem the righteous cannot solve . . . we're the ones she sends. The ones who stopped Duke Marcian, and Duke Constans, and Duke Sabbas from attending this meeting. Believe me when I say—"

"—you'd *much* rather deal with the monk," finished Alex.

There was an uncomfortable silence in which, notably, no one took up recourse to violence. It was Jakob's first contribution to the meeting, and the last he needed to make.

"I'm sure this comes as a disappointment." Brother Diaz smiled at the gathering. "I've been disappointing people all my life and can only apologise, but I've merely scratched the surface. If Her Highness wishes me to continue my work in the Athenaeum . . . I can only imagine what further inequities, grievances, and debts I might uncover."

Duke Michael turned to his niece. "*Does* Your Highness wish Brother Diaz to continue his work in the Athenaeum?"

Alex sat back, thoughtfully pushed out her lips, and slowly tapped the arm of her chair with one fingernail, letting the discomfort of her covetous nobles stretch.

"I am sure those who were willing . . ." offered Brother Diaz, "to promise the princess their full-throated support . . . could, in further negotiations, rely on her generosity and regal forbearance?"

Alex's smile seemed somehow more earnest than before. "The very things I've always been known for."

"Then may I be the first!" Duke Kostas sprang to his feet. "To swear loyalty to our future empress!"

"And I the second!" shouted the Duke of Paphlagonia.

"I cannot *wait* to see Your Highness upon the Serpent Throne!"

A third of the gathering rose to acclaim as their overlord a girl who a few months before had been begging on the streets of the Holy City. Another third muttered and glanced about and hedged their bets. The remainder grumbled and scowled. The duke with all the moustaches turned towards the bottom of the table. "Have you anything to say . . . Duke Arcadius?"

"I do indeed, and it is this." Eudoxia's eldest son swept his feet from the table and stood, propping his clenched fists before him and glaring balefully towards the Serpent Throne. "*Never* fuck with a librarian." He burst out laughing, then chuckled, then sighed, and wiped both eyes with a knuckle. "Now, there is a matter I must settle with Her Highness that may place all of this in a different light. Something best discussed without the representatives of the empire's aristocracy present, and *please* could we spend less time leaving the room than we spent getting in?"

Arcadius need not have worried on that score. As with contestants at a prizefight, there is much strutting about on the way to the ring, but the losers waste little time skulking away.

The moment the doors clicked shut Arcadius slapped the table, grinning over at Brother Diaz. "Cousin, I simply *love* your smiling assassin! I took the knight with the face like an antique anvil for the killer, but it's your monk who committed the murders this morning!" He waved a dismissive hand towards the doors. "Don't mind those idiots, they're like all little dogs, they need a big dog to rally around. The nobles will grind their teeth but, in the end . . . they'll be satisfied if I am."

Alex narrowed her eyes. "I used to buy and sell a little. Mostly sell. You get a sense for when someone has a deal already in mind."

"Well, you know I do." Arcadius looked a little puzzled. "We all have a duty to compromise, and so forth? Meeting you halfway, for the good of the

Empire? I mean, it wasn't my suggestion . . ." He glanced towards Duke Michael, who was looking suddenly uncomfortable, and back to Alex, who was looking nonplussed, then back to Michael. "You didn't *tell* her?" He puffed out his cheeks. "I know you're my uncle, too, but that's a *little* embarrassing."

Alex looked suddenly pale. "What's he talking about?"

But Brother Diaz had worked out what game Arcadius was playing. Or perhaps it had been Duke Michael's game all along. "He's talking about marriage," he said, softly.

Alex's shoulders were starting to hunch again. "Marriage . . . to who?"

"Well, not to me," muttered Jakob.

"I'm sorry, Alex," said Duke Michael.

"*Me?*" she squeaked, staring down the table at Arcadius. "And *him?* And *me?*"

"Well, this has been lovely, but I can see you have a very great deal to think about." Arcadius slapped his thighs and sharply stood. "I keenly await your answer to my proposal, I suppose? I mean . . . I could go down on one knee . . . if that might help? No? No."

The moment the guards swung the doors shut on him, the last of Alex's imperial dignity evaporated. "What the *fuck?*" she snarled, rounding on her uncle.

Duke Michael had the look of a captain steering his ship into a storm. "Please, Your Highness, I worried if I told you, you might refuse—"

"Oh, you *think?* I should have you beheaded! Can I have him beheaded?"

"Now?" Lady Severa calmly considered the question. "I would advise against. After you're crowned? Absolutely."

"Alex!" Duke Michael wrung his hands. "You have to see the *sense* in this. At a stroke you could turn your worst enemy into your best ally! Without Arcadius your grip on the throne will be tenuous at best. You'll be fighting day and night to stay in power. With him as your consort none of those fools will dare oppose you. You can actually govern! You can do some *good!*"

Alex pressed a hand to her stomach. "I think I'm going to be sick. Lady Severa, tell him!"

The Warden of the Imperial Chamber paused, then laid a gentle hand on the tabletop. "Arcadius is not like his brothers. He is thoughtful, subtle, an effective politician . . . popular with nobles and commoners alike."

Alex clutched her head. "Don't tell me you're *for* this!"

"Then there is the delicate question of *issue*. To be secure on the throne you must offer not only a reign but a *dynasty*. There must be the promise of *heirs*."

"Heirs?" Alex's eyes went wider, her voice higher. "Jakob!"

The old knight gave a sour grunt. "Your bed's your business—"

She looked triumphant. "Exactly!"

"But."

Her face fell.

"From a military standpoint . . . Arcadius controls the fleet. Holds key fortresses. He has revenue and resources. You're surrounded by enemies, Your
Highness. This one move could take you from weakness to strength."

"But . . ." Alex was looking more hunched and forlorn than before the
nobles arrived. "I promised Cardinal Zizka—"

"It was Zizka's idea!" blurted Duke Michael. "Before I left the Holy City!"

Brother Diaz grimaced. He'd been rather looking forward to harvesting
some praise for once, but now it seemed as if everyone would have bigger
things to think about. Alex glanced helplessly over at him. He'd given up a
decade of his life wedded to the Church, so he could readily sympathise.

But the thing about sympathy is that it won't save an Empress from an
expedient political marriage.

"Well . . ." For about the hundredth time that day, he spread his hands in
apology. "It would solve a great many problems . . ."

Not Nothing

Fucking Arcadius!" snarled Alex, stalking up and down the bedchamber, which was a fair trek in each direction.

Sunny lay on the bed. Something she'd been doing a lot. How often did she get to lie on the bed where the heirs to an Empire were birthed, after all? Or any bed, for that matter. "I watched him go in," she said to the ceiling. "Didn't seem *that* bad—"

"He's the worst of the fucking four!"

Sunny had run into some really terrible people over the years, but Marcian, Constans, and Sabbas had each, in their way, been right up there. She propped herself on her elbows. "What did he do?"

"Asked me to *marry* him!" screamed Alex, fists clenched.

"Oh." Sunny really couldn't think of anything else to say. It didn't seem to make Alex feel much better. She dropped down on the edge of the bed with her face in her hands.

People are so weird. If Sunny had been one herself, she might have known the right words, but she wasn't, so she didn't. She was very tempted to take a deep breath, disappear, tiptoe out, and pretend this conversation never happened. She was great at pretending things never happened.

Lots of practice.

But Jakob always said, *Life's not about doing the easy thing*, and he should know, he'd been alive for ages and did the hard thing every time. So Sunny took a breath but didn't disappear, and instead slithered over to sit beside Alex.

"I've got something to show you," she said. Alex didn't reply, so Sunny nudged her with her shoulder. "It'll make you feel better."

Alex spread her fingers to peer sideways through the gap. "Is it Arcadius's corpse?"

"Not *that* much better." She took Alex by the wrist, led her across the chamber and into the chapel. Dust motes floated in the coloured light through the stained glass, the Saviour being broken on the wheel by the ever-hungry enemies of God, as usual.

"You're going to lead me in prayer?" asked Alex.

"I am not." Sunny pressed herself against the wall, sliding her fingers down the mouldings till she found the little catches, so very well hidden in the hardest to reach spots, and pressed them together.

With a click, a section of panelling swung inwards to reveal a square of inky darkness.

"A secret door?" Alex's voice had gone a little squeaky with excitement, which was what Sunny had been hoping for. "Don't you only get those in bad stories?"

"And some good ones." There was a lamp inside the door. A clever design, which struck a spark when you lowered the glass hood. Sunny lit it now, and the wick flared up, revealing a passage just high enough for them to stand, and you couldn't have called either of them tall.

"How did you find it?"

"I really have *nothing* to do with my days." Sunny stepped through, drawing Alex after. "So when I felt a draught, I followed it." The passage curved to the left, following the shape of the tower, so narrow even Alex, who hadn't got a lot of shoulders, had to squeeze hers inwards to slip through, ducking cobwebs. "But a place like this? Be disappointing if there *wasn't* a secret passage or two."

A glimmer of daylight kissed the edges of the stones and they slipped into a little vaulted chamber, a dusty bench sitting under a slot of a window.

"Hidey-hole," said Sunny. "In case the Empress has to make a quick escape."

"Exactly what I need." Alex peered into a cramped spiral stairway. "Where does it go?"

"Down to the guest quarters, the kitchens, and storerooms. Up as high as the throne room. Quite the view from up there."

Alex slumped on the bench. "Not sure I can face a climb." And she turned to wedge her back against the wall, slipped her bare feet up onto the bench so her knees were against her chest.

"Never been proposed to myself," said Sunny, slowly, "but surely the thing about it, compared to say, being rammed by a galley . . . is you can say no?"

"In this case, no one seems to think so."

Yet again, Sunny was stuck without the words. "Oh."

Alex peered miserably out of the window into the distance, the faint breeze stirring her hair. "Duke Michael says I can turn my worst enemy into my best ally at a stroke."

"Allies are good," said Sunny.

"Lady Severa says the promise of heirs would bring stability."

"Everyone likes . . . stability."

"Jakob says it makes good military sense, and Arcadius has the fleet, and could starve us out in weeks."

"Jakob's forgotten more about military stuff than I'll ever know. But I have tried starving, and I'd recommend against it."

"Then Brother Diaz says it would solve a lot of problems."

"Right."

"He sounded sorry about it. He always does. But it never changes anything."

"That's a lot of reasons." Sunny got a sense Alex was waiting for her to list some on the not-marrying-Arcadius side of the case, but that hardly seemed her place. After a moment Alex spoke instead.

"You may have noticed . . . I'm not really the marrying kind."

"Not sure an Empress gets that choice."

"Starting to think an Empress gets fewer choices than a thief."

"Better clothes, though."

Alex turned back to the window, jaw working. "Not sure this is the moment to be funny."

"Be serious, then."

"What?"

"It's high time." Sunny shrugged. "You're the Empress Alexia Pyrogennetos, born under the flame!"

Alex sat, curled up in that little embrasure, more like a prisoner desperate to catch a free breeze on her cheek than the destined heir to an Empire.

"No," she said quietly. "I'm not."

"Not yet, maybe, but you will be. You're *Princess* Alexia—"

"No!" Alex shut her eyes, and hugged her knees tight. "I'm fucking *not!*"

Sunny blinked. "What do you—"

"My mother sold cheese!" Alex blurted, looking so angry Sunny took a step back. "She wasn't heir to any fucking throne at all unless you count the stool she did the milking on!"

Sunny blinked again.

"My mother sold cheese, then she died, 'cause that's what people do." Now the anger all bled out of Alex and she sagged again, and turned back to the window, light splashed down one side of her face. "My father dug ditches, and when I was seven years old, he took me to the Holy City on a special trip, and when we got there, he said he couldn't afford to keep me, and he sold me to Gal the Purse to be a thief, and that's . . . that's where I met her."

"Met . . ." Sunny wasn't sure she wanted to ask the question. Wasn't sure she wanted to hear the answer. "Who?"

"Alexia," said Alex.

Sunny blinked yet again. "Oh."

"And one day she showed me the coin." Alex pulled it out, now, on its chain. That half-moon of bright copper, roughly clipped. "And she showed me the birthmark, and she told me who she was. I didn't believe it. Who'd believe that? Serpent Throne, what a crock of shit!" She frowned, and picked at a toenail. "But I could see *she* believed it, and I was so jealous. Because she thought she was *something*. And I knew I was nothing."

Sunny blinked again. Said, "Oh," again. It was getting to be a habit, and not a useful one.

"Then the Long Pox came through, and she was one of the unlucky ones, and . . . she died, 'cause that's what people do." Alex, or whoever the hell she was, had started to cry. "So I stole the coin, because I'm a thief, and I bent a piece of wire to the shape of her birthmark and burned myself behind the ear and stole that, too, because I'm a piece of shit, and I stole her name, even, because . . . I just wanted to be . . . not *nothing*."

Sunny stood a moment, staring. "But . . . didn't the Oracles—"

"All they did was hold my hand and talk fucking nonsense! About towers and elves and fire. Bock decided what it meant. Bock and my uncle, who isn't even my uncle! I suppose . . . they wanted it to be true. What was I meant to do? Tell a duke and a cardinal they got it all wrong?"

Sunny couldn't even manage an "oh" this time, and in that secret room, buried deep in the thick walls of the lighthouse, the silence was like a tomb.

"We could go." Alex sat forwards and caught Sunny's hand. "I don't belong here. We've run this far, why not go further? Find somewhere we do belong." And she looked needy, and desperate, and wild.

Sunny would've liked to hold her, and tell her it would be all right. But she knew it wouldn't be. She saw what had to be done. For everyone's sake.

Everyone's but hers.

She made herself stand still. Made her face betray no feelings. Wasn't difficult. She'd been betraying no feelings for years. "Where d'you think I'd belong?" she asked.

Alex flinched like she'd been slapped. Sunny wondered which of them it hurt worse when she said it. But she said it. So Alex wouldn't have to. "You've a chance to do some good. You shouldn't waste it. It's not like there's too much good around. You wanted to be not nothing?" She would've liked to hold on to Alex's hand. To grip it tight. Instead, she gave it a pat. A limp little friendly pat, then let it go. "Well, you're something now."

Alex stared up at her. "We could still—"

"I don't think so. We always knew . . . this wasn't for ever." Though the truth was Sunny hadn't let herself think about it till now and was seeing it for the first time. "Once you're crowned, the Pope's binding will send me back to the Holy City. It'll be time to get another."

Alex started to reach for her again. "But you're the only thing—"

Sunny stepped back. "You'll find something else. You're a princess. I'm an elf. Sounds like a bad joke. It is one."

Silence, then. In the darkness. The pair of them, so close together but so impossibly far apart.

Then Alex stood. She held herself very straight, the way Baron Rikard had taught her. "You're right." She smoothed the front of her dress. "I can't afford . . . to be silly, any more." And she walked past Sunny, back towards the Empress's chamber.

"Alex!"

She turned back, a glimmer of hope at the corners of her eyes.

"Take the lamp." Sunny handed it to her. "I can see without it."

Jakob knelt in the shaft of light before the window, head bowed and hands clasped, like some old saint in a painting, preparing for martyrdom.

Sunny eased the door a little wider and slipped through sideways, then, so as not to be rude, she picked a bit of warped floorboard she could tell would squeak and set all her weight on it.

Jakob winced as he glanced over his shoulder and his neck gave a noisy click. "Sunny? That you?"

She let out her breath and sat down on the bed with her head hanging. "How many invisible elves do you know?"

"It could've been the Holy Spirit," he grunted, as he slowly stood.

"Why would that visit you?"

Jakob narrowed his eyes at the open panel on the wall, and the slit of darkness showing around its edge. "I've got a secret passage?"

"Place like this, they're everywhere. What are you doing?"

Jakob sighed, as though considering a lie, then gave up. "Praying."

"Thought you didn't believe in God anymore."

"Maybe I was hoping . . . that he still believed in me." He grimaced as he lowered himself towards the bed beside her, then dropped the last distance, he and the frame both giving their own complaining groan.

"Alex has a better bed than you."

"Well, she's a princess and I'm a murderer."

The silence stretched. Jakob wasn't much of a talker, but at silence he was a master.

Sunny took a slow breath. "I think she's going to marry Arcadius."

Jakob took a slow breath, too. "I think, in the end, that'll turn out best."

"Best for who?" whispered Sunny. She would've liked to cry, but didn't really know how. Instead, she leaned sideways, and kept leaning, until she fell over into Jakob's lap with her hands clasped against her chest. After a moment, he put his arms around her.

Gentle was the last thing she'd ever have expected from the old knight, but for a man who'd spent a lifetime killing elves, he was surprisingly good at hugging one.

"I just wanted . . . something," she said. "For myself."

"No one deserves it more."

"But I can't have it."

Another silence. Far off, birds wheeled and cried beyond the window.

"When I was young," said Jakob, "I thought I was working towards something. Building to last. Some perfect state of things. Of the world. Of myself." He gently shifted one leg under her, then the other. "You get to my age, you realise nothing lasts for ever. No love, no hate, no war, no peace. If a thing hasn't ended . . . you haven't waited long enough."

Sunny sniffed. "Is that meant to be comforting?"

"It's meant to be true. You had something. Be thankful for that." Jakob gave a long, pained sigh. "Now you have to let it go."

The Sword and the Book

The Basilica of the Angelic Visitation had hardly changed since Jakob's last visit.

The vast silence, in the deeps of which each footstep, word, or whisper gave birth to a wash of echoes. The bitter-sweet tang of polish and old incense. The endless ranks of benches, seating for thousands, worn to a dark gleam by centuries of pious backsides. The nuns in their crimson cowls, bowed with glowing tapers over forests of candles sprouting from mounds of old melted wax. The star of a hundred spears above the altar, mounted on a great wheel of steel and gold. Spears of the beatified heroes of the First Crusade, fought and won, then lost, before even Jakob was born. And in the centre five glass jars, each holding a pickled angel feather, relics of the angelic visitation that led Saint Hadrian to lay the Basilica's foundation stone, sealed deep beneath the altar. Even now the Patriarch and a whole battalion of priests stood over it, their gilded vestments studded with darkly gleaming jewels, preparing to conduct an imperial coronation and a royal wedding in one throw.

You could hardly see the walls for the acres of icons, crammed in frame to frame from mosaic floor to shadowed dome. Some small as Jakob's palm. Some big as a barn door. Some set in silver and gold. Some mounted in crudely carved wood, polished by centuries of adoring fingertips. Thousands upon thousands of saints, and angels as winged people, and angels in abstract: rings of eyes, spirals of wings, rays of fire, thickets of grasping fingers.

One figure drew Jakob's eye in particular: not painted like a saint, eyes rolled piously to heaven, but scarred and with the slightest smile. As if rather than considering the virtues, he'd come up with a joke, and was trying not to laugh.

"Saint Stephen?" asked Brother Diaz.

"The great protector. Patron of warriors." Jakob realised he'd reached out, fingertip almost touching the frame, and pulled his hand away. "I carried an icon like this for years. Screwed to the back of my shield. Just a daub, not near so fine as this one."

"What became of it?"

"I buried it with a friend." Jakob winced. He was used to twinges, but the one he felt then was sharp indeed. "Or maybe an enemy."

"Whose graves are these?" asked Brother Diaz, nodding towards the shrine beside them, its lectern and its inscriptions and its ranks of time-worn tombs.

"Heroes of Troy, who gave their lives defending the city in the Second Crusade. That's meant to be William the Red." Jakob looked up at the statue, a balefully glaring perfect warrior. "Doubt the sculptor ever met him. You'd never guess he had one leg shorter than the other and the most crooked nose in Europe. Look at him now. Forever young. Forever glorious."

Brother Diaz nodded to a couple of blank stone boxes, still waiting for their own cargo of bones. "Perhaps you'll have a place beside him one day."

Jakob snorted. "God, I hope not."

"What do you hope for, then?"

"To die quietly in my sleep and leave no trace."

"You?" Brother Diaz looked truly shocked. "Surely your life should be celebrated! How many crusades have you fought in?"

Jakob's sigh was deep enough that the old wounds about his chest all stung, each with its own sad story of failures, mistakes, regrets. "Two against the elves. One against the pagans in Livonia. One against the Sarimites in Burgundy. One against the Doubters in Bavaria, though there was scarcely any fighting there, it was straight murder. Then Pope Innocent the Fourth's crusade against the Followers of the Five Lessons." He gave a snort that hurt him, deep in his guts. "We never even reached Afrique. We stopped in Sicily to resupply, and it seemed much easier to sack Messina instead, and skulk home absolved of nothing."

"Even so," said Brother Diaz. "You are a holy warrior, under the personal orders of the Pope!"

"She may not yet be the best judge of character."

"With my own eyes I have seen you, four times at least, risk everything to protect Princess Alexia!"

"He who cannot die cannot risk, Brother Diaz."

"But you've fought great battles, won great victories, suffered great wounds—"

"My greatest battles I fought against myself, and they were all defeats, and I've suffered far less than I deserve."

Brother Diaz considered the statue of William the Red, glaring into the middle distance. "Is that why you're always looking for more?"

"More what?"

"Suffering. Would you presume to find yourself beyond salvation?" Brother

Diaz pointed to the echoing darkness above them. "That judgement is for God."

"He who cannot die cannot be judged."

"He who cannot die cannot run out of time to win redemption. To level your own accusation, reach your own verdict, pronounce your own sentence . . ." Brother Diaz gently shook his head. "That smacks of arrogance, Jakob of Thorn. That smacks of pride."

"Finally you see into my heart, Brother Diaz. You are wiser than I took you for."

"It is easy to be wise about others' lives, others' choices."

"Yet so few ever manage it. I'll admit, when we first met, I didn't have high hopes for you."

"Well, I was soft, naïve, and self-absorbed. I'm not sure things have changed so very much—"

"I think they have." Jakob had never been much for giving praise. In his youth, because he wanted all the praise for himself, like a dragon hoarding gold. In his old age, because he feared his liking a thing might lead to its destruction. But sometimes the right word can nudge a life towards the light, and a life changed is the world changed. By tiny degrees, perhaps. But for the better.

"All my overlong life . . ." he began, "I've been a man of the sword. Prone to judge men on the iron I see in them. Their bravery. Their prowess. I've tried to cure myself of it but, at my age, habits are hard to break."

"I have learned a healthy respect for the sword," said Brother Diaz, "believe me. The sword can cut through dangers and protect the righteous. As Saint Stephen's did. As I have seen yours do."

"On a good day, I like to think so. But all a man of the sword can really do is cut a chance for better men to take. Clear the ground, so men of the book can build something worth raising." He turned from the tombs and gave Brother Diaz a nod. "Let's celebrate them instead. You impressed me a great deal, the other day, in the throne room."

Brother Diaz blinked at him. "I admit I've been . . . somewhat out of my element for most of our journey. That might be the first time you've seen me on my battlefield."

"If that's how you do battle, perhaps it will be you who earns the grand tomb."

"Or me." Baptiste was swaggering up, grinning at the statue of William the Red. "They need some sculpture with a bit of glamour, don't you think?"

"And the inscription would read . . . ?" Balthazar swaggered up after her.

The two of them were like cats and dogs. Always nipping but couldn't seem to stop sniffing each other's arses. "Failed barber's assistant, failed butcher's girl, failed dressmaker's apprentice, failed artist's model?"

Baptiste tossed her head. "I'll have you know I was a *spectacular* artist's model."

"Must be why you kept at it for a whole week," sneered Balthazar. "To earn the big statue you have to *stick your neck out.*"

Vigga stuck her face between theirs. "It'd be easier on everyone if you two just fucked."

"Ugh," said Balthazar, curling a disgusted lip.

"Or one o' you murdered the other."

"Hmm," said Baptiste, raising a thoughtful brow.

Vigga barged between them. "Then *I* can have the tomb!"

Brother Diaz glanced nervously towards the regiment of priests crowding the altar. "I'm not sure how the Patriarch would feel about a statue of a pagan werewolf in his Basilica."

Vigga looked crestfallen. "You've a point." Then immediately brightened. "What if I convert? I mean, what's Odin done for me lately?"

"What's Odin ever done for anyone but Odin?" mused Baron Rikard, lounging on a pew nearby.

"I should be baptised!" Vigga clapped a heavy hand down on Jakob's shoulder and made him flinch. "Oh. Thought your other shoulder was the bad one."

"Mine are all bad shoulders," grunted Jakob, working them around in clicking circles. "And you've been baptised already."

"I have?"

"Twice. Once by Pope Pius, in an effort to drive out the wolf."

"That old woman with the bath?" Vigga wrinkled her nose. "I thought my smell bothered her."

"A not unreasonable assumption," murmured Balthazar.

"I wondered why they didn't scrub me better . . ."

"And then in Cologne," said Jakob, "with the pilgrims, remember? You saw the queue, and said you'd have what they were having."

"Thought they were giving out bread. But that explains why they dunked us in the river afterwards . . ." Vigga blinked. "And why the bread was tiny and not very good."

"That was the body of the Saviour," said Brother Diaz.

"No, no, it was just sort of a little biscuit." Vigga frowned. "Wait . . . am I among the Saved, then?"

Jakob gave a long sigh. "Not in any way that matters."

"And here she is . . ." murmured Brother Diaz. He had a wondering smile on his face as he watched Princess Alexia glide down the aisle, like a proud father watching the bride come in.

"One could almost mistake her for a princess," said Balthazar, if not proud, then at least not scornful.

"Our girl . . ." Baptiste wiped a fake tear from the corner of her eye. "All grown up . . ."

She came ready for her coronation, the "Our Saviour" stitched into her dress in gold thread, her four handmaidens holding up her fur-trimmed train, her jewels flashing as she swept through shafts of light. She came at the head of a regiment of retainers, as befits an Empress, flanked by Duke Michael and Lady Severa, a good deal smaller of stature, perhaps, but far from overshadowed by them.

"Well, well, Your Highness!" Baron Rikard bowed low as she approached, the eyes of her four handmaidens following him fascinated, like cats watching the butcher's cart, "or dare I even say, Your Resplendence? It seems you were attending to my lessons in deportment after all."

"I thought I should make an extra effort." Alex nodded towards her attendants. "Or, let's be honest, they should. A girl doesn't get crowned Empress of the East *and* marry her worst enemy every day, does she?"

Duke Michael leaned close to her. "Speaking of marriage, Your Highness—"

Alex winced. "Do we have to?"

"—I have . . . a favour . . . to ask." He swallowed as he reached out, and Lady Severa smiled, and put her hand gently in his. "You know that Lady Severa and I have been dear friends for many years."

Alex stared at their hands. "Uh-huh . . ."

"Since His Grace returned to Troy," said Lady Severa, "it has become clear that we have always been . . . much more than that."

"God *damn* it," whispered Balthazar.

"Told you," whispered Baptiste.

"I have asked Lady Severa to marry me!" blurted Duke Michael.

"And I have been honoured to accept," said Lady Severa, "provided, of course, that Your Highness approves."

There was a brief pause. Then Alex gave a long sigh. "Far be it from me to hoard all the marital bliss for myself."

"You have made me the happiest man in Europe!" Duke Michael beamed at Severa, then at the rest of them. "On behalf of Princess Alexia. On behalf of myself, and my wife-to-be. On behalf of every citizen of Troy . . ." And he took Jakob's hand in both of his and gave it a brotherly squeeze. "Thank you for all you've done."

"Only the task Her Holiness gave us," grunted Jakob, who enjoyed nothing, but gratitude least of all.

"But what a labour! You will always be welcome here. All of you." Jakob rather doubted that but appreciated the lie. "A ship has been chartered and waits for you on the docks." And the duke clapped Brother Diaz on the arm, and gave Jakob's hand a final shake, and let it go. "I trust your return voyage to the Holy City will be . . . a little calmer."

"Don't *ever* count on it," said Baptiste.

Alex's eyes had gone wide. "You're leaving?"

"Once the crown touches your head," said Jakob, "by the terms of Her Holiness's binding, we have to go."

"Whether we want to," threw in Balthazar, sourly, "or not."

"I was hoping . . ." Alex lowered her voice. "Perhaps, Sunny . . . would be here . . ."

"I daresay she is," said Jakob. "But showing herself wouldn't be the best idea."

"You think elves are unpopular in the Holy City?" Baptiste snorted. "At Easter here they stick fake ears on convicts and hunt them through the streets."

"Right." Alex swallowed. "Then . . . could you tell her . . . that I'm sorry."

Jakob nodded. "She knows."

"I knew we'd have to say goodbye, in the end." Alex looked around at the rest of them. At each, in turn. "I just never thought . . . Brother Diaz, maybe, before the service begins . . . you might give a blessing?"

"Me?" The monk glanced down the nave towards the Patriarch, his gilded robes glittering, then at his own humble habit. "You should have a bishop at least—"

"Wasn't the Saviour herself a lowly shepherdess?"

Brother Diaz grinned. "I shall miss our theological debates."

As the monk walked to the lectern before the tombs, Jakob thought back to the Second Crusade. The blessing before the final sally. The battle that had turned back the elves. The battle from which so many never returned. The knights kneeling, shoulder to shoulder. Patriarch Kosmas, his voice like thunder, calling down the rage of angels on the enemies of God.

Brother Diaz was a different kind of preacher. He laid gentle hands on the lectern, tracing its edges with fond fingers as his congregation gathered in a crescent before him. "I never really wanted to be a priest," he began. "I rather fell into it—"

"Prick first," said Vigga.

"Well." The monk gave a shamefaced grin. "You're not exactly wrong. But they say it is on profane paths that we come eye to eye with God. So it's been with me. I'll confess, I didn't ask for this task. I certainly didn't ask for these companions."

"We all get the ones we deserve," muttered Jakob.

"We took a crooked path, with many . . . dead ends. There were times I thought we'd never reach Troy. Our endurance was tested along the way. We all remember the inn."

"Wish I could forget," said Baptiste.

"The perfidy of Bishop Apollonia."

"One of the most perfidious bishops I ever met," grunted Baron Rikard, "with some stiff competition."

"The illusionist's house, and the talking heads."

Vigga laughed. "They leaked something terrible."

"Then there was the battle at sea."

"I can still smell those crab-men," murmured Alex.

"And the plague pit beneath the Monastery of Saint Sebastian."

"Good times," said Balthazar, with a faraway smile, "good times."

"But at each step somehow, together, we overcame. We may have fought with each other." Balthazar and Baptiste exchanged one of their glances. "But in the end, we fought *for* each other. And Alex . . . Your Highness . . . I have seen you learn. I have seen you grow. From a girl who was once called ferrety. To a woman ready to steer the course of an Empire."

Alex shrugged. "Still a little ferrety, I'll admit."

"A good Empress needs some teeth," said Vigga.

"May God, saints, and Saviour smile upon your reign," and Brother Diaz made the sign of the circle, "as, in the end, they smiled upon our journey. When we set out, I thought you all monsters. I have learned, I suppose, that you are only people. A set of devils, perhaps, but, on this occasion, you've done God's work." And he smiled, and gave a nod, and stepped from the lectern.

Balthazar watched with lips discerningly pursed, like a connoisseur considering a bottle. Then he leaned over. "He's actually not awful at this, is he?"

"All in all . . ." murmured Jakob, "far better than expected."

So Much to Live up To

Vigga was bored out of her mind.

The endless singing and praying and blah, blah, blah by the boring old men. Any desire she'd had to be saved was ebbing fast and she was thinking she'd much rather be a pagan after all. At least when pagans prayed it was over before you needed to piss.

Some bastard with the biggest beard you ever saw had droned on about planting a field so long you'd have thought they were crowning a plough. And when he finally shut up and Vigga was breathing a sigh of relief some other bastard with an even bigger beard got up and told a story about fish.

"What the hell's going on?" she muttered, squirming in her seat. "Are we crowning a fish?"

"It's not really about fish," whispered Brother Diaz. "It's about charity."

"Why not just talk about that, then?" asked Vigga, baffled.

She wasn't the biggest lover of Odin or Freya or Freyr and the rest, they'd done her no favours, but at least she understood them. They were as petty and lustful and greedy as everyone else, if not a bit more so. What's the point of being gods, after all, if you're not a bit more so? But the Saviour was so much to live up to. Vigga stared at her in the coloured glass, arms outstretched on the wheel like she couldn't wait to be carved. All the virtues and sacrifice and forbearance. Vigga could never forbear anything. Even before the bite.

Jakob was a hell of a forbearer. All he did was forbear. Look at him, next to her on the pew, scarred jaw clenched, forbearing away. No drink, no lies, no fucking. He hadn't sworn an oath against fun far as Vigga was aware, but he might as well have. Why live for ever if you're not going to *live*?

Beyond him Baron Rikard lounged, arms spread across the back of the pew like it was a couch in a brothel. The lady on his far side kept glancing at him, breathing like she'd run a mile and sweating like it, too, fanning herself with her hand and doing everything short of begging to be bitten. Vigga had no idea how anyone could want that smirking corpse, and she pretty much wanted anything male when the mood was on her, but then lemmings love cliffs, don't they?

She squirmed again. Hers was not an arse made for warming a pew. "Odin's *fucking* balls, I'm bored. Or wait, if I'm baptised . . . should it be Saviour's tits? Can I say that?"

Brother Diaz rubbed at his temples. "Not in a Basilica, ideally."

Now Alex sat on a stool or something while the priest with the biggest beard of all stood behind her, still droning on. Two of the girls came in and draped a purple cloak around Alex's shoulders, and the other pair pinned it shut with a great square golden brooch. Lady Severa put a sheaf of wheat into Alex's left hand, and Duke Michael put a gilded spear into her right, point wobbling about so Vigga started to hope she might take the Patriarch's eye out, which would've livened things up a bit, but no such luck.

All nonsense but, looking at the rapt faces of the audience, Vigga wondered if she saw a point to it after all. Choosing to be ruled by a seventeen-year-old girl who could scarcely hold a spear just 'cause of the room she'd been born in was, on the face of it, a bit silly. But wrap it in this much gleaming pomp and solemn ritual, you might mistake it for a gleaming, solemn notion.

"What's hard to make," she muttered to herself, "is hard to break."

The Patriarch poured oil from a golden spoon onto Alex's head. Then he took a crown from a boy with a cushion, held it in both hands, and lowered it, slowly, slowly, drawing out that moment, jewels twinkling and winking in the inky darkness, slowly, slowly.

"Drop it on her and let me piss!" hissed Vigga, likely heard from the back row the place was so silent.

She felt a change as the Patriarch settled that weight of gold on Alex's head. That restless tug in the pit of her guts that had dragged her all the way to Troy, dragging her back now towards the sea.

"So that's it." Balthazar rubbed at his stomach, and Vigga knew he felt it, too.

"That's it," said Rikard, closing his eyes. They all felt it.

Four noblemen leaned down and Vigga realised Alex had been sitting on a golden shield, and now they hoisted her up to their shoulders, displaying her to the crowd like the goods at an auction. Everyone shifted from their pews and knelt, sending up a great rustle, and Vigga was grateful at least to get some movement in her legs. Alex teetered under all that crown, eyes flickering up like she was worried it might fall off and she'd end up dropping her spear and wheat and juggling the damn stuff all down the nave. But the crown stayed on, and the girls started singing, and bells started ringing, and Vigga had to laugh, 'cause she'd always loved the bells, since she first heard one being smashed by Olaf on that raid, and the clang of so many filling that grand space made her wonder if she might prefer being saved to being a pagan after all. She'd never been any good at sticking to a choice. Even before the bite.

"Time we were gone." With a pained grunt Jakob stood and led them out in single file. Vigga caught one last look back at Alex, Duke Michael and Lady Severa smiling up at her, and wondered how it'd all turn out. But she never got to see that part. The Chapel of the Holy Expediency was like the corpse cart, and not only 'cause of the smell. People were happy enough to see it in a disaster, but no one wanted it sitting by their front door once the danger blew by.

The bells were still ringing as they stepped from the grand doors, past the many guards and into the dappled daylight.

"Shame we couldn't stay for the wedding." Vigga ducked off the road to wriggle her trousers down and squat among the bushes. "Though this crowd could probably make a boring business o' that, too."

"Must you?" Balthazar rolled his eyes. "Here?"

"Well, I could've gone in there, but I expect it would've pooled on the pew, and no one would've thanked me then."

"She has a point," said Baptiste.

"Why is it . . . when you've really got to go . . . it's sometimes hard to go?" And Vigga grunted as she finally managed it, careful to get her hips at the right angle so she didn't piss all over her own trousers, which wouldn't have been the first time. What with the bells and the binding satisfied and the simple pleasure of a draining bladder, she was quite enjoying herself at last, but no one else seemed to be. With Jakob it was no surprise, but Baptiste could usually raise a smile, and even Baron Rikard looked less smug than usual.

"Freya's arse," grunted Vigga as she slapped the drops off with one hand then wiped it on the nearest leaf. "Look at the long faces on you lot."

"Well, we embark at once for the Holy City," snapped Balthazar, walking on. "To return to captivity, resentment, and contempt. To return to *enslavement*."

"Ah." Vigga frowned. "I forgot about that."

Evil Friends

A lex stood, staring at nothing, her handmaidens buzzing about her. Seemed as if she'd been standing still all day while people buzzed about her. Babbled at her, around her, over her. Wheeled her about like a plaster statue of the Saviour on festival day. Dressed her and stripped her like a tailor's manikin. Plonked different headwear on her like she was a hatstand. It was only that morning they'd been stitching her into this dress, embroidered all over with prayers. Now they were cutting her out of it.

She hardly knew whether she was dizzy from the applause, worn out from the expectations, terrified at the idea of ruling an Empire, or panicking at the idea of enduring a wedding night. She wanted to laugh, be sick, hide under the bed, and run for the docks all at once.

"I'm Empress of Troy," she muttered to herself, for about the hundredth time.

"Without doubt, Your Resplendence." Lady Severa oversaw the undressing the way you might watch an heirloom be unpacked from a crate. Might've been reassuring to think she was now Alex's aunt-to-be, except that right away put her in mind of her own recent marriage, and that brought on a fresh urge to sprint for the door.

"I'm Empress of Troy . . ." She squeezed her eyes shut. "And my husband's on his way."

"I fear this cannot be *quite* how you dreamed of your wedding night."

Alex snorted. "Honestly, I never dreamed I'd live past twenty." Honestly, she still wouldn't have put good money on it.

"You need not worry. Zenonis and Placidia will be outside the door. I and Duke Michael are only on the floor below."

"So if my husband tries to stab me, you'll get here in time to stop the dagger?"

"Your husband will not stab you," said Lady Severa. "Not with a dagger, anyway."

"Not with a dagger . . ." murmured Alex as one of the girls—Cleofa, she thought, or maybe Athenais—sawed through a seam on her dress, and another scattered handfuls of flower petals across the carpet.

Lady Severa delicately cleared her throat. "You are not . . . a virgin?"

Alex snorted even louder. "Not even in the neighbourhood."

"Good. Good."

"Shouldn't a bride be one, ideally?"

"Ideal is not always . . . ideal. You will have some sense of what to expect, at least."

"Bad as that?" Alex took a shuddering breath, and blew it out, to the sound of ripping stitches. "Feel like I've been changing into something new for months. Now I've got to change into something else again. I don't even know what."

"Transformation . . . is a part of life," said Lady Severa. "Frightening, but necessary. Beautiful, even. The caterpillar becomes the butterfly."

Alex swallowed. "Butterflies don't live long."

There was certainly a flavour of doomed moth about the silk gown they draped around her, falling off the moment it was on, wafted about by the breeze from the open windows and leaving precious little to anyone's imagination.

There was a knock at the door. Probably just an ordinary knock, but it sounded as heavy to Alex as coffin nails being thumped in. One of the girls—Placidia, she thought, or maybe Zenonis—glided off to answer while the others went into a frenzy of last-moment tugs, plucks, flicks, and brushes, as if slapping a little colour into her cheeks would make the difference between a blissful marriage and a lifetime of torture shackled to a shit.

They perched a circlet of golden leaves on her head, a thing that couldn't decide whether to be alluring or commanding, which was a highly suitable piece of headgear, since Alex was wrestling with that decision herself and had no idea how to come at either one. So as the door opened, she ended up sort of leaning against one of the bedposts with her arms folded, slightly frowning but also with one eyebrow cocked. Like a grumpy cook who'd been waiting too long for the baker's boy to arrive.

Arcadius stood in the doorway, wearing not a gauzy tissue but the magnificently embroidered tunic, stiffly starched shirt, and highly polished boots he'd been married in. He bowed, very elegantly, which was a relief, as it'd be a shame to be murdered by someone with bad manners.

"Your Resplendence. Or should I say . . ." He glanced up, with the hint of a smile. "My wife?"

"Your Grace. Or should I say . . ." It was somehow hard for Alex to wrap her teeth around the phrase. "My husband."

The last of the girls—Athenais, she thought, or maybe Placidia—tossed a

last handful of petals then whisked the doors shut, sealing the two of them—
husband and wife, Empress and consort, Alex and the man she'd taken till a
few days before for her most dangerous enemy—in her bedchamber, alone.

Great.

"I confess I feel a little . . ." Arcadius cleared his throat, the first hint he
might be suffering from some nerves of his own. "Overdressed." And he un-
buttoned his glittering jacket, tossed it over a chair, and started rolling up his
shirtsleeves. "Perhaps some wine would help us both . . . relax."

Alex hadn't been relaxed for a very long time. In fact, she couldn't really remember ever being relaxed. But she doubted she'd ever been less relaxed than
she was right then. "I wouldn't say no," she muttered as wine gurgled from the
jug into two glasses, glittering red and bloody with the sunset.

He advanced on the bed, holding one out to her. "Hell of a day for you."

She took it, wondering whether you could *see* poison. "And it's not over
yet . . ."

He saw her hesitate. "If it was poisoned . . ." And he took a slurp from his
own glass. "I'd just have killed myself."

"You might've put the poison only on my glass," said Alex.

Arcadius raised his brows. "Exactly the sort of thing my mother would've
done. You're giving me way too much credit." He swapped Alex's glass for his,
then drank from that one, too. "Or perhaps not enough."

She finally let herself take a sip. It did taste rather fine. But then the kind
of poison a duke would use on an Empress you probably can't taste any more
than you can see. She perched herself on the bed. Tried to waft the tails of
her hapless gown so they gave her legs a hint of cover, but it was like using a
feather to hide a side of ham.

Arcadius watched her. "You seem a little . . ."

"Ferrety?"

"I was going to say jumpy."

"Well, your brothers all tried to kill me."

"I heard, and thought to myself . . . how *gauche*." He set off around the
bed to the other side. "My one consolation is that they clearly weren't terribly
good at it. I did try to dissuade them, but though they were very different
men they all three took after our mother in being impossible to dissuade
from anything. But I can promise you, right now, that I . . ." And Arcadius
perched on the far side of the bed and looked earnestly at her. "Will *never* try
to kill you."

"Sort of a minimum standard in a husband, really, wouldn't you say?"

"One that not every imperial consort in history has met, I fear." He hauled off one boot and tossed it aside with a *clonk*. "But I hope to clear it *consider-ably*." He grunted as he strained at the other boot. "I differed from my broth-ers in many respects, but perhaps the most important is that, although I was eldest . . ." He finally got his boot off, and swung his feet up onto the bed, wriggling his toes. "I never had the *slightest* desire to be Emperor."

Alex was a pretty experienced liar. Maybe she was among liars of a higher class than she was used to in the slums of the Holy City, but she didn't think he was lying now. She took another slurp of wine and sat back against her cushions. "So you're marrying me for love?"

Arcadius smiled. "You look ravishing, of course—"

"A turnip would look ravishing with my servants dressing it."

"But a turnip cannot help me save the Empire of the East." He kept look-ing at her with that earnest, slightly amused expression. "For decades now, if not centuries, the leaders of Troy have been their own worst enemies. The city's best children, eating each other. Struggling for power while weakening the whole, all in the shadow of an inevitable pointy-eared *apocalypse*. I want to return the Empire of my forefathers to glory. Together . . . perhaps we have a chance?"

She had to admit she liked what he was saying. And the way he was saying it. God, was she starting to actually like *him*? That never ended well. "Arcadius—"

"My friends call me Archie."

"They do?"

"Believe it or not, I have quite a few."

"I do believe it."

"Why, thank you."

"You're quite a charmer."

"Why, thank you."

"But I've known some very charming, very evil people."

"Well, evil people make the best friends, don't you find? They're prepared to do things for you that *good* friends never would."

Alex, who'd been kept alive for the last few months by a gang of diabolical heretics, could hardly argue with that. "So you want us to be friends?"

"Well, it seems preferable in a marriage to being enemies. I saw my mother make that arrangement with no fewer than four husbands, and it did *not* turn out well. Especially for the men involved. I see no reason to repeat the mistakes of our parents, do you?"

"I barely knew my parents."

Arcadius rolled his eyes to the ceiling. "God, I wish I'd never known mine. Are you trying to make me jealous, Alexia?"

"My friends call me Alex."

"Makes sense."

"Believe it or not, there are hardly any, and most of them just left for the Holy City."

"If ever there were evil friends," said Arcadius, "I think you have some there."

Alex found herself rather nettled by that. "No doubt they're a . . . mixed bag."

"I am told there is a particularly dangerous vampire, as well as a particularly violent werewolf and a supercilious tamperer with the dead."

Alex wrapped her gown, such as it was, a little more tightly around herself. "We've all got our shortcomings."

"Oh, I am *well* aware. Flaws I have aplenty, but hypocrisy isn't one of them." He gave a sigh. "I sense you're not exactly raring to consummate our alliance, and I take no offence, I share your reticence." He held up a hand. "A matter of taste rather than quality, I assure you. Might I hazard a guess that you . . . perhaps . . ." And he raised his brows high. "Prefer rings to fingers, as it were?"

Alex raised her own brows to match. "While you, maybe, are more of a finger man?"

"It seems my wife is as perceptive as she is beautiful."

"That a fancy way of calling me dumb and ugly in one breath?"

Arcadius held her eye. "*Quite* the opposite, on both counts."

"Well, the bed's big enough that we could share it every night and probably never see each other again."

"I've heard it said the secret of a good marriage is a broad mattress."

"We'll have to meet in the middle sooner or later. There's been some talk about . . ." Alex cleared her throat, "*heirs.*"

"Ah, yes. Born here, beneath the flame, as you were. Between the two of us . . . I feel sure we can devise a method that will keep our mutual repugnance to a minimum."

This was turning out more civilised than Alex had dared to hope. "There's more than enough repugnance around without us adding more."

"My *very* feelings." Arcadius plumped one of the cushions with the back of his hand and draped himself luxuriantly against it, looking towards the ceiling, night-sky blue scattered with golden stars. "Perhaps . . . a little assistance from those we find more personally appealing? And a curtain of some sort?"

"With a hole?" murmured Alex, lying back to look at it herself.

Arcadius twisted towards her, making a ring with his thumb and fore-finger and grinning at her through it. "Only a small one. And perhaps some manner of fragranced lubricant."

"Sounds like quite a party."

"Looks like quite a party," said Vigga, gazing wistfully back towards the quay, lit with torches as the sun sank, noisy with raucous music, cheers, and laughter, crowded with colourful revellers celebrating the brave new era. An era the Chapel of the Holy Expediency had helped bring in but could never be a part of.

"Shame we're not invited," grunted Brother Diaz, trudging towards the gangplank. "My name's Diaz! I believe passage to the Holy City has been secured for us."

The man who, by his hat, was the captain, took in Jakob, stonily glaring, Baptiste, jauntily grinning, Baron Rikard, languidly leaning, Balthazar, fastidiously sneering, Vigga, looking exactly like a Viking werewolf would, and finally and with the greatest suspicion of all Sunny, her face hidden in the shadows of her hood but for tufts of pale hair. It would have been far better had she vanished from sight entirely but she seemed reluctant to do it, or talk, or acknowledge anyone at all. In fact, if elves were capable of being depressed, Brother Diaz would likely have put her in that category.

The captain leaned to spit over the ship's side. "Hope I don't regret it."

Baron Rikard sighed. "I fear you will find, as we all must, that hope and regret are sisters eternal."

There was a brief silence. Brother Diaz thought the vampire might have waxed a touch too philosophical for the audience.

"We're ready to go," grunted Jakob, always ready to bring things down to earth.

The captain looked back to a list nailed to a board. "Wish I was. But as you can see . . ." as a sailor brushed past Brother Diaz with a barrel over her shoulder, nearly knocking him into the sea, "we're still loading. All this business with the new Empress. It's held everything up."

"It's held me up for six months," snapped Balthazar, stepping past Brother Diaz and across the gangplank. "We will sit up there on the aftcastle while we wait."

"I'd rather you—"

Vigga grinned down at him. "I can sit on you instead. If you'd rather." As ever with her, it was hard to tell threat from proposition.

The captain took it as a little of both. "No, no, the aftcastle is . . . all yours."

"Grand," said Vigga. "Just sing out. If you change your mind."

"This certainly has been one of the Chapel's lengthier assignments," the baron was saying as he tripped up the steps.

"But our priest survived!" Baptiste slid down the mast till she sat with her back against it. "Has that ever happened before?"

"Mother Pierraud lasted three missions," said Jakob. "But that was before your time."

"What became of her in the end?"

Jakob leaned on the rail, frowning out at the sea. "Best not to dwell on it."

Any feeling of triumph at seeing Alex finally crowned was steadily fading as Brother Diaz considered his future prospects. "What will be next . . . do you think?"

"One thing about life in the Chapel of the Holy Expediency," said Baptiste. "You will *never* guess what's next."

"Demons in Dusseldorf?" mused Jakob.

"Witches in Wexford?" grunted Vigga.

"Goblins in Gdansk?" ventured Balthazar.

"Gdansk is lovely this time of year," observed the baron.

"Maybe I'll put off the retirement." Baptiste looked thoughtfully towards the setting sun, the gold glimmering on the water. "See how one more turns out . . ."

"Every time," said Jakob, shaking his head. "She moans all the way, then stays for one more."

"The only thing we *can* be sure of," said Rikard, "is that it will be a dirty job."

"How could it be otherwise?" Brother Diaz looked gloomily towards the celebrations on the quay. "For the clean jobs, Her Holiness has other servants."

"Well, first step on any successful sea-journey . . ." Vigga slid out a bottle of spirits, and with a flick of her thumb sent the cork spinning into the sea. "Let's get shitfaced."

"First step in any successful alliance," said Arcadius, "I suggest we get *outrageously* drunk."

And he slid from the bed and strode for the door. Alex wriggled into her cushions and drained her glass. She'd always thought she didn't like wine. Now she realised she didn't like bad wine. Turned out she liked good wine quite a lot.

"More wine, if you please!" her husband roared into the corridor, then swaggered back grinning towards the bed. "I find there are few ills more wine won't help with."

"Axe in the head?" asked Alex.

He thought about that and shrugged. "It'll make it no worse."

One of the handmaidens padded in behind him, eyes on the floor. Placidia, Alex was almost sure, a fresh jug balanced on her silver tray.

"What if this one's poisoned?" she asked, drunk enough to joke about it. Or half-joke, maybe. The last thing she'd ever expected from her wedding night was happening—she was actually starting to enjoy it.

"Paranoia would generally be thought deplorable in a wife." Arcadius snatched the jug from the tray and took a swig straight from the spout. "But in an Empress, it's positively essential. Wouldn't you say?" He glanced at Placidia, and his brow wrinkled. "Do I know you?"

"This is Placidia," said Alex. "She's from an unimpeachable family."

"Unlike the rest of us . . . I'll remember in a moment . . ."

Placidia glanced up, and Arcadius snapped his fingers. "I've got it! With black hair, you'd be the absolute image . . . of one of my mother's . . . apprentices . . ."

"Oh." Placidia tipped her head to one side, and tossed her tray away, and it hit the marble with a harsh *clang* and spun round and round on its edge. "How fucking tiresome," she said.

"Wait . . ." Alex held on to one of the bedposts to pull herself up to sitting. "What?"

Zenonis slipped her head around the door. Alex never saw her smile before, but she was smiling now. A bright and hungry smile. And one side of her face was all dotted with blood. "Did they work it out?"

"Wait . . ." Alex almost whimpered. The pleasant warmth of drunkenness was rapidly draining and chilly terror was washing in behind it. "*What?*"

Arcadius took a step back. "Oh no . . ."

Placidia gripped him by the wrist. "Oh *yes.*"

"Ah!" He tried to pull free, face twisting in pain. "Ah!" His arm had turned pale where Placidia held it. A fur of frost, spreading from her hand, veins bulging blue-black on his skin. The jug slipped from his grip and shattered, a slush of half-frozen wine oozing from the wreckage.

He turned to Alex, very slowly, and with a strange creaking. "Run . . ." he whispered, and the word turned to a puff of smoke on his grey lips, ice spreading across his cheeks, eyes turning milky pale.

"Fuck!" screeched Alex, scrambling from the bed, getting tangled in the covers and sprawling across the floor in a shower of cushions.

"Born in the flame?" Zenonis stalked towards her, teeth bared, hair stirred by a hot draught from nowhere. Just like the pyromancer at the inn, and the terror of that memory caught Alex now and choked her. "You can die in the—"

"Fuck *you*!" Alex flung her empty wineglass and it bounced from Zenonis's cheek and shattered on the wall. Alex spun, slipped, scrambled on all fours for the chapel, bare feet skittering on the marble.

"Oh God . . ." She snatched one last panicked look over her shoulder as she stumbled for the secret panel, fumbled for the hidden catches.

Arcadius was frozen, pale cheek glittering with rime, cold fog rising from hair turned furry white with frost. With a snarl, Placidia slapped him, and his whole body shattered into splinters, chunks of pink ice bouncing across the polished floor. She glared at Alex and tossed her husband's frozen hand over her shoulder.

With a click the secret door popped open and Alex blundered through, clutching at the doorframe.

Zenonis was up, face streaked with blood from a gash on her cheek. A tapestry behind her began to blacken and smoke as she raised her hands and a blinding wave of fire shot out.

Alex slammed the door shut as it flickered around her, heat shocking as a punch in the face. She stumbled back through the blackness, slapping at the singed tails of her gown, coughing on the stink of sulphur.

"Oh God . . ." She had just the presence of mind to fumble the lamp from its little alcove. "Oh God . . ." She lifted the hood and brought it down, over and over, till the flame puffed into life. "Oh God . . ." Was the door starting to glow? Was smoke curling from the back? Was it getting warm in the little corridor?

She staggered, clawing cobwebs away, to the little room with the little window where she'd had her last bitter little conversation with Sunny. How she wished Sunny was here now, but they were all gone. Sunny, and Jakob, and Vigga, and Brother Diaz even, all well on their way back to the Holy City—

Duke Michael! His rooms were on the floor below. The guards would still be loyal to him. She ran to the narrow stair, stone cold against her bare feet, and took one step down—

Sounds echoed from below. Scraping footsteps? Was someone coming up?

"Oh God . . ." She could smell burning. A scratch at the back of her throat.

She clutched a flimsy handful of her gown in one hand, lamp in the other, blundering up the steps two at a time, her bare shoulder scraping the wall. The golden wreath had slid down over her eye and she tore it off and flung it bouncing down the steps.

She shoved open a door and tumbled into the throne room, lit by four hanging lamps, sun sinking beyond the great windows and staining the Serpent Throne a bloody red. She scrambled for the great bronze doors, hauled on one of the handles. As it came open a crack, she heard a distant scream beyond, the crackle of flames. Was that delighted laughter?

She backed off, staring wildly around. Tapestries, statues, weapons bracketed to the walls. Nowhere to hide. Beyond the throne, the narrow stair climbed upwards. The stair to Saint Natalia's Flame. She ran to it, dragged herself up it with hands as well as feet, on all fours like a dog. The dog Empress, her panting breath echoing about her.

She blundered blinking into the gallery at the top, brighter than daylight, Saint Natalia's Flame blazing up from the bowl at its centre. She shrank away as a dark figure rounded on her, but it was only a Sister of the Flame in her red hood, sworn to silence, sworn to keep the brazier forever lit.

Nothing else but the cords of wood stacked about the parapet and the two dozen archways beneath the mirrored dome . . . and the dangling chain. The one that would warn the city the elves were coming. Alex stood a moment, staring at it. But it wasn't like there was much left to lose. The nun's eyes went wide as she stretched up to grab the end and jerked it down. The hopper above dropped open and with a pop, a fizz, and a shower of foul-smelling sparks, a stream of powder poured into the brazier.

A stream of black sewer-water poured into the sea, and Balthazar watched, fascinated, as the ripples spread, were subsumed by the incoming waves, slapped against the harbour wall, and rebounded, splitting and merging in an intricate dance.

His mind returned once again to the sorcerous twins they encountered at the Monastery of Saint Sebastian. Their identical technique, with opposite results. Waves. In earth. In air. A common structure to all matter . . . He could not shake the notion. It was so perfect, so beautifully simple, so consistent with the ordered universe in which he still insisted on believing. Could one magically induce a wave through *anything* with the right—

"What's that?" asked Sunny. Balthazar followed her long finger, looking up towards the top of the Pharos. There, at the summit, bright in the gathering dusk, Saint Natalia's Flame was burning blue.

Brother Diaz frowned towards it. "I thought they only did that for an elf invasion?"

And Balthazar experienced that familiar sinking sensation. The one he had felt each time he tried to break the binding and realised he had failed. The one he had felt when the Celestial Court read the verdict. When the Witch Hunters sprang out of hiding in the graveyard.

"Something's wrong," growled Jakob. Some of the revellers on the quay had noticed, too, pointing up, gabbling excitedly.

Balthazar winced. "Nothing that need concern us, surely?"

"Alex is in trouble." And Sunny sprang down from the aftcastle onto the deck, striding past the captain as he ordered the hatches shut on the last of the cargo.

"We don't know that," wheedled Balthazar. "She can't *know* that!"

"If there's nothing to worry about," grunted Jakob, sliding a few inches of steel from his scabbard, then slapping it home with a snap, "we'll soon be back."

"She's Empress of Troy," whined Balthazar, "she'll always be in trouble. We cannot rescue her from every little thing!"

"I won't ask anyone else to come—"

"I'm coming," said Brother Diaz, gripping at the vial he kept beneath his habit.

"It could be dangerous," said Jakob.

Vigga grinned as she stood, slapping the seat of her trousers. "Where's the fun in safe?" Baptiste was clambering up from her place against the mast as well.

Balthazar gave a tremendous snort as he watched. "I can trust that you at least will be taking no risks with your person?"

"The time comes . . ." Baptiste gave her daggers a quick check, then glanced up towards the Pharos, setting her jaw. "You have to stick your neck out."

"*What?*" For a moment, Balthazar could only stare at her. "Well, I am *not* going, and that's *that!*"

"Of course you're not." And she gave him a friendly clap on the arm and hurried down the steps to the deck. For once, there was no trace of rancour in it. No disgust and no contempt. And yet it managed, somehow, to be the most stinging thing she had ever said to him.

"You've been demanding we go for hours!" shouted the captain as he watched them clatter across the gangplank. "Now we're ready you want to stay?"

"Well, we won't bloody wait for you!" Balthazar bellowed after them. He rounded on Baron Rikard, still leaning against the ship's rail, just as he had been when they first noticed the colour of the flame. "I am comforted to see that you at least have retained your perspective."

"Always," said the vampire, watching the others hurry along the quay with his customary faint amusement.

"For *months* I was bound to protect that hopeless girl and struggled with my *every* resource against it. I flatly *refuse* to continue the struggle now I am bound to leave her to her own devices!"

"An entirely rational decision. I would expect no other."

"What are they *thinking*?"

"Who can say? Each of us makes our own choice, in the end, for our own reasons. Alone. With our consciences." Rikard showed his fangs as he grinned. "Such as they are."

"Well, quite," grumbled Balthazar, nodding along. "Absolutely."

"That's why I'm going, too."

Balthazar stared at the baron. "*You?*" He stared at the Pharos. "*There?*"

"Empress Alexia might be in trouble."

"But . . . you're a vampire!"

Rikard laid gentle fingertips on his chest. "So I can't *care*?"

Balthazar gaped even wider than he had at Baptiste. "All this time you studied my efforts to break the binding . . . you *encouraged* my efforts . . . so you could break it yourself—"

"That's what you thought?" Rikard gave a suave little chuckle. "I encouraged your efforts because I found them hilarious. To be fair, you came closer to breaking the binding than any other magical practitioner I have known. Which is to say, nowhere near. But I never wanted to break the binding myself. I never needed to."

"But . . . what . . ."

The vampire rested a gentle hand on his shoulder. "The problem with clever people is they think everything must be clever. The binding works on the *soul*, Balthazar." He shrugged. "I'm a vampire. I don't have one."

"But if the binding doesn't affect you . . ." Balthazar groped for the words like a blind man for the privy. "Then . . . you . . . *chose* to come here?"

"When one reaches my age . . ." The baron gave him a parting pat. "One needs *something* to do with one's time." And he exploded into a cloud of bats that clattered off screeching into the evening.

"Saviour protect us . . ." The captain had chosen that moment to clamber onto the aftcastle. Now he was numbly making the sign of the circle over his chest. "Cast off!" he howled towards his men. "We're leaving *now*!"

Balthazar turned back to the quay. "Well, I won't bloody do it!" He screamed furiously at the evening. "I've done what was asked of me. I've done *more* than was asked of me. You can't make me go!"

Even though no one was asking him to.

The Language of Violence

They were coming.

Alex could hear their footsteps, in the throne room below. The confident tap of expensive shoes on an expensive floor.

She stared wretchedly about the eyrie at the top of the Pharos, bathed now in a sickly blue glare, flashing from the thousand thousand chips of mirror that covered the inside of the dome.

They were coming.

A hideous scream split the night. A hiss like steam below, and the scream became a bubbling whimper, then silence.

Alex stood frozen, sweat tickling her scalp. From the heat of the flame. From the climb. From the abject terror. The nun stood gaping, hard to say if she was sticking to her vow of silence or had lost the power of speech.

They were coming. And there was no way out.

Well, there were about twenty, it was just that beyond each wide archway there was nothing but a spectacular view of her darkened Empire and the longest drop in Europe.

The footsteps had made it to the stair below.

"Oh God." Alex scrambled to the nearest opening, leaned gingerly over the parapet, and her stomach flipped.

A dizzying vastness of dusk yawned beneath her. The side of the Pharos dropping away, the side of the Pillar dropping away below that, the pinprick lights of the city far below *that*, the lanterns of the ships in the bay, the dregs of sunset gleaming on the black mirror of the harbour.

When she fled through the rigging from Constans's fish-men she'd thought herself very high up. How quaint her death plunge into the freezing Adriatic seemed now.

There was only one small mercy. Basil the Builder had clearly loved a bit of decorative stonework. He'd spared no expense on fake pillars, false windows, sculpted plants, animals, faces, and that had left handholds everywhere.

The high, cold wind caught Alex's hair and flicked it around her smarting face, caught her gauzy gown and flicked it around her goosefleshed legs.

She could hear voices on the steps.

"Oh God."

She thought of Arcadius, shattered into a thousand frozen fragments.

No one wants to see doubts.

She planted her arse on the centuries-old names, gritted her teeth, and swung both legs over. She slithered down, clinging to the parapet beside her until the cold stone dug into her armpit, bare feet paddling desperately about till one toe caught something sticking from the side of the tower.

A gargoyle. She'd never seen the point of the ugly bastards before but she was damn grateful for it now. She teetered there, sideways on, perched atop a little stone head too small for both her feet.

She gritted her teeth even harder and peered down, focused on her toes. Not beyond. Not all that swallowing, dizzying beyond. Not the tiny buildings and the pinprick lights and the fall. How long would you fall for?

"Oh God." She told herself that didn't matter. Who cared whether you only broke your neck or your body exploded into soup? It was just like being a thief, climbing up some merchant's drainpipe. She made herself let go of the parapet, palms sliding down the masonry as she bent her knees, slowly, slowly, cold wind chilling one shoulder, cold stone scraping the other, praying for balance.

"Oh God." Heart pounding in her mouth. Pounding behind her smarting eyes. She got her straining, tingling fingertips to the gargoyle, thighs digging into her churning stomach. She worked one foot off it, then the other. Its stubby stone horns scraped her shins, then her knees, then her stomach, then her chest. Her arms trembled and her hands burned with the effort as she lowered herself, dangling over the void, every muscle aching as she stretched out.

She'd always wanted to be taller, but never half so much as in that moment.

The tip of one fishing toe brushed stone, and with a whimper she trusted to fate and let go. Her heels thumped onto a ledge and she stood gasping, plastered into a shallow alcove, one of a set that ringed the lighthouse, matching the gallery of archways at the top.

"Where is she?" The voice echoed from above and Alex pressed herself even tighter to the stone, not daring even to breathe.

"I asked you *where?*"

A sudden gust blew up, trying to peel her from the Pharos, singed sleeves of her imperial bedwear whipping at her eyes, and she dug her fingertips into some carved vine leaves and clung on like grim death.

"You're a Sister of the Flame? I can give you flame."

There was a hideous screech. Alex couldn't hold in a gasp of terror as something plummeted past her, blazing brightly, flailing wildly, shrieking like a boiling kettle.

The nun.

"That was a waste." Placidia's voice, but so cold Alex could hardly believe it was the same girl who'd so gently combed her hair that morning.

"No more talking." Zenonis's voice. "No more plotting. No more picking that stringy shrew's dirty toenails. It's time to take back what's *ours*."

"Then we have to trap our little rat and kill it."

Alex realised with a surge of fresh terror that Placidia was coming towards the parapet, leaning out to look down. She sucked in her stomach and pressed herself to the Pharos, shrinking from the blue glare above, eyes squeezed shut, toes trembling as they clung to the ledge, fingertips worming into the carvings, clutching a handful of her whipping gown close so it couldn't give her away, holding her breath like Sunny would've and wishing she could disappear the same way.

Any moment, she'd hear the cruel laughter, see the fire glow through her eyelids, feel the searing pain, and follow that sorry nun downwards, the shortest and most disappointing reign in Trojan history ending in a human torch—

"Downstairs." Placidia's voice moved away. "Check the throne room again."

Alex let out a shuddering sigh. She yearned to sob or blub or even scream but didn't dare to so much as squeak. She forced her feet to move. To edge along that shelf of stone. She peeled her sweat-sticky back from the masonry, twisting to face the wall, one fishing foot over the void, toes straining towards the ledge of the next alcove along—

Something flapped at her, clattered around her, batting wings, squawking beaks. She lost her grip with one hand, swinging out by the other, clutching at nothing, weight tipping over the drop, swinging, out of control, and she gave a whooping gasp—

Stone smacked into her face, filled her head with stars.

She gripped on by broken, trembling fingernails. Salt in her mouth. Head spinning.

Her feet were on the next ledge, wedged among a wreckage of twigs, slimy with droppings and broken eggs. Birds, nesting high up. She tried to breathe through the dizziness, the pulsing pain in the side of her jaw.

There was a pillar beside the alcove. She shuffled to it, wrapped her legs around it, clinging to the carved leaves at its top. She tried to ease downwards, but right away she began to slip, juddering, shuddering, stitches popping, gauzy material ripping.

She squeezed her eyes shut, growling through gritted teeth as the rough stone chafed her raw—

Her feet hit something, and she realised she was still. A ledge at the base of the pillar. There was a great window beside her. One of the windows of the throne room, the welcoming glow of lamplight leaking out into the dusk.

Alex had spent some bad nights on the streets, but the idea of *inside* had never held so much appeal.

She shuffled her grazed feet towards the window, clung to the frame with her bleeding fingers, peered into the room, and froze again.

There they were. Placidia crouched, long limbs seeming longer than ever, eyes sunken in dark rings and her lips turned pale blue, her jewellery glittering with frost. Zenonis stood tall beside her, streaks of blood down her face from the cut cheek Alex had given her, eyes wide and wild, scorched dress and shining hair stirred as if by a hot draught. Two of the missing members of Eudoxia's coven, right beside her all along.

Alex cursed silently to herself. Beautiful people, tending to a piece of shit like her? She'd forgotten Gal the Purse's last lesson! *Never* trust the rich. They're even more treacherous than the poor.

"How'd she get away?" Zenonis poked at something with her shoe. A heap of bubbling fat and blackened armour that must once have been a guard.

"Rats are clever little creatures," said Placidia, each word with a puff of chilly smoke, "when it comes to finding holes to hide in. Tell the others we'll have to do this the hard way. Scour the palace. Kill anything that might be loyal to her."

Zenonis sniggered. "I like the hard way."

Her shining eyes flicked towards the window and Alex shrank back against the stone, squeezing her eyes shut. Then she snapped them open.

Duke Michael! She had to warn him!

And maybe, just maybe, together, they could get out of this alive.

She clung to the outside of her own palace as another chilly gust whipped around her bare arse . . . could she feel specks of drizzle on the air?

"Oh God . . ." What girl doesn't live in fear of rain on her wedding day?

Though most brides don't have to climb down the outside of a giant lighthouse after the groom's been shattered into a thousand pieces.

Jakob had never been much with words. But in the language of violence, he was a poet.

He'd been steeped in it since he was a babe in arms, speaking it eloquently since before he could walk and—try as he might to learn others—violence was still the language he first thought in. He knew its every dialect, from tavern brawl to pitched battle. He understood its every subtlety and idiom. It was his mother tongue.

So when he heard it whispered on the streets of Troy, he understood the meaning. A wildness in the eyes of the revellers. A shrillness in their cries as they pointed up through the drizzle towards Saint Natalia's Flame, still burning an eerie blue. It was fair to say no one liked the elves, but for most of Europe they were a far-off menace. *Eat your dinner or the elves will eat you.* Here in Troy, where their unearthly savagery had boiled over the edges of the map within living memory, the hatred and terror were of a different order. *Keep your sword always sharp and your eye ever watchful, lest the elves eat your family the way they ate your grandfather.*

A damp crowd had gathered before the lift, held back by a double line of Palace Guard. "All's well!" their captain was bellowing, though his drawn sword wasn't putting any minds at rest. "The elves are *not* coming!"

"No more'n one, anyway," muttered Vigga as she ploughed through the angry press.

"I'm Brother Diaz!" called the monk, stepping from behind her, not at all cowed by the naked steel. "Envoy of Her Holiness the Pope, and I'm concerned for the safety of the Empress!"

"Who's this brash bastard and what's he done with Brother Diaz?" muttered Baptiste out of the corner of her mouth.

"I know who you are." The captain had a twitchy look. "But there's nothing to—"

"Then why the blue flame?" demanded Diaz, and the crowd muttered in angry agreement.

Jakob slid past him and beckoned the captain close, one professional to another. "No one wants to add to your troubles, but we've all got superiors to answer to."

"Let us go up there," said Baptiste, gold teeth glinting as she grinned. "All's well, we can help you put minds at rest."

The captain considered the gathering mob, then glanced towards his men. One shrugged. Another nodded. "All right." And he sheathed his sword as he turned for the lift. "We'll go together."

In the language of violence, Jakob was fluent. He'd had his suspicions, but as the soldiers slotted the rail into place behind them, the captain pulled the lever, the machinery rattled into life, and the city fell away beneath them, the hints he saw left no room for doubt.

How one guard had his weight all in his front foot, body slightly twisted, like a bent bow. How another rested his hand on the buckle of his sword-belt, thumb nervously tap, tap, tapping. How a third watched Baptiste, standing that bit too close, a muscle working on the side of his head.

"Glad to have you with us!" Brother Diaz grinned at the guard beside him. In many areas, the monk had proved himself surprisingly erudite. But in the language of violence, he was illiterate.

Jakob couldn't tell exactly how many guards were around him without turning, which might've given him away, and definitely would've hurt his neck. So he kept his eyes ahead, and took a long breath, and let it sigh out. Strange, how it was only at a time like this that he felt truly calm. Sometimes it's a burden, to know just what's coming. And sometimes it's a wonderful comfort.

"Your Palace Guard must be some of the best equipped soldiers in Europe," he said.

The captain glanced sideways at him. "Every man pays for his own armour, he's that honoured to serve."

"Acacia wood shafts to your spears?" asked Jakob, admiringly. "Must be shipped in from Afrique?"

"The best," said Vigga, raising a knowing brow at the spears of the four guards clustered close around her. She could miss the point in almost any tongue, but when it came to violence, you'd get nothing by her.

"And you carry the paramerion." The captain's left hand was gripping his sword. He had to let go to show off the gold on the hilt. "I've always favoured straight blades." Jakob let his right hand rest carelessly on his dagger, but made sure he left it there, thumb hooked under the pommel. "They're what I grew up with. But I've seen those sabres of yours do deadly work, especially from the saddle. The Empress doesn't skimp in equipping her elite, eh, Brother Diaz?"

"I . . . suppose not." The monk frowned back at him. "You're talkative, of a sudden."

"I'm among men who speak my language!" Jakob clapped his hand down on the wet-beaded shoulder-plate of the man beside him. A sergeant with a scarred face he judged the worst threat within reach. "But I've fought many battles. *Many*. And there's a piece of equipment you don't have. One that can make all the difference."

"What'd that be?" growled the sergeant.

"An invisible elf."

There was a pause. The captain gave an uncertain laugh. A couple of his men chuckled. Jakob stayed stony, though, gripping the sergeant's shoulder a little tighter. Soon enough, as Troy dropped away into the flitting rain, the chuckling sputtered out.

"No," said Jakob. "Really."

They were good soldiers, but when it came to the language of violence, their vocabulary was limited. They were drilled for warfare, not a street fight on a lift. Their instinct was to use their spears, or draw their swords, poor tools for such close quarters.

Jakob had always been as comfortable with a back-alley knifing as a charge of heavy horse. As the captain's hand twitched towards his sword, Jakob was already lifting his boot. Even leaning on the sergeant's shoulder, he couldn't get it near as high as he'd have liked, but it caught the captain around the hips and made him take a step back. That was enough, since he tripped over something that wasn't there, pitched over the railing, and vanished from sight with a high scream.

In many languages a rhetorical pause can be devastating. In a fight you make every point quick as you can, hoping you'll leave your opponent unable to retort. Jakob was already ripping out his dagger to smash the pommel into the sergeant's mouth. As he dropped, coughing on his own teeth, Jakob was whipping the blade the other way. The man on his right twisted so the point missed his eye, only scraped down his cheek guard and gouged off a great flap of his face.

He stumbled back, bloody fingers clapped to the wound, fumbling for his sword with the other hand. Jakob pinned him with it half-drawn, stomped on his foot, then butted him in his bloody face, and finally swung him by his slippery breastplate, flung him into one of his comrades and—with some help from a timely invisible foot—sent the pair of them tumbling over the railing.

Brother Diaz was stumbling about in a clinch with the guard he'd been so happy to have with him. Baptiste was snarling as she stabbed a man, a dagger in each hand. Another stared at her, desperately tugging at his sword. Sunny flashed into view for an instant, heaving in a breath as she hung off his arm. Jakob stepped forwards, rammed his elbow into the man's throat, and dropped him, clawing at his neck.

Three guards lay mangled about Vigga's feet. She caught the wrist of the fourth as he tried to swing a mace at her, grabbed his helmet with the other hand, and shoved it against the back wall as it rushed past. Metal screamed, sparks flew, the man gave a shriek as a great bloody streak was painted down the masonry.

The last guard stood against the rail, one armoured arm around Brother Diaz's neck and a dagger to his throat. "Stay back!" he bellowed, spraying spit. "Stay back, you devils, or I kill him!"

"Can't advise it," snarled Vigga, letting the corpse drop, head a misshapen mass of glistening meat and twisted metal, her tattooed arm spattered red to the shoulder.

"Let's take a moment!" Jakob forced his aching fingers open to show his palms. "Let's do nothing . . . *hasty*."

Sunny appeared from nowhere, hugging the guard's forearm and sinking her teeth into his fist. With a shocked cry he fumbled his dagger and Brother Diaz tore free. When his eyes focused, it was on Vigga grabbing his breastplate with both hands and bending him back over the railing.

"Vigga!" Brother Diaz caught her elbow. "Wait!"

She showed her teeth as she pushed the man towards the ever-lengthening drop while he fumbled hopelessly at her tattooed wrists, his feet leaving the floor. "For what?"

"I order you not to hurt him!" squealed Brother Diaz. "What's happening up there? Is Empress Alexia in danger?"

The man glared at Sunny, at Brother Diaz, at Jakob, who was kneading at his throbbing knuckles. "There's nothing you can do! Your impostor shall not pollute the Serpent Throne for—"

"Oh, *fuck off*," snarled Vigga, hefting him over the rail. He gave a little disbelieving squeak, then tumbled flailing from sight.

Brother Diaz stared after him. "I said don't hurt him!"

"Shit." Vigga scratched her head. "Right. Must've forgot."

There were more guards at the top of the lift, but Sunny wasted no time on them.

Alex needed her.

She held her breath and darted sideways between the points of their levelled polearms as they roared a challenge, off the paved path and through the carefully chosen shrubs of the Hanging Gardens, towards the palace.

To no one's surprise, the trouble didn't end at the lift. Sounds of violence stabbed at her from every direction, torchlight glared as running figures clattered by beyond the trees.

Sunny had helped start two coups, and neither had been any fun at all, and this felt very similar. She stifled a burp, winced as she swallowed acid. The Pope's binding starting to tighten its grip, dragging her back to the Holy City, which was just the extra problem she needed while trying to hold her breath in the middle of a civil war.

But Alex needed her.

She passed a pair of soldiers rolling on the wet grass, struggling over a dagger. She could've tipped the balance, but which way? Who was on the right side, who the wrong, and who was she, an enemy of God, to make the call? So she tiptoed guiltily around them as they fought to the death, mouthing a silent sorry, hid behind a tree trunk long enough to take another breath and hold it, then scurried on.

The doors of the palace stood open, which seemed bad. Unguarded, which seemed worse. Sunny padded down the hallway beyond, dark portraits of gloomy Emperors and Empresses watching her pass. There was a great slick of blood partly soaked into a carpet, a wide spray across a wall then smears leading her on, trails of red footprints down the marble. That seemed, honestly, terrible.

But Alex needed her.

She found the right panel, the catches to either side, popped them open, and slipped into the darkness of one of the secret tunnels, where she could breathe again, and do another sore burp, and wipe the chilly sweat from her forehead.

Then she padded to the nearest stairway and started to climb.

Alex slithered through Duke Michael's window face first, tumbled across his desk knocking things all over the floor, and finally sprawled in a sobbing heap on his carpet.

Her lungs were on fire and her feet caked with bird droppings, every muscle quivering from the effort of clinging to the rain-greasy exterior of her own palace. Her wedding-night gown was ripped and singed and stuck to her with drizzle. Every bony spot on her body—which was pretty much all of it—was scraped raw by masonry, and where her skin wasn't torn, it was chilled to clammy gooseflesh.

She would've liked nothing more than to lie there and cry, but she was still in mortal danger, and so was Duke Michael.

She clambered up, skinned knees trembling, catching the edge of the desk with one blood-smeared hand, absently gathering the things she'd knocked from the top with the other—a quill, a stub of old candle, a sheet of parchment already written on . . .

From the Office of the Head of the Earthly Curia to His Grace Duke
Michael of Nicaea, on the Festival of Saint Jerome, the fifth of Forbearance,
My eyes and ears in the Balkans inform me that our plans have borne

fruit beyond all expectation. Duke Sabbas has joined his brothers Marcian and Constans in hell and the devils are even now conveying Princess Alexia to Troy.

This seemed at first a complication, but I begin to see in it the hand of God, for it occurs to me that an offer of royal marriage might serve to lure Duke Arcadius into a state of vulnerability. A state in which Eudoxia's students, carefully positioned beforehand, might remove him from the board.

It may be that Alexia must be crowned after all but, if so, let it be the briefest reign expediency demands.

It is in the interest of Her Holiness's Earthly Curia, and indeed the cause of humanity, that you are raised to the Serpent Throne, that the schism between the wayward Church of the East and its mother in the West is healed, and that you lead the united forces of Europe in a new crusade against the coming scourge of the elves.

I know you are a man possessed of considerable stocks of the thirteenth virtue, who will not baulk at what must be done. I pray for your success.

Needless to say, it would be best if you destroyed this letter.

Zizka

For a moment, Alex didn't even breathe. Just stared at the paper, while horror flowed to the torn tips of her fingers like ice water.

Duke Michael was in on it, the cheating *bastard*! The man who stood to gain most, in fact! Her own uncle, plotting to *kill* her! Well, he wasn't really her uncle, of course, but he didn't know that, the lying *shit*! She crushed the letter in her trembling fist, smearing it with red from her broken fingernails. And Cardinal fucking Zizka was in on it with him! She'd known the woman was a snake—

"Alex! Thank God!"

She spun to face the door, and there he was.

"We have to get you to safety!" Duke Michael held out his hand, and he looked so earnest, so honest, so worried for her, that she almost reached to take it.

"Most of the Palace Guard will still be loyal, I'm sure of it!" He took a step towards her, and she couldn't help shrinking back. "But we don't know . . ." He noticed the letter in her hand. "Who we can . . ." His eyes flicked from the crushed paper to her face. "Trust."

He looked in her eye and she looked in his. Too late to hide her shock. Too late to disguise what she'd read. In an instant, she knew . . . that he knew . . . what she knew.

"Oh." He puffed out a long-suffering sigh and swung the door shut with a final *clunk*. "Don't tell me someone taught you to read?"

The same nose, the same mouth, the same eyes, but suddenly there was no trace of kindness in his face. No trace of guilt, either. No strong feeling at all. A man unexpectedly assigned an unpleasant chore.

"I should've seen it," she whispered. "I should've guessed."

"Oh, you're being far too hard on yourself." Duke Michael stepped over to a chest where a jug and glasses stood and poured himself some wine. "After all, you're a fucking idiot. It runs in the family. Both my sisters were fools. Eudoxia, a crippled pervert obsessed with parlour tricks. Irene, a preening do-gooder without the courage to dirty her hands. And don't get me started on my nephews—spleen, avarice, vanity, and sloth. The Serpent Throne should always have been mine." He took a sip, then grunted as though he'd tasted better. "I was born in the Imperial Bedchamber, too, don't forget. Michael Pyrogennetos has a pretty ring to it, don't you think?"

"Then . . . why find me?" whispered Alex. "Why bother to bring me here—"

"I needed a decoy. Only that. I hoped you and the devils might distract Eudoxia's sons long enough for me to get a foothold in the city."

"That's how they got the papal bull . . ." muttered Alex. "You gave it to them!"

"I circulated a few copies ahead of time. You'd have made a piss-poor diversion if no one knew about you." He washed another swig of wine thoughtfully around his mouth and swallowed. "Bit inconvenient that Marcian found us so soon, mind you. I was supposed to be well out of the way by the time he tracked you down. Was going to twist my ankle falling off my horse or something." He put on a sad expression. "I can't carry on! Keep going without me, Alex!" And he chuckled, and shook his head, like this was all the height of drollery. "But it turned out pretty well, overall, I'd say, wouldn't you? I never dared dream you'd kill three of the four. Well done!" He raised his glass and knocked it off with a toss of his head. "And *then*, serendipity, you actually got to Troy, and made the perfect bait for my last and most dangerous rival. I was sure I'd have to fight another bloody civil war against Arcadius." And he slung his glass back on the chest where it rattled around on its base. "I can't tell you the effort you've saved me there."

"Delighted to be of *fucking* service," snarled Alex.

Michael's smile faded. "Well, did you really think for one moment . . . that we could have a scrap of rubbish from the gutters of the Holy City sitting on the Serpent Throne? A thief and beggar being mother to a dynasty? A piece of shit as Empress of Troy?" He drew his sword. "Really, really, *no*."

He took a step towards Alex and she shrank back, not that there was any-where to shrink to but into the desk. She clawed at the top for any kind of weapon, but all her grasping fingers found was the quill she'd just put there.

"Sorry to say . . ." Duke Michael came on another step. "When it comes to a fight . . ." He lifted his blade. "The pen really isn't mightier than the sword—"

There was a *thud* and he stumbled forwards. He spun around, slashing wildly at the air. Alex caught a sudden and extremely welcome glimpse of Sunny, ducking low as the blade whipped over her head, then vanishing again.

Duke Michael snarled as he dropped into a crouch, eyes darting about the room. "You fucking—oof!" He bent over, eyes bulging. Alex would've very much liked to follow up with a boot of her own, visible or not, but the point of his sword was still flailing around dangerously, and a moment later she felt her wrist caught, so the best she could do was throw the quill at him as she stumbled out into the corridor and watch it flutter wildly through the air as the door slammed shut behind her. Sunny appeared, turning the key in the lock then flinging it away.

"You came back for me?" whispered Alex.

"Of course I did."

"I don't deserve you."

"Of course you don't," said Sunny, and she pulled Alex down the corridor.

The Right Side and the Wrong

Vigga smacked a guard over the helmet with his own sword so hard the blade broke, the end bouncing away across the cobbles. Here was the problem with swords. Well, that and the silly prices and the endless oiling and polishing. Vigga had always preferred something with more heft. She ducked as another guard swung at her, wind of his halberd ripping at her hair. That definitely had more heft, so she smashed him in the mouth with her broken hilt and left his head flopping, tore the halberd from his limp hand as he fell, and flung it point-first at a third man. He got his shield up in time to knock it wide, send it ripping through the bushes, but by then Vigga was on him, punched him in one side then the other and left him tottering, picked him up by his dented breastplate, turned him upside down, and rammed his head into the ground.

Maybe they deserved it and maybe they didn't, but that was a question to be asked after they were dead or better yet never asked at all. Life is complicated, but a fight has to be simple. The moment you spend mulling the rights and wrongs will be the moment you get a spear in your tit. *Regrets are a wonderful thing after a fight*, Olaf always used to say, *'cause they mean you lived through it.*

"Come on!" Brother Diaz was running on through the slackening drizzle towards the palace, a jagged shadow in the gathering dusk, lights burning at its many windows, Saint Natalia's Flame still glowing blue at its very top.

"Is he actually leading?" grunted Baptiste, wiping a dagger on her sleeve.

"Sticking *his* neck out!" Vigga barked a laugh. "Who'd have thought?" And she snatched up a spear and hurried grinning after him.

Made her think of those heady days, before the bite, when the world seemed bright somehow, and full of chances. Running up the beach with the old crew, taste of the sea in her mouth, smell of the wind in her face, feel of the axe-haft in her fists. Laughing as she pushed her hands into the stolen silver, cool coins tickling between her fingers. Chuckling as she killed a pig just 'cause it was alive. Smiling as she stabbed that fallen monk and he moaned and crawled and bled all over the spilled flour on the bakery floor, white as fresh snowfall. Watching as they herded the squealing nuns into the chapel and barred the doors. Frowning as the others tossed their torches onto the thatched roof. Tossing her torch as well 'cause that's what you did. She'd asked Olaf if they deserved it, and he'd shrugged. *If they didn't, they could stop us.* Staring as Harald pawed at her with one hand while he held his guts in with the other, bleeding a pink slick over the salt sand, trying to say something but only coughing blood, coughing blood halfway back across the sea till he stopped coughing and they rolled him over the side, out of sight of land, the best of them unmarked and unremembered. Sniffing as they divided his share, Vigga's sight swimming with tears as she looked down at her handful of coins, wondering whether it had been worth it.

She felt tears on her cheeks now, and wondered if there had never been a better time, only dead friends and burned nuns and spilled guts and worthless coins and blood on the white.

Had things always been bad?

Had she always been bad?

Even before the bite?

"You all right?" said Jakob, limping up beside her, gripping his leg.

"Me?" She wiped her face on the back of her hand. "'Course." She made herself laugh. "Just rain, isn't it?" Though the rain had stopped.

There'd been fighting in front of the palace. Dead guards lay everywhere. She hadn't killed these ones, she didn't think, though when she saw corpses, she always did wonder. The smell of blood had the wolf up on tippy-toes, spilling slobber behind her ribs again, and she slapped at her breastbone and slapped it back mewling and showed it in no uncertain terms who wore the muzzle.

More guards running towards the palace now, armour glinting in the light of their torches, and you had to hand it to these bastards, they surely kept coming.

"You think these ones are friendly?" muttered Brother Diaz.

"Wouldn't bet your life on it." Vigga jerked her head towards the big lighthouse. "Get up there and find our girls, Jakob. I'll make sure no one bothers you down here."

Jakob leaned back, teeth gritted, to look up towards Saint Natalia's Flame. "Those steps might finally do for me—"

"But it'd be a shame if I got all the way to Alex and ended up killing her." Vigga shrugged. "I mean, I've nearly killed her twice already."

"She has a point." Baptiste pushed Jakob towards the palace with one elbow and stepped up on Vigga's left. "I'll watch your back."

Brother Diaz clenched his jaw as he stepped up on Vigga's right. "And I'll watch . . . the other side of your back?"

Vigga laughed as she shoved the spear into his hand, threw one arm around Baptiste's shoulders and the other arm around his.

Reminded her of those high times, before the bite, when the world was young and brimming with adventure. Just her and a few good oarmates against the odds. And she gave Baptiste a squeeze, and kissed Brother Diaz on the cheek. Not in a sex way, in a comradeship way, although thinking about it, the way his beard tickled her lips, maybe a bit in a sex way after all.

"Never dull, eh?" Vigga watched the guards close in, clenching her fists. "*Never* dull!"

Alex crept like a thief through her own palace, aching with fatigue and trembling with fear, tiptoeing after Sunny as she blinked in and out of sight, from one doorway to another, one corner to another, one staircase to another, picking a careful path downwards.

"Where are we going?" croaked Alex.

"Kitchens," whispered Sunny as she eased to a corner to peer down another flight of steps. "Lots of guards out front. Some have turned on you." She paused. "Most, maybe."

"All?"

Sunny pressed the tip of her tongue into that little gap between her front teeth.

Alex swallowed. "How do we tell who's loyal?"

"The disloyal ones will be trying to *kill you*."

Alex swallowed again. "Probably best we avoid them all."

"That's what I was thinking," whispered Sunny. There was no marble or gilding down here, behind the scenes, only a smell of old food. Must've been the staircase the servants struggled up with Alex's wine, or fruit, or clean clothes, or hot bathwater. She only now realised that she'd never given much thought to where it came from. Strange, even if you grow up in a slum, how quickly you get used to being pampered.

"What about the others?" whispered Alex.

"On their way. Jakob won't give up."

"Long as his knees hold out." Alex's own skinned knees were close to giving way and hers were about a century younger than his. "Balthazar might be some help, I guess." They crept from the bottom of the steps and down a shadowy hallway with walls of old bare brick. Black mould flared from the corner of a rotten window. "The man's a prick but he knows his magic."

"The man *is* a prick," said Sunny. "Which is why he stayed on the boat."

"He stayed on the *boat*?"

"Vigga came. And Baptiste. And Brother Diaz."

"Great. When the werewolf rips me apart the monk can say a prayer over the bits."

Sunny shrugged. "Better than no prayer, I guess."

Alex stared at her for a moment. Then she shrugged, too. "I guess."

Fires burned low along one side of the kitchen—a long vaulted hall with a ceiling stained by decades of grease. A corpse lay face down over a stove, top half-cooked, legs draped across the floor. Another had burst open as if dropped from a great height, guts sprayed everywhere.

Alex covered her mouth as she crept on after Sunny. "Why did they kill them all?"

"Because it makes me feel *powerful*." Cleofa, who used to pick Alex's fingernails so carefully she hardly felt it, stepped through the far door with Athenais behind, blood smeared down one side of her beautiful dress.

"Run!" hissed Sunny, blinking out of sight.

Cleofa spoke a word and fog whipped from nowhere in a spiral cloud, a crouching shadow in its centre.

"There!" Athenais clawed at the air and a blast ripped the mist into swirling tatters. Sunny groaned as she crashed into the wall in a hail of loose food, clattering cutlery, shattering crockery. Alex gasped, splinters raking her shoulder, stinging her cheek. She heaved Sunny up, the two of them scrambling together through a doorway as another gust tore at Alex's gown, a barrel bursting against the doorframe and showering them both with ale. They stumbled into a hallway, lined down one side with shelves holding hundreds of bottles of wine.

"Your Resplendence!" Zenonis stood grinning, no more than twenty paces off. "The stores are for servants *only*."

She raised her hands, heat shimmering around them. Alex caught one of the shelves, shrieking as she hauled with all her weight and brought it over to crash against the opposite wall, bottles shattering.

Fire blazed up, a withering plume of it. Alex was just opening her mouth to scream as Sunny bundled her through a door, flames surging past the fallen shelves and licking hungrily around them as she kicked it shut, heaved across a bolt.

"Oh God!" Sunny's back was on fire and Alex beat wildly at it, trying to slap the flames out with her hands.

"Oh *God*!" She realised one torn tail of her gown was on fire, too, for the second time that evening, and she yelped as Sunny slapped at that, the pair of them squealing and spinning and slapping till the fire was out, ash fluttering around them and Alex's nose stung by the oily smell of char.

"Oh God . . ." There was a fork stuck in her shoulder. Not that deep. But definitely stuck. Blood ran in streaks as she gritted her teeth and eased it out, her burned palms singing with pain, her arm covered in bloody little cuts and scratches, riddled like a pincushion with slivers of wood, with shards of broken crockery.

"There's a passage," gasped Sunny. They were in some panelled boot room, stools and brushes and polish everywhere, shoes stacked up on racks. "Somewhere here . . ." She fumbled at one of the panels, teeth bared.

"Sunny . . ." muttered Alex. She could hear the handmaidens out in the corridor, a crash as they ripped the shelves away, a tinkling of breaking glass. Sunny limped to the next panel, clutching at her ribs. "Sunny!"

"I *know*!" It popped open and Sunny darted in, Alex scrambling through behind her, shoving the door shut. A chink of light crawled across Sunny's bloody face as she backed into the darkness, breathing hard.

"Do they know about these tunnels?" whispered Alex.

"Shush." Sunny narrowed her eyes as she listened. The faintest scraping, then louder. Closer. Footsteps.

"Oh God," whispered Alex. "They know about these tunnels."

"May God have mercy on their souls." Brother Diaz made the circle over the dead and, in one case, dying, as the last of the guards choked on his own blood.

"Mercy's overrated." Vigga wrinkled her nose at her broken spear haft, then tossed it into the bushes. "Souls, too, if you ask me."

"May God have mercy on them anyway," said Brother Diaz as the gurgle became a wheeze, then stopped entirely. "And ours, too . . ."

Wasn't long ago, if asked to guess at the villains of the piece, he would've confidently pointed out the werewolf, the cursed knight, and the elf. Sometimes it's difficult to tell who's on the right side, and who the wrong—

He heard a desperate cry and spun about to see Lady Severa tottering down the palace steps, her eyes wild and a smear of fresh blood across her cheek.

Brother Diaz caught her as she almost collapsed into his arms, gasping for breath. "Treachery . . . the handmaidens . . . the blackest of Black Art . . . Empress Alexia is in danger!"

"Don't worry." In spite of the circumstances, Brother Diaz managed to feel slightly pleased that for once he wasn't the one panicking. "You're safe now."

"No one's safe!" Severa struggled up, catching Vigga's wrist. "But . . . you're hurt."

Vigga touched bloody fingertips to her bloody hair and laughed. "Believe me, I've had worse."

"And given it, too," said Baptiste, staring at the human wreckage scattered about the palace doors.

"No, let me." Severa reached up to touch Vigga's face, but at the last moment twisted her wrist and nimbly flicked her forehead instead.

There was a puzzled silence. With Vigga's back to him, Brother Diaz couldn't quite tell what had happened. But Severa's expression had changed. No longer fearful, or alarmed. She wiped the blood from beneath her nose, as calmly assured as she had been when they first met her on the docks. Vigga slowly turned.

There was a needle stuck in her forehead, with a little square of cloth on it, and stitched into the cloth, a single letter in an alphabet Brother Diaz didn't recognise. A *rune*, one might almost have called it.

Vigga spoke, and Lady Severa spoke, their lips moving in time. "It would be best," they said, both with eyes narrowed in exactly the same way, "if you laid down any weapons."

It was ever so strange, to hear Vigga speak in the cultured tones of a lady of the Trojan Empire.

Ever so strange, and ever so chilling.

Jakob paused on the landing, hardly knowing which aching leg to grab first, and ended up wedging his sword under one arm so he could grab them both, grinding one aching thumb into a cramping thigh, the other into a throbbing hip. The man they once called the Hammer of the Elves, the Judgement of Livonia, the Terror of the Albigensians, laying down his arms so he could massage his legs.

"Some champion," he hissed, through his eternally gritted teeth.

Why couldn't it have been Paris, with that sprawling pile where the rulers of Frankia laid their heads? Hardly a step in the whole place. Or Burgundy, where the lame Emperor David had built his grand suite on the ground floor, and made the servants sleep upstairs.

"But nooooooo—" he growled, cut off in a gasp at a savage twinge through one knee.

It had to be *Troy*. The most vertical city in the known world.

They didn't even have to send warriors. Steps were enough to defeat him.

He looked on, up the grand staircase, one pitiless marble enemy after another, until it switched back and divided on the floor above, switched back again and came together on the floor above that. God, was there no end to it? A question he'd been asking himself for a century or more.

He should've thrown his sword in the sea and stayed on the boat with Balthazar. He should've stayed in the Holy City, for that matter, with his feet in warm water and something easy to chew.

"But nooooooo—" he growled, cut off in a groan at a brutal spasm through his back.

He had to find more unwinnable battles to lose. Limp on forever up this crooked road to nowhere. Wrestle with himself to an endless, agonised impasse in his efforts to redeem the irredeemable—

A crash echoed down the stairway and he nearly fumbled his sword as he pushed away from the wall and ended up in a trembling crouch, trying not to breathe noisily.

He heard voices. Women's voices, maybe? Angry voices, certainly.

He wiped sweat on the back of his sleeve. Wrapped his fingers around his sword's hilt once again.

It fit there, as it always did, like a key into a lock. He set his aching jaw and squared his crooked shoulders. He reached the sad realisation he'd reached a thousand times before: he wasn't really *him* without a sword in his hand.

He pressed on. One boot after another. One step after another. They were like an army. Together they might seem unconquerable, but each man was just one man. Each step was just one step.

He left them beaten behind him, as he'd left so many enemies ruined in his wake.

So many friends.

Sunny eased open the secret door and peered into the private chapel.

"Careful," whispered Alex. She wasn't looking her best—panting for breath, hair stuck to her sweaty face, gown singed and torn, splinter-riddled, fork-stuck, blood-sticky right arm clasped to her chest.

Sunny would've liked to give her an encouraging smile, but she was no good at them, and likely wasn't looking great, either.

"I'm always careful," she said, and held her breath, gripping her bruised side with her burned hand.

She slithered through the doorway and across the room, its walls covered in watchful little icons of the saints. They loved an icon, here in Troy.

Sunny didn't mind them on their own, but they put her off rather as a crowd.

Reminded her of the crowd at the circus, jeering and throwing coins.

The sun had almost set beyond the windows, down to a red clipping over the western sea, and the Imperial Bedchamber was full of tricking shadows. Some of the hangings were blackened by fire and there were dots and spatters all across the marble, as if someone had spilled a cart of butcher's offcuts.

"What is this?" muttered Sunny. "Is it meat?"

"It's my husband," whispered Alex, peering over her shoulder.

"Oh." What else was there to say? Sunny had to pick her spots as she crossed the room so as not to step in all the mush, angling her feet this way or that, going up on tiptoes. "Is that an ear?"

"Oh God." Alex put the back of her hand to her mouth as she followed. "Oh *God*." As she stepped in something, bare foot squeaking on wet marble.

"There may have been messier wedding nights," murmured Sunny, "but this is right up there."

Alex snatched Arcadius's marriage tunic from a chair as she passed, grunting as she pushed her bloody arm into the embroidered sleeve. It was too big for her, and covered in flowers in golden thread, glittering brightly even in the darkness.

"What?" she hissed as she rolled the overlong sleeves up.

"Doesn't exactly fade into the background, does it?" whispered Sunny.

"If it's all the same to you, I'm going to die dressed."

The door was ajar, the darkened hallway beyond empty.

"Where do we go?" whispered Alex.

"Make for the main staircase, try and get down that way."

"Won't they be watching for that?"

"Sometimes people look everywhere but the most obvious places."

"Sounds thin. Sounds thin as fuck."

Sunny glanced around at Alex and shrugged. "You could stay here. With your husband."

Alex swallowed. "Main staircase, then?"

"Good idea." Sunny crept to the steps and peered down. Let go her breath to beckon Alex over, caught her hand as she came close, easing down the steps—

She stopped dead.

"What is it?" whispered Alex.

"Shush."

She heard a board creak below.

"Oh God," whispered Alex.

Then voices. "She didn't come this way." One of the handmaidens. Sunny had never been sure about those girls but lately she had *really* gone off them. "She must be above."

"We herd her, then, upwards. Her and the elf bitch."

"Rude," muttered Sunny, though far from the worst she'd ever heard.

"She's a tricky one," sang out from below, "but I can find her."

"Find her, then." Duke Michael's voice. Sunny really wished she'd hit him harder. Maybe with an axe. "Sooner or later, they'll run out of tower."

"Oh God . . ." whispered Alex. She was backing away, in a tunic you really couldn't miss, leaving bloody footprints on each step, but Sunny didn't have the time or the equipment to mop up after her.

"Back," she hissed. "Up!"

"Up?" Alex stared towards the next flight of stairs. The last one, leading to the throne room.

"Or you could stay here. With your husband."

Alex swallowed. "Up, then?"

Release the Leftovers

Brother Diaz tumbled sweating over the threshold, slipped as he turned, seized one of the doors while Baptiste grabbed the other, both straining against the ancient wood, both growling with the effort, both with boots sliding on marble polished by centuries of pilgrims' feet.

He snatched a glance down the darkened avenue that led from palace to Basilica, saw Vigga approaching with an elegant step quite unlike her usual stomp, Lady Severa at her shoulder. As if their odds against a werewolf and a sorceress hadn't been impossible enough, it looked as if they'd picked up a company of sympathetic Palace Guard on the way.

"They're coming!" he gasped.

"I *fucking* noticed!" snarled Baptiste, elaborate hinges squealing in protest.

"Push!" groaned Brother Diaz, setting a shoulder to his door as it began to shift.

Baptiste twisted around to press her back against hers. "What the *fuck* does it look like I'm doing?"

"Don't swear . . . in *church*!"

The two doors met with a clatter and Baptiste slammed three iron bolts across while Brother Diaz hauled up the great wooden bar that stood against the frame. It had the first line of the "Our Saviour" carved into the back, but that made no noticeable difference to its weight.

"Help . . ." he wheezed, just about getting the end off the ground, every joint trembling with effort as he staggered one way, then back the other, "me . . ."

"What the *fuck* . . ." grunted Baptiste, catching the other end a moment before it toppled and crushed him flat. "Does it look . . ." hefting it onto her shoulder and bending at the knees, "like I'm *doing*?"

They heaved it up together, managed to guide it sideways as it fell, Brother Diaz snatching his hands away as it dropped into the wrought-iron brackets. He was about to flop gasping against it, utterly spent, when a great thud rattled the doors and made him stumble back.

"Will it hold?" he whispered, shuffling away as dust filtered down.

"Against Vigga?" Baptiste shuffled away with him. "I wouldn't want to bet your life on it."

Another blow echoed through the Basilica and made Brother Diaz jump, the bar trembling in its brackets.

"Who beats on the gates of God's own house?"

He reeled around to stare into the lined face of Patriarch Methodius, in full regalia as Supreme Head of the Eastern Church, the very embodiment of spiritual authority. He was accompanied by a retinue of two canon priests, a trio of monks whose lips moved constantly in silent prayer, a boy holding a giant candle and another struggling with a giant, jewel-studded copy of the scriptures.

Behind them, scared little knots of nuns, servants, and bureaucrats were cowering beneath the icons. People who'd fled to the Basilica seeking sanctuary from the violence that had broken out in the heart of Troy. People who'd had the very same idea as Brother Diaz, in other words.

"Your Beatitude!" He felt a surge of relief strong enough almost to produce tears.

"What brings you here in such disarray, my son?"

"Desperate need!" Brother Diaz was obliged to plant his hands on his knees as he struggled to get a proper breath. "Fighting, in the Hanging Gardens. In the palace itself!" As if to add urgency, the door shuddered at another blow. "Treachery and treason, against the rightful Empress Alexia, crowned by you in this very Basilica only hours ago. Lady Severa pursues us and she's . . . she's . . ."

"A very good liar," muttered Baptiste.

"A sorceress!"

Many of the refugees shrank back still further as the word rang out, but the Patriarch looked entirely unmoved by this horrifying revelation. "I am well aware."

"Wait . . ." Brother Diaz swallowed. "What?"

"Lady Severa was the first of Empress Eudoxia's apprentices. Many more followed."

The door rocked again, even more violently. Baptiste gave it a nervous glance as splinters scattered from the shuddering brackets.

"And you are . . ." Brother Diaz swallowed again. "*Fine* with that?"

Methodius narrowed his eyes. "My predecessor, Patriarch Nectarius, was a man of the highest moral calibre. When Eudoxia seized the throne, he objected in the strongest terms. His tomb, downstairs in the crypt, is empty. There was nothing left to bury. When I was selected to succeed him, I was left with no choice but to do what was . . . expedient. Something you should understand only too well."

Brother Diaz cleared his throat. It was true that, when it came to an impassioned stance against the use of Black Art, he didn't find himself on quite the firm theological ground he used to. The door quivered again, and he wondered whether he might be able to hide behind that giant book. He decided yes. But not for long.

"And Empress Eudoxia," the Patriarch went on, "for all her manifold and manifest faults, kept the Black Art in the Athenaeum . . ." he indicated the door, even now shuddering at another blow, "and left the house of God to God. And to his properly appointed servants."

"The ones she didn't murder," said Brother Diaz.

"Well, while those ones are doubtless adorning heaven, they really were left unable to influence earthly events one way or another, wouldn't you say?"

Brother Diaz was experiencing a familiar sinking feeling. "Your Beatitude, all I want—all *any* of us want—is to see the Saved once more united against the enemies of God," he was aware of a needy whine in his voice but couldn't seem to get rid of it, "the Eastern Church joined with the Western as one family—"

"You would see the Eastern Church *subordinated* to the Western!" thundered the Patriarch, in full self-righteous sermonising style. "You would see us bow down to *women*. Be led in prayer by *women*. Be christened, confirmed, and buried by *women*! You would see us kneel before a *little girl*! A puppet in stolen papal white!"

"Our own Saviour *was a woman*!" said Brother Diaz, moving from wounded disappointment towards nettled indignance. Progress of a kind, perhaps. "God's daughter, who gave her life for our salvation." He pointed at the expanse of stained glass above the altar. "She's *on your window*."

"And the window is the proper place for her," said the Patriarch, without so much as a pause, "not dictating Church policy! *No*, Brother Diaz!" He raised his arms towards the thousand thousand images that covered every wall. "The angels look down in despair upon your betrayal of our faith! I will not suffer it! Lady Severa has given me assurances as to the status of the Eastern Church." And he waved his priests forwards as another booming blow echoed down the nave. "Open the doors, my friends!"

Brother Diaz stopped one of the priests dead with a hand on the chest. "The devils are at your gates!" he snarled, spurred finally from nettled indignation to outraged disgust. "And you'd invite them *in*?"

"The devils *are already* within!" bellowed Methodius. "I would admit the broom to sweep them out!"

"Oh, *fuck this*." And Brother Diaz punched the Patriarch right on the point of his chin. He toppled straight back, his expansive headdress bouncing off and rolling down the aisle, his arms spread out wide, just like those of the Saviour on the window above.

Everyone stared, astonished. No one more so than Brother Diaz himself.

"I knocked out the Patriarch of Troy," he whispered.

"I saw." Baptiste peered over his shoulder at the stricken Pontiff. "Maybe there's hope for you yet."

There was an almighty crash behind them and Brother Diaz spun to see the bar, already bending, shatter in a shower of loose fibres, one of the brackets ripping free and clanging away among the pews.

The doors wobbled open and Vigga stepped through, bloody fists clenched, that dangling rune still pinned to her forehead. Lady Severa followed a few paces behind, matching her stride precisely, demonstrating the same impeccable dignity with which she'd followed Alex down the very same aisle to her coronation that afternoon. Palace Guards spread out around the far end of the nave and worked their way through the benches, crushing any meagre hopes of escape.

"Should've stayed on the boat . . ." hissed Baptiste, backing off towards the altar. "*Knew* I should've stayed on the boat . . ."

"I don't suppose . . ." called Brother Diaz, weakly, as he followed her, "if I said we'd taken sanctuary in the house of God . . ."

Vigga and Severa spoke at once, with the same neat little smile. "I have honestly never taken my faith all that seriously, and I doubt your Viking friend goes even as far as lip service."

"She has been baptised, in fact," said Brother Diaz.

"Twice," offered Baptiste.

"Even so. I doubt this would be the first church she has desecrated." The Patriarch's entourage had backed away, now the boy dropped his candle and ran for it, the rest of them scattering beyond the altar, where the nuns and servants had gathered fearfully like sheep herded into a pen. "Now," said Lady Severa and Vigga, together, "I think it would be best if you surrendered."

"We can expect good treatment, can we?" asked Baptiste.

"Let's say better than if you don't surrender."

Brother Diaz swallowed. "A quick death, then."

"It sounds a cliché, but when you've seen the slow deaths I have . . ." Severa and Vigga both puffed out their cheeks. "You really start to see the value."

Vigga stepped forwards, over the supine Patriarch.

"Should've stayed in the Holy City . . ." muttered Baptiste.

Brother Diaz winced, shrinking back, turning his face away—

There was a blast of wind from nowhere, Vigga's hair was blown wildly around, and the needle and its rune-stitched cloth suddenly whipped from her forehead and were whisked away on the breeze.

"It works!" someone yelled. One of the guards had sprung from among the pews, heels of his hands pressed together and thrust forwards. "Earth and air! A common structure to all matter!" The voice, not to mention the tone, sounded strangely familiar. "I am a *genius!*"

For perhaps the first time ever, Baptiste looked surprised. "Balthazar?" she asked.

The guard pulled off his helmet and pushed back damp hair to reveal the delighted face of one of Europe's foremost necromancers. "Saving the day once again!"

"Why are you wet?"

"The ship cast off. I was obliged to swim."

"Wha 'appen?" Vigga rubbed at her forehead like a woman waking from a drunken slumber. "I dreamed I was a lady." She peered down baffled at the Patriarch, lying between her boots. "Who's this bastard?"

"You came *back*?" snarled Severa, glaring at Balthazar in furious disbelief. "Why?"

He gave an airy wave. "Call it a matter . . . of professional pride."

Baptiste slid a dagger from her boot, another from her back somewhere, and dropped into a waiting crouch. "You couldn't let me have the last word, could you?"

"I absolutely could *not*," said Balthazar. "Mistress Ullasdottr?"

Vigga glanced over at him. "I like the sound o' that."

He narrowed his eyes at the guards. "Would you mind giving me some corpses to work with?"

Vigga held one fist with the other, cracked her knuckles, and showed her pointed teeth. "Oh, that'd be my fucking *pleasure.*"

Alex stumbled from the stairway and blinked in the glare at the top of the Pharos for the second time that evening, a good deal more battered, burned, sweat-stuck, and bloodstained than she'd been the first time and at about the same level of mortal terror. Saint Natalia's Flame still blazed in its brazier, bringing a merry sparkle to her dead husband's gaudy wedding tunic. So it looked like she'd die warm, at least.

"We've run out of tower," she mumbled.

Sunny scurried to one of the archways and peered over the parapet. "Maybe we could climb down the side—"

Alex hardly knew whether to laugh or cry at the thought of doing it again. "They'd catch me for sure." And she preferred to die somewhere with a floor. "You go." She put her hand on Sunny's shoulder, blood crusted under the nails. She tried to smile, but it wasn't easy. "You can't save everyone."

"I just want to save you. We can still—"

"You've done more than I could ask for. Far more than I deserve."

Sunny kept shaking her head. "No."

"Please. Let me be noble. This once." She held up her chin, hoping Baron Rikard would've been proud of her bearing. "Let me . . . deserve it. What I stole. Her birthright. Her name."

Sunny shrugged her off. "I said *no*."

"Aw, *please* don't argue." Cleofa came grinning up the steps. So at least someone was enjoying themselves.

"We will *happily* kill you both." Athenais stepped from behind her. "In fact, we might have to insist on it."

Sunny sprang, blinking out of sight, but Cleofa spoke that word again, the flame flickering as mist formed from nowhere. Athenais barked like an angry dog, and Alex stumbled back as Sunny crashed into the pillar beside her and crumpled on the ground in a groaning heap.

"An elf," said Placidia, sauntering between the other two, frosty smoke curling from her blue lips. "Who can go unseen."

"We should take it apart," said Zenonis, coming last into the gallery to complete the handmaidens' reunion, "and see how it works."

Alex stepped in front of Sunny, fists clenched. "Let her go. Please—"

"You're in no position to negotiate," said Cleofa, lip curled with disgust.

"Empress of vermin," spat Athenais as they closed in.

"The only question—" said Zenonis.

Placidia held up her hand, chilly rime smoking on her fingers. "Is whether we should freeze you like your erstwhile husband—"

Zenonis waved towards Saint Natalia's Flame and Alex shrank back as it flared up brighter than ever. "Or burn you to a greasy cinder."

"We could throw her from the tower?" offered Cleofa.

"Let the ground do the work."

"And we needn't dirty our hands with her."

Placidia frowned towards the night sky beyond the archways. "Do you hear that?"

And suddenly the gallery was alive with flapping bats.

Alex clung to Sunny as the tiny beasts circled, tighter and tighter, the four sorceresses ducking and slapping and cursing at them, until they formed a fluttering knot directly in front of her, and became, in an instant, Baron Rikard.

The vampire raised one urbane eyebrow at Sunny, sprawled on the ground, Alex, crouching over her, then at the four sorceresses, ready and willing to unleash all the powers of hell against them. He issued a long-suffering sigh.

"Ladies," he said.

"Fucking took you long enough," whispered Alex.

"I believe I have told you it is *always* considered rude to arrive early to a party."

"The etiquette instructor," hissed Zenonis, in a ready crouch, heat shimmering from her fingers.

"How apposite," said the baron, "since a lesson in manners appears to be necessary." He calmly watched the four handmaidens spread out in a crescent around him. "I take it you are the missing members of Empress Eudoxia's coven?"

"We were once her students," snarled Athenais.

Placidia proudly tossed her head, frosty mist shaking from her hair. "And now we are adepts of Black Art!"

"So you think you know darkness?" The baron gave a sad smile, showing the very points of his teeth. "Then it is only fair that I warn you . . ." There was something fascinating in his tone. Alex couldn't look away from him. "That in the eastern part of Poland . . ." It was as if a light shone from him, so bright and beautiful that even Saint Natalia's Flame seemed dim in its presence. "Where my wife once had her estates . . ." Alex stared, mouth open, desperate to hear each word, each syllable, each breath and inflection. "They serve a certain kind of dumpling . . ."

Jakob hobbled into the throne room, each breath caught between growl and whimper. He half-leaned on, half-collapsed against the nearest pillar, forearm on the cool marble, gasping as he shook one leg out, then the other. He tried to wriggle away from the aches in his hips, and failed, as he'd been failing for years. Finally, he blew out a long breath, and wiped the sweat from his prickling face, and frowned towards the Serpent Throne.

"How very unsurprising," he grunted.

Duke Michael sat at ease where only Emperors sit, his drawn sword placed point down while he turned the pommel back and forth between finger and thumb. "A good twist, once revealed, should seem obvious all along. Should seem . . . inevitable, even."

"The uncle?" Jakob gave a weary snort. "That's your twist? It's always the fucking uncle."

"You must have seen it coming, then?"

"Well . . . no." Jakob had sworn an oath of honesty, after all. "But I've always been suspicious of good people and trusted the evil ones. Maybe I understand them better."

"It's a very human failing," said Duke Michael. "Virtue, honesty, and forgiveness. All fine in theory but just so bloody *boring*. Give me ambition, deceit, and revenge! There's a glamour to them, isn't there?" He gave the serpent-carved arm of the throne a fond stroke with his fingertips. "Deplore the tyrants and conquerors all we like, mouth along with the platitudes with the rest of the hypocrites, but do you think, alone in the darkness, men dream of *doing good*?" He looked up at Jakob. "Perhaps some do. Brother Diaz, and his harmless ilk. But I can tell you I don't. And I'm damn sure you don't, either. Perhaps the lesson is . . . we can't ever really change who we are."

"I've been trying. For a long time."

"Any success?"

"To my great regret, not much."

Duke Michael smiled. "Show me a man who regrets nothing and I'll show you a man who's achieved nothing."

"Where's Alex?"

"Upstairs. Her handmaidens are seeing to her every need. And the rest of your lost, cursed, and damned congregation?"

"Held up below. I'll have to do." Jakob tried to make that last phrase a growling threat, but he ran out of breath and it finished in an old man's wheeze.

Duke Michael didn't laugh, though, as he stood. "The infamous Jakob of Thorn? Grandmaster and Witch Hunter, crusader and Templar, champion and executioner? Who could be disappointed in such an opponent?" He began to come down the steps, sword in hand. "I mean to say . . . how many deaths are you responsible for? A thousand?"

Jakob said nothing, only pushed himself from the pillar.

"Two thousand?"

Jakob said nothing, only squared his shoulders.

"*Ten* thousand?"

Jakob said nothing, only limped towards the throne.

"And there I was . . ." Duke Michael sank into a ready stance. "Thinking *I* might be the villain."

Vigga struck a guard with such colossal force his own mace was left buried in the front of his crumpled helmet. Balthazar caught him, metaphorically, before he hit the ground and, to the consternation of his companions, whisked him back to his feet like a puppet with every string pulled at once.

He proved challenging to operate with his face entirely caved in, but served as an effective meat shield as other guards tried to stab Vigga with their spears, and after a few thrusts ended up a waddling mace-headed pincushion, broken hafts sticking out of him in every direction.

By then Vigga had generated several more corpses and Balthazar was already tossing them leaking, hopping, and in one case biting into the fray. Ah, the joy of the freshly deceased! He could acquire a going concern, as it were, and launch them directly into action. No risk of them falling to pieces in transit, and since they had been intent on violence prior to expiry, it really was the simplest thing to redirect the echo of those urges towards their own comrades.

So it was they fought a running battle through the Hanging Gardens, down tree-lined ways, between neat rows of shadowed greenery, over picturesque bridges and around splashing fountains. They spattered one of the wonders of the world with gore, rent the dusk with screams of fury, groans of pain, wails of horror. They fought through darkness lit by torches, by fire, by flashes of magic. They fought to the death and, in many cases, beyond. They drove Lady Severa and her guards across the top of the Pillar, from the doors of the Basilica towards the darkened outline of the Athenaeum, the dead hopping, crawling, lurching, and lumbering after.

When Balthazar first encountered Vigga, he had considered her a barbarian one cut above, or possibly one below, an animal. But costly experience had forced him to concede that, in savage circumstances, a barbarian is just the ticket. Demanding from people qualities entirely opposite to their nature is a sure road to disappointment. Vigga was entirely fearless, unshakably loyal, and excelled beyond any living thing Balthazar had encountered in causing violent death. Once you scraped away their mutual repugnance and focused on the professional, they suited each other splendidly.

Vigga turned enemies into corpses, and Balthazar turned corpses into friends.

She hurled a man bodily through the air where he crashed into a tree trunk, spraying splinters. Balthazar snatched him up, but he was crooked as a chicken leg, his pelvis pulverised, and in any case Severa slashed furiously at the air and sliced him and another walking corpse in half at the waist. One pair of legs dropped instantly while the other waddled on a few steps. The corresponding top half, meanwhile, clawed its way through the grass towards her wheezing, for some reason, "I found one, I found one," and unwinding a trail of glistening innards.

Baptiste and Brother Diaz skulked along behind, awestruck. Or possibly horror-struck, but really, is there a significant difference? Balthazar had never felt more powerful, his heart pumping scalding steam, his thoughts fast as searing lightning, his senses honed to a razor's edge.

On the lawn before the Athenaeum, Lady Severa spun, searing the darkness with a jet of fire so hot it cooked the stripe of grass beneath it brown. Baptiste gasped, Brother Diaz squealed in horror, but, for once, Balthazar had come prepared. He stepped in front of the helpless pair, whipping out his paper, its circles inscribed using borrowed draughtsman's instruments.

He mouthed the five-part incantation, never halting, never doubting, and Severa's flames were sucked into the centre of the diagram, the runes beginning to glow through the back of the paper. Balthazar's fingertips smarted from the heat, but he refused to let go. Severa's sorcery was raw and furious, but he controlled it, he contained it, he *overcame* it! She might be a true artist, all instinct and passion, but he was a calculating engineer and composed his counterspell as a spring: the more force it absorbed, the more it would deliver. So when the onslaught was finally exhausted, his ears still roaring with its noise, his throat still smarting with the tang of sulphur, he merely had to speak one word and the fire burst from between his hands with thrice the intensity.

Severa's eyes went wide for an instant before she dipped her head and pressed her hands together. The inferno divided, flames roaring to either side of her. Two guards fell incinerated in the smoking grass, their armour glowing as if from the forge. Severa herself staggered back, singed hair stuck to her face with sweat, her dress faintly smouldering. A tree behind her blazed like a torch, pine cones popping, sap exploding from the splintering trunk, casting a mad, flickering glare over the scene of carnage.

Balthazar did not pause. He tossed his toasted paper aside and dragged upwards, the freshly burned bodies already rising, still smoking as they began to stumble towards her, smouldering arms outstretched.

"Sweet Saint Beatrix," whispered Brother Diaz.

The Palace Guard were doubtless brave and experienced men, but even the best of the living have only so much fight in them. The survivors fled, throwing aside their weapons. Lady Severa retreated, backing up the steps towards the doors of the Athenaeum, teeth gritted, hands raised, as the pitiless dead closed in. The dead and Vigga, growling softly in her throat.

"To be so inconvenienced . . ." She curled her lip as she swept them with a deadly glare. "By this . . . *clown show*."

"You are a formidable practitioner!" shouted Balthazar as he watched for her slightest move. "But you must see you are outmatched. It is over!"

"On the contrary, we are just beginning." Without taking her eyes from Balthazar, she turned her head to call over her shoulder. "Release the leftovers!"

There was a grinding of metal from within the Athenaeum, and to either side of the steps those barred gates trembled, then began to rise. Did Balthazar see something glinting within? Something unfurling in the gloom of the abandoned menagerie? Something huge, a throbbing groan emanating from the darkness, neither animal nor human, but less than either.

He had become so carried away with his own power, he had forgotten Eudoxia's failed experiments.

"Oh dear," he said.

As the barred gates rose, another began to drop across the Athenaeum's entrance. Without thinking, he sprang up the steps two at a time, rolling beneath its spiked skirt a moment before it crashed shut.

A War in Miniature

A swordfight is a war in miniature, and wars are often won and lost before a blow's struck. In the training yard, the armourer's workshop, the quartermaster's office. In assessing your enemy, guessing his strengths, predicting his limitations, anticipating his tactics. In knowing your own.

A good swordsman can recognise another before their blades even touch. How they grip the weapon, draw it, present it. As Duke Michael took his guard before the Serpent Throne, he showed neither panic nor passion, neither fervour nor fear. He had the even gaze of a chess master, considering his opening.

His stance reminded Jakob more than he liked of Constans. That losing duel on the sinking galley. Perhaps uncle and nephew had sparred together in happier times. Perhaps the older man had been instructor to the younger. But there was none of Constans's arrogant flourish in how his uncle presented his sword, perfectly still, perfectly level. The discipline of a man who's suffered disappointments. Who knows the precipice of failure yawns always at his heels and takes nothing for granted. He might've been a few years past his prime, but Jakob had been past his decades before Michael was even born.

A swordfight is a war in miniature, and in war knowing the ground is key. Every hill, road, wood, and stream can be a weapon. Must be made into a weapon. Especially by the weaker side.

So as Jakob limped to the centre of the circular floor he glanced about the room, absorbing every detail. The marble columns a skillful swordsman might weave between, breaking up an opponent's attack. Tapestries that could snare and tangle, statues that might be used as shields, hanging lamps that might shower burning oil. The Serpent Throne itself, so valuable yet so fragile, a thing Michael coveted so deeply he might fear to strike towards it. The armoury of captured weapons bracketed to the walls, ready to be snatched down and pressed into desperate service, centuries after they last shed blood.

Jakob came to a halt, maybe the length of a dead man from his opponent.

A swordfight is a war in miniature, and in war one must be ready for anything. Jakob had seen it all, then seen it all repeated, no man alive labouring under a greater weight of experience. As he bent his creaking knees, he spun out a thousand possibilities. The ebb and flow of combat. The likely techniques and the possible counters. He stored up a deadly arsenal of the tricks he might play.

Their blades touched, near the points, with the slightest pressure, and Jakob looked into Duke Michael's eyes.

A swordfight is a war in miniature. There are patterns the veteran never forgets. The tense silences, full of doubt and discomfort, the brief interludes of frenzied terror when everything you'll ever have is risked on one manoeuvre, one charge, one thrust. But no two are quite alike. And the outcome is never certain. That's what keeps men fighting, even against the odds, even after countless defeats. There's *always* a chance.

Perhaps Duke Michael felt the thrill of the gamble, because he smiled, ever so slightly, as Jakob felt his weight shift. Sensed the pressure against the point of his sword ease by a fraction. Felt the first strike coming. He stiffened in preparation for a cut, prepared to twist his wrist at a thrust, made sure he was fully ready for a feint and to turn defence in an instant into attack—

Michael's eyes flickered sideways, the skin between his brows creasing with doubt. "Alex?" he muttered.

Jakob glanced over, winced at the sting as his neck clicked.

There was a scrape of steel as the duke stepped in, lightning quick.

Jakob's legs were sluggish after the climb, he could only push Duke Michael's point down a few inches.

It punched through his shirt just under his bottom rib.

Jakob's eyes bulged as the blade slid though him almost to the hilt, leaving him rocking slightly on his heels.

"Oooooooooof," he wheezed. However often it happens, you never quite get used to the feeling of being impaled.

A swordfight is a war in miniature. Sometimes won by cunning or bravery.

More often lost through a dumb mistake.

Vigga had seen sights to make the bravest shit their trousers.

The first real battle she ever fought, the Gotlanders hurtling naked from the mist, partly peeled and their minds cracked by mushrooms. That mindless blob of wailing demon-meat those witches had been feeding in Germany. When the faces of those villagers split open in the painted cave, and she'd seen by garish torchlight what had been inside all along . . .

But not even Vigga had ever witnessed the obscene like of this, as it twisted, wriggled, grasped, and slithered from the darkness. Eudoxia had made monsters, but the worst by far was the one she threw together from the bits left over.

"God help us . . ." whispered Brother Diaz, tripping on his own feet as he stumbled back and sitting down hard.

It had so many limbs Vigga couldn't count them. Far too many, was the number, sprouting every which way, hooked and crooked and horribly hairy, paws and claws and hands plucking at the night, legs with three elbows and two ankles and arms that were all knees, and it cocked one foot covered in ears, twitching and trembling, as if it heard distant music.

"I should've quit . . ." breathed Baptiste, her eyes going very wide, "after Barcelona . . ."

It wallowed forwards in lopsided lurches, its crooked body sliding through the grass behind as if it dragged an ill-stitched sack of plunder, but the riches within were its own misfiring guts. A great serpent of grafted carcasses, a motley wyrm of grey hide and tawny leather and striped orange fur and spotted yellow pelt. It kept coming, and coming, new horrors uncoiling from the darkness in sticky spasms, a patchwork Jörmungandr, sprouting with horns, tusks, antlers, covered in weeping scars. An almighty slug, leaving a trail of glistening slime, spindly little bird limbs clawing helplessly, huge bull limbs bursting with hoofed muscle.

"Odin's . . . fucking . . ." The broken spear clattered from Vigga's limp hand. Odin's what? Even the All-Father, who knew all tongues, would lack the words for this.

It saw her. So many eyes it must see everything and nothing, and it stiffened of a sudden, and the thicket of limbs at its head end curled back to reveal a round mouth, and that rolled open like a flower to show another mouth within, and another, a well of teeth that cried like a sad baby.

It rushed at her with awful speed and awful hunger, its many-fingered feet some forwards and some backwards and some sideways skittering on the grass, its dozens of hands springing open to grasp her, foul wind farting from the toothed tunnel of its maw, and Vigga remembered, for the first time in a long time, what it felt like to be terrified.

She'd let herself think she had the wolf muzzled. Tricked herself it was her pet. But the wolf was trickier than she, hiding its bulk in the shadows and playing good doggy. Now it seized its chance and tore from its flimsy cage inside her ribs and swallowed her in one bite.

So when Vigga opened her mouth to scream it was the wolf's terrible howl that came, and as she tried to fend off that forest of mismatched limbs it was the wolf's terrible claws that reached out, and as the horror plunged into her embrace it was the wolf's bottomless hunger that it found.

The Vigga-Wolf took a violent tumble through the flowers with this coiling obscenity, wrestling and wrangling. The thing punched and picked and poked with its legion of limbs, but the Vigga-Wolf trapped them in her dagger jaws, twisting in bloodthirsty frenzy, bone cracking and sinew ripping, ruined arms and legs and bits of arms and legs flung all about.

She caught it with her front claws, ripped at its scarred belly bag with her hind ones while it slurped and slobbered at her with its mouths inside mouths, nicked and cut and gashed her with its thicket of teeth. She wriggled about and tore at it, digging, digging, for she knew that if the good meat was anywhere in the world, it must be inside this striped and fearsome offence against God, and she must open it and see what treasures it contained.

It was as she was biting she saw her mistake. While she gnawed at its head end the thing's mass of body had tightened about her, till she was hemmed on every side by horned and scaled and furred flesh. She tore free as it coiled shut on her, raked by spike and bone as she popped from its clutches like a cork from a bottle, fur slick with her blood and the thing's ooze, dancing and flailing and howling with shame.

The leftovers pawed the ground with purple-nailed hands, ripping up grass, showering sod, steam huffing from its clusters of nostrils, human eyes and goat eyes and snake eyes all bulging. It came on, crushing the earth with its great hooves, making ground quiver and trees shake, ploughing a scar through the lawns and bringing down a rain of leaves and twigs and blossom.

But the Vigga-Wolf wasn't just teeth and fury, she was deep grudges and poisonous patience, too, and she slipped away through the trees in a furry spiral, a streak of claws and slather. The horror slowed as it blundered from one trunk, rolled and reeled, limbs flailing as it shattered another, then plunged after the Vigga-Wolf through too narrow a gap and wedged itself between two thick-boled trees, straining towards her with all its many hands, howling and trembling, veins popping, but the more furiously it wriggled the more stuck it got, thrashing up a blood froth as the old bark ripped its patchwork hide.

The Vigga-Wolf slithered beneath its snapping teeth, slipped under its many-nippled underparts, and slit its belly open with one long claw. Black gore poured from inside, full of squirming young, worms big as snakes twisting and snapping at each other, some with mouths and some with hands and some with ears and the mother bellowed its mindless upset at the blind brood it had begot, trampling and squashing them in its rage.

The Vigga-Wolf slid free of its trapped body, howling her victory and taunting her triumph. The leftovers shrieked, every hand and foot and tongue straining towards her, and of a terrible sudden it tore in half, a soup of steaming guts oozing from its tattered midriff, the front part ripping loose, catching her with its dozens of crooked limbs.

The Vigga-Wolf bit at them but there were too many, too strong, and they dragged her in, and its blubbing, bubbling maw peeled open once again and she was sucked and scoured and swallowed whimpering into that toothed tunnel eaten whole and what an irony.

No wonder she could never find the good meat . . .

If she was the good meat . . .

All along.

Balthazar burst through the open double doors and skittered to a halt at the railing, gazing up in awestruck wonder at the darkened rotunda of the Athenaeum of Troy. The giant space was crowded with shadows, lit only by far-off firelight flickering through windows high above, striking here and there a precious gleam from a gilded spine on the ranks and ranks and ranks of books, soaring upwards uninterrupted towards the far-off dome, surely one of the most formidable gatherings of knowledge in the known world.

After the chaos outside the place was oddly silent, worryingly still, Balthazar's every quick footstep and snatched breath raising a chorus of echoes. His heart played percussion as he padded down the steps to the great circular floor, his mouth dry as he crept out across it, the sweat springing from his forehead as fast as he could wipe it, ready at any moment for some lethal evocation to boil from the darkness.

Metal dully glinted in the marble. Conjurer's rings on a vast scale, appended by chiselled sigils, runes scrawled in minute painted verses, preparations for a ritual of daunting scale and complexity. This must have been the venue for the mad Empress Eudoxia's research, merging man and beast in her doomed efforts to locate the soul. And these, as he neared the centre, could only be the remnants of her final, fatal experiment.

A pursuit of the most dangerous sorceress he had ever encountered hardly offered the ideal opportunity for an exploration of arcane theory, but a magician of Balthazar's insatiable curiosity could hardly help glancing towards the abandoned apparatus as he crept past. It was, after all, unlike anything he had ever witnessed . . .

This metallic rod, scorched by fire, or . . . he touched the ashy deposit coating it, rubbed it between finger and thumb . . . by a thunderstroke? These coils, copper stained powdery green as if by an instant of frenzied reaction, still with the lingering odour of acid.

An apparatus designed to harness lightning, that most arbitrary, fleeting, and violent of nature's phenomena . . .

"Impossible," he whispered.

And yet, these jars . . . clamped to either side of the rod with carefully calibrated precision. Was there something floating pickled inside? He wished he had more light, almost pressing his nose to the distorting glass. Feathers? He jerked away, the memory flashing up of Shaxep's visit to the world at his desperate invitation. One jar held a demon quill. The other an angel feather. Opposite spiritual poles, positioned to contain and control the flow of mystic force. To balance the apparatus as the universe was held in balance. He stooped to brush the rune of cleaving set into the floor below it with his fingertips . . . he had never seen it used in such a manner . . . to split an *energy* . . . then direct it towards the two benches, furnished with straps, intended to restrain a reluctant prisoner . . . or to hold an insensible subject?

An apparatus designed not only to locate the soul, but to release it . . .

"Impossible," he murmured.

And yet . . . *two* benches. He frowned at the labyrinthine inscriptions that ringed them, the geometry that both separated and connected them. It put him in mind of a pale chamber he had once seen, assembled then abandoned in haste by the Inquisition in Naples—no doubt using Oracles in their hunt for heretics, good God the irony—but there were differences. The work was passionate, imprecise, he took them at a glance for mistakes, but as he pored over them, he began to see otherwise. Here, aspects of channelling and movement. There, aspects of transformation and exchange. They were wilful alterations. They were intricate improvements. They were ingenious refinements! Sarcomantic elements had been elegantly interwoven—flesh and spirit—his mind reeled as he attempted to comprehend the sheer ambition.

An apparatus designed not only to release the soul . . . but to *transfer* it . . .

"*Impossible* . . ." hissed Balthazar, looking up—

And caught a glimpse of movement, reflected in the curved sides of those two jars.

He spun, throwing up a protective hand, to see Severa crouching, teeth bared, one finger pointed towards him.

There was an incandescent flash, the whole towering book-lined well of darkness made brilliant daylight to its mosaic ceiling, ranks of shelves etched with the pin-sharp shadows of teetering gantries, balconies, ladders.

There was no time for a gesture, nor even a word, only for one thought: that rune of splitting. Balthazar pictured it, so huge in his mind it filled his whole self, and with that rune and his raised hand he cleaved Severa's lightning in two.

The shelves behind him were blasted apart, singed paper fluttering like confetti, two landslides of torn and smouldering books tumbling down to either side of him. His vision was etched with the jagged tree of the discharge, his ears rang with its thunder, his nose stung with an alchemical reek, his skin fizzing with the overwhelming power, jolting sparks still arcing from his outstretched hand to the floor.

Severa glowered at him, her finger still extended, her snarl lit by the flames of burning books, and Balthazar readied himself for another onslaught, his fingers twitching to make the forms, his heart pounding painfully as he wondered whether he possessed the mental wherewithal to withstand her next attack . . .

But it did not come. One more shelf gave way behind him, a few more singed volumes flapping across the rune-scrawled floor like fledglings flown too close to the sun and coming to rest.

"You threw lightning," he whispered, unable to keep the awe out of his voice. His every hair still stood to tingling attention from its after-effects, some of those on his forearm gently smoking.

"And you *caught* it," answered Severa, and did he dare to imagine the faintest admiring inflection of her own?

"Eudoxia's students told me the Empress could do it . . ." Though he had not believed them until he witnessed it with his still-smarting eyes. "She taught you the technique . . . ?" But what practitioner worth their salt, especially one so infamously jealous as Eudoxia, does not keep their deepest secrets for themselves? "Or . . . could it be . . ." Balthazar's skin had gone cold. The back of his neck tingled. He felt he trembled at the brink of some grand revelation. He glanced to the apparatus: the rod, the pickled feathers, the twin benches.

Severa began to smile, eyes glittering with the flicker of burning paper. A smile quite out of place on that usually so dignified face.

Exultant. Triumphant. Irrepressible.

"Eudoxia's experiment . . ." breathed Balthazar, ". . . *worked*."

He recognised that smile. He had worn it himself, not so long ago, when he proved his theory of the nature of matter in the Basilica of the Angelic Visitation. The pride of the arcane explorer, taking the first human step into undiscovered country, plumbing the mysteries of creation, committing bold trespass where only angels and demons were permitted to tread.

"*Your* experiment . . ." he barely whispered, ". . . *worked.*"

"A good twist," said Lady Severa—*Empress Eudoxia*, as she was now revealed to be, wearing her servant's meat like a fine new suit of clothes— "should come from a mystery in a stunning flash, like a stroke of lightning from an overcast sky."

"So, if I now have your absolute attention . . ." Baron Rikard scanned the top of the Pharos to make sure all eyes were turned towards him, and they were, unerringly, in awestruck reverence. Placidia had dropped to her knees, hands clasped, like a nun before a shrine. Athenais had forgotten to close her mouth and actually had a streak of drool at the corner. Alex, kneeling beside Sunny, gave a breathless squeak of excitement as the vampire glanced towards her.

"And I believe I do . . . coming to my *point.*" His skin was no longer perfectly smooth, there were laughter lines at the corners of his eyes, but those eyes . . . as if he looked into Alex's soul, and knew her deepest desires, and was about to give them to her. She sobbed with disappointment as he looked away. "Now *your* name was . . ."

"Zenonis!" She thrust up her arm, hand flapping wildly, like a pupil desperate to show her learning to the schoolmaster.

"And you are a pyromancer?" The baron smiled, showing those beautifully pointed teeth. God, Alex wished she had teeth like that. "I well understand the fascination of the flame . . . so beautiful, yet so deadly, so beautiful *because* it is so deadly."

"He speaks *really* well," murmured Sunny, lying against the wall clutching her ribs, big eyes even bigger than usual as she gazed at Baron Rikard.

"Shush! Shut up!" Alex couldn't stand the thought of missing a syllable. The only other sound was the faint hiss and crackle of Saint Natalia's Flame, and even that seemed a little embarrassed to be getting in his way.

Her eyes followed the baron's finger as it stretched out to point. "I think you should show her—"

"Cleofa!" said Cleofa, eagerly.

"Such charming names for such charming ladies—I think you should show *Cleofa* the beauty of the fire."

"That's an amazing idea," whispered Placidia.

"That's an incredible idea," breathed Alex. She vaguely remembered having some sort of squabble with these girls but that seemed so silly now, all of them happily united in their desire to do whatever the baron wanted. He couldn't be a vampire. That was all a mistake. He was a saint. To doubt him was impossible, to refuse him unthinkable. He was an angel. Alex wished she knew how to burn someone for his amusement. He was a *god*, and she yearned to be burned herself if it would please him.

Cleofa stared at Zenonis and clapped her hands. "This is a fucking *spectacular* idea."

"Me next!" said Placidia, nearly jumping up and down.

"Don't worry." Zenonis gave a blissful smile, the bones glowing white hot through the flesh of her fingers, her sleeves smoking, smouldering, scorching black. "There's enough fire for all of you."

Alex felt the searing heat kiss her cheek as Cleofa's clothes burst into flames. She caught a last glimpse of her delighted face before her hair went up like a torch and her skin started to blacken and peel and she fell singing with joy, which only sounded a bit like an utterly hideous scream, thrashing and rolling on the ground in blazing ecstasy.

Alex felt a tear roll down her cheek. A tear of pure jealousy, that Cleofa should be the one shown the fire.

"Why does no one ever pick me?" she said, bitterly.

"I picked you," said Sunny, through teeth gritted in pain.

"Oh, fuck off." Alex shuffled a little closer to Rikard on her skinned knees, hoping against hope he might pick her next.

"How beautifully she burns!" Firelight flickered in the gaunt hollows of his face. The wrinkled skin about his eye twitched with effort.

"I . . . suppose." Zenonis frowned slightly. "Are you sure we should—"

"*Quite* sure," snapped the baron, "and next you must introduce the joys of the fire to . . ." And he glared over at Athenais.

"Athenais," she said, and her perfectly plucked brows wrinkled. "But I'm starting to think—"

"Think only of those dumplings!" hissed the baron, through gritted teeth, his beard, and the hair about his temples, now shot with grey. "Pork, remember, with a little onion, in oil . . ."

But Alex didn't find the dumplings so utterly fascinating as a few moments before, and her handmaidens seemed to feel the same. Maybe it was the smell of cooking meat that was so distracting, or the sheen of bloody sweat across the baron's forehead.

Zenonis stared at Cleofa's smouldering corpse, then up at Placidia. "Dumplings?" she muttered.

Alex shook her head. Wasn't there something really important they'd been doing?

Athenais's eyes went wide. "Die!" she shrieked, flinging her open hands at the baron. One of the pillars was ripped apart, a section of the dome went with it, chunks of stone hurtling into the empty night sky.

But Rikard was no longer there. He'd become a cloud of black smoke, ripped apart then flowing back together as Athenais spun, blasting wildly. Alex crouched, arms over Sunny's head as plaster showered across the gallery. A lump of masonry, one curved side of it still covered in mirrors, crashed down right beside her. The smoke tore and eddied and gathered around Athenais and was the baron once again, wrinkled face fixed in a hungry grin, pinning her arms as he gripped her from behind, his mouth opening far too wide, his too many teeth too white, too sharp. He sank them into Athenais's throat, ripping half her neck and a chunk of shoulder away, blood spurting from the yawning hole.

"No!" wailed Zenonis, raising her shimmering hands just as Alex staggered up, heaving that block of stone with her, mirrors flashing. "I'll show *you* the—ugh!" And Alex clubbed her on the back of the skull with a dull *crunch*.

Zenonis turned drunkenly, blood bubbling through her hair, trickling down her forehead. One eyelid flickered. One hand dangled, limp. She raised the other, heat still shimmering around it. "I'll . . . show . . ."

Alex smashed her across the face with the rock. She stumbled back and Sunny groaned as she stuck out a boot. A very visible boot, for once, but no less effective for that. Zenonis tripped over it, staggering, falling, made a wild grab for the parapet—but it was gone. She fell through the great hole Athenais had blasted and tumbled out into the night.

Alex heard a snarl of triumph, turned blinking to see Placidia catch Baron Rikard, crystals of glittering frost spreading up his arms. "I *have* you!"

He showed his outsize teeth and gripped her back, flesh creaking and cracking as he wrapped his icy fingers around her arms. "No . . ." Her feet slipped, slid, the skin of his face creasing, sagging. "I . . ." he croaked as he lifted her, his hair withering away to a few frosty wisps, "have . . ." Placidia kicked and flailed but with one last effort he bore her back and thrust her into Saint Natalia's Flame, "*you*."

The brazier had been guttering, the flames no higher than her hips, but now Baron Rikard spoke a word, a puff of smoke from his blue lips, and the fire blazed up white hot, tongues of flame roaring through the holes in the broken dome.

Placidia screeched, clawed at the vampire with burning hands, but he kept his grip, his own arms on fire, his black eyes glittering with the flames. Her cries faded to a rattle and wheezed out. Rikard tottered back, every bit as ancient as the first moment Alex laid eyes on him, but covered now in melting ice and his arms looking like burned sausage. He tripped over his own foot and slumped against the parapet in a smouldering heap.

A column of sparks whirled up from the brazier where only glowing embers remained. Ash fluttered down around the ruined gallery, covering Alex, and Sunny, and the corpses of Eudoxia's apprentices in black snow.

Jakob stood, skewered.

The agony was indescribable, of course.

But he could breathe. So it wasn't through his lung. It wasn't through his heart.

He stayed on his feet. He gritted his teeth. He looked up at Duke Michael, and shrugged. "Eh," he grunted. "I've had worse."

Duke Michael stared back, unsure what to do next. To be fair to the man, running your opponent through is usually enough. He tugged on the hilt of his sword but Jakob caught the crosspiece with his left hand, groaned with pain and effort as he lifted his own sword in his right.

Michael let go, going over on his back with a shocked gasp as Jakob's clumsy swing whipped over his head, heels of his boots squeaking on the marble as he wriggled away.

"My God . . ." he murmured, scrambling up as Jakob limped doggedly forwards with one sword in his hand and another through his belly, blood streaking the hilt and dripping from the pommel, scattering dark spatters across the tiles.

Jakob growled as he lunged again. Duke Michael dodged, nearly tripped, fell heavily against the wall as Jakob's sword—the one in his hand, not the one in his guts—chopped the side from a great pot, chunks of gilded porcelain spinning away across the floor.

Michael caught one of the ancient spears but the brackets wouldn't give. He lurched away as Jakob slashed at him, scoring the wall and sending plaster dust flying, then ducked as Jakob slashed again, leaving a long gash through an emerald-green tapestry.

Duke Michael's fishing hand caught one of the elf-daggers. He dragged at it with all his weight but it came away easily and he nearly fell. He barely dodged Jakob's flailing sword, catching him as they blundered together.

Jakob butted Duke Michael in the face and he stumbled back with a bloody nose, then slipped in Jakob's blood, boot heel leaving a long smear as he went down, then several more as he scrambled up again. Their duel had become less elegant chess match than lethal slapstick. Jakob tottered forwards with something between a growl and whimper but Michael rolled one way, then the other, Jakob's sword clanging into floor, leaving long scars and making his arm buzz.

He sagged against the Serpent Throne with his right shoulder, each breath faintly whooping, and looked down. The elf-dagger was buried in his ribs, bloody grip sticking out sideways. Must've happened while they were wrestling. He would've laughed if he could've got the breath. The elves had spent decades failing to stick him with one, now a prince of Troy had managed it.

"Reckon that . . ." he wheezed, tasting blood on each rattling breath, seeing red bubbles around the hilt, "*is* in the lung."

"Have you even asked yourself," asked Duke Michael, backing warily away between the pillars, "what happens if you win?"

Jakob wheeze-groaned as he pushed himself from the Serpent Throne and doggedly limped after him, each step a new stabbing, each breath a new impalement. Labouring on down that dusty road, lined with bodies, on that endless retreat across the steppe. One foot after another.

"The elves are coming." The room was getting dark. Lamp flames burning low, leaving glowing trails across his vision. "A pointy-eared tide of them, and their one desire is to wipe humanity from the world." The elves are always coming. Jakob had to squint to tell who was talking, who was fighting. Was it Szymon Bartos's face he saw beside a pillar, ducking away before he could swing? "Troy will be the bulwark on which that storm first breaks. Will it be stronger with the *Empress Alexia* on the throne?"

"That choice . . . is for *God*." Jakob spat blood, swung at William the Red, and hacked a chunk of marble from the pillar where his head had been, splinters bouncing across the floor. No one wants to see doubts.

"They say God is blind," said the Emperor's Champion, the Pope's Executioner, the Grandmaster of the Order, backing towards a statue of some long-dead Emperor while Jakob struggled after, leaking air, leaking tears, leaking blood, leaving a pitter-patter crooked trail of all the stuff that should ideally stay inside a body. "I say he is deaf, dumb, and a fool besides. He chooses those who choose themselves."

There was a loud crash upstairs, one of the hanging lamps wobbling, its flame flickering. Jakob stood, wobbling himself, point of his sword on the ground as a crutch. He shook his head, tried to focus. His sight was swimming.

"And that is the sound . . ." Duke Michael grinned towards the ceiling, "of him choosing *me*."

"You sure? I was thinking . . ." The floor was spinning. Tipping, like the deck of a ship in a storm. "Might be Baron Rikard. Bloody vampires . . . always late." Jakob didn't feel much like smiling himself, but he managed to show his bloody teeth. "Makes you wonder. Have you been playing for time . . . or have I?"

He made one last exhausted lunge but the Michael-shaped blur dodged it, stepped behind the statue as Jakob struggled to recover, and heaved it from its plinth. Jakob got his balance back with a stab of agony, just in time to see it toppling towards him.

"Oh fuh—"

He went down under it with a sick crunch, his head cracking against the floor.

Most of the weight wasn't on him, he didn't think. But enough was. His left arm was crushed. And he was stabbed with a sword, of course. Not forgetting the dagger. He was still holding on to his blade. He wafted vaguely at nothing with it. A useless instinct.

"Stay there," called Duke Michael, his voice drifting off. "We can finish this later!"

Jakob slumped back, each breath a bloody effort, and stared up at the ceiling.

It didn't really hurt any more.

"Here's a pickle," he whispered.

Unacceptable Behaviour

Y ou took Lady Severa's body . . ." whispered Balthazar.

"Mine was, frankly, dying," said Eudoxia, or Severa, or the soul of one in the body of the other, "while hers is, frankly, superb." And she calmly smoothed her dress. "And she *had* been betraying me to my brother for years. She died in my withered corpse. Having thought all along I was mad."

"I have no doubt you are," murmured Balthazar. "*Gloriously* so."

No agreement was made and no flag of parley offered but, without their eyes leaving one another, they both, with the greatest caution, straightened from their ready crouches.

"Only *you* have had the vision to realise the truth," she said. "Not one of those narrow-minded ants I tried to teach could even *conceive* of my success. Not my self-serving courtiers, not my self-interested subjects, not those preening vultures, my so-called sons." She gave a snort of disgust. "My own treacherous dunce of a brother was so blissfully unaware of what soul occupied this flesh that he asked me to marry him."

"A proposal which you . . ." Balthazar delicately cleared his throat, "accepted?"

She gave a twitch of one shoulder. Barely even a shrug. "It seemed the smoothest path back to the throne." He supposed once you have usurped an Empire, fused humans with animals, and capped it off by stealing the body of your lady-in-waiting in a heretical crime against God, a little light incest does seem rather a paltry misdemeanour.

"For so many years, all I thought about was taking power. Holding power." She slowly approached, while Balthazar kept every sense sharpened for another attack. "It became a habit. An addiction. But now . . . I begin to wonder if I even want it." She reached out, gently touched the burned padding on one of the benches. "I have had the unique opportunity to see the world after my death, and it is fair to say I was not mourned. My sons wasted no time tearing into my metaphorical carcass. The literal one, incidentally, was incinerated without ceremony." She blinked, as though coming to the realisation for the first time. "The Serpent Throne did me no good. And I certainly did it no good."

"You would let Alexia have it, then?"

Eudoxia looked up at him. "Now you suggest it, why not? I have always appreciated an underdog. And no doubt Troy has had worse leaders. The throne room for me was a place of endless frustration and disappointment. My true victories were won *here*!" She threw up her arms and Balthazar took an involuntary step back, hands twitching to repel her.

There was a brittle silence, and she narrowed her eyes at him. "If we continue this duel, one of us will likely not survive."

Balthazar managed a scornful toss of his head. "This time your death will be permanent."

Eudoxia did the same and, having stolen one of the best necks in Europe, vanquished him utterly, at least as far as head-tossing was concerned. "I beg to differ. But even if you were the victor, what will you have won? Fame? Wealth? Freedom? Knowledge?"

Balthazar gave careful thought to that. "None of the above," he conceded.

"You were bound to see Alexia made Empress."

"I was."

"You are not bound to duel with me."

"I am not." He was bound to return to the Holy City with all dispatch, indeed, his gorge had been rising ever since he dived from the ship.

"So there is nothing to stop us simply . . . letting each other go."

"You could have made such an offer before doing your level best to incinerate me," observed Balthazar.

"It is in demonstrating yourself equal to my level best that you have proved your value."

She made a strong argument. He had never felt so alive as in their struggle to the death, never felt so powerful as when stretching his powers beyond their limits to counter hers. The blinding after-image of her lightning was fading. Her dress was scorched, ripped at the shoulder. Her hair was pinned on one side, hanging tangled about the other. Her lip was split, bright blood smeared across her jaw. Her stolen body was as battered by their struggle as he was.

And it had never looked better.

"How can one achieve greatness," he murmured, "without great adversaries against whom to test oneself?"

"You make a formidable rival." Did her eyes flicker from his face for a moment, down towards his feet, and back? "I cannot help but think you would make an even more formidable ally."

"Do you propose . . ." He cleared his throat, voice ever so slightly hoarse. The suggestion of such a beauty being attracted to him was intoxicating, but paled in comparison to the suggestion of such a genius admiring his arcane talents. "That I join you?"

"Only think of it! A magician of your calibre, a sorcerer of mine? The princes of Europe, the cardinals of the Church, even the elves themselves would tremble before us! The world would lie at our feet!"

He had been unable to think of anything else since she stopped trying to annihilate him. "Your offer is not without its . . . considerable attractions. I will admit I am—or at the very least *was*—an ambitious man—" Balthazar was obliged to swallow a burp. "But there is the troublesome matter of the papal binding."

"Applied by a child?"

"I witnessed the procedure and laughed."

"But it is effective?"

"Ever since, I have laughed rarely if at all."

"Perhaps between us we can find a way to break it, and the last laugh will be ours."

Balthazar licked his lips. "Shaxep herself could not do it."

"You bound a Duke of Hell to the purpose?" He declined to mention that he had not so much *bound* the demon as called then asked *very* politely, but he was deriving far too much satisfaction from the spark of Eudoxia's respect in Severa's stolen eyes. "You are a more audacious practitioner than I dared imagine."

"From a practitioner as audacious as you, those are words I will treasure. There was a time I would have clutched at your proposal with eager hands, but . . . the truth is . . ." Balthazar realised something he would never have thought possible. "I no longer wish to be freed."

"You choose . . . to remain a *slave*?"

"I have . . . by a roundabout and, admittedly, exceedingly unpleasant route . . . found myself in the service of the Second Coming of the Saviour herself."

"You truly believe that?"

"I am a man of science. I have reviewed the evidence." Balthazar shrugged. "What more important place could an ambitious magician find?"

It did lurk rather at the back of his mind that the men with whom Eudoxia had previously associated herself—four husbands and four sons—had not exactly prospered. But there was, even if he would never admit it to her, even if he could hardly admit it to himself, one other compelling reason to remain with the Chapel of the Holy Expediency: the sense of almost choking disappointment at the thought of never getting to rub Baptiste's face in that day's stupendous triumphs.

He would not have particularly blamed her had Eudoxia blasted him with lightning a second time, but she only pressed her lips thoughtfully together. "You have done three things men almost never do. Impressed me, interested me . . . and turned me down."

"I hope I have caused no offence." Without taking his eyes off her he bowed. "And that we may still part on good terms."

"Good terms might be too much to ask." She backed towards the far door-way, torn hem of her dress swishing against the runes her past self had in-scribed. "But alive? By all means."

She paused in the shadows and, for an instant, Balthazar was sure the air was about to explode into flame.

"We should do this again," she said.

He smiled. "I shall count the hours."

"Our Saviour . . ." breathed Brother Diaz.

The Hanging Gardens before the Athenaeum, whose beauty had put him in mind of paradise a few weeks before, had been rendered into a scene from hell that even the master painters of the Holy City would not have dared imagine. Had a tornado ripped through a burning slaughterhouse it could have left behind no greater carnage, malformed limbs, dead guards, and unknowable innards scattered thickly as leaves in autumn, glistening in the flickering flames of burning vegetation.

Merciful Saviour, one of the stately palms was festooned with dripping guts.

". . . at God's right hand . . ." he whispered.

The back part of the horror: a decapitated snake the size of a longship, a harlequin monstrosity patched together from every gaudy skin that must once have been on show in the Imperial Menagerie, was still wedged between two trees, writhing like a worm cut in half, spraying gore. It was, without doubt, the worst abomination ever visited upon creation. Until one's dumbstruck gaze had the misfortune to fall upon the front part: a torn and leaking spider-like sack of horned flesh with a thicket of wriggling, misshapen limbs surrounding the arse-mouth that had just swallowed Vigga whole.

"Though death's breath is upon us . . ." whispered Brother Diaz, "I *will* not fear."

The thing rolled, burped, lurched towards him and Baptiste, unspooling a great welter of misshapen guts in its wake, dragging its ruined body at shocking speed with its lower arms while the upper ones reached out, its maw peeling open to reveal a well of bloody teeth.

Brother Diaz dragged Baptiste back, stepping past her, pulling Saint Beat-rix's vial from inside his collar and closing his fist around it. He had no better ideas.

"I know I am but a weak vessel," he hissed, not mouthing now by rote but putting all his soul into the words, "but *fill* me with your light."

The monstrous conglomeration of leftovers clawed its way towards him, its bulging remains weeping at the stitches, eyes rolling, ears twitching, limbs dancing.

"Deliver me from evil, that I may live by your virtues! That I may do your work!"

He could feel the thing's rancid breath. His nose was full of the charnel stink of it. Here was death, and it was an utterly horrible death, and there was nothing left to lose.

"Deliver me from evil!" he snarled, narrowing his eyes, gripping Saint Be-atrix's vial so tightly it dug into his palm. "Now or fucking never!"

As if repelled by an invisible wall, the thing jerked to a halt.

It shuddered, all its fingers fluttering, and recoiled.

It tilted its mouth towards the sky and made a ghostly whine, every limb flailing.

Brother Diaz stared, hardly able to believe his prayers had at last been an-swered. "It's a mirac—"

The thing burst open, showering him with gore, the patchwork sack of its body tearing at the seams and something digging from inside. Claws, like black glass, and then a snarling snout, and the Vigga-Wolf was birthed from the shredded horror in a flood of blood, howling and gurgling, fur matted with ooze, dragging itself into the glistering firelight.

"Oh yes!" breathed Brother Diaz.

The wolf's eye flicked towards him. A devil's eye, burning with wounded hatred for all that lives. It gave a great snort, blowing a mist of blood, and shook itself with a flurry of trembles. It squirmed from the still-twitching wreckage of Eudoxia's creation, jaws dropping open and its great steaming tongue flopping out to feather the grass.

"Oh no," breathed Brother Diaz. He took a helpless, weak-kneed step back as the great wolf stalked towards him, one bent back leg dragging, matted hackles twisting as its great shoulders shifted, huge paws like human hands clutching at grass glistening with bloody dew.

He felt a hand on his arm, pushing him aside, and Baptiste stepped in front of him.

"Vigga . . ." she growled, fists clenched. She strained forwards, sticking her neck out, and screamed at the top of her lungs. "This behaviour is *un-acceptable*!"

The monstrous wolf shifted back. Away from Baptiste and—thank the Saviour—away from Brother Diaz. Did it seem less a thing, more a person? Did he see, for a moment, behind the tangle of hair, less muzzle, more face?

There was a strange silence, with only the last death throes of the rear half of Eudoxia's most obscene experiment in the background.

Then the Vigga-Wolf curled black lips from teeth big as daggers and let go a growl to make the earth throb, bloody slobber dripping from its jaws to spatter the bloody mud as it eased towards them.

Not Vigga. Still very much the wolf.

"Oh no," whispered Brother Diaz, again.

"Should've quit . . ." Baptiste swallowed. "*Before* Barcelona . . ."

"Can you walk?" asked Alex.

"Can I not?" Sunny let her head drop back against the broken parapet, showing bloody teeth. "Might just . . . lie down here."

"No." Alex dragged Sunny's limp arm across her shoulders. "I'm issuing an imperial decree."

"Thought the one good thing about being an elf . . . is I don't have to obey those . . ." They both groaned as Alex stood, pulling Sunny up with her. It was lucky she weighed about as much as a mid-sized cat because Alex doubted she could've lifted anything heavier. They hobbled together towards the steps, night sky showing through the rents in the dome, the chips of mirror covering the rest of it stained red as Saint Natalia's Flame burned low. Baron Rikard lay crumpled against the wall like a heap of ancient rags, eyes shut, arms cooked. "Our vampire's looked better."

"And worse," grunted Sunny.

"Worse than that?" Alex picked her way between Cleofa's still smoking corpse and the wide pool of blood that had spread from Athenais's throat.

"He spent forty years as bones. He'll get over this."

"Not sure I will," muttered Alex. She was battered and scoured and aching all over, her torn arm stinging from wrist to shoulder under her dead husband's tunic. She heaved Sunny into a better position and started to wobble down the steps. "This has been the worst fucking night—"

"And it's not over," said Duke Michael, coming up the other way.

Sunny's breath whooped in. She blinked out of sight but Michael's fist was already swinging. She blinked back when it caught her jaw and flung her sideways, head cracking against the wall. She crumpled and Alex was dragged down with her, twisting free to scramble back up the steps as Sunny flopped the other way, out cold.

"The state of this place." Duke Michael shook out his fingers as he stepped into the ruined gallery, watching Alex wriggle across the floor with far from imperial dignity, her backside leaving a worming trail through the scattered plaster and gravel and broken chips of mirror. "You've let our blessed beacon burn *low*." Fat sputtered in the guttering brazier. The one recognisable bit of Placidia's corpse was a leg hanging over the side, largely unburned from the knee down and still sporting a very fine shoe. "Poor choice of fuel, perhaps." He tapped that dangling leg with the side of his boot and it broke off, dropping in a shower of sparks and ash.

"I had to improvise," muttered Alex, which was what she'd been doing for years. She clambered up, looking for anything to fight with, anywhere to run to. But Duke Michael had an easy confidence as he stepped over to the neatly stacked logs. There was no way around him, and they both knew it.

"The people look to Saint Natalia's Flame for guidance," he said, heaping new wood on the embers. "They expect to see it always above them—constant, pure, radiant. Just as they expect to look up and see their Empress."

"Or . . . don't tell me . . . their Emperor?"

Duke Michael grinned at her. "You're learning." He took a flask, sloshed oil over the wood, and stood back as fire surged up hungrily, shining bright and white from the mirrors and casting that unforgiving glare across the gallery once again. "The flame rekindled . . . as Troy will be renewed, under my guidance." He slapped his palms clean as he stepped over Cleofa's roasted corpse. "It is *so* hard to find good help. I warned Eudoxia's idiotic harpies to wait until your devils were well over the horizon."

Alex edged back, but she was fast running out of floor. "Guess they couldn't stand me a moment longer."

"They should've waited for this as long as I have. A day or two then would've made no difference." He gazed out of the ragged hole in the side of the gallery. The one Athenais had made. The one Zenonis had fallen through. The one he was herding Alex towards. The side of the lighthouse blasted away, without pillars or parapets, to show a great rent of night sky, the stars ablaze over the dark country. "But sometimes we have to lose everything . . . so we can win everything."

"So you can steal everything, you mean."

"Well, you'd know. You're the thief. Though I have to admit one wouldn't see it now. I was expecting the same sullen street rat I found in the Holy City.

Imagine my shock when *quite* the little princess stepped off the boat. I never expected you to find some *dignity*." He stepped closer, looking her up and down as she edged back. "You actually start to remind me of your mother, you know. She had precisely that expression when she realised I'd poisoned her."

Alex blinked. "When you . . . what?"

"Then I blamed Eudoxia, and of course everyone despised the twisted witch, so they believed me."

Alex hadn't thought her opinion of him could drop much lower but the bastard had found a way. "You started the civil war . . . in the first place . . ."

Duke Michael gave a bored wince. "*Must* we really dig away at who did what so many years ago? All that really matters . . ." He took a satisfied breath through his nose, and let it puff away. "Is that I've *won*. Afraid I left my sword in your friend Jakob, but I could strangle you easily enough. It's a fine tradition with Empresses. Or beat your brains out?"

Alex was not loving either choice. She kept edging back, but another couple of paces would have her heels over the void.

"Or you could always jump." Duke Michael shrugged, as if this was all a sad necessity they had to help each other through. "Then you'd get a few more moments on the way down. I've found when it comes to it, people will do anything for a few more moments. Especially . . . well . . ." And he smiled. A smile with a hint of lazy contempt. As though a hint was all she deserved. "A piece of shit like you."

God knew how many times she'd said it about herself. But for *him* to say it?

This smug fucking puffed-up traitor, a prince born in the Imperial Bedchamber, whining about how hard he'd had it.

This self-pitying sack of lying slime, who'd been given everything anyone could want, then killed one sister, blamed the other, and started a war so he could steal more.

All her life, there'd always been some bastard wanting to put their foot on her neck. But this piece of shit? He was the worst.

Alex had always been able to cry on cue, and now she crushed her face up and let the tears flow. Just the way Jakob once told her to.

"Really?" sneered Duke Michael.

"Please . . ." she whimpered, cringing. She had no knife, but behind her back she squeezed her hand into a trembling fist. "I don't want to die."

"For pity's sake." He stepped closer. "You're a crowned Empress, you could at least try to—"

Alex sprang, catching his shirt with her open hand and smashing her fist right into his mouth.

It was the best punch she'd ever thrown, catching him off guard, snapping his head up. She wasn't a big woman, though, and he was a big man. He didn't go down, only took one shocked step back. Alex had been an Empress for hours and a princess for months, but she'd been a street rat all her life, so she did what they do in the slums of the Holy City and jumped him.

"Fuck!" she screeched as she caught him around the shoulders, wrapping her legs around his waist. "*You . . .*" turning to a mindless growl as she sank her teeth into his nose and bit down hard as she could.

He gave a great howl, clutched at her, dragged at her, scrabbling desperately to tear her off, and finally sank his fist into her side and made her gasp, jaws coming open, losing her grip.

She caught a glimpse of his fist coming, then she was crumpled against the parapet, head full of stars.

She tried to shake them away, groggy.

Up, Alex, *get up.*

God, her face was one great throb. Again.

She rolled over, sort of sitting. Big tunic twisted around her, so heavy.

They might put her down but she'd never stay down. She blinked, groaned, trying to focus. She floundered up to one knee. The lighthouse was made of jelly, wobbling all over the place.

Duke Michael stood over her, one bloody hand clutched to the shredded wreckage of his nose. "You bit me!" he spat, not just hurt, but outraged.

Surely she was going to lose, and likely she was going to die, but fuck this horrible bastard. "You're the piethe of shit," she said, a bit slurred, but he got the gist, and she showed her teeth in a red smile, and laughed at him. "You're the biggest piece of shit in Europe."

"You little *bitch*." And he caught her around the throat and heaved her up.

Couldn't breathe. She twisted and clutched and kicked. Her toes brushed the gritty flagstones. His teeth were bared, like a wild animal. How could she ever have been pleased to see that awful fucking face?

Couldn't breathe. She scratched at his hands, plucked at his shoulders. But her arms were nowhere near long enough. Always wanted to be taller. Blood leaked from his torn nose, ran into his beard.

Couldn't breathe. Her throat squelched and glugged. Face throbbed. Lungs burst. In spite of the blaze, it was getting dark at the top of the Pharos.

Over the rushing of blood in her ears, she thought she heard a tapping. A scraping. Coming from the steps.

Duke Michael's eye twitched. He glanced sideways. His grip loosened a fraction. Enough for Alex to get one foot on the ground. Enough for her to jerk the other up and knee him in the balls.

"Ooof . . ." he groaned, eyes bulging. His grip loosened more. Enough for her to twist closer, get her splinter-riddled, bloodstained arm inside his, and with her last strength dig her broken fingernail right into his eye.

"Gah!" He let her go, stumbling back, towards the broken parapet, towards that inky patch of night sky, just as something burst from the roaring column of Saint Natalia's Flame.

Jakob of Thorn, bloody teeth set in a mad snarl. The hilt of a sword stuck from his stomach. The hilt of a dagger from his side.

Alex tottered back, dragging in a desperate, wheezing breath, tripping and falling as the old knight plunged through the flames like a devil from hell, his clothes on fire, his hair, his beard, even. He took a lurching step, one arm flailing while the other hung limp, more falling than charging.

Duke Michael tried to turn but Jakob hurtled into him first. He was a big man, but so was Jakob, and the old knight held nothing back.

They both left the ground, hanging in space for an instant, wreathed in fire, against the night sky.

Then they dropped.

Alex stared, mouth wide open, quick breaths whooping in her battered throat. Then she twisted onto her belly and wriggled to the brink.

"Oh God . . ." she whispered.

She saw the flaming speck, far below, tumbling down the side of the Pillar, dwindling as it plunged towards the sea.

Then it winked out.

"God damn it," hissed Balthazar, heaving at the crank. He had never been proficient at manual labour and, further, was trembling with a bone-deep weariness following a magical duel with a body-stealing former-Empress. It was only the thought of rubbing Baptiste's face in his glory that was keeping him upright.

"God *damn* it." Arms aching with effort, hands singed by lightning, sweat beading his forehead as the grate over the Athenaeum's gate squeaked up by the most frustrating of gradual degrees.

He pictured her expression when he reminded her of the day's events, something he would now be doing on an hourly basis. *Remember that time I saved your life from a phrenomantically controlled werewolf? Then contended* with one of the most powerful sorceresses in Europe and fought her to a draw? Or wait. *And bested her utterly!* Who would be there to correct the record, after all? *And finally proved myself the one man capable of unmasking her as the reincarnation of the supposedly deceased Empress Eudoxia herself!*

"God damn it!" he snarled as he hauled impatiently at the crank. Here was the final, crushing victory over his chief tormentor of which he had for so long dreamed. A defeat that, however slippery she might be, she would have no choice but to concede!

Balthazar Sham Ivam Draxi . . . she would say, pronouncing each syllable correctly, and then, with a delicious grimace of dismay, *I was wrong about you all along. You are no figure of scorn but indeed rank among the finest magicians not only of the day but of all time.* Not really her voice, he had to admit, but that would be the gist! *Your powers are formidable, your insight unique, and your calves not unattractive!*

She would look into his eyes. *I was wrong about you all along.*

You came back for us. For me. You are . . .

He paused, staring at nothing. "A good man," he whispered.

He let go the wheel, chains rattling, tearing his shirt on one of the spikes in his haste as he slipped under the gate.

"You will never guess what happened!" he cackled as he ducked out into the night. "Severa was—"

Few men indeed had witnessed more of the uncanny, eldritch, and obscene. But the unholy spectacle on the lawn before the Athenaeum was one that gave even Balthazar pause.

It was as if a giant sack of animals, people, and bodily fluids had dropped from an immense height and burst apart. Gore was showered everywhere, the columns of the Athenaeum spattered with blood, scraps of the hides of exotic species dangling from the broken trees, organs that defied identification flung widely across the beslimed grass.

In the midst of this charnel yard knelt Brother Diaz, Vigga on her hands and knees not far from him. The fact that she was largely naked, slathered in gore, and making a strange sobbing whine indicated that she had recently recovered from one of her transformations. That went a long way towards explaining the state of the place. She truly was incorrigible when it came to the generation of dead bodies.

Balthazar wrinkled his nose, clearing the steps of shredded meat with one shoe, kicking a horribly distorted severed arm aside with a grunt of disgust. Brother Diaz did not seem in a particularly receptive state of mind. He had not so much as looked over.

"As I was saying . . ." Balthazar edged gingerly around a revolting conglomeration of dead flesh, misshapen bone, warped arms, legs, teeth, horns.
"You will *never* guess . . . what happened . . ."

He petered out as Vigga made a wailing sob, choking off into a sick gurgle.
It was becoming clear that a not inconsiderable amount of the blood *on* her
was coming *out* of her. There was a great oozing gash in her tattooed back.
One of her legs was torn and twisted under her in a manner that did not look
at all healthy, one of her arms and some of her fingers were far from straight.
Was a flap of her face hanging off? That really looked as if it could use a
bandage.

"Where is Baptiste?" asked Balthazar, glancing around. "Hiding, no doubt,
that bloody woman *never* . . . sticks her neck . . . out . . ."

Brother Diaz slowly shook his head, blood-smeared face streaked with
tears. Balthazar realised there was something stretched out between the werewolf and the monk. A carcass? Horribly twisted, missing much of its skull.
Were those . . . knee boots, on its broken legs?

Balthazar's mouth had turned suddenly dry. He looked at Vigga, shaking,
blubbing, bleeding on all fours.

"What did you do?" he whispered.

She rocked forwards and was noisily sick, sobbing and retching at once,
bringing up a stream of bloody offal. She coughed, shuddering as she dragged
something out of her mouth. Something long and bloody, stuck in her teeth.
Wads of black, curly hair.

"What did you *do*?" he demanded.

She gave a wretched howl, lurched onto her hands, and was sick again,
lumps of black meat splatting down into a widening bloody puddle. Something glinted there. Could it be . . . a gold tooth?

Vigga stared at it, whimpering with each hard breath, tears dripping from
her face.

Balthazar leaned down over her and screamed it. "*What did you do?*"

Deep Pockets

The doors of the throne room were swung open, and Zizka strode in. She wore solemn black, edged with cardinal's scarlet, a silent delegation of a dozen priests shuffling after her with heads bowed. If she was at all intimidated by the dazzling room and its majestic view, or by the awe-inspiring sight of Alex enthroned among the serpents in brooding silence, or even by the stairs she'd been forced to climb, she showed no hint of it.

"Your Resplendence," she intoned, bowing ever so slightly. She glanced over the prizefighter's bruises covering Alex's face and neck, which she'd pointedly chosen not to powder, and didn't so much as twitch. "I bring greetings from Her Holiness the Pope and regret that, as her legate and representative, I am not permitted to kneel."

"Daresay you'd grovel otherwise," grumbled Alex, under her breath.

"And Brother Diaz." Zizka turned towards him, standing on the steps of the throne at Alex's right hand. "I must congratulate you on—"

"Father Diaz, in fact," he said.

Zizka was as unsurprised as she was unintimidated. She briefly took in the priest's cassock he'd traded for his monk's habit, the silver wheel he'd swapped for his wooden circle, and instantly worked it out. "It has pleased Her Resplendence to accept you into the Church of the East, then."

"As my personal chaplain and confessor," said Alex, struggling not to lose her temper too soon. "He's proved his loyalty. And someone in my position can't put a price on *trust*."

Father Diaz was not a man troubled by ill temper. He was all smiles. "The palace chapel's a far humbler affair than my previous benefice, but the role comes with administrative responsibilities I feel are better suited to my talents, such as they are. I hope you will convey my thanks to Her Holiness for the opportunity, but I remember Your Eminence stating that she did not expect vicars of the Chapel of the Holy Expediency . . . to last long in the post?"

Cardinal Zizka did not bat an eyelid. "The Celestial Palace will feel much diminished having lost a theologian of such towering promise, but we will try to limp on without you. So. First of all, I bring a gift from Her Holiness . . ."

Zizka snapped her fingers at one of her priests, who shuffled forward, head bowed, to offer up a jewelled casket. "A relic of the blessed Saint Natalia, returned after centuries to her birthplace and yours. An expression of the Pope's delight to see you restored to your proper place as Empress of Troy, and my own, of course—"

Alex couldn't help tipping her head back to shout, "Ha!" at the ceiling.

The priest froze nervously, casket trembling at arm's length. Her mistress raised her brows by the slightest degree. "After the efforts I made on her behalf, can she doubt—"

"Oh, there's no *doubt* in my mind!" And Alex snapped her own fingers. Father Diaz unfolded the letter to Duke Michael and stepped down from the dais to offer it to Zizka.

She glanced at him, and then at Alex. She took the letter. She gave it a shake. She impatiently waved forwards a different priest, who offered her a pair of lenses on a handle. Zizka held them to her face, tipping the letter until she had it in the right light, moving it back and forth until she had it at the right distance. She squinted at it for a moment. Her own seal and signature. The undeniable proof of her treachery. She lowered the lenses, handed them back to her priest, then waved her away. She held the paper out to Father Diaz between two fingers and gave a weary sigh.

"Well, this is exactly why I told him to burn the letter," she said, calmly.

Alex stared. "That's it?" She hadn't really known what she expected. Slimy denials that she could icily pull apart. Grovelling appeals for forgiveness that she could furiously reject. But this . . . passionless shrug of the shoulders? "You conspired with my uncle . . ." The note of wounded upset in her own voice, as if conspiring with her uncle had been cheating at some child's game, made her pent-up rage boil over. "To have me *fucking killed*!" She ended up screaming at the very top of her voice, which gave her a stabbing pain through her ribs where Duke Michael had punched her, which only made her scream louder than ever.

Father Diaz flinched. The guards stirred unhappily. Zizka's priests shuffled back. The one with the casket cringed, clutching it to her chest. But the cardinal herself seemed as impervious to anger as to shock or intimidation.

"People try to kill me all the time," she said. "Provided they fail, I try not to take it personally."

Alex stared. "You *what*?"

"I fully understand your irritation—"

"Try *fury*!"

"—but I was faced with a choice. I have served five Holy Mothers as Head

of the Earthly Curia. Such a role requires great sacrifices, painful compromises, necessary—"

"*Evils?*" snapped Alex.

"One woman's evil, another's . . . *expediency.* My task is to walk in the
shadows, so Her Holiness may stand in the light. As Empress, you may find
yourself in the shadows more often than not. You will face sacrifices and
compromises of your own, and on occasion may even be obliged to do what
is expedient. That is the price of sitting in the big chair." Her eyes wandered
over the Serpent Throne. "And there are no bigger chairs than this one. What
is it that you want?"

"An apology would be a start!" snarled Alex, nursing her battered ribs.

"I apologise. What else?"

Alex had never gone to see Gal the Purse without working out what she'd
like to leave with. "I want the devils. I want them released from the Pope's
binding and given over to me."

Now, finally, Zizka frowned. "Out of the question."

"You're in no position to—"

"I am nothing, but I stand before you as the representative of Her Holiness,
and Her Holiness is the voice of *God on earth.*" She didn't shout, exactly, but she
had some trick that made the last words almost painful on the ear. She wagged
one finger at the ceiling as the echoes faded. "No matter how lofty your throne,
you will yet find the Almighty above you. I understand your request. It even
does you credit. They have been your protectors. They have seen you through
the fire. But be under no illusions as to what they really are. Vigga Ullasdottr
was an uncontrollable menace before she became a werewolf. How would you
control her now? Perhaps we should ask Baptiste?"

There was an awkward silence. Alex realised she was picking at the bandages that covered her arm and made herself stop.

Father Diaz cleared his throat. "We accept, perhaps, that Vigga is best held
in the Celestial Palace—"

"If you think the others pose lesser threats you are deluding yourselves.
You have been fortunate to meet Baron Rikard in a good mood. His bad
mood wiped out sizeable tracts of Eastern Europe. And do not get me started
on the demon-bargaining grave robber." She snorted. "What would your subjects make of an Empress who entertains such companions?"

Alex swallowed. Sacrifices and compromises indeed. "Sunny, then—"

"Are you sure? The elf has spent her whole life separated from her kind,
tortured and tormented by ours. I, for one, find her hard to read, don't you?
Can you say, with absolute certainty, that if her kind were to find her, she

would side with us against them? And make no mistake, her kind are coming. If elves are feared and hated in the West, they are the subjects of utter loathing and revulsion here, and with good reason. Keep her as your pet, and it is discovered, your subjects will likely burn the pair of you."

Alex tried one more time. "The devils . . . the congregation . . . they're not evil—"

"I never said they were. Evil can be reasoned with. They are far more dangerous than that. They are each, in their way, children, but with the power of monsters, and they must return with me to the Holy City where they can be contained. Better for you, and the truth is . . . better for them. Sooner or later you would have to cage them yourself. Or be destroyed by them. And I think you are wise enough to know it." Alex had known it, if she was honest. She'd never left Gal the Purse with quite what she wanted, and Zizka was a negotiator in a very different league. "Jakob of Thorn is a different case, admittedly," she went on. "I expected to see him here . . ."

"He fell into the sea," said Father Diaz.

"Careless of him."

"From the top of this tower!" growled Alex. "In flames. Saving my life. From your friend Duke Michael!"

"How very . . . *Jakob,*" said Zizka, not at all disturbed by that, either. "For such a grim fellow, he always did have a flair for the dramatic. He may well wash up, sooner or later. If so, he is welcome to join you. He has been convicted of no crime. But be advised, he may be the most dangerous of them all." Zizka took a step forwards. She was not a large woman, but she seemed somehow to fill that room. A black tower of blunt speaking in the midst of all the gaudy splendour. "May I speak honestly, Your Resplendence?"

"Since you've admitted attempted murder, I wouldn't say plain language is going to make much difference, is it?"

"When we were first introduced, I saw a desperate child, a thief and beggar, bereft of breeding, education, or character, entirely unsuited to a place as a chambermaid, let alone an Empress. Frankly, I suspected you would run away at the first opportunity or betray our cause for a crust of bread."

Cardinal Zizka left a lengthy pause, as though inviting Alex to disagree. As though inviting anyone to disagree. No one disagreed.

She came forwards another step. "Duke Michael was a snake. But I know how to deal with snakes. Choosing him over you was a decision that made itself."

Alex lifted her chin, the way Baron Rikard had taught her. "So what do you see now?"

"Breeding can be faked. Education learned. What truly matters is character, and on that . . ." Zizka considered Alex carefully. "It seems I may have rushed to judgement. I see a woman who, if she listens to wise voices, and makes wise choices, may very well grow into her role."

"Not to mention that the other candidates were . . ." and Alex counted them off on her fingers. "Ripped apart by a werewolf, impaled with a sword on a sinking ship, dragged into a plague pit by a legion of the dead, frozen and shattered into a thousand pieces of melting meat, or plummeted in flames down Europe's longest drop into the sea."

There was a pause.

"It seems the decision makes itself again," said Cardinal Zizka, coming forwards another pace. "I fear you will discover that, the more powerful one is, the more often one finds the decisions have made themselves. When we face the inevitable it behoves us, for the sake of those who rely on us for their safety and prosperity, to make the best of it."

"So you suggest I put my feelings aside for the common good?"

"Your words. But, in my opinion, well-chosen ones." Zizka's voice certainly betrayed no feeling as she took another pace, her toes almost touching the Serpent Throne's lowest step. "Speaking frankly, still, your position remains precarious. You have few friends and many rivals, and your Empire is hedged in by enemies. And that is before we even consider the threat of the elves, and their mindless gods, and their terrible appetites, an enemy before whom even the bravest must tremble, against whom even the strongest must seek every ally. Only Her Holiness, leading a Europe united under the one true Church, can give you the support you need."

"Meaning her Earthly Curia, I take it?"

"You show wisdom beyond your years."

There was a pause. Alex glanced across at Father Diaz. He raised his brows, and gave the slightest nod. The way they'd got here was far from pleasing. But she knew they'd been heading there all along.

Thieves and Empresses. They all have to make the best of what they're given.

She took a long breath and slumped back in her uncomfortable seat. "We're prepared to consider a union between the Churches of East and West, and work towards an end to the great schism." Alex fixed Cardinal Zizka with her eye. "But it's going to *fucking* cost you."

There was a silence, as the two of them glared at one another. Then Cardinal Zizka gave the faintest smile. "God has deep pockets," she said.

Another Man's Poison

S aviour's tits, he's alive!"

Jakob dreamed of falling.

Of burning.

Of sinking into the deep.

He dreamed of the very end of things, and the cold that comes after.

But even in his dreams there was a niggling ache, and he tried to shift, and the ache became a throb, and it spread from his chest to every extremity.

"Look! He moved!"

"How could he move, fool, he must've drowned days—"

Jakob gave an upset grunt, but no air moved, and in a sudden panic he twisted over and half-coughed, half-vomited a great rush of raw seawater.

"Saviour's *tits*! He *is* alive!"

He flopped back, each cough a crushing stab through his chest, through his side, right down to the tips of his toes.

He could hear birds. Waves slapped on wood.

The stabbing of daylight was agony. But everything was. The light, the darkness, the birds, the voices.

Two figures stood over him. Angels standing in judgement.

"How can he be alive?" one whispered.

Not angels, as Jakob's eyes began to adjust. Fishermen. A young one and an old, enough beard between them to stuff a mattress.

"That . . ." croaked Jakob, "is a long story . . ."

He retched up more seawater, then dropped back and lay there, on the tipping deck, stabbed afresh by each in-breath, a salty rattle on each out. To never breathe again. That was the great hope. One he could never realise.

Still alive. Every time he came to that realisation, it was with the slightest sting of disappointment.

He could smell fish. Because he was lying naked in a heap of them. Netted along with the daily catch. He could almost have laughed, had it not been for the pain.

"Who rules Troy?" he whispered.

The young one blinked down at him. "Empress Alexia."

"Huh." Jakob let his head drop back. The deck creaked under him. A couple of white clouds moved against the blue. "That's good."

He hoped so, at least.

Time would tell.

Jakob of Thorn—once illustrious Grandmaster of the Golden Order, once indomitable Champion of the Emperor of Burgundy, once infamous General-in-Chief of the Livonian Crusade—hobbled hunched through the Hanging Gardens in a borrowed set of fisherman's second-best rags, sweating and swearing, arms wrapped around himself, trying to take only shallow breaths through his gritted teeth so the half-healed wounds around his lungs wouldn't cause him any more agony than they did already.

The Basilica was a pale blur through his tears and he stopped before he got there, limping from the road to grind his forehead against the nearest tree trunk. All his too-long life, doggedly shuffling back, even more broken than before, to the scenes of old defeats.

"You look like I feel." Baron Rikard was slumped on a bench, sunning himself like an ancient lizard. There was no trace of the young god who had paraded through the city a few days before, turning the head of everything female from laundry girls to stray cats. His raven-black mane had shrivelled to white wisps. His emerald eyes turned milky and bloodshot. Skin like new porcelain had sagged to baggy saddle leather. Not that Jakob's looked much better, puffy and peeling from a few days' pickling in brine.

"Duke Michael impaled me," grunted Jakob. "Twice. Then he dropped a statue on me."

"May he rot in hell," croaked the baron, cheerfully. "Where the three of us will no doubt one day be reunited."

"Though how exactly . . ." Jakob gasped at a particularly savage sting as he tried to straighten, and quickly thought better of it. "The torments of the damned . . . would differ from my usual mornings . . . I've no idea."

"More forks, flames, and, judging by the paintings I've seen . . ." The baron attempted to waft a hand around, but it was bandaged to a white mitten, and he gave up. "Unlikely objects up the anus."

"What is it . . . with paintings of demons . . . and the anus?"

"Says more about the painters than the demons, I daresay. Some people pay good money for that."

"Paintings of demons?"

"Unlikely objects up the anus."

"One man's meat . . ." Jakob groaned as he lowered himself inch by inch onto the bench beside the baron, legs trembling until he could take it no more and flopped the remaining distance onto his arse. "Another's poison."

The shape of that familiar smirk could still be recognised on the withered mask of the baron's face. "We were the terrors of our day, you and I. Now look."

"No matter how you fight, you can't beat time. It lays low every Empire, topples every tyrant."

Baron Rikard's pink-rimmed, red-streaked, yellow-stained eyes rolled sideways, and all trace of a smile was gone. "Did you hear?"

And Jakob felt that familiar sinking. Death never came as a surprise. It had been following him all his life. It just never quite caught him. He wondered about walking away. He wondered about jumping back into the sea. But he had his oaths to consider. He gritted his teeth. Like a man sentenced to a flogging, waiting for the lash to land.

"Who?" he asked.

"Baptiste."

Jakob winced. That one hurt. Hurt as much as any stabbing he'd endured. He'd known a lot of people who'd died, of course. More or less all of them. But Baptiste always seemed so alive. "What happened?" he whispered.

"According to Brother Diaz . . ." Baron Rikard shrugged. "She stuck her neck out."

"She never could help doing that." Jakob gave a long sigh and looked up to the sky. "Always thought I'd go first. But then I think that about everyone. And I'm always wrong." He nodded at a walking stick hooked over the back of the bench. "Could I borrow that?"

"By all means." Rikard closed his eyes. "Next time I move I plan to be carried."

If little had changed inside the Basilica of the Angelic Visitation in a few centuries, why would it in a few days? Still the countless ranks of benches, the countless crowd of icons, the bitter-sweet tang of old incense, the silence in which each scrape of Jakob's shuffling sandals, each click of Jakob's borrowed cane, gave birth to a volley of echoes.

There was one difference, though, at the shrine of the Second Crusade. One of those two empty tombs had been filled, the freshly cut marble of its lid oddly bright among the old heroes. Alex stood nearby, the gold of her circlet, and the jewels on her fingers, and the pearls sewn onto her dress, gleaming by candlelight. As Jakob came close she turned, and saw him, and her eyes went wide.

He paused to catch his breath, leaning on his stick. "Well, don't act like you never saw the dead walk before," he said.

"You're alive!"

"Always . . . ooof," as she ran the few steps between them and caught him in a hug, the feeling as she squeezed him like being stabbed fresh, and he lurched back, only by a heroic effort keeping from going down with her on top of him.

"Sorry!" She let go, holding her bandaged arm. "Ow." Her eyes and her neck were ringed with bruises, a scab across the bridge of her nose.

"The state of we two old warhorses," he muttered, still gripping his ribs.

"You should see the other fucker. Did you lose some of your eyebrow?"

"My own sacrifice to Saint Natalia's Flame." Jakob put a hand to the mottled burn that had claimed half his eyebrow and some patches of his beard besides.

They trailed off into awkward silence, as Jakob's conversations generally did, both looking towards the shrine of the Second Crusade. Both looking towards that new tomb.

"You heard?" asked Alex, quietly.

"I did," said Jakob.

"I'm sorry."

"So am I."

Alex cleared her throat. "I thought I'd have a statue made." She gave a snort of laughter. "Imagine her standing there, next to William the Red."

"She'd approve." Jakob gritted his teeth. "Give the place a bit of glamour."

"Shame she's not here, she could likely have done the sculpting herself."

"I believe she did do piecework as a mason, for a summer. You should send to the Duke of Milan."

"For what?"

"He's got a painting of her. You could use it as a reference."

"Why does the Duke of Milan have a painting of Baptiste?"

Jakob smiled, just a little. "Long story." And he cleared his throat, and nodded towards a pair of young women lurking near the lectern. "I see you've found new handmaidens." The brown-haired one was staring up at the icons, eyes wide with wonder. The blonde one had a slyer look, as if guessing what everything might fetch on a fence's bench.

"Orphans." Alex leaned close to murmur. "I found 'em in the poorhouse."

"They'll have a lot to learn."

"Less than I did, when we started out from the Holy City." Alex sighed. "Less than I still do. But at least we'll understand each other while we're doing it." She beckoned the blonde girl forwards with a bundle in her hands. "I've got something for you." And she started to unwrap it, from what proved to be an old battle flag. "I mean, how many men can say they've given their lives for me more than once?"

Jakob could guess what was inside from the shape. But even he, who must've seen a hundred thousand swords, wasn't quite prepared for what was revealed when she pulled the last scrap of cloth back.

The leather of the scabbard was polished to a soft sheen with age, chased with silver and set with gems. The hilt was bound in a web of gold wire, the pommel was the sacred wheel, carved from some lustrous stone. No one could've doubted at a glance it was a masterwork even more antique than he was.

"They say the charcoal for the steel came from a fragment of the wheel the Saviour died on," murmured Alex.

"Holy *shit . . .*" Jakob reached out to lay gentle fingers on the scabbard. How could he help it? "It's beautiful. As beautiful as a sword can be."

"Belonged to John of Antioch."

"Marshal of Troy. He led the armies of Leo the Blind against the elves . . . in the First Crusade . . ." And Jakob gave a grunt of amusement as he saw the gift behind the gift.

"So you get where I'm going with this." Alex stepped a little closer. "Everyone says, sooner or later, the elves will come again, and they'll be hungry. I need a soldier I can trust. A general to lead the new crusade. Who better than a man who fought in most of the others?"

You had to give it to Alex, she'd known exactly how to pitch it. She'd come a long way from that shifty waif he met in the Celestial Palace. He closed his eyes a moment, then snapped them open. "I wonder, sometimes, how many swords I've carried. How many have been *my* sword. I helped forge my first, long ago, when I was a boy. An ill-formed thing, but I was so proud of it. Thought I'd never need another."

Jakob brushed the golden crosspiece with his fingertips. "Emperor Odo of Burgundy gave me one after I won him the County of Charolais in a tournament. A work of art, the hilt a dragon's body in gold, the crosspiece its wings, eyes two little rubies. More jewellery than weapon, but when you buckled it on . . . you felt like a *king.*"

Jakob bared his teeth as he wrapped his gnarled knuckles around the sword's hilt. "Then there was the one I carried as the Papal Executioner, verses from the scriptures stamped into the blade. A flat tip, no need for a point, and the balance was all wrong for fighting. Too long. Too heavy. But when you drew it, and stood over the convicted . . ." He drew John of Antioch's sword now, a length of rippled steel sliding from the clasp and catching the candle-light, "you felt like a *god*."

He heard Alex swallow, and glanced up. He'd somehow forgotten she was there, and now she looked ever so slightly scared. He forced himself to slide the sword away. To hide that beautiful blade.

"When I first came to Troy, I was a squire no older than you are. Eager for a sight of the elves. Desperate to prove myself to the great warriors." He looked to the statue of William the Red and shook his head. "To wear a sword like this, to lead an army for an Empress like you, would've been more than that boy could've dreamed of."

"Isn't that why you should say yes?"

He gave a long sigh as he let his aching fingers relax. "That's why I have to say no."

Alex shook her head. "But we could do so much *good*."

"That's how it always begins. The just cause. The good fight. Each time, I tell myself it will be different. But for me, as the fight wears on, the good wears off. Before I know it . . . I've made myself a devil. That's why I swore to serve Her Holiness. That's why I have to keep my oath." And with the bitter regret of a drunk pushing away the bottle, he let his lingering fingertips slip from the gold-wired hilt. "John of Antioch was a great hero."

"So they say."

"And a bloodthirsty traitor."

"Eh?"

"After the First Crusade, he turned on the Emperor and tried to seize the Serpent Throne. Unleashed a civil war that was scarcely better than the elves had been. He caused thousands of deaths, lost, was blinded and banished and died in penury."

"Shit. They don't tell that part of the story." Alex wrinkled her nose at the sword. "Well, I expect you'd only leave it stuck in a troll or something." She handed it to her blonde handmaiden, who was smiling thoughtfully at the jew-elled pommel. "I'll be checking that got back where it was supposed to," she muttered.

The girl's curtsey was as clumsy as her smirk was sly. "Very sensible, my lady."

"Who's the joking saint?" asked Alex.

Jakob found he was looking at that icon beside the shrine, no bigger than his hand. "Saint Stephen. Patron of warriors. Protector of the desperate."

"Appropriate."

"The Templars used to screw his image to the backs of their shields. I had one once, but—"

"Here." As simply as that, Alex unhooked the icon and offered it to him. "You're not *bloody* leaving empty-handed."

Jakob glanced about the nave. "Are you sure?"

"It's this or a dukedom. I believe Nicaea's available." She waved the little picture at the echoing space above, the walls covered in acres of saint's faces. "And I think we'll still have a few to be getting on with."

Jakob took one step towards Baptiste's tomb and laid a hand on the lid. "It should've been me. Long ago. In the Second Crusade. Then I could've been buried here. With the heroes. When I still deserved to be."

Alex shrugged. "Then who would've protected me when I was desperate?"

Jakob took the icon from her, in both hands. "Perhaps evil men can do good, still."

"If they do enough, don't they become good men?"

"Maybe," said Jakob. "Maybe one day." Because she wanted to believe it. He wasn't sure he could.

"Well, there's still a grave spare." Alex nodded to the one beside Baptiste's. The last one. "I'll keep it free for you." She leaned close to whisper. "In case you get lucky."

Jakob laughed, then. He put one arm around the Empress of Troy and, however much it hurt, he squeezed her tight. "Good luck, Alex," he said, and as quickly as that let her go, and was limping towards the door.

"You think I'll need it?" she called after him.

He didn't turn back. "We all need it," he said.

All Bad Things

Thought I might find you here," said Alex.

"It's nice." Sunny put her head back to stare up at the chinks of blue sky between the stirring foliage. "The sun through the leaves and the wind through the branches."

"An elf who likes plants." Alex sat down next to her, stripes of sunlight sliding across her bruised face. "What a cliché."

"It's not so much the plants as the shadows. Sometimes it's nice to just . . . breathe."

A silence, then. One Sunny didn't know how to break.

"We're leaving," she said, after a while.

"I know."

"Today, most likely. Cardinal Zizka will take us back to the Holy City."

"She and I . . . had a bit of a disagreement."

"To know Cardinal Zizka is to disagree with her."

"She did try to have me killed."

"You're among some very good company there, if it's any consolation."

"A bit." Alex looked over at her. "Who wants to be alone?"

Sunny stared at the ground. As if there was something very interesting there, between her boots. "Impressed you stood up to her. An Empress can't be scared, I guess."

"An Empress is scared all the time. She just can't look it. I tried . . . to get her to let you go, but—"

"She wouldn't." Sunny was not enjoying this one bit. It was easier, in the end, to feel nothing.

"I wish you could stay," said Alex.

"I know. But I can't."

"I wish I could come."

"I know. But you can't."

Another silence. "Who's going to save me now?"

"Well, if things work out, I guess . . . you won't need saving any more?"

Alex gave her a look.

Sunny winced off into the trees. "Father Diaz, then."

"That fool can't even turn invisible."

"You might have to save yourself."

"I was afraid you'd say that."

A breeze came up, and shook the trees, and washed through the space between them. A narrow space, but one there was no bridging.

"What if . . ." Alex licked her lips, dropped her voice to a whisper. "They find out . . . I'm not the real thing—"

"You're the real thing now. Wherever you came from."

"But I've done . . . I'm not *good*—"

"It's not what you've done that makes you good or bad. It's what you do next."

Alex gave a little snort. "An elf giving an Empress lessons on virtue?"

"Someone has to, and your priest fucked a werewolf."

Alex gave another little snort, of laughter this time, and Sunny was pleased she'd made it happen, but soon enough Alex's smile faded. "Is there anything . . . I could give you?" she asked. "You deserve . . . something."

Sunny thought about it. She could've asked for one last kiss. She got a feeling that's what Alex wanted. But a kiss is the start of something. A doorway to something else. The fun is all the promise of what's on the other side. A kiss, when you know it's leading nowhere . . . what's it worth? It's just a reminder of what you don't have. The first sentence of a story that'll never be told.

Sunny looked away. "I don't need anything."

"Maybe I'll see you again," whispered Alex. Sunny didn't want to look at her. She guessed from her voice she was crying a bit, and she didn't want to see it.

"Maybe." Jakob always said, *People rarely want all of the truth*, and she reckoned this was one of those times. She stood up, slapping the seat of her trousers. "Maybe."

"It's not *fair*," snapped Alex, sounding furious of a sudden. "You risked everything for me, over and over! And I can't do the same for you."

"Do it for someone else, then." Sunny liked that idea. That she might do a good thing for someone, and they'd do a good thing for someone else, and it'd come back around, one day, in a big circle of goodness. Hadn't happened yet, but you could hope. "Do it for everyone else."

"For the people, eh?"

"Why not? I like people." Sunny took a long breath. "I wish I was one."

Alex stared at her. "You're the best person I ever met."

And that was nice to hear, at least. Could've been the nicest thing anyone ever said to her. It wasn't saying much, but still.

"Look at that," said Alex, tears in her eyes but grinning at the same time. "You can smile after all."

Sunny put her fingers to her cheeks. They did seem a different shape from usual, somehow.

"Huh," she muttered. "Who knew?"

Vigga lay in her cage.

They hadn't dragged her in. She crawled in by herself. She burrowed into the straw more rat than wolf, and lay in the darkness, and didn't move, and didn't speak, and didn't think, and was just meat, and not good meat.

She was cut and gashed and chewed all over. Ragged wounds left by giant teeth, stitched closed by an idiot. She'd worried at the bandages and peeled them off, then worried at the scabs and opened her wounds, then another idiot had stitched them closed again, then Cardinal Zizka had put an iron collar on her and said if she worried at the bandages again she'd flog her tattooed hide off, so she'd let them be.

She'd been flogged before and it was horrible.

Her leg was fucked. It might heal. Or not. For now she couldn't stand and didn't care. She was an animal and didn't deserve to stand. She was an animal, and deserved to wear a collar, and crawl on her belly in the filth, and she pissed there in the straw where she lay and didn't even roll away from it.

Baptiste had been her friend and the wolf had killed her. The wolf had killed her, but it was Vigga's nails that her blood was still crusted under. Vigga's mouth that still tasted of her meat. She scraped her tongue raw and spat and sobbed and retched and stuffed her mouth with straw and spat again but that taste was always there. Would always be there.

She'd seen no more terrible and no more pitiable monster than the leftovers that slithered from beneath the library, but she was more terrible and more pitiable yet, because she pretended to be a person, and sometimes, for a little while, even tricked herself.

But then she was a fucking idiot, and easily fooled.

She wasn't clean. She wasn't safe. She was as unclean and unsafe as anything God or gods or whatever was up there suffered to live. If there was anything up there.

She began to doubt it.

There were voices in the darkness. "Does she have to be in the cage?"

"Of course she does, Father Diaz. You've seen what she is."

"The wolf . . . is not *her*, Your Eminence. The wolf is . . . a curse!"

A snort of scornful laughter. "Do not fool yourself that it is one that can be cured. Even before the bite she was a monster. A Viking spreading terror down the coasts of Europe, who burned churches and killed monks for the sport of it."

"She deserves our pity, not our hate—"

"She deserves neither. No more than the dogs who guard the Celestial Palace. She can be made a weapon to smite the unholy, to strike righteous terror into the enemies of the Church. That is why she is suffered to live, and only that."

The pagans had chained her in a cage, and starved her, and goaded her, and used her to kill their enemies. And Vigga saw now the pagans and the Saved didn't hate each other because they were so different, but because they were so alike.

"You saved us," said Diaz. She heard him move closer, speak softer. "You saved me." She heard him slip his fingers around the bars. Softer yet, almost a whisper. "In more ways than one."

"I'm glad," she grunted, into the straw. "But I can't save me." She didn't turn. She didn't want to see him. Zizka was right. She couldn't be cured, and deserved neither pity nor hate. She could feel the wolf inside, whining to be let out. Never sleeping. Never satisfied. Always, always whining to be let out.

"I'm not safe," she said. "I'm not clean." She burrowed into the straw and hid her face. "I never will be."

As Balthazar edged, somewhat gingerly, across the gangplank, he winced in anticipation of some withering barb. As he hopped, somewhat inelegantly, to the deck he glanced up, expecting to see that infuriating smirk, the gleam of the gold tooth behind the scarred lips—

But he saw no such thing, of course, and never would again. How often had he wished for her gone? Now that she was, somehow her absence seemed enormous. He kept thinking of things he should have said. Rehearsing things he might have done. Spinning out ever more unlikely scenarios. He had always imagined he would win some crushing final victory over her. Or that, perhaps, they would come to understand, to respect, to admire one another. Or . . . who knew what? Something, anyway. Some *outcome*. And now there was merely a tantalising prologue, cut off mid-sentence, abandoned in the writing, never to find completion.

Balthazar was obliged to wipe his eye, pretending at irritation by the wind.

He had to shake himself free of these self-defeating, self-indulgent, maudlin meanderings. He was one of Europe's foremost necromancers, for God's sake, a master of the grave's mysteries! Why should a single death perplex him so completely?

He clenched his fists and dragged in a lungful of salt air. In the past, he had always disdained the sea. He had always disdained all outdoor odours save the tantalising miasma of the graveyard, but his feelings on that, as on so much else, had undergone a radical change over recent months.

He was a new-forged man, animated by a new purpose! He realised now that he had made himself small, in his long years of study. He had constrained his potential within narrow jealousies and cramped ambitions. But confinement to the service of the Pope, in a paradox worthy of some antique philosopher, had freed him from his self-imposed imprisonment. Now he stood ready to grow! The world burst forth with possibilities, and he was intent on marching forth to seize them!

He strode over to Jakob of Thorn, leaning against the ship's rail with that perennially pained expression of his. "When can we expect Her Holiness to assign us another mission?"

"When she needs our talents," grunted the ancient knight. "The voyage back to the Holy City will take two weeks at least. Maybe three."

"But never fear!" Cardinal Zizka had followed Balthazar across the gangplank onto the deck, two burly manservants helping with her luggage. "You will be travelling in style."

"Indeed, Your Eminence?" asked Balthazar.

"The best stateroom has been prepared."

"Truly?" He had hardly dared imagine that others, least of all the Head of the Earthly Curia herself, would be so ready to reward his change of heart. "Then, in the spirit of cooperation, I have some momentous information to share! I apologise that, given the events . . . concerning Baptiste . . ." Something was caught in his throat. He thumped his breastbone, and soldiered on. "It did not heretofore seem the proper moment, but it is a revelation concerning Lady Severa—"

"Ah, the one that got away," said Zizka.

"Indeed, though the astonishing thing—"

"The one *you let* get away," said Zizka.

Balthazar awkwardly cleared his throat. "I believe you will want to hear—"

"Then you should be properly dressed while you tell me."

Balthazar's face fell as, with some effort, the older of the two manservants—

who he now realised could, in fact, have more accurately been described as jailers—produced a set of mighty iron fetters, runes crudely stamped into the black metal of the bracelets. Runes of containment and control. Bonds intended to prevent sorcerers from using magic. Or magicians, naturally.

"Hands," grunted the man.

Balthazar did his best to produce a watery smile. "These really are not necessary."

"But they are expedient," said Zizka.

"Your Eminence, please! May I speak briefly?"

"*Can* you speak briefly?"

Balthazar gave that false little titter. Even after all his recent triumphs, it seemed he could not avoid it when nervous. "I have come to a profound realisation, Your Eminence. An epiphany, one might say! I must confess that, on our journey from the Holy City, I three times tried, and three times failed, to escape Her Holiness's binding. On the final occasion, indeed, at a set of standing stones near Niksic—"

Jakob gave a sharp intake of breath, and Balthazar realised, as Zizka narrowed her eyes yet further, that the summoning of a Duke of Hell might not land so very well with a leading member of the clergy. "Well, er . . . let us not dwell . . . on the *precise nature* of the evidence, but I have become convinced that Pope Benedicta is indeed the Second Coming of the Saviour herself!"

His confession did not elicit the delight he had hoped for. Zizka took a long breath through her nose, and raised one lethal eyebrow at Jakob of Thorn. "Our necromancer has found religion?"

"Faith is not necessary, Your Eminence! I am a man of reason, and it is reason that has led me to this conclusion! I no longer *need* to be compelled to serve Her Holiness!"

"Because you thrice tried to break her binding and thrice failed."

"Exactly!"

Jakob gave that sharp intake of breath again.

"Well, no . . . not because of *that*." There was something about Zizka's basilisk glare that made it very hard for Balthazar to keep his thread. He had faced drawn swords he found less worrying. "But because, I mean . . . I will serve her *willingly*. I have been searching, you see, perhaps all my life, for a *purpose*. A *mission*. A *cause* to which to apply my talents!" He smiled. Zizka did not. He had yet to receive any evidence that she was capable of it. "And what higher purpose can there be, after all, than to serve the very *daughter of God*?"

Zizka's eyes did not un-narrow by even a fraction. "At last," she said, "we have found common ground."

"I knew we would!" he replied, smiling wider.

"Well done you." She waved to the jailers. "Now take him to the cages."

Balthazar stood, mouth open. The older jailer held out the weighty fetters.

"Hands," grunted the man.

"Your Eminence, please! The cage really is not *necessary*—"

"Necessary, expedient, convenient." Zizka dismissed him with an impatient wave, as if even that was more than he deserved. "That's hardly the point. The cage is where you *belong*."

The older jailer closed one bracelet on Balthazar's wrist with a scraping of unforgiving ratchets. The younger one stepped forwards silently to make sure they were secure. Balthazar could already feel the effects. Like slipping one's head beneath the water, from a magical point of view, the senses suddenly dulled.

"You are a *heretic*, Balthazar Sham Ivam Draxi," said Zizka. "Tried, convicted, and sentenced by the Celestial Court. You are a summoner of demons and a fiddler with the dead."

"I really must object to *fiddler*—"

"For the crimes you have committed—crimes against God himself—there can be no atonement aside from your death and righteous commitment to hell."

The other bracelet scraped shut, the deadening effect intensified.

"I thought the Saviour rejoiced at the redemption of a wrongdoer . . ." muttered Balthazar.

"The Saviour might," said Zizka, turning away. "But she's not holding your leash."

Balthazar gave something close to a wail of dismay as he was flung onto the straw with entirely unnecessary violence, the gate thrown clanging shut behind him, the keys turned in the several locks, then the hold plunged into almost total darkness as the trapdoor was sealed.

Not merely a cage, but an oppressively small one, lined with dirty straw, deep in a lightless hold. "*Curse* them!" he snarled, and punched the floor, and immediately regretted it, then startled as he heard something shift, peering into the thick shadows. "Who's there?"

"Only me," came Baron Rikard's papery wheeze. Could Balthazar detect, as his eyes adjusted to the darkness, the faint twin gleam of his ancient eyes?

"And me." Pale fingers showed in a chink of light, wrapping gently around the bars opposite. A slice of pale, scabbed, bony face and one huge eye, ringed with bruises. Sunny nodded sideways. "And Vigga."

"Uh," came a grunt. Almost a sob.

Balthazar felt no rancour towards her for Baptiste's death. She was helpless before her own nature. It was the corrupt cardinals, the infant Pope, the whole rotten Church that he blamed! On which he would be *revenged*!

"Treated like *livestock*," he snarled, sucking at his abraded knuckles. "*Worse* than livestock. After all we *sacrificed*! They confine us in the darkness! In *cages*!"

"Where else would I go?" said Sunny, softly, and she slipped her fingers from the bars, and retreated into the shadows, and was gone.

"I should be caged," he heard Vigga mumble. "Best for everyone."

"Suit your *fucking* selves! But Balthazar Sham Ivam Draxi will *not* take this lying down!"

From somewhere in the darkness, the baron gave a weary snort. "By all means take it standing up. But you'll be taking it, that I promise you."

"No . . ." whispered Balthazar. What practitioner worth their salt does not keep their deepest secrets for themselves? As luck would have it, Lady Severa's true identity remained a secret known only to him.

"*No* . . ." He began to smile. The binding worked upon the soul, and who knew more of the soul than the mistress of the arcane who had transferred her own into another body?

"I will find a way free . . ." If he could get a message to her, enlist her aid, perhaps between them, a sorcerer of her talents, a magician of his . . . "I *will* break the binding."

If he had to tear down the pillars of creation, he would find a way. He forced down an acrid burp and clenched his fists around the bars so tightly his knuckles ached. "I *swear* it!"

Jakob clenched his fists around the weathered rail so tightly his knuckles ached. Sometimes it almost seemed, if there was a moment when he wasn't in pain, he had to hurt himself. He frowned back towards the city, Saint Natalia's Flame a flickering pinprick in the evening, casting a faint glimmer on their wake.

"Do we really have to keep them in the dark?" he growled.

"Of course. You have forgotten what they are, Jakob." Zizka glanced across at him. "I begin to suspect that you need to be reminded of a great many things."

"It could've come out worse." Not a statement you could make about every cause he'd fought for down the years. "Troy was a great bastion against the elves once. I saw it. With the right leader, it can be again."

"Oh, I am in wholehearted agreement." Zizka's lip curled. "Which is why I wished to install a dependable ruler. A predictable ruler. One who would bring an end to the great schism and reunite the Churches of East and West. Emperor Michael would have served our purposes admirably."

"Those were not the terms of Her Holiness's binding," grunted Jakob.

Zizka gave a disgusted hiss. "For a man who has sworn an oath of honesty you have turned mealy-mouthed, and for a man who has sworn an oath of poverty your arrogance is astonishing. Were it not for the oath of temperance, one would wonder whether you were *drunk*." Cardinal Zizka worked her mouth and spat over the rail into the sea. "Her Holiness, who let us not forget is ten *fucking* years old, asked you to see Alexia crowned. On that I congratulate you. On that and nothing else, because all that came *after* was your personal project, one that has laid waste to years of careful planning. Do you know your problem, Jakob of Thorn?"

"I was cursed by a witch so I cannot die?"

"Oh, let us be more specific. You were cursed by your *lover* so you cannot die." Cardinal Zizka stepped closer, glaring up at him. "And *there* is the key to it! Despite all your scars, all your bitter experience, all your professed cynicism, you still entirely lack the thirteenth virtue. You remain an *incurable romantic*."

The temptation to bundle the Head of the Earthly Curia over the rail and into the churning sea was very great. As a younger man Jakob would likely have done it, and God damn the consequences. But down the long years, he'd learned to resist temptation. He kept his aching fists locked to the rail.

"As always, it will be up to the pragmatists among us to repair the wreckage the idealists leave in their wake." Zizka turned scornfully away. Back towards Troy, already dwindling into the distance. Into the past. "You would not want me as your enemy, Jakob of Thorn."

"Of course not, Your Eminence." Jakob humbly bowed his head, wincing at the twinge in his neck as he straightened. Then he caught her eye. He held it. He made sure there was no misunderstanding. "But you wouldn't be my first."

"Sorry to bother you."

Brother Diaz turned to see Alex in the doorway. Or Father Diaz turned to see Empress Alexia. He suspected it would all take some getting used to. "Not at all." He waved towards the stained-glass window. "I was just . . . talking to the Saviour."

"Much to say for herself?"

"No more than usual. But she's an excellent listener."

"You've got that in common." She loitered, on the threshold. "Can I come in?"

"Of course!" Father Diaz stood, raising his hands to encompass the chapel. He'd already spent far more time there than in his previous benefice in the Celestial Palace, and much preferred it. It might be modest in terms of size and decoration, but he judged his chances of being roasted by a fireball, or sucked dry by a vampire, or drowned in a giant charnel pit to be a good deal lower here.

His chances of coupling with a werewolf were, for that matter, close to nil. He cleared his throat as he beckoned Alex in. "It is your chapel, after all."

"People keep saying that," she said, stepping through the doorway. "My chamber. My palace. My city. When you grow up with nothing, it's hard to think of anything as yours. Let alone an Empire."

"No doubt that will come. You always struck me as a quick learner."

"I've had good teachers." She ran a fingertip along the arm of one of the high chairs built against the walls, and gave an approving nod. "You've been dusting."

"Clean chapel, clean soul, my abbot always used to say. Not that he did much scrubbing himself. From the state of the place, I've a feeling your predecessor didn't spend much time at prayer."

"Eudoxia? No. But likely more than I have. I grew up in the Holy City, after all. None of the locals go to church. Unless it's to filch from the collection plate."

"What could be nobler than to cut out the middleman, and convey the funds directly to the needy?"

"That's what I always said." Alex grinned, for a moment, but it soon faded, and left her thoughtful. "So . . . they're gone?"

"I watched their ship depart from your window." One more white streak on the dark sea. "I prevailed on Jakob to take a letter for me, in fact."

"You finally managed to send one!"

"Just a short note to Mother. Let her know where I am. How it all turned out."

"What will she think? When she hears you're chaplain to an Empress?"

Father Diaz thought about that for a moment, then raised his brows. "Do you know . . . I find I really don't care."

Alex was looking solemnly towards the stained glass. "I wish . . . we could've done more for them."

"We can pray for their redemption." He lowered his voice. "Perhaps while we're praying for our own."

"They're not beyond it, then?"

"I don't believe so. Even if they do. Who is without sin, after all?"

"Not me, that's for damn sure." Alex frowned at the floor for a moment, then reached up to clutch her head with both hands. "What the *fuck* do I know about running an Empire?"

Brother Diaz would likely have deplored the language, but Father Diaz saved the deploring for when it really mattered. "Running an Empire is hardly the job of an Empress," he said.

"What is her job, then?"

"To pick the people who'll run it for her. In my humble opinion, Her Resplendence has already made one excellent choice." Father Diaz patted the lump on his chest, where the vial still sat against his skin. "I shall pray to Saint Beatrix that she continue to guide your hand."

"I'm surprised you're still sending her prayers. After all we went through."

"More than ever! She delivered, didn't she? How many times did we face death? And here we are, both still standing, both strengthened by our trials, both guided to a place where we can do . . . some *good*. If you cannot see the hand of the divine in that—"

"The divine?" Alex looked far from convinced. "Saint Beatrix didn't save us at the inn. A werewolf did. Remember?"

Father Diaz swallowed, his heart suddenly thumping almost painfully hard. "Not an episode easily forgotten."

"And Saint Beatrix didn't save us at the monastery. A necromancer did."

Father Diaz thought of the plague pit, a chill sweat prickling at the small of his back. "Another moment to linger in the memory."

"Did Saint Beatrix dive through Saint Natalia's Flame to save me? No. It was a cursed knight."

"I will admit—"

"And in the rigging of that ship, and in the war-torn wilderness, and in the secret passages of this palace, was it Saint Beatrix who risked everything for me? No. It was . . ." Her voice cracked, and she took a moment to compose herself. "An enemy of God, supposedly."

There was a silence while Father Diaz considered these facts. "I must admit . . . theology was never my strongest suit. Honestly more of a numbers man, but . . . perhaps the werewolf, and the necromancer, and the cursed knight, and even the enemy of God . . . are the tools Saint Beatrix chose?"

"A saint sent a set of devils to turn a thief into an Empress?"

"Well, when you boil it all down . . ." Father Diaz kept one hand on the vial for a moment. Then he let it drop, and shrugged. "That seems to be about the size of it."

Saint Tabitha's Day

It was the fourth of Generosity, and Mother Beckert was early for her audience with Her Holiness the Pope.

"May God have mercy on their souls," she murmured, making the sign of the circle as the carriage was buffeted by a procession of wailing flagellants, their backs streaked with blood and their faces with tears of rapture, whipping themselves along beneath a banner that read simply, "Repent." There was no need to say what one was called on to repent of.

For are we not all sinners?

The carriage door banged open and the din—of prayers, trade, and appeals for charity—and the stench—of incense, overworked sewers, and a nearby fish market—were both instantly tripled as a young man climbed in. He was tall, slender, flamboyantly dressed and, as he glanced surprised towards her, very handsome.

Mother Beckert did not trust handsome people. They were too used to getting away with things.

"Ever so sorry." He spoke with a rich man's accent. But in a way that made her guess it was not the one he grew up with. "Hadn't realised I'd be sharing the carriage."

"You know the Church," said Mother Beckert. "Always after savings."

He sat opposite her, wiping sweat from his brow, and the carriage lurched on, at the snail's pace that was the top speed of the Holy City's traffic. "You're heading to the Celestial Palace, too?"

"They say everyone is," said Mother Beckert, "whether they know it or not."

"Hope we're not late. Streets are swarming!"

"A crowd out for Saint Tabitha's Day. A list of her registered miracles is being given a formal reading from every pulpit." Mother Beckert shrugged. "But it's the Holy City. Every day is at least one saint's day, and everyone is always late. They shift all the appointments to allow for it."

"You're familiar with the place, then?"

"I was." She winced, as if she could smell something bad. This was the

Holy City, after all. One could always smell something bad, especially at the height of summer. "I lost my taste for it."

"But now it's returned?"

"It absolutely has not." She frowned out of the window at the sweltering crowds. "The cardinals," she murmured. "The so-called Saved. They have made of it the most unholy place on God's earth."

The bells for midday prayers were starting to echo over the city, beginning with a desultory dingle or two from the roadside shrines, mounting to a discordant clangour as each chapel, church, and cathedral added its own frantic peals, competing viciously to hook the pilgrims through their doors, onto their pews, and up to their collection plates. If one had built a giant machine for the fleecing of the faithful, it would have looked no different.

The handsome young man cleared his throat, flapping the collar of his loose shirt. "It's hot even for the season," he observed, with that nervous need some people have to fill the silence.

Mother Beckert had spent much of her life in silence, and even more at one extreme of temperature or another. Carrying the word of the Saviour to the benighted corners of the world beyond the edges of the maps. To the steaming jungles of Afrique and the mountains of Norway where the snows never melted, aye, even to Novgorod, where she had bathed in the freezing waters of the river to the astonishment of the locals, and asked them in their own tongue to bring more ice. Heat purged the body, cold sharpened the mind. The greater the bodily discomforts, the purer became her faith.

"I'm used to harsh weather," she said.

"Oh? Where have you travelled from?"

"From England."

"I'm so sorry."

"Don't blame them, they know no better. And you?"

"From Alexandria."

"You don't look Alexandrian."

He smiled, showing a silver tooth. "I am a mongrel. No two of my great-grandparents were from the same country. I am from everywhere and nowhere."

"And what do you do when you are everywhere and nowhere?"

"A little of this. A little of that." He offered his hand, the nails of which appeared to have been shaped with a file. "My name's Caruso."

She considered his hand, then his smile. No doubt he thought himself quite the special case. Most people do. But she saw to the heart of him. Most people are the same, once you peel the outer layers away. "But I expect you have others," she said.

He smiled a little wider. "When I must."

She gripped his hand firmly. "I am always Mother Beckert."

"A German?"

"If you unwound my guts, you would find them stamped *Cast in Swabia*."

"Like the best armour."

"But made of stiffer stuff."

"I hope your innards won't be put on display!"

Mother Beckert gave a snort and looked back to the window. "We shall see."

The carriage crawled through a narrow square, hot as an oven, busy as a slaughterhouse, and squalid as a shithouse. On one side there was a painted enclosure crammed with licensed beggars and a linden-wood platform for public punishments, on which a set of children were burning elves in straw-stuffed effigy while onlookers bellowed encouragement. On the other side the prostitutes were out in numbers, pouting painted lips and displaying sun-burned extremities to the midday glare.

"I would not have thought it possible," she murmured, "but there may be more prostitutes here than ever."

"You disapprove of prostitutes?" he asked, with a hint of a smile.

It was possible he had merely mistaken her. But it was also possible he was making fun of her. For herself, Mother Beckert had long ago surrendered any vanity, but to mock a priest was to mock the Faith, and to mock the Faith was to mock God, and that was a thing to be nipped in the bud. She fixed his eye, and looked directly into it, without blinking or deviation.

The way she once looked into the eye of the accused, as if she already saw the truth within, and only wished it confirmed.

"My mother was a prostitute," she said. "A very good one, by all accounts. Also a very good mother. One would be a fool to judge a person by their profession alone. Like pox on a plague victim, the prostitutes are the symptom, not the sickness. They merely answer a desire. It is the scale of that desire, of that sickness, that concerns me. Especially here, in the Holy City, among the ruins of the ancient Carthage, in the shadow of the thousand churches, within the echo of their blessed bells, where all eyes should be turned to heaven." She leaned towards him, still with her eye on his, without blinking or deviation. "Tell me, Master Caruso—what is the one sin the Saviour cannot forgive?"

He was starting to look a little uncomfortable, which spoke well of his grit. Most would have mumbled their apologies much sooner, and buttoned their lips for the rest of the trip. "Well, I confess I'm no theologist—"

"A man who's a little of everything should be a little theologist, too, don't you think? The Saviour can forgive any trespass honestly confessed and atoned for. Which makes *dishonesty* the only crime that cannot be forgiven." She bared her teeth as she spat the word. "*Hypocrisy*, Master Caruso. The pretence that you are something better, nobler, holier than you are . . . is surely the worst dishonesty of all. It is *that* of which I disapprove."

A silence then. She let it stretch, until she judged that there would be no more mockery. "So tell me. What brings a man from everywhere and nowhere to the Holy City?" Though she already had her suspicions.

"Oh, well . . ." He slid out a letter and held it up. Fine paper, and a great seal of scarlet wax, stamped with the crossed keys of the Papacy. "I was sent for. By Her Holiness."

"Your appointment may be with Her Holiness," said Mother Beckert, "but your meeting will be with Cardinal Zizka."

"The Head of the Earthly Curia?" He blinked. Afraid and excited at once. More afraid and more excited than if the meeting had been with the Pope herself, which said a great deal, and none of it good. "The letter mentions replacing someone, but . . . it doesn't say who."

"Zizka always loved her mysteries."

"You know Her Eminence?"

"Since we were girls. We shared a cell at seminary."

"Old friends, then?"

Mother Beckert chuckled. She did not laugh often, but that was too rich. "We have despised each other from the moment we met. And admired each other. Because we are each everything the other is not. But we know that what the other is, the Church must have. Zizka is like the sea. Ever hungry, never sated. Always flowing, yielding, adapting, treacherous as the tide. If her principles get in the way, she will make new ones."

Caruso swallowed. Perhaps it shocked him, to hear the most powerful woman in Europe so carelessly slighted. "She's a politician, I suppose . . ."

"Her blessing and her curse."

"But you're otherwise?"

She fixed him with her eye again. The way she had once fixed the convicted, when she spoke the sentence. "I am the rock on which the water breaks. That is *my* blessing." She took a long breath. "And my curse."

"Over years . . . the sea will wear the rock away."

"Oh, I am *well* aware. Zizka sent for me, too." And she drew out her letter between two fingers, and held it up. "As a replacement."

"Who for?" Caruso's accent had slipped slightly in his eagerness. Did she detect a hint of something earthy and German underneath?

"She did not say. But I can guess. She wants me to take back my old bene-fice. A chapel. Within the Celestial Palace."

Caruso frowned. "I doubt a chapel would have use for my talents."

"You might be surprised." Mother Beckert took a long breath. She had surrendered her fear along with her vanity, but she still hesitated to name it. As if, until the word was spoken, it could be avoided, but once named, was made inevitable. "It is the Thirteenth Chapel," she said, softly, already know-ing how he would reply.

"Aren't there twelve chapels in the Celestial Palace? Twelve chapels, for Twelve Virtues."

Mother Beckert smiled to have been proved so exactly right, and she sat back, and let herself be jolted by the movement of the carriage. "You might know a little of this, Master Caruso, and a little of that. But about virtue . . ." She looked back to the crowds outside the window. The pilgrims. And the prostitutes. "You have a lot to learn."

ACKNOWLEDGMENTS

AS ALWAYS, FOUR PEOPLE WITHOUT WHOM:

Bren Abercrombie, whose eyes are sore from reading it.
Nick Abercrombie, whose ears are sore from hearing about it.
Rob Abercrombie, whose fingers are sore from turning the pages.
Lou Abercrombie, whose arms are sore from holding me up.

THEN, THE SENIOR SAINTS:

To those Witch Engineers of British publishing who dared to bring the devils into our dimension, including but by no means limited to Katie Espiner, Anna Valentine, Paul Stark, Paul Hussey, Cait Davies, Jenna Petts, Marcus Gipps, and Brendan Durkin. Then, of course, all those who've helped make, publish, publicise, translate, and above all *sell* my books wherever they may be around the world.

For spreading the one true Church across the sea, aye, even unto the New World: Lindsey Hall and Devi Pillai.

For crimes involving the Black Art of design: Will Staehle and Joel Daniel Phillips.

A dauntless crusader often wounded, never vanquished: Tim Miller.

One of the best three—possibly two—audiobook readers in Europe: Steven Pacey.

For masterful handling of the collection plate: Robert Kirby and Ginger Clark.

Proprietors of that slaughterhouse in Aviles: Diego Garcia Cruz and Jorge Ivan Argiz.

To all the writers whose paths have crossed mine on the internet, at the bar, or in the writers' room, and who've provided help, support, laughs, and plenty of ideas worth the stealing. You know who you are.

AND LASTLY, YET FIRSTLY:

Cardinal Redfearn. That the authors may march all one way when the heavenly trumpets ring out a new crusade . . .

ABOUT THE AUTHOR

Lou Abercrombie

Joe Abercrombie was born in Lancaster, England, studied psychology at Manchester University, and worked as an editor of documentaries and live music before his first book, *The Blade Itself*, was published in 2006. Two further installments of the First Law trilogy, *Before They Are Hanged* and *Last Argument of Kings*, followed, along with three standalone books set in the same world: *Best Served Cold*, *The Heroes*, and *Red Country*. He has also written the Shattered Sea trilogy for young adults, the Age of Madness trilogy for old adults, and *Sharp Ends*, a collection of short stories. He lives in Bath, England, with his wife and three children. *The Devils* is his thirteenth novel.